THE UNREMEMBERED

THE UNREMEMBERED

PETER ORULLIAN

A TOM DOHERTY ASSOCIATES BOOK  NEW YORK

THE UNREMEMBERED

Copyright © 2015 by Peter Orullian

"Stories and Music" © 2015 by Peter Orullian

A Tor Book
Published by Tom Doherty Associates, LLC
175 Fifth Avenue
New York, NY 10010

www.tor-forge.com

Tor® is a registered trademark of Tom Doherty Associates, LLC.

The Library of Congress Cataloging-in-Publication Data is available upon request.

ISBN 978-0-7653-7987-0 (trade paperback)
ISBN 978-1-4299-6086-1 (e-book)

Tor books may be purchased for educational, business, or promotional use. For information on bulk purchases, please contact the Macmillan Corporate and Premium Sales Department at 1-800-221-7945, extension 5442, or write to specialmarkets@macmillan.com.

First Edition: April 2015

Printed in the United States of America

10   9   8   7   6   5   4   3   2   1

For Cheyenne,
in the hope of more Daddy stay-home days

• ACKNOWLEDGMENTS •

You've read it before: too many people to thank. That's true here, as well. But like so many good things in life, the thanks this time come in threes.

First, my family. I remember reading an introduction to a Dan Simmons book by Harlan Ellison that talked about how Dan's writing would affect his family. Competing priorities or somesuch. I've thought about that damned introduction every day this past year. For my part, it's safe to say I owe a forgiving wife and two patient kids more than I can say. And I'm capable of saying quite a lot.

Second, my editor. Claire Eddy and I have been friends about ten times longer than she's been my editor. That's a damned cool thing. She took me on about a year ago, well after the first version of this book was published. And when we began to unlock the possibilities together, well, I hit her up with old ideas about a new edition of *The Unremembered*. Enough can't be said about a writer and editor sharing the same vision for a book. A vision, in this instance, that reshapes the story, adding and subtracting to arrive at the volume you hold in your hands right now. A volume rather different from the first. Claire and the many talented folks at Tor are quite simply the best. Many thanks to them for embracing this project with enthusiasm.

Third, my readers. All of them. Let me enlighten you (yes, that's a Disturbed reference), there's not a better lot. And this includes my beta-readers, among whom, this time out, I'll mention Steve Diamond. Thanks, dude.

I'm incredibly honored and humbled to have the support of these good people. And others besides. My books don't happen without them.

SAECULA FOREST

PALL MOUNTAINS

SOLLEI STRETCHES

SAECULORUM MOUNTAINS

NALTUS FAR

SOTOL WASTES

ELYK DIVAD

•NORHAL

ONITOL

•IR-CAUL

All the rest are walking earth, breath first, enslaving breath in ignorance.

CANTLE WOOD

FALETT RANGE

LUHIN PASS

WYNSTOUT DOMINION

•A'VOTEL

Y'TILAT MOR

NALTUS REY

•REGTYV

BALENS

KUREN

PATER FUL

For there are two eternal truths that may not be put asunder, that force and forces or matter and energy, or body and spirit, can be neither created nor destroyed only rendered changed, made new, and next, that these eternal elements may choose for themselves.

SO'DELL

MAVEN WOOD

THE EAST OF
AESHAU VAAL
IN THE AGE OF
RUMOR

DYNLUL MOOR

MASSON DIMN

RIVEN PORT

DALLE

SOREN SEAS

Prelude to
The Vault of Heaven

One is forced to conclude that while the gods had the genius to create music, they didn't understand its power. There's a special providence in that, lads. It also ought to scare the last hell out of you.

—Taken from the rebuttal made by the philosopher
Lour Nail in the College of Philosophy
during the Succession of Arguments on Continuity

What hadn't been burned, had been broken. Wood, stone . . . flesh. Palamon stood atop a small rise, surveying the wound that was a city. Beside him, Dossolum kept a god's silence. Black smoke rose in straight pillars, its slow ascent unhindered by wind. None had been left alive. None. This wasn't blind, angry retaliation. This was annihilation. This was breakage of a deeper kind than wood or stone or flesh. This was breakage of the spirit.

Ours . . . and theirs, Palamon thought. He shook his head with regret. "The Veil isn't holding those you sent into the Bourne."

Dossolum looked away to the north. "This place is too far gone. Is it any wonder we're leaving it behind?"

"You're the Voice of the Council," Palamon argued. "If you stay, the others will stay. Then together—"

"The decision has been made," Dossolum reminded him. "Some things cannot be redeemed. Some things shouldn't."

Palamon clenched his teeth against further argument. He still had entreaties to make. Better not to anger the only one who could grant his requests. But it was hard. He'd served those who lay dead in the streets below him, just as he'd served the Creation Council. *Someone* should speak for the dead.

"You don't have to stay," Dossolum offered again. "None of the Sheason need stay. There's little you can do here. What we began will run its course. You might slow it"—he looked back at the ruined city—"but eventually, it will all come to this."

Palamon shook his head again, this time in defiance. "You don't know that."

Dossolum showed him a patient look. "We don't go idly. The energy required to right this . . . Better to start fresh, with new matter. In another place." He looked up at evening stars showing in the east.

"Most of the Sheason are coming with you," Palamon admitted.

"All but you, I think." Dossolum dropped his gaze back to the city. "It's not going to be easy here. Even with the ability to render the Will . . ."

Palamon stared at burned stone and tracts of land blackened to nothing. "Because some of those who cross the Veil have the same authority," he observed.

"Not only that." Dossolum left it there.

"Then strengthen the Veil," Palamon pled. "Make it the protection you meant it to be." He put a hand on Dossolum's arm. "Please."

In the silence that followed, a soft sound touched the air. A song. A lament. Palamon shared a look with Dossolum, then followed the sound. They descended the low hill. And step by step the song grew louder, until they rounded a field home. Beside a shed near a blackened pasture sat a woman with her husband's head in her lap. She stroked his hair as she sang. Not loud. Not frantic. But anguished, like a deep, slow saddening moved through her.

Tears had cleaned tracks down her field-dirty cheeks. Or maybe it was char. Like the smell of burning all around them.

But she was alive. Palamon had thought everyone here dead.

She looked up at them, unsurprised. Her vacant stare might not have seen them at all. She kept singing.

Palamon noticed toys now beside the home.

"The city wasn't enough," Palamon said, anger welling inside him. "They came into the fields to get them all."

The woman sang on. Her somber melody floated like cottonwood seed, brushing past them soft and earthward.

Dossolum stood and listened a long while. He made no move to comfort the woman, or to revive the man. His face showed quiet appreciation. Only when she'd begun to repeat her song did he finally speak. And then in a low tone, like a counterpoint.

"Very well, Palamon." Dossolum continued to watch the woman grieve. "Write it all down. Everything we tried to do. Our failure. The Bourne and those we sent there. The war to do so." He grew quiet. "A story of desolation."

Tentatively, Palamon asked, "And do what with it?"

The woman's song turned low and throaty and bare.

Dossolum gave a sad smile. "To some we'll give a gift of song. They'll sing the story you write. And so long as they do, the Veil will be added to. Strengthened."

He nodded, seeming satisfied. "But it will be a suffering to sing it. Leaving them *diminished*."

"Thank you, Dossolum." Palamon then silently thanked the woman who mourned in front of them. Her mortal sorrow had touched his friend's eternal heart.

"Don't thank me." Dossolum's eyes showed their first hint of regret. "Like every good intention, a song can fade."

Palamon looked up at the same evening stars Dossolum had watched a moment ago. "Or it might be sung even after the light of the stars has fled the heavens."

"I hope you're right, my friend. I hope you're right."

• BOOK ONE •

The Unremembered

Stillborn

The Church of Reconciliation—Reconciliationists, so called—
preach that the Framers left behind protections. And these protections were given proper names. Names we've forgotten. Would these
protections cease, then, to serve? Or would we have to question
the origins of the doctrine?

> —Excerpt from "Rational Suppositions," a street
> tract disseminated by the League of Civility

An open door...

Tahn Junell drew his bow, and kicked his mount into a dead run. They
descended the shallow dale in a rush toward that open door. Toward home.

The road was muddy. Hooves threw sludge. Lightning arced in the sky. A
peal of thunder shattered the silence and pushed through the small vale in
waves. It echoed outward through the woods in diminishing tolls.

The whispering sound of rain on trees floated toward him. The soft smells of
earth and pollen hung on the air, charged with the coming of another storm.
Cold perspiration beaded on his forehead and neck.

An open door...

His sister, Wendra, wouldn't leave the door open to the chill.

Passing the stable, another bolt of white fire erupted from the sky, this time
striking the ground. It hit at the near end of the vale. Thunder exploded around
him. A moment later, a scream rose from inside his home. His mount reared,
tugging at his reins and throwing Tahn to the ground before racing for the safety
of the stable. Tahn lost his bow and began frantically searching the mud for the
dropped weapon. The sizzle of falling rain rose, a lulling counterpoint to the
screams that continued from inside. Something crashed to the floor of the cabin.
Then a wail rose up. It sounded at once deep in the throat, like the thunder, and
high in the nose like a child's mirth.

Tahn's heart drummed in his ears and neck and chest. His throat throbbed with
it. Wendra was in there! He found his bow. Shaking the mud and water from the

bowstring and quickly cleaning the arrow's fletching on his coat, he sprinted for the door. He nocked the arrow and leapt to the stoop.

The home had grown suddenly still and quiet.

He burst in, holding his aim high and loose.

An undisturbed fire burned in the hearth, but everything else in his home lay strewn or broken. The table had been toppled on its side, earthen plates broken into shards across the floor. Food was splattered against one wall and puddled near a cooking pot in the far corner. Wendra's few books sat partially burned near the fire, their thrower's aim not quite sure.

Tahn saw it all in a glance as he swung his bow to the left where Wendra had tucked her bed up under the loft.

She lay atop her quilts, knees up and legs spread.

Absent gods, no!

Then, within the shadows beneath the loft, Tahn saw it, a hulking mass standing at the foot of Wendra's bed. It hunched over, too tall to remain upright in the nook beneath the upper room. Its hands cradled something in a blanket of horsehair. The smell of sweat and blood and new birth commingled with the aroma of the cooking pot.

The figure slowly turned its massive head toward him. Wendra looked too, her eyes weary but alive with fright. She weakly reached one arm toward him, mouthing something, but unable to speak.

In a low, guttural voice the creature spoke, "*Quillescent* all around." It rasped words in thick, glottal tones.

Then it stepped from beneath the loft, its girth massive. The fire lit the creature's fibrous skin, which moved independent of the muscle and bone beneath. Ridges and rills marked its hide, which looked like elm bark. But pliable. It uncoiled its left arm from the blanket it held to its chest, letting its hand hang nearly to its knees. From a leather sheath strapped to its leg, the figure drew a long knife. Around the hilt it curled its hand—three talonlike fingers with a thumb on each side, its palm as large as Tahn's face. Then it pointed the blade at him.

Tahn's legs began to quiver. Revulsion and fear pounded in his chest. This was a nightmare come to life. This was Bar'dyn, a race out of the Bourne. One of those given to Quietus, the dissenting god.

"We go," the Quietgiven said evenly. It spoke deep in its throat. Its speech belied a sharp intelligence in its eyes. When it spoke, only its lips moved. The skin on its face remained thick and still, draped loosely over protruding cheekbones that jutted like shelves beneath its eyes. Tahn glimpsed a mouthful of sharp teeth.

"Tahn," Wendra managed, her voice hoarse and afraid.

Blood spots marked her white bed-dress, and her body seemed frozen in a position that prevented her from straightening her legs. Tahn's heart stopped.

Against its barklike skin, the Bar'dyn held cradled in a tightly woven blanket of mane and tail . . . Wendra's child.

Pressure mounted in Tahn's belly: hate, helplessness, confusion, fear. All a madness like panicked wings in his mind. He was supposed to protect her, keep her safe, especially while she carried this child. A child come of rape. But a child she looked forward to. Loved.

Worry and anger rushed inside him. "No!"

His scream filled the small cabin, leaving a deeper silence in its wake. But the babe made no sound. The Bar'dyn only stared. On the stoop and roof, the patter of rain resumed, like the sound of a distant waterfall. Beyond it, Tahn heard the gallop of hooves on the muddy road. *More Bar'dyn? His friends?*

He couldn't wait for either. In a shaky motion, he drew his aim on the creature's head. The Bar'dyn didn't move. There wasn't even defiance in its expression.

"I'll take you *and* the child. Velle will be pleased." It nodded at its own words, then raised its blade between them.

Velle? Dead gods, they've brought a renderer of the Will with them!

Tahn's aim floundered from side to side. Weariness. Cold fear.

The Bar'dyn stepped toward him. Tahn's mind raced, and fastened upon one thought. *The hammer.* He focused on that mark on the back of his bow hand, visually tracing its lines and feeling it with his mind. A simple, solid thing. He didn't remember where he'd gotten the scar or brand, but it seemed intentional. And it grounded him. With that moment of reassurance, his hands steadied, and he drew deeper into the pull, bringing his aim on the Bar'dyn's throat.

"Put the child down." His voice trembled even as his mouth grew dry.

The Bar'dyn paused, looking down at the bundle it carried. The creature then lifted the babe up, causing the blanket to slip to the floor. Its massive hand curled around the little one's torso. The infant still glistened from its passage out of Wendra's body, its skin red and purple in the sallow light of the fire.

"Child came dead, grub."

Sadness and anger welled again in Tahn. His chest heaved at the thought of Wendra giving birth in the company of this vile thing, having her baby taken at the moment of life into its hands. *Was the child dead at birth, or had the Bar'dyn killed it?* Tahn glanced again at Wendra. She was pale. Sadness etched her features. He watched her close her eyes against the Bar'dyn's words.

The rain now pounded the roof. But the sound of heavy footfalls on the road was clear, close, and Tahn abandoned hope of escape. One Bar'dyn, let alone several, might tear him apart, but he intended to send this one to the abyss, for Wendra, for her dead child.

He prepared to fire his bow, allowing time enough to speak the old, familiar words: "I draw with the strength of my arms, but release as the Will allows."

But he couldn't shoot.

He struggled to disobey the feeling, but it stretched back into that part of his life he couldn't remember. He had always spoken the words, always. He didn't release of his own choice. He always followed the quiet intimations that came after he spoke those words.

Tahn relaxed his aim and the Bar'dyn nodded approval. "Bound to Will," it said. The words rang like the cracking of timber in the confines of the small home. "But first to watch this one go." The Bar'dyn turned toward Wendra.

"No!" Tahn screamed again, filling the cabin with denial. Denial of the Bar'dyn. Denial of his own impotence.

The sound of others came up the steps. Tahn was surrounded. They would all die!

He spared a last look at his sister. "I'm sorry," he tried to say, but it came out in a husk.

Her expression of confusion and hurt and disappointment sank deep inside him.

If he couldn't kill the creature, he could at least try to prevent it from hurting her.

Before he could move, his friends shot through the door. They got between Tahn and the Bar'dyn. They fought the creature. They filled his home with a clash of wills and swordplay and shouted oaths. Chaos churned around him. And all he could do was watch Wendra curl deeper into her bed. Afraid. Heartsick.

The creature out of the Bourne finally turned and crashed through the cabin's rear wall, rushing into the dark and the storm with Wendra's dead child. They did not give chase.

Tahn turned from the hole in the wall and went to Wendra's side. Blood soaked the coverlet, and cuts in her wrists and hands told of failed attempts to ward off the Bar'dyn. Her cheeks sagged; she looked pale and spent. She lay crying silent tears.

He'd stood twenty feet away with a clear shot at the Bar'dyn and had done nothing. The lives of his sister and her child had hung in the balance, and he'd done nothing. The old words had told him the draw was wrong. He'd followed that feeling over the defense of his sister. Why?

It was an old ache and frustration, believing himself bound to the impressions those words stirred inside him. But never so much as now.

For there are two eternal truths that may not be put asunder: that Forza and Forda, or matter and energy, or body and spirit, can be neither created nor destroyed, only rendered, changed, made new— yea, and all power within them lies, yea even the First Ones were bound by these very laws in framing this world as in all the worlds that came before and all those that will come after; and next that these eternal elements may choose for themselves.

—Drawn from the apocryphal writings of the
author Shenflear, during the Age of Discord

A grave I traveled past, and stopped to look upon the stone.
I read the tribute words aloud.
My voice seemed an intrusion in the silence
For a brave man gone to his earth fighting the Quiet.
And I despised myself for feeling reverent.
What then was his death about?
So I recalled a jest and spoke it to the stone
And laughed great loud, yawped a bit, and honored him with noise.
The grave's only power is this: that therein dies the laughter.
For this is life, and life is loud, or else the Quiet's you.

—"Reflections from an Ossuary,"
attributed to the poet Hargrove,
during the Age of Hope

CHAPTER ONE

Old Words

It is the natural condition of man to strive for certainty. It is also his condition not to find it. Not for long, anyway. Even a star may wander.

—From *Commentary on Categoricals,* a reader for children nominated to Dimnian cognitive training

Tranquil darkness stretched to the horizon. Small hours. Moments of quiet, of peace. Moments when faraway stars seemed as close and familiar as friends. Moments of night before the east would hint of sunrise. Tahn stepped into these small hours. Into the chill night air. He went to spend time with the stars. To imagine dawn. As he always had.

There was a kind of song in it all. A predictable rhythm and melody that might only be heard by one willing to remain quiet and unmoving long enough to note the movement of a star. It could be heard in the phases of the moons. It was by turns a single deep sonorous note, large as a russet sun setting slow, and then a great chorus, as when showers of shooting stars brightened the night sky. They were harmonies across ages, heard during the brief measure of a life. But only if one paused, as Tahn did, to watch and listen.

He stood at the edge of the High Plains of Sedagin. The bluff rose a thousand strides off the flatlands below. Stars winked like sparkling bits of glass on a dark tablecloth. His breath clouded the night, and droplets hung like frozen tears from low scrub and sage.

He looked east and let his thoughts come naturally. Deep into the far reaches of the sky he let them wander, his emotions and hopes struggling for form with the stars. He traced the constellations, some from old stories, some from memories whose sources were lost to him. A half-full moon had risen high, its surface bright and clear. The pale outline of the darkened portion appeared a ghostly halo.

Tahn closed his eyes and let his thoughts run out even further, imagining the sun; imagining its warmth and radiance, its calm, sure track across the heavens. He imagined the sky changing color in the east from black to violet to sea blue and finally the color of clear, shallow water. He pictured more color as sunlight came to the forest and touched its leaves and cones and limbs. He envisioned those first moments of dawn, the unfurling of flower petals to its light, its glint on rippling water, steam rising from warming loam. And as he always did at such a moment, Tahn felt like part of the land, another leaf to be touched by the sun. His thoughts coalesced into the singular moment of sunrise and another hope risen up from the night, born again with quiet strength.

He opened his eyes to the dark skies and the foliate pattern of stars. In the east, the first intimation of day arose as the black hinted of violet hues. A quiet relief filled him, and he took a lungful of air.

Another day would come. And pass. Until the beautiful, distant stars returned, and he came again to watch. Until someday, when either he or the sun would not rise. And the song would end.

He lingered, enjoying a moment's peace. They'd been on the road more days than he could remember. Chased by the Quiet. Chased since the night he'd let Wendra down, failed to shoot when she'd needed him, when the Quiet took her child. Tahn shook his head with guilt at the memory of it.

And now here he was. Weeks later. Far from home. Just tonight they'd climbed this plateau, arriving after midnight. After dark hour.

He took a long breath, relaxing in the stillness.

The sound of boots over frost-covered earth startled him. He turned to see Vendanj come to join him.

Even the shadows of night couldn't soften the hard edges of the man. Vendanj wore determination the way another does his boots. Carried it in his eyes and shoulders. Vendanj was a member of the Sheason Order, those who rendered the Will—that melding of spirit and body, energy and matter. The Sheason weren't well known in the Hollows, Tahn's home. And Tahn was learning that beyond the Hollows, the Sheason weren't always welcome. Were even distrusted.

Vendanj came up beside him, and stared out over the plains far and away below. He didn't rush to clutter the silence with words. And they watched together for a time.

After long moments, Vendanj eyed Tahn with wry suspicion. "You do this every morning." It wasn't a question.

Tahn returned the wry grin. "How would you know? You follow me everywhere?"

"Just until we reach the Saeculorum," Vendanj answered.

They shared quiet laughter over that. It was a rare jest from Vendanj. But it was a square jest, the kind with truth inside. Because they were, in fact, going to the Saeculorum—mountains at the far end of the Eastlands. Several months' travel from here.

"For as long as I can remember," Tahn finally admitted, "I've gotten up early to watch the sunrise. Habit now, I guess."

Vendanj folded his arms as he stared east. "It's more than a habit, I suspect."

And he was right. It was more like a compulsion. A need. To stand with the stars. Imagine daybreak.

But Vendanj didn't press, and fell silent again for a time.

Into the silence, distantly, came again the sound of footfalls over hard dirt. The chill air grew . . . tight. Dense. It seemed to press on Tahn. Panic tightened his gut. Vendanj held up a hand for Tahn not to speak. A few moments later, up the trail of the cliff face came a figure, unhurried. Directly toward them.

Soon, the moon brought the shape into focus. A man. He wore an unremarkable coat, buttoned high against the chill. No cowl or robe or weapon. No smile of greeting. No frown. It was the man's utter lack of expression that frightened Tahn most, as if feeling had gone out of him.

Twenty strides from them, the other stopped, returning the bluff to silence. The figure stared at them through the dark. Stared at them with disregard.

Softer than a whisper, "Velle," Vendanj said.

My dying gods.

Velle were Quiet renderers of the Will. Like Sheason, but followers of the dissenting god.

The silence stretched between them, dawn still a long while away.

Into the stillness, the other spoke, his voice soft and low. "Your legs will tire, Sheason. And we will be there when they do." He pointed at Tahn. "Send me the boy, and let's be done."

"It would do you no good," Vendanj replied. "If not the boy, there are others."

The Velle nodded. "We know. And this one isn't the first you've driven like a mule." The man's eyes shifted to Tahn. "What has he told you, Quillescent?"

Tahn didn't really understand the question, and didn't reply. He only took his bow down from his shoulder.

The Velle shook his head slowly in disappointment. "You don't have the energy to fight me, Sheason. You've spent too much already."

"I appreciate your concern," Vendanj said, another surprising jest from the usually severe man.

The Velle hadn't taken its eyes from Tahn. "And what about you, with your little bow? Are you going to ask your gods if I should die, and shoot me down?" The expression in the man's face changed, but only by degrees. *More* indifferent. Careworn to the bone, beyond feeling.

He knows. He knows the words I speak when I draw.

The Velle dropped its chin. "Ask it." The words were an invitation, a challenge. And the chill air bristled when the Velle spoke them. Grasses and low sage bent away from the man as though they would flee.

Vendanj held up a hand. "You've strolled onto the Sedagin plain, my Quiet friend. A thousand swords and more. Go back the way you came."

A slow smile touched the Velle's face. A wan smile lacking warmth or humor. And even that looked unnatural, as though he were unaccustomed to smiling at all. "I don't take care for myself, Sheason. That is a *man's* weakness. And there'll be no heroes this time." He raised a hand, and Vendanj let out an explosive exhale, as if his chest were suddenly being pressed by boulders.

In a single motion, Tahn raised his bow and drew an arrow. *I draw with the strength of my arms, but release as the Will allows.*

The quiet confirmation came. The Velle should die.

Tahn caught a glimpse of a more genuine smile on the Quiet's lips before he let his arrow fly. An unconcerned flip of the Velle's wrist, and the arrow careened high and harmless out over the bluff's edge.

Vendanj dropped to his knees, struggling against some unseen force. Tahn had to disrupt the Velle's hold on the Sheason somehow. But before he could move, a deep shiver started in his chest as though his body were a low cello string being slowly played. And with the resonance rushed the memory of his failure to shoot the Bar'dyn that had come into his and Wendra's home, taken her child.

Except it seemed more raw now. Like alcohol poured on a fresh cut.

And that wasn't all. Other memories stirred. Lies he'd told. Insults he'd offered. Though he couldn't recall them with exactness. They were half formed, but sharpening.

He was maybe seven. A fight. Friends. Some kind of contest to settle . . .

Tahn began to tremble violently. His teeth ached and felt ready to shatter. His mind burned hot with regret and self-loathing. He dropped face-first beside Vendanj, and curled into a ball against the pain.

Vendanj still wasn't breathing, but managed to thrust an open palm at the Velle. The Quiet man grimaced, and Vendanj drew a harsh-sounding breath, his face slick with sweat in the moonlight.

Tahn's own inner ache subsided, and the quaking in his body stopped. Briefly. The Velle dropped to both knees and drove its hands into the hard soil. Blackness flared, and the Quiet man looked suddenly refreshed. This time, it simply stared at Vendanj. The earth between them whipped, low sage tearing away. But Vendanj was prepared, and kept his feet and breath when some force hit him, exploding in a fury of spent energy. The Sheason's lean face had drawn into a grim expression, and he began shaking his head.

The Velle glanced at Tahn and tremors wracked his body again. With them came his insecurities about childhood years lost to memory. As if they didn't matter. As if *he* didn't matter, except to raise his bow and repeat those godsforsaken words, *I draw with the strength . . .*

As the Velle caressed him with this deep resonant pain, a shadow flashed behind the other. Light and quick.

A moment later the Velle's back arched, his eyes wide in surprise. Tahn's tremors stopped. Vendanj lowered his arms. The Velle fell forward, and standing there was Mira Far, of the Far people. Her pale skin awash in moonlight. Only a Far could have gotten behind a Velle without being noticed. Looking at her, Tahn felt a different kind of tug inside. One that was altogether more appealing.

For the third time that morning, boots over hard earth interrupted the dark morning stillness. A hundred strides behind Mira three Bar'dyn emerged on the trail. At first they only walked. Then, seeing the downed Velle, they broke into a run, a kind of reasoned indifference in their faces. Their massive frames moved with grace, and power, as their feet pounded against the cold earth.

Tahn reached for an arrow. Mira dropped into one of her Latae stances, both swords raised. Vendanj gasped several breaths, still trying to steady himself from his contest with the Velle. "Take the Bar'dyn down," he said, his voice full of hateful prejudice.

Tahn pulled three successive draws, thinking the old words in an instant and firing at the closest Bar'dyn. The first arrow bounded harmlessly off the creature's barklike skin. But the next two struck it in the neck. It fell with a heavy crunch on the frost-covered soil.

The remaining two descended on Mira first. She ducked under a savage swipe of a long rounded blade and came up with a thrust into the creature's groin. Not simply an attack on its tender parts, but a precise cut into the artery that ran alongside them—something she'd taught him during one of their many conversations.

The Bar'dyn shrugged off the blow and rushed onward toward Tahn. In a few moments it would grow sluggish from blood loss, and finally fall. Tahn had only to keep a distance.

The other Quiet pushed ahead faster, closing on Tahn. Mira took chase, but even with her gift of speed wouldn't reach it before it got to him. Tahn pulled a deep draw. The Bar'dyn raised a forearm to protect its neck, and barreled closer.

"Take it down!" Vendanj began raising a hand, clearly weakened. The Sheason had rendered the Will so often lately. And he'd had little time to recover.

Tahn breathed out, steadied his aim, spoke the words in his mind, and let fly. The arrow hit true, taking the Bar'dyn's left eye. No cry or scream. It stutter-stepped, and kept on. Its expression was as impassive as before—not fury, reason.

Tahn drew again. This arrow struck the Quiet's knee, as he'd intended. But it shattered against the armor-hard skin there. It was almost too close to fire again, but Tahn pulled a quick draw, Mira a half step behind the creature, and fired at its mouth. The arrow smashed through its teeth and went out through its cheek.

The Bar'dyn's face stretched in a mask of pain. Then it leveled its eyes again and leapt at Tahn.

It was too late to avoid the Quiet. Tahn braced himself. The massive creature drove him to the ground under its immense weight. Tahn lost his breath, couldn't cry out. He could feel blood on his face. The Bar'dyn shifted to take hold of him.

It propped itself up with one arm, and stared down at Tahn with its indifferent eyes. "You don't understand," it said with a thick, glottal voice.

The Bar'dyn began to roll, pulling Tahn with it, as if it might try to carry him away. A moment later, it stopped moving. Mira. She pulled her blade from the creature's head. Then she turned on the wounded Bar'dyn, who was now staggering toward them, weak from loss of blood.

The last Quiet fell. It panted for several moments, then went still.

• CHAPTER TWO •

Keeping Promises

And a Sheason known as Portis came into the court of King Yusefi of Kuren, and demanded he keep his pledge to the Second Promise and send men to help the Sedagin in the far North. But Yusefi denied him. Whereupon Portis rendered the king's blood boiling hot and burned him alive inside. To my knowledge, this is the first recorded instance of Sheason violence against man.

—An account of the Castigation, from the pages of the Kuren Court diarist

Warm Bar'dyn blood steamed in the moonlight. Tahn scrambled away from the dead Quiet and sat heavily on the cold ground. His heart hammered in his chest. There was no getting used to this.

And now a Velle! What had it done to him? He still felt it. Like vibrations of thought or emotion. Deep down.

"All the way to the Saeculorum," Tahn said, repeating the joke Vendanj had made before this latest Quiet attack. Now it just sounded exhausting. Impossible.

Vendanj eased himself down to sit near Tahn. "It's good you're handy with a bow."

Mira crouched in front of them, keeping her feet under her—always ready. "Velle. That's new." She was looking at Vendanj.

He nodded. "But not surprising. And not the last we'll see of them."

"There's a happy thought," Tahn said without humor. "Seems like every damn day another storybook rhyme steps from the page. What was it doing to me?"

Vendanj eyed him. Tapped his own chest. "You felt it in here."

Tahn nodded.

"A renderer of the Will can move things," he explained. "Push them. Sometimes you'll see what he does. Sometimes you won't." He took a long breath. "Sometimes it's outside the body. And other times," Vendanj tapped his chest again, "it's in here."

"I don't feel the same," Tahn said.

"It's Resonance." Vendanj said it with obvious concern. "It'll linger like a played note. Won't ever go away completely. But it'll stop feeling like it does today."

Tahn rubbed his chest. "I felt like I was remembering. . . ." But it hadn't completely come back. Mostly the *feeling* of the memory remained. He turned to Vendanj. "What did it mean, 'There'll be no heroes this time'?"

Vendanj took a storyteller's breath. "This plateau used to be part of the flatlands below." He gestured out over the bluff. "The Sedagin people here are known as the Right Arm of the Promise. Masters of the longblade. They've always kept the First Promise; always marched against the Quiet when they come."

"What about this time?" Tahn asked, looking at the dead Velle.

Vendanj didn't seem to hear him. "First time the Quiet came, the regent of Recityv called a Convocation of Seats. Every nation and throne was asked to join an alliance to meet the threat. And most did. The Sedagin were the strongest part of that army. And the Quiet were pushed back.

"Ages later, the Quiet came again." Vendanj shook his head and sighed. "But by then Convocation had become a political game. Kings committed only token regiments. So, the regent Corihehn adjourned Convocation and sent word to Holivagh, leader of the Sedagin, to march toward the Pall mountains. He told him there was a Second Promise from this Second Convocation. He told him an alliance army would meet them there."

Tahn guessed the next part, disgust rising in his throat. "It was a lie."

"It was a lie," Vendanj echoed, nodding. "Twenty thousand Sedagin soldiers cut a path through the Quiet. They reached the Pall mountains where Bourne armies were crossing into the Eastlands, but by then only two thousand Sedagin were left. Still, they held the breach for eight days. They waited for Corihehn's reinforcements. But the army of the Second Promise never came. And every Sedagin bladesman perished."

"But we won the war," Tahn added, tentative.

"When Del'Agio, Randeur of the Sheason, learned what Corihehn had done, he sent Sheason messengers into the courts of every city. They threatened death to any who wouldn't honor Corihehn's lie. The Castigation, it was called."

Vendanj looked up and down the edge of the bluff. "When the war was won, the Sheason came into the high plains. For several cycles of the first moon they linked hands and willed the earth to rise, built an earthen monument to the Sedagin. Gave them a home. These plains are known as Teheale. It means 'earned in blood' in the Covenant Tongue."

Tahn sat silent in reverence to the sacrifice made so long ago.

"Seems our Velle friend doesn't think Sheason and Sedagin can turn the Quiet back again." Vendanj's smile caught in the light of the moon. "No heroes."

In many ways, Vendanj reminded Tahn of his father, Balatin. Serious, but able to let worry go when he sensed Tahn needed to laugh or just let things lie. Tahn suddenly missed his father, a deep missing. His da had gone to his earth a few years ago, leaving Tahn and Wendra to make their way alone—their mother, Vocencia, had died a few years before Balatin. He missed her, too.

"It'll look something like this." Vendanj gestured away from the high plateau again, shifting topics. "The Heights of Restoration, Tahn. On the far side of the Saeculorum."

"Because you think this time *I'm* the hero?" He stared at the steam rising from the dead Bar'dyn's wounds.

Vendanj sighed. "I'm inclined to agree with the Velle. And I don't think like that anymore." He paused, his eyes distant. "If I ever did."

"He said there were others," Tahn pressed. "Called me a mule."

Vendanj gave a dismissive laugh over that. "We're all mules. Each hauling some damn load, don't you think?"

Tahn waited, making clear he wanted an answer. He'd agreed to come. He was bone weary, and scared to think Vendanj had pinned too much hope on him.

Tahn could hit almost anything with his bow. There'd been countless hours of practice supervised by his father. Even before that, he'd had a sure hand. Somewhere in those lost years of his young life he'd obviously learned its use; fighting techniques, too—his reactions were like Mira's Latae battle forms, just less polished. But against an army? Against Velle? That thing had taken hold of him somehow. Not just his body, but *who* he was. It had stroked painful memories, giving them new life in his mind. It was a pain unlike anything he'd yet felt. This was madness.

What the hell am I doing?

The Sheason seemed to know his thoughts, and put a hand on Tahn's shoulder. "There's a sense about you, Tahn. Like the words you use when you draw your bow." He paused. "But no, you're not the only one we've taken to Restoration. Remember what I said at the start: We believe you can stand there. You've not passed your Change, so the burdens of your mistakes aren't fully on you yet. That'll make it easier."

"Why would you need *me* if you've taken others?"

Vendanj let out a long breath. He settled a gaze on Tahn that spoke of disappointment and regret. "None have survived Tillinghast." He paused as if weighing Tahn's resolve. "That's its old name. Tillinghast is where the Heights of Restoration fall away." He gestured again toward the cliff's edge close by. "Like this bluff."

Before Tahn could comment, Vendanj pushed on. "And that's those who went at all. Most chose not to go. Your willingness. It sets you apart from most."

"He's right," Mira added, approval in her voice.

Tahn looked up at her, finding encouragement in her silver-grey eyes. She showed him the barest of smiles. And warmth flooded his chest and belly, chasing out some of the deep shiver still lingering inside him.

"Tahn," Vendanj said, gathering his attention again. "The thing you need to remember is this. Standing at Tillinghast isn't just about whatever mettle's in you to survive its touch. It's more about whether or not you can suffer the change it'll cause in you once it's done."

Tahn shook his head, panic fluttering anew in his chest. "What change?"

"Different for everyone who stands there," Vendanj replied.

"If they *live*," Tahn observed with sharp sarcasm. "And then do what?"

"If the Quiet fully break free of the Bourne"—Mira nodded as though it was only a matter of time—"they'll come with elder beings. Creatures against which steel is useless."

Vendanj got to his feet. "And my order is at odds with itself. Diminished because of it." He looked down at Tahn. "This time . . . we've asked *you* to go to Tillinghast. The Veil that holds the Quiet at bay is weakening. Could be that the Song of Suffering that keeps it strong is failing. I know there are few with the ability to sing Suffering. But whatever the reason for the Veil's weakness, we think—if you can stand at Tillinghast—you can help should a full Quiet army come."

Tahn shook his head in disbelief. And fear. "All because of the damned words I can't help but say every time I draw." He shook his bow. "And because I have a *sense*. Maybe it's time you restore my memory. Give me back those twelve years you say you took from me when you sent me to the Hollows."

He wanted that more than he let on. His earliest memories began just six years ago. *Twelve years. Gone.* And until Vendanj had come into the Hollows, Tahn had thought maybe he'd had some sort of accident. Hit his head. Lost his memory. But the Sheason had taken it. To protect him, the man had said.

"You may believe you're ready for that. But think about it." He pointed at the Velle, which had surfaced searing memories in him. "You don't remember your young life . . . but it was a hard one. Not *all* hard. But most of it was spent in an unhappy place. And now, you're far from home, chased by Quiet, asked to climb to Tillinghast, and you're coming soon to the age of accountability."

Tahn had been eager for his Standing and the Change that came after his eighteenth year. Eager for what, he didn't exactly know. To be taken more seriously was part of it, though. And because he'd thought he might somehow get his memory back.

Tahn stood, shouldered his bow. "Wouldn't that suggest I'm old enough—"

"No, it wouldn't," Vendanj cut in sharply. "I took your memory all those years ago as a protection to you. It still is. Before we reach Tillinghast I'll return it to you. You'll need it there." He put his hand again on Tahn's shoulder, his hard expression softening. "But not now. Trust me on this. I've seen what it does to a mind when so much change comes at once."

Tahn thought about the pressure in his body and mind when the Velle had taken hold of him. The things it had surfaced all in a rush. Jagged, ugly things to remember.

Images of young friends, though he couldn't see their faces. A fight, though he couldn't remember why. Except they were settling something. The feeling of betrayal lingered. A sad pain in the pit of his stomach.

Tahn walked to where the Velle lay. Something glinted on the ground near its body. He hunkered down and ran his fingers across a smooth surface glistening with moonlight. Felt like glass. At its center were two fist-sized holes.

"What's this?"

Vendanj came up beside him. "Velle won't bear the cost of rendering the Will. They transfer it. Take the vitality of anything at hand so they can remain strong."

The Velle had thrust its hands into the soil. Darkness had flared. It had caused the formation of this thin crust of dark glass. Tahn stepped on it. A soft *pop*. A fragile sound. If Vendanj hadn't been here, what else inside Tahn would the Velle have taken hold of?

He finally gave a low, resigned laugh. "You win. Why complicate all this fun we're having, right?"

He stole a look at Mira, who showed him her slim smile again. That, at least, was helpful. Hopeful, too. Like the lighter shades of blue strengthening in the east behind her.

Just before he turned away, he caught sight of low fogs gathering on the lowland floor. He pointed. "You see that?"

Vendanj looked, and his expression hardened. Soon Mira stood with them, as they watched a cloud bank form around the base of the plateau.

"Je'holta," Vendanj said.

"What is it?" Tahn asked.

"Another form of Quiet." He paused a long moment. "And something we'll now have to pass through when we leave here."

Mira's smile was gone. "Good test for Tillinghast."

Tahn gave them each a long look, and said without humor, "I just came out to watch the sunrise. . . ."

• CHAPTER THREE •

Invitations

The Oath of the Sodality is an oath to defend the Sheason, to lend aid. To a sodalist, a book means as much as a blade. And he'll raise both with vigor. But his oath isn't compulsory. It's not a blood rite. It's stronger than that. It's his choice.

—*Explications and Comparisons of Oaths Real and Imagined*, by Relin Corinat, archivist at the Library of Common Understanding

The sun had just cleared the bluff as Vendanj led his companions through the Sedagin city. A city that had the feel of a town. No tall buildings. Few stone structures. But it sprawled across the great open plain risen from the flat-lands with a mild sense of impermanence. The Sedagin people had long been a wandering army—lived where they were needed—before Teheale. And even now, with a home of their own, they hadn't bothered with the arrogance of architecture.

Vendanj and the others crossed near a wide tract of closely cropped grass. On their left, hundreds of young boys stood in short lines before men who were demonstrating precise moves and attacks with the great swords the Sedagin carried. Their attention never drifted to Vendanj and his friends. In turn, each boy executed the move and returned to the end of his line. The swords themselves were taller than their wielders, but the boys carried them and performed their drills without any apparent difficulty.

As they moved past the drills, homes grew in number, wood framed, and modest in appearance. But it was the absence of street barkers that Vendanj relished most. There were no handcarts filled with food or handmade trinkets; no beggars sat in the shadows of the buildings petitioning passersby. No loud, confusing din clouded the air, no smell of refuse rotting behind and between the homes and buildings.

"Not one house of bitter," Tahn's friend, Sutter Te Polis, remarked behind him. "I don't trust sober minds."

Vendanj kept the smile off his face. Sutter liked to run his mouth. But there was strength in him. A friend's strength. As well as the sense and steadiness of a root farmer—Sutter's trade. It's why Vendanj had allowed the lad to come with them. Though, headstrong as Sutter was, he'd likely have followed them anyway.

They passed a group of men standing beside a house. Each wore a sword and exuded an air of calm and confidence. As they continued down several lanes, they could see more of the Sedagin at their doors and windows, and gathered in small groups outside, regarding the Sheason with a quiet respect.

They stopped in front of a particular house. No less than fifty Sedagin stood close by.

Sutter nudged Tahn. "Did you notice that none of them looks like fat old Yulop?" He mimed a round belly in front of him.

The door of the house opened, and a man emerged. His hair and eyes were the brown of brushed saddle leather. He too wore his long sword at his waist, but sported no cloak or cape. The other Sedagin bowed noticeably as he stepped outside, but Tahn could see nothing to distinguish him as their lord or king. The man made a quick survey of his guests, stopping to note their weapons. At a look, all the men dispersed, save a few who relaxed and began to talk quietly.

"Vendanj, my friend," the man said. "You always surprise me when you return from the lowlands." He offered a lopsided smile and stepped down from the short portico to the grass road.

Vendanj embraced the other. "I imagine that's true."

"My scouts tell me the Quiet follow you, but I suspect their report leaves the best of it unspoken."

Vendanj nodded and smiled. "You've a talent for understatement."

The man laughed. "Come in. I have cold water and hot bread."

Inside, a large room lay awash in sunlight from windows on every side. The smell of fresh loaves beside the hearth to the left gave the place a relaxed, homey feeling. Against the rear wall, sketches in charcoal of several men hung in a perfect line. Beneath each sketch, a sword stood buried in the wood floor. To each side of the door, bookcases reached to the ceiling.

"Please, sit," the man said, raising a hand to several chairs set around the hearth.

"Thank you," Vendanj replied, and sat nearest the fire.

As his companions each found a chair, Vendanj made introductions. "This is Jamis Costnar. He leads the Sedagin."

Jamis offered a gracious smile. "Let's say I'm more of a guide."

"It's been a long time since you've come into the High Plains." Jamis began pouring glasses of water from a sweating pitcher. "Refuge from the Quiet?"

"Too long," Vendanj said to the first comment. "And we're not here for refuge. We're here with a request."

Jamis stopped pouring, staring down at Vendanj. He then resumed, saying nothing until all had a glass of their own. "Introductions first," he said, regaining his smile as he sat with his guests.

"Of course." Vendanj nodded to his right. "This is Braethen Posian. Took the sodalist oath not long ago."

—"To stand with *you*?" Jamis leaned forward toward Braethen and whispered like a conspirator, "Brave soul."

Braethen smiled.

"He's an author's son, from the Hallows," Vendanj added. "Had his nose in books most his life. You'll like him."

Jamis showed a surprised expression. "I didn't think the Sodality had people in the Hallows."

"They don't," Braethen chimed in, sounding a bit defensive. "But I've studied the Sodality most of my life. Tried to understand how they serve with the Sheason."

Jamis leaned forward again, wearing a peacemaker's look. "Any reader of books is a friend of mine."

Mira was suddenly behind Jamis, leaning down and taking him in a rear embrace. "Good to see you."

Jamis started. "One of these days I'm going to catch you sneaking up on me," he warned with good humor. He then patted her hands and nodded toward Vendanj. "I'm surprised you're still with him and haven't gone mad."

Mira smiled, then took a spot beside a window, where she kept watch along the rear of the house.

Vendanj went on with introductions. "This is Tahn Junell, his sister Wendra, and their friend Sutter Te Polis. All from the Hallows, as well. And the lad"—he gestured toward the boy sitting beside Wendra—"is Penit. Joined us a few days ago out of Myrr. Pageant wagon player. Only member of his troupe to escape arrest by the League of Civility for playing an old rhea-fol. Has pluck. We'll see him safely to Recityv."

Wendra put a protective arm around the boy.

Jamis nodded greetings to them all. Of Penit, he asked, "You have parents?"

"No, sir. Just the pageant wagons." Penit sat forward, not a whit intimidated. "And it's getting harder to play the stories. The troop was only going to survive if we did well in Myrr. There's not enough money in the smaller villages anymore, and the larger cities all have the League and their laws. A scop's got to get paid."

Jamis smiled. "Another brave soul." Then he turned back to Vendanj. "So tell me. Why do the Quiet chase a Sheason, a Far, a child, and several Hollows folk?"

Vendanj took a long draught from his glass of water. He let the coolness fill him. Then he explained about Tahn and Tillinghast. There was more he could have shared, like Wendra's gift with song, like the ingot of steel he'd had mongered into a new shape—a sword this time. But none of that was important for Jamis to know. And Vendanj finally came to his request. "The regent is going to recall the Convocation of Seats."

Jamis held up a hand. The genial look on his face soured. Became grave. A very old wound shone in the man's eyes.

"We won't come." Jamis returned Vendanj's stare. "Anything after the First Promise you can keep."

The man had the right to his anger. But Vendanj wasn't finished. "The Veil is weakening. It hasn't yet fallen, but some Quiet are passing through." He paused. "I fear it will fail again. And when it does, Quiet will reach every doorstep."

"Quietgiven have always escaped the Bourne," Jamis argued. "But only twice with invasion numbers."

"And both times," Braethen interrupted, "in the months before they came, the records show the frequency increasing. People fleeing for the protection of city walls."

Vendanj put a hand on Braethen's arm. "We've seen this on our way here. And an increase of illness, too. Supal disease. Chrondia. To say nothing of produce markets selling half bushels of bad crops. It all points to the same thing."

Jamis looked at each of them in turn. "If the time comes, we'll defend our friends. As we always have. Your Convocation is filled with horses' asses. And liars. I won't see a single Sedagin die to protect them."

Vendanj had no argument for that, and a heavy silence followed. It hung for several long moments. "Come with us anyway," Vendanj asked, his voice soft but clear. "To Recityv. Convocation can be different this time."

Jamis stared back at him a long while. "You're brave, too. The League's Civilization Order will see you killed if they find you rendering the Will. You know this."

"I'd like to have them try." They weren't idle words.

The Sedagin leader gave him a sympathetic look. "How are you, really, my friend?" He paused, then spoke softly enough that only Vendanj might hear. "Illenia would have wanted you to fight hard. But she'd have wanted you to be happy doing it."

Hearing her name brought that familiar ache, that empty feeling, that sense of being unmoored. Alone. Dear gods, he missed her. The fight helped. Her death wasn't the only reason to go to Tillinghast. But for him it was the most important.

Vendanj looked back at Jamis. "I think it's the only time I *am* happy." He gave his old friend a half smile.

That restored some of the good humor between them.

"You're like your brothers of old," Jamis said, returning the smile. "The ones that held the Second Convocation of Seats accountable for the death of an entire Sedagin brigade. That's why I like you."

They shared a quiet laugh, even as Jamis reminded Vendanj why he wouldn't be attending this new Convocation.

Jamis sat back, and looked over all his guests with new warmth in his face. "We'll talk more later. Tonight a dinner will be held in your honor, Sheason, for the home your order gave us here on the Teheale." He lifted his own cup and drank a solitary toast to Vendanj.

"And in remembrance of your sacrifice for the First Promise," Vendanj replied, reminding him of his commitment.

"Just so," Jamis agreed.

• CHAPTER FOUR •

Release of the Shrikes

It is simply time to put away superstition. It makes men and women dependent, rather than aspirant to their own greatness.

—From the new Creed of Civility, issued
by Roth Staned in his second year as Ascendant

Helaina Storalaith, regent of Recityv, ruling seat of Vohnce, threw open the doors to her High Office and stormed inside. Close behind came Roth Staned, Ascendant—the highest officer—of the League of Civility. Soon General Van Steward and Sheason Artixan followed. These four members of the High Council, which had just concluded a bitter season, stood in the sunlit office.

The argument had followed her unbidden to her sanctuary.

"It's foolishness, my lady," Ascendant Staned said. "Don't be baited into action by rumors. It sets us back as a people to fall victim to outdated beliefs and false traditions."

"Watch how you speak to the regent," Van Steward cautioned.

Roth cocked an eye at the general. "We are in open debate. Deference is set aside."

"Not while I'm in the room," Van Steward said.

"The High Council hasn't ruled on this, Helaina," Staned reminded her. "You cannot call a Convocation of Seats without a unanimous vote of the Council."

Artixan lifted a finger. "That's not entirely correct. The regent alone holds the power to call a Convocation. She may seek the wisdom of the Council, but it is not a matter to be voted on, let alone requiring unanimity. You know this, Roth."

The leader of the League glared at the Sheason. "It's not an authority the regent can claim in these times. Once, yes. But that was long ago, when superstition ruled the wits of men . . . and women. Calling a Convocation of every ruling seat, nation, and kingdom cannot be the capricious act of a single individual. Right actions must come by the consent of even the most conscientious objector. If they're right, they will prove out. That is the civility we've grown to. Let us not devolve because of a few stories out of the west."

The regent finally turned. "You don't believe Quietgiven have descended into the land, Roth? Didn't you hear the stories related to the High Council just now? What else explains them?"

"Dear lady." The Ascendant softened his tone, resuming a politic air. "Fear of the Quiet runs deep in the race of men. We were all raised on the stories. But what we heard could be a hundred nightmares confused with Quiet. Will you displace so many kings and rulers without certainty? Suppose you recall the Convocation after so many thousands of years . . . and you are wrong. What then?"

"I should rather think that prudence and solidarity would make an acceptable reason," the regent fired back. "Whatever the threat, a broad agreement throughout the Eastlands would serve all interests."

"Except the interests of a man who would have that power for himself," Van Steward offered.

Roth turned on the general. "Do you wish to say something to me directly?"

Van Steward stared back with the glare of a man who could no longer be threatened. "When at last I wish to do anything concerning you, it won't be to talk."

Roth Staned turned back to the regent, undeterred. "I appeal to your wisdom, Helaina. The other members of the Council are deferring to you out of respect and duty. They're well meaning, but they are not rulers, or even leaders. They're caught in the fear that grips a tiller or fisher, because these are the people they represent. But reason today resides in the places of learning and progress. Don't let all we've worked for pass away with a choice that smacks of superstition or shibboleth."

The regent didn't immediately speak. She noted the thoughtful look of her most trusted advisor, Artixan, whose heavy brow told her all she needed to know of his opinion. Then she cast her gaze at her general, an iron-willed man the left side of whose face bore three severe scars that ran down his forehead and cheek like white runnels. Van Steward was harder to read, since his place was to receive an order without question. But when the man dropped his chin ever so slightly in a half nod, she knew his mind, too.

Leaving only the Ascendant, Roth Staned.

He was an intelligent man, one she believed always represented the people's best interest, at least as he saw it. And for that, she was grateful. But he'd not been successful in turning the Council to his view of the rumors. And so he'd stormed after her when the Council was dismissed. He challenged her now because she had rejected his proposal to wait for evidence of the Quiet before committing to recalling the Convocation of Seats.

He did this, she knew, because when it was all said and done, he wanted to possess the chair of the High Office, and couple his rule of the League with the regent's seat.

Political maneuverings. *I'm too damned old for this.*

An oppressive silence had settled over the room. It bore the weight of choices that would take a heavy toll on the lives of countless men and women and children. Today, the people had no worry that the darker side of history could come back upon them: no fear of Quietgiven returning to the land, no concern that legends might actually be true. Most of the tales were no longer even recited in the streets of Recityv; the League had a hand in that.

She finally returned Van Steward's nod. The general swept past Staned to the door and spoke a soft summons into the hall. Shortly a dozen young boys entered with caged shrikes.

"Roth—" she began.

The Ascendant held up a hand to stop her. "Do this if you wish," he said. "But you should know I intend to formally call for an end of the Song of Suffering. I may not be able to stop Convocation, or agree with your reasons for calling it. But the superstitious practices in *this* city are something I *can* do something about."

Roth showed them all a condescending smile and strode out, his heels tattooing the marbled floor in a quick, mocking rhythm.

Roth's intention struck a new fear in her heart. Convocation was an attempt to prepare a military response *if* the Quiet somehow breached the Veil in force. If Suffering ended, there could be no doubt. The Quiet would roll into the east like a tide.

Artixan and Van Steward held grave looks at this new League plan. She needed them focused. "We'll fight Roth on Suffering in the Council. For now, we need to concentrate on preparing for Convocation." Artixan and Van Steward nodded.

She signaled to the boys holding their bird cages, and the shrikes were set free from the windows of her High Office. The flutter of wings echoed from the hard marble walls as the birds escaped into the sky, angling in every direction from her eight windows.

"Send the riders and criers, as well," she said to Van Steward. "Every nation and king will be offered their seat again. And let's hope this is the last time."

Together, the three watched the birds fly until they could no longer be seen.

Will the rulers of men answer the call? she asked herself. The answer to that question was less certain than she might have hoped.

• CHAPTER FIVE •

Hot Water

Your effectiveness in battle will double when you come to understand that your weapon isn't what you hold in your hand. It's you. And your effectiveness will double again when you lose regard for yourself.

—Preceding Principle to the Latae combat dances of the Far

*T*he sun burned low in an azure sky. Tahn coughed and spat up blood. Waves *of pain rolled across his chest and back and made him sick again. He dry heaved several times, most of his dinner already spewed beneath him. He shifted on the ground among dead sage, raising plumes of dust into his mouth and nose. He coughed up more blood. Looking west, past the legs of his attackers, he saw a figure. A silhouette of a man stood against the horizon. Watching.*

Heat shimmered as it rose off the plain. Was the silhouette a mirage?

Anger grew inside him.

He crawled toward the figure. He didn't get far before boots laid into him again. They knocked the wind from his lungs. He collapsed to the ground, tasting the fallow, barren soil.

What he wouldn't give for his bow right now.

Dust filled his nose and throat, and the sweat on his brow ran dirty into his eyes, biting with salt and grit.

He blinked against the sting, and wiped his face with his sleeve. The stumps of a few trees long dead, bleached white and forming jagged patterns, jutted up like gravestones amidst patches of dry grass.

The dreary plain continued, heat shimmering at the line of earthsky. Shimmering around the silhouette . . .

"You bastard!"

Someone grabbed and shook him.

His scream died in his throat and he looked up into Sutter's questioning eyes. "Must have been one hell of a dream, yeah? Who's the 'bastard'?"

Tahn stared, disoriented. "I'm not sure."

He'd been in a fight of some kind. But against who? For what? His mind reeled in the wake of it . . . begun when the Velle had found a resonant note inside him.

"How are you feeling? Still sore from your tussle with the Quiet?" Sutter asked.

Tahn had gone back to bed after their talk with Jamis. He sat up, wincing some with the effort. "I feel like one big bruise. Inside and out."

"Wonderful," Sutter said, mischief in his eyes. "Wait until you see what I've found us."

Half an hour before sundown they slipped naked into a natural hot-water spring not twenty strides from the bluff's edge. It felt damn good to ease muscles they'd been working for weeks without rest. Not to mention the deeper ache and shiver inside himself.

Sutter splashed Tahn in the face. "Silent gods, it's like water boiled over the pit." He leaned back, his head lolling against the bank. Together they watched the water steam in the evening sun and let the strains ease from their bodies.

"I wish my da could be sitting here." Sutter smiled sadly. "He could use a good hot soak."

"Earns it every day," Tahn agreed.

"Can hoe a furrow faster than any two other men at the same time," Sutter quipped.

Tahn scrubbed his face. "That's not what I meant."

"I know. But it's still true." Sutter grinned, and stretched his arms. "It's a good ache, don't you think?"

"Oh, yeah, wonderful, Nails." "Nails" was Tahn's nickname for Sutter, whose fingernails, on account of him being a rootdigger, always looked like dark crescent moons at the tips.

"Truly, Woodchuck," Sutter replied. "Woodchuck" because Tahn spent so many hours in the woods hunting. "I haven't used the sword skills the townsmen taught us . . . well, since they taught us. Makes me wish I'd kept practicing."

Tahn was still sharp with his bow. Constant use. But he knew what Sutter meant.

"I know this is all serious." Sutter pointed back toward the Sedagin city. "But wasn't that what the Change is about? Things getting more serious?" He stood, raising his arm in theatrical fashion, like a pageant wagon player might. "Taking life in hand. Being responsible." He laughed and sat back down. "Did you intend to put meat in Hambley's storehouse forever?"

Tahn raised his brows in thought. "And who's going to play the part of First Steward at your Standing? Now that you're off your da's farm and finally have your adventure."

The question caught Sutter off guard. "Hadn't thought of that." He tapped his lip. "But I'll figure it out. What about you? Maybe our charming Sheason?"

Tahn laughed. "Was going to ask your da," he said as their smiles faded. Then he finally asked, "Why didn't you tell me you were adopted?" The fact had come up unexpectedly as they'd left home.

The question hung in the air between them, and for several moments Sutter didn't respond.

"Not sure how to say it," Sutter began. "Sometimes I felt ashamed. Always felt lucky to have a home at all. I wanted to tell you. But what do you say when your parents leave you because they have something else they'd rather do? Because they play skits on a pageant wagon and can't be bothered." He paused, shrugged. "What difference does it make, anyway?"

"None to me . . . *Nails*," Tahn said, trying to lighten the mood. "But all this time I could have been calling you 'orphan Nails,' or 'vagabond Nails,' or 'Nails, the homely abandoned waif.'"

Sutter laughed. "Believe me, I have names for the shitheaps who left me behind."

Tahn saw something in Sutter's eyes when he said it. He got the feeling maybe part of Sutter's desire to leave the Hollows was to track his birth parents down. Or maybe it was something else he saw in his friend's distant look. Whatever it was, Sutter kept it to himself.

They fell silent, until approaching footsteps brought Mira into view. She came to the hot pool, and without a word started removing her clothes.

Tahn and Sutter could do nothing but stare.

If Tahn had thought she was beautiful before, this defied every dream he'd ever had. He became suddenly aware of his own nakedness, and his bodily reactions to seeing her this way. Sutter gaped, wide-eyed and slack-jawed. Tahn wanted to cover Sutter's eyes, but realized how stupid it would look.

Despite their gawking, Mira didn't appear the least bit inhibited or embarrassed. Nor was she clumsy or rushed. She placed her things out of the way and set her blades near the pool's edge, within reach. She then slipped into the hot water, and traded looks with them. Her expression was one of confusion or wonder over Tahn and Sutter's sudden silence and attention.

She gave a patient sigh. "I see neither of you are used to seeing a female bare."

Sutter said something unintelligible.

Tahn caught that slightest of smiles on the Far's lips. He looked through the steam rising off the water between them, and could think of just one thing to say: "Subtle."

It was the first time he'd ever heard her laugh. The sound of it could break a man's heart, or make of him the best self he had to offer.

When her laugh had receded she explained. "The unclothed body is not as . . . *noteworthy* in my country as it is in the kingdoms of men. Our customs aren't the same."

"Suddenly glad the Quiet chased us out of the Hollows," Sutter quipped.

Which reminded Tahn of something he'd heard Vendanj say that morning. He looked at Mira. "Why did Vendanj call the Hollows 'the Hallows'?"

Mira eyed them both.

"Tell us already; I'm getting to look like Merid Lavia's sunned fruits in here." Sutter held up his fingers, showing them his wrinkled skin.

"The First Ones knew the Quiet might eventually breach the Veil." She nodded at the logic. "So they consecrated a place where the Quiet couldn't walk, or Velle render. The soil was sanctified."

Mira paused, cupping a handful of water and dripping it back into the pool.

The Hollows had been Tahn's home since he could remember. *Sanctified by the Framers?* He stared, a bit dumbstruck, and more than a bit chilled.

Sutter seemed to have forgotten his concern for his shriveled fingers, examining them instead like newly found jewels. "The soil . . ." he muttered.

"With time, the Hallows lost its name. Became the Hollows." Looking at Sutter she added, "I suspect its purpose was mostly forgotten, too."

"I suspect its purpose was *lost*," Tahn countered. "The Quiet walked right into my home. Nearly killed Wendra."

Sutter shook his head with irritation. "You two are ruining my hot soak." He shared a quick look with Tahn: *Going to give you two some time alone. And naked!* Then he climbed from the hot spring, clumsily hiding his manhood as he pulled on his trousers, and headed back toward the city.

Before Sutter had disappeared, a dark bird flew into the light of the setting sun. At a fair distance, it still seemed headed toward them. They watched it for a few moments.

Tahn had managed a handful of private conversations with Mira in the weeks before. He'd even stolen a kiss. A wooden, clumsy thing on his part. But he'd made her smile. Damn good wages. But right now, his head spun with stories of the Far.

"Is it true you live a short life?" He stopped, wishing he'd framed his question better, and started again. "I mean, the stories say the Far are fast in life and fast in death."

She smiled in that slight way that made her look beautiful and dangerous all at once. "That sounds like an author's pen. But it's essentially true. My people keep an old covenant. We watch over the language of the Framers."

The Covenant Tongue is real. It still struck him. Every time he heard it, it struck him. A language with inherent power. A language used by the First Ones to create the world. Tillinghast might be their destination, but Vendanj had told them they must also find a way to bring the Language back. To use it against the Quiet. That meant a few stops along the way, including Mira's home in Naltus Far.

"We keep it safe," she continued, "until it might be needed."

"Like now," Tahn said.

"Perhaps," Mira replied, seeming less sure than Vendanj about it. "And in trade for protecting the Language, we never pass the age of accountability—what you call the Change."

Tahn gave her a sympathetic look. "I'd say you're cheated of your best years."

"It lets us do what's necessary to protect the Language without worrying about the costs." She nodded matter-of-factly. "We move on to the next life before accountability. I like the trade."

The bird grew larger against the russet hues of dusk.

"Then, you really are . . ."

"I still have a few years left." She made it sound like a lifetime.

All *his* life he'd just wanted to reach the damn Change so that he could be taken seriously, could have his choices *matter,* could find a girl. . . . "Maybe it's the Hollows in me, but it doesn't sound like much of a bargain."

She gave him another patient look. "Most folk I meet, whatever their race, only fight *not* to die. Or to keep others from dying. Maybe that's because they don't have a sense of what comes after death." Her patient expression turned quizzical. "It's not that I don't value my life. But I don't fight in fear of losing it, either. The undying life after this world will be a sweet refrain." In the soft shadows of the failing light, her face looked peaceful.

Tahn gathered the image of her in that moment to hold in his mind.

"You sound eager to get there," Tahn observed. "I'll take my time, if you don't mind." He smiled and rubbed at his bruised ribs.

Mira slid closer and corrected his motion. "Rub from the outside in." Her hands on his skin made his heart pound along like a barrel drum.

Then she looked up and caught his eye. "Man's problem is he's selfish. Try not to be like the rest, will you?" She smiled, but he knew she meant what she'd said.

She looked away at the approaching bird for a moment, her gaze mild in a way he hadn't seen before.

He'd never spoken to a girl or woman like this, except for maybe Wendra. And when she looked back, he kissed her. Less awkward this time, despite sitting nude in a hot spring in the full light of sunset. And she didn't let go the kiss, either. Instead, she looked back at him with a mix of understanding and approval . . . and amusement.

Still smiling, she said, "Not a selfish kiss—"

"Because you wanted me to," Tahn finished, and offered his own smile.

The bird began to descend toward them. Tahn hefted a nearby stone to chase it away. But Mira put a gentle hand over his to lower his arm. He thrilled again at her touch, though a bit confused. The raven lit upon the edge of the hot spring, and cawed into the twilight.

"Do you also have some husbandry gift I don't know about?" Tahn laughed as the bird shifted around to look at him.

Mira stared at the raven. "It's a message from home."

"There's nothing tied to its feet." Tahn looked more closely to be sure he hadn't missed it.

"The bird itself tells the news." The look in Mira's eyes changed again. Not the quick, appraising cast she most often wore, nor the softer faraway look Tahn had just seen. This was the look of grief, and the difficult choices that often follow it.

"What does it mean?"

"It means my sister, the Far queen, has passed this life. It means I have a choice of my own to make. And it might mean you'll go to Tillinghast without me." She said it with new weight in her voice, as one mourning more than mere death.

She said she didn't fear death, though.

Mira shooed the bird back into the sky and they watched it wheel away north and east.

When the bird had faded from view, Mira climbed from the warm pool and began to dress. She would miss Lyra—her sister had possessed the good sense to go slow. Not an easy thing for a Far. Lyra went slow when reassurance was needed, or when memories were being made. It was unique wisdom.

But more than missing Lyra, Mira felt like a hypocrite. She'd told Tahn that mankind was selfish. But she wished her sister hadn't died because the woman hadn't produced an heir. And the last thing Mira wanted to do was perform that task.

The short life of a Far meant she would never truly be a child's mother. Give birth, perhaps. But never live to raise that child.

There had been a string of caregivers who'd used that term—*mother*—with Mira all her life. But each was only around a short time before going to her final earth, replaced by another *mother*.

By every silent god, she would not do that to a child. It's why she'd left the Soliel with Vendanj years ago.

She glanced at Tahn, who was pulling on his boots as he watched her. He said nothing, though his eyes were alive with questions. She liked him for that. For keeping quiet when he itched for answers.

Moments later, they walked back into the heart of Teheale: *earned in blood*.

• CHAPTER SIX •

Dances

Remembering is a weapon. Sadly, we mostly use it on ourselves. Damn shame, that. But it doesn't have to be so. You can put a deep hitch in a man if you'll just remind him of something he's forgot.

—Captured in the thin volume known as *Barstool Wisdom,* a collection of battlefield insights compiled by Timmony Sewel, chronicler of the Wynstout survivors from the fight at Luhim's Pass

The sun danced on the treetops, filling the plain with golden hues and sepia shadows. To the west, smoke rose from countless fires. Braethen and the others followed Vendanj toward the smoke, and shortly the plain opened up onto a broad expanse of closely shorn grass. Large pits had been dug into the ground, each one tiered and lined with stone. Great fires burned there, and tables, filled with food and pitchers of drink, were set around the flames. Children chased one another about the tables, sounds of their merriment giving it all an easy feeling—the family kind.

They drew near the table where Jamis sat holding a small girl on his lap.

"My daughter," he said as they approached. A woman came forward and took the girl from Jamis. "And my love, Sonja," he finished, introducing her.

The woman bowed her head slightly. "Sheason," she said, then turned to Braethen and bowed again. "Sodalist."

It was the first time someone had shown him any deference for being a part of the Sodality. It put him a bit off balance. Beside him, Sutter stuck a thumb in Tahn's back to take note—not of Sonja's acknowledgement, but her striking beauty. That righted Braethen, seeing something normal.

"Let's begin," Jamis announced. He went to the fire and raised a pole bearing the Sedagin banner—one of their longblades held aloft by a right arm. In turn, someone at each fire raised the same standard. "Tonight, we celebrate the company of one who wears the three-ring symbol, and his sodalist companion. They remind us of our oath."

The entire company fell silent. Thousands of Sedagin. Even the children quieted. There was no movement, no cough, no whisper. All eyes turned west. And Jamis himself, leader of the Table of Blades, watched the horizon, patiently waiting for something.

Vendanj watched, too, the fading sun catching the three-ring sigil in the hollow of his neck. Three successively smaller circles, each inside the next, all joined at one point. Almost like ripples on water. The glyph indicated inner resonance, vibrations moving outward from one to touch many.

Staring at the symbol, Braethen fingered his own emblem, newly taken—a quill dancing along the flat edge of a blade. Knowledge and might.

A moment later, the sun dipped completely below the horizon, and blue shadows fell across the plain. In the long silence, only the fire could be heard, though Braethen felt reverence all around him.

Jamis lifted his cup. "Drink now," he said. "And enjoy this moment of peace."

Every glass was lifted into the twilight, and all drank.

Braethen and the others were invited to sit at Jamis's table. They ate roast pheasant and potatoes, speaking of uncomplicated things as night came on. The sky lit with stars. The fires glowed brightly and kept the chill at bay. Laughter rose from the plain with sparks from the flames.

"So, you're new to your oath." Jamis filled Braethen's cup for him.

"A few weeks," Braethen admitted. "But I've been studying it all my life."

"Son of an author. An author of some reputation," Vendanj added, putting a hand on Braethen's shoulder.

Jamis's eyebrows rose. "Surprising that you didn't follow the Author's Way, then. Most authors' sons do."

They couldn't know how raw a topic this was for Braethen. His father, Author Posian—A'Posian as tradition went—had indeed wanted Braethen to follow the path. Had groomed him for it. Twenty-six years of grooming. Braethen could still see the disappointment in his da's face when he'd told him he was leaving home to go with a Sheason. In hopes of becoming a sodalist.

Braethen half-smiled, trying to end the conversation. "I suppose I just preferred a different oath."

"A fighting kind," Jamis pressed, wearing a half grin of his own. "Binding you to this one." He raised his cup toward Vendanj. "You have interesting luck."

Vendanj laughed softly. "Braethen's oath is binding in the same way yours is." He raised his cup back to Jamis. "It's the extent to which you keep it." He turned to Braethen, and added an advisement. "It's not compulsory."

Braethen knew as much. But he suddenly needed to be sure they understood his reasons for leaving his father behind, and taking up steel—something Hollows men learned but rarely needed to master.

Quietly, but with firmness he recited: "Change is inevitable and necessary, but the traditions of our fathers need to be preserved. Some must watch. Some must remember. Some must defend. And some must die."

When he looked up, the whole table was staring at him. He didn't shrug or offer a sheepish smile. He might not yet be masterful with the blade-half of his own emblem, but he knew its quill like he'd pulled it from his own skin. So, he met their eyes with steadiness. He even kept a private smile from his face. *How many of them know that "some" is the Dimnian root for the fraction "one-fourth." Thus the oath tells of the four parts of being a sodalist.*

When most of the table had returned to conversation, Jamis and Vendanj were still staring at him. "I think you tied into a good one, here," Jamis offered, nodding toward Braethen.

Vendanj's face held its familiar hard and scrutinizing expression. The Sheason then slowly placed something on the table between him and Braethen. Long and wrapped in aged leathers, it wasn't hard to guess what it was. In general, anyway.

Braethen gently folded back the edges of the wraps to reveal the sword. Even in the dim firelight, it appeared unfinished. The metal was dark, as though left in the midst of being tempered. It gave the impression of being half forged. Portions of its edges were clearly blunt.

And yet Jamis's jaw hung slack. "Dear dead gods. Is that what I think it is?"

Vendanj kept focused on Braethen. "The Blade of Seasons, Braethen. I want you to wear it. Use it."

He'd read about the weapon. But honestly, it had seemed a fiction. "What should I know about it?"

"You're remembering storybooks," Vendanj said. He placed a hand on the weapon's handle. "This won't make you a slayer. Not its purpose, anyway." He looked down the long, unrefined edge of the thing. "That's why it's forged and refined only so far. The blade is more about remembering. Goes well with your histories. The ones you brought with you. The Reader's books." He smiled and flipped the leathers back over the blade, covering it.

Braethen felt a pang of loss for the Reader, Ogea. He'd been a good friend who'd died not long ago, leaving him his satchels of books to care for. Braethen's emblem took new meaning: the sword and quill.

"Much of its value," Vendanj said, speaking softly, "will be clear to you when you put it to use." He gave Braethen a reassuring pat on the arm.

Jamis gathered both Vendanj and Braethen's attention. "I'm not sure *any* weapon is going to keep you safe from the League, if you insist on going to Recityv." He waved his hand in a circle around his head. "Every city near the Teheale has seen Sheason executed on the authority of the League's Civilization Order. I think," he added, "the regent's Convocation comes too late. The League, in ways that matter, is already the law."

"That's bitterness talking," Vendanj returned sharply. "Helaina's no dog to be led. And we're going through the Scarred Lands. To ask Grant to come with us. He keeps his own counsel about the law."

"Keeps his own *law*," Jamis corrected. "The League won't have much use for him. Any more than it had for your pageant boy here."

Penit had been listening intently to everything they said.

Vendanj sighed, seeming to remember he was the guest of honor, but added, "Need I remind you I'm not much for good citizenry anyway."

Jamis laughed. "It would seem we *both* have a gift for understatement."

"Truer than you know." Vendanj leaned closer to the Sedagin leader. "And Grant is only part of it."

Jamis sat listening, his eyes on Braethen.

"I want Convocation to succeed"—Vendanj spoke with reservation—"but we can't place all our hope there."

Understanding entered Jamis's eyes. Wonder and worry. He turned, speaking as though this were an old conversation. "The Covenant Tongue," he said softly.

Vendanj nodded.

"Have the scriveners deciphered it?" Jamis asked, his tone cautiously hopeful.

"Small pieces," the Sheason replied. "We'll visit the library at Qum'rahm'se on our way to Recityv. They keep the Tract of Desolation there. It's our best source of the Language."

"But it's still not everything we'll need to know," Jamis said, as one reminding a friend.

"Which is why we're going to Naltus after we've spoken to the regent." Vendanj looked at Mira. "The Far still keep their part safe."

Jamis eyed Vendanj closely. "Do you think Elan will let it be used?"

Vendanj scrubbed his face with his hands, as one might who's considering a long road. "I don't think he has a choice. But between the scriveners and the Far, we may have enough to retranslate the Tract of Desolation, and hopefully strengthen the Veil."

"But even that's not all, is it?" Jamis said.

Vendanj stared across at his old friend. "If the Quiet break free, perhaps the Covenant Tongue can be used . . . as a weapon."

When the food was nearly gone, several musicians began to play and people started to dance near the fires.

"Woodchuck, I could get used to this." Sutter popped several raspberries into his mouth.

"A man who sniffs the dirt is an easy man to please," Tahn said, distracted by a sudden idea.

Sutter poked him in the side and resumed his meal with vigor.

Taking his lead from other tables, Tahn got up and went around to Wendra. "Care to join me in a dance?"

She looked up at him, reticent.

"Please," he added. He'd been waiting a long time for a good excuse to talk to her, figuring out what to say. Or maybe *how* to say it.

A reluctant smile touched her lips and she took his hand. A few strides away, they began to imitate the dance steps of the others.

He watched her as they turned in slow circles. It took her a while before she met his eyes. Then, he said simply, "I'm sorry."

Firelight caught in her eyes, which welled with tears. She shook her head.

"It's these damned words, Wendra. This . . . feeling." He paused, realizing he'd never shared any of it with her. Partly because he'd sensed he shouldn't. Partly because it was embarrassing. "Every time I lift my bow, it's like I have to ask if I can let the arrow go."

Her eyes shifted from pained remembrance to something hotter. More angry. "And you decided not to shoot the Quiet that took my child."

"I'm a horse's ass," Tahn said.

Wendra gave a sudden burst of laughter. There was something slightly manic about it.

"I wind up caught in the grip of the feeling that comes," he explained. "I hate that part of it."

They turned a few steps, and as always happened with Wendra, she found some compassion. It didn't mean her anger went away. She was a rare woman, capable of sympathizing with, even understanding, someone she didn't care for.

"It's why Vendanj asked you to come." She sniffed, settled into an easy rhythm. "And before you got to the cabin . . . my baby came still."

"Because of the Bar'dyn?" he asked.

She shrugged. "But by every abandoning god, I wanted you to shoot the bastard."

"You didn't have to come with us." Tahn looked into her eyes again. "Or did you come in hopes of seeing a Bar'dyn crush my neck?" He showed her a conciliatory smile.

Her laugh came more naturally, though not quite with full forgiveness. "I think maybe your neck is too stiff for crushing." She gave him a wry look. "The whole world isn't waiting around for you to shoot your bow. Vendanj asked me to come. Wants me to visit Descant Cathedral. It's a music conservatory. Said he'd heard I was fair with my voice."

Tahn nodded appreciatively. "You sing as well as Mother ever did."

They fell into a mutual remembrance, dancing slow. Wendra not quite ready to forgive, it seemed, but warmer. And Tahn relieved to have explained what happened, but still feeling a bit shackled by those words. *I draw with the strength—*

Sutter tapped Tahn on the shoulder. "I'd like a round with the lady. Stop being a hog." He looked to Wendra. "You game?"

She smiled and nodded.

"Here," Sutter said, and took Wendra's hand, spinning Tahn away and into Mira, who he'd been dancing with.

Seeing her so suddenly in front of him, she gave him the impression of purple logotes, a small stubborn wildflower that flourished where nothing else ever could—on the rocky, windy hills of Cali's North. He smiled at the image.

"You think you can keep up?" she asked.

Tahn took her hand just as the music changed to a slow tune played on a deep-pitched fiddle. He put his arms around Mira and they swayed in time with the music.

"You're not very good at this, are you?" Mira looked down where Tahn's feet had pinned her own to the grass.

"Just need more practice. I'd think you'd be used to that with me by now."

She smiled and they turned slowly under a canopy of stars.

"Your sister," Tahn asked. "Did she have children?"

Mira drew her head back and looked him in the eye. "You're a clumsy dancer, but you're perceptive."

"If she's a queen, and she's childless . . . you'll be expected to bear the line an heir. That's the decision you were talking about, isn't it?"

"It's possible. Authority means something different to the Far than it does to others. It's not dominion. Or even just leadership."

Her eyes held a distant look. She usually lived so completely in the present that to see her so distracted unsettled him. A young boy and girl, no more than eight, danced by, a bit fast and not in time with the tune.

"Do you want a family?" he asked.

The Far looked down at the children passing them. "It's not a question of what I want. I am Far. For us, even the most favorable conditions leave a mother but a very short time with her child. And our idea of family is different than yours."

Tahn caught her attention. "I didn't ask about all the Far. I asked about you."

Mira stared back at him. They'd stopped dancing, and now were sharing a set of impossible questions without speaking. And except for when she sat vigil in the depths of the night over his sleeping friends, it was the only time he could remember seeing her motionless. He believed her heart stirred, mostly because his own told him it must.

A desire and ache for what one might wish but could never have.

For them both.

But Tahn wouldn't let go the hope that had begun in his heart. Not yet.

Just before Sutter set to impress Wendra with his dance skills, he saw her rub her stomach with her free hand. It was a habit she'd developed while carrying her child. Was she even aware she was doing it? The motion clearly comforted her, and mentioning it would be a bad idea.

He smiled, took her other hand, and found the rhythm of the song. As good as he was with his fingers in the dirt, he thought his sense of dance was better. Hopefully it would put him on good footing when he came to his question. He'd wanted to ask about it for the better part of a year.

"How are you?" he began.

Wendra's gaze sharpened on him, her mouth almost a smile. "What do you really want to know?"

Sutter executed a perfect turn to a fiddle run. "You know how I feel about you—"

"You're not even through your Change yet," she said, letting her smile come.

"Yes, yes. I'm melura, sure. But . . . I want to set things right, Wendra. The man who . . . the man who . . . He needs to be held responsible. And I want to be the one to put his name before the townsmen."

Her smile faltered. And he wished he hadn't brought it up. What in all the names of dead gods had he been thinking, reminding her of her rape. She seemed angry, but also to understand his desire to help. She shook her head. Then her expression changed, softened. "If you want to do something for me, make me laugh. Here, sing me something to the fiddle. Your voice is awful."

He didn't waste a beat, and began to sing, making his usual bad attempt at song. And she did laugh, the sound of it musical in the midst of his own several clumsy efforts.

Over the next moments, he felt closer to her than he ever had.

Then someone tapped his shoulder. He turned to see a Sedagin man he didn't know.

"I'll have a turn with the lady," the other said, and started to move in.

"Not this time." Sutter angled between the man and Wendra.

The Sedagin raised a hand, and the music stopped. He stepped close. Sutter gently dropped Wendra's hand.

"You are low born," the Sedagin said with derision.

"I don't know what that means to you," Sutter replied, "but it sounds like an insult." He modulated his tone to threaten action.

"So the lowlander can reason," the other mocked. "But you don't deny a blades-man a turn with a woman." The man spoke like a court counselor.

Sutter looked for Tahn. He found him, locked eyes. The silent message was clear: *If you need help . . .*

Then he looked to their table, and found the face of the Sedagin lord—a ready contempt for what might come next. That turned Sutter's anger more black.

He'd throttled men for mocking his trade—always there were jokes about his dirty hands. But this. This somehow made him angrier. The interruption, the presumption of it.

"Hoping to find a friend to take your challenge for you?" the bladesman taunted, following Sutter's gaze.

Sutter shut his eyes, his jaw working as he bit back a retort. Another word and he might explode. He knew the foolishness of it, standing here in the middle of a plain *filled* with Sedagin. But by all hells, he would not yield on this. Not because he meant to prove himself a man to Wendra. Not because of the Seda-gin's arrogance or any of that.

But because he had to believe that a boy left by his parents to a life of root farming wasn't any less than a member of a blessed, vaunted nation with a glori-ous history of promises and honor in war. Otherwise he could have, should have, stayed in the Hollows.

A hush fell over the company, the plain now quiet as it had been during Jamis's toast. Only the sound of burning wood filled the air.

Sutter opened his eyes and shifted his gaze to the Sheason. Vendanj didn't appear ready to offer assistance. But somehow looking at the man he was reminded of his da, of something he'd taught Sutter a long while ago. *A good farmer lets the land tell him when it wants to yield.*

Sutter's jaw relaxed. His fists unclenched. A smile softened him further, and he looked back at the Sedagin standing close.

"And what of the *lady's* choice?" Sutter asked in a low voice, his words nearly lost in the crackle of the fire.

"You're suggesting she would rather dance with you than with one who is high born, given in blood to the Promise." The man chuckled.

Sutter choked back more anger, then shook his head. "So close to the sky, the sun has withered your wit," Sutter offered dryly. "I'm suggesting that *she* ought to have been asked, not *me*." He stepped closer, his face only the width of his fist from the Sedagin's nose. "What is this First Promise that you claim gives you rank above me? Is it possible that it was meant for such a use?" It was Sutter's turn to chuckle. "I think I've learned more honor nurturing life from my soil, than you have in all the grandeur of your sword and oath."

"You tread close to death, lowlander." The bladesman's face tightened, and he took a wider stance.

"Then we will have ourselves a fight," Sutter said evenly. "And either your arrogance will come to an end, or my dirty hands will fall defending the *will* of another. Poetic that it's a lowlander to do so, don't you think?"

Sutter counted himself a good fighter. Threshing-strong from eighteen seasons on his da's farm. But he was no match for the Sedagin's skill with a blade, if it came to that. Fear rippled through him.

The longblade reached for his sword.

Tahn was moving fast toward them.

"Hold," Vendanj said, speaking to Tahn.

"Or," Sutter said, his smile returning, "you could ask *Wendra* if she'd like to dance. Does your Promise allow for such civility?"

The man paused with his hand on the hilt of his blade. He looked across at Jamis, who nodded. The man unhanded his weapon and turned to Wendra. "Anais, would you care to dance?"

"Anais," the old term of respect for a woman. That's more like it.

Wendra's face shone as she looked at Sutter. Then she diplomatically answered, "Yes." The longblade took her hand and the music started again, as festive as before. Sutter was turning to leave when the bladesman grabbed him by the wrist. Sutter wheeled about, ready to fight. Before he could think to strike, the man forced something into his hand. Sutter looked down, confused. When he glanced up again, the Sedagin nodded and returned to his dance with Wendra. Sutter ambled back to the table and sat, inspecting the present.

Tahn was there a moment later, and leaned close, looking at the gift—one of the Sedagin gloves. A wide leather bracelet of deep green, a thin cord meant to loop up and around his third finger.

"You're expected to wear it," Jamis remarked. "Mutual respect."

Sutter put it on, and flexed his hand into a fist. Jamis appeared pleased, but he didn't speak of it again, returning to food and conversation.

"I thought you were going to lose your nails," Tahn said, as Sutter continued to study the odd glove. "You're lucky it didn't come to a fight."

"Maybe," Sutter replied, finally picking up the last of his wine and finishing it. "But they've never fought a man from the Hollows before." He laughed and re-filled his goblet.

Tahn shook his head, then shook Sutter's arm, splashing wine on them both. "What happened?"

"He wanted Wendra to dance. Forced himself in," Sutter said, trying to sound incredulous.

"So you defended your love," Tahn remarked, as one deducing a great mystery.

"What else?" Sutter smiled.

"And what if she takes a stronger liking to the longblade?"

"I'm sure his blade is the only thing about him that's long." He laughed. "Besides, I won the challenge, didn't I? I used his own virtue to defeat him." Then, softer, "I wish my father could have seen it." He flexed his hand again, pull-ing the string tight over his fist. "I think he'd have been proud."

The night deepened. And sometime later the musicians laid down their in-struments and took a break. In the lull, Wendra turned to Penit. "Let's have a story," she said. "Play one of the rhea-fols for us."

Sutter groaned. He'd never cared for the pageant wagon plays. Not since learning his birth parents had been troupers.

Penit's face lit up. He stood and rushed to the fireside. "What story do you wish?"

"Anything," Wendra said. "Something stirring. Something funny. Oh, you choose."

Penit eyed Vendanj and Jamis, as though something they might have said gave him an idea. He cleared his throat. Raised his chin, just as Sutter had seen him do atop his stage-wagon in Myrr. Then the words came, taking a form scripted by a gifted author, no doubt.

"Years ago," Penit began, with the tone of a storyteller, "the Great Court of Recityv convened to rule on the life of a man condemned, the people said, be-cause he held no *regard* for life." Penit took a step toward the fire, adopting an orator's pose.

Wendra chuckled enthusiastically. Tahn and Braethen smiled at the words so eloquently fashioned. Vendanj and Mira watched. The fire cast shadows around them.

"Go on," Wendra enthused.

With another tilt of his head, Penit resumed, this time raising an open hand to dramatize the tale. "Our man in this account stood beneath the weight of his accusation, while the gentry, the ruling seats, and the merchant classes all looked on." Penit lowered his voice to a whisper. "And the words he spoke are said to reverberate still in the Great Court of Recityv.

"And so it goes," Penit said, as if ready to tell one of the greatest rhea-fols he knew.

• CHAPTER SEVEN •

Rhea-Fol

A Sheason's authority to render the Will—to cause change in body and spirit—isn't license to do as he pleases. For example, the dead should remain dead, no matter how painful to those left alive. To do elsewise is to arrogate to godhood.

—From *The Tenets of Influence,* a mastery work
in the Sheason canon

And so it goes," Penit said, and turned a circle where he stood. When he'd made one full round he held a grave expression and tightly folded arms, his eyes stern and turned earthward toward the fire. The flicker of the flames lent much to the look of condemnation the boy wore.

"You are accused here of high treason, Denolan SeFeery," Penit said with a surprisingly authoritative voice. "You are aware of the crimes that bring you here?"

Penit turned a circle—a character change—and stared upward into the starry night, defiance clear in the set of his chin. "I know why you've brought me here, my lady," Penit said with firm resolve and a second adopted voice, this one calm but implacable. "But it's your arrogance and ignorance that call my actions *crimes.* Stop these proceedings before you condemn yourselves in your haste to place blame. I'm no traitor."

Penit whirled, again with arms folded. "Enough!" The vehemence of the command caught Tahn off guard. "You will answer as you are asked, and nothing more." Penit pointed an accusatory finger toward the fire, disgust curling his upper lip.

"There is ample evidence that I might wish to forgo these . . . pleasantries . . . but *I* will obey the law before all else. Counselor, lead on."

Penit turned again, dust pluming at his feet and drawn into the stream of heat now rising from the fire. He spun to a new stance two paces from where he'd been, a calm, calculating expression in his features—the counselor. "Two nights ago our good and noble regent gave birth to a child. Trumpets heralded the arrival. Celebrations had begun. But a secret was kept by the regent's closest servants." Penit paused, his eyes narrowing further. "The child arrived without breath."

Penit spun in one long turn back to the place of the accused. With an upturned face and the poise of one beyond his years, he said, "These words weave a deception meant to demonize me, my lady. No such jubilation existed in the city. The regent's child is not heir to her seat—"

Penit shuffled in a tight spin to his first position. "Silence." Clear hatred shot from Penit's eyes toward the fire. "You'll have your chance to speak. Now, go on, Counselor."

Again Penit turned, the cool, intelligent gaze returning. "Yes," he began, confident. "The child had no birthright to rule. That's not our way. But it's not the threat of losing a monarch that brings you here." Penit grinned with malice, and shook his head. "Rather, you must answer why you felt it your place to stop the restitution of that child's life by the benevolent abilities of the Order of Sheason. I might add, trying to stop the Sheason from saving the child is not so different from murder. For to take life and to prevent its reclamation are close cousins, are they not?" A snide look passed over Penit's face.

In the darkness, Vendanj appeared to scowl, his own arms crossed in front of him as he watched Penit's dramatic telling.

Penit again performed his circular dance, and landed in the guise of the accused. "Though framed as a question, sir, I take it you didn't mean it so. I'll leave the question to its own destruction by every man's common sense."

Once more the boy twisted around to the place of prosecutor, a thin haze of dust floating in the circle around his feet near the fire. "Very well. A semantic discussion for another time." Penit paced back and forth a few steps before cocking his head and staring inquisitively into the flames. "How is it that you knew where the ceremony would take place?"

Penit turned, this time more slowly, his form casting shadows. As a defendant he spoke toward the sky, "I lead the regent's Emerit guard."

Penit turned. "I see." His eyes shone as a child's that had captured something with which to play. "Then by her confidence, you knew when and where the Sheason would minister to the child to give it a chance at life. And with this knowledge you undertook not only to deny that chance, but to contravene the wishes of the regent. Is that," Penit said, raising a dubious brow, "also a weave of deception? Or have I fairly described the circumstance and your intentions in its regard?"

Tahn watched the change in expression take place as the boy came to the position of the accused. "It is . . . incomplete. It's true that there's little I didn't know about the affairs of the regent. And I became perhaps the only one able . . . or willing," Penit said as he looked back to where his questioner might be standing, "to tell her she was wrong."

Wendra and Sutter let out a gasp. Tahn found himself looking in the direction Penit did when addressing the judge, attempting to see the object of Penit's fancy.

For a long moment Penit let the words hang over the fire and his rapt listeners. When Tahn spied Vendanj again, the Sheason had not moved, shadow playing across his darkened features as the fire spat and surged, glinting dully over his three-ringed pendant. He knew the story; recognition was clear in his eyes. But something more rested there, something inexorable like floodwater in a spring of heavy rains.

Penit then stepped twice, gracefully completing his turn to change his guise back to the counselor. A thin smile spread on the boy's lips. "Tell her she was wrong, you say. With an adversary like you, SeFeery, I hardly need to present evidence here." Penit let his grin fall. "And in any case, wide is the gulf between the liberty to provide strong counsel . . . and taking measures to obstruct the regent's wish. We have witnesses to your actions. Do you wish to hear their testimony, or will you concede their words as truth?"

Penit twisted back and raised his eyes in calm compliance. "I've read their written testimonies. They are accounts of what *they* saw." One eyebrow rose as Penit said, "But I admonish the Court of Judicature on this point: They are of no use in determining whether my actions were *right*."

With a short step and a quick turn, Penit returned to his first position, a harsh glare on his face. "We're not here to determine if *you* believe in the correctness of your actions. Should we ignore the law in exchange for a criminal's earnest belief that he was justified in his crime?" Penit approached the fire and bent close. He glared down with disdain. "You, fellow, would be a handful of coins in an assassin's purse if I . . . could feel justified in my *actions*."

"It was *her* child," Wendra whispered in realization. "The judge is the regent herself. It was *her* child the man tried to keep dead." She looked over at Tahn, her eyes wide.

"The particulars are irrelevant," Penit continued as counselor. "You are privy to the most delicate information in the realm. You admit to speaking in open defiance to our lady. You accept the testimony of witnesses that describe your actions as contrary to the lady's wishes. And even now you place your ethics above the peaceful traditions of this Court of Judicature." Penit waved a hand as though to erase the insufferable image of the defendant, and stood up slowly from his slight crouch. "Do you deny any of this?"

Penit rounded deliberately, his face slackening to near tranquility. "Yes."

Braethen looked on at Penit, marveling at the story.

As the accused he explained. "This chamber hasn't been house to peaceful traditions since the First Promise. Solath Mahnus is a monument to possibilities, but today many of its chairs sit vacant in the council rooms. Bloodlines run diluted with the cowardice of *civility*." Penit widened his stance and looked heavenward, even more defiant. "We are men, women, and children. We are hopeful and able. We are grown in our understanding and have enjoyed peace for generations." Penit stopped. His eyes seemed to gather the light of stars. His voice softened, deepened. "But we are *not gods*."

A chill ran down Tahn's spine. Penit stood resolute, maintaining his fiction, eyes peering up at a judge no one could see.

A scowl rose on the Sheason's face.

Penit then whirled violently, his feet throwing rocks and dirt in a shower as he forced himself to a stop. "Such impudence! Such disrespect! How dare you say such things to our lady. You're a mule. I'll have you bound—"

Penit leapt, forgoing the turn. "Why do you assume I speak only of your lady? *No* one should claim the rights and powers of the First Ones. Such arrogance has consequences."

Penit slid to the spot of his fiction's regent. "We return to pride so often, it seems." Consternation slipped from his brow, replaced by pity. "Have you considered that trying to prevent the Sheason from restoring a life (as you did) is the same attempt to control life and death of which you accuse *us*? *You*," Penit shoved a regent's finger toward the fire, "are the one guilty of claiming godhood. You are a hypocrite. . . . You are a traitor."

A brief turn, and Penit raised his head. "To your law, perhaps. But I am not selfish."

Again Penit paused. Wood crackled and popped in the flames. Embers rose in orange flares against the night and winked out. The boy's words froze them all, the severity of the indictment casting a pall over the plain.

It's a simple rhea-fol, Tahn thought.

Penit completed a wide circle as he resumed the role of accuser. "Let us put an end to this," he said with a note of finality.

The boy gracefully took the place where he spoke in the voice of the regent, and frowned toward the fire with a look of melancholy. "You may make rebuttal if you so choose. I call on you to use discretion. But you mustn't feel constrained from sharing any information you believe has bearing in this Dissent. No matter the costs to others." Penit raised his brows, deeply furrowing his forehead. "You may speak freely. Do you understand?" Penit looked into the fire expectantly.

Then, another proud turn, and his head inclined toward the stars low on the southern horizon. He nodded, and adopted the most steadfast demeanor Tahn could imagine. "I tremble at what is about to take place here," Penit said in low, resigned tones.

"Hour after hour, for years I studied the art and tactics of combat. Became a student of the body: its movement, its capabilities, its purpose. My preparations made me valuable to the men and women who occupy Council seats. I've stood in attendance during court sessions and heard the life of a single man blithely dismissed. In higher, grander rooms, it was the lives of scores of men. And not soldiers alone, but the innocent people of a nation. People whose livelihoods turn on the decisions a few make around a banquet table." Penit swallowed, his throat thick with emotion. "All this I witnessed, but kept my hope in the simple balance of life, believing we yet choose our paths, and that the only real measure of our lives is our response to it."

Sutter was nodding. Wendra and Braethen, too. Vendanj waited, focused, as if wanting Penit to get the words right.

"But our attempts to define law are miserable," the accused declared with firm resolve. "They grow out of the mistaken belief that one group of people knows better than another. And we fail when we assume more authority than is rightly ours. It's inconvenient, this life. But to rob it of its sting is to deprive it of the very *reason* to live." Penit took a deep breath and looked about, capturing the eyes of each of his audience in turn, ending with Tahn.

Looking back to where the regent might be, he said, "I don't acknowledge the authority of this court to pass judgment on me. It's a body of men and women too steeped in their own traditions to acknowledge a higher law. I hereby grant myself amnesty from its ruling. Its deliberations have no bearing on my life. You do as you will. But I will grant myself freedom and liberty from this mockery."

Jamis sighed in sympathy for this man Penit played.

Vendanj stroked his beard with thumb and forefinger, a mix of admiration and disagreement in his face.

Penit turned a final time, retaking the first position of his narration. A resolute look stole over him, a look different from those of the other characters he'd portrayed. Staring at the fire, the boy began to speak in the voice of the regent. "I will excuse your blasphemy because I know you face a great challenge in reconciling justice with your own actions."

Glaring, Penit said, "You're no different than the host of men and women brought here who try to cover up their crimes or justify them because they fear their sentence." In an angrier tone, he continued, "I only regret that I took you into my confidence. Would you be so bold had you never been my Emerit? You've become the very sanctimonious nobility you despise."

Penit waved a dismissive hand. "I will abide no removal of the Council for deliberation. By a raise of hands I want a vote now on the dissenter's guilt." Penit cast his glance around. The boy's haunted expression as he looked about the fire circle chilled Tahn to the bone. Without seeing a single juror, he knew the vote.

With pleasure Penit announced, "The record will indicate unanimous conviction. Set the rest down as I now say." Penit raised his chin so that he might look down his nose at the flames, at the convicted. "For the crime of treason it is hereby declared that Denolan SeFeery is unfit for citizenship in the free city of Recityv. It is further known and witnessed to in this writ that Emerit SeFeery has willfully committed treason against the stewardship entrusted to him and against the right order of progress as held by the Higher Court of Judicature and the League of Civility.

"Denolan SeFeery is thus remanded to permanent exile, and in the interest of justice will be given a sentence in the emptiness known as the Scar.

"Anyone known to abet Denolan SeFeery will be adjudged a traitor like unto him and punished accordingly.

"From this day forward, Denolan SeFeery will no longer be referred to with the Emerit honors of his former office. And return to the free walls of Recityv shall be construed as an act of aggression and punished by immediate execution.

"And so it is," Penit ended, his final word at once the crack of a gavel and the sound of a closing book. All that was spoken hung in the air, daring contradiction. It came as an epitaph, like words one reads on the gravestone of a dead man. The night swallowed the feeling, absorbed it. Deafening silence remained, broken only by the hiss of wood.

Then with a touch of familiarity Penit leaned forward. He spoke in a sweet, conversational tone. "Death is too good for you, Denolan. In exile you will feel the weight of your crimes, and the barrenness of the Scar will remind you of the barrenness of my womb. There you will live. And what will keep you there? Your honor? A guard? An army?" Penit laughed caustically. "Hardly any of these. No, it will be the establishment of an orphanage for foundlings, castaways, the children of unfit parents. The very thing you hoped to prevent will be the tie that holds you to your heated rock. Derelict guardians will be forced to surrender their offspring to the Council, which will decide where the babes are to be reared. And to you will be sent a share. A tree will be hollowed as a waypoint and cradle at the edge of your domain. On an appointed day a child will be placed there, given into your care."

Penit went on with severe reproof. "And if you don't rescue these children from the tree, you will become the murderer you conspired two days ago to be. My officers will be watching; anyone other than you attempting to retrieve the children will be killed. What honor you still possess will fetter the sentence to you. If not," Penit's smile faded, his eyes blank in the firelight, "then the deaths of countless innocents will be yours.

"*Grant* yourself amnesty? *Grant* yourself freedom and liberty from this mockery? The mockery is yours, Denolan SeFeery. Mockery of life itself. I am done with you." Penit stopped and stared into the fire.

Glassy eyed, the boy did nothing more than raise his head heavenward, a last character change. "And I am done with you. My name in your mouth and the gossip of your court is like the sting of vipers. I won't answer to it again. I'm not accountable when your law is corrupt. When you violate the basic Charter of man. My obligation to you is done. I am free. I am clean . . . I am *Grant*."

A long silence stretched when Penit was done playing the rhea-fol. Eventually, it was clear he'd finished.

Tahn shared a look with Sutter, who whispered the questions he was thinking. "Is it true? Or is it a lot of exaggeration? And who's the child this Grant tried to keep dead?"

Tahn shrugged, and conversation lulled for a time. Eventually, the music started up again, and the somber rhea-fol was replaced by songs that gave a different voice to the same feeling.

CHAPTER EIGHT

Payment in Oaths

You know everything you need to know about a man by the way he treats his wife and child.

—Engraving in the lintel above the door at Hambley's Inn,
the Hollows

Grant walked in the early morning light, a cloak wrapped around his shoulders. He usually had no need of the garment. Not in the Scar. But here in the frost-covered hills at dawn, the chill had its bite. And the child he cradled close to his chest would have gotten cold.

The babe slept. And Grant neither hurried nor lingered, as he moved up the road beneath the overarching branches of sycamore, hemlock, and oak.

He knew his destination, and would arrive soon enough. So he kept a careful eye and a measured pace. When he came to the place, he wanted the infant rested.

He'd stopped to feed the babe several times a day. It made for slow going. But an end to that drew near. The man felt the pangs of relief and loss. As he always did.

He topped a rise and spied the small farm on a gradual slope a league distant. "Almost your time, little one," he whispered. "We'll see how you're received today. I hope you don't have to come back with me."

The child woke, as if knowing it was being spoken to. Quiet and thoughtful the way a babe can often be, it stared up into Grant's sun-worn face.

"But we must talk with them first," Grant continued. "Let's pray they have means."

The child, still less than two weeks from its mother's womb, stared, content. For the briefest of moments it appeared to understand his words. But her unfocused eyes soon turned in a new direction, and he turned himself to the path ahead. He tried not to let the softness of the child's skin soften his resolve. This was the best thing for her.

Dew caught the radiance of dawn and shone back in a hundred points of bluish light. Long ago, in another life, he would have at least paused to consider the difference between his own life and that of the family he now approached.

He didn't stop.

A small road blocked by a meager gate announced the farm he'd been angling toward. Up the path he went, the child tucked close to his chest. Moments later he came to the back steps of the dwelling.

He always rapped at a home's *rear* door. Women and men who earned their way by the use of their hands rarely used the front entrance. Life turned on the axis of a home's back door—closest to the kitchen and fire and stories. And while some didn't recognize his subdued calling card (rear door and light knuckles), he felt it important that his errand have the appropriate level of solemnity and discretion.

Life: traded at the back doors of the world.

There were bargains to be made.

He rapped at this lintel, turning hard eyes on the yard as he cradled the child who began to stir. No chickens scratched at the packed earth; no cattle lowed in the field nearby. He worried these people didn't have the resources to meet his demands. But then, there were many forms of payment.

The door drew back and a young wife dried her hands on a towel hanging from her belt before taking his hand in greeting and fingering the token of the hillfolk. Then she glanced down at the child in his arms. The look in her eye told him all he needed to know. This woman would love and teach and protect this child.

This may go well, after all.

She stepped aside, indicating that he should enter.

Inside the house, he sat, resting his legs from his long journey. He surveyed the modest home, noting cleanliness, books, food. Shortly, the woman's husband stepped in: a large man with large hands. *Good.*

They bore each other company in silence for a long moment.

The woman spoke first. "Would you like some hot tea?"

Grant shook his head. "No. But the child could use some milk."

The woman turned to a table behind her and took up a carafe. She crossed the room and waited for him to surrender the little girl. With interest he did so, and watched as the woman took the child in her arms, sat, and removed her towel. She twisted it at one corner and dipped it in the milk, then offered it to the babe in imitation of nursing. The child went right to it.

Grant nodded with satisfaction.

Then her husband spoke. "We can't offer you much for the child."

Grant turned to gather the man's attention. "Payment isn't always made with coin. What's she worth to you?" The intimations were many, and Grant let them all hang in the air, ready to judge.

The hill-man stared back, seeming to consider. "She'll have a hard life here. Many . . . most don't live to see their stripling years."

"So your payment is uncertainty?" Grant looked back at the sure hand of the woman feeding the infant.

"The child won't go hungry," the hill-man replied. "I'll see to it. But beyond that, we've few promises here. And anything we give *you* will mean less for the child."

Grant stared with eyes that might have looked faded from so long under a heavy sun. His *own* wages in this affair were hard won. "Your assurances aren't grand, friend. There are others who have need of a healthy child like this one. A few days more on the road and I could return home with fuller pockets."

The hill-man didn't hesitate. "Choose that if you will. I've little use for quick hands to make a prize of a child. And at least you know I am no slaver. Some families would take the child and sell it to a highwayman. I can offer the little one my home, and the knowledge of the hills besides. I've no delusions. This is meager. And perhaps not the best place for the child after all. We'll have our own questions to answer about how she came to us and from whom. These won't be easy to avoid. And the truth brings its own risks to our home, if you take my meaning."

Association with Grant was a crime. "I do at that. But I've my own balances to keep." He stood. "For payment I'll have your oath. And trust that I'll call that marker if it's broken. The child's true parents, her origins, even me . . . we're all irrelevant now. No questions will you ask, or answer. And your commitment to the child will be the same as if she was your own."

The hill-man took three steps and put out his hand. The two clasped, and the hill-man wrapped his finger around Grant's thumb in the hillfolk token to seal his oath. The woman likewise nodded her assent. Grant went to the woman, whispering low, "She'll grow to greatness, if treated better than was her start." He put a hand on the child's head in farewell.

He then strode from the room without another look at either the new father or mother. Into the first light of dawn he went, his weathered skin warmed by the sun. He set his feet back upon the road.

He had leagues to go.

The hard light of midday beat down on Grant. But it couldn't injure his skin any more than his years in the Scar already had. He walked contented through the rolling hills, glad for the moment to be out of the Scar.

His contentment was shattered by angry shouts from the cottage he'd come to visit. He hastened his step, feeling an awful certainty of what he might find. He mounted the front stoop. Three voices—two belonged to adults, the other to a lad.

As he stopped to listen, a loud crack shot from inside the cabin. A fist striking the face of another, followed by the thump of someone falling to the cottage floor. A scream ripped through the windows and cracks in the cottage walls— the wail of a woman. Then another crack . . . and silence.

Grant pushed open the door.

Angry surprise registered on the face of a husband and father who stood panting at the room's center. On the floor to the right lay his woman, crying now, her head buried in her hands. On the left sat a boy of ten—a boy Grant had brought to this family long ago. The lad struggled to suppress his anger and fear and helplessness. A heavy welt purpled one side of the boy's face, the skin there also split. Blood dripped slowly down his cheek.

The lad lifted his gaze to Grant, and the two shared a long look. He knew its message. The boy wanted to be rescued. This moment of anger and abuse wasn't the first. But any intervention would have to be permanent, because anything less would only bring more beatings after Grant left the cottage.

Indignation flooded him. Grant had entrusted this boy to the man's care and safety.

He slowly turned his glare on this unworthy father, who stared back with defiance.

"It is *my* family. I will do as *I* see fit," the abuser said. "You've no authority here. Get out!"

Instead, Grant drew close, his arms alive in anticipation of violence. He allowed his nearness to be his threat, staring, saying nothing. The abuser's breath reeked not of bitter, but of some recent meal. This cruelty hadn't even the excuse of drink.

"Do you know how close you are to death?" Grant said softly. "Were it not for the family you've thrown down at your feet, I would end you here."

The abuser didn't yield his own ire. "I don't owe you anything. I've fed and clothed my own well enough. Don't you show up and play the hero. I've my own way of keeping things right around here. And you gave up any part in it the day you left the brat." His eyes darted at the lad. "So you can take yourself back to your desert. And you'd better hope I don't share it around that you've been here. Violation of your sentence, that is."

Grant shook his head in disgust and leaned in toward the man so that his nose touched the other's. "You're a fool. If I'm the criminal you suggest, what makes you believe I won't kill you to silence your gossip?"

"You've a double tongue," the abuser shouted back. "I won't be trapped—"

"It's your *family* that's trapped," Grant cut in. "Bound to you for food and safety. But instead you feed them fists and fear, when they would have the better part of you to learn and grow by."

Grant's wrath seethed in his words. "You'd be better to them dead than alive. At least then they'd have hope."

The abuser sneered. "Hope?"

In his mind Grant recalled countless children he'd carried into the care of others. It was always the same, hoping and fearing he would make the right choice of their guardianship.

This abuser was not the first to betray Grant's trust.

If his banishment could be more bitter, it was in moments like these.

And it was in these moments that the soil of his heart grew stonier, when he sought—with all his training from so long ago and honed by decades of practice since—not to protect, but to destroy.

Destroy a man that would harm his own family.

With that thought, guilt pricked the edges of his conscience. But he wouldn't let it stop him.

Grant gave the boy another long look. "Which is your father's strong arm?"

The lad's brow wrinkled. "His right."

Grant seized the abuser and ran him from the cottage. The other had no time to react or defend himself. Grant steered the derelict father deep into the trees and out of sight. The abuser protested loudly, swearing oaths and calling for help. His cries echoed back into the grove and were lost around knotted trunks and deep ravines.

Then Grant let him loose, his indignation boiling over.

The abuser whirled, whipping a fist around at Grant's head. Grant ducked and punched the man's chest, knocking his wind out.

But the abuser didn't give up so easily. He kicked at Grant's groin. Again Grant avoided the blow and drove a fist into the abuser's cheek—the same place the boy had been hit.

The other howled in pain and frustration, his eyes bright with rage.

Grant had lost his patience. He barreled the man to the ground, and in one lithe motion drew out his sword and cut off the man's left arm.

As the abuser screamed in shock and pain, Grant quickly cut a swath of the man's shirt and used it to stanch the flow of blood spurting from the stump of his arm. He then tied it off and stood up. The abuser groaned and cried for some time. Grant watched with unfeeling eyes.

When he thought he could be heard again over the abuser's softer cries, Grant took up the severed arm and held it between them. "You'll either redeem yourself with the arm I've left you, or I'll come again and find you. Don't fool yourself that you can take vengeance on your family and run. There's no place far enough I can't track you. And I've no other cause in life. If you ever trusted anything, trust that."

Grant then tossed the arm into the high grass and returned to the small home. He paused at the steps again, considering what he would say. But that was a brief moment, since he now knew only one way to speak, even to a woman and child.

He strode in and found the boy comforting his mother, who had gotten herself to a chair. The lad knelt before her holding her hands. Grant took one knee beside them, and sought their frightened eyes.

"He'll never lay another hand on you. And if ever you fear he might, remind him of this day." He then fixed his gaze on the lad. "You're going to be all right. I'm sorry for what's happened. But even that will give you mettle when you're grown, if you use it well."

He put a hand on the boy's shoulder to reassure him. Then he stood, nodded to them both, and returned to the road that had brought him to this shattered home. His only consolation was that at least these homes—and his own ward in the Scar—kept these children from the highwaymen who trafficked in human stock across the east.

• CHAPTER NINE •

Crones

A womb does not a mother make.

—Reminder spoken by highwaymen as they assess value

Jastail J'Vache led the woman and his men at an easy pace on the dark road. The stars shone bright enough to navigate by. And Jastail was close enough to his destination that he didn't want to set camp and waste another day. Besides, the night revealed yet another guise of the road, one he liked to savor.

A few hours more and they turned off the road. They followed a path so obscure that he'd never have seen it if he didn't know it was there.

Many times he'd come this way to visit the crone in her cottage. A place set back deep in the whispering aspens.

The night air rattled the leaves, lending their arrival the music of nature's applause. A dim glow could be seen behind heavy curtains at the window. A streamer of smoke rose in a silver wisp from the chimney above. She couldn't have been expecting them, but as they dismounted, the door opened quietly on a shadowy room.

Jastail ordered his men to tend the horses and pitch camp, as he took his captive by the arm and led her inside. He closed the door and turned, his keen eyes already adjusted to the dimness. The crone now sat in a rocker near the fire with knitting needles held in her knobby fingers. She worked bland yarn into what might become a shawl. The room seemed to press inward, confining them. It smelled of old age, of one who rarely gets beyond her door.

"Greetings," he said.

"And yourself, highwayman. What prize do you bring with you tonight?" The crone didn't turn, her eyes fixed on her knitting.

"I don't need much of you, and I apologize for the hour—"

"No you don't," she interrupted. "You're eager to have your answers. That's why you steer yourself through the shadows with this woman. But no matter. What will I have for your intrusion to make it worth my time? And don't play at lying with me. You're a good one at it, but I can see your deceptions, lest you forget why you come to me to begin with."

In the shadows of the crone's knitting room, the highwayman smiled to himself. He appreciated her directness and lack of moralizing. She'd removed herself from the company of others precisely because she lacked the grace of polite society. That, and her special talents, which he was sure others hadn't understood.

Special talents. The very reason for his visit.

"I have three bolts of fine cloth that are yours. And I've got a horse you may have if you've a use for it." He waited to see if his offer would prove agreeable.

"You've some ale, too, no doubt," she said. "I'll have everything you carry."

"Done."

Her fingers stopped, and her milky eyes turned. The woman recoiled from the crone's awful stare, and Jastail put a bracing arm around her shoulders.

"Bring her close." The crone's voice came softly, but cracked and thin, as if it had been abused somehow in her youth.

Jastail had to use some earnest force to get the woman moving toward the crone's rocking chair. Finally, he whispered in her ear, "Consider the old woman a healer. She'll do you no harm. Think carefully, what would it profit me to come all this way only to allow something to happen to you now?"

The woman stopped fighting, and he eased her toward the crone's chair. So close, in the glow of the firelight, he could see the hair on the crone's upper lip, which obviously meant nothing to her. The hag stared up at them both, her clouded sight never seeming to quite look either of them in the eye. Still, he knew a kind of *seeing* was taking place. Then she motioned for the woman to stand directly in front of her.

Jastail let the woman go, and stood back as the crone put her knobby fingers on the woman's stomach and began to grope around her breasts and hips and loins and thighs, slowly returning to the woman's navel with an awkward caress.

"What are you doing?" the woman finally asked, and tried to step away.

The crone's bony hand shot out and grasped the woman's wrist, holding her tight and near.

"This highwayman took me from my husband!" the woman yelled. "Why are you helping him? Where's your womanhood?"

The crone cackled dryly into the confines of her small room. Her milky eyes were almost youthful again with the light of humor. "Womanhood? Child, you're old enough to see the folly in claiming gender as a common bond with a stranger. No kind of defense, that."

"And *you're* old enough to know that I can find my way back here . . . with my husband. Who will not be kind." The captive stared at the crone with bright defiance and anger.

"Where was this husband of yours? Why did *he* not defend you?" A slight smile drew at one corner of the hag's mouth.

The woman looked at the highwayman, who stared back evenly. "He chose to live in hope of my rescue."

"I see. Well, if you come to ill use, then you both will revisit the prudence of that choice, won't you?" Then the frown of the aged and bitter stole over the crone's face. "I don't have time for this. Come closer or our highwayman will force you to it. Either way, child."

Several moments passed. Jastail relished the battling emotions he could see in the woman's face. The contest of indignation and acquiescence. He remembered it well from his own life. His mood darkened briefly at the thought. Then finally the woman approached the crone, who again put her hands on the woman's stomach.

As the night waned, the old woman began to mutter to herself as she slowly moved her wizened hands in circles over his captive's navel. The scene struck him as ceremonial after a fashion, the two women locked in a strange union. But it also smacked of rape in a way he couldn't describe.

Despite his need of both his captive and the crone, revulsion touched his mind in long remembrances of other women in small, dark rooms. Other women who used or *were* used in unholy transactions. He recalled the tight, painful feeling of those rooms. He could almost feel in his throat the unanswered sobbing prayers that he'd offered in them so long ago.

Those memories were interrupted when the crone stopped muttering and dropped her hands. His woman collapsed to her knees, spent. The hag took up the half-knitted shawl and used it to wipe at her brow and hairy lip before turning her clouded eyes back to Jastail.

"Get the bolts of cloth and the ale," the crone said.

"And the woman?" asked.

The crone shook her head. "Her womb is ruined. She'll not bear children. Never has. Never will."

"Are you sure? She doesn't look too old. And she has fire in her." Jastail didn't like to think that for all his effort he'd come up empty.

"Did you happen to notice any children when you snatched this one from her husband?" The crone's loose, wrinkled skin shrugged into an awful smile that showed gums bereft of teeth. "Something makes you hasty this time, highwayman. It's dirty work to seize the living. And it's worse when you get it wrong. Sometimes that can't be helped. But there are signs that may be read to increase your odds, eh, besides just seeing children about. You know them, I think. Make your gambles, but do it wisely." Her smile faded as she asked, "What makes you careless?"

Jastail looked deep into the milky eyes of the crone, his anger mounting. "Damn." He took a threatening step toward the hag and stopped. She wasn't to blame. He whirled on his captive, raising a fist. Someone must pay! His creditors wouldn't be lenient with *him*.

He nearly struck the woman down before realizing that damaged goods fetch lesser prices.

Jastail shot a glance back at the crone. She was right. He'd been working too fast of late. He'd gotten sloppy. But there were still bargains to be struck. Oaths to be fulfilled.

"Get the bolts of cloth . . . and the ale," the crone repeated, and went back to her knitting.

He stepped into the darkness beyond the door, where the aspen leaves whispered in the soughing wind. The slow, chill breeze touched his skin, cooling his anger. Already he yearned once more to take his chances. Tomorrow he'd go back to the road, where he would try again.

CHAPTER TEN

The Bottom of Pain

The difference between a player and a musician is honesty. Not craft or ability or experience. The listener hears it every time. And honesty is more quickly understood through suffering.

> —From the "First Lecture on Attunement,"
> taken in a Lyren's first cycle of music
> study at Descant Cathedral

Late in the night, when her companions had wandered off to bed, and all the Sedagin had done the same, Wendra remained, listening to the musicians. Scops. They were the last to leave a fire. Just like back home. They stayed on to play for each other. For themselves. Songs that they didn't air in the company of crowds.

The fire burned hot, but low, keeping her in shadows, unseen.

She listened. The songs were unlike any she'd heard in the Hollows. When they were bright they were boisterous; when proud, courageous; and when sad, they were piteous and plaintive. Here, it seemed, the music became more than a performance, it grew into an accusation or challenge. There was boldness in it that she hadn't heard before. Even through the troubles and madness since fleeing the Hollows—and before, back as far as her rape—Wendra was entranced by this new sound.

It made her think of the simple, dark melodies she'd found in recent months.

When the night at last found its end, the scops began to pack their instruments to leave. Wendra slid from her chair to catch the last two before they were gone.

"Thank you," she said. "You're very gifted."

A woman, still packing, looked over her shoulder at Wendra as her male counterpart turned to receive the accolades.

"You're most welcome, my young woman. Was there a particular song you liked?" He smiled and bowed in thanks for her praise.

His companion shook her head without turning again.

"The songs of loss. There was something soothing or comforting about them. I don't know. It seemed—"

"They didn't simply accept the pain, but demanded answers and retribution," he finished for her.

"Yes," Wendra said. "The music offered relief because it didn't simply wallow in grief and resentment."

"You're an astute listener. Are you a musician yourself?" The man looked Wendra top to bottom.

She understood then his designs, her stomach roiling at the thought. So, she was grateful when the scop woman chimed in. "If you are, don't waste any more breath on him," she said. "You'll want to talk to the composer, which would be me."

The woman hefted a lute case over her shoulder and came to stand beside her companion. "He's quick to accept the credit, however he can get it." She gave him a look of amused disgust. "But he's never around to help write the music we earn that credit by. What's your name, my young lady?"

"Wendra."

"I'm Solaena. This is Chrastof. He's got packing to do. Why don't you and I sit so I can rest my feet, wet my lips, and I can give you the advice my father never gave me." She waved a hand to dismiss Chrastof, who mocked being hurt, and went to put away flutes and drums.

Solaena and Wendra sat together, as the woman poured a tall glass of steaming tea from a pot she'd gathered from the fireside. She sipped, the warmth seeming to ease her features, and relaxed into her chair.

"If you find any fascination in playing songs to a crowd"—Solaena swept a hand toward the empty tables—"well, let me tell you, find another way to earn a coin. Most times we aren't paid. And precious few even listen. Around here, it's swords and oaths." She offered a tired smile. "Keep your music, my girl, but don't make it your life's path."

Wendra nodded appreciatively. But her questions weren't professional. "How do you make them? The songs that feel like anguish, not for its own sake but for justice."

The scop smiled. "I see. Well, that's just writing from my own heart's desire. I guess so late in the night it's tolerable to admit that I don't believe in the same things I did when I was your age. And maybe because I don't, I write about them in my songs to remind me of a time when I did. What I mean is, the songs are a place where I can give voice to my inmost wishes, even if the world around me doesn't hearken to my words. You understand?"

"I believe so. But the world does hear you. The Sedagin. Me."

A grateful smile touched Solaena's lips. "You're a dear heart, my girl. Thank you. And because of your gracious praise, I'll tell you the trick of it—as I think that's what you'd like to know." She leaned over her tea, and spoke in a sincere tone. "When you make your sad song, you mustn't be afraid to go to the bottom of your own pain. Any power in those tunes comes from the well of your own torment, and it's from there that the demand for relief will come. Anything else is simply a lament. And personally, I don't see a lot of point to that."

Wendra nodded. She was done with laments.

"And one more thing besides," Solaena added. "Those songs don't always need to be brayed out. We do it for crowds because they're noisy." She looked around the broad plain. "But what I'm sharing with you here can come with the same power and meaning in a lullaby. If you doubt it, listen to a mother singing the hope of her heart for a child born into a dangerous world."

She stared back at the woman, whose words struck Wendra. Her own recent melodies were, in fact, lullabies for a child that would never hear them. But she thought she might still put them away. And sing louder this bottom of her pain.

• CHAPTER ELEVEN •

Partings

Some say the Quiet's only real power is to show you what you hate most about yourself. But those are sophists who haven't seen the working end of a Bar'dyn flail.

—Interview taken by a League recorder of a footman
in the forward waypoint of Northwatch

Countless points of light glinted as sun reflected off the dew along the plain. The horses stood nearby, shiftless. Tahn was closest to the cliff's edge, where he could see the cloud like a broad grey sea surrounding the plateau.

Vendanj had been quietly talking to Jamis for several moments. He turned toward them. "The North Face of the High Plains is a difficult descent under the best of conditions. . . . We have many leagues to cross before reaching the Scar. Save your strength because we'll be moving fast."

With that, the Sheason motioned them to mount.

"Any idea why we need this Grant fellow's help, Braethen?" Sutter asked. "He sounds like a lot of fun, for sure. But you know, details would be great."

Braethen shook his head. "Don't know. Sounds like he knows his way around an argument. And he was Emerit. Training for that takes more years than you've been alive."

Sutter rolled his eyes.

Before they got under way, Jamis wheeled to face them. "It's been my privilege to have you here." He nodded to Vendanj, who nodded in return. Clearly a signal. "Sutter, will you come forward?"

Sutter put a hand to his chest in question. Jamis waited while Nails rode forward, casting a skeptical look back at Tahn.

The man retrieved his longblade and flipped it into the air, catching it by the edge of its shaft. "Last night, Tylan made a present to you of our hand."

Sutter looked at the glove he still wore.

"Now I make a present to you of our arm." Jamis extended the sword to Sutter. "Faced with a challenge to fight, you spoke the truth of the First Promise. We haven't heard that from a lowlander in a long while."

Sutter didn't reach for the blade, appearing confused.

Jamis sidled closer. "Please take it," he said in a respectful tone. "It's as much a blessing to give as it is to receive."

Jamis held the blade out so that Sutter would have to reach out to claim it. Hesitantly extending his arm, Sutter grasped the blade by its hilt. Before letting go, Jamis maneuvered the blade so that the point pierced the tip of his own middle finger. He kept it there as Sutter continued to hold the blade, connecting the two men in a precarious position.

The sword had to be heavy, and Sutter's arm soon began to tremble. Jamis didn't remove his finger, but pressed more firmly to steady Sutter's hold. As he did, blood welled up over the tip of his finger and dripped to the plain below. For several moments Jamis helped Sutter hold aloft the blade. Sutter's arm began to shake more violently, and he started to sweat. When Tahn thought his friend was about to drop the weapon, Jamis pulled back his hand, and the sword swooped down harmlessly.

"Thank you," Jamis said, and bowed his head.

Sutter opened his mouth to speak, but found no words. He managed to bow as well. Vendanj watched closely, seeming pleased. Admiration shone in Mira's eyes, too.

Jamis turned to Vendanj. "If there are changes . . ."

"Thank you," Vendanj replied. Then he turned to the others. "Remember that we've been pursued by a Quietgiven tracker. It can feel the connection of Forda

I'Forza in the land and air—*your* Forda I'Forza." He pointed at each of them. "It's how it tracks. Now that it knows of us, we won't be free of it until it lies dead."

The Sheason turned to start down the path.

At the cliff's edge, they each saw the dense mist enshrouding the lowlands. "Lovely," Sutter said.

The path wound more narrowly than the one they'd ascended on the south side of the High Plain. Switching back on itself at sharp angles, the route became more circuitous, dropping hundreds of strides in a short distance. Before long, they dismounted and walked the horses down.

Tahn watched his feet, but found it difficult to look away from the roiling mists below. The mists bore the look of a storm cloud, charcoal and pregnant with thunder and sleet, except they moved in silence, as if patient.

Vendanj stopped several strides above the fogs. Tahn looked out across the tops of the clouds, feeling like he stood at the shore of a vast dark sea. He kicked a rock from the edge of the path. It tumbled downward, and Tahn jumped when a number of tendrils rose like tongues and licked at the rock as it disappeared into its folds.

"Empty your minds," Vendanj said. "Find a single, pleasant thought and fix upon it." He stopped and looked away at the menacing bank of dark clouds. "It is Je'holta. The caress of the Male'Siriptus. Be focused on whatever brings you comfort. Anything else will tear at your reason. Je'holta will inspire panic and madness by exaggerating your own fears. Mira, tie the horses together in a line. Slipknots, so we can get them free quickly. Braethen, you'll lead the animals; they'll be unaffected by the mists. Each of you will hold the hands of those next to you. The mists don't have the power to separate you."

Sutter shook his head and muttered, "Here we go, come Quiet or chorus."

While they waited for Mira to secure the horses, Tahn noted Vendanj. The Sheason looked tired. His cheeks sunken, his eyes rimmed with dark circles. Like one who hadn't slept. It was all his rendering of the Will. They'd not had time to really rest since leaving the Hollows. And now they were dropping into a Quiet cloud.

Mira finished linking the horses, and Vendanj took her hand, each of the others joining in turn. Together they walked into the darkness.

The mists folded around them, thin streamers reaching out to wrap them and draw them in. The sun became a pale disk in the sky. The damp and cold instantly chilled Tahn's skin. The mist touched his cheeks and fingers like icy velvet. Mira's hand firmly gripped Tahn's own, while Wendra's grasp tightened painfully on his other. Vendanj led them slowly, peering into the depths around them.

Tahn could see Penit on the other side of Wendra. But Sutter blurred to shadow. And Braethen appeared as nothing more than a figure that might have been mists shifting and shaping themselves. The hoofbeats of the horses came as muted, dull clops. The horses themselves completely lost to sight.

Noises echoed in the depths of the dark cloud, faint sounds that Tahn felt more than heard—echoes like cries or laments, or death-side prayer offerings. Desperation began to seize him, manic and wild. He fought an almost irresistible need to turn and race up from the dark cellar, though he'd seen nothing. He'd go mad if he stayed long in these velvet folds.

The shadows deepened as they descended the North Face. Soon, the sun disappeared completely. Charcoal-hued light encircled them, and Tahn began to feel like part of the mist itself.

The Sheason didn't waver or slow—their progress cautious but steady. Mira constantly searched the fogs, seeming uncomfortable without a free hand to hold a sword.

Gradually, pressure built, constricting Tahn's chest and making it difficult to breathe. The mists plumed in successive shadows, pushing in on them as soft as cottonseed, but as oppressive and suffocating as a dozen wet blankets.

Tahn gasped, drawing in gulps of the dark mist. From the blackness, he heard others coughing and fighting for breath. Suddenly, a wave of warmth coursed through him, entering from Mira's hand and passing to Wendra in an instant. His lungs expanded, and he breathed more easily. The Sheason had sent something through them, from hand to hand. The coughing stopped.

Vendanj pressed forward.

Tahn had no idea how long they'd been in the mists. His hands cramped from clutching Mira's and Wendra's fingers. His eyes ached from the strain of trying to peer through the clouds that enveloped them. Finally, the path leveled out. They had returned to the lowlands.

In moments they were encircled by the mists on every side. Tahn lost all orientation.

The languid calls from deep in the mists grew louder, more urgent. Tahn thought he heard voices calling his name. Then again. The words were shapeless and vague and sounded as though uttered from lips too pained to form them completely. Finally, the mists fell utterly quiet and calm.

Then distantly, a sound like tree roots pulling free from the ground rose on the mist. Deep, thunderous tones, like the splitting of bedrock, resounded all about them.

"What is it?" Sutter asked.

"Silence," Vendanj ordered. Under his breath the Sheason added, "Je'holta's gotten stronger."

The sounds grew louder, accompanied by wretched cries in a cacophonous din. The chorus was somehow visible in the mists around them. It began to swirl in tight, angry eddies. Through the dim light, Tahn saw forms darting at the edges of his vision, moving in every direction and vanishing as quickly as they came.

"Do you see them?" Sutter called out, his voice desperate.

"Quickly!" Vendanj commanded.

The Sheason pulled them forward into a jog. Something like saplings whipped at their feet, the mists swirling in a frenzy as they rushed blindly ahead.

"Hold on!" Vendanj called back. But his words scarcely reached Tahn over the sibilant rush of the wind and the dark song of rending earth and tortured cries.

Then came the beat of a drum, struck only once, but with a sound so deep and resonant that some god might have struck the very land they rushed to escape. The air throbbed with the beat, which echoed out and back from the North Face. The pulse came at them from above and below, like a quake disrupting the fabric of things. The Sheason abruptly stopped. Again everything was still. Tahn could see mist frozen in the air before his face, un-moving.

Then the mist began to take form.

The darkness swirled in front of him, coalescing into an image of . . . himself. The disembodied mask mouthed words. Its eyeless sockets looked nowhere, but also inside Tahn. Then its features were gone, and the face hung before him like a canvas to be written upon. Tahn averted his eyes, turning to Wendra for reas-surance.

Before he could find her eyes, a scream erupted in the mist. Penit's high, shrill voice pierced the cloud banks. The boy pulled his hands free and raced into the dark fog. Without hesitation, Wendra took off after him.

"No!" Vendanj commanded.

Wendra didn't listen.

"Find her," the Sheason said to Mira.

The Far jumped into the roiling clouds and was gone.

A flurry of movement exploded in front of Tahn, as the misty face before him found its own voice. "Draw and release as you choose, dead man." The words came without inflection.

In his mind, Tahn suddenly saw sunrise after sunrise, but the sun was mov-ing backward, retracing its arc back into the east, time and time again. It was as though a thousand days were being taken back, and each time the sky became blacker, more blurred. He saw a desert wasteland, where children walked on dry ground in endless loops. He saw crags and dried roots, and himself standing at the mouth of a stone canyon, tearing at its walls with his bare fingers. He saw a young girl falling into the canyon. Burning pages floated in the wind, becoming cinders and sparks that winked out against a violet sky. He saw himself speaking, but the toneless words lived only in his mind. He saw broken swords lying like kindling. And bodies. So many bodies. Under a double moon. He saw a great white mountain thrumming and quaking. Then he saw the face of a man, the same face that twisted and writhed in the mists before him. And the face was his own. But somehow different this time. Tahn screamed.

"Don't betray yourselves!" Vendanj yelled.

But it was too late.

Tahn bolted from the line to escape the image. He rushed through the mists, branches whipping, black clouds licking at him as he raced aimlessly. He could hear Sutter chasing after him. Holding his arms over his face, he thrashed through the foliage and undergrowth. He stumbled and went down hard, smashing his leg against a rock. He clambered back to his feet and rushed on, unsure which direction to go, only trying to escape the face.

"You can't outrun the consequence of another's choice." The words resonated in the mists around him, throaty and hushed. "Or your own . . ."

Tahn screamed again and pushed his pace. The mists grabbed at him. He ran, careening off trees and falling over boles. Images became stronger and more searing.

Finally, the darkness began to break. The charcoal light softened to grey, and soon Tahn could see the faded disk of the sun through the mists. He lost his footing again, but scrambled on hands and knees toward the light, the pull of the cloud strong in his mind. But he began to break free. A rushing scream of failure grew behind him, and with a cacophony of rushing noise, he leapt from the mists into the full light of day. And collapsed.

Distantly he heard Vendanj call: "To Recityv!"

Gasping, Tahn touched his head and pulled away bloody fingers. The world turned and his eyes filled with blackness.

Wendra chased after Penit. Dark grey clouds swirled and thickened, obscuring her sight. She crouched as she ran, and could just make out his feet as he sprinted through the mists. The boy dodged in and out of low alders and lunged through tight stands of bottlebrush. Images and forms moved maddeningly at the edges of her vision. Masses of dark fog leapt, tendrils trying to wrap her arms. They lacked the substance to hold her, but their touch filled her mind with thoughts of failure, of never catching Penit, of losing him as she had lost her own child.

"Penit, wait, it's me!"

The rush of wind and distant anguished voices rose and swallowed her pleas, their cries indistinguishable from her own. Penit pushed on at a manic pace. Then from the left two huge hulking shapes materialized out of the mists. They weren't like the other shapes constantly rising and dissipating in the fogs around her.

These were Bar'dyn.

The first dove, launching its huge body in a powerful arc to intercept her. She jumped forward to avoid the attack. The Bar'dyn crashed into the trees behind her and rolled to its feet. The second closed in fast.

The mists thinned to a lighter shade of grey. She could see the boy now. "Run, Penit!"

He didn't turn, pushing at breakneck pace through the mists. She was gaining on him, but the Bar'dyn was now only two strides behind her. It stretched a massive arm toward her. The heavy footfalls stopped, and she turned in time to see the Bar'dyn diving at her legs. She tried to push herself faster, but she had little left. The Bar'dyn's large hand clipped her hip and ankle and sent her tumbling into the grass and brush. It landed with a heavy thud, but quickly regained its feet and bore down on her.

She rolled over, pulling a small knife from her belt. She'd never fend it off with this!

A moment later, the Bar'dyn's back arched. Its broad features pinched, the mists churning as though themselves wounded.

The Bar'dyn fell, and there was Mira standing close behind, a blade in each hand. She whirled, setting her feet as the second Bar'dyn emerged from the mists at a frightening pace.

Mira lunged so quickly the fogs appeared to pass through her rather than around her. In a crosswise motion, she pulled her blades through the Bar'dyn's neck. Her swords scarcely pierced its thick skin. She backed away as the Bar'dyn drew a pair of axes and started for her.

"Go!" Mira yelled. "Find the boy! We'll look for you beyond the mist. But you know our destination, if we don't find you."

The Bar'dyn lunged forward, aiming with one ax at the crown of Mira's head. She easily sidestepped the blow and brought her right sword down on the Bar'dyn's shoulder. It let out only a sigh of pain. A moment later, the sound of many feet were pounding through the mists toward them.

Wendra didn't want to leave Mira to fight alone, but she'd be little help with her knife. She stood, wincing from the gash in her ankle, and hobbled as quickly as she could in the direction she'd seen Penit go.

She heard a clash of steel, muted by the mists behind her. She pushed on. The sound of battle faded and the mists receded until the sun penetrated the darkness. Wendra caught sight of several broken stems and followed them. Her entire leg began to throb, and she slowed as the pain washed over her in nauseating waves.

She limped ahead, the mists growing lighter. She could see several strides ahead of her now. A few limping steps further, and she saw Penit, crouched near the base of a large elm, shivering. She fell to her knees beside him. His hair and clothes were drenched with sweat. He clung to the tree like a child holding his mother's leg.

"It's all right, Penit. I'm here."

The boy didn't respond, didn't even look at Wendra. He trembled more violently, spittle falling from his lips. She removed her cloak and wrapped it around him. Distantly, the sound of footsteps thrashing through the undergrowth cut through the thinner fog.

"We have to go," Wendra whispered, trying to help Penit to his feet.

The boy resisted, his small arms bulging with the effort to remain rooted to the spot.

"Please, Penit, trust me," Wendra pleaded. She knelt again, coming face-to-face with him. "I will protect you." As she spoke the words, she silently wondered how she'd do such a thing. *I wasn't even able to protect my own child.* But in that moment, she vowed she would do so, or die trying.

The sound of footsteps grew louder. She looked over her shoulder, and saw the mists moving frantically, parting in anticipation of something it might not care to touch.

She looked back at Penit. "You must play the part of someone brave."

At that, Penit's eyes focused on her. He seemed suddenly to be aware of who and where he was. He released the tree. His inner arms were marked with the pattern of the tree's bark. He blinked away the tears in his eyes, and nodded.

Ignoring the wound in her own leg, Wendra helped him up, and nearly fell as she tried to stand. Penit put his arm around her waist, and together they started toward the lightest break in the mist. The dark fogs stilled, and a moment later they stepped into the light of day.

CHAPTER TWELVE

Escaping the Darkness

The great tragedy of the Placing—if not an elaborate fiction to begin with—might be that races were sent into the Bourne not because they were corrupt, but because they were peculiar.

—Supposition made by social theorist Amada Sellut in her treatise, *On Divergence,* used by the League of Civility in the formulation of its modern creed

Braethen drew his sword, and looked at Vendanj. "What happened?"

"Penit saw the face of Male'Siriptus," Vendanj explained.

"I didn't see it."

"A child sees with simpler, truer eyes, and his feelings are closer to the skin. The mist laid hold of these things and used them."

"What now?" Braethen asked.

"We'll hope there isn't an entire collough of Bar'dyn at the edge of Je'holta."

The mists continued to form strange shapes. Braethen paid them little attention, focusing on an image of him and his father, reading together on the porch at day's end. His da had wanted him to be an author, too. . . .

The fogs began to solidify in front of him, forming deep, wide holes where eyes might have been, and a slack jaw gaping in a frozen scream.

"Steady, Sodalist." Vendanj put a hand on Braethen's shoulder.

Braethen started, blinked, and the face was gone.

The mists began to list and heave, moving first one way, then another, but more slowly, as though dancing to a silent, mournful dirge. Vendanj put a hand to Braethen's chest and pulled him back. The mists parted like a curtain, creating a clear, dark path before them. Soft steps over the dank ground. Braethen felt suddenly cold. A shape made its slow way toward them, draped in shadow. A simple inclination of its head spoke a chilling disregard.

The mists undulated in a series of waves at its passage. This was a different kind of Quiet.

How many nights had he sat at his table reading, trying to understand what he might one day face if he became a sodalist? His elbows had worn thin the varnish at the table's edge, and the smell of candle wax had become his closest friend. And yet no book, no imagining had prepared him. His hands trembled as he held forth the Blade of Seasons.

The mists erupted in a din of snapping wood and rustling leaves and the roar of a thousand whispered voices from the dust of the earth.

The horses broke free from Braethen's grip, the slipknots pulling loose. They dashed into the mists. He tried to keep control of the one closest to him as it reared and whinnied and kicked its forelegs, but the horse got away and went to ground.

"Forget the mounts," Vendanj said. "They'll find safety."

Braethen turned as the Quiet emerged completely. He shivered, and pointed the Blade of Seasons at it.

The world turned black and he could see nothing.

He turned in circles, and soon felt weightless, having no idea which way was up or down. He still held his blade, but couldn't see it. He reached out, hoping to feel the Sheason. Nothing. He crouched, sure he would find the ground beneath his feet . . . but it was gone.

Braethen reeled. Was this death? He tried to speak; no sound came. He shouted; still nothing. He pressed his fingers to his lips to be sure he was opening his mouth. The only thing real, touchable, was his own flesh.

And the sword.

In his hand the solid feel of the hilt reassured him. Inside the blackness, he and the sword were all that remained. Its weight comforted him. And though he still couldn't see it, he lifted the blade before his face.

What's happening?

Braethen began to fall. He couldn't see the passing of clouds or rocks or birds, but his gut wrenched as though he were plummeting from the North Face to the lowlands below. A feeling grew violently in him that he was rushing somewhere. Toward his own end, maybe. He needed to solve the riddle of this darkness or be pulled apart. His heart hammered in his chest. He gripped the hilt of the sword with both hands.

What am I meant to learn here? The question seemed to hasten his fall.

An elusive awareness danced at the edge of his understanding. His father. The porch. A look of disappointment. His mother dead in the other room. He sensed that his fall and the dark would end there. Was he retreating in his mind? To his mind? His shoulders and legs began to cramp.

Then a simple thought. *It's me.* Beside Vendanj. In the dark. Or with my da on the porch. *I . . . am I.* Somehow the sword made them all true. At the same time.

The world rushed in. The darkness retreated. The ache and cramps were gone. He was back in the mist beside Vendanj as though not a moment had passed.

Vendanj gave Braethen an approving look, and turned to meet the Quiet. It lowered its chin and a pulse of darkness rushed forward in a thick wave, cutting a path through the mists and knocking them both off their feet.

A low, soft voice followed. "Mal i'mente, Therus."

"Maere," Vendanj said. "It's a Maere."

Braethen felt a deeper chill. Behind his eyes he saw the memories of his youth. Cherished and formative memories. Memories that were being rewritten and unwritten, taken from him or re-formed into painful scenes he would never want to revisit. Bit by bit, he was losing his da. Losing his love of the Sodality.

Braethen howled at the loss, and jumped to his feet. Unbidden, something rose in his throat. "I am I!" he screamed. The cry repelled the darkness and the shifting in his own mind.

He turned to see Vendanj rise to his feet, his hands coming up. The Maere whipped its cloak back off its broad shoulders, its long form rearing like a horse. But before it could do more, Vendanj thrust his hands at it. The mists parted as an unseen force struck the Maere. Its mouth widened in a silent scream.

Braethen lunged and brought his sword around with all his strength. The blade tore into the creature, and the Quiet's cry finally erupted in a deep, slow, undulating pitch. The sound pulsed on the fog in visible waves. One muscled arm took Braethen in the side of the head, and sent him sprawling. He landed hard on the ground, his ears ringing. But he didn't let go his sword. Hot blood ran down his neck. He tried to stand, but the world turned at dizzying speed, the force of it pulling him down. He collapsed back to the soil.

Vendanj placed one hand on his chest and extended the other. He spoke something in low, quick words. Instantly, the mists withdrew from around him, and a rush of light descended from the sky. Braethen looked up and saw a long, wide opening through the dark cloud. The sun streamed down, catching the Quiet in its light. The Maere began to thrash to and fro. Steam rose from its body and holes opened in its flesh, as though it were completely insubstantial, a construct of their minds.

In desperation, the Maere charged Vendanj, whose eyes were shut as he focused his energy and words into the Will.

Braethen struggled to his feet, but fell forward onto his hands. He scrambled ahead, using one hand on the ground to keep his feet under him. The Maere closed on Vendanj, but staggered, losing substance with each step.

Vendanj's eyes were still shut, and he stood, unaware. Braethen pressed on, gaining speed and resolve. He pushed away his dizziness, focused on the Maere, and rose, bolting ahead. The Quiet raised its hands, just two strides from Vendanj. Braethen cried out, and Vendanj opened his eyes as the Maere blew from its torn lips a rank breath across its blackened hands. Darkness leapt, flashing forward in jagged arcs toward Vendanj.

With the last of his failing strength, Braethen brought his sword up into the belly of the Maere. The blade thrummed as it met the Quiet. The creature doubled over, its dark magic dissipating as it crumpled, writhing, to the ground. The sun continued to stream down on them, and in moments the Maere was nothing more than steaming ashes at their feet.

Braethen looked up again at the marvelous tunnel carved from the mist straight up into the light of day. The Sheason slumped to the ground, and Braethen sat down hard beside him.

Tahn lay facedown on the ground, gasping for breath. Sutter collapsed on his hands and knees beside him, drawing his own ragged gulps of air. The smells of dirt and rocks warming in the sun filled his nose. After a moment he turned over and propped himself up on his elbows. The mists remained just a few strides behind him, small plumes puffing outward, threatening to expand and engulf them again. Distantly he thought he heard a shriek, but his heart still throbbed in his ears; he couldn't be sure.

Their horses had bolted from the fogs a moment ago and stood fretting and stamping ahead of them.

"Abandoning gods, what is that?" Sutter exclaimed, looking back at the mist. Tahn shook his head.

Sutter slapped Tahn's chest. "Why did you run?"

The images flashed in Tahn's mind—the young woman falling from a cliff of broken stone, singed sheets of parchment rising on hot winds. He saw an image of himself tearing at stone with bloodied fingers. Tahn held up his hands and looked at them, but saw nothing save the old hammer-shaped scar on the back of his hand.

The images didn't make sense to him. Countless suns folding into nothing. The gentle voice of Balatin teaching him on a summer porch with light flies winking in nearby pinions. It all disolved into a mirror of desert brush, waterless wastes, a barren tree.

He was left with only the litany he recited every time he drew his bow, and that meant no more to him than before. He took fists full of dirt in his hands and shuddered beneath the growing heat of sun on his back.

Sutter gently grabbed his arm. "Tahn, what's wrong? What did you see? Why did you break the line?"

Tahn stared at the bank of dark fog. "It got inside me. I don't know how, but I could feel it reading my memories like pages in one of Braethen's books. And then it was like something was writing the story forward." Tahn paused, trying to understand the feeling. He shook his head.

Sutter stared at him for several long moments. Finally, he said, "We've got to go back for the others."

Suddenly, Tahn remembered Wendra. "Silent hell, what have I done?"

The sound of pounding feet rose from the fog. Tahn sat up, hoping to see Wendra emerge from the grip of the dark cloud. Several feet inside the mist the large shapes of several Bar'dyn appeared.

"Run!" Tahn yelled.

He scrambled to his feet and headed for his horse, Sutter at his heels. The stamping of heavy feet shook the earth behind them. Sutter quickly drew abreast of Tahn, matching his every step. Tahn looked back and saw the Bar'dyn emerge from the mist. Their eyes fixed on him and Sutter, massive legs carrying them with impossibly quick strides.

Tahn's chest burned. He'd not gotten his breath back. As he struggled up a low hill, something pierced his foot. In his haste, he'd stepped on a spine-root. Several needles shot through his boot and entered the soft flesh of his sole. He almost fell, but Sutter caught him, grabbing his waist with one arm and jerking him forward.

As they struggled toward the horses, something hit Sutter in the back. Nails pitched forward, breaking his fall with his hands. Stuck in his back was a spiked iron ball. Sutter got up. Blood spread in circles around the spikes. Tahn glanced behind them, and saw a Bar'dyn hurl a second ball. The Quiet threw the weapon with its bare hand; its fibrous skin keeping it safe from the spikes. The ball hurtled with tremendous speed. Tahn dove to his left, his foot jolting with pain as he hit the ground.

The Bar'dyn closed on them, eyes set and determined, an intelligence burning from within. Two drew swords without breaking stride, a third shifting a long ax into its other hand. But the look in their large eyes frightened Tahn more than the weapons they carried—patience, reason.

Sutter stooped and helped Tahn up, arching his back against the ball lodged there. Leaning together they hurried through the dry grass. Tahn could hear the labored breathing of the Bar'dyn, like horses going full on. Any moment the steel of a blade or huge, gnarled hand would rip at them. The mounts were close, but each step grew heavier, more difficult. Tahn's legs threatened to give out. His hair fell in wet strands over his eyes and face. His friend's cheek and jaw dug into Tahn's own as they pushed forward, heads together. Even the heat of the sun fell like a weight on him.

They reached the horses. Sutter climbed on his mount and rode around, putting himself between Tahn and the Bar'dyn. He lifted his sword as a challenge. The Bar'dyn came on undaunted.

"Hurry, Tahn!" Sutter yelled. His friend ducked, another ball sailing past his head.

The mounts began to sidestep, tugging at their reins. Tahn couldn't get his foot in the stirrup without stepping on the barbs that had broken off in his foot. Putting pressure on his foot to mount would be agonizing.

"Hold!" one of the Bar'dyn called. "You run only from lies!" Its voice rasped powerfully, the words glottal and hard to understand.

"You can go to every hell!" Sutter cried in defiance. But even in his stupor, Tahn heard his friend's fear.

There wasn't time to move around Jole to mount from the other side, and he couldn't jump into his saddle with only one foot. Tahn gritted his teeth and thrust his boot into the stirrup. Intense pain filled his foot, ripping through his entire body. Something snapped in the middle of his sole as one of the spine-roots in his foot met bone.

Tahn screamed, and put his full weight on his foot to hoist himself up. The force drove the spines deeper into his tender flesh. Seated, he let go the reins and put his arms around his horse's neck. His old friend ran like canyon wind.

Sutter swiped down once with the flat of his blade and kicked his mount into a full run. They raced away, looking back warily. Another ball hurtled past, missing badly over their heads. Each time he bounced in his saddle, Sutter's face twisted in agony at the sharp spikes in his back.

"Faster!" Tahn yelled.

The Bar'dyn kept pace with them, one gaining ground. Glancing back, Tahn marveled at their graceful gait despite their immense size. Powerful muscles rippled beneath their thick, coarse skin. Their faces had eased into a terrible, placid expression, though their arms and shoulders pumped vigorously.

"We'll have you," one of them announced with an even voice—not a threat but a comment. "Then your lies and the lies of your Fathers will we show you." The Bar'dyn's face remained unchanged as it called after them, the eerie calm not unlike the Sheason's.

"They're gaining!" Sutter yelled over the fury of hooves and the pounding of Bar'dyn feet.

In moments they'd be overtaken. *What can I do!* Just then a cry shattered the air. The Bar'dyn all stopped and looked back to the mist hundreds of strides behind them. The Quiet looked momentarily confused and without direction. They looked at one another, then back at Tahn and Sutter, who were now well beyond their reach. One of the Bar'dyn pointed, and they began to run again, this time south, toward the North Face.

Tahn and Sutter didn't slow, and gradually the High Plains faded in the distance as they raced east toward Recityv.

CHAPTER THIRTEEN

The Help of Young and Old

The failing of most adults is that they mistake size for capacity, especially in the person of a child.

—Assertion made by opponents of the League's seizure and operation of orphanages in Rectiyv, and elsewhere

Wendra stepped into the light and saw six Bar'dyn with a figure in a plain buttoned coat: The Quiet watched the mists further to the North, and didn't see her or Penit duck behind a rock formation twenty strides from the mist's edge.

Her wounds bled freely, the blood pumping madly and coating her entire left leg.

Penit looked at her with horror. "Are you dying?"

"No," Wendra said, suppressing a nervous laugh. "But we have to be quiet," she whispered.

Penit nodded and looked around, grabbing a rock and holding it with his arm cocked and prepared to throw. Wendra let him alone in his protective pose, and gingerly touched her cuts. The wound burned hot, feverish. It would get into the rest of her soon, she guessed. A few drops of blood fell to the soil in the shade of the large rock.

Will the Bar'dyn smell the blood and track us down?

She searched about, and realized they were only paces from the North Face. The dark cloud held steady, rising several hundred strides up the cliff. But on this side of it, the face of the sheer bluff shone red, orange, and white in jagged striations that looked like lightning. The summit was lost beyond sight, too far for help. But close by, at its base, she saw her answer.

A cave.

Wendra pulled the strapping from her left boot, tore a strip from her cloak, and bound her wounds as tightly as she could bear. Then she tapped Penit and pointed to the hole at the base of the cliff. The boy understood immediately. He helped her up, and using the large rock as a shield they stepped as quietly as they could toward the cave. Wendra watched closely for drops of blood on the ground, but soon lost her concern in the flashes of pain that stole over her.

Strange sounds emanated from the mists, but Wendra didn't stop. She fixed on the dark mouth at the cliff base and pushed all other thoughts out of her mind. She hoped the Far had fared well against the Bar'dyn. She hoped Tahn and the others were all right. But even her concern for her brother fell away under her determination to find shelter for herself and Penit.

They reached the cave and guardedly entered, stopping to sit only when the shadows hid them completely. Penit eased Wendra to the cave floor. She felt the cool invitation of the ground there on her cheek and lay down.

Sometime later a great rushing wind howled against the cave entrance. Moments later rock and debris fell from the cliff, sealing the cave's entrance and dropping them into blackness.

She awoke to the same darkness. "Penit," she whispered.

"Right here," the boy replied. He reached out and touched her arm.

She jumped at his touch, causing a twinge in her leg. Sweat coated her face and neck. The fever had spread. She sat up and leaned back against the cave wall.

"Any sign of the others?" she asked.

"The rockslide covered the entrance." Penit scooted closer to her, his boots and bottom scraping the cavern floor. "Can we start a fire?" he asked. "It's getting cold."

"Is there wood?"

Penit stood and returned a moment later with an armload he laid on the cave floor beside her. She pulled a flint from her coat pocket and handed it to the boy. Soon enough, they had a fire. His face, streaked with dirt and tears, glowed in the orange glare of the flames with a thankful smirk that warmed Wendra's heart.

When she felt rested, she tried to stand, but her leg had grown stiff and numb. She sat again and looked at Penit, who appeared content despite the events that had brought them here. She thought she could see circumstances and night-mares leaving him as he put himself in the present moment, tending a healthy fire. She envied him this, living so contentedly, even for a few moments, without concern for tomorrow. She smiled, thought of her father. He must have looked at her this way. It made her glad. Perhaps she had offered him some respite from his own hardships.

"When do we go find the others?" Penit said, interrupting the silence.

Life on the pageant wagons had certainly instilled persistence in him. "To-morrow. My leg is stiff and I have the sweats. After I sleep, and it's light, we'll dig our way out and search for them. They may well find us; Mira knew which direction we were headed."

"Good," Penit replied.

They steadily fed the flames and remarked softly about unimportant things, the way she and Balatin and Tahn had done. Sometime later in the evening, she began softly to sing, her song a perfect counterpoint to the crackle of the fire and the low hum of wood being consumed by flame. Penit crawled closer and rested his head on her lap. Long before the fire had burned to coals, Wendra followed the boy into sleep.

Wendra woke to the sound of Penit fussing over kindling and flint. A faint light streamed through a small crack or two in the rockslide at the mouth of the cave. She sat up, several drops of sweat falling from her nose and forehead. The fever was worse. And she'd lost a great deal of blood. Even without standing she knew her leg would be no use to her.

Propping herself up, she wiped her face and sat a moment as Penit finished relighting the fire. What she must ask of him was too much. But she must ask. Merely sitting up had exhausted all her strength.

"Penit, I need your help."

"Sure." He showed her a helpful expression.

"I can't walk." She swallowed hard to keep her emotions from welling up. "I'll need help if I'm to make it to Recityv." She paused, looking into the boy's large blue eyes.

Penit didn't hesitate. "I can crawl through the rockslide and find someone." Then he surprised her. "It was hard for you to ask me that, wasn't it?" The smile he gave was older by far than the face that made it. "I can take care of myself. Have for three years now. I'll find water and follow it. Water always leads to people."

"Be careful. Even if the Bar'dyn are gone, a child . . . a young man alone on the road isn't safe."

Penit smirked knowingly. "I've seen my share of scalawags. They're always close to the wagon pot trying to lift a coin." His smile faded and he looked distantly into the fire. "I'll be careful. I don't want to see any more dark clouds."

He offered no explanation, and Wendra chose to hold her questions. "You'll be all right, Penit." Her voice broke with emotion. She wiped her brow and eyes with the hem of her cloak.

"You, too," the boy said.

Penit gathered a great stack of wood for her. When he'd finished, he knelt beside her. "You're sick because of me, because you came after me and got hurt. I won't fail. I *will* come back."

Wendra put her arms around him and kissed his cheek. "Go safely."

He rose and walked to the mouth of the cave, where he stopped and looked back. "I lied before. Right after you let me come with you from Myrr. I do care about the pageant wagon, the troupe. And I miss them." He stopped, seeming to reflect. "But I had to get away. I saw what happens after a life on the boards."

He left off there, and climbed the rockslide to the top. He worked at the smaller boulders until he'd opened a thin window. He didn't look back again before he crawled through and was gone.

Wendra lay back down in the cool loam of the cavern floor.

Over the next several hours, she drifted in and out of consciousness. Too weak to even lift herself up, she lay on the ground and watched the last dances of fire shadow on the uneven surface of the rocky ceiling. Fever sweat drenched her clothes, and her lips dried and cracked from panting and dehydration.

As the fire died, the cave grew quiet and cold. Dim light shone from the entrance as the day came fast to a close. Chills shook her violently, alternating with hot waves of fever. She lay listening to the sound of her own heart in her ears.

Perhaps the Sheason or the Far would find her before Penit could return with help. But she'd been here more than a day. If they hadn't come to her yet, they'd likely turned east toward Recityv.

She was alone.

Worry and frustration brought sobs to her throat. She coughed from the thick emotion. The convulsions from the coughing tore at the wounds in her hip and ankle.

Lying on her back worsened the coughing. She managed to roll onto her side to try and calm the spasms. Her coughs now stirred the fire ash into small clouds that settled and clung to her sweat-slickened face. The smell of spent alder and soot nauseated her, but the wracking convulsions stopped, and she breathed easier. Lying still, Wendra felt an uncomfortable lump protruding into her side. She reached into the folds of her coat and removed the box she had brought with her from beneath her bed back home.

Carefully, she placed the song box beside her head. A wan smile touched her lips at the memories the box's cedar smell evoked, and the gulf that separated her from the life when the box had been so important. Then her thoughts turned bitter, and she considered how much better this token might serve as wood for her fire than as a reminder of what was no more. Salty tears stung her eyes and ran over her nose and cheeks. She liked the feel of them and did not wipe them away, tasting them as they ran onto her lips.

The song box reminded her of home, but also of Vendanj's insistence that she accompany them to Recityv. To meet the Maesteri at Descant Cathedral, where song was everything. Where they sang the Song of Suffering, to keep the Veil strong.

She fingered open the box's clasp and lifted its lid. Softly, its melody played, small gears turning the roll inside, which plucked a tune through the tiny tone prongs. The delicate song was too soft to ring as high as the cave's ceiling. But it fell on the fire pit, and the cavern floor round her, and her own tired ears like a memory. She closed her eyes. The gentle notes called out their melody like a wounded bird, and Wendra felt herself falling into a fevered sleep.

Suddenly, she had the feeling that she was not alone. Opening her eyes, she saw seated across from her a kindly-looking man in a brilliant white robe. Between them, the fire had been rekindled. Distantly, like wind causing chimes to jangle, she could hear the melody of her box.

A fever vision?

Maybe. But despite not feeling any immediate fear, she sensed that her life had just irrevocably changed.

• CHAPTER FOURTEEN •

The Rushing of Je'holta

A man or woman has only so much life. At an abstract level, if it was possible to give it all away, death would occur. We agree that energy is not destructible, only transferable. But where we disagree is on the notion that man has any such ability.

—From *A Defense of Mortality,* an academic response made by the Society of Philogists at Ebon South to the esoteric notions of Will; often quoted by League leadership

Braethen lay on the ground staring up through the great hole in the mist. His chest heaved from exertion. He clutched in his left hand the sword Vendanj had given him. The Sheason remained still, one hand to his chest, the other extended. Around them, the ashy heap that had been the Maere still smoked in the bright shaft of light that broke through the gloom.

The sound of hurried footsteps could be heard in the cloud; vague, retreating sounds. The cries and moans deep within the fog bank slowly faded, leaving Braethen and Vendanj in a deep silence. The hole torn in the mist began slowly to close, but for several moments the two sat in the sunlight catching their breath.

"Do we wait for the others?" Braethen asked.

Vendanj shook his head tiredly. "I heard heavy strides, Bar'dyn probably, chasing them when the line broke. The Quiet will feel the death of the Maere, gather quickly, and come for us. We'll wait for Mira to return, then try to find Tahn and the rest."

"What of the voices in the mists?"

"They're no longer alive in the flesh. The mist gives them shape to the eye, but their influence is in the mind. Souls lost while serving Quietus."

"The Bar'dyn aren't affected by it?"

"The Bar'dyn and other lost races don't feel hope the way you or I do. The taint of Male'Siriptus has no hold over them."

The Sheason's words drew Braethen's thoughts back to the black world that had enveloped him when he'd tried to use the sword Vendanj had given him. "Darkness swallowed me. . . ."

Vendanj looked first at him, then at the encroaching wall of mist. Cautious footsteps rose in the quiet. The Sheason put a finger to his lips to silence the sodalist, stood, and turned in the direction of the sound. From the bank of darkness, Mira slowly emerged, her swords drawn, her face flushed.

"Wendra?" Vendanj asked.

"Bar'dyn found her and the boy deep in the mist. She fled while I fought them back."

Vendanj nodded. "Are you all right?" he asked.

"Out of patience," she said sternly.

The mists followed her as she approached, and quickly Je'holta filled in the large hole above, blocking out the sun. She stopped near Braethen and appraised him carefully, her gaze alternating between him and the sword in his hand. Under her scrutiny, Braethen got to his feet and replaced the sword to its sheath. Around them, plumes of mist rose and fell, their touch feeling as a willow bud in early spring.

"We'll go north to the edge of the cloud," Vendanj said. "Perhaps the others have reached safety." The Sheason extended a hand. "The power of Male'Siriptus still surrounds us. Be watchful."

It took time, but eventually they emerged from the low, dark cloud, into the light of day. Braethen raised his arms and turned to face the sun.

"I'll find the horses," Mira said. "Je'holta will not go quietly."

Vendanj nodded. "It will rage soon."

Mira left at a run, covering ground with incredible speed. In a moment she disappeared from sight.

"We need to find shelter." Vendanj got moving. "The rushing of Je'holta is painful to the point of death. It will howl like a storm dropping off the slopes of the Pall. Come."

Vendanj hastened up a low hill. A dense copse stood halfway down the lee slope, the rain and weather having hollowed a space beneath the gnarled root system on the downhill side. Braethen and the Sheason ducked beneath it.

They sat silently in the protection of the hollow, looking out on the day and watching cloud shadows move across the land. Then a wind rose up, mild at first, nothing more than the breeze that precedes a summer shower. But soon it became a gale, carrying leaves and dust in streams down the hill below them. The trees swayed, low oak and sage rippling in the fierceness. Above them, the sky darkened, and the wind screamed in horrible gusts. Braethen squinted at the mists rushing past them at incredible speed. Branches were torn from their trunks and smaller plants uprooted entirely. Small sticks wheeled into the sky like feathers as the dark cloud rushed out.

The gale raged for several minutes, the tree roots around them groaning and straining against the onslaught of wind. The noise was deafening, like standing beneath a waterfall during spring thaw. Braethen grasped a root nearby to anchor himself, and hoped Mira had found cover. Vendanj sat with his cowl drawn up, a shadow in the rooted hollow, patiently waiting out the rushing of the winds.

The angry cloud expanded outward, dissipating to nothing. Soon, the howling died and the wind grew still. Light filtered through, replacing the darkness, and revealed the terrain around them, ravaged in the passing of Je'holta.

"Silent gods," Braethen muttered.

"Let's go," Vendanj said, and stepped out from under the trees.

They hiked back to the top of the hill, and watched as Mira appeared over the rise to the west, leading four horses. Moments later, she arrived with their mounts, and Penit's besides. Her hair had blown free of its band and fell in long, silken strands about her face and neck. Braethen hadn't seen Mira like this; the difference surprised him.

"We may find the others traveling east toward Recityv," she said. "But the winds have erased any trail we might have followed for leagues in any direction."

They mounted and rode east, Mira constantly scanning the ground and horizon. All the rest of that day they rode, stopping finally when the light became too dim.

Mira secured the horses, then started a fire. Braethen helped her gather wood before sitting near the blaze and placing his sword in his lap to look it over. It was entirely unremarkable. No polish or finish. No markings. No edge to speak of. The metal was unyielding though. Tarnished, but strong.

Vendanj took a seat near the fire and removed his small wooden case from his cloak. Opening it, he took two leaves from a stem and placed them in his mouth. Then he settled in, clearly exhausted, to savor the fire's warmth.

Mira left for some time, returning without a sound. She seated herself on the trunk of a fallen tree. "There's no sign of them. But there's no sign of Quiet, either," she reported. "Perhaps the others moved further north before turning east."

They shared a companionable silence for a time before Vendanj turned his attention on Braethen. "Tell me what you know of the Will."

Braethen cleared his throat. "The Will is the power of creation." He thought a moment. "It's what moves us. It's body and spirit. My father liked to say it's the power that resides in all matter, and the matter that resides in all power."

The Sheason lifted the symbol fastened to his necklace: three rings, one inside the next, all joined at one point. "It's the nature of how one thing connects to another. Through space. Even through time." He paused. "Through consequence."

Vendanj ran his finger around the circles toward the point where they were joined. "It's inner resonance with outward things."

"And Forda I'Forza?" Braethen asked.

"Old words that mean the same thing: energy and matter," Vendanj answered. "Sometimes called Ars and Arsa. All things are a marriage of the two. They list and heave under pressure from one another, becoming new, sometimes refining each other into beauty and balance, sometimes becoming discordant and unstable in a struggle to reach harmony. To reach Resonance."

Vendanj let out a tired sigh. "To be confirmed a Sheason is to accept the responsibility of wielding the power of the Will. The authority cannot be claimed; it must be given."

Mira tossed two pieces of wood into the fire. "It's a noble call, but not all those who receive it live long with the blessing." She stared at Braethen across the fire, her grey eyes bright and knowing.

Vendanj tapped his chest. "We, ourselves, are Forda I'Forza. Our physical bodies are one half; thought and feeling the other. For some this second part is known as the spirit or soul. The idea of the First Ones was that this life would teach both halves."

He lowered his eyes and took a handful of dirt from the earth between his feet. "When the Framers held council at the Tabernacle of the Sky, one was asked to create opposition to test and refine the races. But that one—Maldea was his name—grew cankered in his efforts. Swollen in his pride. The First Ones saw no way to reclaim the world, and so abandoned it."

Vendanj looked away, the words seemingly distasteful in his mouth. Flaring eyes returned to Braethen. "It was the Sheason who kept the dream of the Fathers alive. The Sheason were those who served the First Ones. Sheason means 'servant' in the Covenant Tongue."

He took a deep breath and let the dirt slip from his palm. Then he gathered Braethen's attention with a hard stare. "The world became craven. The Veil was thin and those who followed Maldea wrought havoc and destruction over most of the kingdoms south of the Pall."

"Maldea was given the name Quietus," Braethen added—something from his history books.

"And when all seemed lost," Vendanj went on, "a Sheason named Palamon rose in battle against Jo'ha'nel—Quietus's first dark messiah. Palamon defeated Jo'ha'nel with the power to render the Will given him by the Framers."

Vendanj paused, lending weight to what he said next. "That victory came with a price."

Several long moments later, he continued. "To render the Will requires an expenditure of Forda I'Forza. Palamon would only draw that from himself. All Sheason after him have honored this covenant of personal sacrifice."

Braethen stared as understanding grew inside him. "Then each time you draw on the Will, you die a little?"

Vendanj said nothing, but Mira's eyes answered Braethen plainly. "Joining this cause may hold a price for you, too." She stopped, the sound of her words replaced by the yowl of coyotes in the prairies to the west and the crackle of pine boughs in the fire between them.

Braethen's hand tightened instinctively on his blade. "When I raised this . . . I was caught in darkness."

Mira shared a look with Vendanj. The Sheason then gave Braethen a reassuring nod. "It will take time for you to understand how to use it. Be patient. This blade is about remembering. And the fold that exists between now and then."

"Then I was stuck in the fold," Braethen figured.

"That's as good a way of saying it as any." Vendanj took a deep breath. "We need our rest. We have a longer route to Recityv than the others."

"By way of the Scar?" Braethen said.

"And before that, Widows Village." Vendanj's voice became thoughtful, soft. "We have names to record. . . ."

The Sheason lay down and soon his breathing slowed. But Braethen's mind would not be quieted. He thought only of the fold between now and then.

CHAPTER FIFTEEN

Tenendra

If you can't find it in a tenendra camp, you don't need it.

—Familiar call of the tenendra barker

The land and sky turned bronze as the sun fell toward night. Shadows lengthened and the hazy light of end of day stretched over the full-bellied roll of the land north of the High Plains. The trees became dark shapes, and the whir of cricket song came as the stars rose again.

But Tahn and Sutter didn't fully stop until Sutter fell from his saddle.

Tahn jumped from his horse's back, taking care to lessen the impact on his damaged foot. He got to Sutter's side. His friend lay on his stomach, his nose in the dirt, the spiked ball bloody and still protruding from his back. But the bleeding was relatively light. Sutter's fall wasn't from loss of blood.

"I feel weak." Sutter's words came too soft.

Something on the spikes?

Tahn looked around, panic mounting. There was no help in sight.

"Let's sleep here," Sutter said. Something in his voice struck Tahn's mind like a warning. *Don't let him sleep. Keep him talking.*

"How about you stand your lazy ass up? I could use some help. My foot's killing me." Tahn jostled his friend.

Sutter managed to look up with a tired smile. "Ah, Woodchuck, stuff that swollen foot of yours into your mouth so I can't hear you complain."

Tahn needed to get Sutter back on his horse. But he'd never do it still hobbled by these spines in his foot. He gently removed his boot and stocking. The coppery smell of blood rose from the wool sock. In the dim twilight, his wound didn't appear too serious. He slowly probed the sole of his foot, wincing when his fingers brushed the entry marks.

"How about some help with this little prize in my back?" Sutter spoke from behind Tahn, his words slurring a bit.

"I think it suits you fine. I say we leave it for a while and see if it grows on you."

Sutter laughed, and immediately groaned. "Don't make me laugh. It hurts too much."

"Never thought I'd hear those words from you." Tahn stood on his one good foot.

"Only when you're telling the joke, Woodchuck. Now, about my back."

Tahn drew his knife and used it to pry the ball loose. It rolled to the ground with a thud. Sutter bit back a curse as Tahn tucked a cloth in Sutter's shirt to cover the wound. "Good as new. You'll be stooped over the dirt again in no time."

Sutter returned a wry half smile and stood. The pain seemed to have dispelled some of whatever had gotten into his blood. Tahn sat and took a drink from his waterskin, then washed his foot.

"Ah, my hells!" Tahn exclaimed.

"What you whining about now?"

"I can't even see the spines. They're too deep inside." Tahn continued to probe, grimacing as he touched each buried needle.

"I can get them out," Sutter said. "But your cries will be heard all the way back to the Hollows if I do it." Sutter's lips tugged into a lopsided grin.

"It's all those marvelous years plucking twigs from the ground that qualifies you to do surgery on my foot. Is that it?" Tahn waved a dismissive hand. "Forget it. I'd rather burn the foot off. It'd be less painful."

"Your will is your own, Woodchuck." Sutter made a show of two good feet by stomping down hard on the ground. "My father taught me how to use a short knife to remove the slivers a professional rootdigger such as myself is bound to get working the soil. And those spines are a great deal larger than thorns I've coaxed from my hands."

"Do you have some balsam root to dull the pain?" Tahn asked.

"I think there's a bit left if your womanly foot is too delicate."

Tahn smiled defeat through gritted teeth. "Find the balsam root."

As Sutter looked through the saddlebags, Tahn had his first moment of quiet and calm since they'd entered the mists of Je'holta.

He looked west, as though he might see Wendra even now in her own flight from the Quiet. Only the hues of sunset there. He thought of her, of the simple life they'd led in the Hollows, of the awful moment of her childbirth. . . .

He chastised himself for allowing the mists to get inside his mind, send him fleeing recklessly away from his friends. He wanted to go back and find them, make sure Wendra was safe. He owed her that much.

But he needed to get Sutter and himself to a healer. And he wasn't sure which way to go.

With unexpected suddenness he missed Mira. He'd become accustomed to the sureness with which she moved and spoke and knew what to do. He'd grown used to her certainty. He missed her small smile.

Sutter returned, hefting two roots in his hand. "Here," he said, and threw one at Tahn.

The root hit him in the stomach. "Such compassion."

Tahn stripped the shoots from the main root, then broke it in two. He ate the first half, grimacing at the bitter taste.

"You're a picture of loveliness," Sutter said, pulling a short knife from his own boot.

"And you're a credit to dirt everywhere, Nails—" Tahn gagged on the root. He forced himself to swallow.

"Eat the other half," Sutter admonished. "It's a thin root. You'll want it all if the pain is as bad as you're making it look."

Tahn frowned and put the second half in his mouth.

"Chew it," Sutter said. "It works faster that way." Sutter took his own root and gobbled it up.

Tahn bit into the balsam and quickly chewed it into small pieces before swallowing. "How long until you can start?"

"The balsam won't dull the pain of getting them out, just the throb once we're done." Sutter was slurring his words again.

"Come here," Tahn said. "Let me check your back."

Sutter turned. "Why?"

Tahn slapped Sutter's wound, eliciting a yowl. "What, in all hells, was that about?"

"You're slurring your words and your hands are trembling. Something was on those spikes. The sting keeps you sharp. Now, get these spines out, and try not to enjoy causing me pain. Then let's find us both some help."

A look of disbelief on his friend's face quickly changed to worry. Sutter sat, lifting Tahn's foot to the last light of day. The smile left Nails's face as he carefully put the blade against one thumb and started on the punctures near the toes. His friend folded back a flap of skin, and pressed the knife into the wound. Exquisite pain shot up Tahn's leg. He muzzled a cry, and in a second, Sutter lifted the first spine for Tahn to see.

"Not bad for a rootdigger, wouldn't you say?" Sutter commented, though his face held no hint of humor.

Tahn gritted his teeth against the next operation. One by one Sutter removed the other spines, and as he did he began to speak in a faraway voice. But this, Tahn thought, wasn't the poison on the spiked ball, but remembrance.

"This was my father's knife when he was a boy," Sutter said, holding up the bloodied blade with another spine dug from Tahn's foot. "He gave it to me when I saw my tenth Northsun. Told me a good knife and a bit of root knowledge was all a man needed."

"He's a good man," Tahn offered.

"I know." Sutter nodded, returning to his task. "Was always good to me. Never said a bad word about the parents that left me. Never asked more or less of me than he did of Garon." Sutter was quiet a moment, as if thinking of his stepbrother. "He needs me on that farm," he said, mostly to himself.

Tahn heard guilt beneath the words.

"We'll go home eventually," Tahn assured him.

Sutter looked up and caught Tahn's eyes, a question passing unspoken between them: Neither of them knew if they'd ever get home again. His friend worked another spine out of Tahn's foot. Then he stopped, and stared at the knife. "It wasn't for shame of him or my mother that I never said anything about being adopted, Tahn. I want you to know that. Never of them. It was . . . it was the parents who left me to begin with. That's what I didn't want. . . . I love my father, my mother. I wanted to come with you, yes, but I love them . . . I do."

"You're a good son to them."

"Am I?" Tahn's friend squeezed back sudden tears. "They don't deserve the hardship of that farm without my help." Then softer, "Maybe Vendanj was right. Maybe putting my hands in the loam should have been noble enough."

Sutter's words were painfully clear. No poison, Tahn thought, could have dulled them.

"Your secret may be new to me," Tahn said, "but it's not the reason you left the Hollows. Remember what Vendanj said. Staying there would have put them in danger." Sutter looked up. Tahn nodded. "They know you love them."

In the dying light, Sutter looked at Tahn a long moment, then nodded. Soon, his grimy face showed the vaguest hint of a smile.

"Now, can we get on with it?" Tahn concluded, pulling them out of the past. Sutter's smile came on full.

The two last spines felt as though they slid from bone deep inside his foot. The pain in Tahn's sole was excruciating. When Sutter finished, Tahn's body fell limp. His foot throbbed while his friend gently wrapped it with several lengths of cloth torn from the hem of his shirt. Nails then helped him into his saddle, and the two friends turned east and rode hard enough that the jouncing of their mounts kept their pain fresh.

The terrain undulated in long, rolling hills and vales. As night became complete they came upon a road stretching north and south. Tahn looked both directions, as Sutter handed him another balsam root.

"Eat and be well, Woodchuck." This time his friend's words slurred badly.

"Your face is pain enough to need this bitter medicine."

"You're feeling better, I can tell. Any thoughts?" Sutter pointed up and down the road.

"Yeah," Tahn replied. "But your face would still be ugly." Tahn looked both directions again and turned north. After another hour, they crested a low rise and found a town nestled in a narrow valley. Firelight flickered in windows like light-flies, and people ambled along the streets. A few rode in overland carriages—the type built strong for long journeys that might encounter highwaymen.

At the far end of the town, several large tents glowed like the hollow gourds fitted with candles at the commencement of Passat each Midwinter. But these were grand tents, decorated with stripes that flowed from their pinnacles to the ground. Tahn could see six tents in all, and from a distance could hear the thrum of voices and activity. People were entering and exiting like bees coming and going from a hive. And in the air hung the scent of animals sharing close quarters.

"A tenendra?" Sutter asked.

"Looks like it," Tahn said. "I've never seen one."

"My father says they're low entertainment, unworthy of coin." But Sutter's eyes were alight with curiosity. "I don't suppose it would hurt to test the wisdom of our elders." His smile was lopsided, as though the left side of his face was numb.

Tahn looked back at the brightly lit town below. He wanted to see the tenendra. Stories of the feats and wonders exhibited at such events were widely known. And the bright tents looked warm and welcoming, the kind of thing he and Sutter had talked about finding ever since he could remember.

But more importantly, they needed a healer.

"We'll go," he concluded. "But we find a healer first. And remember there's no one to stand behind us if you rile up trouble."

"You couldn't even stand behind *me,* gimpy," Sutter mocked. "Come on, before we miss all the fun."

But Sutter looked unsteady in his saddle. They were running out of time. Whatever had gotten inside him had gone deeper, and would continue to do so.

Sutter clucked at his horse and Tahn hurried to catch up.

Tahn led Sutter through the center of town. To his surprise, no one seemed to take note of them. Men and women crossed in front of their horses without care. More than once, he and Sutter slowed or wound their way around pedestrians who stopped to share a greeting or an insult with one another. Even through his stupor, Sutter gave Tahn a look of delighted, unrestrained glee as comic as the scop masks they'd seen in Myrr. But his friend's eyelids drooped, giving him the look of one deep in his cup of bitter.

They needed to hurry.

The varied fashions made it clear that the town hosted travelers from near and far. Every third building either let rooms or announced itself as a full-service inn to this town called Squim. Brightly painted signs nailed to building façades listed what could be purchased within and at what price. More than a few led their menu with blandishments like "Fairest Anais east of the Sedagin," and more plainly, "Bed Company."

And if there were a lot of inns, there were scads of taverns. Loud laughter and the sound of challenge poured from open doors, and the jangling strains of poorly tuned citherns and badly carved pipes and flutes floated on the air. Each of the taverns had one or two large men sitting near doors propped open for ventilation. Dull expressions hung on their faces, and their massive arms rested in their laps. The Hollows' own Fieldstone Inn had never needed such men to control clientele, but Tahn felt sure that was precisely these fellows' purpose.

Most of the buildings were wood, built with little care for appearance. Rough, ill-fitted planks showed slices of the light within. Narrow alleys ran alongside many of the shops and passed through to secondary streets. Shadowy forms huddled in the darkness of those alleys, the wink of lit tobacco stems flaring orange in the dark.

They passed a long building with multiple entrances, each lined with signs two strides high. The signs were large slabs of slate. Upon the black surface long lists of sundry items were scrawled in white chalk. As Tahn and Sutter passed, a short man with thinning hair and wearing an apron bustled out and used a cloth to erase a number of items on two of the slates.

Men and women in various states of agitation entered the store. Tahn watched some who carried wrapped parcels, whose heads twitched around nervously as they passed through the doors. A few women went in looking distressed and mournful, their gait halting as they neared the entry. One woman strode briskly up to the door, her face heavily painted and her bosom threatening to free itself from its constraining bodice. She carried a man's belt over her shoulder like a hunter returning with game-hide. The buckle glinted in the light from the shop's windows, casting shards of blue and violet and red on the ground behind her. She disappeared inside without a backward glance.

"What is that place?" Sutter asked.

"I would guess it's some kind of skiller's shop."

Without realizing it, they'd stopped in the street to watch the traffic in and out of the many doors to the long store. Dirty men with knotted beards carried soiled bundles into the place. At one point, Tahn was saddened to see a young boy and girl sneak into the first door on bare feet, holding something together in their small hands.

They got moving.

Further into town, narrow streets were filled with horses hitched to posts and overland wagons unloading large barrels and chests. People gathered together in storefronts and windows, their shadows falling in long, jagged shapes across the road.

The byways were dry, and from their shadows emboldened beggars reached up toward the street's edge to harangue passersby, their cant like so much iturgy. The repetition of their pitches soon combined into a deafening roar that made Tahn want to cover his ears.

That's when Tahn saw it: *Body Healer,* the sign read.

Tahn and Sutter moved as fast as their injuries allowed, hitching their horses with double knots in this questionable place, and going right in. A diminutive man with stubby fingers and thick spectacles sat in a chair against the back wall. Seeing them, he said simply, "You pay first," and pointed.

A metal box with a thin slot in its top stood bolted to the floor in the corner.

"Three handcoins. I'll need to see them first." The little man waddled over and looked up at them.

"How do we know you can help us?" Sutter slurred.

"Sounds like you just need to sleep off some bitter, except your eyes look funny. Come now, my fee."

Tahn found the payment and showed the healer, who snatched up the money and rushed to put it into his box. His face lit in delight at the clanging sound of the coins as they rattled inside his vault. He then turned back toward them. "Okay, what ails you?"

Tahn looked at Sutter, who began to weave now that he'd come to a full stop. "Get him a chair."

The healer scooted a seat up behind Sutter, who sat heavily.

Tahn considered what to say. He didn't think he had time to lie. He didn't know what was at work in his friend's body, and caution might kill him.

Tahn knelt to be close enough to speak low and directly into the little man's ear. "We were attacked by Bar'dyn. One hit my friend in the back with a spiked ball. I pulled the ball free, but in the last several hours his speech is slurring, his eyes are heavy, and his balance is off. I think he's been poisoned."

The short fellow buried his face in his stubby fingers. "The first fee of the night and this is it? What, by the deaf gods, did I do to deserve you two?" He stabbed a finger into Tahn's chest, and immediately went back to his lock box. He produced a key from inside his shirt, opened the vault, and drew out Tahn's money. Stumping back, he lifted Tahn's palm with one hand and slammed the coins into it. "I can't help you!"

Tahn stared, slack-jawed. "Can't? My friend is sick. What do I do?"

The diminutive fellow went back to his chair to resume his vigil. "He's got Quiet poison in him. You need a healer from the Bourne. Good luck."

Tahn's ire flared. "But I don't know where to find that. Can't *you* do something?" Tahn stood, feeling for the first time the kind of righteous anger he remembered of his father. Things had grown serious, and now so was he.

The small man seemed to hear it, too. He puffed air from his wide nostrils. "The tenendra. They have a tent of low ones at the far end. They say there's a creature from the Bourne caged inside. Good luck."

Feeling a speck of hope, Tahn thought about the road beyond Squim. Vendanj had called for them to get to Recityv. But from the beginning, the Sheason had said they'd pass by a library on their way. There were papers there he said they'd need. Scholarship about the Covenant Tongue.

Tahn turned back to the short healer, and held out one of the handcoins. "You can keep it if you can tell me where to find Qum'rahm'se."

"The library?" the little man said, incredulous.

"The library," Tahn confirmed.

The man jumped from his chair and snatched the coin. "North road. Ten hours maybe. You'll see a mountain to the east. Looks like a fine set of breasts. No road that way. But go until you see the river. Follow it north. None of it's marked. You'll find it if you root around."

"You're sure it's Qum'rahm'se?" Tahn questioned.

The short healer scowled. "Brother's a scrivener."

"Will it take us out of the way if we're headed to Recityv?"

"You're pushing the value of a single handcoin," the healer said with heavy insinuation for more pay.

Tahn couldn't afford any more. Instead, he took a threatening step toward the little man.

All in a hurry, the fellow said, "Hells, no. It's all north, lad. Roads are faster. But the roads and the river heading north all pretty much lead to Recityv. Now, can we please be done?"

Tahn nodded his thanks. Then with some difficulty, he got Sutter to his feet, and the two stumbled back into the street. The peaks of the several tents to the north glowed like beacons, luring folks to come and pay the admission fee. Tahn and Sutter followed the crowds in that direction.

The closer they got to the brightly lit tents, the stronger the many sweet smells: honey, molasses, and flower-nectar creams. But with them rose, too, the acrid smell of people long without a bath, massed together for whatever entertainment the tenendra brought to this shady town.

"There," Sutter said, getting Tahn's attention.

They rounded the last large building near the end of town and stopped at the massive tent swelling before them. It rose to at least the height of Hambley's Fieldstone. Ropes the thickness of Tahn's arm anchored to great iron stakes held the tent in place. Great swaths of color ran in wide stripes to the peak—red, green, yellow, blue, violet. Straw had been laid all about. But in the heat, there was no mud to cover, so chaff rose from the trampled straw, filling the air with the smell of a dry field.

Along the perimeter of the tents were carts filled with honey-glazed fruit, sugar-wines, and rolled flat-cakes filled with berries and dusted with powdered sugar. Men and women and children all clamored for a taste. Torches blazed all around the tents, casting rope shadows here and there. From within the tents came applause and roars of approval and gales of laughter. Outside, those still standing in line for their food looked anxious to gain admittance to the tents and join the fun.

The tide of the throng took them around the first tent. Two more tents rose against the darkness like enormous, pregnant light-flies. One of these glowed a peerless aqua blue color; the other was covered with sketches of faces in exaggerated expressions of pleasure, pain, joviality, sadness, anger, and orgasmic content. Booths were erected in the thoroughfares that ran between the tents. The intoxicating smell of food and drink wafted over the crowd like an invisible cloud.

Several booths were manned by men and women who hollered the merits of one game or another. Tahn passed one woman wearing an eye patch who barked about the ease of tossing a small dart through a hole in a plank of wood set fifteen feet from the front counter of her stand.

Further on to the right stood three more tents like the first, all in a row. But on the left, out of the way, sat a long, square, dimly illuminated tent. Tahn caught a whiff of something more acrid from that direction.

No one stood in line there.

This had to be the tent of the low ones, with a creature from the Bourne.

CHAPTER SIXTEEN

Song Box

All things have a song in them. All things. If you're wise, you'll listen for it. If you're blessed, you'll hear it. And if you're able, you'll resonate with it.

> —From the study of progressions and their relationship to Absolute Sound, Descant Cathedral

"D on't be alarmed, Anais," the gentleman said.

His long white hair was drawn back in a tail. Clear blue eyes shone beneath thick white brows, and the clean smells of sandalwood and oak leaves seemed to emanate from him. He sat with his elbows on his knees and his fingers laced, smiling paternally at Wendra across the fire.

"Who are you?" she asked, looking around for Penit. Perhaps this was the help the boy had brought back with him.

"A friend," the man said.

Wendra shook her head and tried to push herself up. She collapsed quickly from the effort.

"Don't exert yourself," the old man said. "I'll do you no harm, and you must conserve your strength." He took a piece of firewood from a pile nearby and stirred the coals with it before tossing it on the rest. "It's a joyous sound, is it not."

Wendra looked at him, confused. "What sound?"

"The fire." He closed his eyes. "If you close your eyes it sounds like the wind luffing a sail, the rush of water over a falls. Yet it's gentler than these. And stronger." He smiled with his eyes shut. "The life of the wood is consumed, reborn into flame and warmth. The force that gives the tree its form, still deep within the wood long after it ceases to grow, is offered up in a bright flame that warms our meals and soothes our skin."

Wendra licked her cracked lips, but said nothing.

"It's an old song, older than the races, and one they've forgotten." He opened his eyes. "Its power is still harnessed, but the sacrifice of the touchable becoming untouchable is no longer appreciated. The song is no longer sung." He didn't speak reproachfully, and the same kindly smile remained on his lips. "This is the way of things," he concluded, and rested his gentle eyes on Wendra.

"What do you want?" she asked. "Are you here to help me?" Her voice trembled with emotion.

The man wasn't really there. He couldn't help her. She was having fever visions, death dreams. She remembered her dying father holding entire conversations with the empty chair that sat beside his bed. Tears welled in her eyes. Distantly, the tune of her box continued to chime.

"You don't need my help." He looked down at his hands, then held them up without unlacing his fingers. "What is their song?"

"I don't understand."

The man unlaced his hands. "I may use them to fashion a home, cup the face of a child. I may even use them to take up instruments of war." He turned his hands over each time he listed an example. "I can even put them before the light and create forms of things which are not."

He joined his hands in odd ways and cast shadows of animals and people on the cavern wall behind him. Slowly, the images there became more distinct, moving independently and taking on color and sound. Suddenly, Wendra was watching Balatin playing a cithern on the steps of their home while she and Tahn danced. Her father, laughing, showed them how to perform the next step in the jig, while his fingers plucked the strings, and the yard rang with a lively tune. Tapping one foot, Balatin finally stood and joined them in their dance, continuing to play. Fresh tears escaped Wendra's eyes as she remembered the tune her father played—the same as the tune in her box.

She gave a manic laugh, and the images disappeared, replaced by the old, white-haired gentleman sitting death watch with her at her fire.

His smile never wavered. "Do you understand now?"

Wendra shook her head, then stopped. "Yes. Maybe. These are my comforts as I go to my final earth."

The old man's smile broadened. "Dear Wendra, death is a song worth singing, but not yet for you." He again rested his elbows on his knees and settled in as if preparing to tell a story. "With my hands I can create many things, many good things. But the things I touch and shape are only my best interpretation of what I see and feel inside." He touched his chest.

"These things can be glorious, like Shenflear's words or Polea's paintings. They may ascend into the sky with magnificence as Loneot's great buildings that arc and rise on the banks of the Helesto. But"—the man leaned forward, excitement clear in his features—"can you imagine what thoughts, what images existed in the *hearts* and *minds* of such men and women, but were not perfectly reflected in the efforts of their *hands*?"

Wendra began to feel cold inside. The fire burned on, but held no warmth for her. Its flames, even the old man's kindly face, blurred and wavered before coming into sharp focus again. Beyond it all, her wood box played on, slower now as it wound down. She tried to fix her attention on the melody, to grasp something she knew was real, something she could understand.

The old man sat up and flung back his great white cloak. In the firelight, his white hair and beard looked regal. He again fixed his stare on her, never losing his warm smile. "You, Wendra. The instrument you must play is *you*. It is the first tool, the first instrument. It is a uniquely wondrous symmetry of Forda I'Forza. It is Resonance. And I can teach you. But you'll have to get up off this floor." He patted his leg. "So, how will you do that, Anais? Tell me, what song will serve your need?"

"I'm too weak to get up," Wendra said. "I've sent a boy to bring me help, and I worry that he's lost. Or hurt."

"The Quiet aren't looking for you or the boy."

"My brother . . . they came to our home . . . my child . . ."

"Indeed," the old man said. "And these are strains of a song that should be sung with reverence . . . and hope, because they create in you what only you can voice. Learn from them, Wendra. I have stood in places for days at a time to hear and know the voice it sings with. Even this place, this dark cave, knows a song. And it's inside you now. The rocks and fire and ash. Penit, too, for what you see in him that is forever lost to you. It's a lament, Wendra. One you may sing of this place, this moment . . . but what joy there is in that, too."

"Joy?"

The old man smiled. "Yes, joy. Because your lament can someday be your empathy for someone else, someone who can't express such things for themselves. Not unlike your box." He motioned toward her music box. "What's captured there that causes you to return to that simple melody? Why, it's things forever lost to you in flesh, but alive to you in spirit. Like the wood expending its form to exist as something brighter. We create as we can, Wendra, but the end must be to fashion something finer of ourselves."

For the first time, the old man's eyes grew distant. "But Suffering is changing, and there are few anymore who can sing it. It's the call of Descant. A call that some are trying to end. And so you must get up." He smiled kindly, and focused her on this moment. "I ask you again, what song is it?"

In a moment, the old man was gone, leaving Wendra in the darkened cave, drenched with the sweat of her fever. The smell of ash rose in cloying waves. But more clearly, more intimately, she could hear her box plucking its tune in the darkness. The soft click of the gears hummed just beneath the melody. In the shadows, Wendra parted her lips to hum in time with the song of her box. And her chills began to fade.

The natural resonance in the cave carried Wendra's soft intonations further than she projected them. But as she sang, she found her voice gaining strength rather than tiring. Her humming grew louder, and soon she was adding words. And memories. Every few minutes, when her box wound down, she rewound the cylinder and sang again to its accompaniment.

She listened to her own voice echo and re-echo off the rock walls. In the welling sound that filled the cave, she found unique comfort . . . and more. Her fever broke. She wasn't sure how long she'd been singing, but she knew it was because of her song. She didn't leave it there, though.

She began to turn subtle changes in the melodies, creating counterpoint to the original tune. But faster and more filled with challenge. The new rhythms and harmonies to the music excited her and she found strength to rebuild a fire to keep warm as she continued to sing changes on Balatin's simple song.

She sang all night, continuing to compose her own lyrics and countermelodies. The weave and flow of her music swelled and quickened her heart. She was facing down her illness. The vaulted cavern resonated with a score that wrapped Wendra in its bold embrace. The sun had not yet risen before feeling in her side and leg returned.

And despite the lack of sleep, her arms felt light, her eyes alert. Without thinking, she stood and felt only the faintest trace of pain in her wound. She lifted her voice in a strong, roughened note and then stopped, listening as her final word echoed into the recesses of the cave.

Carefully, she walked to the rockslide, climbing up and through the hole Penit had made. Outside, she squinted in the light, allowing her eyes to focus. Early-morning haze hung over the lowlands, leaves and grass glimmering with dew. The sweet smell of vegetation washed over her, and she took it in gratefully after the old earth and ashes of her fireside bed.

The dark mists were gone. But she could see no sign of Penit. And the others would be on their way to Recityv. She had little choice but to try and make it to Recityv herself. But how long should she wait for the boy to return? He'd promised he would. How he was young.

Then suddenly, the image of the old man with a white beard and cloak surfaced in her mind, startling her. *Fever visions!* But it had seemed so real. A smile touched her lips when she realized what had just happened: She'd healed herself by doing nothing more than what came most naturally to her.

Music had always been a central part of her life. But what had happened in the cave was something spoken of only in rumor, a story repeated more in legend than history. A metaphor or symbol, the power of song to affect the way of things.

What had the old man called it? Resonance?

Wendra lifted her blouse, then her pant leg, examining her wounds. The cuts had closed, only thin, pale scars now. They looked years old. She touched them, and felt nothing. "My skies," she muttered. "How can this be?"

But she didn't spend any more time thinking about it. In the distance she could see a small river. Penit would have found it and followed its course. She set out that moment.

The river took Wendra east until dusk. Tired, she made camp, lit a fire, and managed a few green roots for supper. The sun dipped below the horizon, and gentle shades of brown and red streaked the sky, leaving sepia shadows on the land. She filled her waterskin from the river and washed her face.

Kneeling at the river's edge she listened. She heard as she hadn't before the musical cadence of the current, the babble and chuckle of the water over stones, the rush of it around stems and branches growing or dangling in its flow. Wendra thought she could also hear the deeper, quieter pull of the current from the bottom of the river, where cold, blue water moved more slowly, more powerfully. The several voices of the river merged into a lulling requiem, its soothing power sweeping away the fatigue of the day.

She returned to her fire and sat as day gave way to night. Softly she began to hum, creating her own tune in dual harmony with the fire and the river, her concentration so complete on her song that she didn't hear the approach of feet. Before she knew what was happening, three figures stood opposite her, smiling devilishly in the glow of her fire.

"What fortune," the man in the center said. "This place is like a garden; we leave it and it grows new fruit."

The two other men chuckled, their eyes appraising Wendra the way she'd seen herders do with new breed stock.

The man who spoke had rough, handsome features, two days' growth of beard, and thick brows. His eyes shone with an intelligence the others lacked, and his clothes were simple but better cared for.

Their intentions weren't charitable, but Balatin had taught her never to show fear. "Half the battle is what they don't know," her father had been fond of saying. She composed herself, allowing a bit of an edge to her voice, and inclined her chin smugly, preparing to ask the only thing she cared to discuss with these men.

"I'm looking for a child, a boy, about ten years old," she said. "He would have been traveling this way a day ago." She leveled her eyes at each man in turn. Their stares were filled only with greed and lust.

The man on the left spoke up in a voice bruised by too much tobacco. "You ought to be worried—"

"Silence," the first interrupted. He looked at Wendra, his eyes appraising her in a different way than the other two. A softer look spread on his handsome face. "Indeed, lady, we've seen the child." He paused as though he had more information and intended Wendra to know he was holding the rest back.

Wendra steadied her eyes in an unflinching stare on the obvious leader of the small band and gave a knowing smile. "Well, perhaps you also know where I might find him." She reclined a bit to show her lack of concern.

Straightaway a wide grin spread on the man's lips. "I think we might, my lady, but how could we ask you to travel these dangerous roads alone." He paced past his men to one side of the small clearing.

"Do I look like I need your help?" Wendra asked. "Unless, of course, *you* mean me some harm." She lowered her gaze to the man's sword, holding her smile. Inside, panic gripped her, but she knew she mustn't show it. "I seem to be doing just fine in this suspicious land you describe. Not a jot of trouble, not a curious word . . . until now."

The man bowed persuasively. "Well said, my lady, well said. Allow me to introduce myself, and then you and I will no longer be strangers. Jastail J'Vache." He held his bow, but inclined his head to watch for Wendra's approval.

Wendra nodded. "A man of breeding," she said, her words laced thinly with sarcasm. "How fortunate that I met you, if, as you say, the world about is so corrupt."

"My lady," Jastail said. "You've not yet given *your* name." He stood, his devilish smile too large on his rugged face.

"I'm Lani Spiren," Wendra said. "Make yourselves warm." Wendra knew they would have stayed regardless. Whatever their intentions, her game with Jastail would at least allow her to retain some freedom, for a while anyway.

Because these were highwaymen. She could feel it.

And if they did know where Penit was, then she'd have to convince them to tell her where or take her to him. She rubbed her stomach from habit.

Jastail eyed her closely. He then motioned his companions to a fallen log. The men appeared disgruntled, but obeyed. One of them produced a bottle of wine, and the two began to whisper in harsh, sibilant exchanges. Jastail sat with a flourish near Wendra.

"Be true, my lady. Why would you travel alone in open country?" He looked away thoughtfully, relaxing as though he shared a fire with an old friend.

"I've told you," Wendra answered, not needing to pretend. "I'm searching for a small boy." She turned to him. "But you've not said where I might find him."

Jastail laughed aloud, and his two comrades reached for their weapons in a start. When Jastail stopped, they resumed their muffled whispers and sidelong stares. "A sharp eye and reason besides, Lani," Jastail said. "But would you also expect me to share with you all my secrets so soon?" He grinned suggestively, the smirk a mix of wit and wisdom Wendra knew must serve him well. "And would you have me believe that I know all I must of you?" Jastail continued. He held up his hands to stop Wendra from repeating her objectives.

"Yes, yes, I know you seek a boy. But how carefully you dance around the fact that you're alone in this endeavor. Something, lady, is missing in your story, and I forgive you for not coming straight out with it. Just as you must forgive me for guarding *my* secrets from a stranger. However," he leaned in and spoke in a low, conspiratorial voice, "my friends there are not as inclined as I am to extend courtesies. They listen to me *most* of the time, but as with men who walk the roads, they don't trouble much with questions of civility or morality. They understand what they can touch, what they can take, what they can buy, and the work that brings them money to do it."

He put a hand gently on Wendra's leg. "I may even grow to be fond of you, Lani. But paid men mutiny when their salaries are threatened. And gifted as I am, I can neither remain awake all the time, nor predict their true intentions."

Her mind raced with Jastail's veiled threats. This highwayman was clever. His eloquent language always traveled two steps away from its truest meaning. But she forced herself to wear her own smile.

"You undersell your persuasiveness," Wendra began. "You convinced me to invite you to my fire. And your concern for me," Wendra raised her voice so that the others would hear her, "makes me confident that these hirelings will obey your wishes when it comes to me." She put her opposite hand over Jastail's own. "You're right that I keep secrets. A lady is allowed."

Jastail's eyes narrowed. "I believe you're right, Lani. How clumsy of me to forget. You must never allow me to interrogate you further about such things. My concern for you, however, is quite genuine. Whatever brought you here alone, and whatever the boy flees from or runs toward, is beyond our control." He placed his other hand over Wendra's. "But I must insist on conveying you safely to your destination."

Wendra spared a glance at the men across the fire. They had ceased talking, dazed expressions on their faces, their eyes fixed on her and Jastail's clasped hands. She couldn't be sure that they would lead her to Penit, or that they had even seen the boy. But playing Jastail's game might afford her an opportunity to escape.

The dark memory of her rape threatened to surface, but she pushed it back.

He had started by saying that this place bears fruit, perhaps his only mistake, suggesting that they had discovered someone, maybe Penit, here, just as they had discovered her.

Finally, her forced smile became natural, widening, and she put her second hand over Jastail's, trumping him and coming out on top. "And together we will find the boy," she concluded.

One side of Jastail's weathered face tugged into a bright, fetching grin. This one, Wendra thought, had more the look of real humor. "And we've better than a gambler's chance at that, my lady," he said, noting the final position of their hands before withdrawing his own and beginning preparations for supper.

But something in the way he used the word "gambler" left disquiet in Wendra's heart.

• CHAPTER SEVENTEEN •

The Wall of Remembrance

The thing for us historians to remember is that King Baellor believed Layosah would cast her child down on the steps. If he hadn't, he'd never have rushed out. Never have established the first Convocation. There's something more to these "wombs of war" than we're seeing.

—Transcript notes from the Conclave on Democratic Response held at Dalle in the wake of the third Mal War

Helaina took private counsel in the darkness before the dawn. With her walked her most trusted advisors, the Sheason Artixan and General Van Steward. Somewhere out of sight, shadowing them, were a half dozen of her Emerit guard; they would never be seen, but were always as close as a word.

They walked the street that encircled Solath Mahnus. They walked the Wall of Remembrance. The wall rose the height of three men. Fashioned of granite, its face depicted the history of the city. Or perhaps it was the history of the world. Carved in relief were events that should not be forgotten.

Beyond the wall rose the Halls of Solath Mahnus, a palatial expanse at the center of Recityv. At its pinnacle, her High Office stood outlined against a spray of stars. But walking the wall helped focus her thoughts. Her own High Council stood in disarray. Unless she put it right, she would lead from a weakened position when Convocation commenced, and when she needed to defend the Maesteri and their Song of Suffering.

That's what bothered her most now. She needed to find a way to secure Suffering against Roth.

"The League has begun to politick with those still loyal to you," Artixan said. The Sheason kept his voice low in the stillness. "Some will remain faithful regardless. But others have weaknesses that Roth will exploit. And though they'll hate themselves for doing it, they'll vote against you when Roth asks it of them."

Van Steward nodded. "League lieutenants have been lurking around our garrisons. They're taking inventory of our strength."

"Are you concerned about a coup?" She continued to walk, noting the histories in the wall to their left.

"No, my lady. We'll hold. But anyone gathering information on the size and readiness of your army should be seen as more than a political adversary. . . ." Van Steward let the rest go unsaid.

"The inns of Recityv begin to fill with the retinues of those answering your call to Convocation," Artixan added. "They're taking their own inventories."

"Of what?" she asked.

"Of you," Artixan replied. "Many of them know you by reputation, some only by name. But all will want to take their seat at Convocation knowing your own seat is strong, that you have the support of your High Council."

"They'll want confidence that you have the strength to draw them together," Van Steward added.

Artixan made a noise of agreement in his throat. "There'll be alliances, Helaina, even before Convocation begins. Indeed, in some ways Convocation has *already* begun."

Helaina said nothing. She'd guessed as much. But hearing it from her friends made it real.

She stopped on the stone-cobbled road, and surveyed the Wall of Remembrance. Scenes from the Wars of the First and Second Promise played out forever upon the stone. She could see Layosah with her child raised above her head, ready to dash it against the steps of Solath Mahnus rather than send another child to war. The sculptor had given the figure an attitude of resolve Helaina could see even in the darkness.

Layosah. A *womb of war*. Willing to take any measure . . .

"Your recommendations?" Helaina asked.

"Dispatch Roth," Van Steward said without hesitation.

She looked around at her general, at his uncustomary joke. The three chuckled lightly in the darkness.

The general spoke again. "Put the call out to bolster the army. As peacekeepers we're competent. But we haven't taken to the field in war in a long time. If that's coming, we should train a contingent twice the size of what we have. It will also give you more weight against the League's politics."

"Are there men in Recityv to answer such a call?" she asked.

"No. But I would invite the whole nation of Vohnce to our ranks. And if we still fall short, I'll recruit beyond our borders." Van Steward spoke with passion. "There are men who have no allegiance to their crown. I can find them."

She heard secrets in her general's words, and considered pursuing them, when Artixan placed a gentle hand on her arm.

"You would expect me to ask you to try and rescind the Civilization Order. But it's not the time. The League needs to believe it remains in control of the Court of Judicature. Roth's propaganda has convinced the people that the League is their advocate. While you fortify the Halls of Solath Mahnus with alliances, don't give your people cause to question you."

"It's an immoral law, Artixan. You know how I feel." Her anger rose.

"I know. And the time will come. But not yet." The Sheason himself looked at the Wall of Remembrance, his gaze growing distant. "Begin with your own council, Helaina. Roth is right that many of its members are not leaders, certainly not if war comes."

"Are you suggesting that I remove members of the High Council?" she asked.

"Replace," Artixan corrected. "Many of them will be relieved to go, I promise you. And you'll have the advantage of *qualifying* their replacements. You need to employ the shrewdness that won you the regent's mantle to begin with. We need you to be the *fist in the glove* more now than ever."

As he said it, they again passed the carving of Layosah. It stirred Helaina. Her own womb had been barren until the miracle of one child. The thought of dashing her baby against hard steps to rouse a king to his duty . . .

Helaina's legs were tired. Silver hair and arthritic hands were reminders, too. But she would be the iron fist of Recityv again, by Will or War.

"General, begin your recruitment," she said. "I'll draw up the Note of Enmity before the day is done. But don't wait for the Note to begin; get started the moment you return to your offices." She turned to her closest friend, and most powerful ally. "Artixan, find those who have come already to answer the call of Convocation. I will see each privately to either discover their allegiance or create a new alliance. I'll take those audiences in the High Office, where the glory of Recityv can be seen from the windows to inspire their honesty . . . and choice."

She thought a moment, considering her next words. "As for my own High Council, these are old friendships. I'll speak to them myself, in their homes, to see if they have the will to lead."

Helaina nodded with her own renewed purpose. A firm council would help her when Convocation began, but it would have an equally important role regarding Suffering.

"And we will fill again the council chairs that have been vacant too long," she said. "The authors will be recalled. And the Maesteri. It'll be good to have them when Roth brings his argument to silence the Song of Suffering."

Helaina then considered one last seat at her table. "And announce that we will once again seat the Child's Voice. Prepare for the running of the Lesher Roon. The winner of the race will speak for the children, as it used to be."

Artixan smiled in the darkness. "Roth will take exception to it as another false tradition better left in the past. He won't care to listen to the opinions of a child."

She spared a last look at the Wall of Remembrance, where she saw the granite image of the Lesher Roon being run by countless children. "I don't give a tinker's damn what Roth cares to listen to."

• CHAPTER EIGHTEEN •

Widows Village

Did it ever occur to anyone that while we go round and round trying to unlock the secrets of language and the literal power it might hold, that its simplest, most important purpose is a name? Not a name with inherent power. But something we might use with affection toward someone who needs our care.

—From the journal of the ranking scrivener over
the investigation of the Tract of Desolation
at the Library of Qum'rahm'se

Braethen's muscles ached. He, Vendanj, and Mira had ridden hard for three days, sparing little time to rest. Late the third day, under gathering clouds, the hills rose up to the north and east. Through a dispersion of oaks they entered a village of humble dwellings thatched together of tares and plant husks and rough wood. The shacks huddled against the ground.

The threat of rain came with peals of thunder. Perhaps the storm would sweep away the smell of neglect. The sparse village looked abandoned. The residents had likely retreated indoors to escape the coming downpour. Yet the windows held no lamp or candle, cold and unfriendly in the grey twilight. A gentle breeze tugged at their cloaks. The sizzle of rain falling on the hills began to drone like a distant hive.

They passed through the center of the village, coming to a longer building at the far end. A woven rug hung from the cross-brace to serve as a door. Vendanj lashed his horse to a post and rapped on the lintel as rain cascaded into the streets behind them. Nothing stirred, and no light or fire shone through the windows. Mira and Braethen tethered their mounts and came up behind the Sheason.

Vendanj rapped again, the sound of it meek and hollow, nearly lost in the hammer of rain on the thatch of the small building.

Several moments later, a woman drew back the rug and stared coldly at them. She wore a featureless smock the color of clouds at night. Around her shoulders she'd wrapped a shawl of the same shade. Its weave was so coarse it looked incapable of holding any warmth, and appeared abrasive besides. But it was her face and eyes that evoked Braethen's pity. Her ashen skin lacked the flush of womanhood. The plain, unexpressive face could be described only as haunted.

She looked at each of them with indifferent eyes. Then she stood back, and held the rug aside, motioning them in.

The room within seemed smaller than it appeared from the outside, and yet might be a town common room. A table with a few bottles set to one side served as a little bar or kitchen. The hearth opposite the bar sat cold and silent, the hollow sound of rain echoing down its flue. One lone table stood at the room's center, three chairs at each side and one on each end. A gourd in the middle of the table held an unlit candle. In the rear wall there was a second doorway, also hung with a shabby rug. The floors were clean. And despite the abandoned feel, he could see no cobwebs or dust anywhere. A feeling of habitation resided there, but not life.

Penaebra, he thought, an old word that described the disembodied spirit. This place felt like a body, a husk, left behind when its panaebra had gone.

Vendanj took a seat at the low table. Mira sat beside him. Braethen at the end. The woman shuffled past him and sat opposite the Sheason. The rain began to fall hard, pounding the world outside. The hollow sound of drops hitting the window filled the room. Middle-aged, the woman made no attempt to speak, only stare.

Vendanj showed her a look of understanding. "How are you, Ne'Pheola?"

"Too young to suffer your pity, and too old to do anything about it." It wasn't a joke.

"Not pity, empathy." There was something new in Vendanj's voice—deference, kindness.

She accepted that with a nod. "Why have you come?"

Vendanj hesitated a moment, looking long into the woman's eyes. "A list of names. Every Sheason spouse who's come here."

"The residents of Widows Village have no use of names. You know this." Ne'Pheola lit the candle between them. The flare of light made Braethen squint.

"You still answer to yours," Vendanj observed softly.

"So I can take such grand company as yours," she returned. "The severed halves of Sheason marriages come here to live quietly. It's a desolate heritage, Vendanj. Leave them be."

Long moments passed before Vendanj said simply, "I can't."

Braethen thought he heard a tremor in the Sheason's voice. A personal note.

Ne'Pheola reached out a hand and patted Vendanj's fingers. "You've taken a sodalist to your side." She then turned to Braethen. "What do you think of this place, my young man?"

Her question caught him off guard. But he felt this wasn't a place for false flattery. "Anais, I'm in a dreary place. And forgive me, but one I hope soon to leave."

The woman coughed a bitter laugh. "You're a good one for Vendanj, all right." The woman turned more fully toward him, her nose, chin, and brow throwing the right side of her face into shadow. "I once walked the Vaults of Estem Salo, where the Sheason make their home. Twelve years I lived there, not as a renderer, but as a wife to one. Our life was happy. But that ended when the Quiet killed him. Twenty hellish years ago."

No emotion cracked her voice as she spoke of her loss. "Yes, Sodalist, this is a dreary place. Because we here are Baenal."

Braethen knew the word, had read about it. It meant "eternally left behind." But references to it in the books he'd read didn't give a lot of information, and even then had been found only in the oldest texts his father owned.

Her eyes narrowed. "And now that you have placed yourself alongside those who walk into the breach," she waved at Vendanj, "the burden is yours to share."

Braethen sat, waiting, wanting to understand this burden.

Ne'Pheola turned and looked ahead, staring at nothing. "More than once the Quiet have nearly overwhelmed the world. As protection, an early Randeur of the Sheason found a way to bind a husband and wife together. Even beyond death. Do you see?" She turned back to look at him. "Every Sheason could die, but they would go knowing they'd be reunited with their love in the next life." She laughed dryly. "The Undying Vow, it's called. Made Sheason bold. And it did defeat what the dissenting god stood for . . . for a time."

Braethen put the rest together. "The Quiet have found a way to sunder the vow." *Panaebra, eternally left behind.*

"My love was killed by the League under the Civilization Order." Her eyes turned distant again. "Sanctioned by a council of men with greed in their fingers and wine in their gullets."

The candle danced slowly in the quiet of the room. Vendanj appeared lost in thoughts of his own. But Mira gave Braethen a searching look, and he remembered what she'd said: *Joining yourself to this cause may hold a price for you, too.* His own vow was starting to mean more than he'd imagined.

He returned Mira's long gaze, then also recalled one of the truths written by his father's own hand. Softly, to them all, he said, "And this is the great gift of life, is it not? That I may choose to go where others have found sorrow."

He stood and walked out into the storm, needing to clear his head.

The rain descended in great drops, hammering the ground like stones. Braethen pulled his hood up and strode through the downpour. There was no place for him to go, but he needed some time alone. He slogged south, the way they'd come, watching his feet kick through the gathering puddles. Then the splatter of the rain changed as hailstones replaced the drops, beating the sodden ground more heavily, tapping an endlessly complex rhythm against the earth. The hail fell on his shoulders, and quickly stung him through his cloak.

In moments, the world filled with a dizzying white roar, hail striking the ground so hard it jounced up at odd angles and skittered against other hailstones like the glass balls children roll in their games. The hail fell in sheets, shortening his vision. The hovels of Widows Village became nothing more than low, hulking shadows through the gloom. He looked desperately about for a place to take cover. Tree branches rattled, bare. He almost turned to dash back to the little room, when a voice rose through the storm.

"Here," came the voice, "quickly." The invitation was muffled by the beating of hail upon the earth.

Braethen peered around him, shielding his eyes as he searched for the owner of the voice. He could see nothing, and the hail bit at the flesh of his hand.

"Quickly," the voice repeated, "to your right."

Braethen still could see no one, but he followed the directions, finding himself in front of a dwelling a short distance away. Drifts of hail had already collected against the outer walls. The shutters had been latched tightly against the storm. A rug door similar to Ne'Pheola's hung from the lintel of this even smaller hovel.

A hand drew back the rug, offering entrance to a darkened room. Braethen hesitated. In the darkness he could see no face. Hail continued to pelt down in painful waves, covering the ground in a blanket of white. Unable to stand the thrashing, he dashed inside, away from the onslaught.

The room was utterly dark. The sound of feet became Braethen's only evidence of his rescuer. Slowly, his eyes adjusted; dark shapes showed themselves against lighter shadows. Behind a table stood a figure patiently looking at him through the darkness.

"Thank you," he said. "I'd nowhere else to go."

He wiped his face with his cloak and looked around. A small bed, cupboard, and desk furnished the modest home. In one corner stood a trunk half covered with a piece of some delicate fabric. Atop it a slender vase held a number of green stems. It appeared to be an attempt to brighten the spartan room, though the stems bore no flowers or buds.

"How often I've said the same thing," the figure said. This time Braethen heard the soft inflection of a young woman, different from Ne'Pheola's even tones. He guessed this voice hadn't been in Widows Village as long, her remark almost witty.

"Do you have a candle?" Braethen asked.

"Yes," she answered, "but the dark might be preferable to you."

"Nonsense," he said, adding a single laugh.

The woman went to the hearth behind her and struck flint to a bed of straw. When the straw flared, she added several small sticks before taking one lighted stem and touching it to a candle wick. The room brightened, but seemed emptier in the light.

"That's better," he observed with good humor. Then he looked back toward the woman. Terrible burn scars had ruined one side of her face, the disfigurement running from her forehead across one eye to her cheek and jowl. Scar tissue had grown completely over her left eye. She refused to look at him with the other.

She couldn't have been much older than Wendra. She wore a shapeless grey dress. Her hair and skin were as drab as her clothing. Over her ear she had tucked a green stem like the one in the vase. It was all the color she held, apart from the blue of her one good eye. Around her delicate shoulders, she had wrapped a shawl. Her hands trembled, as if unfamiliar with visitors.

"You may leave if you wish," she said, still not looking at him.

"But I may stay, too?"

Her eye finally found him. "Yes." Braethen thought he saw a thin smile touch her lips.

"Well then, I am Braethen. What may I call you?"

"Names have no—"

"But I am not from here," he interrupted. "Please."

The woman's one eye grew distant. "I was called Ja'Nene."

"Ja'Nene," Braethen said cheerfully. "It suits you."

"You don't understand," Ja'Nene said.

Braethen looked about and lowered his hood. He spoke loudly, deliberately filling the room with sound. And he paced as he spoke, filling it with movement. Ja'Nene stood still and did not speak.

"I haven't seen a storm like this in ten years," he said. "In the Hollows, we wait for the hail to stop, then rush into the streets to gather it into balls. Hail fight. Usually only the young ones play the game. But can there be anything funnier than someone getting hit in the ass with a snowball?" Braethen chuckled.

Ja'Nene may have smiled weakly, or it may have been a trick of the light.

He went on. "Wait, there *is* something funnier. We have a grand inn at home, and the roof is not quite even on one side. In the winter, melting snow falls at the foot of the kitchen door. When the skies clear or the night comes, the water there freezes. Our good man, Hambley, can never seem to remember it. I've waited in the morning cold for him to come out his kitchen door to fetch eggs from his coop. The funniest sound is a man slipping on the ice and *falling* on his ass."

Braethen laughed more genuinely, seeing Hambley in his mind's eye pinwheeling to stay on his feet before landing hard on the seat of his trousers. This time, Ja'Nene clearly smiled, the smile turning to laughter, and the look and sound of it stole his breath. It was beautiful and weary and sad, like the first touch of yellow in autumn leaves.

The laughter faded to smiles.

"It's been a long time since I laughed. It feels strange." She motioned to her scarred face.

"What happened?" he asked.

"The League came for my husband. When I tried to stop them, they threw an oil lamp at me." She faltered, a tear escaping her good eye before she resumed. "It struck my face and shattered. The oil lit. I ran into the street to find a water trough to douse the flame. By then, the damage was done. And when I returned home, Malichael was dead. I felt it even then; I knew we would never meet again. And so I came here."

"You've no family?" Braethen asked.

Another weary smile pulled at the ruined half of her mouth and cheek. "Who would want to look at this?" She gestured at her face. "More than that, I guess, I needed the company of others who knew what I was feeling. And yet," she paused, "with time, even empathy dies from the burden of grief, doesn't it? For me," she looked away from Braethen, "well, a woman wants to feel womanly. The night they killed Malichael, they stole that from me, too."

Braethen went around the table and took her hand in his own. "I think what a woman is has very little to do with how she looks, Ja'Nene. On this topic, I'll suffer no argument."

She looked up at him, another tear falling from her useful eye. "Would you kiss me?"

Braethen stared back at her. A delicate hope and plea etched her gentle, ruined features.

"Is that proper?" was all Braethen could think to say.

The disappointment in her face was painful to see. And he flashed on another look of disappointment—his father's—not when he left home, but when his mother had died. Braethen had disappointed them both. . . .

Braethen held up a hand. "Wait—"

"Questions are the last effort to avoid action . . . or honesty. I know I'm ugly."

He felt as though he'd been slapped. It brought him back to himself. "I've come a great distance in a very short time," he began. "And I've seen things I'd only read about in books, some things I didn't believe were more than tales created by gifted authors." He looked her straight. "And today I come into this sad and dreary village of people who've removed themselves from the company of others. People who believe their lives are over. It isn't proper—"

She shot him a scathing look. Braethen bit back his words, and painfully watched as her anger turned first to sadness and then quickly to apathy. He much preferred her scorn. She sat and ignored him, the shadow of her head cast large upon the table.

Braethen looked around the room, searching to find something to talk about, something to say. He lit upon the thin, green blades of tall grass, the stems sitting in the vase. They too cast long shadows, like ethereal fingers trying to claim purchase upon the physical world. The image struck him.

Finally, in an emotionless monotone, Ja'Nene spoke. "Forgive me. I forgot myself. They say I'll eventually come to understand, to accept . . ." The haunted sound of her words was more disturbing than Ne'Pheola's. Perhaps because of her youth.

"Accept what?"

"It was rash of me. But I didn't ask because I'm love-starved." She turned her one good eye on him, her lips quivering to smile. "Though that's certainly true. And I'm not looking to make a memory to warm me on bitter nights." A tear fell gently down her cheek from her one eye. "I sense a gentleness in you. A kind of caring. I've always been fast to know such things about a man. And I . . ." She swallowed, tears coming more freely. ". . . I just wanted to remember . . . the closeness."

Braethen looked from Ja'Nene to the long blades of grass and back again. He understood. They weren't just color for her drab hovel. They were a bit of life. A stem of hope. In a simple godsdamned blade of grass.

He put his hand on her scarred cheek. She jerked away at first, but a moment later inclined her cheek toward his hand, a warm tear falling on his knuckles. Braethen looked at her, and in that moment did not see her ruined face. Or rather he saw it for what it was. Leaning in, he kissed her tenderly on the lips. And before pulling away, he shifted and gently put his lips to her scarred face.

When he drew slowly away, he saw the wonder and gratitude in her eyes. He smiled and nodded to her. Then, gazing around the room, Braethen memorized the look and smell of it all. Fixing on the blade of grass, he turned back to speak directly to her. "It won't always be this way. A blade of grass might sire a forest."

He could have found better words, but he hadn't bothered to consider them first. And she understood him, in any case.

He stood and crossed to the rug-door. When he looked back, she was sitting in the shadows of her small fire and candle, staring after him. He remembered the darkness he had felt when he took the sword, and his cry when he lifted that sword to defend the Sheason's life. It stirred in him the one thing more he could leave her with.

"You *are* beautiful. And I will not forget your name . . . Ja'Nene."

He stepped back into the hail and strode toward the others with a smile and a purpose. Good things both.

• CHAPTER NINETEEN •

Reputations

There's a no-bounty list kept by guilds and gillers and assassins. Oh, the list changes by trade. But the top name is always: Grant. Former Emerit to the regent. Master of combat and ethic. Defier of courts. An exile. Survivor in the Scar. The man who takes him down will be a king among killers.

—Firsthand account recorded in a canvass
by the League to determine influentials

Solencia squatted against a low hill, little more than a collection of merchant shops and a smithy. The town did trade with overland travelers. A waypoint, was all. A few homes dotted the road into and out of the place, and some few tents and wagons had been set up along the highway—travelers taking a day of rest while they gathered supplies. Grant headed directly for the general mercantile where he always purchased what we needed. Except today he'd brought his ward Mikel with him.

"Don't speak to anyone," he warned Mikel.

Thirteen now, and old enough to come on these trips, Mikel nodded.

But in truth, it was a town of little talk. Prices weren't negotiated and pass-ers didn't stop to trade greetings. The one tavern hunkered small and quiet at the end of the main road—a place to get a drink, nothing more. And the sound of wagon wheels and horse hooves seemed loud for the lack of human voices.

They stopped in front of the mercantile and went in. Grant handed a list of items to the shopkeep and dropped exact payment on the counter without a word. They waited patiently while the order was filled, then began to shoulder the provisions out to their small wagon for the trip back.

On their last haul, voices finally interrupted the solitude of Solencia.

"So our outcast comes to take our food and water back to his desert home. And he brings with him one of his bastards this time."

Grant turned. Three men stood in the road several strides away. Challenge in their stances. Weapons in their hands. Grant took a survey of the scene. He noted the men's positions, their full complement of weapons, the ground itself, onlookers, everything.

This wasn't the first time someone had called him out, hoping to make a reputation by killing the exile of the Scar.

"Go home," Grant said. "We've no quarrel with you. We'll take our supplies and go. There's no need to fight."

His challengers laughed. The leader said, "It's not enough that you take our goods, but the word is you also take our arms. I think you've much to answer for. And we won't wait on the courts and councils to put it right."

Grant recalled the child abuser whose arm he'd cut off, then placed his sack of oats in the wagon bed and spoke softly to Mikel. "Stay calm. I'll talk with them. If it comes to it, remember your training. You're young, but practiced."

Despite his confidence in the boy, Grant didn't want to see him tested on the road of Solencia. He approached his challengers, his weapons still sheathed.

He gave them each an even look, no pride or fear—something he knew a wise fighter could use to gauge what would follow. "You're not the first to call me out. There's no reputation to earn from killing me."

The lead man returned a menacing grin and deployed his men to circle Grant. "*Your* reputation is for betrayal. And now for crimes against the innocent."

"Don't be a fool," Grant replied. "But I won't ask again. We're packed and ready to leave."

Grant could see his words had fallen on deaf ears, and clenched his teeth in anger. His sentence had made of him other men's ambition. *Kill the exile and make oneself a name.* And their reasons were always the same: notoriety at hav-ing killed the regent's Emerit, the defiant Grant.

There'd been almost twenty years of daily drills since then. He'd sent more men to their earth than he could count. He didn't lament a one.

The attack came fast, but predictable. A knife shot out from the lead man's left hand, meant to put Grant off balance, while he brought a hammerfall stroke with a heavy sword.

Grant dodged the knife and in a fluid motion stepped, unsheathed his own blade, and removed the challenger's arm. A deliberate irony.

A scream shot out across Solencia.

But it didn't belong to his attacker. Grant spun in time to see the two accomplices fall upon Mikel. The lad defended one stroke, but took a second in the belly.

Grant rushed toward the boy's attackers, calling out to distract them. But they each raised their blades to finish Mikel. The lad ducked and rolled, grimacing with the pain of his wound. Mikel brought his short sword up to deflect another strike and managed to stick one of his attackers. His sword hung in the other's flesh. As he fought to pull it back, the man gave a wicked smile and used two hands in his final swing.

"No!" Grant cried, now only a stride away.

The man's blade tore out Mikel's throat. The lad's eyes showed awful surprise at his own death, followed fast by a look that longed for home.

Then the boy fell, his head striking the edge of the wagon bed before he landed on the hard road.

In a fury, Grant laid into the killer. With a single raging stroke, he took the man's head from his body. He followed the momentum of his sword, doing a complete turn, and brought it around on the second man, ripping his throat out as the other had Mikel's.

The challengers fell simultaneously, their heavy bodies thudding against the road and bleeding out. Grant dropped to his knees beside Mikel. He had a few precious seconds to hold the boy and look some comfort into his eyes before the light there went out forever.

It was once again quiet, terribly still, as he sat alone on the road of Solencia, holding a child he had been entrusted to protect. Mikel was dead because prideful men had sought Grant's death to build their own esteem.

No matter where he went, he never escaped his condemnation. He frowned. That condemnation would spread further now as word of Mikel's death passed like rumor. The poor boy, dead so young. His heart ached at the sight of him. But his heart also grew harder. Stonier.

Something had to change.

Such pettiness. Such selfishness. These things had banished him into his desert to begin with. And now they threatened him and those he watched over, even when buying a bag of godsdamned oats.

He had his own set of sins. But they were long in the past, and more than atoned for.

Grant picked Mikel up and gently placed him in the wagon, covering him with one of the blankets he'd just purchased. *I shouldn't have brought the boy,* he thought. Alone, he could have killed all three and been done.

He hung his head over the boy's body. "I'm sorry."

Then he went back into the mercantile. He stepped up to the counter and looked across at the shopkeep. The thought in his mind was heresy. But he'd reached a final outpost in the land of his heart. And he might be the only one, given his vantage, to consider such impossibilities.

For what he contemplated might well be impossible.

But the act alone would ease his troubled mind.

"Parchment," the weathered man said.

• CHAPTER TWENTY •

Emblems

The victim of cruelty often loses some primary ability to feel. To empathize. One without empathy is given to greater cruelty toward others. It should not be viewed as an excuse for deviant behavior. But it naturally leads us to the conclusion that, once begun, cruelty escalates indefinitely.

—From *The Syllogism of Resentment,*
first used as a resource to identify valuable recruits
to Mal ranks; later adopted by reformists

Wendra was given her own horse to ride as Jastail led her and his two men east along the same river she'd been following. For two days they rode through several valleys, fording rills that joined the main waterway. Toward nightfall of the second day they came to a great wide river. Two hundred strides across at its narrow point. They followed it south for several hours before coming in sight of a sizeable dock awash in moonlight. Jastail smiled as if seeing an old friend. He sent a man to the dock's end where a lantern fastened to a piling was lit.

Jastail then moved them into the cover of nearby trees, where they waited and watched. The river shone with a thousand ripples of shimmering moonlight. And it carried a low musical hum, hypnotic in its passage.

Not an hour later, another sound joined the river music. A sound like geese honking floated across the water. Jastail looked north. Soon a large riverboat, multiple lamps flaming from its runners, rounded a bend in the river. The sound of laughter came more clearly now, still sounding like geese.

The riverboat angled toward the dock, the maneuver a slow one—the boat was immense.

Several stories rose from the main deck, an entire second building clearly a stable for livestock. At the rear of the craft, a team of oxen had been yoked to a thick crossbar fastened to a revolving post. As the animals walked a never-ending circle, they turned a set of large wooden gears that powered the rear paddle-wheel.

Men appeared on deck with ropes in hand, and guided the vessel to a deft stop beside the dock. The sailors, six men in all, brandished long knives. One extinguished the lantern. Jastail seemed to take this as a signal. He spurred his horse from the cover of the trees and led them all to the pier's end.

The clop of hooves on the wooden planks drowned out the sound of the river, but not the jollity streaming from the brightly lit decks of the boat. The incessant chatter reminded Wendra of the Northsun festival back home. Animated laughter, punctuated shouts, and constant bickering.

Jastail brought them to a stop before the sailors. He lifted his hand in greeting, folding one finger down.

"Name it," said the deckhand who had doused the lantern.

"Defiera," Jastail said, and the men relaxed the angle of their daggers.

"What is wanted?" the other asked.

"Passage downriver to Pelan," Jastail said. "We've business there." His head turned slightly, and Wendra had the impression Jastail was indicating her.

The sailor, his face lost behind a protuberant nose, shifted and peered around Jastail at Wendra. He nodded appreciatively, then sized up the two men who bore them company.

"And these?" the sailor added.

"Hirelings," Jastail replied. "Honest enough if they're paid. Sullen enough on an empty gullet."

At that the sailor laughed, joined by a number of the other deckhands.

"Three horses, three men, one woman," the sailor leered at Wendra, "a hand-coin, no less, and a stem for each man here so that their lips are occupied when asked about the business our new fares have in a place such as Pelan. Putting in there is hazard enough. You'll not want the captain poking into your merchandise."

Raucous laughter fell hard upon the wood dock.

Jastail didn't join them, but reached inside his cloak and pulled out a handful of coins. The sailor came forward and greedily reached for them. Jastail pulled back his fistful of money. "I've ridden your vessel before, fish, and find that I tend to . . . lose things. I'll pay you for boarding, but the rest will I give when we're safely on the dock near Pelan. If I'm complete at that time, twice your price will you have. If I'm not, then all the money will I give to but one of you and say nothing to the others. You may then share the money as you see fit."

The sailor glowered at Jastail, who dropped a single silver coin. The man snatched it from the air with a quick hand and walked away, muttering under his breath.

"Why do you spar with them?" Wendra asked. "They outnumber you, and you've no place to hide on the boat."

"Ah, my lady, it's good that we paired together in this enterprise," Jastail said as the other sailors stood aside to let them pass. "It's unwise to pay in advance. And with rivermen there are precautions to be taken. They'll think three times before stealing what is ours, because I would then give all the tongue-money to just one man. The distrust and danger created when each believes the other is holding money that belongs to him will insure us against pilfering while we travel."

Wendra surveyed the sailors. "I think you're too confident."

Jastail smiled. "Rivermen are as greedy as the river is cold. The one I would pay would never share it with the others. The result would be that each of them becomes a target for the daggers of the others while he sleeps. Do you see my point?"

She had to concede his ingenuity.

They boarded the great ship and passed into the building used for stabling horses. There they dismounted, unsaddled their horses, and climbed a stair into the glare of the middle deck.

She followed Jastail around odd tables that held sunken pits bottomed with slate. Between gamblers standing around the tables, she caught glimpses of grids drawn across the slate with different numbers marked in soapstone. Men and women moved colored markers in a flurry of hands until a man in a bright yellow shirt cast several triangular rods into the recessed area of the table. He then quickly counted the numbers scrawled on the stained surfaces of the rods.

Jastail pulled Wendra along. The two hirelings they'd been traveling with quickly found room at tables and tossed coin onto the slate to enter the games. On the left, a handful of large men stood stoically overlooking the whole of the room. They wore swords menacingly on their backs, the handles protruding in bold advertisement of their function. A black-and-white patch had been sewn to the left breast of their tunics. Next to them, a very small man, perhaps only three and a half feet tall, stood on a raised platform serving bitter and wine. He waddled in a strained gait, having to throw his left shoulder up to lift his right leg, and his right shoulder up to move the other. His pants were held in place with strange belts looped over his shoulders and fastened to both the front and back of his trousers. He looked terribly uncomfortable, but he smiled constantly.

They wound past several more games Wendra had never seen. And around them all, general hilarity swirled. Many of those gambling were dressed in unrefined wool. A few even wore pelts. Beside them were players adorned in silk and twilled cotton, linens of extravagant color and design. Their wagers often flashed of gold, sometimes several coins high. And their cups were just as full as the rest.

The participants seemed to share a familiarity. It was common for a man here to put his hand on a woman's breast, or she to cup another man's loins. Even men and women who appeared to be here together laid hands on others. The gestures fetched bouts of laughter and calls for more bitter. Sweet-leaf tobacco stems flared and puffed like small cloudmakers, filling the room with a pungent haze. The revelry never abated, but fed upon itself as the boat moved down the river.

Jastail took hold of Wendra's hand to guide her more surely through the throng. Toward the back of the great room, a few round tables sat partitioned off from the rest by a low wall. One of the swordsmen stood at the passageway into the area. Upon seeing Jastail, he stood aside and let them pass.

Only a few men sat at these tables, most of the seats empty. Jastail led Wendra to the last table, where just one man sat with a stack of thin wooden placards. He wore a smartly tailored russet tunic, with golden piping and a double column of silvery buttons down the front. Rings on each forefinger bore weight, elegant gems. And his beard had been frosted to match his buttons. The fellow didn't rise, didn't take note, but sat shuffling the plaques over and over. Jastail's tall shadow fell across the table. The man surely knew they were there. But he refused to immediately acknowledge them. Jastail waited, holding Wendra by the wrist.

The seated man took a tobacco pipe from the lining of his jacket and tamped fresh weed into its bowl. He pulled a straw from a wooden canister beside the table lamp and lit one end in the lamp's flame. With deliberation, he applied the flame to his bowl and puffed his pipe to life. With his head wreathed in the sweet smell of perfumed tobacco, he looked up with smiling eyes and greeted Jastail.

"Hello, my friend," he cooed. "Come again to test your luck, have you?"

Jastail flashed his standard smile. "You're a temptation to me, Gynedo. How can I resist the game?"

"And you play well for such a young man," Gynedo said. "But young men should not be so willing to pay the price of the game, I think. Old men like me haven't the . . . concern for reputation or consequence that young men should. How say you to that?" One brow rose in expectation of a response.

Jastail motioned to the chair opposite Gynedo.

"Please," the older man said, puffing at his pipe.

Jastail sat, pulling Wendra to the tableside where he could see her, and let go of her wrist. "In any other time, Gynedo, I would say you're right. But the days we live in are filled with rumor. This isn't a time for a man to lay stores by in the hope of surviving the winter. I—"

The old man pointed his crooked finger at Jastail, arresting his answer mid-word.

"You're a philosopher, my young man," Gynedo said, his eyes narrowing. "But leave the rhymes and riddles for those you intend to betray. Tell me why you come tonight." The old man tapped the table with his finger, seeming to indicate not the boat, or even the room, but the very table at which he sat.

Jastail's smile failed him. Wendra liked the look of his face plain, absent the attempt to distract or deceive. He appeared to earnestly consider the question. His eyes looked thoughtful and directed despite the confusion throughout the room.

"Because it thrills me," he said finally. "It's a base logic, I'll grant you. Fah, no logic at all. I play because it's the only game that speeds my heart."

Gynedo sat appraising Jastail, seeming to consider his answer. Finally, he nodded. "A pity for you, I think. Your trade in human flesh has dulled your senses." The old man looked at Wendra.

Jastail said nothing.

Wendra leaned forward. "I'm not his to sell. I'm here because I choose to be."

Gynedo's brows went up in pleasant surprise. "She's got fire."

The highwayman nodded agreement.

"But it *is* a thrill." The old man turned excited eyes back to Jastail. "None greater that I know; no paltry game as what the herds come to play." He motioned in disgust at the outer room. "With their pittance on the slate, their heads dulled with watered bitter, their wanton hands all over the damn place . . . I need my wall." He gave a wan smile and tapped the low wall separating them from the rest of the chancers.

Jastail seemed eager to begin. "Let's make our accountings."

Gynedo clapped his hands together and stood up, leading Jastail into a small anteroom.

"Stay here," Jastail told Wendra. She sat, glad to finally rest.

But she watched through the open doorway as the old man, Jastail, and a woman she couldn't see too well took turns holding up various items. They pointed and touched the objects as they seemed to describe to one another what they were. Wendra couldn't hear what was said, but solemn faces and appreciative nods followed the presentation of each item. Assessing value, she imagined. It seemed clear that the various articles would be what the players wagered in their game.

What Gynedo called "the accounting" took an hour, and Wendra had nearly nodded off when the group came out of the anteroom.

Gynedo sat, as did Jastail. The two men stared at each other for some time before the young woman sat between them. She made a show of sitting in her beautiful satin dress. Her hair had been tied up above her head, exposing the delicate, white flesh of a neck that had never been exposed to the workday sun. Gold earrings dangled delicately against her skin, and on each thumb she wore a gold ring with a large white stone.

"Set three ways," she said, speaking to Gynedo, but looking at Wendra as if with some private knowledge.

"Just so, Ariana," the old man said. "Take a chair and three will play." He looked up at the other men who'd followed them out of the accounting room. "But no more."

Gynedo divided the placards and pushed one pile toward Jastail, another to Ariana. "Pick them up, my young friends, and let us see where the chances take us this night."

Jastail picked up the thin wooden plaques and fanned them out, studying each with great interest. Wendra could see a number of designs on the plaques, but couldn't understand what they meant or what game they might be used for.

As the game began three other men gathered around. All were elderly like Gynedo, and all puffing pipes as though in imitation of the man. But it was Ariana who made Wendra uncomfortable. She leered at Wendra, appraising her hair, her lips, her bosom.

Over her shoulder there were more gamers and gamblers watching the development of the contest.

None of this was getting her any closer to Penit, or to Tahn, and her frustration mounted. A stirring of song came darkly to her mind and fought for release. But she held herself still and thought of Balatin and his words concerning patience: *Luck serves a patient woman.* She turned her attention to the game, trying to understand how it was played.

After several minutes of consideration, Gynedo put a plaque down on the table in front of him. Both Jastail and Ariana betrayed a look of surprise at the play. The plaque held the image, rendered in red, of a serpent with great wings.

"To you, then, Jastail," the old man said, taking pleasure in his pipe and smiling around its stem.

Jastail spared a look at Ariana, touched one plaque, then quickly removed the leftmost wood in his hand and set it before him. It was Gynedo's turn to show surprise, but only in the raising of one brow. The old man nodded, then shook his head, still smiling around his pipe.

Ariana's face showed nothing, and she didn't hesitate in making her play, immediately putting down a wood bearing the same symbol as Jastail's.

"One round," Gynedo said. "What have you to carry you to the next?"

Jastail removed an earring from his belt that bore the likeness of a tall woman.

"Most impressive," the old man said. "It was you that did it, then." He nodded appreciatively.

Ariana turned baleful eyes on him. Jastail didn't favor her with a return look. The woman's composure failed for only a moment, though, before she removed a glove from a small silken bag tied to her wrist. Woven of metal shavings, the warrior's glove shimmered in the light.

"He went to battle for you, dear Ariana," Gynedo said. "How better suited to play the game is a woman, don't you agree, Jastail?"

Wendra's captor looked at Ariana, whose obvious hatred now burned through cold, inscrutable eyes.

"We shall see," Jastail commented.

The old man laid a small drawing on the table, rendered in an unpracticed hand. As a child might. A hush fell over all who saw the wager. "That gets me to round two. Does anyone disagree?" No one spoke. "I will accept that as an invitation to continue."

Another round of plaques was laid down, and again each of the players produced an item that seemed to shock those gathered to watch. Wendra didn't immediately grasp the significance of the objects, but she guessed that they represented people in some way. The literal value of the item seemed secondary to what it signified.

Around they went, laying six placards on the table. And each time they followed with some token that appeared to be the personal effect of someone the wagerer had known.

Then Wendra understood. Looking at the pile of items on the table: a mourner's kerchief, a child's diary, an author's quill, a worn doll, a stringless fiddle . . . Things she'd seen them presenting and discussing in the back room before the game began. These were symbols of loss, of emotional pain, of death, tokens whose voices were the sounds of silence and sorrow, of life's sacrifice and bereavement.

And somehow these gamblers were the cause or custodians of these moments of grief and regret, gamblers whose souls were stirred only by the despair and tragedy represented in such offerings.

Wendra's heart ached at the tokens heaped at the center of the table.

"Young friends, you've played well," Gynedo said with a hint of condescension. "But your plaques don't make a strong bid against your last play." He leaned back and drew deeply on his pipe. "There's only small shame in getting up from the table. But to do so, I require you to take back your wagers."

The onlookers gasped. Gynedo seemed to be demeaning Jastail and Ariana's efforts to play the game, devaluing their wagers. Wendra guessed that if a gambler stood up, he lost more than the game. He lost reputation. Gynedo was mocking them.

Then Jastail smiled, as wicked a smile as Wendra had yet seen on his lips. "Not me, old friend. I will turn my last plaque."

Ariana studied the plaques on the table, appearing to weigh her chances. She looked at Jastail and Wendra, then nodded that she too would play to the last.

"Your will to do," Gynedo said. "What shall be the prize that gets you your last turn?" He took his pipe from his mouth and watched Jastail with curious eyes.

Jastail smiled at the old man, his cunning looks holding back something, a secret that he seemed to enjoy not immediately sharing. Ariana leveled her icy gaze on him, an angry beauty in her that Wendra admired. The entire room again fell silent, players pausing to hear the last turn even if they couldn't see the play.

As he leaned forward, Jastail's chair creaked loud in the suddenly quiet room. He seemed to want a close look at Gynedo's face as he put in his last wager.

He slowly reached for Wendra, taking her again by the wrist and drawing her toward the table. "And with this, I buy my last turn."

CHAPTER TWENTY-ONE

Names of the Dead

In all the scholarship on the topic of language and names, the most often overlooked is the layer of intention. On its own, it may be nothing. But I'm convinced that without it, none of the rest of our findings mean a tinker's damn. If true, reports of Mor Tongues ought to excite us more.

—Portion of a letter sent by a Divadian linguist
to the Scrivener in Residence at Recityv

Vendanj sat across from Ne'Pheola in the darkest, smallest hours of the night. By the light of a solitary candle, they worked. Through the rug door, the cold encroached, leaving his writing hand more cramped after putting the stylus to such long use.

But he would have no one else write these names.

And it took time, because he wouldn't add a name to the parchment until Ne'Pheola had related the story of both the one that was gone and the one left behind. In soft tones, Ne'Pheola shared the stories of the fallen, and the barren lives of widows and widowers that remained behind. The long hours stretched, but Ne'Pheola went on, and Vendanj thoughtfully recorded the names.

Not all names. But recent ones. The last thirty years. As many as they could remember.

At second hour, Ne'Pheola drew a tepid cup of water to wet her dry throat and steady the emotion that crept there as she gave the names of friends. As she gave even her own name. "I still don't understand, Vendanj. How does the Civilization Order end our vow?"

Vendanj paused, laying down the stylus and putting his fingers near the candle's flame to urge some warmth into them. "I don't know," he answered. "Not fully, anyway."

"Not fully?"

He gave her a long look, then placed a finger beside a name on one of the sheets of parchment. Then another. And another. "When Sheason and their spouses take the vow, the suffix 'yan' is appended to the end of their family name. It's a phoneme from the Covenant Tongue. A root part of the speech that carries a binding power when spoken properly."

"You know the Covenant Tongue?" she asked.

He smiled wanly. "No. Only select Far know the Language. But parts of it are studied during the years a Sheason learns Influence." He put his hand down, covering up the column of "yan" suffixes. "Something has happened to rob this phoneme of its power. In effect, the names of all these people . . . have changed. They are not who they were." He looked at her. "None of us are."

The widow stretched a cold hand across to him, and they locked fingers beside the candle. They remained unspeaking for some time.

"If the Civilization Order was rescinded," Ne'Pheola asked, "would it remake the bonds that have been severed?"

Her eyes were etched deeply with lines of grief and sorrow felt over many years. She'd once been the flower of Estem Salo. He wanted to give her hope, wanted to see her vibrant again.

"I'm not sure," he admitted. "I'm not sure how they're related. If at all." He paused a long moment. "And some things can't be remade. A nail can be removed from a piece of wood, but the hole it has created remains."

Despair etched itself deeper into the lines of her face, and he couldn't leave her with that. "I think someone has found a way to manipulate the vow and perhaps the Language itself to rob us of the promise," Vendanj said. "We're going to Naltus. I'm going to ask King Elan to put the Language to use. Against the Quiet." He tapped the names on the parchment. "I intend to find out what's happened, and if I can, restore these names and vows."

Ne'Pheola smiled small. And briefly, he saw it. The flower of Estem Salo. For that small hope, he was doubly paid for any loss he might suffer further down the road.

"So, it's not just a list to buy leverage with others," she observed.

Vendanj had told her he would use the list when he found Grant. "It has many uses," he said, and returned a half smile of his own. "And you. You have much to give, my friend. Why don't you return to the Vaults of the Servants?"

Ne'Pheola raised a hand, cutting him off. "Kind words, Vendanj, but my heart couldn't bear it. And more than that, these here"—she tapped the parchment on the table—"have need of whatever strength I have left. Some days are a struggle to convince them that they should want to live another day."

Vendanj didn't press. He understood well enough.

They held hands for several long moments. Then he took up his stylus and they resumed recording names. With each one the magnitude and toll of service mounted, the document growing.

The list they created whispered of the abyss, and he wished that there'd never been need to create it.

Wished especially, as the last name he put to it would be his own.

I'm trying, Illenia. Gods know, I'm trying.

With the thought of the woman he loved, a woman taken from this life by the League, Vendanj wrote on. Name by name. And the last thing he did was carefully go back over the entire list and draw a thin line through the phoneme "yan." Of every name. To make the point clear.

Mira leaned against the outer wall of Ne'Pheola's home in the dark of predawn. She surveyed the street, the land beyond the last homes, the sky. She thought she understood why Tahn took to the dark for his moments of solace. The peace of a sleeping world before lying tongues and dire threats came into the day was something to be savored.

In those few moments Mira forgot the Quiet, forgot even the changes coming for her and the Far. Mira stood in the still serenity with no need to do other than breathe and listen.

"You don't sleep, do you?" Ne'Pheola shuffled into the street to stand beside her. Her voice, though soft, seemed loud in the silence.

"Return to your bed. I'll watch here," Mira said.

"I've been up at this hour for more years than you've drawn breath, Mira Far. That's not going to change now." The old woman leaned against the wall with her, and stared out upon the unwaking world.

Together they shared the calm for some time, before the widow spoke again, her words so soft that Mira had to strain to hear her.

"Do you know where your road ends, my girl?"

Mira understood that she meant the journey they all had undertaken. "If it ends prematurely, no."

Ne'Pheola might have smiled in the darkness. "You will go into the belly of the Quiet if you would see this thing done. And for my part, I hope that's where you go. It's selfish of me, but I believe I've earned a wedge of selfishness for my own burdens."

"I think we're *all* going to the belly of the Quiet before we're through." Mira didn't say it lightly. She'd thought on this.

"We might at that," the widow said, nodding. "We might at that. But here's the question: Is it your intention to stand at the Sheason's side to see it done?" Mira started to answer when Ne'Pheola held up her hand. "I don't need an answer, my girl. I only want you to have considered the question. Vendanj will make an enemy of himself to most before this is through."

"Enemy," Mira repeated. It wasn't a word she'd ever attributed to the Shea-son. He was a hard man at times, driven and uncompromising. But those quali-ties were the reason she'd joined him some four years ago.

Ne'Pheola looked up, surveying the stars above Widows Village. "The world is changing. The things a Sheason stands for, his service and sacri-fice, are considered by many to be at best irrelevant, at worst criminal. The Quiet stirs. And this, Mira Far, isn't simply another war. The very instru-ments we've always had to protect ourselves—the Song of Suffering, the Tract of Desolation, the Will itself—are under attack from within our own borders."

Mira followed the widow's gaze skyward. "You speak of the League."

"Not only the League." Ne'Pheola sighed. "If you intend to stand beside Ven-danj to the end, you'll stand not only against the secrets held deep inside the Bourne. You, child, will stand against nations and kings. Yes, the League, as well. But before it is over . . . the Order of Sheason itself."

Mira stared intently at the old woman, waiting for her to explain.

Ne'Pheola remained silent for a time, taking in those stars as if she'd never seen them before. Then she looked at Mira again. "I've seen and felt it this last evening as I sat with him. A terrific burden he's placed on his shoulders. You must decide if you're going to help him to carry it. Yes, you've brought hope out of the Hollows." The widow paused, a grave look passing over her eyes. "But hope often fails. Vendanj knows this. He seeks to surround himself with those hard-ened enough to come against these threats even when hope is gone. And that, my girl, will mean looking into the faces of those you've esteemed as friends and being willing to do what is necessary."

Ne'Pheola stopped. She rubbed her eyes slowly then looked heavenward again. "Before it's done, our friend will likely become a fugitive, and yet . . . his heart will remain fixed on the goal. This is why he can be cruel. There's no middle ground for him. And it's why this old woman will carry a thought of hope when you leave here."

Mira pondered all Ne'Pheola said. At times she and the Sheason had dis-agreed. And while he trusted many things to Mira, if he set himself on something, there was no further debate. In fact, it was part of what made them compatible. Mira was woven of the same cloth.

But Ne'Pheola's words were unsettling: Standing against Sheason; looking into the faces of those she'd esteemed and doing what was *necessary*—these were dark portents to Mira's heart. It amounted to a war against both sides of the Veil. There could be no victory for them in such a cause. How the widow could feel hope in that escaped Mira.

But that wasn't the question she'd been asked: Had Mira considered where this ended?

The answer came when Ne'Pheola spoke again into the stillness. "And what of your own family, Mira Far? You are come to the age to bear your own heritage a child, are you not?"

Mira remained undecided on the choice her king would put to her when next they spoke. And the thought brought fresh sadness about her sister's death.

She did want to go into the belly of the nightmare to stand beside the Sheason and her new friends out of the Hollows. But part of her motivation was selfish: She didn't want to bear a child she would never live to raise, a child she would never hear call her "mother."

• CHAPTER TWENTY-TWO •

Inveterae

When a child brings you their first drawing, do you cast it in the fire for its lack of refinement? Pity then for Inveterae, who burn.

—Colloquial expression heard in the Sotol Wastes

Cheers continued to erupt to the right, noise and laughter and applause rising from the great luminous tents. Tahn shuffled Sutter away from the throng. The feeling of the tenendra changed as they approached a distant part of the field. The low tent. Chills rose on Tahn's skin. If the physic healer was right, there was a creature from the Bourne inside.

"Some taste in entertainment you have," Sutter slurred, and nearly fell.

Sutter hung on Tahn, making it difficult to walk. But Tahn managed to get them to the flap of the tent, where he stopped dead, staring at the most captivating woman he'd ever seen.

She stood leaning against the stand at the tent's entrance. A sign nailed to the front of the makeshift podium read: *Stay two steps from the cages.*

Her long, curly hair was drawn back in a tail. Tight-fitting leather trousers, cut extremely low across her hips, clung to her calves and thighs. Her blouse plumed at the sleeves, but stretched across her bosom and ended above her ribs, showing a lean stomach. She was maybe a few years older than Tahn and Sutter. But there was experience in her face. Knowledge. It gave her an exotic look. Her brow rose with impatience over large, brown eyes and a delicate nose.

"Find what you're looking for?" The woman flashed a dangerous grin, hardly looking at them as she used the tip of a knife to clean her nails.

He'd been gawking. But beyond her raw beauty, he'd seen the lucre in her eyes. She was tenendra folk. If she sensed his desperation, he'd never afford the admission price she'd quote him.

In those few moments of hesitation, she sized him up. "I suggest you speak true words when you open your lips, boy, or your friend here is likely to gather some scars." She used her dagger to delicately caress Sutter's lips, which hung loose and wet with spittle.

Tahn pulled Sutter back out of reach and shot an angry glance at the tenendra girl.

She laughed. "I'll wait a moment or two, and then the price will double." She pointed her dagger toward the tent flap to their right, then spun the blade in her hand and sheathed it against one trim thigh.

Tahn decided on the truth. "My friend is sick. The healer in town said there's a creature here that might be able to help him." Tahn nodded toward the tent. "Which means I'm going in."

A wicked smile crossed her lips. "I hear the hope of free admission in your voice. Are you appealing to my sympathies?" She leaned forward, studying Sutter's sweaty face. "Either your friend is feigning his sickness, in which case I really will make you pay double. Or you tell the truth, and you'll pay triple." She laughed. "So, which is it?" She tapped the dagger at her thigh.

Tahn stared back. "How much?"

"I'll take you in, and three local marks each."

Tahn shook his head. "Four. We may need to get close." He nodded toward the sign on the front of her stand.

The woman's eyes darted to the sign and back to Tahn, measuring him closely. Then her face lit with savage amusement, a dangerous humor that lent her a raw sensuality. She stepped close, her lips brushing his ear when she said, "Well enough, boys. I believe I know what you need."

Tahn felt flushed, swallowed.

She drew back, looking at his lips, and back into his eyes. "To have the beast's cooperation I'll have to threaten it. Dangerous business." She pulled her dagger from its sheath, and laid the flat edge over Tahn's lips. "And you take the risk knowing I won't help you if you come to harm. The beast isn't human, and mad as the Kaemen Sire when he marched upon the Sky."

The girl twirled her dagger in front of his face. "Pay now, and you'll have your chance with the low ones. No tricks. Real coin. I can smell alchemic ore a league away."

Tahn looked past her dagger into her sultry eyes. "Four now. The rest when we're done."

The girl slowly laid the point of her dagger on Tahn's chin, just barely pricking him. The wicked smile widened, arousing Tahn even over the threat of her blade. "Another time I might put you into your earth for such a veiled insult to my honor." She leered at him, a wanton look that made him ache in a surprisingly pleasant way. "But I'm feeling generous tonight. We are made," she said, sealing the deal. Before sheathing her dagger, she reached down and gave Tahn's manhood a gentle squeeze. Then she lifted that same hand, palm up, to be paid.

Tahn fetched the fee from his pouch.

"You may call me Alisandra, lover," the girl said, hiding the coins in a pocket of her trousers. "It's not my true name, but it will help you find me if you have further . . . desires." She again studied Tahn's lips, still smiling her seductive smile.

She then strode toward the long tent, her tight leather pants showing a firmness Tahn couldn't ignore.

"That girl is all greed and muscle," Sutter slurred as soon as she began to lead them away.

Tahn continued to look after her, noting the hint of sinew beneath the smooth skin of her back—lithe as a mountain cat, and just as dangerous. He rubbed his chin and hurried to follow her, when Sutter collapsed for the last time.

Alisandra reached the tent and pulled back the flap. "In you go, boys," she said, wearing a half smile.

Tahn hoisted Sutter over his shoulder and ducked inside. The humid smell of caged life hung in the air with the thick, rich scent of straw and unclean skin. Alisandra came in after them, passing to lead them forward.

Inside, small lanterns lined the far right-hand wall, the light scarcely more than a candle might give. Straw had been thrown down to cover the mud. The fetid smell of mildewed canvas permeated the tent. To the left sat darkened cages fashioned of close iron bars. The smell of animal waste and unwashed flesh mingled with the smell of the moldy canvas. Tahn's stomach turned at the stench. Above each cage another dim lantern burned, fastened well out of reach of whatever might occupy each stall.

The first cage stood empty. Tahn walked ahead without speaking. Rustling sounds, as things shifted in the straw, inspired his anxiety. He swallowed and slowly passed the first cage to view the second. There, two young girls, naked, huddled together in the straw at the back of their stall. The flickering light played delicately upon their skin, but seemed somehow intrusive.

Tahn didn't immediately see why they might be caged. Then they moved, as one. The girls were joined at the hip, sharing a middle leg and part of the same stomach. Dirty, ratted hair hung over soft, supplicating faces. They looked away and cowered into a corner, gathering up straw to hide their nakedness. Tahn noted a bowl of wormy fruit and another of filthy water. The sight unsettled him. But he wasn't uncomfortable. He was angry.

His anger burned behind his eyes. Somewhere, these two girls had parents who surely loved them. Yet here they were, an attraction meant to disturb or cause ugly wonder (maybe disgust) in the looker.

Staring at the girls, a different, hopeless thought occurred to him. Maybe the parents of these poor girls had been glad to be rid of them. Perhaps even at a price.

He sighed and moved quietly to the next cage, Sutter grunting on Tahn's shoulder with each step.

The lantern above the third stall had burned out, casting the cage into deep shadow. Tahn peered into the darkness, but could see nothing. Then a hoarse cry shrieked from the back of the cage and a form rushed forward to the bars. Tahn recoiled, tripping and sending both him and Sutter sprawling. They landed heavily in the straw.

He turned over and looked back. Vaguely human, the creature flesh was little more than scar tissue. It must have been pulled from the belly of a fire. Its features ran like liquid. It made noises with its tongue through one side of its mouth. Its shortened limbs bore no hands or feet. It beat at the bars with its stubs, one good eye fixing Tahn with an imploring stare. The thing lost its balance and fell back into the straw. It made no effort to get up, but sat whimpering with its lipless mouth.

Despair and pity joined Tahn's indignation. He glanced up into Alisandra's face, and saw an inscrutable look. Did she find him pathetic, or was there a touch of guilt buried inside her?

He looked back at the burned man. And after a moment, Tahn crawled to the bars.

"Careful," Alisandra warned.

Tahn put a hand inside the cage, palm up. And waited. Several long moments later, the man dragged himself close. Tentatively, this low one put a clubbed hand in Tahn's. It looked up at him.

Slowly, deliberately, the man formed a few whispered words with its ruined lips. "Kill me. Please."

Tahn stared back, grieved at the earnestness of the request. The stink and silence grew thick around them. And somewhere in that long hush, Tahn thought the old words.

Certainty spread in his chest like the warmth of a summer wine. This unfortunate man *should* die. It made Tahn wonder if the tenendra folks had burned him deliberately to create a low one worth paying to see.

"Please," the man said again. This time, spittle ran from the corner of the man's mouth.

It would be a mercy. He could draw his knife and end the man's suffering. And it was right. He felt that as surely as with every Quiet, as with every animal, he'd ever shot at . . . after speaking those words.

The burned man nodded, a hope in his eye. Perhaps he thought the hesitation meant Tahn would help him.

And Tahn wanted to.

But he couldn't do it. It wasn't a fight. Or an animal. Or the Quiet.

And his heart ached that he would leave the man in his suffering.

"Let's go, lover." Alisandra kicked him playfully in the ass.

The burned man shook his head, seeming to hope Tahn's hesitation wasn't a denial.

Then a thought. Tahn made a clumsy job of sitting up, and drew his small knife out in a quick motion, tucking it in the deep straw near the bars.

The man's good eye saw it, and flicked back up to Tahn as he stood. The fellow made a single, almost imperceptible nod. *Thank you.*

I helped you kill yourself, Tahn thought. It might have been right to do, but it still left an ache inside him. *These godsdamned words.*

It was more than that, though. Deep inside he understood the man's need to end himself. Some part of him resonated with it, as though this sad fellow wouldn't be the first Tahn had known to do it. Though, he could remember none.

He grabbed Sutter's arms and dragged him forward, following the tenendra girl onward, staying close to the outer wall.

She stopped at the last cage. Tahn let Sutter's arms drop. His friend was now unconscious.

The sheer size of whatever lay captive in this last stall drew Tahn's attention. The bars restraining it were double the diameter of the others, casting vague shadow-stripes on its rough skin. Sitting in the pen, something very like a Bar'dyn patiently watched them. It was broad in the face, but the bones beneath its eyes didn't protrude as far as a Bar'dyn's. And its skin didn't look like elm bark. Its legs though, and chest and neck, were immense like the Bar'dyn. Muscled and threatening. Its fingers rested as passive and hard-looking as stones. And it stared, unmoving.

Tahn stared back, and shivered to realize the one certain similarity between this thing and the Quiet that had been following them: the reason and intelligence reflected in its eyes. Tahn stepped closer.

Pity swelled in him, just as it had for the girls a few cages away, and for the burned boy. This last cage was meant to inspire the most fear and awe, culminating the wonders of the low ones. Tahn dropped his eyes to his hand, looking again at the mark there, tracing its familiar pattern with his eyes. They were prisoners, these low ones. Trapped in a routine. He shook his head and looked up again.

He was startled to see the creature standing at the edge of the cage, just a hand's length away. The beast had moved soundlessly while Tahn looked away. His senses swam and clouded as he stared face-to-face with the creature, its eyes still placid. It could kill him with one hand, but Tahn did not budge. He studied the intelligence in its eyes.

Then, softly, in a deep, proud voice it very clearly said, "Lul'Masi."

Tahn blinked in ignorance. Was that its name? The word came so quietly, Tahn wasn't sure he'd heard it correctly. Before he could ask a question, Alisandra pulled him back.

"All right, back up, back up." She waved her hands at the beast, who slowly stepped backward to the far side of its cage. "Here's how it's going to go. You," she said, pointing at the creature, "are going to stay where you're at while I open this door and let our young friends here inside. They want your help. And you're going to give it to them or the beatings on this little family of yours are going to start back up again." She pointed toward the other cages.

The Lul'Masi's eyes never left Tahn while she spoke.

Alisandra lifted a lantern from one of the poles behind her, and shined it deeper into the cage, her face more stern. "Do you understand me?"

The creature nodded.

"You may have come here to dig your own earth," Alisandra said to Tahn. "This beast may tear your arms from your body. You're either brave or foolish."

Tahn looked down at Sutter, whose breathing rasped over open lips. His friend was still alive, but for how long? "Hurry. Fetch your key and let us in."

The girl turned reproachful eyes on him. "Don't grow brave with *me*. I may feed you to it for half our agreed price, just to amuse myself." She replaced the lamp, and retrieved a set of keys from a flap in her boot.

"Mark me, lover. Nothing can be done for you once you're inside." She tapped the bars with her knife. "It takes five men to cage the beast. So take your chance. And either I will increase my fortune, or one less low one will need feeding when the supper bells chime."

"Open it," Tahn said.

Alisandra stepped forward and inserted the key in the lock. A small click sounded as a tumbler fell back. Alisandra kept her eyes on the beast at the back of the cage as she slowly opened the door.

He'd paid to take himself into the company of a creature from the Bourne. This was mad. But a glance at his friend bolstered his resolve. He took Sutter's arms and dragged him through the straw and into the cage of the Lul'Masi.

Alisandra closed the door behind them.

As Tahn turned his attention to the beast standing back in the shadows, sudden helplessness filled him. A chill raced down his back.

A chuff of breath came from the great shape in the shadow. Tahn laid Sutter down and began to creep toward it. Its sides heaved as it stared at him in the dimness. Its thick skin rippled with muscle. One of its hands could easily encircle Tahn's neck. He stared up into its broad face.

The beast stared back, and bent toward him. The ground vibrated with its shifting weight, and Tahn's legs locked in fear. His heart thumped in his ears and chest. The creature's arm measured at least the size of Tahn's leg. He began to feel claustrophobic and started to pant. Waves of hot and cold ran over him, threatening to tumble him to the floor. He turned to look at Sutter, trying to recapture his resolve. His friend moaned, eyes shut tight against unconscious poisoned dreams. A moment later, Sutter cried out in witless pain.

Tahn whipped around and stood face-to-face with the beast. Its glassy eyes were like large black pools, so close that Tahn could see himself in them. He thought he saw a pain-fed apathy in its expression. Its presence was dizzying. Its silence more menacing than any shriek or cry it might have uttered. Intelligent eyes peered at Tahn, assessing him.

For several moments the thing stared, unmoving, unspeaking. Then it said in its deep voice, "We are Lul'Masi. I am Col'Wrent."

The creature said it as if it should mean something to Tahn.

The beast continued to look back, seeming to consider behind its intelligent eyes. Then its features tightened. "I am Inveterae."

Warmth rushed into Tahn's body, like the thaw of winter all in an instant. He knew this word from the Reader's stories. This creature had escaped the Bourne. But it wasn't Quiet. It was Inveterae. One of the *unredeemed*.

CHAPTER TWENTY-THREE

The Stakes Are Raised

A woman's tolerance for pain and degradation surpasses a man's, particularly when you have something she cares about. But pushed too far, she will unwind. After that, praying doesn't help.

—From *The Subtle Art of Manipulation*,
by Rema Olana, in her first essay on odds;
copies found in League barracks and the
private libraries of riverboat men

Jastail smiled across the table at his opponents. Gynedo's face fell, making him look every year of his age. Murmurs erupted throughout the gambling deck. Wendra struggled to breathe, panic and smoke and stares rushing in on her. A dark tone stirred inside her, but before it found form, her knees buckled and she fell to the floor. No one moved to assist her. Over the lip of the table she could see Ariana, who showed Wendra a blank stare.

"And now you, Ariana," Jastail said softly.

The beautiful young woman looked a moment longer at Wendra. With steady hands she turned over her plaques. She did not speak, but sat with quiet dignity, waiting for the game to finish. She was out.

Gynedo found his composure, his face twisting into a semblance of the amiable smile he'd worn before. He took a long drag at his pipe before speaking. "More than a fair price," the old man said. Then he bent forward and peered into Jastail's eyes. "You were too young to learn such a game, friend. You've gone past me. Silent gods, I hold no value for your life."

Jastail didn't avert his eyes, nor blink at the strong condemnation. "Will you try to match me, Gynedo?" he asked with a mocking reverence.

The old man sat back, looking over the plaques, the wagers, and then all the faces surrounding them. "No."

A collective gasp sounded in the room, mutters slowly filling the silence. Jastail sat back in his own chair. He and the old man locked eyes, each searching the other. Ariana wore open disdain, but it seemed a self-loathing. Like she should have thought of such a wager before Jastail did.

The thought of what had just happened left Wendra breathless and tasting acid bile in the back of her throat. She had been the last raise, the last wager. And something told her it wasn't merely her life. That vague thought churned like panic in her throat, trying to coax a song.

The roar of the gaming room rose to its previous volume, clouding her mind.

Two gentlemen clapped Jastail on the back before taking their seats again at their own game behind the low wall. The old gambler stared at the heap of tokens, shaking his head. Soft words fell from his lips like prayers to broken stones, but Wendra couldn't make them out. Jastail swept the pile of tokens into a bag before extending a hand to help Wendra up.

She slapped his arm away and pulled herself up using the wall at her back. Blood rushed to her head, and she steadied herself, waiting for the pressure to ease. The din of wage-makers calling odds and gamblers squealing delight or shouting misfortune rose in dizzying cacophony. Laughter and angry barks punctuated the chorus of voices. No one looked twice at her now, involved in the play of their own chances.

"It's time we go," Jastail said.

Wendra stared. Her attempt to play this man's game, to salvage control over her circumstances, had failed in one raise of the stakes. She wanted to jump at him and tear at his eyes, but his companions stepped behind the wall as her balance finally returned.

"Jastail," Ariana called with soft seduction.

Jastail half-turned and smiled wanly. "Not tonight, Ariana. I haven't the patience for it."

The woman pushed back her chair and started to exit the rear gambling area.

Wendra grabbed her arm. "He takes women? Sells them? And you sit and do nothing? Play games with men like this?"

Ariana stared back. The woman's face shifted from anger to impatience to something like pity. Mostly she seemed irritated to have lost the game. She leaned in close to Wendra, her expression cool. "You need to find your strong suit, dear. Until you do, every man," she paused, "every*one* will see you as an item to bid."

Without another look at any of them, Ariana departed.

"Bring her." Jastail nudged Wendra toward his men, and started to leave.

"Too far," Gynedo blurted.

Jastail paused but didn't look back at the old man.

Gynedo's words were weak against the noise in the room. "Take care. You and I, we know the lie of the wager. Wine and tobacco . . . they'll sate a man in a way. What you play at now . . . it will never satisfy—"

"You're a poor loser, Gynedo." Jastail jingled his bag of winnings.

The old man's face sketched itself in stern lines. "Don't forget yourself, boy." The old man reclined into his chair. "I judge that the game has more of you than you of it. You're too enamored of the stakes to maintain control. You're reckless." He took his pipe to his lips. "Do your trade and leave me in peace."

Jastail left, briskly striding through the game room and out onto the deck. His companions urged Wendra to follow, and reluctantly she made her way past the revelers into the night air.

She found Jastail leaning against a rail watching the moonlight ripple on the water. Without turning, he dismissed his men, leaving Wendra at his back, unguarded.

"You're thinking to attack me," he said calmly. "Take your chance."

Wendra's fingers clenched and unclenched. She could shove him over the railing into the river. *No.* She'd lost sight of her goal: Penit. Jastail had used the promise of taking her to the boy to manipulate her. Maybe it was all a lie.

A dark pressure filled her lungs, burning from within. But it also warmed her against the night, against this place, this man. She took a step toward Jastail and raised her arms.

"Do you suppose you can do it?" he asked. His words stopped her. "I mean to say that you don't strike me as one acquainted with murder." He spoke conversationally, as he might to a friend. Still he hadn't turned toward her.

"You're wrong," Wendra answered. "I've seen it." An image flashed in her mind, and she rubbed her empty belly. The dark pressure in her lungs grew. "I've had it coaxed from my body and torn away from me before I might give it a name."

At that, Jastail turned. His eyes looked strange as he searched Wendra's face. His lips parted as if he meant to pursue her comment, a wary concern folding the lines of his mouth and eyes. He looked at Wendra's stomach, seeming to understand a part of her story. But he left unspoken whatever questions he had. After a few moments, the same smile as he'd given Ariana played across his features.

"Acquainted, perhaps," Jastail conceded. "But not done it yourself."

Wendra came to the railing beside him and looked out at the expanse of river. Moonlight rippled on its surface, a silent dance accompanied by the music of small waves lapping at the prow and the wailing of gamblers inside the game room.

"No, not myself . . . Unless the boy dies," she threatened. "I will find him. Either you'll help me, or you won't. But you *will not* stop me."

"Anais—"

"Anais?" Wendra interjected. "I don't want to hear that word from your lips. You may be smart at the table, and more than a match of wits for those two dogs you keep with you, but I'm not blind to your lies and empty promises. You've made a mistake in bringing me into the company of others as greedy as yourself."

Bitter laughter escaped Jastail's tired face. It fell flat on the deck and river.

"There's fire in your belly," he enthused. "The dust won't take you easily. But there's no help for you on this riverboat." He considered a moment, a more wry smile returning to his weathered features. "In truth, I'm your only friend here. You may have need of my protection against other, less . . . friendly passengers."

"And what if I just cast myself into the river and swim to shore?"

"In this water?" Jastail asked, his smile lingering. "Not likely. Your legs would seize and drag you down before you stroked half the distance."

"And if I kill you while you sleep?"

Jastail regarded her. "Then you will never find the boy." He took up his vigil on the river, his amusement gone.

Wendra couldn't divine the truth. Did he know where Penit was? Or was he playing her false to the last?

The chill off the water bit at her skin, while she kept her captor company and the river carried them south. On another night, the sweep of stars in the sky above the wide river basin would have caused her to sing. But the song she wanted to give voice to would sound like a dissonant rasp, like a cough from winter winds.

They watched the river together in silence for some time, and the tranquil rush of water along the side of the boat nearly caused her to forget the strange relationship she shared with him. And as she stared into the cold depths, she heard a new sound; not the water sluicing down the side of the riverboat.

Wendra heard water splashing.

And the zip of arrows penetrating the river's surface.

The Bar'dyn? Could they have tracked her here?

Fearful voices suddenly barked commands.

"Bring her!" Jastail yelled, calling his men to action.

They rushed down the side of the boat, deckhands firing arrows into the night. Wendra followed their aim. *Bar'dyn!* Massive bodies swimming toward them. Wendra looked up to the shore where dozens of Bar'dyn rushed south to get ahead of them. Hundreds of strides downriver, the Quiet splashed into the water and began swimming to intercept them. The large creatures moved swiftly, their long, powerful arms pulling them with ease against the current. Arrows continued to strike the water, some bouncing off thick Bar'dyn skin. Two men manned the front ballista, firing spears with little accuracy.

Jastail led her toward the stern. The riverboat yawed as the wheelman turned to try and put some distance between the watercraft and their attackers. The oars and paddlewheel worked wildly, slapping the water and pulling with the current to increase their running speed. Celebrants lined the gambling room windows, their moon faces peering into the dark with concern. Wendra ran past them, and at the back of the boat saw Bar'dyn beginning to climb aboard.

She and Jastail came to the stable. The highwayman threw the door wide. His men came from behind and darted in, leading four mounts out in a hurry.

"The other side!" Jastail barked.

The men led the horses to the far side of the riverboat. The hull sliced across the current, angling toward the east side of the river. The clash of metal chimed in the night air. The Bar'dyn were aboard. Strangled cries rose and echoed out across the water. Men and women streamed from the large gambling rooms, filling the deck with chaos and desperate screams.

The large sword-bearing guards emerged, jumping to meet several Bar'dyn who were rounding the corner. Quiet eyes found Wendra, and the creatures broke into a run toward her. Jastail physically threw her into her saddle, jumped into his own, and slapped her horse's rear. Together they vaulted the railing. Their mounts crashed heavily into the freezing waters. The two hirelings came directly behind them, splashing into the river at their back.

The instant cold forced a cry from Wendra's throat. But her horse began working toward the opposite bank.

Already, her legs were growing numb from the freezing water. The horses chuffed and swam, struggling to make the far shore. Behind them on the riverboat, the Bar'dyn cut down a few more guards before setting the boat to burn. Gamblers who escaped the blade and flames jumped into the river and swam for the near shore.

Countless heavy splashes rose behind her—Bar'dyn diving into the water, pulling after them with long-armed strokes. She glanced ahead. The east bank wasn't so far away. But the Bar'dyn were gaining. The slowest of Jastail's henchmen was snatched from behind and pulled from his horse. His scream ended in a gurgling sound.

Could the horses outswim the Bar'dyn? Downriver, dozens of Quiet had seen their escape and now swam swiftly for the shore.

The riverboat became an inferno of swirling flames on the water, men and women trying to swim away from the heat, their arms succumbing to the freezing cold water and slowing their flight for land. More than a few slipped soundlessly into the depths.

A close splash behind them. Wendra turned to see a Bar'dyn crush the second of Jastail's men before sending him adrift, blood flowing from a wound to his neck.

Then Jastail's horse lurched from the water, jumping onto the bank. The Bar'dyn said something she couldn't discern and kicked harder toward her. Before it could close the distance, her own horse gained the land and pulled her from the river. In a heartbeat, she followed Jastail north along the riverbank into the trees, the feeling in her legs all but gone.

The wind cut at her as she raced to stay close to Jastail. Tree limbs and tangled roots whipped past as they forged a path through the dense wood that clung to the riverbank. Twice, her horse nearly went down—the swim had exhausted its legs. But the animal righted itself and raced forward.

The forest rose like a series of dark columns frosted with moonglow. Wendra clung desperately to her reins. They splashed through an estuary and up into a dense stand of firs. Jastail slowed at the top of a short rise and cocked his head toward the river to listen. Wendra looked in the same direction and saw a shape moving among the trees.

"Run!" she screamed, and kicked her mount hard in the sides.

The horse bolted forward past Jastail just as a Bar'dyn dove from a thicket of saplings. Jastail scarcely had time to draw his sword and turn. The Bar'dyn's immense body sailed through the air with strange grace, hitting Jastail's mount full in the side. The horse, Bar'dyn, and Jastail all went down in a knot of arms, legs, and drawn weapons. The horse was up fast, and bolted into the trees. Jastail rolled and tried to scramble away. One large Bar'dyn hand clasped his ankle and yanked him back. Wendra could see blood on Jastail's pant leg where the beast's razor-taloned hand held him.

The highwayman struggled, but to no avail. Still clenching his sword, he tried to grab a tree root to pull himself away. The Bar'dyn's grip didn't slip. Jastail stopped trying to escape. He twisted his sword in a quick spin and with two hands plunged the weapon at the beast's head. The Bar'dyn shifted, and the blade took it in the shoulder.

It didn't yowl, but let Jastail go and got to its knees. Jastail's sword rose like an ornament from its body. The creature touched it tentatively then pulled it free. A soft, wet sound accompanied its removal. One of its arms hung slack, but the other lifted the weapon to its eyes and surveyed the blood streaming in runnels down the blade's flat edge. It grunted and tossed the sword aside, fixing its cold eyes on Jastail. The highwayman scrambled backwards, kicking with one good leg.

Wendra realized she could flee. Either Jastail would die, or he would find a way to defeat the Bar'dyn. But either way she could be several thousand strides north of here when the fight ended. She looked north, ready to kick her horse into a run.

The Bar'dyn took a menacing step toward Jastail, who couldn't get to his feet. In a moment, it would pounce on him and Jastail would be dead. To the right, water suddenly splashed at the river's edge. More Bar'dyn had reached the shore. She had to decide. Now!

The forest trees and low growth and Jastail and the Bar'dyn all swam in her eyes. Her lungs burned with the breath of violent song. She shook her head, dismissing the strange irrelevance of that inclination, and thought. Her legs were still numb from the river cold. She couldn't stand to defend Jastail.

Dead gods, am I doing this?

The Bar'dyn took another menacing step. Jastail clambered back, butting up against a tree, turning on his side to crawl around its base. The Bar'dyn grew still, a serenity entering its face that frightened Wendra more than anything she'd seen yet. Heavy feet pounded the forest floor, growing louder from the direction of the river.

Wendra slapped her horse with the reins and plunged forward, placing herself between the Bar'dyn and Jastail. The Quiet looked up in surprise, its death mask gone, replaced by a reasoned indifference.

"Sa'hon Ghetalloh," it said, compacting the very air around her. It turned at the sound of its brothers racing to its side. "It's time for you, Womb. No more children for dead gods."

The coarse sound of its voice caused her horse to rear, kicking with its front legs. One hoof caught the Bar'dyn in its wounded shoulder, forcing it to double over in pain. A second hoof landed on its head, driving it back into the saplings.

Wendra yelled to Jastail, "Get up!"

The highwayman struggled to his feet, leaning against the tree. She pulled her mount backward by his reins and Jastail struggled to the saddle. As Jastail put his arms around her waist, three more Bar'dyn emerged from the trees behind the saplings, where the first Bar'dyn had recovered its balance. Wendra kicked hard, spurring her horse into a dead run. Through the trees she pushed, gathering speed. Behind them, the Bar'dyn pursued, their feet pounding the ground. But slowly they outdistanced them, and before the first moon fell west of the river valley, Wendra was alone again with her captor, who sat slumped against her back.

She didn't stop to tend Jastail's wound, or to warm herself or eat. She followed the riverbank, keeping it just within sight, but stayed far enough away to avoid being seen by anyone traveling by boat. Jastail still claimed to know where Penit was, and the promise of finding the boy had filled up her mind.

The cool smell of evergreen softened the heat of their flight. And at dawn Wendra finally did stop. They all needed rest. She hoped the Bar'dyn did, as well.

Birdsong filled the strengthening daylight, and Wendra pulled up Jastail's pants leg to check his wound. He muttered incoherently, flinching at her touch.

His leg was purple and black, lined with several deep talon cuts. She cautiously made her way to the river, and wetted a length of cloth from her cloak. Crouching at the water's edge, she looked both north and south along the smooth surface that reflected a clear morning sky. No boats or Bar'dyn interrupted the perfect glass image in the water.

Silent, she paused there, listening to the lapping of water at her feet and watching swallows dart close to the surface, gathering food. The steady burn in her lungs subsided, relieving her need to rasp a song from her swollen throat. She finally wrung the cloth out and returned to find Jastail more coherent.

"Why did you save me?" he said as she knelt and gently cleaned his wound.

"The boy," she said evenly.

"And if I'm lying, you've made a very bad wager."

She lifted her face from dressing his bruised and cut leg. "It'll be the second time my life is the stakes, won't it?" she replied. "But this time, I choose it."

Jastail frowned at her words. "Who is this child to you? You could have left me to the Bar'dyn and been free. Or you could leave me now. I'm too weak to stop you." He gave a low, incredulous laugh. "But you tend my leg . . . haven't you considered how the child came so far? Who brought him or why?"

Wendra returned her attention to Jastail's leg. She finished cleaning the blood, and wrapped the cloth around the bruised and damaged flesh, tying it firmly.

"You're a highwayman. You took him. Just as you took me," Wendra reasoned. "I don't know why. But you'll have the chance to repay this kindness." She tapped his leg.

Jastail's hard, angular face betrayed no softness. In his eyes she saw the same look as she'd seen at the game table the night before. She played a dangerous game. But she had no choice.

"Come," he said, "we've lost much time."

Jastail struggled to his feet, favoring his hurt leg. Wendra stood beside him and allowed the man to lean on her as they got to the horse.

Wendra clucked softly, walking the horse to walk at an easy pace. They made their way slowly along the river valley. Shafts of light filled with motes and chaff fell through high boughs of fir and towering hemlock.

"Tell me why Bar'dyn would swim a cold river after a girl," Jastail asked, cocking a quizzical brow.

"Just help me find the boy, and you'll be glad of it, I assure you."

"Clever," Jastail said, squeezing Wendra's waist affectionately. "Making a partner of me. You've seen how well my companions fare, my lady. Be careful how you make your alliances. I expect that a time will soon come when we have fewer secrets from one another. But the time in between is fuller for the ignorance, don't you think?" Jastail smiled.

That night Jastail made a fire from wood that Wendra gathered. Her chill ran deep, having lingered in her flesh ever since the river. The bones in her legs felt brittle and shaky. Jastail had led them off the road to avoid contact with travelers. He warmed his hands at the fire, the mellow glow softening the angular shape of his face. Despite the clear sky, the air didn't grow overly cold, and slowly the chill ebbed from her body.

Jastail warmed some dried meat and bread on a rock beside the fire, giving half to Wendra and settling back against a low boulder to eat his supper in silence. The gambler and highwayman stared into the flames, his eyes distant and flickering with the light of the fire.

The lines in his face were the work of sarcasm, mockery, and deceit. His handsome features used a smile or laugh less because of amusement and more to paint the picture he wanted another to see. The sallow, tired mask he wore at the close of such a rough day was as close to anything Wendra might consider natural to him. In her mind she heard the words of the old man on the riverboat, "Too far." And yet when Jastail laughed it looked and felt genuine. The thought caused Wendra to shiver in the heat of the fire.

"Are we close to the boy?" she asked.

"Indeed, we are," Jastail replied. "Tomorrow we'll come to the place where I believe he may still be." He tossed a dry piece of cedar on the fire. "I can't guarantee it, but the odds are likely that he's there. And I'll have kept my part of our bargain by helping you find him."

Wendra eyed him suspiciously. "And what is your price?"

The same wry smile creased his face. "Isn't it possible that I have done this for charity's sake?"

"Honestly," she said, "I would bet against it."

"That's not a wager worth taking," Jastail answered. "We'll come into Galadell midday. You should sleep."

"I thought we were going to Pelan?"

"That's what I wanted the deckhands to believe," Jastail said, smiling.

The name of the town—Galadell—was unfamiliar to her, but it was Jastail's unwillingness to say what he stood to gain that unsettled her. He hadn't asked for money in exchange for information about Penit. And he hadn't sought intimate pleasures from her. His desire must be more fundamental. Or more extravagant. The riddle of it led her back to the certainty that there existed no bargain between them. His promises were possibly lies, but he'd not made a habit of overtly lying to her either. What was she not seeing?

Jastail covered himself in his blanket and closed his eyes. The last rays of light escaped the sky and gave birth to a thousand stars. Wendra persisted in trying to discover Jastail's intentions. Then suddenly, something struck her.

"What were the tokens?" she asked, her voice tremulous and louder than she'd intended.

Jastail opened his eyes and looked up into the night. "You should sleep," he repeated. But he didn't close his eyes again.

"You made me a final trump in a game of chance," she said, emotion tightening her throat. "I don't know the game, but I saw their eyes when you drew me to the table. I want to know what you made of me." Something stirred in Wendra's chest. A dark melody.

Jastail peered upward, ignoring her indignation, as though threats held no barbs for him. "No you don't, my lady. About this you should trust the liar."

"Liar?" Wendra asked, confused. "What game are you playing? Tell me!" Her voice rose, rasping in her throat. At her words the campfire pitched like a dervish stirred by the wind. The change was slight, but she'd seen it.

Jastail remained unmoved. He continued his gaze into the sky, his face slack and still.

"Very well," he finally said. "But mind you, the land east of the Lesule Valley belongs to an unrestrained few. Alliances are all that matter, and I am known in Galadell. Without me, tomorrow won't go well for you. Remember that when I tell you."

He continued to stare into the heavens, half of his face lit by the fire. Cricket song whirred in the night around them, as Wendra waited.

"I care nothing for money," he began. "Coin is the currency of the ignorant, those imprisoned in the delusion that it elevates them. The earth provides food, the animals clothes, the timber and mountains wood and stone to build homes and cities. With flint we warm ourselves, and the birds teach us music. All this is given freely. The world is plentiful, and each age inherits something of the age before it." Jastail's voice quieted. "But the deeds of men, the measure of their lives, these are things that can't be obtained from the land."

Jastail slowly turned his head toward Wendra. "The great game is to know the offering in these deeds, these sacrifices people make; to weigh their price, and barter them. To hold them in token is a dear thing." Wendra remembered the many items upon the gambling table, and her feeling that they represented actions, choices, sacrifice.

"Dearer still," Jastail went on, "is the one who can *direct* the choice, up the wager, hold the deed suspended in his hand. It's no less than holding life. For what is life but choice."

He held up the metal glove won from Ariana. "Our fair lady at the table spoke but a wish to a doting warrior, and sent him to his death, knowing he would die." Jastail's smile flared. "Do you see, his was the choice, but by her influence he chose a path of ultimate sacrifice. The glove became an emblem of his life, his will offered to another."

Anxiously, Wendra rubbed her belly. Only vaguely did she note Jastail's observant eyes as she did so. Her mind raced to remember what other tokens had lain on the game table. But she went quickly past them to Jastail's final play—pulling her toward the table's edge. A dark revelation came.

My silent gods, he does know where Penit is! That was his wager. It wasn't my life. It was my chance to find Penit.

She risked everything for it. And had Jastail lost, she'd never have found the boy.

Wendra rose from the fireside and crawled into her blanket, taking long, deep breaths of crisp night air to cool the fire that burned inside her.

• CHAPTER TWENTY-FOUR •

The Scar

We know the Velle draw life to sustain themselves. If the Veil falls,
the number of them that walk into the east . . . could be staggering.

—Ponderings on the effects of rendering,
during discussion on the topic of Imparting
in the Vault Halls of Estem Salo

Vendanj led Braethen and Mira to the top of a low hill. Over the rise stretched an endless waste.

"The Scarred Lands." Vendanj didn't wait, descending onto the long plain.

The sun grew hot, the heat also rising off the baked soil all around them. Rocks and earth were a patchwork of white and the color of soot. And everything was still, empty, quiet. What grass Braethen saw was dead. Only the hardiest sage grew, and that sparsely. Fissures yawned like sores in the arid expanse of hard-baked soil and stone.

Occasional wind dervishes licked at the earth, small flurries tugging at the brown grass that bristled with their passage.

"What caused this?" Braethen asked.

Vendanj stared into the wastes. "Velle."

"But so much?" The Scar would take days to travel through.

Vendanj waved Braethen to his side. "The First War of Promise lasted four hundred years. Not constant battle. Years of peace passed here and there. Then the Quiet would come again. Generation after generation watched their fathers go to war. Schoolrooms focused on combat strategy, whatever knowledge could be had of the Quiet. Literacy belonged only to those children whose mothers sang and read to them. Women forged weapons and bore the men that would wield them. Before the war was over, they were known as the Wombs of War."

Braethen lifted his face to the sun, wanting to shake off the chill of that term. *Wombs of war.*

Vendanj took a drink from his waterskin. "But steel alone couldn't put down the Quiet or drive them back into the Bourne. And they came with Velle and other creatures from beyond the Veil." He nodded to the landscape around them. "But this is the work of Velle."

"Dead gods, they drew this much from the land?" Braethen asked.

"The First War of Promise ended here. Called the Battle of the Round. The army of the Promise was outnumbered four to one. In the end, they formed a great circle, leaving no flank. Velle drew the life from the earth to fuel their renderings. Used it to try and end the war. But Maral Praig, Randeur of the Sheason, gathered his fellows together at the center of the round. While the army held the line, all the Sheason joined hands. Praig uttered a cry, and a light flared like the sun. Thousands of Quiet fell. Every Velle." He paused. "And every Sheason standing in the round."

Braethen was dumbstruck. "He used the life of the Sheason for his rendering. . . ."

Vendanj cast his gaze from left to right, finally looking back at Braethen. "It's an ugly wound, but a good reminder."

Across the barren landscape lingered the smells of dry sage and dirt like that of a burial cave. But there was something more. Ever since they'd come into the Scar, the quality of light, of movement, seemed strained. A lethargy permeated the place, like the broken spirit of a man.

"All this time, and still so little grows here," Braethen observed.

Vendanj took a deep breath of the dry air. "Some have tried to cultivate crops in the Scar. Gave up. The Forda is nearly gone."

"But Grant lives here," Braethen said.

"What if he says no?" Mira interjected.

Vendanj showed them each a blank stare, but said nothing.

The rest of the day they traveled in silence. The earth rolled in dry stretches. Low spots where rainwater had pooled had left behind alkali flats. Juts in the land showed coarse streaks of limestone. Other spots had turned red from long exposure to the sun, their surface rough like the dry tongue of a mongrel dog.

That sun dipped low on their left near the horizon, its weak light casting violet shadows. The Scar might have been the most barren place Braethen had seen, but the stars shone brighter here than anywhere he'd ever been.

Before full dark they stopped to set up camp. Mira saw to the horses. Braethen built a fire against the chill. And Vendanj consulted a map, using the bright stars to check position.

In those brief moments of distraction before a watch could be set, four shadows converged on them from four directions.

Mira dropped into a Far Latae stance, both swords drawn. Vendanj began lifting a hand. Braethen fumbled for his sword.

A moment later, the weak light revealed youths. None of them could have been more than sixteen years old. Two held drawn bows. Another had hands filled with knives. The tallest, like Mira, carried dual swords.

"Easy, Mira," Vendanj said, and lowered his hand.

"Forgive us, Sheason," the tallest boy said, looking at the three-ring symbol at Vendanj's neck. "There's really just one type of man that enters the Scar."

"Is Grant with you?" Vendanj asked.

"No."

Braethen let go his sword handle, which he hadn't managed yet to free from its sheath.

"How far?" Vendanj asked.

"Another day," the boy said, pointing east and north. "I can take you there. It's not easy to find."

"I know the way." Vendanj gestured to their fire. "Join us."

The four youths cautiously entered their camp, eyeing Mira and Braethen. They didn't sit, instead squatting, keeping their feet under them. Braethen guessed their leader was the oldest. The two girls were maybe fifteen. The youngest was a boy no more than thirteen.

"I'm Meche," the tall boy said, speaking to Vendanj. "We're running the south patrol toward Parley's Gap. Setting markers . . . Watching for intruders. Shall we go ahead and announce you?"

"Not if it takes you off your patrol," Vendanj replied.

A lull fell between them. "What type of men come into the Scar?" Braethen asked.

Meche looked over at him. "Those seeking to bolster their reputation by killing its warder."

Braethen followed the logic. "You live with Grant?"

"We're his wards." Meche ran a hand through his short hair. "We live here much of the time. Train." He raised the swords he still had in his hands. "And patrol."

Braethen recalled Penit's rhea-fol at the Sedagin fireside: . . . *an orphanage for foundlings, castaways, the children of unfit parents.*

Meche stood up fast. Mira a half moment later. Then the other three wards. All were looking southwest.

Moments later, over the lip of a small knoll rose nine silhouettes.

CHAPTER TWENTY-FIVE

The Wages of a Kiss

The Veil has been breached by great numbers more than once. It is typically forgotten that some Inveterae houses have come through. And largely left men alone.

—Observations of a census taker, who refused
a commission to Y'Tilat Mor

A hundred tales of caution filled Tahn's mind. Inveterae. The unredeemed. Races formed by the hands of the *noble* gods, but found somehow lacking. Races sent into the Bourne ages ago with the Quiet.

Tahn stood, frozen, scared to move. Chills ran down his arms.

Abandoning gods, Inveterae.

The oldest stories said the Inveterae and Quiet had been herded together out of the east in a mass exodus known as the Placing. But the Inveterae weren't like the creations of Quietus. The Inveterae were initially good peoples, but simply those who the First Ones had no faith in, no belief in their potential.

Because of it, they'd grown as hateful as the Quiet. That was the assumption.

But *this* Inveterae, Col'Wrent, didn't seem to be *lacking*. Not that Tahn could see. And Balatin had taught Tahn that a good greeting went a great distance. Tahn offered his hand. "I'm Tahn Junell."

The Inveterae didn't respond. The two stared at one another in the dim light of the cage. Then the creature spoke, but low so that only Tahn could hear. "The Lul'Masi have no friends in the land of men."

Tahn spared a look at Sutter lying in the straw. Returning his attention to Col'Wrent, he raised his hand higher. "Then let me be the first."

A strange look passed across the Lul'Masi's thick features. And with some hesitation, it raised its immense arm and locked hands with Tahn, his fingers were lost in the massive palm. When they joined hands, the Lul'Masi's face softened.

Tahn leaned closer still, the sharp smell of the creature strong in his nose. "The tenendra girl threatened you to force you to help us. I make you a different promise. Help my friend and I will free you from your cage."

The Lul'Masi's grip on Tahn's hand tightened uncomfortably—reflexively, Tahn thought. The creature closed its eyes for a moment, the way Tahn did when he thought of the sunrise. It breathed deeply, its chest expanding, the air it drew producing a deep rumble in its chest as it exhaled.

Finally, Col'Wrent nodded, its face as unreadable as the moment before. But gratitude passed across its eyes. "What is wrong with your friend?"

"He was struck with a spiked ball thrown by a Bar'dyn. He lost his balance, his speech, and now he's unconscious. I think he's been poisoned. The healer in town said you may know what to do."

Panic filled Tahn's chest again, as Col'Wrent did nothing more than stare at him for several long moments. Perhaps there was nothing he could do, and Sutter would die in the straw of the low one's cage.

"Bring him to me."

Tahn dragged Sutter to the back of the cage, the straw heaping around him.

Col'Wrent knelt over Sutter like a mass of boulders. "Your friend will not die. The poison in him is meant to slow, not kill. But without a cure, he could sleep for days." Col'Wrent put a finger in his mouth and drew out a thick stream of saliva and mucus. He gently pried Sutter's mouth open and wiped the viscous fluid on the tongue of Tahn's friend.

Then together they waited several long minutes in the hiss of the lantern and stink of the tent. Sutter lay unmoving for some time. At length, his eyes opened and he began to writhe in the straw and spit foulness from his lips. "What in all hells did you put in my mouth?"

"You don't want to know." Tahn put his hand on Col'Wrent's shoulder in appreciation, feeling the strong, rough skin of the Lul'Masi.

Suddenly, Sutter realized where he was and looked up into the broad face of his healer. He scrambled back against the side of the cage, trying to free his sword, but fumbling with the weapon.

"Easy, Sutter." Tahn pointed at Sutter's blade. "You were poisoned by the Bourne, and you've been healed by the Bourne. Maybe a thank-you is in order."

Sutter stared, incredulous. "Thank you?"

"Good enough," Tahn said.

From behind them, Alisandra called, "Looks like you're finished. I'll take my second half now."

With his back shielding their exchange, Tahn spoke in low tones. "She won't let you approach the door. I'll get the key from her—"

"No," Col'Wrent said in a deep whisper. "She won't trust you. Tent folk thrive because they are greedy and assume all others are like themselves."

"Then how?" Tahn asked.

"What's going on?" Alisandra asked, impatience edging her tone. "Your friend looks fine. Get out here."

"What bribe got you into my cage?" Col'Wrent asked with a hint of distaste.

"Three and six," Tahn replied.

"You were wise enough to hold back full payment?"

"Half before, half after."

Col'Wrent looked over Tahn's shoulder. Patient eyes surveyed the cage door, then returned to Tahn. "Tell her how low and stupid I am. Tell her you believe you've already trained me to perform simple tricks, like a dog. That you got me to lift my hand, and that you are going to have me hold out the balance of her payment in my servile palm for her to take. The tent folk are wary, but infected with greed and pride beyond their caution. I will play my part, until her hand is close enough to grasp."

There was no murder in Col'Wrent's eyes, but Tahn hadn't yet seen any real emotion in them, either. Caging the Lul'Masi was wrong, but he didn't want Alisandra killed.

"I can't help you if you intend to kill her," Tahn said.

Col'Wrent's brow tightened. Tahn craned his neck back to look up at the towering creature. Slowly, Col'Wrent extended a hand and placed it on Tahn's chest. "I will do as you ask."

Tahn took out his money pouch and dropped the coins in Col'Wrent's large hand. He then whirled, adopting a self-congratulatory grin, and strode confidently to the door.

"He is indeed low," Tahn said to Alisandra as he came close to her. "But hardly the monster you described. He has the mind of a child."

"But the body of a Slope Nyne," Alisandra put in.

"I've never seen such a thing," Tahn answered. He leaned casually against the inner bars of the cage. "A dog bites when it's threatened or beaten into a corner," he explained. "But let the dog smell you, show no fear, and it welcomes you into its home. Will even perform tricks for you."

"Tricks?" Alisandra said suspiciously.

"Nothing as fancy as the feats in your larger tents, but I have given the beast the rest of your money, and some extra besides, and asked him to bring it to you."

Alisandra took up a dagger.

"There's no need of that," Tahn said. "The creature wants to serve. A kind word and second meal bowl will earn you his trust. Think of the money to be made by bringing people to this cage and letting them inside to pet its hoary skin. You could train it to do small tricks." Tahn leaned in conspiratorially. "Your mastery over it will make you rich."

Alisandra's eyes danced with the prospect. She appraised the Lul'Masi, greed written large upon her face. Then her lust for lucre gave way to the guarded look she naturally wore. "Why tell me this? What gain is there for you? Do you want a partnership?"

Sutter laughed, causing Alisandra to frown. "No partnership," Tahn said. "A kiss."

The request startled the girl for a moment, and she drew her head back in obvious suspicion, a grin teasing at one corner of her mouth.

"I don't care for the beast, and I don't seek my fortune," Tahn said confidentially. "My friend is healed, I have what I want . . . mostly."

"Mostly?" Alisandra's beautiful, dangerous smile returned.

"I'll have a kiss from you without price, and then I'll carry the memory of winning your favor without lightening my purse. It will warm me when my fires grow cold."

Sutter laughed from behind him, but this time Alisandra regarded Tahn with appreciation.

"Well, boy," Alisandra said, "you may have your kiss, and that will put paid to all future claims you might make." She inclined toward him, stopping short. "And you'll take this information with you when you leave Squim. Should another come to understand the gentle nature of the beast, I'll find you and show you your earth."

Tahn shook his head and puckered clownishly. Alisandra put her soft lips to his own, and Tahn's pucker melted beneath the heat of her mouth. She moved her lips across his for several moments, taking, he thought, some pleasure in the kiss. The touch and taste of her lips, the danger and mystery of her, the striking beauty, all of it raced through Tahn. He thrilled with the ruse, and his own fledgling desires. He'd never forget this kiss. Alisandra gave a soft, submissive sound before pulling away. Tahn's mouth hung open as she called the beast toward her.

Col'Wrent walked sheepishly, cowering but advancing at her call.

Tahn could see Alisandra had bought his story. A wild light shone in her eyes like that of a child waiting to be given gifts. Hesitantly, Col'Wrent approached until he was within arm's reach. He turned his head, looking away with mock fear as he proffered his palm filled with coins. His fingers trembled as the girl reached to take the money. In her confidence, she made no haste in gathering the coins.

In an instant, the Lul'Masi took Alisandra by the wrist, her hand going white fast. He yanked the girl toward him, and wrapped his mighty arms around her. He squeezed until her face reddened to the hue of summer apples. She lost all her breath before she could utter a cry, and moments later slipped to the floor.

Tahn dove to his knees to check her breathing. She was alive, merely unconscious.

"We should hurry," Sutter slurred, still woozy. "The town won't be safe once they find out what we've done."

Tahn stood, dwarfed beneath the Lul'Masi. "Thank you."

"The debt is mine," Col'Wrent answered. "Now go. Your friend is right. I will free the others."

Tahn and Sutter raced to the end of the tent. Sutter ducked outside, but Tahn looked back to see the Lul'Masi take the key from Alisandra's hand and begin to open the other cages. Col'Wrent looked up and caught Tahn's eye. A look of gratitude passed between them, and it made Tahn wonder about the nature of the Inveterae. This one, anyway. It didn't seem to *lack*.

Then Sutter pulled Tahn through the tent flap and they ran back past the tenendra toward town.

They rode most of the night north out of Squim. They didn't speak, putting leagues between themselves and the tenendra. In the waning hours of night, Tahn turned his attention east and thought about the coming of dawn, about another day of life. He imagined the rays of sunrise striking a more peaceful world, one where Wendra hummed over morning bacon. The thought of his sister ended his ritual predawn reverie. Skies, he missed her. There seemed a hole inside him. He couldn't remember a time without her in his life. Not where he couldn't go to her if he needed to. Or if she needed him.

And again he recalled the moment when he hesitated in releasing his draw on the Bar'dyn hovering over his sister's birth bed. *I'm so sorry, Wendra.*

Those maddening words—*I draw with the strength of my arms . . .* —Tahn's frustration returned.

Sometime later, full day lit the sky.

Near midday, Tahn spied the double mountain in the east. "That way." He pointed.

Sutter's brow creased. "There's no road."

"We're going to Qum'rahm'se," Tahn explained.

"Even though Vendanj said to get to Recityv," Sutter argued.

"We might find the others there," Tahn reasoned. "If not, we can at least collect whatever Vendanj meant to find. Papers on the Covenant Tongue. Make sure it gets to the right hands."

"You mean if Vendanj even made it out of those nasty clouds. . . . What am I saying? That man's too thorny to die by cloud." Then, like a man remembering his own purpose—*adventure*—Sutter jumped from his horse. "Let's go."

Tahn did the same, wincing when he hit the ground—he'd forgotten his wounded foot.

"Watch those delicate toes," Sutter ribbed. "I have it on good authority that they intend to dance a turn with a quick-footed Far. You'd better stay on the mend."

Tahn half-smiled.

Sutter put his hand on Tahn's arm, his smile fading. He turned to face Tahn. "Thank you."

"What?"

"Don't get me wrong. It's no treat to taste the snot of a brute from the Bourne. Thing gave me the crawls." He paused. "But you went into that cage and could've been its next meal. You didn't know what it might've done."

Tahn tried to dismiss it. "You'd have done the same—"

"Yeah, I would have," Sutter cut in. "But . . . there's only a few who'd take that risk for me."

Sutter was surely thinking about the man and woman who'd raised him, and about his actual birth parents, who'd given him up. Maybe a lot of who his friend had become had to do with trying to reconcile himself with—or maybe leave behind—the choices those people had made. Maybe Sutter felt dispensable. And suddenly some of the jokes they'd shared all their lives echoed back a touch darker.

Tahn thought. "I won't be caught on the wrong side of helping a friend, Sutter. Not ever again."

They traveled the rest of the day, mostly walking. The ravine led to a river running south. They turned north. Near dusk, they descended a low ridge. The hum of the river rose beside them, a soothing, familiar sound. They stopped to let their mounts drink. An orange sun reflected its double in the glossy surface, river flies and other insects darting to and fro over the calm water. The ripples of fish surfacing to feed briefly interrupted the languid smoothness. Near the shore, the river bottom tapered gradually, the water clear enough to see the sands in the shallows.

Tahn looked out over the river with relief. This, at least, was good fortune—rivers meant food, water, and always met a road if you followed them far enough. He let his horse drink, and laid himself in the shallows facedown to do the same. The chill water felt good on his skin.

After a few mouthfuls, his head was forced down into the water.

A dark certainty filled him. This hand around his neck didn't belong to his friend.

CHAPTER TWENTY-SIX

Dust on the Boards

I grind the rocks. I've nothing to do with who makes a stick of chalk, or dry-powder for a slave's foot. I grind, see. That's all. But now that you mention it, I'm not sure why we're worried about Quiet when our own kind are selling folks.

—Investigation interview conducted
by League surveyors into reports about
human trade in the upper Balens

The day after the riverboat fire, Jastail led Wendra north. They left the road at midday, and traveled an hour of unmarked terrain before cresting a knoll and looking down at a makeshift town. No real roads. No stone buildings. Worry stole over her as they went slowly into Galadell.

Not a single man or woman failed to take note of them. A few nodded to Jastail, but didn't verbally greet him. He nodded in return, an air of authority in the angle of his head. Something bothered Wendra about the place. It felt impermanent, as though it could be abandoned at a moment's notice. She sensed no sort of commitment, or community, or tradition here.

They stopped at a ramshackle establishment near the center of town. Beside the door hung a weathered sign nailed to the wall announcing the "Overland Bed and Cup." Jastail looked both ways along the street before entering into the dimness beyond the door. Wendra shot a glance over her shoulder at the passersby, catching one of them in a long, appraising gaze that didn't flinch at being caught. Quickly, she followed Jastail inside.

The room stood weakly lit by a few sparsely placed candles inside glass lanterns, and by a bit of daylight that crept through cracks in the poor carpentry along the outer walls. The smell of stale bitter hung in the air, along with boiled roots and a meat odor unfamiliar to her. The tables were empty save for two nearest the back where a set of wine barrels had been fastened to the wall. Drips fell from spigots into cups placed on the floor to catch them. A man in a long leather apron sat beside the barrels with a short-brimmed hat drawn low on his brow. His chair stood tilted back against the wall and his chest rose and fell in the slow, steady rhythm of sleep.

Jastail moved soundlessly across the floor and made as though to take up one of the cups catching the spillage. The chair legs came down fast and the man's hand latched onto Jastail's before he could lift the glass.

"You're slowing down, Himney," Jastail said.

The other laughed. "I'm old. But there's not a thief swift enough yet to take bitter from me."

Jastail put the cup back under the drip, and pulled Himney to his feet. They clasped each other by the wrist and shook in two deliberate up and down motions.

Himney let go Jastail's hand and nudged the cup the highwayman had put back so that drips hit its exact center.

Jastail dug into his cloak and pulled out a coin, walking it along his knuckles with deft skill. He then tossed the coin up. Before it could finish rising, Himney snatched it from the air. The little man licked the coin, running his tongue over its surface and along its edge, then rolling his eyes up as he concentrated and wagged his tongue just behind his teeth. Satisfied, he hid the coin so fast Wendra wasn't sure where it went. He then picked up two fresh cups from a shelf between the wine barrels and filled them for Jastail and Wendra.

"Still the best nose in open land," Jastail said with bemusement.

"Can't run risks with the dreck that scuttles through these parts, my friend." He led them to a table away from the few patrons and put their cups on one side, positioning himself on the other with a clear view of his wine barrels. Once seated, he eyed Wendra with a long, hard look, making her feel like a coin held in his sweaty lips. "You've been busy lately, friend. The open country is treating you well."

Jastail took a long drink. He wiped his mouth and leveled his gaze at Himney. "Must be my honest face."

The two chuckled.

When their chuckles had faded to smiles, Jastail said, "Things haven't been"— he looked at Wendra—"easy," he finished. "Tell me the news, Himney, and leave the garnish for the next man. I've no patience for tales, and no money for lies or rumors."

The other man raised his hands before him and waved them to shush Jastail. "I understand. Earth and dust, but you do go on. Drink your bitter and let me do some talking." Himney leaned forward in his seat and rested his elbows on the table. One eyebrow cocked upward quizzically. His tongue lashed out in a quick motion, licking the sweat from his lips. He then drew a breath, paused dramatically, and began in a cautious voice.

"Dust is up, dust is up," he said.

Something about Himney's use of the word "dust" unnerved her.

"Men come into Galadell two and three a day, north out of Ringstone, south from Chol'Den'Fas, even from the east, the coast of Kuren. But you," Himney said, pointing at Jastail, "you go to the west. What do you know that the others don't?" He pondered for a moment, then went on. "But less than a handful know the trade like you, Jastail. Not like you."

"Any strangers come to the lowland?" Jastail tapped the table, as though meaning Galadell.

"We haven't seen any. Though there's talk of a three-ring. Some say the Quiet press close." Himney nodded dismissively. "Nothing new there. But most of the new traders have no sense of what they do, only itchy palms for coin."

"A different breed entirely," Jastail agreed, looking directly at Himney's waist belt, from which hung several leather purses. "Tell me more of the Quiet."

Himney bent forward toward them and talked so low that many of his words were nothing more than the movement of lips. "There's talk of a full collough come across the Pall as far south as Vohnce." Himney swallowed. "And rumors that the Velle lead them." He stopped, seeming to think about what he'd just said.

"Anyone seen it with their own eyes?" Jastail asked.

"One," Himney said. "The others like to prattle about it, though. As for myself, I take the talk as truth. The skies are not as friendly as they were ten . . . five years since."

"Your barrels empty sooner with less coin in your purse," Jastail said without humor.

"No!" Himney barked, immediately quieting himself. "I mean that the night holds longer. Cycles seem confused of their proper time. Winter comes early. Spring comes late. Summer falls like the bake of the smithy's forge."

"Dreadfully poetic for a bitter salesman in a leaky Galadell tavern," Jastail said, the mockery still dark.

Himney made a vulgar gesture. "Fah, you asked for the recent news. This is it." Himney pointed a finger at Jastail. "We don't go to the Bourne. But now it comes to us."

A grim look tugged at the lines in Jastail's weathered face. Wendra couldn't place it. His usual cynicism remained, but now it appeared broken, tentative. She thought about the Bar'dyn on the riverboat and their fight near the bank of the Lesule River. Jastail perhaps understood more of the truth in the rumors than he let on. And he already assumed that Wendra was keeping something back from him. Sooner or later he'd force the issue: why Bar'dyn chased a girl with nothing of apparent value.

"Has the dust gone up today?" Jastail asked.

"Not yet," Himney said. "You'll know when. The tables fill with men who take a cup before heading to the boards."

Wendra finally had to ask. "What is the 'dust'?"

Himney's gaze shifted to her, and he retracted his head the way a turtle does when it feels threatened. Wendra met the look squarely.

"Shut her up," Himney said emphatically. "She has no business asking."

"Calm yourself," Jastail replied. He returned his attention to Wendra. "My lady, this, too, is something you'll understand when you meet the boy. I must ask you—"

"To hells with you," Wendra said, rising from her chair. "I played your game. From the North Face to the river to this godsforsaken place. I came because of the boy. I was a token for your gambling. And I saved you from the Bar'dyn." She glared, losing patience, feeling tones shifting in her chest. "Now take me to him! If he's in this place, then now. If not here, then let's go. I warn you."

Jastail regarded her with little concern. But something did rise in his face. Something that might have heard the notes churning inside her. Even just hearing these fragments of melody in her mind made her skin tingle. *The bottom of pain.* She stepped closer to him.

Jastail stared back evenly. "You may be right, my lady," he said, sounding deferential. "But haven't you learned that *chance* is all that matters to me? If your threat is more than simple desperation, then maybe there are odds to play. I'd like that. And in any case . . ." He sat forward in his chair, so that his face was directly beneath hers. "You could be dead long before any risk presents itself." He smiled calmly. The look of it was the most natural thing Wendra had ever seen on his rough face. "Hold your tongue and you'll have your answers soon enough."

Wendra's song stirred inside her, and she shuddered under its intensity. She grasped the table's edge to stop herself from collapsing and eased herself back into her chair.

Slowly, she blocked out the continuing conversation, focusing on the thrumming in her head, a pulse that emanated from every part of her. A pulse that felt like the sound of a musician's bow drawn slowly across the strings of a bass fiddle.

An hour later the tables filled, just as Himney had predicted. The tavern remained quiet, with low chatter as people took one cup, drank it quickly, and left the way they'd come. When the tables emptied, Jastail stood and shook Wendra to follow. She got to her feet with the hope of finding Penit. Jastail put a coin on the table and gave Himney a watchful stare. Then out he went, not looking to be sure Wendra followed.

Into the street they strode. Men and women were running past them toward a square where all the town seemed to be gathering. Wendra could feel excitement in the air; nothing spoken, but nonetheless singing in her nerves as if everyone in town knew the same secret. The crowd didn't jostle for position, but found places from which to see. And then they waited. Many of them held colored sticks, marked with numbers. An ominous feeling crept over her.

Jastail led her to a place near a raised wood platform. "The boards," he said, indicating the single most finely crafted structure in the ramshackle town. Long slats of oak lay neatly fitted together to form the raised platform six feet off the ground. On either side stairs ascended to the boards, which stretched thirty feet long. A short table and chair stood near the left edge, a locked ledger and quill set there.

Moments later the crowd parted and several individuals were led toward the platform by a tall man, thick in the waist and shoulders. Wendra couldn't see who they were, but the procession stopped at the foot of the stair. The tall man bent to do something before escorting a bound woman to the desk. A second man clasping a key fixed to a chain he wore around his neck rushed up the stairs and took a seat at the table. Quickly, he put the key to a lock that sealed the book, and opened it. Dipping the quill in a reservoir of ink, he inclined his ear as the big man said something softly to him. Then the big man ushered the bound woman to the center of the platform and turned her toward the crowd.

Looking on, Wendra now knew what "dust is up" meant. The woman's feet had been powdered with talc or chalk, and with each step dust rose in a faint blue-white cloud.

The big man raised his hand and gestured with several fingers. Members of the crowd lifted their colored sticks with the painted numbers on them. No one spoke, the mild breeze whistling through cracks in the poorly built structures around them. The woman stared at her feet, her bedraggled hair hanging limp from her scalp and obscuring her features. She wore a shapeless smock, drawn in at the waist with a length of rope. The man pointed to one of the many sticks, then raised his hand again, performing a complicated series of hand gestures. More sticks went up, but not as many as the first time. Again the pattern was repeated, each time fewer sticks rising into the air, until but one stick rose above the crowd. The bullish man pulled the woman to the stairs at the right, where she met the woman who had purchased her.

The officious little man at the table wrote in his ledger, dipping his quill feverishly to record the transaction. Then the large fellow descended the stair, again bent out of sight before rising and escorting a young girl to the boards. Information went into the book under the small man's quill, and powdered feet trod the boards to the center, where frightened eyes looked out on the bidders.

Wendra's gorge rose. *This is madness! People can't be bought and sold!* But Jastail stood beside her, a living rebuttal to the notion that even Wendra was free. And something more lingered beyond her awareness, something awful, something that her mind shielded her from, wouldn't let her see. She tried to recall a melody or lyric to give her comfort, but at the sight of the young girl her throat swelled shut. Jastail put a hand on Wendra's arm to steady her. She didn't shrug it away.

Again the large man lifted his hand and declared some unknown price. All sticks went up. The man smiled, showing a mouthful of bad teeth. He'd grossly underestimated her value. This time his hand fingered a simple gesticulation. Half the sticks remained up this time. The cycle repeated, and the girl on the boards watched in dawning horror at the event unfolding around her. The rounds of bidding extended further, but still only the wind talked, ruffling the girl's downy hair and kissing her chalked feet with delicate plumes of dust over the neatly manicured lengths of wood.

As the auction wound down to two bidders, one of them waved his stick. At that, the auctioneer removed the young girl's dress so that her buyers could view her naked body.

Wendra fell weak against Jastail. But a song stirred deep inside. The tingling began to crawl into every part of her, leaving her disoriented—weak but angry, unable to act but desperate to do something.

More came to the boards. Chalked feet. Vacant eyes. Mostly women and girls, occasionally a frail man, but never the old.

And then a young boy was put upon the boards. . . .

• CHAPTER TWENTY-SEVEN •

Wards of the Scar

For me, calling them Quiet is as much about the way they look and feel and die as it is about them following Quietus. What scares me more is wondering how they got this way.

—From a missive written by a Reaper,
sent home two days before the Battle
of the Hand, in which he died

The nine silhouettes were too tall to be more of Grant's wards. But not thick enough to be Bar'dyn. They came. Unhurried. Directly toward Braethen and the others.

Meche and the other wards fanned out into a staggered line. They'd never let go their weapons. Mira took several steps forward, putting herself between the strangers and Vendanj, who squinted against the dusk to try and see who approached.

Braethen pulled his sword from its sheath, reticent. *I am I,* he thought, trying to steel himself.

Moments stretched. The nine drew nearer. And when they came into close view, they looked like . . . men and women. Braethen glanced at Vendanj to gauge his reaction. The Sheason stared ahead, a severe expression on his face. Disgust and readiness to kill. As he always had when facing the Quiet.

But the only remarkable thing about the nine, besides the fact that they had weapons in their hands, was the indifference in their eyes. The cool reason and lack of regard. There seemed something ruined in them, *turned.* They wore no armor. No cloaks. Only well-used, practical coats, buttoned high.

"They look like an autumn harvest crew," Braethen muttered.

Vendanj shook his head. "They are Quiet."

The air thickened. The early evening chill deepened.

They spoke no words. Never paused. Simply walked to Mira first, staffs and steel coming up only when they were finally necessary.

Mira ducked under a clever feint and thrust, then struck the first in the stomach with both blades. The Quiet never cried out or showed the pain of death. The man folded to the ground.

To the right, each ward met one of the Quiet. They moved with grace, anticipating strikes and sweeps as if they'd seen them two moments earlier. Mira engaged a stout-looking woman who, like her, carried two swords. The three remaining Quiet came at Vendanj.

Braethen stepped in to defend the Sheason.

Vendanj pulled him back. "Not these ones," he said. Then he pointed at the closest Quiet man. The stranger's neck cracked, his head falling at an odd angle. And he slumped to the ground.

A Quiet woman made a quick throw of a knife, trying to catch Vendanj off guard. He swept his arm to the right and the knife went sailing off into the sage. But she followed close, lunging at him, and taking him to the ground.

As they rolled, the third got in close to Braethen. He raised his sword, wondering if the darkness would take him again and hint of another place and time. Hint at a painful remembrance. There wasn't time. As the Quiet woman stepped close, her face plain and unexpressive, he began . . . *not* to feel. A kind of apathy came from being so close to her. He suddenly cared less about succeeding as a sodalist, cared less about his books, about his father. Even Vendanj and getting to Tillinghast, it all cascaded down to nothing.

And he began slowly to lower his blade.

The woman stared at him as he lost his own regard for things, including his own misspent life. But it wasn't sadness he felt. It was nothing. It was a *lack* inside. And he didn't regret the loss.

In those long moments, he saw the four wards fighting the Quiet back. They moved in easy rhythms almost as if the battle were choreographed. And though they were outsized, one by one, the wards took the Quiet down. And not a single one cried out or showed emotion as they fell to death.

Beyond the woman standing in front of Braethen, Mira finished off the Quiet woman she'd been fighting. And to his right, Vendanj pinned the woman to the ground and placed a hand on her chest. Another time, it might have looked like a gesture meant to calm a panicked mother. Tonight, it made her body go still, her eyes glaze.

He had an instant to wonder why only he seemed susceptible to the feeling emanating from this breed of Quiet. Then the Quiet woman in front of him pulled back her arm, set to run her steel into his gut. He fought the lethargy. He fought the apathy. He tried to remember A'Posian and reading on the porch. Something warm.

It was no use.

Only in the last moment did it occur to him. Disregard. Disregard for this Quiet woman. Not anger. Not defense. Not better cause. He simply took in the waves of indifference and turned them back on her. And to be safe, instead of his sword, he drew his short knife and put it in her belly.

He'd expected to see surprise in her eyes, staring at him from a hand's length away. Maybe a grimace. But he didn't even see a storyteller's gratitude for release. She carried her disregard with her to the hard earth and her eyes lost their sight in her expressionless face.

A rush of feeling came in his body. Painful. Running hot and cold. He fought not to laugh then cry then scream. He sank to his knees beside the Quiet woman and saw feet gather around him.

"What happened? What were they?" he asked, staring at the dead Quiet. Softer, "Did you feel it?"

Vendanj put a hand on his shoulder. "I'm too much a bastard to have felt it deeply," he said. "And these," he nudged the woman with his boot, "are just another Quiet race. Sometimes called 'heedless.'"

Braethen looked the same question at Mira, then the wards of the Scar.

Did you feel it?

Mira only frowned.

Meche stared at the Quiet woman. "We are a long time in the Scar."

CHAPTER TWENTY-EIGHT

Tracker

All things have a signature inside them that may be identified. No matter where. Or when.

—Last-level study of the Leiholan
—*Rudiments of Absolute Sound*

Tahn struggled to get free. He pushed his hands into the soft river bottom, trying to rise up. No use. Whatever had him was much too powerful. His lungs started to burn, and he thrashed from side to side, twisting his neck and bucking his feet. The water around his head clouded red, the fingers digging into his skin and cutting his neck.

He collapsed his arms, hoping to surprise his attacker and win some advantage. His face quickly met the bottom, his nose filling with wet sand.

His chest spasmed, trying to force a breath. He stifled the need, but would soon suck water in and start to drown.

Around his face, the water clouded, obscuring his vision. He reached back desperately, hoping to grab his assailant's arm and pull him into the water. He couldn't get hold. The water roiled. Murky light bent and shadowed in his eyes. He twisted, and began trying to kick the man off his feet.

The legs didn't give, rooted like iron in the river bottom.

The urge to draw breath became too much, and Tahn heaved a huge rush of cold water through his nose and mouth. The feel of it down his throat came like a dagger. He immediately began to cough. Panic swelled in him, and he thrashed, trying not to breathe again.

Getting his feet under him, he pushed up with all his strength, and broke the surface. He gasped a breath, and saw a water-blurred image of Sutter rushing to his horse twenty strides away, just before the creature thrust his head back into the river.

He clawed at the hand around his neck, beating at the fingers and wrist. The man's grip held him. Tahn's lungs began to burn again, and in his eyes he could see red dots flashing. His resistance ebbed, his arms tired, grew heavy.

Then vaguely, the sound of rapid splashes echoed under the water like dull thuds. They grew nearer, deeper, louder.

His lungs began to spasm, and then suddenly the hand pulled free, the fingernails tearing away thick strips of his skin.

Tahn shot to the surface, gulping air in a loud, hoarse rush. He retched and fell back down, coughing and choking. His gut still felt like ice, like he was drowning.

He whirled and saw a figure in simple charcoal-colored clothes regaining its balance. The tracker that had been following them since before the high plains. Sutter had been thrown aside in the shallow water. Tahn realized the splashes he'd heard were Sutter's running steps as his friend had thrown himself at the tracker. The figure lashed at Sutter, who scrambled out of the way and fell back into the river. The creature wheeled around, fixing its eyes on Tahn. Its pale skin glistened with water beneath a drenched cloak that clung to its emaciated frame.

"Patience, child," the creature admonished. "I've no intention of killing you. Just breaking your spirit before taking you back."

Tahn scrambled away like a river crab, trying to regain his feet and reach his bow. He stole a look over his shoulder at the horses, which had run some distance away and milled nervously near the trees.

The tracker came on, its feet gliding through the water without breaking the surface.

A bare smile spread on its face as it fast closed the distance between them. The grin drew rough, unnatural lines in the tight, thin skin, which threatened to split over the tracker's sharp, angular features. It came on, hunched, bent as though stooped forever to the ground. Its fingers coursed across the river's surface, likewise making no mark.

Tahn tried to stand, his wet cloak catching beneath his foot and tripping him back into the shallows. He flipped over to meet the tracker, who rushed at him.

The keening of a blade drawn from its sheath.

Sutter's longblade lodged itself in the tracker's right shoulder. A grimace of anger and hatred twisted on its lips. It swung around to deal with Sutter, giving Tahn time to get up. Pain shot through his foot with each running stride, but he forced himself to move faster.

Reaching his horse, he pulled his bow and wheeled about, knocking an arrow.

The tracker was almost on Sutter, who knelt at the riverside, blood on his hands, staring helplessly toward Tahn. The Quiet raised a hand. Tahn drew, the old words racing through his mind. One arrow, a second, and a third whistled from his string, biting the tracker in the back one after the other.

A scream split the air, waves welling in the river, leaves quaking on their branches.

The tracker slowed, turned toward Tahn, and came on. Tahn backpedaled, fumbling for more arrows as he retreated. The sound of running footfalls came across the riverbank. The tracker turned again, to meet Sutter's charge.

Nails skidded to a stop, using his momentum to swing his sword with reckless abandon. The sound of steel biting the air echoed across the water. But the tracker evaded the blow and shot one long arm at Sutter, taking his neck in its powerful grasp. Sutter dropped his blade, using both hands to try and loosen the tracker's grip. His face reddened. The veins in his neck and forehead swelled with blood. The Quiet lifted Sutter from the ground. A terrible stream of clucks and choked words fell from his friend's lips.

Sutter's legs flailed, trying to kick the tracker. But he only feebly hit the body wrapped in the wet folds of its cloak. His friend's mouth gaped open, trying to draw air. Blood welled onto Sutter's lips and began dripping from his nose.

At last, Tahn fingered some arrows. Already speaking his cant as he nocked them, he let three more arrows fly into the tracker's humped back. The creature reared, releasing Sutter, who fell to the ground clutching his throat.

The wizened visage turned on Tahn, bloodied lips rasping curses Tahn didn't understand: *"Je'malta yed solet, Stille. Sine ti stondis roche."* It crumpled to the ground, one withered hand creeping forward toward him. Then it ceased to move altogether.

Giving the tracker a wide berth, Tahn rushed to Sutter's side. His friend sat huddled, wheezing, his hands working ineffectually at his throat. Lifting his wet cloak, Tahn wiped Sutter's face and helped him lie back on the ground.

"Slowly, breathe slowly," he instructed.

Sutter shook his head, gulping air. His neck had already purpled from the attack, dark blood suffusing the skin. Tahn began taking exaggerated breaths in a slow, steady rhythm to lead Sutter in his own breathing. After several moments, they both calmed, lying wet and bloodied in the shade of a river tree just strides from the dead tracker.

When the pounding of his heart eased beneath the sound of the river, Tahn looked at his friend, whose eyes seemed lost in the nearness of his own death. "Would it be too much to ask you to find that balsam root now? I'm kind of sore."

Sutter rolled his head over to look at his friend. "Foot still bothering you, is it?" Neither laughed. "The tracker wasn't interested in me, Tahn."

"Not until you picked up that sword of yours," Tahn said in a grateful tone.

Sutter shook his head. "Even after I knocked it off you, it just turned back." His friend's eyes darkened momentarily. "What did it want?"

Patience, child, I've no intention of killing you. Just breaking your spirit before taking you back.

Tahn looked at his friend. "I think it wanted to take me into the Bourne. But I'm not the first. And I doubt I'll be the last."

Sutter studied Tahn's face for several moments, his eyes moving over every feature as if he'd never seen Tahn before. Then he propped himself up, grimacing with the effort. "We'd better get moving. Where there's one, there may be more. I can't promise to save you more than once a day."

While his friend looked for more balsam, Tahn filled the waterskins and gathered the horses. Sutter quickly mashed his harvested roots into a paste, and he and Tahn both spread it liberally over their abrasions and cuts, wrapping them with strips of cloth. They grinned at the similarity they bore one another with their necks thickly swaddled. Sutter applied poultices to cuts across each forearm. And Tahn took some of the paste under his tongue, sucking the bittersweet juice to ease the throbbing in his foot.

Before setting out, they dragged the tracker to the river and cast it facedown in the shallows. Tahn fell to his knees beside the body, the panicked feeling of not being able to breathe still aching in his chest. He dropped his bow and looked toward Sutter, who stood over the Quiet, a grimace twisting his lips.

"It's dead," he said, sounding like he was trying to convince himself. "It's dead."

Then Sutter pushed the shape from the shallows into the deeper water, where the current began to pull it downriver. The tracker floated away into the scarlet-tinged water of sunset. Soon, the lump might have been nothing more than a fallen log pulled from the shore during a heavy rain. After another moment, the body was gone, swept south and away.

"I didn't hear it coming," Tahn said.

Sutter continued to watch the river where the figure had disappeared. He shook his head. "It didn't make a sound. Even in the river." His friend's hands and arms shook, trembling from cold and fright and weariness, the blade in his hands dangling in the water. "We were lucky."

Tahn followed Sutter's gaze. "Part lucky, part brave."

Sutter shook his head again. "Instinct. Survival."

"That, too," Tahn admitted. "But we got the best of it the way we always beat Maxon Drell or Fig Sholeer."

"Yeah, but you were under a long time. I thought you drowned for sure."

"Me?" Tahn said with mock confidence. "I was just letting you test that sword of yours."

Sutter turned back to Tahn, and the two shared nervous laughter in the waning light of day.

When quiet returned, Sutter looked Tahn in the eye. "You know what I thought about?"

Tahn didn't understand the question.

"When I thought it might kill us? When I thought this was truly the end?" A pained look drew Sutter's eyes and mouth taut again. "I thought of that root farm. I thought of Father and Mother, and that they must think they failed making me feel loved. And when I thought it, part of me wanted to kill that thing so I could go back and tell them the truth." He stopped, swallowing back emotion. "But part of me wondered if dying today . . ."

Tahn looked out at the river, letting the admission pass without comment or judgment.

But Tahn's friend had struck a chord. "You know what *I* thought about?"

Sutter wiped moist eyes and shook his head.

"I thought about my parents' funerals. The sound of the earth covering them over one shovel at a time. And Wendra, and how I wasn't there to protect her when she was raped." Tahn shook his head in self-reproof. "But then I saw her grow happy as she became excited for her baby. She's all the family I have left, and it was good to hear her sing again." Emotion thickened in his own throat. "Then I thought about that Bar'dyn taking her child."

And Tahn finally shared a secret of his own, the very old compulsion to utter those words before he could release a single arrow. He shared how it had kept him from his own sister's defense in her time of greatest need. And when he was done, he hung his head for a long while.

When he looked up at his friend, he saw him bleeding beside him, a gift sword laid across his knees, less than a day removed from Bourne poison in his blood, and remembering the two people who had taught him to farm the dirt.

They shared wan smiles.

Under a crimson and violet sky, they led their horses north, taking a course just inside the river tree line, each carrying his weapon in hand. A few hours later, they returned to the river, and found a shallow cave in the high bank from which the water had receded. They made camp there, eating a cold meal to avoid the smell of fire on the wind, too weary even to jest. Alternating their watch, they finally slept.

Images from the mist spun in his dreams like bits of flotsam in a river eddy. And under it all was the vague dream of scorched earth feeling bruised by an endless, savage sun and touched by the taint of the Bourne. And a faceless man teaching him how to aim, how to focus . . .

Tahn awoke to stars that still held their places in the heavens.

Despite his exhaustion, he propped himself up on his elbows. He looked east and wondered if the sun would ever cease its cycle, and why each day he paused to consider the dawn. Maybe it was more than mere solace.

The smell of dew rose from the ground. The comforting fragrance eased into him, and he closed his eyes to envision the dawn. The moment stretched out as he watched in his mind's eye the path of the sun. Suddenly, the image flooded with red. The sun shone a bloody hue, and the mountains, clouds, treetops, everything in his mind turned scarlet.

The world ignited, the air burning and the rocks melting into rivers of blood. The sun shimmered in hues of crimson and sable, flickering like a man blinking blood from his eyes. Tahn began to choke, the horror in his mind making it hard to breathe. He couldn't open his eyes, couldn't free himself from the images in his head.

Strangled pleas gurgled from his throat. Then hands were on his shoulders, shaking him. Words cascaded down to him as though spoken from very far away.

"Tahn, wake up!"

But he *was* awake. He tried to say so, only his swollen tongue wouldn't obey.

Hands slapped his face, but the vision held. His heart thumped in his ears and behind his eyes, the rhythm slowing, growing louder, like the single, great beat they'd heard in the mist. Then stillness. The scarlet sun faded.

"Silent gods!" he screamed. But the sound of it echoed small and only in his head.

A hand struck his back, batting him. Soon after, water splashed his face. But the sensations were distant and soft the way a bird's wing sounds across a lake, or the cry of a loon comes muffled by the cloak of night.

"Tahn. Breathe," he heard, and thought he knew the voice, but couldn't place it.

He gasped a breath as if he *was* that loon, surfacing from a long dive, and a painful rush of air seared his lungs. He panted as a jumble of fiery colors streaked through his mind. In their wake a solitary disk of light hung in a blue sky. He opened his eyes and looked into Sutter's worried face.

"What happened? Are you all right?"

Tahn stared at his friend without answering. When his breathing returned to normal, he again felt the throbbing in his foot.

"That must have been some dream you were having," Sutter said. "I hope there was a girl in it, at least."

Tahn looked over his friend's shoulder at the break of dawn on the horizon. He hoped there were answers in Recityv. He hoped they *reached* Recityv.

He hadn't yet passed from melura to adulthood, and he'd never felt further from it.

They followed the river north for two days. The afternoon of the third day, something curious fell from the sky and settled on Tahn's cheek. He wiped at the bit, and drew back a finger smeared with ash. They rode onward. And soon flakes of black and grey were falling like snow.

Sutter held out a hand to catch one. "Forest fire?"

"I doubt it," Tahn answered.

Sutter nodded. "Then let's stay near the river. My neck is too sore to fight today." He smiled weakly.

Ignoring him, Tahn maneuvered his horse in the direction of the smell.

"Of course," Sutter said with a shrug, falling in behind him.

Soon, the smell of fire filled the air, but what burned was something more than wood.

They climbed the wooded hill that rose from the river valley. The ground grew carpeted with soot and ash, the rain of spent embers coming like a strange, quiet storm. Tahn checked his fletching, and urged his mount upward through a tight bank of spruce.

On the other side, blackened trees stripped of foliage spired like bony fingers. Some still smoldered, smoke lifting lazily to the sky. The ground stood charred with intricate patterns of burnt needles like tight embroidery. But the number of burnt trees didn't explain the fall of ash that piled now at their feet, the flakes continuing to descend softly around them.

They dismounted, drawing their weapons. They emerged into a small semi-circular clearing. Sutter's eyes widened as Tahn whispered denial.

Ahead, the face of a short granite cliff hung in graceful, molten waves, like a banner sagging where it had lost its mooring. Steam issued from pockets of the liquefied rock, sending tendrils of smoke up against the blackened face of the escarpment.

"Abandoning gods," Sutter muttered. "What makes rock run like honey from a hive?"

Tahn surveyed the ground, searching for something specific. To their right, a circle of earth glinted dully in the light filtered through the ash-laden sky. His heart fluttered in his chest. He took four long strides and bent to brush ash from the glazen surface. At the center of the black-glass ring, two holes burrowed into the earth. Holes the size of a man's hand. Surveying the rest of the clearing, he noticed several more dark rings, some larger than others, some at the center of depressions in the clearing around them.

Brushing ash from his hands, Tahn stood, again pulling his bow to half draw, and continued forward. Dark ripples in the cliff hung like stone curtains, and appeared to seal a doorway into the granite where an obvious footpath ended at a puddle of cooling rock.

"That'll do." The voice rang out over the clearing and startled Tahn, causing him to fumble his arrow from its rest.

• CHAPTER TWENTY-NINE •

Heresy

The gods were wise. They never wrote down their intentions.

—Rebuttal to the concept of the Charter,
given in the Dissent of Denolan SeFeery

A lone candle lit Grant's home. He sat at his table in its glow, the silence and emptiness wrapping about him. His hands still bore the dirt of Mikel's grave—the lad buried next to the others. Too many.

In his dirty hands he held a charm the boy had always carried with him—a token left to him by a mother he'd never known. The lad had never worn it, but still had never been without it. Maybe it had been Mikel's hope for reunion, or a reminder of the neglect that had brought him to the Scar to begin with.

The boy had never shared its purpose, nor had Grant asked.

But now he turned it over and over in fingers soiled with the boy's final earth, and thought about choices. And death. He thought about his many wards. And he thought about the soil of his own soul.

He held little use for men. Little hope. The few who bore their burdens well had his esteem. But they wouldn't last against the tide that was coming. The tide of bad choices.

He'd known it when Helaina had sent him here.

He knew it better now.

He couldn't stand against it without thinking boldly, even if what he considered was only an exercise to ease his battered mind and spirit.

He looked about, taking in the modest home. It held no touch of warmth. They only *existed* here. Basic necessities, shelter, nothing more.

It seemed barrenness had gotten into everything. And yet, there was a seed of hope. He thumbed the parchment on the table before him.

He gave a bitter smile as he considered that his hope would to others be heresy. The world had been stood on its head. So it might take heresy to set down what he dared now to write.

The patter of small feet interrupted his thoughts. He looked up to see one of his young wards standing at the mouth of the hall, staring at him. She was four. She'd been born with a disfigurement of the lips. She couldn't quite smile, or close her mouth. You could always see her upper teeth, crooked as they were.

He'd not tried to find her a home. The life she'd have known in the company of cruel children and adults who traded on such disfigurements would have been dreary. He imagined tenendra camps where oddities were caged. And he thought of panderers with base clientele.

My good fortune. Her sunny spirit often proved the only cheer he knew in a day. In the absence of the jeers and cruel jokes she'd have known elsewhere, here she had all the confidence she deserved. He waved her over, and she ran and leapt into his lap, hugging him close.

"Where did you go this time?" she asked, always eager to hear stories.

"Just supplies, dear one." He would not tell her yet of Mikel, who she considered a brother.

She smiled with her ruined lips. He smiled back.

"Did you get any molasses sticks?" Her voice slurred around the name of the confection, her lips unable to make the sound. She looked up expectantly.

He took two from his breast pocket and handed her one. "Make it last," he said.

She nodded. "Did you meet any interesting people?" In addition to the stories, the girl always wished to know of others, as she'd only ever known the other wards—she longed to meet new people.

The man returned her nod. "Some interesting people indeed. But not anyone you'd have liked. You're much nicer than them."

"You always say that," she replied. "Maybe sometime someone will come to visit *us,* and then we'll know who is the nicest."

The man smiled. "Yes, maybe."

The girl then looked at the tabletop. "What are you doing?"

Finally, he set aside the charm and put his own molasses stick in his lips. "I've got some things to write down," he said, and ran his hands over the parchment laid flat on the table before him.

In the sallow light of his single candle, the parchment looked brown, like his skin. He was no author. His profession and skill came first of the body. But he had a keen appreciation of ethics. And he lived by wit as much as skill. He knew how to write this. Whether it would come to anything, he didn't know. But, he *did* know the act alone would comfort him.

And just now, that more than anything was what he needed.

"Can I help?" the girl asked. "I know all my letters."

Grant looked into the girl's eyes and wondered if it wouldn't be most appropriate, after all, to have a little one help him write such a thing as he was set to write. After all, it was for her and all those like her that he meant to do it.

"I will write, and you will ensure I make the letters well."

She put her molasses stick in her mouth and leaned forward to begin.

He took up his pen and dipped it into a phial of black ink. He paused a moment, and looked into his candle. Once he was finished, could he find a way to give it purpose?

He knew but one way. And access to that power remained a myth and mystery to most. Going to where it lay guarded was a fool's errand.

But pausing with his ready pen, a man watching after the world's orphans, an outcast with the audacity to even consider writing what he now planned, he thought himself the perfect fool. For only fools went where courage and reason would not. And that was where he would need to go if tonight's scribblings were more than simply his need to purge his anger and frustration and sadness.

With one rough hand, he stroked the honey-colored hair of his young ward. With the other, he put ink to parchment and began to write.

He penned deep into the night, thinking of a better world for the wards that came into his care. A better world for this girl with the beautiful, ruined smile. On and on he wrote, pouring out the quiet thunder of his heart.

CHAPTER THIRTY

Reunion

Poetry. Real poetry. One neither writes nor reads it well, unless she's suffered. And arguing the point just proves you're too happy to know the difference.

—Defense of the Nallan poets made by Julia Hipwell during the Curration Conference, Recityv

Penit came alongside the muscled auctioneer. He held his head straight. His feet had been heavily chalked. As he strode the boards, with each step a large dust cloud plumed. He took his place at center stage—so different from his pageant wagon. This time the auctioneer's hand did not even fully rise to indicate a price before sticks flew high against the late-afternoon sun.

Seeing Penit put up for auction, a flood of strength ripped through Wendra.

The auctioneer's hand gestured convulsively, acknowledging the raised bids, his eyes wide with the number of slavers determined to purchase Penit. All were bidding, except Jastail.

The song she'd been hearing in phrases leapt inside her now. Strong. More fully formed. Dark, disturbing melody. She wanted to unleash it in this auction yard. *On* this auction yard.

She struggled with painful memories, and lurched from Jastail's grasp. When she tried to sing out her anger, instead of song came a torn wail. It rose, shattering the silence. And she fell, her scream echoing harmlessly above the crowd.

Jastail helped her to her feet. His eyes carried a hint of delight. But she was too angry to worry about him. The blinding rage began to build again inside her. She looked at Penit, who stared at her now from the boards, a grateful smile on his lips. He raised his bound wrists to wave to her, and was cuffed by the auctioneer.

"Be still, my lady," said Jastail. "You've no need of any of this. I intend to purchase the boy."

Wendra looked with a strange mix of revulsion and gratitude at the highwayman, who slowly lifted his stick and did not drop it again until only his marker remained high against the pitiless sky.

Wendra awoke before she opened her eyes. She lay quiet, aware that she wasn't alone.

The back of her throat throbbed, as though a bruise were forming there. She needed a cool drink. But she lay still and continued to regulate her breath in the slow cycles of sleep. A slight movement made her conscious of another hand in her own, and reality crashed in upon her in happy, bitter waves. Penit.

She took several deep breaths, then opened her eyes. The boy slept in a chair with his head against the bedpost, his small hand curled around her fingers. He looked peaceful, a vague smile on his dirty cheeks. She squeezed his hand. Tears ran from the corners of her eyes. Soon, Penit awoke, and the smile grew on his lips.

"You're all right," he said with bright enthusiasm.

"And you," Wendra said. "I thought I'd lost you. What happened?"

Penit's smile faded as quickly as it came. "I followed the river," he said, avoiding her eyes. "Sooner or later, you always come to people if you follow water. I made good time, too. No dawdling, no sidetracks. Kept to my script, you know. I kept thinking of you alone in that cave with the fever. No one ever depended on me that way," he said, trailing off.

Wendra put her other hand on top of his, pressing it between her own. "You did all you could," she said softly. "Don't be ashamed."

The door to the small room opened and Jastail walked in. "You're awake, good. You look weak, but we must leave. Be about it." He went to a dresser opposite her and pulled it back from the wall. He pried the back panel off and began loading a satchel with items hidden there. He smiled at her with one side of his mouth, and went back to his work.

Penit stood from his chair and squared his shoulders to Jastail. He kept Wendra's hand, but raised his chin. "Let us go."

Jastail didn't look up. "Boy, for the trouble this is turning out to be, I almost agree with you. And I admire your asking. Now, see that you help the lady, and save your comments on me until we're clear of this place. I don't want to have to gag you."

Penit fumed, shaking with pent-up anger. Wendra raised herself on one elbow. "What now?" she asked. "You bought Penit's freedom. It's time for the boy and I to be going."

Jastail looked up. "You can't buy what you already own." He cinched the satchel shut. "You're an insightful woman, but your belief in people cripples your judgment."

A hint of regret edged his words, but Wendra couldn't tell if it was for her or for hopeful people in general. He rose and shouldered the parcel. "Don't dawdle. Get up and come to the rear door. Mind my warning; we're not among friends here. And they'd have the *use* of you before the chalk is put to your feet.

"I need to buy a horse. I'll be at the rear door in a meal's time. There's bread and root for you at the table, and clean water. Eat and be ready."

He closed the door and left them alone again.

"He's the one that brought me here," Penit said. "I'd followed the river half a day when he and four others found me. I tried to explain about you, I told him you were sick and needed help. He asked me for directions. I told him I would take him there. But he said I looked ill, and that he'd send me with his friends to a safe place, and bring you back himself. He wouldn't listen to me. So I finally gave him directions to the cave." Again Penit trailed off. "And now he has us both."

"What do you mean?" Wendra asked. She sat up on the edge of the bed and pulled Penit around to face her.

"You saw it," Penit said. "He intended to sell me. All of us were being sold. That's what he meant that he couldn't buy what he owned."

"He doesn't own you," Wendra said firmly. "Or me. We're leaving here together, right now."

Penit backed away, shaking his head. "No. I don't like him, but the others know we aren't *traders*. They'll capture us as soon as we're in the street. The others . . . they do horrible things . . . and it would've been worse if it weren't for Dwayne."

"Dwayne?"

"I met him when they put me in the pen. That's where they keep everyone that will go to the boards with chalk on their feet. They put me and him together and made us fetch things, running all the time. Racing. Dwayne helped the younger ones."

Wendra took a short breath. She didn't want to think about how young the children he spoke of might be.

"He helped the older people, too, kind of showing them how to deal with the traders in order to get better food, or at least more food. He made it all kind of a game. And it kept me from getting too scared."

Wendra drew Penit close and hugged him. "If we could take him with us, we would." She thought a moment. "We'll let Jastail take us away from here. Once we're far enough away, we'll decide what to do. But I won't let him sell either of us." She swallowed against the fear and rage that battled inside her.

Before they went out into the outer room she pulled the dresser from the wall and pried back the panel she'd seen Jastail get behind.

A hollowed compartment held a small handwritten note:

Meet me at the wayhouse two days from the final auction. Bring every man you can trust for five handcoins. We'll set the balance right, and you may have yourself a route of your own for the trouble. Watch that you're not followed. And should you feel ambitious, know I've taken precautions against your greed.

Wendra tucked the note inside her bodice, and checked to be sure she hadn't missed anything. Satisfied, they went out to the table. They were eating stale bread when Jastail returned.

"Quickly, and hold your tongues," he said.

Outside, they climbed onto their mounts, and Jastail led them casually down a vacant alley toward the east. The sun lay low in the west, sending their shadows in long, dancing rhythms on the ground before them. Penit fought to ride alongside Wendra even through the narrowest lanes.

We could make a break now.

She dismissed the thought. They might be able to break away, but it would have to be once they reached the open road, and even then would need to be planned. If Jastail caught the boy, Wendra couldn't leave him again.

They passed a cluster of tents and rode into a field dotted with cook fires. Shallow ditches had been dug to catch the rainwater as it rolled from oiled canvases stretched over wooden frames. The smells of grouse and prairie hens rose on the dusk air. Wendra's stomach growled at the savory smell.

"What is this, then?" said a man, stepping into their path.

A group of men joined him.

"I've business elsewhere," Jastail said, looking past the men at the open land along the horizon.

"So pressing that you would leave at suppertime?" the man asked with a smile. "And taking your stock with you." The others laughed, their eyes passing from Wendra to Penit and back with a dark lust. "How far the great Jastail has fallen that he buys his own wares. Damaged goods, my friend." The man shifted his head to the side to affect a sidelong glance of reproof.

"Business elsewhere," Jastail repeated.

"Is that so?" the leader of the group replied. "Well, perhaps. But I don't like what this means to those of us you leave behind." The man raised his hand to his mouth and bit a fingernail before continuing. "Why did you forfeit the price of a boy on the block? It isn't like you." His eyes narrowed. "And it isn't fair to those prepared to pay good money for him, either. And what of this one?" He walked past Jastail and laid his hand on Wendra's thigh. She kicked him in the chest, and would have put her boot in his face if the stirrup hadn't caught. The man stumbled backward.

When he regained his balance, he rushed toward her, one arm brandishing a deeply curved knife. Orange sun glinted in the beveled edge as Wendra tried to shy away from the charge. Instantly, Jastail was between them. He ducked beneath the man's arm and drove a leg into his ankles. The other went over on his face, his jaw slamming the hard-packed earth. The report rose in the mellow evening like the striking of river stones together.

Wendra had seen men cower when their leader was put down, but these men rushed in on Jastail the instant he swept the first man off his feet. Two smaller fellows tried to flank him as the largest among them came directly on, a moronic grin showing five existing teeth. Two more drew short blades and skirted the edge of the fray like dancers anxious for a turn with a courtesan.

Wendra needed Jastail to win. Whatever the highwayman had planned for her and Penit, he was their only chance of escaping Galadell.

Jastail lunged for the largest man, feigning an exaggerated roundhouse toward the man's face, and drove his knee into the fellow's groin. The lout doubled over with an airy whoosh. One blade swept near Jastail's face. But before the man could recover to strike again, Jastail drew his own sword and struck a deft jab to the man's sword arm. The wounded brute dropped his weapon and turned tail.

The other swordsman rushed at Jastail's back. He fell into a forward roll and narrowly missed a jab at his spine. He came up and whipped his sword around in a deadly, level arc, catching the man in the neck.

The fight had drawn the attention of nearby traders. Troubled shouts rose, and the faint clink of blades and armor accompanied bellowed questions sounding from the tents.

Wendra turned her mount on one of the men trying to flank Jastail and spurred the horse. In a burst, the animal leapt, trampling the man before he could cut Jastail. A frenzied whinny erupted to her left. Penit had followed her lead, knocking the other thug to the side with his horse's broad chest.

As running steps and calls of concern flooded the street, the last man slowly backed away. Jastail jumped into his saddle and rode toward the shadows. Wendra and Penit raced at his heels. She'd saved her captor's life again. But she expected no gratitude from the man leading them past the last tents of Galadell.

They rode another three leagues before stopping for the night.

Jastail said nothing, tethering the horses and throwing his blanket near the base of a tree. He tied Wendra and Penit's hands and feet, but let them sleep close together.

When Jastail had fallen asleep, Penit nudged her. "You awake?" he whispered.

She nodded, but kept her eyes closed.

"If he ties us every night, it's going to be hard to get away." He paused until he heard Jastail make another sleeping noise. "I'm going to play a part. Like a dumb kid who needs a da. To make him trust me. It might give us a chance."

She wanted to argue, but it made sense. "Be careful," she whispered back. "This isn't a pageant."

That was all he said, and sooner than she might have thought, he was asleep beside her.

A rough boot at her calf awoke her the next morning. "Pack and eat," Jastail said, untying them. "Stretch your legs and arms before you mount."

Jastail had already seen to his blanket, and had allowed a small fire over which a pot of black tea heated. Wendra saw a handful of juniper berries laid on a clean rock near the pot to spice the tea once it brewed. He sat reading from a book, making notations with a thin piece of graphite.

Penit insisted on packing both his and Wendra's blankets and fetching food from their packs. She allowed him the task and sat opposite Jastail on a low rock, watching him.

Jastail lifted his eyes. "Did you assume a ruffian like me couldn't read?" he said with a hint of sarcasm.

"No," Wendra replied. "I just didn't expect to see you reading poetry."

Jastail partially closed the book, his brows rising in interest. "And how did you know it was poetry, dear lady? Have you been rummaging through my things without my knowledge?" His voice held a bit of humor.

"No. Your eyes move unevenly to each line. History and fancy run the width of the page."

"How astute. And why do you wonder at my choice of literature? No wait, let me guess. Is it because the dreams of a laureate would be lost on one like me, who kidnaps women and children? Because if it's so, lady, then you make an ardent case. And I may be at a loss."

Her silence seemed to disconcert him more than her words might have. His charming demeanor fell like an ill-fitted mask.

"I wasn't born near the blocks, dear woman." The words came bitterly from his lips. "And not every scop looks heavenward when he contrives his rhyme."

"You want me to believe in the noble savage," Wendra said tersely.

"Not at all." He rubbed the binding of the book the way Balatin used to touch Wendra's hair before he kissed her goodnight.

"What you think of me is none of my concern. And the differences between nobility and savagery aren't as clear to me as they are to the gentry. I've sat at fires where a man who doesn't read is distrusted and shunned. In other lands my poems wouldn't earn me the shoveler's spot in the court wastery." Jastail's eyes flared. "But that's precisely why I read these works. Precisely why I don't care what you think of me."

"I see," Wendra observed in an even tone. "Your books have confused your morality." She sent Penit back to the horses to retrieve the waterskins. "What about being taken into the company of thieves by one who wagers you on the table like a loose coin, or watching a child marched onto the blocks before a crowd to be auctioned like a hog at breeding season?" Her voice continued to rise as she lashed out at him. "Tell me how as a child you offered your hand to your elders to find an ally, elders who then used you to cheat another, as you did the boy." She stood, dark stirrings in her chest.

Jastail showed her a flat, dead stare. "My answer to that might surprise you. But, you forget yourself, woman. Take care."

"And what about you?" she asked. "Not concerned about your fellow tradesmen pursuing us anymore?"

The highwayman smiled. "They'll wait their chance upon me. For now, they'll return to their trading." He carved a slice of cheese. "When we meet again, they'll remember what their efforts earned them, and I'll be wealthy enough to have them whipped for harboring ill thoughts of me."

"The shine of a copper has long since lost its luster for you," she observed.

He nodded as if it might be so. "My poet might agree with you." He tapped his book, easy enthusiasm in his eyes. "His lines open a spyglass to the farthest reaches of what man is. And where the lens blurs on too distant an object . . . there, there is where I long to be. To know what I am capable of . . ."

Jastail looked into the distance, as though he were recalling words from his poet.

> The bird that uses wings only to gather insects,
> No matter how finely plumed,
> Is a meaningless creature.
> The horse that uses hardy legs
> To but pull a plow through the soil,
> Is a meal waiting to be prepared.
> What then of man, so noble in reason, fine in particulars, crafty with wit,
> Who rests his body and rises again at dawn to weed a furrow,
> Draw a mug, or argue over the shifting of a line upon a map?
> How lesser is he, to have been endowed with such capability
> And yet negotiate each breath to the breeding of yet another man,
> Who will but eat and drink and argue until his own rest is come.

His smile returned. "So now you have it . . . the all of me."

"Bitter words for a poet."

"The truth always sounds bitter to an unfamiliar ear." Jastail put his cheese away, and pointed at Penit. "It's forgivable in the boy, but you'd do better to understand the poem."

Wendra regarded Penit for a long moment. "I understand it well enough," she asserted, still watching Penit. "And they're a coward's words, written with his own grave at the back of his mind. Some men come to nothing because they aspire to nothing."

"And this is how you value an author?" Jastail said, interest arching his brows.

"No," she said sharply. "It's pity for one who thinks so little of his own contribution that he must do like the starling and soil his home for those that come after him."

Jastail stood, staring at her with that look of apathy she hated so much. "When our verse is written, my lady, you will be a notation writ in small script, and that will be a good deal more than the grave marker will say."

Wendra opened her mouth to respond, but just then Penit returned. Jastail grinned a mouthful of smiling teeth.

The highwayman used people the way his poets used their words, each stroke, each action carefully placed, to carry off the intended meaning. It was maddening. Her head ached with the constant effort to hold her melodic stirrings at bay.

He rose and kicked dirt into the fire. His broad mouth and bright eyes again shifted to the inscrutable expression he'd worn at the card table where he'd wagered Wendra's hope of finding Penit. The look sent a shiver up her back, robbing her of her anger.

Without a word, he mounted and led them north. He wasn't going to give them a clear opportunity to escape. Sooner or later, they'd have to make a gamble of their own.

CHAPTER THIRTY-ONE

Scars—Disappointment

Easily 60 percent of asylum patients claim no physical abuse, but instead say they've failed someone they care about.

—League report on the state of noncontributing citizens

Braethen moved deeper into the Scar.

Meche and the other wards had continued southwest on their patrol. Vendanj and Mira alternated leading and trailing their group toward this man Grant.

It left Braethen with little to do but stare into the waste around them. And remember.

Maybe it was the Quiet woman and the way her utter lack of empathy had gotten inside him. Or maybe it was just the feeling of the Scar. Whatever the reason, his mind kept returning to a moment. He'd been thirteen.

"Braethen?" The pained cry came from his parents' room.

He looked up from his book of Sodality tales. His da was away at Kali-Firth sharing the stories of winter's pen—those written during the long cold months.

"Braethen?" Weaker this time.

Braethen got out of bed and rushed to the room. "Ma?"

He lit the lamp and found her coated with sweat. Her hair was drenched with it, her clothes soaked through.

"You've got winter fever," he said. "We need to get—"

She shook her head. "I've had the fever," she gasped. "This is different."

He now noticed red splotches on her cheeks and neck. Her eyes were bloodshot. And her hands quaked like old Nezra's.

Braethen reached down and grasped her hand to steady it. "Da won't be home until tomorrow," he said. "I'll run get Hambley. He may know—"

She squeezed his fingers. Shook her head. "Don't leave me. Fetch me some water."

He pulled his hand from her grip and dashed to the kitchen, returning with a tall cup of water. She drank thirstily, spilling half the cup over her face and chin, but seemed glad of the coolness.

"Ma, you need help," he insisted. "Let me go find Hambley."

She shook her head again, as she began to stir more anxiously beneath her blankets. She rolled onto her side and curled into a fetal position, but managed to take his hand in her own again.

"Ma?"

"Sweet one, my stomach." Her face pinched in pain. "Cramping."

Braethen tried rubbing her back to soothe her. She seemed not to feel it. Perhaps some willow leaves, he thought. He pulled away again, and rushed to his father's study, where a shelf of dried herbs sat in earthen jars. He threw off the lid of the willow jar and took a handful of the crushed leaves. Racing back to his ma's room, he grabbed the pitcher of water.

At her side again, he poured her cup full and mixed the leaves in with his finger. It wasn't boiled, so didn't dissolve well, but he thought it would work just the same. He propped her head up and helped her drink again. She got half down before vomiting it all.

"Don't leave again," she said, her voice now feeble, pleading. Her eyes pinched shut.

Braethen's mind swam. She needed help. Help he couldn't give her. But she needed his comfort. He glanced desperately at the door. He could get to Hambley's in a few minutes. They could be back in ten. The Fieldstone Inn owner might not know what to do, but Braethen was out of ideas.

His ma whimpered. "I'm so hot."

Braethen grabbed her blouse from the chair and soaked it with the water, then draped it over her neck and forehead in a horseshoe shape. She exhaled with momentary relief.

She opened her eyes and looked up at him. "I love you, Braethen. Whatever happens, I love you."

"Ma?" he said, panicky. "Don't say that. It's just fever. We'll break it."

A weak smile touched her lips. "Your warrior soul."

He stayed at her side, her body drenching the blanket and sheets and pillow. Her cries growing weaker. Some few words coming, soft and incoherent.

If she could sleep, maybe that will help.

She kept hold of his hand through it all. Until the firm grip loosened.

"Ma?" he said, fear spreading in his chest. "Ma?" He gently shook her shoulder. Her chest wasn't moving. And her face was relaxed. Peaceful.

Sitting beside her, his hand held loosely in hers, he silently began to weep. He didn't know how long he'd been that way when the front door opened. Morning. Da was home.

His father came into the room, a satisfied smile on his face. His readings of his winter's pen at the festival must have gone well. He'd be brimming with stories to tell.

His face fell slack when he saw them. A'Posian dropped his satchel and rushed to her side. He felt her neck with his fingers. Worry passed to shock. Shock to grief. He shook his head, and looked at Braethen, tears streaming down into his beard.

"Oh my boy, what happened?" his father asked.

Braethen looked into his father's wounded eyes. "She called to me in the night. I came in." He broke down, crying. "Da?"

His father put a comforting arm around him, patting his back.

Into the man's chest he hitched several sobs, and sputtered out what he could. "She was sweating. I thought it was fever. But she said no. She had belly pain, and red cheeks, bloodshot eyes. . . ."

When Braethen had collected himself, he drew back, and found grief and confusion on his father's face.

"What, Da?" he asked, wiping his face.

"It sounds like Dagen gripe." His father's expression turned questioning.

Then something else settled into his father's face. Something he didn't speak. But the look wasn't mistakable. Disappointment.

But his father never spoke it. He only bent over his beloved and wept. A long while, he wept.

Riding through the Scar, Braethen's chest heaved with guilt and sorrow.

In the months after, he'd realized the origin of that look on his father's face. That disappointment. As part of his apprenticeship, his father had given him physic books to read and understand. Not advanced learnings. But more than general knowledge like willow leaves or balsam root.

Dagen gripe was one of many ailments that had a simple remedy. A combination of herbs. Herbs he knew sat in earthen jars on his father's shelf.

A'Posian never said anything to him. Braethen might have preferred the man's wrath or reproval to the quiet consequence of that mistake. Instead, Braethen lived with the memory that he might have saved his mother. And with the memory of that awful look of disappointment and loss on his father's face. In truth, he'd disappointed both his parents.

Nothing feels worse than disappointing someone you love.

It was the feeling of the Scar.

And someone *lived* here—this Grant. It left Braethen's heart cold and anxious. What kind of man could endure such a place every day? What penance could keep a man here? He wanted to meet this man as badly as he wanted to flee the Scar and never return.

CHAPTER THIRTY-TWO

Qum'rahm'se

It's becoming increasingly clear that simply knowing the meaning of a word as it's written in another tongue is the least part of translation.

—Dispatch sent by the Tract investigator to scrivener leadership

Tahn looked up the escarpment and saw a man sitting high above. Sutter raised his sword toward the destroyed cliff face. Tahn pulled a full draw.

"And what damage would you do that hasn't already been done?" the man asked with sad sarcasm.

The fellow had seen maybe fifty years of life. He wore both an unkempt greying beard and spectacles perched on a protuberant nose. A feather stood tucked over his ear and several more had been fixed into his vest, which buttoned over his right breast. Beside him lay a staff. Not far behind him, plumes of smoke issued continually, flakes of ash rising into the air in a steady stream.

They waited for the man to speak again. Instead, he just sat, saying nothing. He only lifted a small book secured to his waist by a rope and heaved a sigh.

Whispering, Sutter said, "Let's get out of here. He may be more dangerous than he appears."

Tahn stepped over the black crust of glass at his feet. "What happened?"

The fellow's head cocked, then made a long survey of the world around him. "I should think it was evident."

Tahn nodded. "The Quiet?"

Hefting a small stone, the man threw it at them weakly. "Go away."

Sutter laughed in spite of himself. "I like him."

"Are you all right?" Tahn asked.

Tahn seemed to have unnerved the stranger. The fellow glared back at him, then began to pick his way carefully down the cliff. As soon as he got to level ground, he stomped across the charred earth of the clearing, crusts of glass cracking beneath his boots.

He stopped directly in front of Tahn and stared up in open defiance. "You mean 'how did I survive, when no one else did,' don't you?" the man said, his voice a mix of self-loathing and anger.

"That's not what I—"

"I'm Edholm Restultan," the man said, giving his name as if to the strong law. "I was a scrivener here at Qum'rahm'se."

"Silent hells, Tahn."

Tahn was feeling it, too. A sense of helplessness and loss.

The scrivener looked back over his shoulder, and was quiet a few moments before telling the story.

"Early this morning three Velle came into this clearing. I supposed they were couriers from Recityv as have come more frequently this last cycle. I was there." Edholm indicated the cliff. "I stood watch as they passed our wards. Passed our guards. Burned them all."

The scrivener's eyes grew distant. "But before they could get into the library, the ash began to fall."

Tahn looked up at the ash still falling.

"Those inside had begun destroying the library . . . to keep it from the enemy. The Quiet were denied their prize. So, they raised their hands at the cliff face. Unleashed a white fire and lightning. Everything burned. The mountain, the trees . . ."

Edholm shook his head as a man trying to disbelieve. "It sealed the door closed in moments, and I thought I heard . . ." The scrivener fell silent.

"What?" Tahn prodded gently.

"I thought I heard the cries of my fellows inside the library."

The scrivener became silent for a while. Then he spoke with a tone of confession. "I laid on the ground to hide. I'll be remembered as a coward."

"Was everything *inside* burned?" Sutter asked, resheathing his blade.

The scrivener looked back at the charred earth and rock, seeming to judge if even now it were appropriate to share. "I'll have your names first."

"Flin," Tahn blurted, "and Crowther." He nodded to Sutter. "Just hunters."

"I see," the scrivener said with clear skepticism. "Well, if not your names, at least something to call you. Have you been hunters long?" the man asked.

Neither Tahn or Sutter answered.

"You understand my question, since seasoned hunters know that animals flee fire." A tone of condescension drifted on the man's words.

Tahn put away his arrow. "Fire doesn't melt stone."

"And common hunters don't deduce the Quiet so easily." The scrivener gave them each another solemn look, gathering their attention. "The library was dedicated to deciphering the Language of the Covenant. Our commission since the first Convocation of Seats has been to gather any document we could, and try to piece together what remains of the Covenant Tongue. Scholars committed their lives to this place, this work."

"And now it's all gone?" Sutter asked again.

The scrivener seemed not to hear him. "Each generation, the library has grown, expanding deeper into the safety of the mountain, filling new shelves with theory, commentary, bits of translation.

"It was thought that the Language would be needed if there was another great war." Edholm laughed caustically. "The Bourne seems to have similar ideas."

The scrivener sighed. "We hadn't yet pieced it together. Not even close. But we'd made *some* progress. Mostly with the Tract of Desolation." A bit of ash fell between them. "Damn waste . . ."

Tahn tried asking this time. "But if you weren't inside the library when the attack came, how do you know it's all been burned?"

The scrivener pointed to the top of the cliff, at the vent of steam and ash issuing into the sky. Tahn understood now why his first whiff of fire hadn't been of burning pine alone.

Tahn watched the ash spew into the mountain air and waft lazily south on a gentle breeze.

"Orders are to burn everything rather than let the Quiet get their hands on any of it," Edholm explained. "If we just could have killed them before it was all gone."

Tahn pitied the man. "You couldn't have made a difference in the battle to save the library."

The scrivener shot a fierce look at Tahn. "I could at least have died with them. I wear these emblems and tools," he said, lifting the book tied to his belt.

Tahn had no more words of comfort for the man. He understood too well the guilt of not rising to the defense of someone or something you care for.

As if sensing his sympathy, Edholm said, "This is none of your concern. My apologies." Then abruptly, the scrivener asked, "Where are you going?"

Reluctantly, Tahn admitted, "Recityv."

The man nodded. "No more games," he said. "A hunter you may be, but it's not what brought you to Qum'rahm'se. And I'm going to ask you a favor."

Edholm knelt in the blanket of ash that covered the clearing. "Come close," he said in a broken voice.

Tahn and Sutter obeyed. Without looking up, the scrivener lifted the book from his belt and tore free three clean sheets. He handed them out, adding a stick of graphite, too. "Do you know how to write?"

They nodded.

"Good," Edholm said. "Write what you've seen. Leave nothing out. Describe the destruction, the smell, the ash, the burnt rock. Write of me, my shame. But mostly, write of the fate of the books and the library. The fate of the Tract. And put your name to it at the bottom."

"But why—" Sutter began.

"Don't cross me, boy." The scrivener spoke sharply. "I won't be a coward twice."

Sutter raised his hands in surrender.

With the stink of so much soot and burnt timber about them, and a layer of ash as deep as Tahn's ankle, they did as he asked.

Nails finished first, his page half written upon.

Tahn filled his sheet, noting the smell of burnt flesh he could now smell, as well as the char of wood and stone and iron.

Edholm used three pages to make his account, his fingers moving lithely, tracing words in quick, elegant strokes. Tahn watched letters and symbols fill the parchment, lines being written in alternating directions—left to right and then right to left—and all in a language foreign to him.

The scrivener then rolled his parchment tightly. He bound it with several strands of what Tahn thought must be hair. He then produced three ordinary-looking sticks from an inner pocket of his tunic. Taking the first in hand, he opened one end, revealing a hollow compartment. Into it he stuffed his letter.

He sealed it again, the seam undetectable. Reaching for Tahn's and then Sutter's parchments, he read each with amazing speed, seeming to take it all in at a glance. Afterwards, he likewise placed their letters in the remaining sticks.

"They succeeded, Tahn," the scrivener said. Tahn immediately realized that he and Sutter had signed their real names to their parchments. Edholm didn't draw attention to the uncovered deceit. "The Velle destroyed countless years of accumulated thought and wisdom."

Standing together, the two of them shared wary looks, before the scrivener handed the sticks to Tahn. "Never let these out of your sight. You'll take them with you to Recityv. Give them to someone with authority. Someone on the High Council. The regent, if you can. Do you understand?"

"Why don't *you* take them?" Sutter asked.

"I won't need them," he replied. "If I make it as far as Recityv, my presence and testimony will be proof enough that Qum'rahm'se has fallen."

Focusing again, he said, "The Quiet are still close. So I'll head west for a time, travel obvious roads, burn bright fires, sing loudly. Draw attention away from you."

"You should come with us," Tahn pressed.

Edholm stepped up close to him. "Why did you come here? The truth."

Tahn stared down at the scrivener. He hesitated. Then said it. "We were on our way here with a Sheason. He meant to collect whatever you had on the use of the Covenant Tongue."

"Where's this Sheason?" Edholm questioned with obvious skepticism.

"We lost him in some Quiet clouds," Sutter put in. "That satisfy you?"

The scrivener's face fell slack. "My last hell, Je'holta. Then your Sheason friend is probably trying to find a way to strengthen the Veil." Edholm looked away to the dark glass rings in the soil. "Time is short."

"Yes, so why don't you just come with us," Tahn said again.

The scrivener shook him off. "You follow the river north. Make no fire. In a few days, you'll come to an old overgrown road. Any other time, I'd tell you to follow it west to the main road north." Edholm shook his head again. "Not this time. Follow the road east back to the river. There you'll see a grand old bridge arcing toward high cliffs. That's the way for you. It's an old road, a forgotten way."

Tahn could feel the scrivener building to something. "Where are you sending us?"

Edholm motioned them close and whispered so softly they almost couldn't hear him. "It'll still get you to Recityv. Through an old city. Abandoned now. But it's been said the people there had a codex for the Covenant Tongue."

"And you want us to find it?" Sutter asked with his own skepticism. "If you've known about it, why haven't the scriveners tried to find it?"

"Some have," Edholm shot back. "Never found any kind of codex, unfortunately." Then, his face softened. "But in all honesty, lads, it's not a place you visit often unless you have a damned good reason."

"Why?" Tahn asked.

The scrivener's face became thoughtful. "Old places attract old things."

"That's helpful," Sutter quipped.

"It'll be safer than the main roads, I can guarantee you that. And main roads are where the Quiet will be watching." Edholm looked them each in the eye. "I don't know that you'll find a codex. Maybe that's a myth. But if it's real, you may look for it in a way we haven't. See with different eyes. I think that's worth a try." He paused a moment. "Take care and you'll be all right."

As an afterthought, the scrivener reached for one of the books at his belt. He tore out several written-upon sheets, and rolled them as he had the others before stuffing them inside yet another stick—this one larger. "Take this with you, as well."

Edholm fell silent, looking weary. "It's an imperfect plan, but likelier to succeed than the three of us going together."

The scrivener extended one hand, which Tahn took willingly. He did the same with Sutter, then set out through the still-smoking trees and spared no backwards glance.

"What do you make of all that?" Sutter asked.

"I don't know," Tahn said.

Sutter watched Edholm disappear down the hill. "Are we really going to do this?"

"Sounds like it gets us to Recityv just the same." Tahn looked at the smoking ruins of the library. "And with the library burned, I think the scrivener's right: We have to try."

Sutter nodded. "Well, if it gets us away from the Quiet, that's good enough."

Tahn stuffed the sticks into an inner pocket of his cloak. "I think we should get going."

They rode two days, speaking little, each caught up in their own thoughts. Evening meal and night watches were more of the same. On the morning of the second day, they broke through to a road choked with holly brush. High grass grew at its center, nearly obscuring the wheel ruts. Tahn angled east toward the river, stems brushing his legs and the bellies of their mounts. In the breeze, the air filled with seeds blown from river cottonwoods shedding their plumage.

The ripple of leaves rustling together in the wind reminded Tahn of the Hollows, and he relaxed in his saddle. Slowly, the sound of running water grew. The dappled light gave way to an open sky above them as Tahn and Sutter suddenly found themselves at the edge of a bridge arching up and over the river.

The bridge was bordered by balustrades and supported by stout pilings of seamlessly fitted larger stones. The architect had invested great care in fluting the masonry posts that rose at even intervals on both sides of the bridge. Beveled edges marked the side ledges. The stone had darkened from long years of river moisture and sun, but stood stately in the light.

Across the river, the bridge dropped to the base of a sheer cliff, a chasm there opening like a rift in a risen plain. It was hard to tell if the chasm had been built to service the bridge or the bridge to service the chasm.

Sutter smiled and started across. The clop of hooves on stone seemed loud. Tahn swung his head about like a thief wishing not to be heard. A moment later, he followed.

The great arching bridge ended at a stone gate. Sutter pushed on it with his left hand. The huge block wouldn't budge.

"Your assistance?" Sutter invited in a sarcastic tone.

Tahn rode to the gate and together they pushed. The gate gave, slowly. A moment later they had opened it far enough to pass beyond.

Before going through, Sutter asked, "If the cycle turns and there's no one around to witness for us at our Standing, do we still become men?"

"You won't," Tahn jibed. Then more seriously, "I don't know. I'd always thought Balatin would stand for me. And when he went to his earth, I chose Hambley. But I don't think we'll be home in time for that to happen. . . . I guess one way or another we'll get older."

Sutter brushed his hands. "Well, Woodchuck, I think it might be okay if we don't." He grinned with mischief and went through the gate.

CHAPTER THIRTY-THREE

Scars—Mothers

A child will choose what you have in your hand now. An adult will
wait if promised more later. Which is wise and which is selfish?

—Dimnian thought riddle

Mira had been to the Scar before. She understood its secrets and silences.
Not as well as Vendanj. And not like the man Grant, who lived here. But
the way of the Scar visited her the way the Soliel Stretches did when she walked
the shale plains of her homeland.

This place was an emptiness, save the lives of some children. Grant's wards.
Castoffs who knew no real mother or father, like the common misfortune that
all children of the Soliel knew.

"I don't understand," Mira said. "I thought you were my mother."

She stood in the warmth of her home, going over basic movements she'd been
taught. The Latae dance forms. And only arms and feet so far—she was only four.
She'd get to start practicing with weapons the next turn of a cycle.

She repeated the forms again and again, taking correction from Genel, the
woman she'd been calling "mother" for two years.

"Mira, you need to listen closely. I am your mother because I'm taking care of
you right now. But I didn't give you life. The woman who brought you into the
world was called Mela. She fulfilled her call in your first year."

Genel cautioned Mira that her foot was too far back for proper balance.

Mira corrected her stance. "What do you mean 'fulfill her call'?"

"When a Far reaches the age of accountability, she's called home, into the next
life. This is the honor given us for our oath. We will never taste the fear or pain of
reckoning for misdeeds. It's a great blessing."

"It's a blessing to go to the earth so young?" It confused her. Mira naturally
thought that doing well meant the reward of pleasant things, not dying.

Genel interrupted Mira's next movement, and took her face in her hands. "Yes.

You must understand. We protect a very important knowledge. To do so means we must be willing to do anything necessary to keep it safe. And that will mean doing things that seem wrong to you. But in the service of our oath," she said, commanding Mira's attention, *"nothing is wrong. And so when our life is done, we go unblemished."*

Mira looked back, understanding dawning in her young mind. *"But accountability is when you have eighteen cycles. Does everybody die then?"*

"If they are Far, they do," Genel said.

"How old are you?"

"Seventeen. I will go into my next life in but a few months."

Mira began to cry. *"I don't want you to go. Please. Can you stay? I will be very good. I won't beat up on any of the boys anymore."*

Genel smiled. *"As long as you don't really hurt them."* Then she wore her serious face, her teaching face. *"Mira, this is who we are. You will have many mothers in your life. And they'll all love you and take care of you. And then one day, you'll do the same for a child. Many, in fact. And then you can tell her it's okay to beat up on the boys."*

Mira didn't smile. *"I don't want to. I just want you to stay. I don't want any more mothers. One is enough. Just until I'm old enough to be by myself."*

Her mother held her close, and hugged her. And rocked her. *"One day, you may even have a child of your own, Mira. It's such a blessing when that happens. Especially for you, because you belong to an important family for our people. And when that child comes, you'll be happy to know that there'll be Far to take care of the child when you're gone. Just as I am doing for you."*

Mira shook her head. *"But then the only way she'll ever know me is because someone else told her my name. And we'll never be able to sing the Soliel songs or Run the Light as you and I do, because I'll be gone before she is old enough to do those things."*

The woman who called herself her mother tried to hug her again. But Mira didn't want her hugs right now. She didn't want to love Genel anymore, because she was going to die and give her to another mother. And she couldn't understand why this was a blessing. So she ran. Ran out the door and into the city and moved as fast and long as her small body would allow her.

Why do I have to be a Far? *she thought.* Just train and learn and fight and . . . die. What if I just want to be a mother and keep being one?

The memory receded, leaving her unsettled. For a Far there was life and love and duty, and these were all supposed to mean the same thing. And included caring for another woman's child at some point. But she had left her city, and made peace with her own brief, childless life.

Until her sister died.

Vendanj rode beside her, watching the horizon. "Does it remind you?"

Mira had shared the Sheason's company for too long to be surprised at his ability to guess her inner thoughts. They'd shared parts of each other's past over the last few years. "Yes."

"Remembrance isn't always cheerful." He paused, letting those words linger. "But it's a good test for what may come."

Mira stared back, nothing to say.

"It's harder, though," Vendanj added, "when new feelings stir inside."

It would be pointless to deny her feelings for Tahn. "It has no bearing on what I must do, or why I came," she said.

Vendanj showed a wan smile. "I know. But be careful that in spending so much time *with* me, you don't become too much *like* me. Your future may be short, but it's worth living. Don't let anything, even a Sheason, ruin that for you."

She looked back at him for a long moment, then offered a crooked smile. "You say that now. . . ."

Under the weight of the Scar sun, they shared between them a rare laugh, low and even and mild. She had the thought that it might likewise be rare that laughter was heard by *anyone* in this place.

• CHAPTER THIRTY-FOUR •

Stonemount

What I find interesting is that the Stonemounts didn't seem to prepare to leave. Things you'd expect they would take still lay about their homes.

—From the first commissioned expedition to Stonemount

The chasm reminded Tahn of a box canyon near Jedgwick Ridge in the Hollows. Except this passage felt . . . constructed. It stretched into the rock until its walls seemed to meet. Birds had managed to build nests high up the sheer facings, using small imperfections to gain purchase. The walls rose more than a hundred strides. Beyond them, the sky appeared as a river seen from high above. The sensation of peering up and seeming to look down caused Tahn to swoon in his saddle.

He steadied himself, and noticed figures carved into the stone on either side of the canyon, one showing a man, the other a woman, both with tightly shut lips.

"Come on," Sutter scolded. "We're wasting time." His friend pushed his horse into a gallop down the chasm.

They rode for some time before the narrow canyon came to an end. The shadows of evening were falling fast, casting the gorge into darkness. When the rock at last gave way, it was as though the mountain before them had been hollowed out. In the belly of a great depression lay a city, stretching a league wide. In a great circle, sheer cliffs rose around the basin, the whole thing looking like a vast crater. From where he stood, Tahn could see no other entrance, no chasms like the one they'd just traversed.

The westering sun caused a sharp line of light and shadow to fall across the city, leaving its western half in darkness. But nowhere could Tahn see the flicker of a lamp.

The city definitely seemed abandoned.

No smell of cooking fires or livestock. No voices. No dogs barking. Nothing. An unsettling quiet held over the city. Outer buildings were covered in creeping vines that had covered their timbers. Deeper into the city, smooth white walls rose in lonely majesty as though seeking the light that fled the sky. But even these showed cracks and fissures. This city's protection—the great cliffs—had also become its tomb.

"Look at this place," Sutter said in wonder. "It must be a thousand years old, two thousand. I've never heard Ogea mention it in his stories."

Maybe some places are left to the dead.

"Come on."

The soft loam in the chasm ended, letting them into a shallow gully that dipped to a natural spring before rising again to the city plain. Along the crater wall in both directions, forming an outer band, lay a cemetery like a circle of defense. *Or warning,* Tahn thought.

They rode around grave markers and stone tombs erected like small bath-houses. The line of shadow falling across the city seemed to move out of the crater, leaving them in deep shadow. They moved slowly over long-untended grass that bristled in their passage. The peculiar smell of old earth and leaning stones accompanied the fragrances of night-blooming flowers that seemed to grow only where bodies were gathered in death.

The sound of crickets began to whir, arythmically at first, but soon in a common pulse.

Then above it, Tahn heard a scratching.

He froze in the deepening shadow of a stone mausoleum, raising his finger to his lips to warn Sutter not to speak.

The scratching came again, like bare, winter tree limbs blown by the wind, scrabbling against one another or scraping the side of a barn. No wind blew. Tahn nocked an arrow and Sutter slowly drew his sword. Tahn eased forward and peered around the corner of the stone monument. Through the dark night he squinted.

It came again, stealing his breath. Hunched over a grave, a shadowy figure examined the writing on a marker. It gently touched the ground there, its long, thin fingers moving easily into the earth as it seemed to ponder.

A mourner?

It raised an arm against the night and then plunged it deep into the earth. The ground moved only slightly as the shape cast its arm back and forth as though searching, feeling, digging toward something. It stopped, perhaps having found the object of its desire. The figure's cowl slid directly over the place in the grave bed, and it lowered its head so close to the ground that it might have inhaled the dust of it.

There it remained still for a moment.

The form huddled but fifty strides from them, and Tahn feared that even a breath would reveal them.

Suddenly, the figure raised both arms to the sky. Its long, thin fingers curled into knotted fists that shook in defiance as it tilted back its head and screamed an airy hiss. Tahn's skin rose in chill bumps, and his muscles weakened. His fingers and toes began to tingle and his temples pound with the beat of his own heart.

Tahn held perfectly still, waiting, worrying the creature would turn and discover him.

Finally, the thing stood and rushed north, vanishing behind a forest of grave markers. Tahn relaxed in his saddle, resting his head against his horse's neck.

Reflexively, Tahn then traced the familiar pattern of the scar on his left hand. The hammer. The shape calmed him, and slowly his breathing came under control. He remained silent for several moments, shaking off Sutter's questioning gaze. The light had completely drained from the sky, showing a bright tapestry of stars on a sable backdrop that ended in a wide circle where the cliffs rose against the night.

"Something," he said, when it felt safe to speak. "I don't know what. It was digging at the graves." He didn't explain that the being hadn't needed to remove the dirt to put its arm freely into solid earth.

"My kind of *something*," Sutter said, a bit nervous.

Tahn pulled an arrow to half draw, then he led them through the cemetery to the low wall on the other side, and into the city.

The first buildings they encountered were houses—most of them single-story structures. Near the walls rested a few produce baskets and water barrels, blown by winds and chewed in the mouths of rats.

Further on, the buildings rose two, three, four stories, blocking more starlight and blurring the edges of the buildings in deep shadow.

Tahn pointed to a towering building on their left. "Let's bed down."

They rode directly in. Ceilings rose the height of two men, rough chunks of stone fallen from the walls, the lonely smell of dust blanketing everything. Bits of glass lay strewn near the windows. A few paintings dressed the walls, appearing to have become sepia-colored from endless days of exposure. And a handful of tables and chairs littered the floor in jumbled masses, broken and marred.

After tethering the horses in an adjacent room, Tahn headed for an inner wall. There, he swept the rubble aside with his boot and sat with his back against the firm rock. Sutter sat beside him, laying his sword across his legs and exhaling tiredly.

"Is this the adventure you wanted?" Tahn asked.

Sutter emitted a single, low chuckle, and was fast asleep, leaving Tahn with the darkness. How much more comfortable he would have been knowing Mira watched nearby. He fingered the outlines of the sticks stuffed in his cloak, and wondered if the others had reached Recityv yet, wondered if they had escaped the dark clouds at North Face.

His mind turned, raced, with the images and events just since leaving the Sedagin. He huddled against the wall, staring through the empty, darkened window at the abandoned streets. So many unfamiliar things swam in his mind and in his eyes, he soon had no power to discern if he were awake or asleep, dreaming.

His legs dragged over the harsh terrain, carving shallow furrows in the dusty trail. The height of the sun put it near the meridian. Its heat fell like the yoke of a peddler's pack on his shoulders. No wind stirred. Around him was the patient smell of aging sage and earth left baking under a cruel sun. The horizon wavered with heat, blurring the dips and rises in the land.

Tahn stumbled, catching himself with his hands on the hot ground. He allowed himself to kneel and rest, raising weary, half-shut eyes to the glare of light from a pale blue sky. The firmament appeared washed and bleached and absent of clouds.

And there he stood, learning to shoot his bow out over a precipice from a man whose face he couldn't see. . . .

The dream ended, and Tahn awoke in the darkness beside his friend.

"My last hell," he muttered, and knew he would get no sleep that night.

He left Sutter sleeping and ambled through the first story of the building in search of a window facing east. Around the corner, a stair rose through shadows into the upper levels. Gossamer threads hung between the posts supporting the dust-covered stair rail. Tahn warily climbed through successive stories—the stairs ending after six flights and letting him out onto the roof.

Under a veil of starlight, he could see the beauty of the hidden city. Its surface rose and fell across rooftops and streets silhouetted against the outer cliff.

He faced east and started to recite the names of stars. He knew them like friends, friends met of necessity each morning. He couldn't remember a time when he didn't rise to see them. It was a quiet, peaceful time. Voices left the silence alone. His thoughts could run outward without interpretation, without resistance.

He remembered sitting on the front stoop with Balatin and Wendra and trying to describe how far the sky went, the speculation soon becoming so preposterous and cumbersome that they all laughed and turned their attention to the light-flies and songs. But there were moments, Tahn thought, when that furthest point could almost be understood, almost glimpsed. He braced himself against a breeze sweeping in from the tops of the cliffs and thought of dawn.

He shut his eyes, and imagined again the image of the sun, elegantly slow as it rose into the eastern sky, the gradual strengthening of the light an unassuming, wakeful promise.

After a moment, he opened his eyes and saw the strengthening light at the eastern rim of the cliff. A wave of relief stole over him. He nodded a greeting toward the dawn and descended the stair the way he'd come.

As Tahn reentered the room, Nails woke. "Find anything good to eat?" he said, with a sour morning smile.

Tahn laughed in spite of himself. "Let's get moving. I don't think we can spend more than a half day trying to find this codex. We need to get to Recityv."

In the watery light of predawn, they stepped into the street. Their mounts' hooves clopped loud against the hard stone and morning silences.

"Hello, gentleman," a voice greeted, as they cleared the door.

Sutter pulled his sword in a clumsy movement, his eyes trying to fix on the owner of the voice.

Tahn nocked an arrow and made a full draw, bending at the waist and swinging his bow in a full circle. He could see no one.

"Those aren't necessary." A man stepped from between two of the buildings. "May I ask what brings you to Stonemount?"

The fellow wore brushed leather breeches and tunic, with an embroidered belt done in scarlet colors of varying hue. Gold rickrack graced the collar and cuffs of his loose white shirt. A tricorne hat, likewise garnished with gold thread, sat at an angle on his head. His cloak—really more of a cape—was bright red, and gave the impression that the man cared more for fashion than warmth. And at his hip he wore a rounded blade in a jewel-encrusted sheath.

"Come now," the man insisted, "cease your careful scrutiny of my sword and answer my question." He spoke with a merry expression on his face, as though the things he said were of no consequence at all, things charming and lightly conversational.

"I know you crossed the Lesule on the Ophal're'Donn bridge. So, you're not men of the valley or you'd never have set foot upon it. And I don't take you for trophy hunters, because you brought no cart." All the while the man's face remained jolly, unconcerned.

Tahn relaxed his draw and dropped his aim to the ground. He started to speak when Sutter chimed in. "We're adventurers."

"On our way to Recityv. We're just passing through," Tahn amended.

"But a grand place to pass through," Sutter added with thick irony.

The stranger seemed to like Sutter's response better. "Grand, indeed," he echoed.

Sutter removed a waterskin from his horse and took a draught from the skin, then offered the stranger a pull.

"No, my young friend. But thank you all the same."

Sutter corked the skin and refastened it to his saddle.

Tahn put away his arrow. "May we ask what business brings *you* here?"

"I'm an archivist and historian, good fellow," the stranger replied with enthusiasm. "Where else should I be?"

"In a school or library?" Sutter retorted.

The other's waxen smile dipped, but only for a moment. "Fah, no. This is my school." He pointed to the ground. "This is the place to find what matters."

"Not for us. We're on our way *through*," Tahn repeated.

"Well," the man exclaimed in a calm but commanding voice, "there is but one passage out of Stonemount besides the one you entered by. And energetic as you are, you're not likely to find it alone." His smile returned. "Come with me, and all your better deeds I'll add to my histories. Then away you'll go to continue your adventure. I'm known as Sevilla Daul. What may I call you?"

Sutter sheathed his sword. "I'm Dulin. This is Renn," Sutter lied.

Sevilla bowed, and started to amble up the street.

The light strengthened on the eastern rim of the cliffs that encircled the city, bathing the walls and immense towers in bluish hues. In the dawn of another day, the city felt safe, protected.

"A marvel of engineering," Sevilla was saying. "Everything you see was sculpted, erected, and fashioned by the hands of the Stonemounts. An industrious people, gifted as few in the raising of stone to art." He scanned the city with appreciative eyes.

Smaller buildings at the edge of the city had given way to towering structures that rose near the city's center. The sun was now striking the immense gables and beautiful archways that joined the high buildings hundreds of strides up. In the distance they looked like flags unfurled from parapets into these man-made canyons of stone. Despite the wear of time and cracks creeping into the walls, the symmetry mesmerized him.

"Makes you wonder why they left," Sevilla said, following Tahn's gaze.

"They left?" Sutter remarked, incredulous.

"It's fodder for scholars, and theories abound. I, of course, have my own." He paused dramatically. "I believe they found a harmony between death and life, like the circle of stone that surrounds the city. They found a way past death, past life."

Tahn raised his brows at Sutter. *The Covenant Tongue?* He turned to Sevilla. "'A way past death, past life'? Sounds like you're talking about the Language of the Framers."

The man eyed Tahn. "That's an astute inference for an adventurer." Sevilla smiled.

"I know my stories," Tahn said dismissively. "Have your archivist studies here taught you anything about the Language?"

Sevilla laughed. "You're not so very clever, are you? You're wanting to know if I've found the codex of Stonemount. That sound familiar?"

"Now that you mention it," Tahn said, maintaining his part, "I do remember a story about a codex."

"So, you're actually treasure hunters," the man said, nodding. "I suppose that *could* be considered a type of adventurer."

"You know of it, then?" Tahn said, keeping them focused on the codex.

"Oh, I know of it," Sevilla said, laughing as though it were a childish question. "But it doesn't exist. Not that I've found. I've scoured every corner and surface of Stonemount."

Tahn hid his disappointment.

"I tell you, though," Sevilla kept on, "I'm not entirely sure it ever existed. And even if it did, even if the Stonemounts learned command of the Covenant Tongue, I'm not convinced that's how they found their way past death."

The archivist grew quiet. And they walked in silence for a time.

"I intend to find it," Sevilla said so quietly that Tahn wasn't sure he heard him correctly. The words sounded like a secret uttered in the shadow of a dying tree.

Whatever else the man was, or whatever lies he might tell, Tahn believed him about the codex. And if it *was* here somewhere, finding it would obviously take a lot more time than he and Sutter had to spare.

"How do we find our way out of this place?" Tahn asked, impatient now to get going.

"What, so quick to leave so remarkable a place?" A wry grin spread on Sevilla's lips. "What adventurers you are proving to be, young friends."

"Will you help us, or not?" Sutter asked bluntly.

Unsmiling, the man pointed to the northeast. "Between those two towers."

Tahn spotted a dark, vertical line in the distant cliff wall.

"Must be a gap like the one we came through, huh?" Sutter remarked.

"Indeed," Sevilla said. "But it's a great deal more difficult to find than it appears. The streets in that direction are not square, and the cemetery there is less . . . habitable."

"We'll just follow the rim around until we come to a break in the cliff," Tahn stated matter-of-factly. "We should be able to reach it well before dark."

"And so your eyes would deceive you." The stranger stared at both Tahn and Sutter. "The envy of the outside world forced the Stonemount people to protect themselves. In the west there is the Canyon of Choruses. In the north"—he looked again to the dark line between the towers—"the canyon is bordered by wild growth. People here learned to navigate the wilds, but foreigners often found their final earth trying to pass through them without a guide." He turned a mirthful eye on Tahn.

"Don't tell us. You know the way through these wilds."

CHAPTER THIRTY-FIVE

Scars—Arriving Late

The art of governance isn't writing laws you know are right. It's writing laws you believe people will follow, and that have a measure of "rightness." Strict control breeds revolt.

—Excerpt, *Practical Governance*, from the private library
of Roth Staned—a book now banned

Vendanj never slept well in the Scar. More than the land's loss of Forda, or the memory of war that lingered across its barren surface, the Scar had a way of reminding one of their own wounds. Sheason were no exception.

Looking up at the hard, dim flicker of stars, he knew what dreams awaited him.

Vendanj ran. Black scorchmarks on the sides of buildings, homes razed to the ground, smoke in a distant part of the city. The Quiet had attacked.

But all he could think about was Illenia, his wife. And their unborn child.

He tore through the streets at a maddening pace, cursing himself for being overlong in his journey to Recityv. He'd helped bring a Dissent against the new League law forbidding Sheason to render. There had been some time before their baby was due, so he'd felt safe in leaving for a few days. And Illenia was also Sheason; she could serve equally well without him.

He turned into their street. No!

The mortar stood in rubble. He raced to their doorway and stepped past the half-broken door. Fragments of wood and fallen stone lay all around. He picked up long crossbeams and peered beneath piles of broken rock. She wasn't here.

But his panic wouldn't let up.

He raced back into the street, thinking to try the homes of people she knew, when Amalial called. "Vendanj!"

He followed the voice, and saw the woman. "Where's Illenia?"

"She was taken to the League's hospice, yesterday, when the attacks came."

He sprinted toward the far end of the quarter, where the League's healing ward stood. His lungs burned and his head pounded with dark suggestions. Please be all right, Sweet One.

He slammed through the hospice door and shouted her name. A scholarly-looking gentleman in a dark brown tunic bearing the League's emblem came right up.

"Calm yourself, my friend. We have sick people here. Tell me the name of your friend or family member and we'll see what we can do." The fellow smiled paternally.

Vendanj hated the impertinence and grabbed the man by the arms. "My wife's name is Illenia. I'm told she was brought here. Please, I must see her."

The man then spied the three-ring sigil Vendanj wore, and his countenance visibly changed. He asked to be unhanded and then called to a standing guard, who came forward with his palm on the hilt of his blade. Vendanj let the healer go and implored them to tell him where his wife lay.

"Please, she's with child. I need to see her." Panic rose in his chest. He thought he would scream soon and keep screaming.

Shortly, three more guards came to reinforce the first. They didn't snarl or curse, but simply barred him from two shadowed hallways that led to several private rooms. The healer then took Vendanj gently by the hand and patted his knuckles.

"You are probably a fine man. And I understand your worry. These fellows will accompany us, and we'll take you to see your wife." He pointed down the left hall. "They're a necessary precaution in these troubled times. That seems most reasonable, doesn't it?" He smiled his patronizing smile again.

Vendanj barely heard him.

The four sentries went first, directed by the healer through the third door. Vendanj came after, the healer still holding his hand. The gentleman may have thought this a supportive gesture, but Vendanj was going to need his hands free soon, and the grip of this League healer began to irritate him.

But it all faded when he saw Illenia lying in a bed of white linens. Her face had been heavily bruised and her arms were completely bandaged. She turned her head, and when she saw him, a pained smile rose on her purpled lips. "You came."

Vendanj tore free of the man and rushed to her side. "Silent gods, Illenia, what happened?" He put his hand on her stomach, as he had grown accustomed to doing, and stroked slowly.

She spoke softly, just a few words at a time. "Quiet came. They had Velle with them." She swallowed. "The guard failed. Didn't know what to do. League"—her eyes darted to the men behind him—"ran. The people started to fall, Vendanj. Fall." A tear coursed across a yellowed bruise at her temple.

He shook his head. "Don't talk. You're going to be all right."

"Had to do something. I went to the gate. Called the Will." Her voice cracked, and she squinted against some pain.

"I think this is not helping her," the healer said. "She needs rest. This whole affair has been most . . . unbelievable. We need to assess. And she's taken serious—"

Vendanj silenced him with a stare. The guards moved closer to him. Their presence angered him all the more. He didn't need them; Illenia didn't need them anymore either. Vendanj could care for her now.

"Wasn't enough," Illenia said. "Too many. I'm sorry, Ven. I'm sorry. I wouldn't have gone. The baby. But no one could stop them. . . ." She ceased to talk, crying openly now, her tears silent and hot and painful, he knew, in more ways than one.

"Leave us," Vendanj said. "Thank you for everything you've done. But we don't need your help any longer. I'll care for my wife now. If we owe you anything, I'll pay when I'm done. Please give us some privacy."

No one moved.

And then the healer came forward. "Sheason. These are troubled times. I am a man committed to healing the sick. And I will continue to watchsafe your wife. I hope you'll have confidence in me, as I've taken her to my care while you've been away." The indictment in his voice was gentle but clear. "But there are two things that are certain, and not easy for you to hear, which is why my colleagues are present." He indicated the League guard.

The leaguemen drew their weapons. Behind him, he heard Illenia whisper, "No."

The healer looked up passively. "Your wife, sick as she is, did nevertheless violate the law. When she is well, there must be a trial. And despite your grief, Sheason, you must entrust her care to me. You will not be allowed to call upon whatever arcane rituals you practice. And I will tell you true, I believe they hold more danger for her besides. The best thing for you is to go home and get some rest. It would seem you've been on the move for quite some time."

Vendanj stared into the man's bespectacled eyes. "No man or army that is going to stand between me and my family, Leagueman. I'm grateful for the care you've shown my wife. But that is over. What I do now has nothing to do with you."

Then it all unraveled so quickly.

"No," Illenia cried again.

This time, Vendanj heard the message in her voice—the baby was coming . . . and something was wrong. The leagueman bustled past Vendanj. "Get him out of here!" In an instant, the guards grabbed Vendanj by the arms and legs and began forcing him from the room.

An anguished cry rose from Illenia's bruised lips. "Please, no. Vendanj. Vendanj!"

He fought to free himself, or at least his hands, so he could call the Will. But he couldn't muster enough strength to outman four guardsmen.

He thrashed, kicking and yelling for assistance, for someone to take pity on him. He could save his wife and baby, if he could get free. "Help me! No. Illenia! Illenia!"

As he was dragged from the room, he caught one last look at his wife. Her bruised, tear-streaked face; her eyes shut tight against pain and grief; one bandaged arm raised toward him.

He fought and fought. Screamed until his voice sounded like stalks brushing each other in the wind. And then he was struck on the head and all fell to blackness.

Illenia died.

Their child died.

As Vendanj looked up into the bitter skies over the Scar, he thought again—as he had countless times—if he'd had the experience he had now, he could have saved his wife. Saved their child.

They were a fool's thoughts.

All those years ago, he'd strictly followed the path of the Order—never rendering the Will to harm another man in anger or frustration or fear. It was a path most Sheason still followed. Not Vendanj. Not anymore.

He shook his head. No good could come of reliving the past. The choices today and tomorrow were all that mattered. He'd learned as much at a dear price. Others didn't see it so clearly. But on important matters, like the Quiet, the choices ahead for himself and now some few others . . . were clear. He would make them see. Not simply because of the scars of *his* past, but because someone must, else the value of a man's wounds would be as nothing.

And Vendanj couldn't let that be true.

CHAPTER THIRTY-SIX

Ta'Opin

The Mor Nations are several Inveterae Houses. But it is believed the Ta'Opin Mors are the keepers of the Refrains. And they don't leave their homeland, save they have a purpose.

—From the *Register of Isolationists,* a demographic study

Jastail and Penit rode side by side ahead of Wendra, talking like uncle and nephew. Jastail patted Penit's head, the boy laughing at some comment. The highwayman glanced back at her. His expression said everything: *I control the lad, so I control you.* And it galled her. Even though she knew it was a ruse, it galled her.

Colors swirled in her vision. She could feel blood coursing through the veins at her temples. She could hear the blood, coming in rushes like the reprise of a song, ebbing and flowing with regret and violence as each beat of her heart pushed it along. She fought for balance as the fading harmonies of rhythmic sound, like strings being plucked by callused fingers, brought tears to her eyes.

These were not the peaceful tunes of her childhood, or her box, and she couldn't remember their melody, only the rough feel of them at the back of her throat, and the images of broken glass on cellar floors.

At dusk, Jastail called them to a stop, and led them fifty strides from the road. He asked Penit to build a fire. The boy eagerly took to the task. And soon, the crackle of burning wood echoed up into the woods nearby.

They hadn't been there long before the sound of metal clanking echoed to them from the road. She could see two lanterns swaying with the gentle motion of a large wagon. The slow clopping of hooves came next, and then the sound of song, evenly measured, and hummed low in the chest of a large man.

Before she could think, Jastail was beside her. "On the high roads it is unwritten grace to share a man's fire and offer him a cup of tea. When he comes, remember what I said. And besides he may be yet a rougher man than I." Jastail sniffed. "But even if I'm taken down, you may be sure I won't go down alone. And you know where my first strike will go."

Wendra marveled still at the indifference in his voice. "You'd sooner we die than let us go free?"

"I'd sooner you keep your manner as cordial as when we first met," Jastail said. She couldn't see his eyes, but he'd already put on his gambler's charm.

The wagon creaked to a stop at the crossroads. "Hail there," a voice called.

"And you, traveler," Jastail said in a raised voice. "Come off the road and share our fire."

Penit jumped through the high brush toward the wagon as it turned from the well-worn ruts. The horses' muzzles emerged from the darkness into the dim glow of the flame. Their tack and harnesses jangled and yawed until the driver pulled them to a stop and tied the reins down to the hitch. A tall man with a deep chest hopped spryly to the ground. His buckle gleamed in the flicker of the firelight, but his face remained obscured until he came close.

Nearer, Wendra realized the man had dark skin. And he'd shaved every last bit of hair from his head and face and wore no tunic. He was bare-chested.

She'd never seen one, but he looked like Ta'Opin, one of the Tilatian peoples of the eastern shores. The Ta'Opin were rumored to be Inveterae, to live six generations, and to end their lives with a strange madness, such that most took their own lives before the dementia beset them.

Jastail strode confidently past her and put out his hand.

"Off of the road when the sun has failed. Share our tea." Jastail said it with a strange rhythm. It carried the sound of a routine greeting.

"And a tale when our tobacco is lit," the other replied as if by rote.

They clasped hands, giving Wendra the thought that she might communicate her predicament to the man without alerting Jastail. As the two approached the fire, Penit flitted about their legs like a light-fly.

Jastail produced two tin cups and poured steaming tea into each. He handed one to the traveler. "What name do you carry across the high roads?" Jastail said, settling himself again on his rock.

"Seanbea," he answered, and sipped his tea. "Thank you for the tidings. Not every fire near the road is the welcome it used to be."

"Truer words were never spoken," Jastail said, nodding. He pointed his cup of tea at Penit. "This is Penit, a fine young man I'm escorting to Recityv to run in the Lesher Roon." He raised his other hand with his open palm up. "I'm Jastail. And this is Lani," he said as Wendra came into the circle near the fire.

The Ta'Opin stood and bowed slightly at the waist. The deferential gesture took Wendra by surprise. She nodded in return and sat on a fallen log next to the boy. She nudged him subtly with her elbow.

"I meant to tell you," Penit whispered. "Jastail told me about it today. The Lesher Roon is a race with a great prize. And we need to go to Recityv anyway, right?"

Jastail cleared his throat with the obvious intention of ending their exchange. "Have a seat," he invited the Ta'Opin. Seanbea sat directly on the ground close to the fire and drank his tea. "You drive your horses late," Jastail said over his own cup.

"And would have gone on another hour or two if you'd not welcomed me to warm my hands," Seanbea replied.

"What makes a man brave the roads at night, and without protection?" Jastail said, refreshing his own cup of tea.

"I go myself to Recityv. And my haul is waited on." Seanbea put his cup out to be refilled, and spoke as Jastail filled it to the brim. "But it's hardly a bounty for a highwayman: music instruments and census records, collected for Descant Cathedral."

Descant! Where Vendanj had wanted her to visit. And where the man in her fevers had been from. She looked away at the wagon. Its load had been tied down with thick cords.

The Ta'Opin went on. "The instruments are old; serviceable maybe, but only to the hand that remembers how to play them. Your man around town wouldn't have any idea how to go about it with any of these. As for the rest, moldy parchments and rotted books, little to interest a thief."

"Still, to ride alone is risky," Jastail commented as he settled himself comfortably with his mug.

"Right you are," the wagoneer agreed. "But an escort would draw attention, and really it isn't the kind of haul that needs extra riders. Besides, the legends of my people make average men wary, and dull men faint of heart." He snickered. "And it's my good luck that a *smart* man rarely takes to the road to earn his fortune."

Wendra gave Jastail a vindicated look.

Returning her expression, Jastail spoke, his pleasant demeanor undisturbed. "To your good luck," Jastail said, raising his cup in a toast. "Luck to have found *us,* and not the kinds of men you describe." Wendra despised the way the highwayman relished the irony that the Ta'Opin couldn't appreciate.

Jastail then proffered his cup toward both Penit and Wendra in a kind of toast. The boy smiled, and Wendra forced herself to do the same. Seanbea hummed a few happy notes as he took another drink of his tea. A comfortable silence settled over them for a few moments. Finally, Wendra had to ask.

"Tell me of Descant Cathedral." She tried to disguise her interest, but she wanted badly to hear about this place that the white-haired man had spoken of in the cave.

Wendra immediately sensed Jastail's anger. But right now she didn't care.

"Ah, Descant, it's a grand place," Seanbea said. "There was a time when it was the pearl of Recityv, the very reason for it. The city lived for the music they wrote and performed there. It was the city's heartbeat, the pulse of all Vohnce. Children like young Penit here are entrusted to the Maesteri, who teach prodigies the art and passion of song."

Seanbea stood. "Its spires rise above vaulted ceilings." He pointed into the sky as though he could see them even now. "Brass cupolas that once blazed like fire in the sun, now colored by rain, dress the cathedral like green crowns." He stared a moment then dropped his gaze, as if looking at the street-level memory of the cathedral in his mind. "Its stone walls are dark now, and many of its colored-glass windows are boarded against vandals. It lies in the old district of Recityv, where rent is cheap and boarding houses stand next to brothels for convenience. The stench of goat pens can be smelled from its ironwood doors."

"You've been there, then?" she asked.

"Been there, lady?" Seanbea said with good-natured incredulity. "I sing there." He sat again, draining his tea in a gulp.

Penit's face glowed. "I've done the skits in many cities," the boy said. "But never in Recityv."

The wagoneer looked across the fire at Penit. "You're a player?"

"For a while," Penit answered. "But only on the pageant wagons, never in the theater houses."

"All the same," Seanbea said, beaming. "What a chance meeting is this: a child of the stage, a brother to give me haven at his fire, and a woman—"

"Indeed," Jastail cut in. "But we've traveled long today and I think—"

"We should travel together," Wendra suggested over Jastail's attempt to put an end to their camaraderie. "We're faster on the horses than your wagon, so we can keep your pace, and it would be a blessing to hear you sing, Seanbea."

"I don't see why not," the Ta'Opin answered.

"No." Jastail spoke harshly. The edge in his voice silenced them all. She turned on him and found him glaring at her. The searing stare lasted a long moment. When Jastail realized he'd momentarily dropped his façade, the anger melted from his face. "My apologies," he said. "We *are* going to Recityv, but we must stop at a friend's. That will take us off the trail. I don't suppose you can spare the time, my friend. Though I too would have liked to hear you sing."

Seanbea held an affable expression on his face, but Wendra thought she saw concern in the set of his jaw. He took a lingering look at Penit and then at Wendra before looking back at Jastail. "I cannot, you are right."

"A shame," Jastail said, his control reestablished. He offered his cup to Wendra, and she fought the urge to push it back into his face.

"I've no stomach for it," she said tersely.

I could snatch the boy and dash to the wagon. The Ta'Opin would defend us.

The thoughts pushed her to her feet, and she carefully eyed Penit, who watched the two men, his elbows propped on his knees and his head held in his hands. She took half a step toward the boy, but Jastail rose to his feet and cut in front of her. He took a quick seat next to Penit and wrapped an arm around him.

"We think Penit's going to win that race," Jastail said. He turned to the boy, his fingers riffling Penit's hair. "Isn't that right?"

Penit smiled, slightly embarrassed, then put his own arm around Jastail's waist.

"He's your boy, then?" Seanbea said, careful eyes studying them.

Wendra knew Jastail would register the curious way Seanbea eyed them as he asked. And she suddenly feared for the Ta'Opin.

"Closer than that," Jastail added quickly. "We're like brothers, right?"

Penit nodded with enthusiasm.

The Ta'Opin looked at Wendra. "Then you—"

"Will you sing with me?" she broke in.

Seanbea's confusion seemed plain. He slowly shrugged his massive shoulders.

"What shall it be," she asked.

"'The River Runs Long'?" the Ta'Opin suggested in a distracted tone.

She could see that behind his eyes he still worked at the problem of the relationships among the three.

"I don't know it," Wendra said. "But sing it through once, and I'll join you."

Seanbea eyed her, then looked back over his wagonload once before putting his cup aside and clearing his throat. She heard a deep hum in his chest, like water on a whetstone to prepare it for use. Then suddenly, the concern that had tensed his jaw relaxed and the Ta'Opin began to sing. The melody settled low around them, as though hugging the earth and rising only as far as their ankles. It came softly, and soothed out in legato strains that flowed effortlessly from his throat. Wendra heard the refinement in his voice, the sweet richness and clear call of each phrase. He sang slowly, allowing each note a life of its own. After but a moment, Seanbea shut his eyes and followed the song where it led him.

Across the fire, Wendra glanced briefly to see Penit paying rapt attention, a smile of wonderment lifting his cheeks and arching his eyebrows. Jastail listened, too, but the deep resonance seemed to capture something different in him, leaving the highwayman to stare at things he alone seemed to see. The blank look of indifference she'd learned to hate in him hung heavy in his lids, drawing the lines at his mouth taut in an expression that bordered on sadness.

The melody slowly rose, coaxed by brighter tones from Seanbea's voice. The tune quickened, and in her mind Wendra could see the river for which the tune was named. She could almost feel its current, visit its shores, and see the world reflected in its smooth surface. The melody didn't inspire dance, but filled Wendra with a kind of hope. Not for herself exactly, but in general, the way spring brings hope after a cruel winter.

Seanbea moved into an elegant passage of music, calls from one voice in the song's story, and responses from a second voice. The first rose like simple questions, a child's questions about the river and where it led, to be answered by the second voice in a deep register, the voice of experience, of a parent, teaching the child the beauties and dangers and destination of the water's path.

Wendra's mind flooded with the image of a Bar'dyn standing over her, coaxing her unborn baby from her womb. The thick smell of copper filled her nose as she saw again the wide, unsmiling face of the Quiet standing at the foot of her birthing bed. She listened to her own unanswered cries for Tahn to come to her defense.

Seanbea's song went on. It grew lightsome in the sharing between a parent and child of such a simple wonder as a river. But every note in the Ta'Opin's song made Wendra's remembrance more vivid. The beauty of the melody ached inside her, describing the child she lost to the rain and night, but proving the hope inherent in birth.

Then, without thinking, she began to sing. Seanbea's song repeated with new questions, new answers, and deeper metaphors for the river. And Wendra wove her own harmonies of aching beauty to his lines. She sang without anticipating what she would sing next. Distantly, she was aware of Seanbea turning to look at her. But she sang past him, giving voice to the single cruelest moment of her life. Her lament rose up in a long echo like a loon's call at dusk.

The image changed then, and in the Ta'Opin's song-fashioned world the skies emptied rain into the river, somehow further darkening Wendra's countermelody. She lifted her song higher, but softer, a delicate huskiness edging the timbre of her voice. She'd never sung like this before, but it seemed right.

The Ta'Opin's melody sank to a whisper, falling to his deepest register, holding long notes with open lips to keep the river running while Wendra wove her dark tale above it. The rush and rasp in her throat sputtered and dipped like an injured bird, falling toward the river mud of Seanbea's vision.

And when she thought her song was ended, when the pain of the voice given to the wound of losing her child might close her throat, a crescendo of song filled her chest, and reached a height of pitch she'd never imagined.

The bottom of pain.

Seanbea followed, in perfect time. Wendra's chest vibrated with the powerful basso of his voice. But she ascended higher, a piercing note rising and turning in melodic groups until the moment of her loss became as real as this moment by the fire.

She sustained the note, the sound of it pounding in her head, making her aware of every beat of her heart, while she felt the explosive power of Seanbea's pulsing rhythm beneath. Then she stopped. Seanbea did the same, anticipating the moment as though they'd rehearsed the duet. The brutal memory departed. And she sat next to the Ta'Opin, listening to the echo of their final notes into the alder and out upon the hard roads that had brought them both here.

When the sound was gone, and all that could be heard was the fire, she looked at Seanbea and saw anguish in his face like that of a father agonizing over a lost son. Had he seen what she saw?

She glanced quickly at Penit, relieved that the awe in his face remained. But she didn't meet Jastail's gaze. Quietly, on weak legs, she left the fire.

• CHAPTER THIRTY-SEVEN •

Hidden Jewels

Thousands apply every year to Descant. A handful are accepted. Of those, maybe one in a hundred has Leiholan gifts. And very few of those ever learn Suffering.

—Lettered response to the Randeur of the Sheason
on the topic of Leiholan

Helaina slid through the shadows of Recityv's worst slum. Fires burned openly in the alleys, where animals lapped at muddy puddles and nosed through refuse on the ground. The alleys reeked of human waste, besides. She held her shawl up over her face, but mostly to guard against being recognized. She'd risked her visit to Descant Cathedral to visit an old friend and ask a favor.

The Cathedral had once rivaled Solath Mahnus as the jewel of Recityv. Its marble gables and towering vaults had risen at the same time as the palace and courts. Now, it lay surrounded by a rough working class that scarcely noticed its remaining splendor. And the coarser among them tended to vandalize or deface the cathedral. Heavy boards had been secured against the lower windows, and its base showed the stain of men who stood against it to urinate.

She smiled sadly. All this came in an age when the League proclaimed that civility had rescued them from the superstition and myths of the past. Free of such *burdens*, apparently men's civility amounted to pissing wherever they pleased.

Even on the symbols of things they once held dear.

She ascended the Descant steps and quietly knocked. A moment later, the door cracked open wide enough for a pair of eyes to see out, and surprise lit the doorman's eyes when Helaina lowered her shawl to reveal her face. He immediately stood back and motioned her inside.

The door shut smartly behind her. "I wish to see Belamae."

Helaina's use of the Maesteri's first name—Belamae Sento in full—startled the doorman. He would not have heard it often used.

"Of course, my lady." The man bustled ahead, retreating into the dim halls of the cathedral and motioning her along.

Only a few steps inside, the distant sound of song rose as a hum emanating from the marble pillars themselves. Among the things she must discuss with Belamae, this song was the most important.

The doorman led her beneath great vaulted ceilings, until they came to an unremarkable door. The man knocked and bowed as he stepped back. Shortly the door opened, and her old friend with his snowy white hair offered his wide smile in greeting before wrapping Helaina in a firm embrace.

"You don't come to see me often enough," Belamae said.

"Nor you me," Helaina countered. "But mine is the greater sin. Your cathedral is a more pleasant place to spend an afternoon."

"Yet you've come after dark hour." He nodded satisfaction to the doorman and sent the man away.

Together, Helaina and Belamae went into his brightly lit office and took chairs beside each other before a cold hearth. She relaxed back into the leather, made for comfort and not ceremony—a fine treat. And for a brief moment, she closed her eyes, concentrating on the distant hum, before coming to her purpose.

Before she spoke, Belamae said, "You've come about the Song of Suffering."

The regent sighed, then nodded. "There are rumors, Belamae. And if they're true, there's likely only one cause. I know you won't lie to me, and I need the truth."

The Maesteri patted her knee, then stood and went to his music stand. There he fingered several sheets of parchment. He gathered them into a pile and sat once more. "I read it every day." He handed the sheets to Helaina.

She took them in hand. "What is it?"

"The music that accompanies the Tract of Desolation." He sat back into his chair. "The Song of Suffering. This is what the Leiholan sing in the Chamber of Anthems."

"Your translation of the Tract is safe?" she asked.

"I would have come to you if it were not," Belamae said.

Helaina grew thoughtful. "How long have you been its steward, my friend? Since long before I became regent, I think."

Belamae laughed warmly. "I hadn't even had my own Change. And I sang the Song for twenty years before I began to teach."

"Responsibilities fall too much to the young these days." The regent looked into the flameless hearth.

"If I recall, you were rather young when you were called to be regent," Belamae said. When she looked up again at him, he was smiling. "Daughter of the wealthiest merchant family in Recityv. A year, maybe two, beyond your own Change, when the commerce guilds asked you to represent them on the High Council. What was it, a year later, when you took the regent's seat? We were both young once," the Maesteri said, wistfully, "both making far-reaching decisions at a tender age."

Helaina nodded, thinking that she was here now, at not-so-tender an age, with more far-reaching decisions to share. "I've called for a running of the Lesher Roon."

"That's what I hear," Belamae replied. "You're filling your table in preparation for the Convocation. Wise of you. And you'd like me to sit again on your council, I'm guessing."

"That's only part of it, but yes."

"The others don't care much for the opinions of the Maesteri, but I'll return to my seat there if you wish it." He patted her knee again.

"Belamae . . ." She hated having to say it. "I want you back on the Council not just because of Convocation." She paused. "Roth is going to formally call for an end of the Song of Suffering. He's gathering Council votes."

The Maesteri returned a serious look that slowly warmed to a smile. Then a warm laugh. "Oh my," he said. "What a fool. He and his League have been talking about that for some time now. Well, I'll come be a vote, then. But rest easy, Helaina. We musicians aren't a soft bunch. And if Roth really wants to square himself against Leiholan, well . . . let's just hope he's not that much of a fool."

Helaina smiled back. Her old friend was unshakable.

"So now I must tell you the truth about these rumors," he went on. "There's word of Quiet in the land again. That's at the heart of it, yes?"

"They're not rumors. Not to my mind."

Belamae uttered a weary sigh, and scrubbed his wooly brows. "The Song of Suffering is meant to keep the Veil strong. But the Leiholan who sing it are tired. And there are few of them left, Helaina. The gift to create with song doesn't come as often to men and women as it once did."

"But you've so many students here," she said with fresh concern.

"And not all those who possess the ability are able to learn Suffering," he explained. "And of those who can, only a few are able to endure the horrors it describes. The act of singing it takes a heavy toll. It's a portion of the Tract of Desolation, for gods' sake. And the song is long. Sung without pause, it takes seven hours. One Leiholan rests a full day after performing it."

"Belamae." She stared him straight, coming to the question that had gotten her arthritic bones moving late this night. "Do the Leiholan falter?"

Her old friend looked back. "Some days . . . yes."

Empathy swelled in her for the keeper of the Tract, even as dread gripped her. "Then the Veil weakens, and the Quiet slip through."

Belamae said nothing.

Helaina handed back the parchments. This last bulwark against the Quiet, hidden among the rags and filth of Recityv, had begun to fail.

"It's time," Helaina finally said, breaking the stillness that had settled around them.

The Maesteri met her confident gaze.

"Time for what?"

She cleared her throat and spoke as the iron hand. "Suitors with dangerous ambition will begin to flood our gates, looking for position and alliances. And the League has its own agenda. I've instructed General Van Steward to begin recruiting to reinforce his army. But our best defense against the Quiet has always been the Veil . . . which means there may be more to do."

"More from Descant?" he asked.

"More from the Ta'Opin," she clarified. "Maybe all the peoples of Y'Tilat Mor."

Belamae showed the smile of a hopeful skeptic. "So, you've come to exploit my heritage."

Helaina returned the smile, briefly. "I won't leave any request unmade . . . however dangerous."

His eyes grew serious, again seeming to understand the implications.

She took a deep breath. "It's time that we consider asking for the Mor Nation Refrains. Their warsong is written of in the Tract itself, is it not?"

Belamae stared a long, serious time at her. "Helaina, once we start down that path . . . Are you sure?"

The regent fell quiet, listening again to the distant hum of the Song of Suffering. She'd started down this path long before she'd come to the cathedral. She reached out and placed a hand over his. "I'm sure." She thought a moment. "We don't need to send our request today. But soon."

"You know the Refrains are just a part of the need. You'll still have the problem of finding Leiholan to give voice to those hymns. The Mors won't do it for you." He glanced down at the parchments of music—the Song of Suffering.

Then he offered a gentle smile. "But perhaps that won't be necessary. I've not been neglectful of my stewardship . . . or the changes lately in the Song of Suffering. Even now, I have voices on the roads seeking records that might help us find those endowed with the gift." He squeezed Helaina's hand. "And there's at least one bright hope out there, my lady. I've seen her."

• CHAPTER THIRTY-EIGHT •

The Wilds

Some hold that even the Quiet aren't the worst off. Some of the Framers' work were never even given form. That's a damn hell, if I ever heard one.

—From *Tabernacle Speculations,* a consideration of creation

The thick hardwoods of the wilds were coated with damp, mossy lichen, and the air rolled with the smell of rot. Root systems snaked along the ground, as though unable to find purchase deep in the soil. It made for uneven footing and labored walking. Branches didn't naturally grow skyward, seeking the sun, but reached in strange directions. Many grew back toward the ground, where they took root or continued to grow laterally.

Soon, the sun was completely obscured by the densely interwoven branches overhead. The trees bore small, budlike leaves that inched skyward.

And underfoot, in places, the ground went soft. Mud pots. Quicksand. Sevilla had been right. They needed his help navigating the wilds.

The natural sounds Tahn had become accustomed to in any forest were absent. Instead, occasionally a low sound rose deep in the woods, like a mallet striking a hollow tree. Infrequently he heard the song of crickets, but the chirp never lasted, cutting off for several moments before repeating the same halting cadence. As they passed deeper into the wilds, a musky fog began to rise from the loam.

"Never mind the fogs," the man assured them. "The heat and cold battle in the topsoil; it'll settle soon."

"You said this was Stonemount's defense against attack?" Sutter asked, picking his way over a confluence of roots.

"Effective, don't you think."

"Seems to me it offers an enemy cover while he sneaks closer," Sutter observed.

"There's more to the wilds than trees, adventurer." The man stopped and turned a full circle, nodding as he surveyed the branches overhead. "The wilds have a way of turning a man around, making him forget himself. Many graves lay within the wilds. But none are marked, because none were planned. There are glyphs in the city that say the city came first, and others that say the wilds came first. Whichever is true, this dark grove has stood here a long time." Sevilla smiled. "How glorious a people. How enlightened. They allowed this grove to grow untamed, its natural state a marker to measure the height of their advancement."

Sutter gave the man a curious stare.

"Or, perhaps they're just trees," the man said unconvincingly. "Perhaps I'm too long in my documents and studies here to have remained objective."

The man whipped his cloak around as he spun and continued deeper into the wilds. His route wound like a snake. And Tahn, even with his woods skills, soon felt completely lost. The land dipped and heaved, the roots growing more closely together and leaving little ground between. All about them was wood: roots underfoot, dark bark upon the trees, and a low ceiling of branches. A cavern of it. In every direction, Tahn could see nothing but the deep dark of endless trunks, grown black in the shadowy confines of the wilds. The smell of rotting wood hung thick in the air.

Then, in an instant, the dim half-light fell nearly to utter darkness. *The sun's gone behind the western rim.* Distantly, the strange sound of wood striking wood echoed again. And strangely, the cricket song ended, leaving a deathly quiet in the grove.

"That's great. I suppose we aren't going to make it to the north canyon," Sutter said with weary sarcasm.

"It isn't far," the man replied. "But travel at night in the wilds is . . . ill-advised. Don't fret. I'm a cautious one, and I'll see you through."

"I'll build a fire," Tahn said. The abrupt darkness had brought with it a chill.

"If you must," the man answered.

Carefully, Tahn shuffled his feet, seeking a clear bit of ground. Sutter gathered a few fallen limbs and shortly they had light again, and warmth. Tahn sat on a humped root and pulled out some bread for himself and Sutter. The firelight glistened darkly on the nearby bark. Sparks from the fire drifted up on the heat, and winked out against the tight weave of low branches. Their guide sat close by, watching the fire and looking alternately at Tahn and Sutter.

"So, where is home?" the man asked.

Tahn studied the easy smile on Sevilla's face. The man likely suffered from a lack of companionship, and was intrusive only because of it. His jeweled scabbard, long cloak, and tricorne hat were the affectations of a man not sure of himself. He spoke with an elegant confidence, like the polished way a trader spoke. But he hadn't anything to gain from helping Tahn or Sutter, and Tahn could sympathize with the feelings of loneliness.

Tahn shared a look with Sutter then, his friend shaking his head in a nearly imperceptible motion to warn him off. "Reyal'Te," Tahn said.

The man nodded to the small reservation. "At the edge of the Mal. You're a long way from home. Maybe there's a bit of adventurer in the pair of you, after all."

Their guide sat comfortably, looking rested after a day's walk, and vital without a speck of food. The night air grew colder still. Tahn and Sutter circled closer to the fire, warming their arms and chests and cheeks while goose bumps from the cold rippled on their backs. Their guide seemed equally content in the dipping temperature.

Something had been bothering Tahn about their route through the wilds, and it occurred to him as he rubbed his hands near the flame. "How do you mark your passage through these woods? You can't have learned the way after just a few trips."

"Oh, I've been in Stonemount a very long time," the man said. "The disservice we do to the past is distilling an entire generation into the notes on a single page. If history is properly studied, I believe it may take as long to learn it as it did for others to live it. And if I'm to discover what became of them, what led them to vacate this beautiful city, I must learn all the things a citizen takes for granted: the multiple meanings of words that are used to insult; the unwritten standards of behavior that show respect or intolerance; the attitudes of their populace that were harmonious with their poets; poets who wrote of rebellion."

"I don't see the purpose in it," Sutter chimed in. "I mean no disrespect," he offered cautiously. "But they left, one way or another, and the world went on without them."

Sevilla's face fell slack, the convivial look gone. He shifted his eyes to Sutter without turning his head. "You've answered your own question. How does it escape you? Today we stood in the most glorious civilization ever erected. From its central fountain to the edge of the graves around it, you walked the streets of a city that showed no despair in the architecture of its least citizen. The whole of it is a lasting tribute to unity, equality. And then they disappeared without a trace of contention or a single indication of where they went."

The man stared at Sutter with wide eyes, clearly feeling as though his point should be obvious.

Sutter shook his head silently. "Maybe they were invaded. If they were over-whelmed and taken captive, they could all have been led away somewhere. That would explain the city being deserted but showing no signs of war."

Their strange guide continued to stare quietly for some time. It was his turn to shake his head.

"Boy." It was spoken with utter evenness, an insult more searing than a curse. "Look at you. Far from Reyal'Te, searching for a codex, and keeping your little secrets because you don't trust me." Sevilla gave a piteous laugh.

"You crossed the Ophal're'Donn bridge," Sevilla rushed on, "and went saun-tering down the Canyon of Choruses as though you'd earned the right. And yet you fail to see the miracle of Stonemount." He paused to make it clear. "Those who lived here overcame the kind of arrogance that makes you feel deserving of more than you have. They overcame the combative nature such arrogance creates. The Stonemount people outgrew their own city of rock and mortar, and left for something better, nobler." The man paused again, the crackle of wood seeming suddenly very loud in the silence. "I want to know what they knew, go where they have gone. I am tired. . . ." He stopped, a genial smile re-turning to his lips. "My apologies. I get very passionate about my studies."

Sutter was frowning with anger, his hand on his sword's handle.

In a soft voice, Sevilla said a few words more. "All the rest are walking earth, upright dust, consuming breath in ignorance." The words were familiar to Tahn, but he couldn't place them. He finished his bread, and later fell asleep watching the guttering fire, his hand on the sticks hidden within his cloak.

Tahn couldn't see the man's face. He never could. But he could feel the figure behind him, prepared to correct an errant move or loss of concentration.

The horizon rose pale blue at the break of day. Tahn stood on a precipice of rock, looking out over an ancient canyon carved by a slow-moving river deep in its valley. The red stone and baked earth appeared tranquil in the gentle light of pre-dawn. The man shifted his weight to his other foot, the crunch of pebbles beneath his sole accentuating the quiet that had settled over the canyon. The air remained still, and Tahn held his breath as he aimed his bow over the vastness of the chasm below.

"Breathe naturally," the man said. "A rigid chest makes weak arms, causes anx-iety. To hit where you aim, you must shoot your arrow without fear. And each ar-row is important. It must fly with the fullest intention of your heart."

"But there's nothing here to shoot," Tahn said, confused.

The man came close to his ear. "You need to learn how to focus on yourself, not the quarry." His voice came softly, but firmly. When the man spoke in such a way, Tahn knew he was expected to listen and remember. "You create the energy of the weapon by making your pull. You can feel the force of it suspended in the string and the give of the haft. None is yet given to the arrow. This is the moment of balance between Forda and Forza, the bow and the energy you give it. In this moment you have the potential to take life or save it. Your intentions are everything, Tahn."

"How will I know when to shoot, and when not to shoot?"

The man let a slow breath through his nostrils. "You'll ask each time you draw whether you should release . . . or not."

Tahn shook his head in confusion.

The man went on. "It will sharpen your sense of the Will, keep you aligned with it."

"But why?" Tahn asked.

The man stretched an arm past Tahn's face, pointing at the emptiness of the sky above the great canyon. "You must learn and remember the power of the draw itself, not the arrow. It is potential power, just as a boulder perched at the top of a hill. You'll need that power, Tahn. Against enemies with bodies as real as yours or mine. And against some . . . who'll come after you to inhabit your body. They're old enemies. Out of the Bourne."

The man stopped speaking, and Tahn knew it was time for him to shoot. He looked into the gathering light of dawn and sought a target: a blackened tree a thousand strides distant on the far side of the gulf, then a mountain peak at the edge of the horizon, then a cloud gliding low across the hills to his left.

He could hit none of these things, and his fingers, wrist, arm, shoulder, and chest began to ache from the constant tension of his draw. He took a deep breath, exhaling as the man had instructed. His young arms began to quiver. The pain of maintaining the draw burned in his shoulders and ached in his knuckles. But he would not release until it was right. Was this the lesson, learning the strength of his own will?

He let go the string, and realized as it relieved the tension in the haft that he held no arrow. The string hummed. The sound of his bowstring rose like the tolling of a great bell, the vibration turning his hand numb. He lost feeling in his arm and dropped the weapon. Beneath him the soil turned white, spreading outward to rob everything of color.

In a frenzy, he thrust his fists against the rock of the outcropping and screamed to hear anything but the awful hum. Hearing nothing, he stopped. Quickly, he took two large rocks and smote them together. No crack. There was nothing in his head but the ringing buzz of his bow's last release, and nothing in his eyes but colorless earth.

Tahn looked up and screamed into the sky. . . .

He started, and came awake in the wilds, a scream dying to echoes in the trees around him.

"Keep it down, Woodchuck," Sutter complained.

Sevilla sat poking at the fire with a slender stick, his eyes on Tahn as he probed the embers. The flame burned low, casting deep shadows over the man's eyes, but hinting with reddish hues at the dark pupils.

Casually, Tahn checked for the sticks. They were still safe in his inner pocket.

Getting to his knees, he took several small pieces of wood and cast them into the fire. The man gave him a quizzical look. "You sleep restlessly. You've got things on your mind."

"We all have things on our minds," Tahn replied.

"So I've noticed." The man settled a thoughtful gaze on Tahn. "Some of the old texts say that sleep is our preparation for death: a day of life and light followed by a quiet, restful end in a night's slumber. Rehearsal, you might say. A pattern we follow often enough to accept when our time is gone and we must return to the earth that makes us. So, it's a riddle why men tussle with it. But a noble fight, I say. I wouldn't easily give in to my barrow."

Something flashed in Tahn's mind: a figure, little more than a shadow itself, hunched over a grave.

Without turning his back to their guide, Tahn stood and shuffled to where Sutter lay. He nudged his friend's shoulder with his foot.

"Don't tell me you're kicking me just as I was about to fall asleep," Sutter protested in a thick, surly voice.

"Get up," Tahn said softly. Something in Tahn's tone must have struck Sutter, who stood up fast and shrugged off his blanket.

"Are you ready to go?" Sevilla asked, rising gracefully. "I sense you're quick to be shut of these wilds and on your way to wherever fortune next takes you."

Tahn cautiously picked up his bow and caught Sutter's gaze before looking down at the sword at his friend's hip. Sutter understood and rested a hand on the handle. If their companion noted their apprehension, he didn't show it. Sevilla's gaunt cheeks held shadows in the flickering firelight, but his eyes remained easy. The jewel-encrusted sheath caught the light in colorful prisms, and he pushed back his tricorne hat on his head as Tahn stepped back from the fire.

"We'll be on our way from here," Tahn said. "Without you."

Sevilla slowly stood, his easy smile faltering. "That won't be necessary."

CHAPTER THIRTY-NINE

A Primrose

It isn't when a man picks up his sword that you have to worry. It's when he picks up his pen.

—From *The Difference Between Anger and Change*,
a philosophical construct, Aubade Grove

V isitors," Braethen heard someone say.

Vendanj stopped, and Braethen came up beside him. Ahead in a broad, shallow bowl was a house, standing like a lone waystation in a very long route. And beside it several forms were silhouetted against the westering sun. A tall man stood at the center, and to each side of him were several shorter figures. *Grant. And his wards.* Braethen raised a hand over his eyes, but the light was too low against the horizon to be blocked out.

They'd been moving since before sunrise, Vendanj continuing to lead them north and east. All day they'd walked in the oppressive heat. Beads of sweat ran down Braethen's neck. He clutched his shirt and mopped them away. Mira's hair and shirt hung wet with perspiration. Her face, too, ran with sweat, but she didn't wipe it away. The heat didn't seem to affect her the same way. And Vendanj simply seemed too stubborn to be bothered.

But their water was gone. Their horses had begun to stumble, and behind Braethen one of the mounts lay down, chuffing from its nostrils with the exertion. In a moment, the other two animals had done the same.

Braethen licked dry lips.

"And a sodalist." Grant's shadow fell in a long line toward them. "He wears his sword like new shoes."

Vendanj stared ahead at the exile. "We have news."

"Of course," Grant replied, a hint of condescension in his voice. "And you believe it involves me." The man took several steps closer. Braethen could now see the dark brown of his weathered, sun-worn skin, and the deep lines at the corners of his eyes.

"I do."

Grant frowned.

"Don't become what they accused you of," Vendanj said.

Grant shook his head. "You should let me be." His words sounded like both command and plea. But also, resignation.

Vendanj began walking toward the man. Mira moved with the Sheason, her hand resting on her sword in an unthreatening way. Braethen followed.

Several days' growth of beard peppered Grant's jaw. Vendanj took the man by the hand, the grip unfamiliar to Braethen.

The Sheason looked down at their bond. "I'm glad to see you, Denolan."

Grant stared at Vendanj. "I've not heard that name in a long time. You must really need help." A long pause stretched between them. "But don't use the name. It's not who I am anymore."

Vendanj nodded to the request.

Grant raised a hand. Four young men and two young women came around to face him. Each of them, skin as deeply tanned as Grant's, wore a sword and carried a bow. All had long hair tied back with strips of cloth. They weren't much younger than Mira, and they wore the same stern look he saw on Grant's face. The Far seemed to appreciate them in a way Braethen hadn't seen her admire anyone before.

"See to their horses," Grant ordered. "Take water and salve."

The six left at a run, and Grant turned toward the house. "There are questions in your eyes, Vendanj. Let's answer them and send you on your way. You don't belong here." The man brushed past Braethen without acknowledging him.

Following them, Braethen stepped over a circular depression that ringed the house at twenty strides. It occurred to him where they must be: the ring where Maral Praig and his Sheason had stood to call the Will in the Battle of the Round. His heart jumped at the thought of being at the center of where it took place.

A light wind whistled around the chimney and stirred dead grass here and there. Large red masonry bricks stood at each corner of the house. They looked like the baked clay of the Scar. Wood planks ran in vertical rows, bleached and coarse from exposure. The roof had been leaved with thin pieces of sandstone, and several ladders stood against the roof's edge, giving Braethen the impression that it was used as a lookout.

At the door, Vendanj put a hand across Braethen's chest. "It may be hard to respect this man," Vendanj said softly. "But hold your tongue. His bitterness is earned."

Inside the home, a cooler, settled air eased the heat in Braethen's cheeks. Shielded from the sun, the trappings of the home nevertheless appeared sun-worn: a washbasin; a book cabinet largely empty; a rough table attended by four rough chairs; and open cupboards with a few dishes.

No art adorned the walls, only bow pegs and a narrow weapons rack near the door. A greying rug, its pattern faded to almost nothing, covered much of the floor.

Vendanj was looking over sheets of parchment laid across the table, while Braethen noticed something fixed to the wall beside the door. An elaborate sigil had been scrawled at the top of what looked like a formal letter:

> *This writ shall serve as witness that Emerit Denolan SeFeery has willfully committed treason against the stewardship entrusted to him and against the right order of progress as held by the High Court of Judicature and the League of Civility. It is hereby declared that Denolan SeFeery is unfit for citizenship in the free city of Recityv.*
>
> *In the interest of justice he is thus permanently exiled into the emptiness known as the Scar. With the exception of the First Seat at the regent's Table, he alone will know the trust this sentence represents.*
>
> *Any known to abet Denolan SeFeery will be considered a traitor and judged accordingly.*
>
> *From this day forward, Denolan SeFeery will no longer be referred to with the Emerit honors of his former office. Should he ever return to the free walls of Recityv, he shall be punished by immediate execution.*

A dozen names marked the bottom of the page. The parchment itself drooped with sepia tiredness. Only the seal at the top indicated the official nature of the document.

"Emerit," Braethen whispered with awe. An Emerit was a Recityv guard with sworn fealty to the regent. The physical prowess of such men was said to be matched only by their intellect. It was a title accorded to only the greatest fighters by only the highest mantle of government.

Grant lit a table lamp and started a fire against the coming of night. From a hidden basin beneath the rug he drew a jug and poured them each a cup of cool water. He waited while every cup was drained, then refilled them. He left the jug with Braethen and took a seat beside the fire.

"You bring a novice sodalist," Grant said. "Does he realize what danger he must be in, simply traveling with you?"

Mira's and Vendanj's eyes fell on Braethen. Another awkward smile twisted Grant's lips. Braethen looked at the wall again, where the edict had been placed. "I know there's danger. It appears to be no less than what you've done in your own past."

Grant's laughter caught in his throat, his smile not looking natural on his face. "Astute words for a boy just out of his books. Before the three-ringed man and his fleetfoot ask me what they must, let me explain something to you." He pointed a finger at Braethen. "I chose to be here. That parchment on the wall reminds me of that. The Scar's an ugly place, and not for any of the reasons you think. But because *I* am here, these young ones aren't sold on the blocks. And I show them how to keep from having their own choices taken from them." Grant sat back, his face relaxing again. "By physical defense; all is coming to that. Or perhaps you knew this, since you wear a sword of your own."

The fire hissed in the silence that followed.

Against the quiet hum of burning wood, Vendanj added, "Then why redraw the Charter?" The Sheason tapped the parchments lying on the table.

Dead gods. The Charter wasn't even something that had been written. Spoken stories said that it was the principles the Framers had put in place for this world before they'd abandoned it. The right way of things. It wasn't scripture. It wasn't even fiction. It was a kind of common ethic that all men were said to feel in the fabric of their lives. An ethic that some said had lost its meaning. And relevance.

Grant gave Vendanj a bleak, unsmiling look. "Perhaps only to better understand what we've become." He paused, his eyes distant. "And what lies ahead."

"For that no Charter need be written," Vendanj countered.

"Or maybe having no written Charter is precisely our problem." Grant stood and went to the table where the parchments lay open. "It's my primrose in this desert. *Not* writing this . . . it would be like admitting the League is right. And if *that* were so, then I couldn't remain here." His eyes seemed to look far away again. He muttered, "And the cradle would be more merciful as a casket."

Again no one spoke, the only sound the popping of sap in the flames. Mira stood as still as a statue. Outside, the sound of hooves approached. Grant went to the door and gave a few instructions. Three of the six wards ran back into the dusk; the other three came inside and stood near the hall entrance.

Vendanj put a hand on Grant's arm. "The regent is calling for a Convocation of Seats."

Grant frowned, unimpressed. "And the Nations of the Sea, those across the Aela, the Mal?" Grant asked. "Do they care about the Second Promise any more than the First? Do they even remember? It's political posturing of the same brand that brought me here. Your Court of Judicature will fatten themselves and squabble over appointments to military stewardships and land resources. And those are the ones that even attend. The rest defend their own farthest borders if they can, and have no use for Convocations."

"You may be right. But it's different this time." Vendanj paused, looking like he'd rather not say what came next. "A call has begun to end the Song of Suffering."

That statement silenced the room.

The Song of Suffering was said to be a gift from the Framers. A song that kept the Veil in place, kept the Quiet in the Bourne.

Softly, Grant asked, "Who asks this?"

"The League." Vendanj took a drink from his cup.

"Ah," Grant grunted.

"There are Quiet deep in the east," Mira added. "I think the Song is already faltering."

Grant sat himself back by his fire. He watched the flames a moment. "I know. But they won't engage *us*. They either fear us . . . or they use us as bait." Grant shifted his attention to Braethen. "How long before they come through that door, Sodalist? You don't care much for yourself to be standing beside a three-ring man. You're a fool."

"Enough," Vendanj said.

"And you, Mira," Grant pressed. "What covenants do you break by coming into the lands of men? You're either more like me than you'll admit, or the mysteries of your people are about to be laid bare for a tribe of Velle too fast for even you."

"Enough!" Vendanj yelled. His voice boomed in the house, seeming to crash down from the crossbeams and echo off the floor. "These are not the words of the man who defied his accusers in the Recityv courts. Don't let your sentence make you foolish."

"Speak softly to dead men, Sheason," Grant returned. "There's no threat that moves us." His gaze never moved from Vendanj.

The Sheason returned the stony stare. "We went to the Hollows to find Tahn."

Grant's expression changed, though it was hard to place. Recognition?

"Through Myrr and over the High Plains we came," Vendanj related. "But on the North Face we were separated. We don't know where he is now, but hopefully moving toward Recityv."

Grant clenched his jaw. "I belong here," he said. "The world beyond the Scar is not mine anymore."

Vendanj sighed in disgust and frustration. "Then answer me one question."

Grant looked him in the eye.

"Why do you look like you haven't aged since you came here?"

CHAPTER FORTY

The Untabernacled

If you're suggesting a legion of ghouls, then I counter with the Dannire. Sanctioned murderers in the name of dead gods. You see? I have devils, too.

—From the rhea-fol *Tell Them by Their Hats*,
a parody of meaningful war

Sevilla showed a toothy grin and stood up. "There's so much to learn here. Perhaps we can find your codex after all. But in any case, I think you're staying here with me."

In a startling rush, the man rounded the fire and tried to take Tahn by the wrist. Tahn felt a chill where Sevilla's hand passed through his arm without so much as a bump. Tahn stared at his wrist in disbelief.

Sevilla snarled at himself in disgust, seeming to have forgotten his true nature. In an instant, his body began to change. The fine garments fell to loose rags, worn with holes. The fine hat and scabbard became a filthy sash and a shock of unkempt, knotted hair that hung like the dark strands of a mop. Behind him, Sutter drew his sword.

Sevilla looked up at Tahn, a strange mixture of bitterness and regret in his eyes. "So long in that dark country, little hunter, digger of roots." Anger surged in his face, pure hatred contorting his features. "I want my own body!"

Sevilla leapt forward with startling speed, his hands rising toward Tahn's throat. Tahn dropped into a backward roll. Sevilla raced through the air where Tahn had stood, then turned, a shriek of frustration tearing through the wilds. Sutter jumped between them as Tahn struggled to his feet.

"Little man with a steel toy," the thing barked in savage mockery. "If I could I'd take your strike to know the glory of the sting."

Sevilla launched himself again. Sutter started to swing, but had only cocked his blade when Sevilla shot an arm into his chest. The creature's gnarled fist plunged deep into Sutter's flesh. Nails dropped his sword, his body tensing, writhing.

It can touch a man when it means him harm.

Cords stood out on Sutter's neck as he twisted and fought to free himself. But it appeared the creature had hold of his friend's heart. Around them the air began to whip and swirl, stirring sparks from the fire in dervishes and tugging at their cloaks. Sutter sputtered calls for assistance, his movements starting to slow.

Tahn nocked an arrow and made his draw before he realized his weapon couldn't harm the creature. There was nothing he could do. So, he charged at Sutter and Sevilla, diving into his friend and wrapping his arms about his waist. His momentum tore Sutter from the creature's grasp, and Nails uttered a weak, throaty cry as his connection to the beast was severed.

Sutter fell to the ground beneath him like a loose bag of grain. Quickly, Tahn turned over and sat up, again drawing his bow and pulling his aim down on the dark creature.

The being slowly came forward. Its withered features contorted with rage and menace. Words hissed from its lips, but Tahn couldn't understand them. It was circling close. How could he destroy something he couldn't touch?

His mind filled with the image of himself standing on a precipice, prepared to fire into emptiness.

You must learn and remember the power of the draw itself, not the arrow.

Tahn stood and uncertainly faced Sevilla. He cast his arrow to the ground between them and drew back his bowstring again. The creature paused, concern narrowing his contorted features. Distantly Tahn heard Sutter howling in pain, but the sound of it was lost behind another sound like the hum of a potter's wheel turning. His entire body began to quake uncontrollably, as though vibrating with the same strident hum he heard in his head. The resonance inside him thrummed, seeking release.

In his mind, he spoke the old words. Nothing. No feeling that Sevilla should die. No feeling that he shouldn't.

My dying gods. What is this?

With no sense of his draw, Tahn felt lost. He stared, paralyzed. *I'm going to die.*

Then it came to him. *Sevilla was never alive.*

The air continued to howl about them as Sevilla took another guarded step forward.

Tahn drew his string further, his heart pounding in every joint of his body. He glanced at the shape of the hammer on his left hand to steady himself, and whispered the old words. Despite the terrible tremors wracking him, his strength and thought and emotion coalesced as he'd never felt before.

The small camp became a maelstrom of embers, leaves, twigs, and dust. Eddies of the mixture swirled in the crevices of trees and large roots. Tahn's hair whipped about his head, flailing at his eyes, but he kept his arms up, trying to hold steady on the figure of Sevilla. He saw the ledge from his dream, the impossible targets of a cloud, a mountain, a horizon, and closed his eyes against them. He felt close to the precipice, and was ready to release, wanted to release, and give way to the feeling that welled inside him.

Then abruptly the wind ceased, the fire fell to a slender flame. Tahn opened his eyes. Sevilla took a step back before turning and starting to walk away.

Tahn watched, unable to stop his own shaking or release his draw. His muscles ached but would not obey. At the edge of the light, Sevilla half-turned and looked back. His clothes still hung like mottled rags, but his face had again become that of the amiable, sure man they'd first seen. He appeared ready to say something, his lips working silently. Then he was gone among the trees. Tahn collapsed, still gripping his bow and staring into the low ceiling of tightly woven limbs.

Sutter writhed.

His soul ached.

The moment Sevilla had put his hand into Sutter's chest, it had taken hold of something inside him. It hurt differently than a cut or broken bone. And the creature's icy touch had taught Sutter an awful, immutable truth: His spirit could be separated from his body. Not death. Displacement.

For a terrible moment, he was sure Sevilla—some kind of disembodied spirit—wished to possess him. It would force Sutter's soul into the empty existence in which *it* had lived. And then he realized what Sevilla—or whatever it was—sought. It hunted for the Stonemounts. Their secret of life and death. It wanted to be alive. It was trying to find a physical form for its spirit.

It's damned.

It wailed at the thought—*damned!*—somehow through its connection with Sutter able to hear his mind.

Then the struggle began in earnest.

Sutter could feel his spirit wrestling, shifting inside himself, trying to stay joined with his body.

His vision swam, one moment looking into the creature's terrible rictus, the next awash in blue where images of the countless dead walked, watched, or wailed. With the eyes of his inner self he could view the unseen world. It was filled with the untabernacled—spirits with no body. It haunted him. He thrashed harder to free himself of Sevilla's hold.

Only vaguely was he aware of Tahn—movement somewhere nearby.

Then his soul began to slip.

An awful comfort stole over him, a dreadful serenity in leaving behind the uncertainty of future choices. He looked about him, embracing the final reality, ready to join the countless spirits he could see with these new eyes. He caught the violet and black and cerulean world in snatches through the creature's mortal embrace.

And at the farthest reaches of his mind, a wry thought halted his surrender: *I'm being plucked from my own body like a root from dry ground.* And on its heels came another thought: *I'm better than this.*

He fought back.

But the burn and tear of spirit from flesh became too exquisite to bear, and soon real death beckoned him.

Then Sevilla's hand was ripped free of its grasp upon his heart. Dark thoughts and dreams receded in a blinding rush, and he crumpled to the forest floor with his friend, who'd forced the creature's release.

He knew in his agony that a part of him had been lost, stolen.

And something else gained.

Drops of rainwater struck Tahn's cheek. He woke and more rain fell into his eyes. The knit of branches obscured his view of the sky, and caused the rain to gather in leaves before falling. The fire had burned out, now hissing as rain plopped into the cooling embers. He wiped his face, spreading the moisture to try and refresh himself.

He lay unmoving and listened to the sizzle of the storm as it struck the upper leaves of the wilds.

Tahn wanted to lie and let the rain fall on him and lose himself to the sound. But Sutter let out a weak moan, and Tahn forced himself to sit up. Nails was a familiar dark shape in the recess of nightshadow beneath the canopy of trees overhead. Tahn tried to stand, but his legs cramped under him. So he rolled over, and dragged himself to Sutter.

His friend lay clutching his chest. No wound marred his clothing; no blood stained his hands.

"Are you all right?" The words sounded foolish as soon as they got out.

Sutter drew breath to speak, but coughed in the attempt and winced in pain, grabbing his chest with both arms. He rolled onto his side and curled into a ball until the convulsions passed. Weakly he whispered, "Cold."

"I'll get your blanket," Tahn said, and tried again to stand. His legs refused, and he sat hard next to Sutter.

"Inside," his friend added, touching his chest.

Tahn looked back to where Sevilla had disappeared into the trees. *What if he returns? What if I had tried to release an empty bow?* He scanned the trees around them and satisfied himself that they were alone. They couldn't stay here, though.

"We've got to get out of here," Tahn said.

Sutter nodded, his eyes still shut tight. He peeled his lips back and spoke through gritted teeth. "I can't ride."

The rain began to fall in earnest, growing louder in the flat leaves and running to the ground like miniature waterfalls. The coals of the fire hissed and steamed more loudly, sending waves of smoke into the air. Tahn folded his knees under him again and sat up. He looked around for long branches to build a litter, and spotted a deadfall not far from the horses.

He tried a third time to stand, but his legs held him only a moment before tumbling him forward into the gnarled surface roots of the wilds' trees. One knee cracked hard against a large, knotted root. His head pulsed with the rapid beating of his heart, blurring his vision. Each breath seemed to rush into his blood and push his heart faster. He shook his head and dragged himself through the mud and mulch to the dead wood. Lying on his side, he pulled two long limbs and one shorter piece from the tangle.

Working against the growing pain, he retrieved a length of rope from his saddle. He lashed the wood together in a slender triangle, and rigged a sling between the poles before laying his blanket across it.

He then gathered their horses' reins, hoping to secure the litter and find the northern passage.

The wilds lit as lightning flared in the sky above. A mere second later, a powerful clap of thunder boomed around them. The air exploded with a hot smell, rushing as if propelled by the boom. Sutter's horse bucked and tried to tear free. Tahn held on, the reins pulling him up like a puppet whose leg strings have been cut.

The horse reared again, this time tearing the leather from Tahn's hand, and slicing his palm as it tore away. In an instant, the horse sprinted into the darkness of the wilds and was gone. Tahn's horse rolled wide eyes and stamped about, but didn't jerk its reins from Tahn's hand.

When he got his mount back to Sutter, he attempted to hitch the litter to Jole's saddle horn. But when Tahn stood, his head swam, and he fell to the ground. He beat at his legs, but could feel nothing, the numbness spreading into his fingers and back. *I don't have time for this.* He buried his face in the mud and screamed his frustration, tasting the richness of the soil and the decay of last year's leaves.

Tahn crawled back to Sutter to roll him onto the litter. As he pulled at his friend's shoulder, Nails opened his eyes, a pained but clear look in them. "Tahn . . ."

He pulled Sutter's shoulder over and laid his friend on his back. Tahn then worked himself onto his knees and heaved Sutter into the litter. He retrieved the blanket and covered him. His friend was wet, but the wool would keep him warm. Tahn looked back at his horse. How would he hitch the litter and mount his horse?

Another burst of light flickered, the thunder seeming to come before the light faded. The noise eclipsed the patter of rain and the sound of his own heart in his ears. Rainwater ran into his eyes and plastered his hair to his cheeks and neck. In his mind he tried to recall the words of the man from his dream, and touched the familiar shape on the back of his hand.

His friend began to lose coherence, babbling: "The spirit isn't whole, Tahn. It's not whole. It can be divided. Given out. Taken. Small portions separated . . ."

Then Sutter passed out.

Tahn dropped to his belly and inched his way to his horse. Clenching the other end of a rope between his teeth, he cut another length of it and tied the end to the apex of the litter. Then he took hold of the stirrup and hoisted himself up. On his feet, he couldn't feel his legs. He hooked his arm under his knee and lifted his foot toward the stirrup. He jabbed his boot in and took hold of the horn. His hands went numb and he couldn't feel the jut of the saddle against his chest. With one great effort he thrust himself up over his horse's back, and shimmied around until his leg fell onto the other flank. He managed to get his second boot tucked into its stirrup, pulled the rope from his teeth, and wrapped it around the horn. With clumsy fingers, he tied it, then took a deep, searing breath.

On the ground, water now tracked in small streams, pooling in low hollows. Tahn was glad Sutter had fallen unconscious; he wouldn't feel the jouncing of the litter across the roots.

Last, Tahn cut another piece of rope and fastened it around his own waist. He then tied the other end to the saddle horn, as well.

Clucking to his horse, he let down the reins. He would trust his old friend to take them ahead and out of the wilds. It was all he could do. Trees passed, one the same as the last. His eyes burned as if they too had fever, and moments later he could no longer feel his arms or chest. He slumped forward and tried to keep his balance, whispering encouragement to his horse until the numbness entered his face and took his ability to speak.

On they went. Tahn remained awake, but felt like little more than a scarecrow in his saddle. The rain didn't let up, and the thunder shook the forest floor as though the lightning shot up from the ground. Flood pools accumulated in low areas. His horse trod through them, casting his head about, seeking direction in the absence of a path. The wind soughed in the trees, stirring wet leaves and dropping rain in sheets over them. Tahn hoped Sutter wouldn't be thrown off the stretcher, because neither of them would ever know.

After what seemed like an endless number of hours, Jole emerged from the trees. Less than four strides away the northern rim rose up into the blackness.

Tahn made a thick sound deep in his throat to urge the animal on. They turned right, following the cliff face. Shortly, the wall opened on the left into a narrow canyon like the Canyon of Choruses they'd come through into Stonemount. Rainwater ran in a shallow river from it and into the wilds. Tahn moaned again, and his mount turned into the canyon and took them away from Stonemount.

The sound of the rushing water reverberated up the high stone walls along the narrow road. The shadows were deep in the canyon, leaving the rushing of water to guide them. The roar of the rain and current blotted out thought, and only the constant ache that cycled in Tahn's head remained. Each pulse of his heart reminded him he was alive, and soon that ache became a grateful prayer.

But would Sutter live?

The night stretched out.

Finally, the canyon ended. Tahn moaned again, and his horse understood to stop. The storm had softened a bit, the heaviness of the drops lighter and their fall less pounding.

Tahn turned his head as high as he could and looked east. He imagined the sun burning away the clouds, touching the treetops with orange light and steam rising from the soil as the rain evaporated in the early-morning sun. He imagined the smell of green things and the stirring of bird wings. The familiar image might have warmed him in a time before the Bar'dyn came to the Hollows. Just now, it held no such power.

He wanted the sun to come, but not with the same earnestness as in days past. He simply cared less.

He needed to get Sutter to shelter, but had no feeling in his body. He fell from his saddle as wind began to riffle his sodden hair.

Sometime later a voice came. "Ho, there, it's night soon. Do you intend to sleep in a ditch?"

CHAPTER FORTY-ONE

Fever Dreams

A man claiming visions I can do nothing for, except to lock him up.
But a man with nightmares, him I can help.

—Testimony of a counselor in the formulation
of the Civilization Order

Tahn gasped and opened his eyes to a darkened room. In the small bedchamber, the smell of drying wool and pine floorboards filled his nose. Across from him, the window showed sun. He tried to move. Nothing. He was completely numb. He couldn't even turn his head. The sound of boots approached. Tahn began to panic. He was helpless. Who was coming?

A set of legs strode into his field of vision. The boots were hard leather, lashed with black cords that had been tipped with silver links to prevent fraying. Rolling his eyes, Tahn looked up into a rotund face.

"Do I look like an angel, my friend?" the man said, his voice gentle but crisp. "Because you have the look of death in your cheeks still. You weren't capable of assisting in your own rescue. So, I brought you here. No man sleeps in the mud when he has power to avoid it."

Tahn rasped something out.

"And coherent, too," the man replied genially. "Never mind, you'll be wanting to know about your friend. He's in bad shape, but no worse than you."

The man hunkered down beside him. The gentleman's rich, russet cloak parted as he squatted, and Tahn saw the brocade of the League clearly over the man's left breast. The stranger put a hand to Tahn's brow. A worried expression touched his eyes.

"I've no interest in alarming you, my friend. But I've pulled up children from the river who feel more alive than you." He smiled, seeming to think better of verbal diagnosis. "Grunt if you understand."

The suspicion Tahn had seen in the eyes of leaguemen wasn't in this man's gaze. But the thought lessened his concern only slightly. He lay powerless against the man's any whim. He might discover the sticks in Tahn's cloak, misuse them in any manner, turn them over to a higher League authority.

Tahn grunted.

"Good. I'm Gehone." He took hold of Tahn's hand and gave it a shake that Tahn couldn't feel. "When you're dry, warm, and able to speak, I'll be interested to hear how you came to travel north on a road that goes through the mountains." One eye cocked. "This will give you time to construct a lie, so craft it carefully." He smiled wryly.

From a pouch at his belt Gehone produced a small jar. With one thick finger he took a generous portion of a green salve. "Hold this under your tongue," he said, and deposited the goop in Tahn's mouth. He then took another fingerful and gently applied it to Tahn's lips.

Gehone stood and left the room. In the silence that followed, Tahn heard the thin rasp of his friend's breathing and caught a glimpse of a second bed on the other side of the room.

Peppermint and parsley cooled his tongue, and a mellow feeling crept over him, inviting him to sleep once more. Before he succumbed to weariness, he looked around for his cloak, and saw it hanging on a peg beside the door. He couldn't see if the sticks were still there, but he hadn't seen Gehone rummage through his things. Satisfied for now, he fell down to sleep.

Tentatively, he opened his eyes. The same room. It hadn't been a dream.

"It's about time, Woodchuck."

He tried to raise his head, and was relieved that he could do so, if just a little.

"Don't strain yourself. Heroes always push themselves too hard," Sutter said from across the room. "But don't go thinking this means I owe you. Hero or not, I'm still a naked man who chafed all night beneath itchy wool blankets."

Tahn licked his lips and attempted to speak. His voice cracked. He swallowed, beginning again more slowly. "You all right? Sevilla . . ."

His friend's face lost its smile. "I feel like one of your arrow tips is lodged inside my chest. Just talking is sending little spikes of pain into my neck. But it means I'm alive and away from Stonemount." Sutter shifted to face him. "What happened to you? Some large fellow walks in this morning and spreads some disgusting goop on my lips. Before I could ask, he put a hand over my mouth and said you needed to sleep."

Tahn tried lifting his arm, and got it mostly up before dropping it back to the pillow. "It's all hazy. After Sevilla left, I started going numb. Before my arms went, I built a litter and started out of there. Eventually we found the canyon. Somewhere along the way I passed out. I woke up here."

"Where is here?" Sutter interjected.

"Don't know."

They fell silent. Beyond the door, the occasional sound of boots over wood reminded them that they weren't alone.

"Did Sevilla poison you?"

Tahn considered the question. Perhaps he did at that. He might have had the opportunity while Tahn was sleeping. But it didn't ring true. He shook his head, still happy to have some movement back. "But whatever happened, you should know we are now guests in the home of a leagueman."

Tahn heard a quick intake of air. "Does he know about us? We'd better get out of here." The rigging under Sutter's bed squeaked as his friend tried to rise. Sutter took a deep breath and held it before grunting and trying again to hoist himself from his bed. Finally, Sutter flopped down and gave up. "All this way," Sutter said, "and it ends like this."

Tahn tried twisting his torso. Mostly worked. "It's all a blur, but Gehone seems decent."

"You're delirious. Do you hear what you're saying?" Sutter's voice became simultaneously vehement and quiet, as he attempted not to be overheard. "I'm grateful for a warm bed, but how many stories do you remember in which the accused are nursed to health so that they may walk the gallows?"

Sutter trailed off, and quiet returned to the room. As they held a companionable silence, light ebbed and returned as clouds passed over the sun. Then down the outer hall, someone began to approach the door.

Tahn spoke quickly. "You're right. We'll leave as soon as we can. Don't let Gehone know you've regained your strength."

The door opened and Gehone entered, carrying a tray with two small bowls and two narrow mugs. Steam rose from all four. He put the tray down on a dresser and crossed to Sutter, propping him up with his pillow. He put a bowl and cup at the stand beside Sutter's bed. "Don't waste a drop," he admonished. "The blend of herbs will give you strength and the broth will heal whatever ails you."

Gehone came to Tahn and sat at his side. "Any movement in these arms of yours?" Tahn shook his head. "Ah, but your neck has returned. Good." Gehone lifted Tahn easily and propped his back against the headboard. He lifted the bowl and scooped a spoonful. "Are you ready to tell me what business you had in Stonemount? And don't deny you've been there. Your boots are caked with soil that belongs to that place." Gehone put a mouthful of the broth in Tahn's mouth. The savory potage tasted good on Tahn's tongue.

"Adventure," Sutter said around a mouthful of the hot broth. Gehone turned a questioning look on Sutter. Under the leagueman's gaze, Sutter pulled back a bit. "Accident, really," he added.

Gehone turned again toward Tahn. "That the truth of it, lad?"

Tahn simply nodded.

"Indeed." The man spooned another bite into Tahn's mouth. "Well, you're lucky to be out of it alive, then. Lore holds that the Stone belongs to the Walkers since the hour its residents abandoned it. If that's so, you two are lucky indeed." Gehone watched Tahn closely.

"What are Walkers?" Sutter asked, his voice tense.

Without shifting his careful gaze from Tahn, Gehone explained. "As lore goes, they were the first creatures to suffer the consequence of the Whiting of the One. Half formed. No bone or muscle to house their spirit. And so they seek to take it from other men. They're the revenants of Stonemount because the bones of the dead there are believed to be able to give life to vagabond spirits. Silly, superstitious stuff, but creatures out of the Craven Season are creatures of appetite, so the stories go. They wouldn't have allowed you to leave, if they exist at all."

A careful smile crossed Gehone's lips. "Can you speak yet, my boy? You see a Walker?"

"No," Tahn said, slurring it a bit on purpose.

Gehone ran a hand through his beard and spied a look at the leather piece on Sutter's hand given him by the Sedagin. "Let me be honest. I've seen you both without your breeches, and if you're not melura, you're not far from it. I know you came by way of Stonemount, so then I wonder what brought you through. Seems there's something different about you lads, and I'm hoping it isn't your penchant to lie. Because tomorrow my commander pays his usual visit to gather my reports and bring me orders. He'll want to know about you, and he'll be a good deal more insistent than I am." Gehone turned around and began again to feed Tahn.

When Tahn was finished eating, Gehone gathered the dishes and bustled out. They sat looking at the door as the sound of the leagueman's boots retreated down the hall.

Sutter got out of bed twice that day, quietly pacing the room to test his strength. The first time, Tahn had him check for the sticks in his cloak; they were still there. By evening, Tahn found himself capable of moving a few of his toes. Gehone came again at dinner, this time bringing thin slices of pigsteak and quartered tallah roots covered in meat drippings. With it he served a mild bitter. "Good for your circulation," he said, and held the cup to Tahn's lips.

The leagueman didn't again mention their travels or the impending arrival of his superior the next day. Instead, he limited himself to idle banter, allowing Tahn and Sutter to enjoy the meal, and taking his leave without a further word when he was done. After supper, Tahn found he could ball his fists and raise his arms with more vigor. As night descended, Gehone left a lantern burning for them, the flame just barely taking the chill off the air and lending warmer tones to the room.

Looking at the hammer scar on his hand, Tahn spoke. "He never went through our things."

"What?" Sutter asked with a preoccupied voice.

"As far as I know, Gehone hasn't gone through our clothes." Tahn looked up at Sutter.

"Maybe that should worry us," Sutter answered.

Tahn shook his head. "He's helped us. Green goop, remember?"

"Yeah . . . And if that thing was a Walker like he said, then he'll be wondering how we got rid of it. All my hells, Tahn, that thing was Quietgiven. How *did* we get rid of it? It had its godsdamned fist in my chest."

Tahn sat quietly, thinking of an empty bow and an aimless pull over a vast canyon. He clenched his fists and pounded the mattress. *What do the images mean?*

Sutter waited for his anger to dissipate. Through the hiss of the lantern his friend said, "I've been thinking about the Bar'dyn, Tahn, when we were separated from the others. They said things, something about lies. Do you remember?"

Tahn nodded.

"And I was just thinking," Sutter continued, "Gehone doesn't speak like a member of the League, and offers to help us. . . . I don't know what the hell to think."

Tahn had no answers to Sutter's observations. He was missing home quite a lot.

Shivering, Tahn awoke to the sight of moonlight pooling on the floor. Chills raced across his skin. He could feel his legs, his whole body. He could feel the wind.

He turned to see the window stood open. Then quickly checked the rest of the room.

"Sutter," he whispered. The sound of his own voice fell flat. No response. He couldn't tell if his friend was in bed, or if the coverlet and sheets had been rolled back in the semblance of a body. Tahn propped himself on one elbow. "Sutter, this is no time for games."

No answer.

Tahn scooted back. His arms were still weak, but he was happy to have their use. He sat upright and squinted intently across the room. The bed lay empty. Then outside he heard the crunching of stones beneath boot soles. A shiver passed down his spine and prickled the hair on his legs. It might be Sutter, but something warned him that it wasn't.

Where's my bow?

Still watching the window, Tahn swung his legs out of bed. He'd started to stand when he realized that he wore no bedclothes. His body cast a thin shadow against the rear wall. He forced himself up, only to collapse on weak legs at the side of his bed. He shot a glance at the window, hoping his fall had been soft, and listening for the stranger's approach.

Silence.

Tahn looked around, searching for his weapon, and spied Sutter beneath his bed, as naked as Tahn. Nails was shivering, wide-eyed and searching.

Over the hard, cold wood, Tahn crawled to retrieve his cloak. Forgetting his bow, he then scuttled toward Sutter, who pushed deeper under his bed as Tahn approached.

"It's me," Tahn said. No recognition touched Sutter's eyes. Nails clutched at his chest, his eyes darting toward the window and back at Tahn. The grit on the floor scraped Tahn's knees and palms, but he lay on his belly and crawled under the bed. Sutter drew up to the wall, his eyes darting to and fro like a ferret's. "Put this on," Tahn said, proffering the cloak. Sutter didn't seem to hear.

A roll of bootheel and toe over hard soil came again. It was more distant this time, but perhaps only because he was now under the bed. He scooted up close to Sutter, and covered him with his cloak. His friend remained skittish, as if he expected Tahn to produce a blade and open his throat.

"What is it?"

Sutter just looked about, his eyes rolling wildly.

Tahn grasped his friend by the arms and shook him. "Tell me." Sutter came to himself as though he'd been asleep. He stared at Tahn, perplexed, then past him to the moonlight falling in a long rectangle from the window.

"I saw it," he said. Tahn was about to question him further when the sound of bootheels came again. The air grew colder.

Tahn listened for several moments, looking back to his friend and wondering if Nails had seen the owner of the boots they heard. His skin prickled, the cold getting into his bones. But nothing moved for a long while.

He took Sutter by the hand and led him out from beneath the bed. He cautiously looked around the room, then rose to his knees. Together they stood, and Tahn had started helping Sutter into bed when Nails again collapsed to the floor, pulling Tahn down with him.

Sutter gasped and pointed at the window. Tahn instantly looked up, but saw nothing there.

"What?" Tahn asked, the sound of it louder than he'd intended.

"Don't you see it?" Sutter cried. "All hells, Tahn, don't let her take me." Sutter began to crawl away, the cloak slipping from his shoulders. He stood, his bare skin full of chill bumps. He held his hands up to ward off nothing more than the pale light of the moon that poured through the window. His mouth opened in a silent scream.

Tahn's attention was pulled back fast to the open window, when it began to hum as though the ground shook with the flight of a herd of swift horses. A thin mist floated over the sill, into the room, and onto the floor. Tahn scrabbled back, bumping into Sutter's legs, but still he could see no one. The freezing mist licked at Tahn's toes as it roiled across the floorboards. He tried to stand, but weak legs sent him to the floor again. In an instant, Sutter snapped out of his fear. He swung around, took up the lantern from the table, and hurled it toward the window. With a loud crash, the upper pane blew outward. A spray of shards littered the sill, the broken glass clattering on the hard ground outside. A rush of wind twisted in the fractured portal as Gehone, clad only in a nightshirt, threw open the door and stepped into the room. Across his chest he carried a large war hammer, his hands in well-worn grips along its haft. He spared a look at Tahn and Sutter before stepping over them toward the window, where small shards of glass whipped in the air like cottonseed in a summer funnel wind.

With a flick of his wrists, he spun the hammer in a practiced movement and reared one arm with the weapon. The muscles in his legs bulged, his thick waist ready to accept a blow. Gehone waited, a cat ready to strike, but the mist evaporated. The wind whistled out into the eaves and was gone.

As soon as it had left completely, Sutter lunged for his sword and clutched it to his chest. Tahn picked up his cloak and wrapped himself. Gehone advanced cautiously toward the window and studied the wreckage. When he turned, he looked blankly at Sutter. "Put on some clothes, and gather your things. I'll put you both upstairs."

Tahn shuddered in the lingering cold. Gehone came close. "You need help?"

Tahn nodded. One bulky arm grabbed him around the waist. "I'll let this pass tonight, lads. But on the morrow, I'll need more answers from you. Nothing sounds so suspicious as the truth, and I'd better know the whole of it, or close to, when my commander comes to call. Hear me?"

Again Tahn only nodded. Still naked, Sutter had picked up his belongings, and with his eyes fastened on the broken glass, waited at the door to be ushered to a new room.

CHAPTER FORTY-TWO

Revelations in Parchment

We need to start considering the messages of written works. People find their own meaning.

—Area of consideration put forth by the leader
of the League's Political Jurshah

In the predawn light, Wendra lay still, listening to birdsong high in the trees and the deep melodic imitations the Ta'Opin made of them while he packed his bedroll and hitched his team. The smell of dew and coffee hung in the air, the latter a gift from Seanbea as he prepared to depart. For the time being, Jastail left her alone, saddling the horses and continuing his charade of friendship with Penit. He hadn't been able to tie her or the boy up the last evening, so he'd had Penit sleep next to him—the threat subtle but clear. Wendra tried to ignore it all, focusing on birdsong. But the melodies of last night's fire lingered, a refrain of the saddest sort.

When she could stand the inner songs no more, she rose. Seanbea sat at the fire, hunkered close to the flame, sipping a mug of coffee.

"Have a cup, Anais," he invited. "My beans are fresh from Su'Winde. I ground them myself this morning." He poured her a cup from a pot, and returned it to its rock beside the fire. "Is there a better smell when day is young?" He tilted his head back and closed his eyes. "There are advantages on the highways."

Wendra wanted to plead for help. Seanbea was sitting close. She could whisper their trouble, ask him to intervene. Just when she thought she might do so, Jastail and Penit joined them.

"A fine day. Good fortune to our separate enterprises, Seanbea. Hardly a worry on a day such as this."

"Right you are," the Ta'Opin answered, lifting the pot of coffee to offer a second cup. Jastail amiably declined. "I'm hitched and loaded. I'll be off when my cup is empty. Is there any message I can carry for you?"

Wendra hoped the offer would raise concern in Jastail's face. The highwayman didn't blink. "How good a man you are. Thank you, but we're fine. Is there more we can do for *you*?"

"There is."

This time Jastail's expression faltered a moment. Wendra could see her captor mentally working the positions of each of them at the fire. How the physical exchange would develop if he were forced to draw. She knew he'd cut the Ta'Opin's throat in an instant if what the man said next jeopardized whatever business he meant to conduct with her and Penit.

She and the Ta'Opin locked eyes. To her right, Wendra heard the soft squeal of a tightened palm over a leather hilt.

"I've something for you," Seanbea said. He reached into his coat, and Jastail began to move. Seanbea produced a rolled parchment. He ignored Jastail's movement and passed Wendra the sheet with both hands. "It's your song, Anais. The one you made last night in harmony to mine." He smiled paternally. "I've rarely heard instant song so beautifully made. The lines of your music played on in my head and demanded to be written down. Keep this. The notation is for only a single voice, but when you have such a gift of music, you share it." Wendra took it from his hands. "Study it. And when you get to Recityv, show it to the Maesteri. They'll recognize it for what it is."

With light, thin strokes the Ta'Opin had marked a series of vertical marks, interrupted by small circles with varying numbers of tails like ship rudders. She rose from her seat and put one arm around the Ta'Opin's neck, squeezing until she thought she might be suffocating the man. "Thank you."

Penit came over to look at it as Wendra sat beside Seanbea and took his hand. Jastail seemed more at ease, and he dropped his hand from his sword. "How foolish of me," he said. "You do my fire honor. You have my gratitude as well." He bowed, but not so deeply that he lost his vantage on all three. "We should be going," he said.

"And I," Seanbea added. "Safe haven to you at your . . . uncle's, did you say?"

"Safe haven to you," Jastail responded.

Penit helped the Ta'Opin gather his last few things from around the fire. Seanbea ruffled Penit's hair and squeezed Wendra's hand. He said to her, "I hope one day to hear you sing again," then mounted his wagon and drove to the road, where he turned north, raising a streamer of dust.

"Wait," Penit called after the Ta'Opin. He turned to Jastail and held up a coffee cup. "He forgot this."

"Never mind that," Jastail said.

"It's bad luck not to return it," Penit insisted. "Everyone on the road knows it."

Jastail's smile frayed at the edges, but only slightly. The highwayman maintained his good humor. "Go on then, but hurry."

Penit ran and caught up to Seanbea, spoke a brief moment, and returned the cup. Then he rushed back. In moments, dirt had been kicked over the fire, and Jastail led them back to the road.

For half a day they rode, Penit tirelessly asking the highwayman questions. The two becoming pals. Wendra stayed behind them, and fought back the sounds that struggled to escape her lips. Angry music. Snatches of song she worried to make, after what had happened in the cave beneath the High Plains of Sedagin. But she did wonder what these sounds would look like in Seanbea's beautiful script.

Shortly after meridian, the highwayman turned them west off the road. No trail. But Jastail seemed to know his way.

Night had just come full when they emerged from a thin grove of aspen into a flat hollow at the base of three mountains. In the center of a clearing, a small log cabin sat low and virtually hidden by several holly bushes. A large moon shimmered on a narrow stream that wound through the flat and near one side of the cabin. In the dark, the smell of wild honeysuckle and high-mountain lilac hung heavy in the air.

Jastail surveyed the basin before going ahead, his sharp eyes searching the dark. He appeared more skittish than she'd ever seen him. The furtive look on his face pleased her. But what might make a highwayman jumpy?

Jastail left the horses saddled while he checked the cabin. A moment later he reemerged into the moonlight. "Come," he said.

Penit slid from his horse and went inside. Wendra climbed down with stiff legs and wrapped her reins in a nearby shrub, then did the same with Penit's. Jastail skulked like a shadow to her side. He rolled a tobacco leaf into a small wrapper, and lit it with a sulfur stick. He puffed his tobacco stem alight, and stood drawing deeply of the sweet leaf.

"We're almost done, you and I." He spoke like a merchant describing a business arrangement.

Wendra smelled the smoke on the air, and watched it, silver and dreamlike in the moonlight. She remembered Balatin striking alight his pipe, the gentle soap-and-tobacco smell of his beard and sleeves as he pulled her to his chest and rocked back in the shadows of their porch. Years ago this night, this moon, and this smoke would have meant something entirely different.

She took out her music parchment from her pocket, and followed the graceful strokes as she remembered her melody. Snatches of song cooled her heart.

"Nothing to say," Jastail mocked, and drew near. His face a finger's breadth from her own. The smell of sweet-leaf soft as a lover's kiss between them. "Dear me, what can this mean?" He puffed again on his tobacco. "I gave the boy a bed. Tomorrow will bring revelations for which he'll need his strength. You should sleep, too."

Wendra said nothing.

No anger, no regret, no fear, no expectation showed in Jastail's hollowed cheeks or slash of a mouth. He stared at her, his eyes focused and unmoving. He recited from memory:

> Some lift prying eyes to discover the motive hands.
> Some toil daylight hours to rest and dream their days a different end.
> Still others make brash sounds,
> And many tormented supplication say on bended knees.
> Youth scrapes and hides and practices for its own time to stare the wall.
> I these things observe and name them wounds,
> And by so doing create my inmost salve,
> With which to rise and watch it all again.

He held her gaze a moment more. Then he tossed his tobacco into a bulrush and unsaddled the horses. But his words leapt to spontaneous melody inside her. They felt like song that mustn't be sung. Until something subtle *shifted* inside her. And the poet's words became her own. The song they *inspired* became her own.

Light fell through the windows, streaming through the ungainly branches of holly bushes growing beside them. Wendra lay in a fetal position, Penit curled up against her chest. The soft intake of his breath against the blanket made her smile with regret.

His smooth brow and downy cheeks glowed just a finger's breadth from her own, his face a portrait of unconditional trust. The memory of sleeping this way with her father, especially in the months after her mother had died, stole over her. His broad chest and strong arms had made her feel safe. Back then, she'd woken first, but lain still so the spell of morning could linger.

This morning, she watched the sun strengthen in the sky, wondering.

In another part of the cabin, she heard Jastail up and moving.

Penit moaned softly, like a response to some fanciful childhood dream. He squirmed and settled again, even closer. Wendra fought the urge to hug him. He might wake if she did. In her softest voice, she began to hum, the sound so delicate that Penit's breathing could be heard to keep time. She found phrases from her song box in her mind and wove them into variations as bright and promising as the light from the window.

He opened his eyes and turned to look at her. "We never had such a good voice on the wagons."

Wendra smiled. Then settled him with a more serious look. "I know you're playing a part, but be careful around Jastail."

"I know," Penit said, a much too grown-up look on his face. "I've known men like him my whole life. They're the ones that take coins out of the hat on the wagon wheel. Or like to beat on players for sport."

The bedroom door opened with a thick, heavy crack against the wall. Jastail came in, untied them, and said simply, "Let's go." Wendra and Penit shared a knowing look. Then he leapt from the bed and pulled on his boots.

"Will we make it to Recityv today?" Penit asked, following Jastail and resuming his ruse.

"Not today, lad." Jastail put an arm around the boy and the two walked into the hall toward the kitchen.

"Maybe never," Wendra added, alone in the sun-bathed room.

She joined them in the foreroom, where Penit was eating a mash of salted brownroot. Jastail stood near the door, beyond which many feet could be heard approaching. Wendra came up beside him.

"Why do you suppose I purchased my own lot?" He motioned at Penit without looking at him. "I saw what happened in you at the auction. And I heard it again when you sang with the Ta'Opin. It will help me fetch quite a price."

"No price will be enough for you," she said, thinking of the riverboat game.

Jastail did smile then, an awful twist of his lips. "You might be right about that."

He fastened his sword belt, slipped two daggers into his boots, and called for Penit. The heavy sound of many feet grew close. He half-bowed. "It's been a pleasure, my lady." He then opened the door.

Wendra looked out. Bar'dyn. Her hands started to tremble, her heart pounding in her chest. Penit took hold of her, his own body shivering against her leg.

Worry filled Jastail's face. *He was expecting reinforcements to arrive first.*

In an instant, his smile returned, and he strode out to meet his buyers.

CHAPTER FORTY-THREE

Public Discipline

Taking no action when you know you should is a greater crime than deliberate harm.

—An unspoken tenet from the Charter

Tahn never fell back to sleep after what happened at their bedroom window. In their new room, Sutter slept fitfully, muttering and calling out, hugging his sword close, the handle locked into the hollow of his cheek like a child's doll.

What had he seen? The mists, what were they?

He stood at this new window, testing his strength. Waiting for dawn.

Over the rooftop of the next building he could see the tail of the serpent stars, dipping now below the horizon. They shone, telling their stories. He felt a moment's peace, watching the stars turn.

Then he imagined he could see the morn, a gentle warming of color at the farthest end of the land. "The song of the feathered," Balatin used to say.

"You're up." Gehone's voice came softly, but startled Tahn nonetheless. "Looks like you have your legs again. Let your friend sleep, and join me in the kitchen."

Bright lamps gave the kitchen a cheerful look. A brick oven warmed in one corner, fired with ash logs that lay in a wood scuttle beside it. A black skillet rested on an iron grate, and the fragrance of cooking apples filled the air. Gehone took a seat at the table and poured a mellow-colored cider. He pushed one mug at Tahn. "Goes good with warm apples," he said, and drank.

Tahn sipped and rubbed his legs, which still tingled the way they did when he'd sat cross-legged too long.

Gehone raised a finger the way Balatin often had, looking ready to speak. But as he opened his mouth, he seemed to think better of it, and smiled sympathetically with his eyes. He said only, "Apples first."

The leagueman went to the cupboard and took down two bowls. From the skillet he scooped two large portions of sliced apples warmed in what smelled like cow's cream. Gehone returned and set the dishes on the table. Before Tahn could take his first bite, Gehone spooned a brown powder over the warm, sliced fruit. Tahn ate, disappearing into the taste of cinnamon and molasses. Gehone was right; apple cider was the perfect complement. They endfasted in silence, while outside the sun blued the sky.

With his last morsel, Gehone licked his lips and studied Tahn's face. "I'm not an old man. Still have use of my arms like a man twenty years younger, but I'm old enough to know *young* men have no business in Stonemount. Old enough to have seen sensible boys cower at the sight of an empty window, or like to it. Now, you can keep it from me, lad, and I'm bound to respect your right to do it, but if there's trouble, I need to know. The League needs to know."

"The League," Tahn parroted before he realized he'd said it.

"Is the name sour on your tongue?"

Tahn returned Gehone's careful stare. "I've no reason to trust *or* distrust you."

"I see, other than me dragging you out of a rainy ditch and giving you a warm, dry bed," Gehone said with a guileless smile.

So far, I've come so far. Maybe he can be trusted.

Tahn wanted to tell Gehone everything, to unburden himself of it all. But behind his need to confess lurked Vendanj's warnings. But Tahn sensed he could trust Gehone, and decided to tell part. He related their run-in with Sevilla in Stonemount, withholding the part about the empty bow; of the library, but not of the sticks in his cloak; of Alisandra and the great striped tents, but not of the Lul'Masi. And he told of Bar'dyn, but not Vendanj or Mira. Gehone sat, paying close attention. The smell of warm apples hung in the air. And when Tahn came to the last, Sutter appeared in the door, a weak smile on his lips.

"Smells good," he said, the question clear in his voice.

"Have a seat, lad." Gehone got up to the endfast fire. "We'll all eat. And then you'll prepare to leave. It won't be good for you to be here when Commander Lethur arrives."

The clatter of hooves interrupted them. Gehone rushed to the window and looked out. He hurried back, showing Tahn a troubled brow.

"To your room, quickly." He gathered the bowls and stuffed them back in the cupboard unwashed. "Get ready to leave, then hide in the closet. Be quiet and stay away from the window."

Gehone dashed past them and down the hall toward the front door. Sutter turned an ashen face to Tahn. Nothing needed to be said. The League of Civility had arrived, and by the sound of it, Gehone's superior hadn't come alone.

They dressed quickly. Sutter buckled his sword and Tahn took up his bow. Near the window, Tahn paused and eased forward, hoping to catch a glimpse of the new arrivals. Several horses stood tethered to a hitching post, their flanks steaming in the crisp morning air. A thin coat of frost still clung to the ground where the sun hadn't yet touched. And above it all, the sky stretched in a perfect lake of unbroken blue. Then came the sound of many boots on the porch. Tahn crept forward, hoping to catch sight of the men.

Then he saw her.

Bound at the wrists, legs tied to the saddle straps, sat a woman, holding her chin at a defiant angle. A soiled dress gathered about her waist and thighs exposed her calves, which bore a cake of mud from her horse's hooves. Her cheeks hung slack as though from lack of sleep, but Tahn thought he knew the look: resignation. She might hold her head up, but her expression held none of the determination she affected.

A firm knock came at the front door and Tahn stepped back from the window. Sutter grabbed his arm and pulled him toward the closet. The smell of moths and disuse clung to the tiny space. Tahn and Sutter quietly sat in the small closet as voices rose from below.

"We are all one," a deep, clipped voice announced.

"And therein lies our strength." Gehone's words seemed a routine reply. The exchange came muffled, but understandable through the floor.

"To protect civility in every form, the surest call," the other finished on cue. A rattle of armor came next, and a series of cordial exchanges.

"You're early," Gehone said.

"First Commander Cheltan thought it best that this business come to a swift conclusion."

The other voice worried Tahn. The man spoke with eagerness, but slowly, as if he might rush toward the exacting of a long, painful punishment.

"What business do you mean?" Gehone answered. "I've had no reports. Is there news?"

"Indeed," the commander said in an odd tone. It reminded Tahn of a man with a surprise to share, but one he knew would displease Gehone. His speech carried a sense of perverse delight.

"What news then?" Gehone asked.

The gleefulness disappeared from the other's words. "A public discipline—"

"But we—"

"I have authority to exercise, Gehone. Make your complaint if you will, but even by courier bird it will arrive too late." A shuffling of feet followed, and Tahn imagined the commander walking to the door to point to the woman he'd seen. *Public discipline.*

"Can you really mean to do this?" The desperation in Gehone's voice concerned Tahn more than the undercurrent of delight in the commander's words.

"The shadow of civil disobedience grows long, Gehone. It spawns insurgence everywhere. The League must stand against it."

"By disciplining a woman in view of children? What's her crime?" Gehone's ardor grew.

"Keep your place, man," Lethur snapped. "All of us have unpleasant tasks to perform. Remember your oath."

Gehone didn't answer.

Several moments passed before Lethur spoke. "You're a good leagueman Gehone."

"When?" Gehone asked flatly.

"As soon as the town is awake," Lethur replied. "I'll expect you to be there. Perhaps I'll even leave the discipline to you. It may help folk here pay you the proper respect, cause reflection in those who do not fully understand the common interest."

Gehone's next words seemed to come through gritted teeth. "It's not really discipline at all, is it, Commander?"

"What do you mean to say, Gehone? Speak up. I won't listen to mumbled words."

"Discipline ought to mean a chance to change," Gehone said.

"Ah, astute as ever, Gehone," Commander Lethur replied. "But you miss the point. You see, it's not really the woman we will be disciplining at all, is it? The spectacle of her discipline will educate a hundred, a thousand, ten thousand. The world is changing, Gehone. Superstition has no place anymore."

The commander paused a long moment. "I smell cream and apples. Do you have guests?"

Tahn held his breath.

"I take it alone these days. I've few who warrant the effort." Tahn heard the veiled insult in the leagueman's voice.

The sound of receding feet rose through the floorboards, and the party of leaguemen exited, pulling shut the door.

Tahn panted in the musty confines of the closet. He finally had to open the door to catch his breath. Crawling to the window, he peered over the sill. Eight men led the woman away up the street, townsfolk stopping to stare and point.

"Away from that window, you imbecile." The command was soft but direct. "Tahn, your horse is in the stable. And an old mare is yours for the taking," he said, nodding to Sutter. Then he handed them each a sack with bread and dried fruit. "That's the last help I can be to you."

"What are they going to do to the woman?" Tahn asked.

Tahn watched a slow burn etch red lines in the leagueman's face. "It's none of your concern. Take advantage of Lethur's preoccupation and leave town. You'll have several hours if you go now. I don't know what his next orders will be, so don't travel directly on the road. If he spots you, you'll be questioned, and Lethur will find any petty grievance to haul you before an authority if he thinks you're hiding something from him. And you two don't look to be good liars."

"But we've done nothing wrong," Sutter said, irritated.

"It won't matter. The principalities are afraid to challenge an argument from a League commander in open court. Lower councils and mayors are men and women with families, easily pressed." He clutched the brocade at his neck. "This wasn't the course we set," he muttered, and turned to leave.

"Wait," Tahn called.

Gehone stopped and turned back.

"Thank you," Tahn said.

Solemn eyes searched Tahn as he approached Gehone and raised a hand in gratitude. The leagueman looked down at Tahn's fingers with an odd expression, as though the gesture were foreign to him. Then, with a growing recognition in his face, Gehone took Tahn's hand in his own. Tahn cupped his other palm under their handshake, as Balatin had taught him to do, emphasizing his thanks. Gehone seemed surprised at the token.

"Go in safety, lads," the leagueman said, a peaceful look smoothing his brow. He clapped Tahn's shoulder and descended the stairs.

"Can we go now?" Sutter said with slight exasperation.

Tahn led them out of the stable and turned up the street. Sutter rode up and leaned close. "This is the way the League went. Shouldn't we find another way out of town?"

Tahn didn't answer.

"Oh, no. You can't be serious. What do you think you can do about it? It's you and me against a whole band of them."

Tahn looked an answer at Sutter this time.

"You're right. What do I care about odds?"

Further on, pedestrians crowded the streets. Fine-chipped gravel had been laid down across the main avenues. Boys gathered in clumps, taking turns running and skidding through the loose rock. The sound of so many feet across the tiny stones reminded Tahn of the Huber at spring runoff, a low white roar.

Several streets up, they came to a broad avenue, nearly twice the width of the others. Instinctively, Tahn turned the corner and kept close to one side. A hundred strides on, a crowd had gathered. High in his saddle, Tahn saw past them to almost a dozen leaguemen in their rich, russet cloaks, preparing some kind of structure at the midpoint of the broad central concourse. Tahn could see the woman still sat her horse, the same resignation weighing in her features.

Tahn angled to a nearby hitching post and dismounted. He and Sutter tethered their horses and blended into the crowd. Tahn positioned them in the center of the pack, not close enough to be clearly seen by the League, but close

enough to have a good view of the proceedings. They'd been there for only a moment when Commander Lethur came forward to address the crowd.

"We live in a glorious time, good people." Lethur looked the crowd over from
one end to the other. "Our knowledge grows every day, our civility improves the
quality of our lives." His voice rose stridently over the mob, which began to
stretch further and further back each passing moment. "It's your birthright, each
of you, to lift yourselves up, despite the superstitions and flawed ideas of seasons
long past."

The space around Tahn became more crowded. He and Sutter found themselves pinched in as the crowd pressed forward. He pushed back, clearing a small
space for himself, to some disgruntled muttering.

"So today, we do what is right by law. How great a reminder is this, that you
are all free to act as your conscience dictates, and not as another would have
you do."

Sutter harrumphed. "I'm a rootdigger, and I can smell a cowflop when I
cross it."

The leagueman behind Lethur finished his preparations and stood back. A
tall pole stood at the center of a raised dais. Several bundles of sticks had been
placed around its base.

"Sutter . . . they mean to burn her."

Sutter looked, a string of curses muffled in his hand.

From the left, Gehone arrived, four men in tow. Each of the others wore the
chestnut-hued cloak of the League, the brocades at their throats dazzling in the
morning sun. Tahn noted that each brocade had been fashioned of a slightly
different design, emphasizing the four separate disciplines of the League. Gehone
climbed down from his steed, and reported directly to Commander Lethur, who
nodded and motioned for Gehone to stand with the rest behind him.

"A great commonwealth is Ulayla," Lethur said, puffing out his chest at the
name of the town. "A marvelous and industrious place, and known for its high
ethics and allegiance to the kingdom's will. It's for you that the League works;
for you we put our flesh and steel where no other would ever go. Because your
concerns are our concerns. No vaunted, meaningless philosophy or tricks of the
light."

The commander nodded, and a second leagueman pulled the woman from
her perch and took her to the pole. Three others assisted him as they lashed her
to the log. All returned to their positions but one, who struck flint to a torch and
carried it to Lethur.

Tahn looked desperately at Gehone, whose face showed the same awful resignation as the woman's. He would not look. He stared at the ground, his hands
clasped behind him.

A fevered excitement passed through the crowd as Lethur raised the torch. There were whispers and speculations and a few gasps. Tahn looked hard at the woman and spoke the familiar words, seeking an answer.

"If there weren't so many of them," Sutter muttered.

"My friends," Lethur continued, "this is a great day. A day for casting off the past and embracing your future. For seeing the work of justice and the truest meaning of the *cleansing fire.* It is us, friends. Not the myths of First Ones. But each of *us.* In the way we support each other, and enforce what is most right and civil among us."

Lethur strode to the platform. He stood beside the woman, who looked with longing toward the heavens. Tahn followed her gaze, wondering if any help existed there. Only the great blue empty sky above. Tahn clenched his fists, the words of the man from his dreams, the old words, the assurance of the right kill, rising in his mind.

He dropped his eyes to the woman, who continued to look up on an endless sky.

"This woman has broken the law. She is Sheason, and has persisted in spreading superstitions that hinder our civility. And so with proper authority, and a clear conscience, I carry out this sentence."

Sheason. She could save herself. This is self-destruction, then . . .

With that thought, a familiar feeling tightened Tahn's gut. Like he'd felt with the burned man in the tenendra camp. Dead gods, he hated this!

The torch began to descend, a slow endless moment. And Tahn looked deep into the woman's eyes, his body thrumming with every pulse of his racing heart. Hot waves of protest curled his fists like a man preparing to fight, and he lunged forward. Sutter caught him, wrapping Tahn and anchoring him down. He struggled against Sutter's grip, but his friend showed uncommon strength and kept him still. The sound from the crowd swelled, muting Tahn's cries. He twisted and tried to pull free, but his friend held him.

He turned his eyes again to the woman as the flame struck kindling into life. Wood dust laid by the practiced hands of the League ignited almost instantly, and the fire mounted around her. Lethur stood back a pace and watched the crowd, a satisfied look on his sharp features. Tahn cast a hopeful glance at Gehone. But the man's eyes never moved from the parcel of ground he watched.

"Look," Sutter whispered. His friend let him go, looking like he'd seen a ghost.

Tahn followed Sutter's gaze back to the woman, who'd lifted her face in pain. The words started to burn in his mind, the same old words he always spoke. He thought them now. For the woman. Wondering if she should die. Or if he should try to save her.

Silent hell, what am I thinking? We'd never get past the League.

But he wouldn't have to try. A calm settled in him. He knew she was innocent . . . but yet meant to die. He hated that this time—unlike the burned man—he couldn't offer her any mercy. Not without taking a chance that would jeopardize Tillinghast.

Could he watch her burn, then? Could he *let* her burn?

Before he knew what he was doing, he'd unshouldered his bow and drawn an arrow.

Sutter was on him again in a second, wrapping his arms around him and shuffling him to the back of the crowd. Bystanders cussed and shoved them along.

Out of earshot of the others, Sutter finally let Tahn go. "We didn't come all this way to die in a small-town prison. Or get burned ourselves."

"I wasn't going to try and save her." Tahn heaved a breath, trying to settle his anger.

"I know," Sutter said. "I know what you were trying to do. But it would have ended the same for us either way. I hate it, too, Tahn. More than you know." He paused a long moment. "But we can't."

Before the sound of the fire could unnerve them further, they got to their horses. He and Sutter left unobserved as the smoke of flesh rose into the bright, shining sky.

Once safely beyond town, Tahn felt more himself again, and finally asked, "What happened last night? You were ass naked and blubbering."

Sutter gave him a long look. Shook his head. "I don't know. Nightmares, I hope."

"You seemed awake," Tahn pressed. "Maybe you're still sick from Sevilla's little trick." He tapped his chest.

"Maybe," Sutter said, sounding unconvinced. But his friend said nothing more, his eyes still troubled.

Tahn let it go for now. Sutter would talk when he was ready.

CHAPTER FORTY-FOUR

Reluctantly Used

There's a vibrant relationship between all proximate matter. Just as gravity exerts itself when two bodies come nearer one another.

—Initial postulate shared in the College of Physics during the last Succession on Continuity

W hy do you look like you haven't aged since you came here?" Vendanj asked.

Braethen stared back at Grant. Was Vendanj really suggesting that the man hadn't aged in almost twenty years?

Grant looked away at the fire, a sad smile rising in his cheeks. "Oh, I've aged. Not the same as you, but I've aged. The Scar"—he pointed aimlessly—"formed when life was stripped from these lands. It appears *time* is part of the *life* inside a thing. So it seems the Quiet took both from this place during the Battle of the Round."

Vendanj's brow drew down in worry.

"But there's no blessing in it." Grant looked at his hand, turning it over to view his palm. "I stay here only because of the cradle."

Braethen heard himself ask about the cradle before he realized he'd done so. The exile again offered his sad smile.

"Each cycle of the first moon, I go to the end of the Scar." Grant rose and went to the window, pulling the shutter open. "Most times, a child is left there in the hollow of a dead tree. It's part of my sentence. Keeps me here."

He looked back at Braethen. "I find a home for that child, a place where it can escape the fortune of the streets or the traveling auction blocks that sell women and children. But some I can't find a home. Those I bring here." Grant looked to his wards at the back of the room. "I teach them to fight, to make choices wisely, and along the way to distrust the best intentions of others." Grant set his eyes on Vendanj.

"An unfortunate education," the Sheason said.

"They share the curse of the Scar, the endless march of days," Grant said. "So I send them to the border often. They patrol, watch for strangers, practice the skills I teach them."

"How do you care for infants? Grow food? Water?" Braethen asked.

"I'm an exile, but there are a few at the edge of the Scar," he said, his voice rough but filled with gratitude, "who believe in the truths I mean to protect. Between them and waystations on the border, I get the help I need.

"But this is my home now," Grant went on. "And these wards . . . some are orphans, some are left by parents too selfish or afraid to keep them."

Several long moments passed. "Grant," Vendanj said, "we've come to ask your help."

"I guessed as much," the man said. "But I can't."

Vendanj pulled several parchments from his cloak and placed them on the table beside Grant's papers. "The names of dead Sheason and their widows."

Grant picked up the parchments and scanned the names written there. For the first time, Braethen thought he saw sadness touch the man's eyes.

Grant looked at Vendanj, a deep frown on his face. "Killed by the Quiet?"

Vendanj shook his head. "Most of those died at the hands of the League."

"How's this possible?" Grant asked, still reading names.

Vendanj leaned in on the table. "To alter a name, to sever the Sheason vow, would require knowledge of the Covenant Tongue."

"The Far?" Grant shook his head at his own suggestion. "The Tract of Desolation is the only meaningful document we have that's written in the Language. Do you think the scriveners have deciphered it?"

"Only small parts. And mostly what was used to create the Song of Suffering," Vendanj said. "We'd planned to go to Qum'rahm'se. Gather what's known about the Language, and possibly the Tract itself, and take them to Naltus with us—"

"To see if we could better translate it," Grant finished. "Strengthen the Veil."

"But we got separated." Vendanj rubbed at his eyes. "There's no time now. We'll get to Recityv. Hope the others have arrived there safely. Then move fast to Naltus. And Tillinghast."

The word made Grant look up. His stare showed understanding. The same look he'd worn when they'd mentioned Tahn before.

Vendanj didn't linger on it. "We'll ask Elan to make use of the Language against the Quiet," he said. "And we'll gather the Tract when we return to Convocation."

Grant returned to scanning the list of names. He reached the last sheet. His eyes hung on the last name. "You and Illenia," he said softly.

Vendanj met Grant's eyes when the exile looked up again. "I think someone has manipulated the vow, or perhaps the Language itself. If so, that ability has broader consequences than the names on those pages." He showed a humorless smile. "I'm not sure even a new translation of the Tract would help. We'll try, of course. But . . . it's time for Tillinghast."

Grant made a noise as one who has deduced something. "Names seem to start about the time the Civilization Order was ratified."

"If this is happening because of the Civilization Order, then sooner or later we're going to come against the League," Vendanj said. "Gods willing, it won't be in war, but in the courts. And no one's ever argued there as eloquently as you. We're going to need that kind of assistance." The Sheason took a breath and exhaled sharply.

Grant seemed to ignore the appeal. He was fixed on the implications of the modified names. He put the list back on the table beside his half-written charter. "Perhaps there's a way to give my primrose a voice, after all. Make it real—"

"Don't even utter such a thing," Vendanj cautioned.

Grant looked back at Vendanj, his expression hardening over several long moments. "I can't leave the Scar. I can't return to that place. That part of my life is over."

In final, humble request, Vendanj asked, "If not for these," he tapped the list of names, "and if not for Convocation . . . then do it for Tahn."

Again Braethen saw a flicker of recognition in Grant's eyes. Regret stole across the man's face. He and Vendanj shared a long look, each man searching the other.

Finally, Grant said simply, "I can't. This is where I've made my home. This is where I was sent to serve sentence for my crime of conscience. Your horses have been rubbed down, your skins filled. I'll give you food and directions. But I won't go back. I've no patience for politics. And if the Quiet are coming, Vendanj, I don't think there's any way to stop them."

Disgust showed plainly on Vendanj's face. He went to the door, Mira close behind. Braethen started to follow.

"East by the Dog Star," Grant said. His voice rough but even. "Your horses are still weak. Walk them if you want them to live. You've water for three days."

Vendanj went into the night. Mira paused at the door a moment, then followed. Braethen spared a glance at the wards, the document nailed to the wall, and the exile poised near the small hearth. Then he rushed to join the others, these stories heavy in his mind.

As they found their horses, Vendanj cursed, "Fool," then gave each horse a sprig from his cedar box. The moon rode high in the night sky, accompanied by the brilliant glitter of countless stars. The day's heat had fled, leaving a brittle cold in the clarity of night.

Braethen glanced back once to see a pale square of light cast from the exile's window. Vendanj rode away at a sprint. Braethen and Mira rushed to catch up.

They traveled an hour, silence across the rocks and dry grass broken only by the sounds of their passage. They couldn't run the horses anymore, and dismounted. After walking a few minutes, the Sheason stopped. He turned and searched the terrain in a full circle about them. The air grew suffocating, dense.

Connected.

That was the feeling. Like swimming in a still pool—the ripples giving away one's presence. Vendanj raised a hand to his chest and moved forward. Braethen took hold of his sword, remembering the last time he'd raised it in his own defense, and grimaced a little at the touch.

They walked over a knoll, moon shadows vague and ghostly around them. Then the world turned to fire. Seven great hulking shapes rose from the ground. They stood against the darkness of the sky, their massive silhouettes blotting out stars. Behind them stood two smaller shapes wearing buttoned coats *Velle!*

Beside each of the Quiet renderers stood shorter figures, slumped and beaten. The Velle stirred, and that feeling of connection, of being close, part of everything, part of them, rippled like heated tar.

Only Mira seemed unaffected. She rushed in, dancing close to the Sheason, and crouched. She held one sword before her, the other cocked back over her shoulder.

One of the figures uttered a command in a deep, rasping voice, and the Bar'dyn fanned to the sides: three moved left, three to the right, and one stayed directly before them. Mira turned to face the three on the left. Vendanj took two steps out and threw back his cloak to free his arms, preparing to face the three on the right. Braethen caught a glint in the blades of the Bar'dyn facing the Sheason. The massive creatures out of the Bourne hesitated.

"Step in, Sodalist," Mira said without looking. "Fill the gap and remember what I've showed you. Balance. Fight quick, not rushed."

Braethen took three long, careful strides and held his sword out at an angle.

The Bar'dyn directly ahead of him pivoted into a defensive posture, and spoke. "All this way. How fitting that you will come to an end here." Its voice rasped as though damaged by smoke.

Braethen's muscles tightened and suddenly the grip of his sword felt sure and right. He looked past the Bar'dyn to the Velle behind them. They stood still, their calm disquieting.

Then each Velle reached to the closest hunched figure beside him, and took vicious hold of its flesh. Weak cries came. In a breath, the air thickened again, grew hot.

"Roll," Mira screamed.

Braethen reacted instinctively, falling to his left and scampering. Mira leapt back, and Braethen heard the sound of the Sheason's thick cloak snapping as he dashed aside.

A white burst of light tore past them, erupting in an explosion of earth and stone a few paces away. The ground shook violently.

Vendanj scooped a handful of earth and threw it into the air. It fanned into dust and lit the night as bright as day, particles like impossibly small suns illuminating the area.

Two Bar'dyn rushed Mira, nearly taking her by surprise. A pike whirled through the air toward her head, another at her knees. She ducked and leapt in the same movement, landing on her feet just when the Bar'dyn were upon her. She pivoted sideways and dove between them, just escaping a second blow from a quick blade.

Braethen rolled to his knees, dust rising in his throat and forcing him to cough. He still held his sword, and got his second hand to its grip as the third Bar'dyn dove toward him. He had no time to roll again, and tried to raise the blade to defend the charge. He was too late. The force of the massive creature bowled him back and under, a gout of saliva spraying his face with rank-smelling mucus. Pain bloomed in his chest, taking his wind. He heard bone snap beneath his coat and drove the thought of it away. The Bar'dyn clutched his throat.

Something unbidden rose in him, then. He looked into the face of the Bar'dyn and wrapped his free hand on the hilt of his sword, gripping it savagely. His chest heaved, and he roared, "I am I!"

The force of the words stopped the Bar'dyn for a moment. Braethen brought the sword up, pulling its edge across the beast's neck. The thick, armorlike skin gave under the blade. It fell back, trying to stop the blood that coursed from the wound. A frightened surprise touched its eyes as it stared at Braethen and pulled away, growing slower with each scrambling step.

Braethen turned to Vendanj. The Sheason made a long sweeping gesture with his arm toward the closest Bar'dyn. It toppled forward, and struck the ground like a great piece of ironmongery.

The men being held by the Velle let out strangled cries. Braethen realized that in the Scar, without Forda in the ground to draw upon, the Velle were using real men, stealing their spirit to fuel their fight. Braethen whipped his sword in a harsh arc toward the Velle, then moved fast to join Vendanj.

Around him, a yellow mist rose, spreading quickly in every direction. Each breath he took seared his lungs. "Vendanj!" he cried, swatting at the air with his blade.

The Sheason spun at the sound of his name. Two Bar'dyn rushed in from behind him. Braethen tried to yell a warning, but the mist stole his voice. He pointed. Just when the Bar'dyn raised their swords to strike Vendanj, the Sheason lifted both arms, his fists clenched. Thunder bellowed from his mouth and struck the Bar'dyn like a battering ram, casting them back several strides. The impact drove the yellow haze from the air in an instant.

A moment later the soil began to bubble, then started to flow like mud. Braethen and Vendanj began to sink. More cries screeched into the night. The first men used by the Velle fell to the ground, spent. The sound they made was ghastly, as if even their dying breaths were stolen from them. Braethen fumed and struggled to wade from the mud in which he was now knee-deep.

Mira leapt over the growing quagmire to meet the advancing Bar'dyn leader. The beast's great sword swept toward her. She feinted back and threw a small knife at the Bar'dyn. The Bar'dyn raised a quick hand to ward off the attack. The dagger pierced his palm, spattering drops of blood into the creature's face. The Bar'dyn shook the knife loose and continued to sweep its steel at her.

As Braethen fought the mud, Vendanj touched his arm. Together, they began to rise from the sludge, which continued to boil and spurt. The Bar'dyn to the right had regained their feet and rushed around the mud toward Mira.

Then, several hollow pops sounded from behind them, and the whistle of fletching tore past their heads. Some of the shafts broke against the armorlike toughness of the lead Bar'dyn's skin. But many pierced its massive body, driving it backwards in a stumbling fall.

Vendanj got free of the mud as another volley whistled through the air. The Bar'dyn tried to scramble away, arrows showering their backs and legs. Those Bar'dyn that could still move scurried off into the night. But the Velle stood firm, keeping hold of their human vessels to draw more Forda.

Braethen turned to see Grant and eight wards standing back with bows aimed and drawn. The youths gasped at what they saw. Braethen turned in the mud and saw it, too. The figures the Velle held to draw their Forda . . . were a few of Grant's own wards. The first two had already fallen; the second two appeared alive, but firmly in the hands of the Quiet.

"Your brothers," Grant said evenly. Some of the wards looked at him with horrified expressions; others nodded gravely. "See what will become of them. It is your mercy." He raised his own bow and held his aim.

The Velle were preparing some dark use of those they held—their last vessels.

A moment of dark regard stretched.

As Grant began to shout, "Fire," the Quiet renderers drew the remaining life from the wards they gripped. Like shadows when the sun dawns over a barren plain, the Velle vanished. Several arrows sailed harmlessly against the night. The two wards slumped when the hands of the Quiet disappeared.

Braethen sat tiredly in the mud, his legs weakened to exhaustion. Several of Grant's wards wandered off to mourn, some went to their fallen brothers. Others examined the bodies of dead Bar'dyn.

When Braethen regained his breath, he tromped from the mud to see for himself what Vendanj had done to the first Bar'dyn. Freezing cold emanated from the corpse. The soil around it white with frost. Braethen imagined that the Sheason had frozen all the fluids in its body. He turned to see Mira run into the dark. The Far never ceased to amaze him with her endless energy.

Vendanj knelt where the Velle had been, looking over the emaciated corpses of Grant's fallen wards. Grant came up beside the Sheason, Braethen came to Vendanj's other side.

They stared at the lifeless bodies.

"They were your own," Vendanj said through labored breaths. The Sheason finally succumbed to his exhaustion from the battle and sat directly on the ground.

Grant took a parchment from his pocket and handed it to Vendanj. "Your list of names. In your haste . . . You win, Vendanj. I'll come along."

"Thank you," the Sheason said, holding up the list of widows.

Grant looked at the paper in Vendanj's hands. "I have my own reasons for coming along," he said. "But you might regret trusting my diplomacy."

Vendanj nodded, still looking at the dead youths lying in front of him. He then lay back on the hardpan of the Scar to rest. He looked not so different from the corpse beside him. He took a sprig of herb and laid it on his tongue.

When Vendanj stood again, they reckoned by the light of the Dog Star and started on their way to Recityv.

• CHAPTER FORTY-FIVE •

Recityv Civility

The Civilization Order is working in Vohnce. We will establish the law wherever we are garrisoned. Attach the Recityv report on crime and commerce as evidence.

—Charge issued by League leadership in the ninth year of the Civilization Order

Tahn and Sutter traveled north for three days, passing towns with greater frequency. On the fourth day, the road widened and became more pocked and rutted by the hour. Then, a great wall appeared in the distance, rising twice as high as any Tahn had seen before. It extended so far to the east and west that trees concealed the ends. Above the wall, Tahn could see great domes and spires and vaulted roofs, gables pitched like the tip of a spear, each one higher than the last. The city was immense. *Recityv.*

More and more travelers joined the stream of people moving toward the gate, some walking, others riding as he and Sutter, still others in ornately decorated carriages. He felt for Edholm's sticks in his cloak. Their touch reassured him, until he thought of Wendra. He only hoped that she and the others had arrived safely.

"Well, Nails, this is what you came for." Tahn gestured ahead. "That's more adventure than I think even you can handle."

A distant look passed over his friend's eyes before the familiar smile returned. "We'll find out, won't we, Woodchuck."

As the road widened, it also became more congested. A few hundred strides from the city wall, houses sat nestled among hosts of tents woven of bright-colored, expensive-looking canvas. Cook fires burned, the smoke settling like a low cloud over everything.

Along the road, merchants had staked out space for their carts. Standing before their wares, they held samples of their goods, pitching anyone who looked their way. Everything Tahn could imagine was on display by well-manicured traders. Some hawked exotic foods, claiming origins as far west as Mal'Sent and as far south as Riven Port.

Many of them looked about with hawkish eyes and weapons on their belts. Others huddled in shadows, raising dirty hands for alms.

Tahn noted pairs of soldiers adorned in burgundy cassocks and cloaks, a white circle prominent over the left breast bearing the sigil of a tree with roots as deep as its boughs were tall.

The chaos of countless merchant barkers, squealing children, stock and pets braying and barking, laughter, insults and curses, quarrels, all of it rushed at Tahn in a swirl of humanity.

Tahn took it all in, and thought more longingly of home.

In many ways, though larger, this city outside the city was like others he'd seen of late. But in *one* way it proved different, unsettling: street prophets.

Calling as enthusiastically as their trading counterparts, these men and women—and children—looked at everyone with astounded eyes and seemed to see no one. Matted, dirty hair hung from tanned scalps as they gestured maniacally and spoke their rants.

"Every son and daughter is an abomination, a curse from the Whited One." The man calling out a wild-eyed screed shouted through cracked lips. Scabs looking like dried leeches riddled his lips, but didn't stop his raving. "The end of Forda I'Forza has long since passed, and we live in a hollow time, a dead age. A dry wind blows south from the farthest places, starting at the other end of the Bourne and passing over us like a whisper. Don't you see!" The man began to jump up and down, accentuating each word with the pounding of his heels on the soil. "We are Quiet already. We are come to our earth and haven't woken yet to taste the worms. No Sheason, no leagueman, no regent or general, no one can undo what has been done. Our Song of Suffering is over, it is the echo of it from a distant cliff that we hear. And when it's gone, we'll have been dead a generation."

Tahn and Sutter swung wide of the man, tramping close to a woman seated on an elaborate rug, who clicked her fingers together and spoke in words that rhymed every third phrase. She spoke of lands west of Mal'Sent, whole worlds on the other side of the oceans. She told of a place that hid beyond the Bourne like the forgotten child of orphan parents. At the end of each rhyme, she opened her eyes to see if anyone had placed a coin in the hat at the edge of her blanket. Her substantial belly hung over the waistband of her skirt, and a slender wrap that hung loosely from her shoulders more than hinted at a full bosom beneath. Straight, dark hair had been gathered in a brass ring at the crown of her head, pointing skyward like a harvest bale.

But perhaps the strangest of all was a child, standing on a wooden box, who tapped answers to questions with a wooden peg leg. They paused to watch. A man standing behind the boy interpreted the responses for those who paid for knowledge. A small wooden sign leaning against the boy's box announced his ability was a gift from the First Fathers, and that he'd been rescued from the mountains fabled to house the Tabernacle of the Sky, where the Fathers had sat at Creation. When he raised a hand, exposing a long tear in the seam of his shirt, Tahn could see clearly the child's rib cage. *What must he do for food,* Tahn thought, as the boy tapped out another answer to some riddle.

These strange and desperate people intrigued Tahn the most. He didn't know if he felt sadness for them, or kinship. Was his own sense of whether a thing should live or die any different?

A chill ran up his back. And worry that he could wind up here, too.

He and Sutter moved on.

Focusing on the wide gates, Tahn pressed through eddies of milling shoppers and travelers toward the city. At the south entrance, one line of wagons and carriages waited to be inspected; another line moved more quickly, where people on foot or horseback were scrutinized briefly before being allowed to go in. When he and Sutter reached a uniformed attendant who held a small copybook in one hand and a quill in the other, panic rose in Tahn's throat.

With a tired monotone, the man asked, "What brings you to Recityv?"

Before Tahn could answer, Sutter declared, "We're hungry."

A crooked smile crossed the man's lips as he visually surveyed them both. "You're not aspirants to any seat?"

"What?" Sutter asked.

"Move along," the soldier replied, "and keep out of trouble."

Relief washed over Tahn as he passed beneath the thick red stone wall of

Recityv. He heard a distant cry in his mind—the voice of the Sheason telling them to get to this place. And now they'd arrived safely. In the shadow of the gate, he no longer felt like a child this side of the Change, regardless of whether he'd had his Standing.

Inside the great wall, buildings towered several stories high. Storefronts gleamed in the daylight, the stone of their facings polished smooth, showing pale reflections of the street they faced. Others were rough-hewn. On the rooftops, a variety of animal statues perched atop the stone, peering down like unmoving familiars.

Windows varied in size and shape and color. Fancier inns seemed to have been crafted in straight lines and angles, fitted with rectangular panes of glass. Other edifices had round windows, long and narrow or polygonal windows. And many were tinted various shades of rose, azure, or gold—those on the east side of the road refracting colorful rays of light.

Some men walked the street in mail, others in cotton twill. Many wore tight leather breeches, mid-calf boots, loose-fitting coats that laced at the neck, and hooded cloaks of various lengths. Women strolled in gowns that shimmered or were oversewn with lace in intricate and delicate designs. Those that didn't have such finery seemed mostly to go about in work dresses, often bearing stains deep in the fabric. Most of the women wore hats; the brims of those worn by the more stylishly dressed women were long and curved subtly downward in the front and rear, while the brims of many others were short and generally flat, and often the hats had no brim at all.

A host of richly ornate carriages lined the streets, their owners seeming to be bustling from one shop to another in pursuit of some item to purchase. A charged feeling buzzed in the air, as everywhere standards flapped in the wind.

Tahn and Sutter kept riding, hoping to see someone they recognized. Perhaps Vendanj would have someone watching for them. Deeper into the city they went, passing arbors and warehouses and multi-floored taverns, past fountains and inns, and offices boldly marked with the sigil of the tree and roots.

At the center of a broad, grassy common rose a tall, narrow building, crowned by a glass dome. Tahn could see tall cylinders within the bubble, pointing skyward. Near the foundation of the building stood a rooted pavilion with several rows of chairs facing a lectern. At the back, a tall dark slate showed diagrams in yellow chalk. These had a certain pull on Tahn.

The city was intoxicating.

And Sutter, agape at the marvels about him, wore an impossibly broad smile, making him look entirely conspicuous.

"Perhaps, Your Majesty, you might close the royal mouth. It makes you appear a commoner," Tahn joked.

Clearing his throat, Sutter sat straight in his saddle. "Just relishing the gems of my domain, boy. It's wise for a man to reflect upon his success and importance."

"A man, you say? And important?" Tahn laughed. "My lord, the only thing *man* about you is your scent, which I find important indeed. You might consider washing the royal ass."

"A job for a chambermaid," Sutter said, leering. "Delicate work for a delicate girl." Dropping the conceit, Sutter added, "Where *are* we going to stay tonight?" He then resumed craning his head at impossible angles to see every height and story of architecture around them.

"I don't know. Maybe the others have already arrived." Tahn looked around at the sheer number of people bustling through the street. "But we'll never find them without asking someone."

"And how do you intend to do that?" Sutter chided. "Saunter up to someone and ask them if they've seen a grim-looking Sheason and a gorgeous young Far?"

Tahn considered. "We'll look for the symbol of the three rings," he said. "If we can find a member of the Order, they'll be able to help us find Vendanj."

"I don't get the feeling Sheason are welcome here much more than they are anywhere else. Maybe we should find a sodalist."

Sutter started to say something more, but choked it off just as they came to a densely packed crowd. The street had suddenly become a wall of humanity too congested to negotiate with a horse. Ahead, and beyond the congregants, Tahn saw a raised scaffold.

"Move over!" a gruff voice demanded.

A portly man with mottled skin over most of his face sneered at Tahn and tried to shove his horse aside. The crowd amassed behind them. Tahn reined left and led Sutter to the edge of the street and out of the way. Then above the tumult, a loud voice echoed down the stone of the building fronts.

"It is with solemn regret, but by authority of the Court of Judicature, that we bring sentence here today."

Tahn squinted into the distance. It looked like a gallows. The thin man announcing from the platform wore the color of the Recityv guard. He shouted through a cone he held to his mouth. But it was so far away that it was hard to make out. As the man continued to speak, two figures climbed a stair and stood behind him.

"Let it be understood that justice will not be denied. The regent will not be swayed by any threat." A protest went up from some; others cheered. "Today treason will be answered as befits the crime."

People jockeyed around for a better view. Tahn looked past the man at the front of the scaffolding at the two standing behind him. And had a feeling hit him about the man on the right. He'd scarcely thought the old words. But still . . .

a horrible certainty. "Ah, my last hell," he whispered, "this just isn't getting any easier, is it?"

But he couldn't stand idle and do nothing.

"Come on," he whispered urgently to Sutter.

Sutter saw Tahn's eyes on the prisoner. "Are you doing this again? Really?"

Tahn jerked his horse's head about. "Out of the way!" he yelled, hurrying back through the tightly packed crowd. Insults flew, a few swinging at Tahn's legs as he gained speed, racing away from the gallows.

Sutter came abreast of him as they dodged around others. "What are you planning?"

Tahn didn't answer. He focused on avoiding the various obstacles in the road. Apple cores sailed past his head and rocks struck his chest and shoulder. Sutter yelled at those hurling things toward them, promising to answer their hospitality. At a narrow alley, Tahn turned left. They leapt overturned barrels and broken crates, the clatter of hooves echoing off the walls. Sutter's nag struggled to keep up.

Emerging into the next street, Tahn reined in and looked left again. Several intersections north, the crowd had just started to gather.

"There," Tahn shouted, and spurred his horse.

Carriages careened to one side or another as Tahn screamed for them to move over. Children clapped at the spectacle, and he saw two soldiers look his way as he passed. He didn't turn to see if they pursued him. Near the cross street where people gathered closest to witness the hanging, he reined in. Hooves slipped and scraped over stone as he fought to keep balance. The mob backed away as he came to a reckless stop near the street corner.

Sutter came in behind him, his old mare dumping him to the ground with a loud thud. Tahn quickly looked around, and found that some second-story windows had short balconies that overlooked the street. He eased to his feet to stand in his saddle, and jumped. Catching a balustrade, he hoisted himself up. A few people appeared to disapprove, but also understand Tahn's desire for a clear view of the hanging. Sutter began climbing the building, using the deep grooves in the stonework as footholds.

Tahn knelt on one knee at the side of the balcony nearest the gallows. Though sixty strides away, it was much closer than they had been before. He could see the fear in the faces of the condemned.

". . . resolve is absolute," the guard was saying. "We are all subject to the rule of law and the discretion of the regent." A continued mix of approval and scoffing rose from the crowd.

Sutter reached the balcony and took a knee beside him. "Hells, Tahn, are you serious?"

"This isn't the League," Tahn said.

"No, it's the Recityv Guard." Sutter tugged at this sleeve.

"Stop," Tahn scolded. "Don't bother me now."

"Tahn, what's this about?" Sutter's voice now held genuine concern. "You can't save them. And hanging's quick. Quicker than your arrow."

Tahn eyed the gallows crossbar.

"And there are two of them," Sutter added. "You'll never get off two shots. This isn't the kind of attention we need. You can't afford—"

"To what," Tahn interjected. "To help them?"

"You don't know what's going on here," Sutter said reasonably. "Those men may deserve this."

Tahn looked his friend in the eye. "One of them doesn't."

Sutter stared back, confused. "How could you know that? Do you recognize—"

Tahn shook his head. "Please, Sutter, just shut up for a minute." He wanted to say more, but he knew that anything he might say would sound crazy right now, and there wasn't time to explain.

"All right," Sutter said softly. "But you seem to be taking over my godsdamned adventure."

The throng of watchers pressed even tighter as their numbers increased. A line of guards three deep extended in a horseshoe around the gallows, the first row pointing spears outward to keep the crowd back. The officer made an end of speaking and stood aside as each of the two men was fitted with a noose around his neck. A horn trumpeted the moment, calling from some high promenade above the yard where the bulk of the mob stood waiting to witness these deaths. A hush fell over the crowd as a blackcoat spoke privately with each of the convicted. Tahn wondered what the man could possibly say to them at this moment. When he left them, Tahn saw the gleam of tears on one fellow's cheeks.

At one side, a second guard in Recityv crimson stood with his hand on a lever, his eyes on the front-most officer. The yard grew quiet enough to hear the birds chirrup in the eaves of a nearby building. The dart and swoop of swallows was the only movement. The sun felt suddenly heavy and too bright, exposing this scene in glaring clarity.

Tahn took his bow from his back and pulled an arrow from his quiver. He moistened his fingers with his tongue and checked the fletching. He traced the hammer scar on his hand, reminding himself not to clutch his weapon too tightly. Then he stood, holding the bow at a perfect angle to the ground. His heart raced in his chest, pounding an impossible rhythm. But he breathed easy and recited the oldest words he knew. And exhaled.

Shouts of alarm rang up beneath him as the crowd became aware that he stood there, aiming a bow. But Tahn might have been standing at the edge of some promontory, like a wide, empty chasm before him . . . and nothing else, save the scaffolding and those condemned. The officer looked at the guard who manned the lever release. At that moment, the guard nodded and performed his task.

. . . *as the Will allows.* Tahn let his arrow fly.

A hatch opened and the two men fell. The ropes tightened with the weight of their parcels, and when the rope holding the man on the right drew taut, Tahn's arrow sailed into the sunlight of the yard and sliced the rope a fist's length from the high beam that held it. The man plummeted to the ground. A gasp of horror and shock erupted from those gathered. And several thousand heads turned to see Tahn standing with his bow still pointed toward the gallows.

Moments later, a squad of soldiers swarmed onto the balcony and put Tahn and Sutter into irons.

"I guess we won't be needing to look for a room," Sutter said. But there was no humor in his voice.

The guards led them away. Tahn could think only of Wendra, her lifeless child, a moment of indecision, and how much better *this* moment had been.

• CHAPTER FORTY-SIX •

The Bottom of Pain Reprise

When two things are brought into Resonance with one another, each is changed.

—*Fourth Precept of Sound,* authored and taught
by the Maesteri of the Descant

Wendra stood inside the cabin, just a pace back from the doorway, peering out at Jastail and eight Bar'dyn. She shivered at the sight of them, recalling the feel of coarse hands tearing her undergarments away and the incredible power in the beast's grip as she was forced to drink a pulpy fluid from a bone vial. Guttural voices responded to the appeasing tones of the highwayman, who motioned toward her.

"Come out here," Jastail said, glancing toward her. "And bring the boy."

Wendra looked despairingly at Penit, who returned a terrified expression. He grasped her hand and together they eased out the door. Wendra shielded her eyes against the brightness of the sun as she tentatively approached Jastail, keeping the highwayman between her and the Quiet. She saw cold appraisal in the heavy brows of the Bar'dyn, their attention shifting from her to Penit and back again.

"Did I tell you?" Jastail said in a confident, pleased tone. He looked back at Wendra and gestured toward her with splayed fingers, as one might do to invite inspection. "And this is why I ask my price."

The Bar'dyn didn't speak at first, running another emotionless gaze over her and the boy. "Perhaps we will just take them," the foremost Bar'dyn said with its rumble of a voice.

"Ah, Etromney, you test my patience with this needless litany each time we meet." Jastail turned his back on the Bar'dyn and paced around behind Wendra and Penit. "You come to me because I deliver goods no one else can."

"Not every time," the Bar'dyn said pointedly.

"Perhaps," Jastail admitted, unruffled. "But I have access to"—He looked at Wendra and seemed to alter his words—"circles that the pedestrian traders never will. But you know all this. I've explained to you my connections many times. So why begin with threats?"

Etromney's expression never changed, remaining as flat as Jastail's had ever been. "The times are changing." The Bar'dyn paused, raising its thick nose to the air as though it could smell what it described. Wendra remained still, feeling as much as hearing the deep resonance of the creature's voice, like a single, thick chord drawn by a heavy bow.

"More threats?" Jastail submitted.

"No," the Bar'dyn answered. "Soon, there will be no need to meet here. No need of any trader or highwayman." The Bar'dyn seemed to frown, but the lines in its folded skin hardly moved.

Jastail let a strange smile crawl over his face, but said nothing.

"Is the boy hers?" Etromney asked.

"No," Jastail said. "But she's still capable of breeding."

"Can you prove her womb is not barren," the Bar'dyn went on. "And what of—"

"See for yourself." Jastail violently ripped Wendra's dress upward, exposing her belly and hips, and pointing to the stretch marks in Wendra's skin from her recent pregnancy. "The marks of one recently with child. Now, no more accusations or doubt! She will suit your purposes well enough. And the child is a suitable receptacle, I'm sure. And I'll share this advice: Control the lad, and you control the girl."

Wendra's legs trembled as she stood exposed to Bar'dyn again. She locked her knees to keep her feet. Jastail held up her dress for several more moments as the Bar'dyn looked on. Finally, he dropped the hem and took a wide-legged stance in front of her, facing the Quiet. Jastail's zeal and confidence in the face of the Bar'dyn surprised her. The creatures out of the Bourne stood two heads taller than he did.

"What of this *ability* you mention?" Etromney asked. "You demand an unheard-of price. I must know the truth of this to grant what you ask."

"Sing him something, Wendra," Jastail said with a near hint of fatherly pride.

The request caught her entirely off guard. "What?"

"A song, let's have a song." He turned, irritation creasing his brow.

"Like a trained animal." She stared at the highwayman, confused. And angry. "To raise my stock for your purse." She gritted her teeth.

But the intimations of a melody did come. It boiled up from her belly like acid. She found it suddenly hard to breathe, and began to pant.

"Don't make me use the boy to encourage you," Jastail warned.

"Enough," Etromney said, shuffling mighty feet. "We did not come to trade today. We will take what we like."

Jastail snapped his head back to the Bar'dyn leader. "Hold there, Etromney." He raised a finger in objection then used it to point toward the trees. "Don't forget that I'm not alone. A party of men stands all around us. To keep things honest, you understand."

The Bar'dyn didn't bother to look. Instead, it came a step closer to Jastail, narrowing its eyes. Wendra recoiled, pulling Penit back. The little clearing became thick with the threat of violence. "I could pinch your head from your neck, grub. I would sooner watch you die than listen to you lie."

"Have I ever come alone before," Jastail said, staring up into the broad, thick musculature of the Bar'dyn's face. "And my stock ought to honor you."

The Bar'dyn stared, then finally looked toward the trees. "Done."

"Wait," Wendra cried. "He's lying. No one will come." She let go Penit's hand and stepped forward, shivering with fear. Her legs betrayed her, and she fell to the ground. But she got to her knees amidst a cloud of dust.

Jastail whirled, lashing her face with his fist. "Silence, cow! You've not been given permission to speak."

Wendra swallowed blood, her vision swimming with tears risen suddenly from the blow. She reached into her dress and pulled free the parchment, clenching it tightly in her hand. "At Galadell he left a note for these men he says will come. But I found the note and took it, hiding it until now. You see. No party is coming. He trades alone today." She raised the note toward the Bar'dyn.

From blurry eyes she saw Jastail raise his hand again. Before he could hit her, the Bar'dyn swept its arm across the highwayman's back and drove him savagely to the ground. "You lie and then abuse the stock." Jastail remained on the ground, spitting dirt from his mouth as Etromney took the scrap of parchment from Wendra's hand. Revulsion rose in her throat at the touch of its rough skin. So close, she caught the scent of carrion on the creature. Etromney examined the note, then let it fall to Wendra's lap.

"She creates this lie for revenge against me," Jastail quickly offered. "And regardless, I have brought you a woman and child. I might have brought you . . . Leiholan." Jastail crawled to Wendra, and thrust a hand into her blouse. He wrestled from her the parchment she kept there from the Ta'Opin—her song. He held it out to Etromney. "So, this time, I'm coming with you."

The highwayman's request stunned Wendra. Perhaps the only thrill left to him was gambling with his own life.

The Bar'dyn leader snatched the parchment from Jastail's hand, and returned to his band, speaking to them in a tongue Wendra didn't know. He then paused to look over the rendering of Wendra's song. With each pass of his eyes over the page, Wendra thought she saw a change in the Bar'dyn's face. At last, Etromney lowered the written song, and whispered to his companions. Immediately, two of the Bar'dyn came toward her and Penit. Wendra's eyes still stung from her tears, but she scrambled back on her hands and feet. Penit stood transfixed as the second Bar'dyn lifted him up and placed him on one great shoulder.

"Please, Etromney," Jastail said stridently. "I've much to offer. I know things."

At that, the Bar'dyn stopped and seemed to consider. He then motioned to one of his party, who went to Jastail and helped him to his feet. The highwayman clutched his own shoulder with one hand as he strode to join the other Bar'dyn.

In front of Wendra, the Quiet moved quickly, grasping her wrist with one clawed hand. With a jerk, it brought her to her feet, turning to drag her back to the others. Wendra blinked the dust and tears from her eyes and found Penit gulping air from his perch as he fought the need to cry. He was terrified.

In that instant, Wendra recalled a conversation with a Sedagin scop on songs sung from the bottom of pain, and felt a hundred moments of isolation and frustration and dark melodies coalesce in her chest and rush like a flood through the gates of her teeth.

The song burst from her virtually unbidden. Tortured sounds that ascended in powerful crescendos, notes turning in and over one another in sharp dissonance. The dark song came in a series of screams that rasped like moving stones without the cushion of mortar.

The terrible sound resonated through her, from her; yet she listened to it and watched, through eyes that saw nothing but white and black, the world all a stark mosaic. She saw the skin of the Bar'dyn begin to blacken, smoke rising from it. The beasts yawped with their chesty voices, a few dropping and rolling through the dirt and brush.

The strains of her song filled the entire meadow with a mighty roar. With every note she grew angrier, the contrast in her vision more severe. Grey deepened to black, white glowed in fiery brilliance. She sang to bring it all to darkness, divest everything of its light. Distantly, she felt her arms and legs tremble with the power rushing from her mouth. Her skin burned, but the feeling of it pleased her, and she smiled around terrible song as it shot forth into the meadow and fell upon the Bar'dyn.

The glory of the harsh sounds enveloped her. At the sight of Penit—a white form on a dark canvas—the tenor of her awful song moderated slightly. And in an instant, she couldn't remember his name. She recognized the shape, the rounding of his chin, the thin chest and legs, but his name was gone to her.

The sadness and frustration of forgetting the child welled in her, cycling toward her song like a reprise, when a sweet, low counterpoint joined her. Wendra whirled toward it, seeing a shining light in the shape of a tall man. She recognized this, too, but likewise had no idea who it might be. The harmony coming from the figure soothed her, eased her own melody, reshaped it, and she found herself naturally working to follow the progression of his simple, beautiful tune. Some phrases threatened to ride away from the new song, to take her back to the soothing certainty of singing everything black. But the gentle insistence of the countermelody assured her, guided her. Gradually, what she felt and heard became one, color coming again to the things she saw.

When their melody joined in a soft unison, she saw Seanbea walking toward her, a paternal smile on his full lips. She sang until her breath forsook her, and collapsed into the Ta'Opin's arms, her dark song at an end.

Wendra woke to the creak of axles and the jounce of hard wheels over stones in the road. A sour taste lingered in her mouth, like curdled milk and soot. Slowly, she opened her eyes to see a leafy world passing by lazily overhead. The slant of the sun said that night would soon come. The thought unsettled her, reminding her of the darkness in her vision when last she'd sung.

She then felt the press of a warm, small hand clinging to her own. Adjusting her head on a blanket rolled for a pillow, she saw Penit sitting in the wagon bed beside her. The boy stared into the forest beyond, a troubled look giving his young face an age beyond its years.

Wendra squeezed Penit's hand, drawing his attention.

"Hey, she's awake!" he hollered at Seanbea, climbing to his knees and scooting forward to huddle over her. "You passed out," Penit explained. "Are you all right?"

Wendra smiled at the concern. "I'm fine, but I could use some water."

Penit kept hold of her hand while he reached forward and lifted a waterskin from a jumble of gear stowed to the side. He uncorked it for her and raised it to her lips the way she'd done for Balatin with her own small hands when her father had taken ill. The connection of the two events eased the aching in her limbs as much as anything could. The water washed the bile from her mouth, and she rested back on the blanket.

"The Bar'dyn?" she managed, coughing the word.

"Mostly dead," Penit answered. "The rest crawled into the trees before you stopped singing."

The memory of her song came back to her, the forceful, angry melody inviting her to give it voice again. But her heart felt none of the former rage, and the feeling passed.

"Jastail?" The thought of the highwayman made her anxious.

It was Seanbea who replied. "When his deal was broken, he made a quick escape. Got away from your song."

The Ta'Opin's deep, resonant voice soothed her like honeyed tea. It lilted and trailed in easy lines, unlike the horrible evenness and clipped speech of the Bar'dyn's deep tones. She wanted him to keep talking so she could listen, could breathe in the music of his words.

"He won't come after us," Penit assured her. "He's afraid of you now. And Seanbea is with us."

Wendra looked at their rescuer. "How did you know?"

The man laughed, and pointed with delight at Penit. "This one's crafty."

She turned her eyes on Penit. "How?"

"Seanbea's cup, remember?" He grinned with pride. "I got Jastail's trust. So, he didn't worry too much when I asked to run Seanbea's cup back to him."

"The one he conveniently hid," Seanbea added, "so he'd have the excuse to do just that."

Wendra began to grin herself.

Penit eagerly shared the rest. "When I handed Seanbea the cup, I told him about Jastail. About the auction blocks. I told him we were being taken to be sold. I asked him to help."

She laughed at that, and squeezed his hand.

"And now, Seanbea's taking us to Recityv so I can run in the Lesher Roon." Penit smiled again, as if the rest was already the distant past.

But it seemed Penit still clung to one of the lies Jastail had told, that he would take part in some kind of race once they reached Recityv.

"The boy might win, too," Seanbea added. "Saw him run to you when that Bar'dyn dumped him to the ground. He's got quick feet."

Wendra looked back. "You mean there really is a race in Recityv? That wasn't just something Jastail made up to trick Penit?"

"You really haven't a notion, do you?" Seanbea said.

"I'll get to meet the regent," Penit exclaimed.

"True enough," Seanbea said. "Whole thing started a long time ago. King then considered a number of tests to qualify one child to sit on the Council. But knew these would favor noble children, who could afford tutors. He settled on a simple foot race. Some still grumbled, because the older children would have a clear advantage, so the king limited the race to those twelve years of age and younger."

Penit shook Wendra's hand to get her to look at him. "I do run fast, you know."

She smiled. The race might mean good things for Penit, after all.

"And if I win," he added, "then maybe I can tell them all about the Bar'dyn. They can send their army to save your brother."

Worry leapt inside her at the mention of Tahn. She hoped he would be safe in Recityv by the time they got there.

"The regent has called a date for a running of the Lesher Roon . . . and she's put out a call for the Convocation of Seats. Whole thing has to do with the Quiet, if you ask me. I suspect that's why the Maesteri sent me out visiting cities and towns, collecting instruments and looking for singers." He gave her a knowing look.

Wendra let the discussion of the race end, and looked about her at the instruments and parchments pushed aside to make room for her. She remembered there being a great deal more in Seanbea's wagon when she'd seen it a few nights before.

"What happened to your cargo?" she asked.

"My cargo is still in the wagon," Seanbea answered, the sound of a smile on his face as clear as laughter.

"Yes, but not all of it," Wendra persisted.

"Right you are," the Ta'Opin conceded. "I had to stow some in the hills so that you could rest. But don't you—"

"Seanbea, you can't do that. Those instruments were old, they'll—"

"—concern yourself. I'm still carrying an old instrument." Again the wagon bench creaked. This time he cranked his head around so he could see her face. "There's nothing in this wagon as important as you, Anais. I think I knew it when you joined my song beside the fire. That's why I pretended to leave, then tracked you into those mountains where the highwayman took you." He paused, his voice sounding far away. "I've not heard those sounds in my life. I've seen them written on parchment, but that's about all."

"How could you have heard—"

"Music is a response, Anais," he said reverently. "A response to what's in our heart. There've been some who put those feelings to parchment. Not exactly the way you did, but enough that I recognized the sad beauty of them . . . the danger in them."

He reined in and stopped the cart. He turned all the way around, putting his feet into the back of the wagon, and looked down at Wendra, commanding her attention. He knitted his fingers, and leaned forward, bracing his arms on his knees. "You'll want to listen close, Anais. Think back and you'll probably remember a time when your songs seemed to do more than just tickle your tongue. A time when they did more, when they *caused* more. Don't bother to tell me about it, and don't try to deny it to yourself."

Seanbea looked at Penit, as if trying to decide whether to go on. He gave the boy a wink. "What you do, what you are, is more an instrument than anything Descant is expecting me to bring. Never you mind the stuff I left behind. It's covered and will keep. You, my girl, must do neither. The changes that prompt the regent to call Convocation are likely the same that sent me into the land to find and haul these records and rusted items to Recityv. And now that I've seen Quiet so deep in the land, I'm almost sure of it. And they almost had you . . . makes my blood cold." He gave her a sympathetic look. "What I saw you do to them . . . You've never done it before, have you?"

"No," she managed. Dark memories flared in her mind. She wondered if her song would have grown dark enough to steal Penit's light. "I'm not even sure what happened."

"This thing in you, Anais, is a rare music indeed," Seanbea said. "In my training at Descant, the Maesteri warned me of it." Seanbea reached down and placed his hand over her forehead. "Having such music is a responsibility you must learn to shoulder. That's why we're going to Recityv. Maesteri there can help. You rest. We should be there tomorrow."

Wendra looked up at the leaves and sky passing in a mosaic against the failing sun. She could smell the brass and wood of the wonderful instruments Seanbea still carried, the dusty smell of old parchment, too. As the wagon creaked northward, Wendra kept firm hold of Penit's small hand.

"Just wait," the boy said, his smile unfailing. "I'll take care of you."

Wendra placed her other hand over Penit's sturdy fingers.

CHAPTER FORTY-SEVEN

A Quiet Cradle

If the gods left. If we're doomed. Or damned. What do we care if the
Quiet come?

—Polemic raised by the Dimnian king during
the First Convocation

G rant motioned to the right and angled his horse in a southeasterly direction. Braethen, Vendanj, and Mira followed. He'd given his wards instructions before coming with the Sheason and his friends. *Use the Scar to hide, if it
comes to that. You know it better than anyone.* They descended a short slope into
a featureless plain that ran outward in a pattern of grey and white earth less
populated with sage and barren of trees . . . save one.

A hundred strides from the base of the hill stood a lone dead tree. The trunk
rose in a gentle twist of bleached wood—like bone left in the sun. Thick limbs
snaked in every direction, ending in jagged snarls as if snapped off long ago. The
bare branches offered no shade from the sun, which rose hot in the morning
sky.

The Cradle of the Scar.

Grant stopped and slid from his saddle. He crossed to the tree, where a
hollow had been carved directly into the trunk. He paused there a moment,
looking up at the tree the way another might an old friend. He then looked inside. His heart fell and he let out a slow sigh of anger and frustration, turning to
look away.

Mira and Vendanj dismounted and started toward the tree. Grant held up a
hand to stop them. "The cradle is my responsibility."

He hardened his heart and reached carefully into the hollow. With a quick
snatch, he grabbed and ripped the snake from the hole. It writhed in his hand.
A snarl twisted his lip before he simply squeezed the serpent so tightly that it
stopped moving. After several moments of death throes, the dead serpent hung
limp in his hand.

The sodalist slipped off his horse and strode to where Mira and Vendanj stood watching. Grant finally dropped the lifeless creature to the ground. Blood coated his fingers. He stared at his hand a moment before turning back to the tree.

"Oh, no," he heard Braethen whisper behind him, the sodalist already understanding.

Tenderly, Grant removed an infant.

The child's skin was pale, cold; dark rings circled its eyes and mouth. Grant kneeled on the hard earth beneath the dead tree and cradled the dead babe in his arms.

None of them moved, observing silent reflection for the passing of a life that never knew a hope. The thought of the baby wriggling its arms in ignorance as the serpent coiled close by seared Grant's mind. He shut his eyes to the image. He wanted to avenge the child, but the culprit already lay dead close by.

A horrible feeling of helplessness gripped him.

The unrealized possibilities of the babe weighed on his mind. And as he did every day in this wide, dry place, he considered the injustice and cruelty of abandoning a child to the Scar. And hated those who had sent him here.

But he put that away for the moment. This child deserved to be mourned for its own sake.

Mira went to the snake and knelt to inspect it. She and Vendanj exchanged a knowing look. "Hostaugh," she said. "Not a serpent from the Scar. You won't find these south of the Pall . . . unless someone brought it here."

"What are you saying?" Braethen asked.

"The serpent was placed in the tree by Quiet," Grant answered.

Mira stood and kicked the snake away with a flick of her boot.

Grant turned, catching a glimpse of the sun, low in the eastern sky. "We're not late. This is the day, the hour. The child is already cold." He pulled the infant's blanket around its shoulders.

"It's the poison," Vendanj said. "The hostaugh bite does more than kill. It steals life . . . like the Velle do when they render."

"Why would the Quiet do this?" Braethen asked. "Wouldn't they have taken the child?"

"It's a warning." Vendanj stared down at the child, his face looking heavy. "Those who left the child would have checked the cradle before placing the child inside. No. The serpent was put there after they left. The child was left to you as a sign."

"A sign of what?" There was a hard edge in Grant's voice.

Vendanj waited a long moment. "Not to help us."

"They're mistaken if they think I'll be frightened or discouraged over the death of one. . . ." Grant looked away into the vastness of the Scar, grief and anger pulling at the creases in his weathered face.

"It isn't your care for this one child that they're threatening," Vendanj added. "They'll come after them all."

Grant nodded. Before leaving them the night before, he'd given his wards new instruction. Discontinue patrols. Leave the home. Remain together in the safe places deep in the Scar. "I told them what to do. They'll be all right."

Mira climbed to the top of the hill, and checked their backtrail. She returned quickly and shook her head—no one followed them.

He gave the babe a final look. *You went too early, little one.* He then gently passed the child to Mira to hold and began digging a grave. Vendanj dropped down beside him to help. Braethen, too. The three men dug together in silence. Beneath the dead tree, they scooped the barren earth that would be the final ground for the infant. The young sodalist drew his sword and began chipping at the baked soil with it. Vendanj seemed to approve of the use.

Pray the abandoning gods this is the last child I have to put into the Scar.

As the three men worked at the earth to create a grave, Mira looked down at the child in her arms. She cradled it close, feelings maternal and mournful touching her in quiet waves. The face of the babe was pallid but peaceful. And looking at the infant girl, the promise of her future frozen forever in her delicate features . . . Mira fought a rising wrath that sought escape.

There would be a time for that.

For now, she honored this small life with the care and attentiveness she deserved but had never received in life. Mira thought about her own mother— her birth mother—whose face she couldn't remember. She wondered at providence that had kept her from being like the child in her arms.

The abandonment of a small life, whatever the cause, ached in Mira's chest. It made the decision awaiting her beyond Recityv a heavy burden, a decision that might affect the success of the Sheason's ultimate plans.

Staring into the unrealized promise of this child galvanized Mira's need to act, but put her further from understanding which path to choose. Only one certainty filled her under the hard sun of the Scar: If she could have given her life to save this little girl, she would have.

Vendanj stared down to where the child lay in its final slumber. The others stood beside him in the stillness.

Then Grant mounted. "You have until the next child comes to the Scar, Vendanj." He looked at the Forgotten Cradle. "Then I come back to my tree." He raced to the east, leaving the others to catch up.

Mira and Braethen mounted.

Vendanj lingered a moment. He looked down at the small patch of dirt that humped slightly above the earth around it. In the barrens of this inhospitable place they had laid to rest a life come unnaturally to its end. The hope and path that had lain before this little girl had been stolen. Indignation surged inside him.

To send a message, a defenseless child . . .

In his mind he saw the helpless little girl being struck by the viper. He saw her crying in pain and confusion and the desperate need of comfort. Comfort she deserved in this life . . . but she'd been abandoned to this tree. This Scar.

Vendanj fell to his knees and silently wept.

This was why the Fathers had placed the Whited One and those who followed him inside the Bourne. This was what awaited them if they failed to keep them there.

Infants . . .

He raised his head and screamed into the pale blue sky. With the sound of it still echoing out on the hard, barren waste of the Scar, Vendanj thrust his hands into the grave of the babe and spoke the words of his heart, giving this little plot of land a portion of his spirit.

And spontaneously from the gravesite came grass and flowers, with their living smells.

The burn of his grief subsided. He pulled his hands out of the soil. "Good-bye, small one."

Vendanj took his knife and found the serpent. He cut off its head and put it in his pouch. He also picked up the fold of the child's blanket they had torn away before burying her, the bloodstained part.

He put the tokens in his pouch and left the babe to its rest.

Just after dusk, they passed the boundary of the Scar. Braethen took a deep breath of the cool breeze that blew across green trees and undergrowth. He could smell life. Bark and needles and fallen leaves and moist earth. They stopped near a small brook to rest for the night. Mira left almost immediately, scouting ahead.

Grant sat staring into their fire, his mind seeming far away.

Braethen finally had to ask the question that had been on his mind since leaving the man's Scar home. "Why are you rewriting the Charter?"

Grant looked up over the flames at him, eyeing the Sodality emblem—the quill dancing over a sword. "How long have you been a sodalist?"

"Not long," Braethen said with a bit of reluctance.

The man smiled, the look of it more appreciative than mocking. "Your sword-work isn't good, but it's better than 'not long.'"

"All youth in the Hollows are taught basic techniques," Braethen explained.

"And your books?" Grant pointed to the satchel Braethen carried.

"All my life," he said more confidently. "My father's an author."

"You care more for books than steel," Grant stated matter-of-factly.

Braethen wouldn't argue it. He hated the idea of becoming comfortable enough with a weapon that it came as easily as reading.

Grant fell silent for a long moment. "And my own feeble efforts at writing . . . are because I'm tired of fighting," he said, just above the sound of the fire.

Braethen recalled the weapons racks at Grant's home. "Then why teach it to your wards?"

"Because sooner or later they'll need it." He sat on the ground, leaning back against a fallen tree. "They'll need it because my little charter holds no weight."

Braethen understood the need to write things down for one's own good.

"A lot of time is what I have, Sodalist," Grant went on, staring at the flames. "A lot of time to think about the ways a man brings angry hands against you. Days and years to teach my wards that freedom is a myth."

"A cynical view," Braethen countered.

Grant laughed, the lines in his face creasing. "Maybe. But I teach my wards to keep a promise. The way the Charter meant us to." He paused. "Maybe I'm just writing down the intentions of the Framers as I understand them. The training, though . . . that's because my scribbling has no power to change things. And I won't send my wards into the world unprepared."

"So you teach them—"

"To *anticipate*," Grant finished. "A thousand days I've walked through the strokes and counterstrokes of fight after fight. Different weapons, different opponents of varying sizes and ability. I've imagined every terrain over which battles might rage, compensated for wounds to myself and my enemy. All up here." He tapped his temple twice lightly. "And when I could think of no more, I considered them again, and again, seeing the results each time, varying the ability in my enemy and anticipating his next stroke based on a hundred factors. And when I was done, I taught my wards. And we practice. It's all there is to do in the Scar."

"Except draw a new Charter," Vendanj put in.

"Well that, too," Grant conceded, his smile a tad more bitter in the concession.

"You still haven't answered why, though," Braethen pushed.

Grant's smiled faded entirely. He turned a hard look on Braethen. "Maybe I want to believe this world has hope, could change. Maybe I want to believe there's a way to give my words the power to do it. . . ."

Like the Language of the Covenant.

Vendanj frowned but said nothing.

". . . so you see, Sodalist," Grant finished, "we're both fools."

Braethen shivered. It was the world's foolish men who made the most sense, and caused the greatest sorrow.

• CHAPTER FORTY-EIGHT •

A Servant's Tale

The point of an oath is to direct behavior. Its potency lies in a man's need for virtue.

—*The Psychology of Oaths*, from the personal
library of Roth Staned

Sutter sat in the dark, his wrists and ankles chain-bound, staring across at a troupe of scops.

My godsdamned luck. I don't get thieves and murderers. I get troupers.

His hate helped keep his mind from the beatings, though.

He stared through one eye, the other swollen shut from where a guard boot had caught him. In the shadows opposite him sat two men and two women shackled to the wall. Their jailer had painted their faces in rough mockery of their profession. From time to time the guard came in and made them dance or prattle out some rhea-fol. Didn't seem to matter if they did it well or not—the whip came with the same intensity either way. One of the women had lost an eye to that whip.

Wonder if she left any kids to village farmers.

Old wounds.

Far back in the crook of the stair, someone moaned. Someone he hadn't noticed before. The dark corner fell silent again.

"Who's there?" Sutter asked.

"What does it matter?" a rough voice answered.

Thank the silent gods, someone to talk to besides a player. "Why are you here?"

The man remained quiet for a time, then finally said, "I was deemed unfit for my throne." A sad laugh followed.

Sutter liked the genuine sound of it. "You're from Recityv?"

"Not hardly. You won't have heard of my homeland: Risill Ond. We're nestled against the eastern ocean beyond the Wood of Isiliand."

"You're right. Never heard of it. And you're the king?" Sutter's skepticism rang in his words.

Again the easy laugh. "My people put away courts and high politics so many generations ago that we had to consult old books to remember our own sigil."

"And what was that?" Sutter found himself grateful for the sudden conversation down in the dark.

"A scythe," the man said.

"Really? A scythe?" Seemed lame to Sutter.

"We're farmers."

A full silence settled between them.

"What's your name?" Sutter finally asked.

"I'm Thalen Dumal. But I'm no king. Risill Ond lives by the cycles of planting and harvest. Not coronations and military parades. We did once have royalty of a kind, though." He paused in his dark corner. "I'd rather have stayed with my crops."

Sutter could relate. "I'm Sutter. I'm familiar with dirt myself." He probed at his swollen eye. "Why'd you come, then?"

"We were obligated. I was obligated. When the Second Promise was issued long ago, we were asked to come. We had no army, so a vote was held. Unmarried men were asked to go. They marched to Recityv, carrying the only weapons they knew, scythes." The man gave a weak laugh. "Soldiers they fought with started calling them Reapers. They were among the few that honored the Second Promise. And so here I am."

"In a dungeon?" Sutter said, confused.

"We don't have a ruling class in Risill Ond. My mother stitched our emblem to an old, thin carpet." There was no shame in Thalen's voice. "When I arrived, I was taken in by some leagueman and questioned. They didn't like my answers. Imprisoning me leaves our seat at Convocation unclaimed. The League will claim it, and a *civil* contingent will come to Risill Ond—something we've been able to avoid until now."

Sutter glanced over at the troupe, who were listening to Thalen's story. Then he turned back. "I don't understand how they can hold you here."

Thalen laughed again. "That's the irony. They looked at my hand-sewn banner and clothes and accused me of being a false applicant to the Seat of Risill Ond."

"Godsdamned horses' asses." It didn't help that this fellow accepted what had happened so temperately.

Thalen spoke again, his voice sad and wistful. "I just want to go back to my fields. Morning dew on the crops and soil. Tilled earth. Long harvest fields. That's my court . . . I'm no king."

The words stole some of Sutter's anger. He could see the things Thalen described. He could see his father and mother ankle-deep in turned soil. He could see himself and Tahn hiding in the deep autumn wheat, having smaller adventures.

He shook his head in frustration. He hoped Tahn was all right—Recityv guards had separated them after they'd been captured—but damned hells, had Tahn gotten them into a mess. All because of a *feeling*.

Two days without food or water. Tahn sat still, aching from beatings. The dank smell of sweating stone lay just under the stench of waste and filth and stale straw. A clink of chains jounced around the room as his cellmate squatted over a waste hole in the corner. A shaft of torchlight fell slantwise from a barred window in the door, growing weaker as it met the floor down a set of stone stairs.

In the night the man in the corner moaned in his sleep. Whatever dreams Tahn's unseen companion had, they caused him to thrash about, scraping his chains across the stony floor.

The manacles around Tahn's wrists and ankles had rubbed the skin raw. The iron stung. His ribs were bruised. His lips cut. And his cheeks throbbed with the beating of his heart. A gash in the back of his head made lying down intolerable. He slept sitting against the wall, his chin on his chest. His left eye had swollen nearly shut. And though he didn't remember it, he thought someone had stomped on his fingers, leaving the joints too bruised to flex.

No outer window freshened the stale air. When he or his cellmate shifted or sighed, the sound of each movement reverberated loudly off the high ceiling.

They'd stripped him of his bow and belt, ripped his cloak from his shoulders. He wished they'd left him that, at least. The cold stone chilled his flesh through his clothes. They had taken Sutter somewhere. Just now he could use some of Sutter's wit.

He pressed the back of his left hand to his one good cheek and felt the familiar shape across his skin. The scar comforted him, if only because it was still his.

In another time, Wendra would have sung to him, the soft sound of her voice easing his mind. But he'd failed her. . . .

"Two days and not a word. Where are your manners, son?" The voice broke the silence. Tahn didn't flinch, paying it no more attention than any other dream that fevered his mind.

"There's just the two of us here," the other said.

Tahn raised his head in the direction of the voice. It came calmly, with patience and clarity.

"You've not spoken to me, either," Tahn said. He tried to peer beyond the shaft of light with his one good eye.

"That's a matter of caution," the other replied. "The League has sent informants pretending to be prisoners."

"Then why speak now?" Tahn still couldn't see the man.

"Because no free man has ever suffered two straight days of beating." The man softly chuckled, and his chains rattled in the shadows.

"So you've decided to trust me because I've been beaten?" Tahn was too weak to lend his incredulity any bite.

"I didn't say I trusted you." The man's voice changed to become flat and precise. "I'm interested."

"In my beatings?" Tahn said.

"Well, yes. What makes the League lay into you with such enthusiasm. I don't think they beat *me* with such zeal." Tahn again heard chains rattle, and imagined the man tapping his chest.

Tahn considered. If he told the man what he'd done, the fellow might want to know why, and what would Tahn say?

"Still cautious," the man said with appreciation. "Then consider this, my young friend. I'll have no reprieve. No second stand before the Court of Judicature. When my turn is done here—a long turn to be sure—I'll stand to face my death and wonder if my final earth could be any colder than this damned stone."

"At the gallows?" Tahn asked.

"Whatever they deem appropriate," the man said. "So you see, your story, whatever it is, will never reach another soul. But down here it may offer us each some entertainment for a few moments."

There was an earnest undertone, a *need*, in the man's voice. A need to hear a story, something to carry him beyond the walls of this cell.

Still, Tahn asked simply, "Why?"

The sound of the man standing came out of the dark, and Tahn saw a shadow rise near the shaft of light that slanted in from the window up the stairs. "Because the League doesn't brutalize simple lawbreakers." The man let that hang a moment. "A young man who smells of the road, whose face is new to a razor, but who excites such passion from his captors . . . you've angered the League, son. That's a story to melt the walls of this place. And I'd like to hear it."

Tahn swallowed against the thickness in his mouth, and suddenly felt the pains of thirst and hunger. "My mouth's dry."

"You'll be fed your fourth day. Moldy bread. And it'll run through you like rain down a spout." Tahn thought he heard a smile. "Still, it tastes good. Careful though. The rush of it into an empty stomach will give you pain."

Tahn groaned and drew himself up against the wall at his back.

"I'll split my ration with you," the man said, still angling to hear Tahn's story. "To keep your strength up."

Tahn meant still to refuse him, when an arm stole into the light, pushing a metal plate with a slice of bread and cheese toward him. A moment later came a cracked decanter. The face and shoulders of the man remained in the shadows.

Tahn ate in silence.

Never had stale warm water tasted so good. He hardly noticed the sting of his shackles over his raw wrists. When he was done, he simply started talking. He spoke just above a whisper. His voice reverberated against indifferent stone.

It felt like confession.

He held back only two things: the sticks entrusted to him by the scrivener, and drawing an empty bow at Sevilla.

He finished by recounting his arrival at Recityv and discovering another public punishment about to be carried out. He described the division in the crowd that watched the hanging, and his feeling that one of the men shouldn't be put to death.

"And here I am," Tahn said, ending his story.

His mouth and throat were again dry.

The cell was silent until his cellmate exclaimed in quiet amazement. "Dear dead gods, son, who are you?"

Tahn's chains clattered on the stone paving, but he couldn't stop his arms from shaking.

The man didn't seem to notice. "And now for my story," the man said in a slightly more genial tone. "I'm Rolen. And I am Sheason."

Tahn's head snapped in Rolen's direction. "Sheason," Tahn echoed. "But then you could free yourself. Why do you—"

"Easy, son. Patience."

Tahn sat up, wanting to know how a renderer could be held against his will. A guard came to the door. The man looked in, letting out an oath before passing by, satisfied that they were sufficiently miserable.

Rolen stood and began to pace slowly. The lengths of chain swayed almost musically in time with his steps.

"The food I shared with you," Rolen began, "always comes in small portions. My rations keep me weak. And what energy I have, they make me render to heal leagueman and the like." Rolen paused, and stared at Tahn. "But this isn't why I stay."

Rolen panted with the exertion of relating his story. The rasp in his lungs reminded Tahn of winter pox. Rolen coughed with a wet tearing sound that made Tahn wince. The man spat something thick onto the floor.

When Rolen's breathing had calmed, he chuckled again, inviting a few more stifled coughs.

Tahn shook his head at a troubling thought. "You choose to stay, don't you?"

• CHAPTER FORTY-NINE •

Maesteri

To sing Suffering is to feel suffering. You live it all. What most forget is the last movement: Reclamation.

—Admonition offered by Maesteri Kyle in his aria
on "incomplete understanding"

Wendra looked up when she heard Penit gasp. The boy's eyes were impossibly wide, staring into the distance before them. Turning, she saw what no reader's description could ever do justice to: a wall more than a thousand strides across, rising from the plain as high, it seemed, as the cliffs of Sedagin. The encampments along the road and at the base of the wall would fill the Hollows a hundred times and more.

"There she is," Seanbea announced. "Recityv. The jewel of Vohnce. House of song and floor of debate." A wide grin split Seanbea's face—the grin of a man returning home.

"How big is it?" Penit asked with evident awe.

"Why, how big does she look, lad?" Seanbea spoke through his smile. "Mountains have fallen to quarry her stone. And forests have been harvested and replanted more times than a man can count to fuel the forges that built her." The Ta'Opin swept his gaze from far left to right. "She's a jewel," he repeated.

Seanbea drove them through the thronged highway to the expansive gate. Soldiers there questioned him, and eventually waved him through.

Wendra thrilled at the size of the buildings, her own surprise as vocal as

Penit's. Seanbea pointed out certain inns, shops, merchant exchange houses, sometimes adding a bit of history in the telling. Wendra sat in the bed of the wagon, clinging to the side and gathering in one sight after another as they rolled onward.

They pressed through a throng of people that parted like waters around an island.

Then gradually, the elegance of the buildings diminished. Stonework seemed older, more often in disrepair and stained from seasons of rain and sun. The buildings themselves weren't as tall, their mortar crumbling and leaving gaps in their facing, like missing teeth. Awnings tilted over entries to various establishments. Many windows looked like sharp-toothed maws where shards of glass rimmed an opening.

Even the livestock here seemed old and broken—horses with deep-swayed backs and ungroomed manes and tails, dogs coated with burrs and muddied bellies. People went about with heads bowed. Coats and breeches were puckered from poorly mended tears. Boot creases showed too many strides to remain comfortable. The streets themselves were unpaved here. Muddy pools stood in potholes. And shallow ditches stood at the edges of buildings where rain fell from rooftops and beat their own stale troughs. Slop was thrown from windows— the smell of human filth rose in waves.

Between buildings, pigs had been penned in narrow alleys waiting to be butchered. Flies buzzed in clouds. Her delight and Penit's fell to disappointed silence.

They turned down a cross street, and like a bit of magic, at the end of the avenue rose a grand building in the midst of the squalor. Four times higher than the closest building, the majestic cathedral ascended in a series of spires and pitched gables that left Wendra with the impression of a castle. The roof and cupolas shone green in the afternoon light, resplendent and luminous.

"Wow!" Penit remarked.

"Descant Cathedral. I told you," Seanbea said.

High in its darkened stone, colored glass caught the sun and glinted violet, crimson, gold, lapis, and emerald. Nearer still, the green cupolas disappeared from view. The spires seemed to angle toward the sky like spears thrown at heaven.

The wagon creaked to a stop, and brought Wendra's gaze earthward. At eye level, the windows showed none of the magnificence of those higher up. Slats of wood boarded them over, either protecting the creation of the colorful mosaics, or filling gaps left behind by a vandal's work.

But despite the unbeautiful windows and the aged stone covered in patches by lichen and withered vines, the cathedral made Wendra forget its surroundings. Descant pressed up and out like a monument of strength and nobility.

A large set of double doors swept inward and two men bustled out and down the stone steps toward them. Each wore loose breeches tied with a wide crimson sash knotted on the left hip, and a simple coat with a pocket over each breast.

"We'll bring you in," one said cheerfully, ignoring Penit and Wendra as he pulled off the tarpaulin and hefted some of Seanbea's load.

The second man paused on the bottom step, taking note of the extra human cargo. "What's this, Seanbea? I hope you don't expect additional pay for these." He pointed fingers toward Wendra and Penit, and smiled.

"And hello to you, Henny, Ilio." Seanbea jumped to the ground. "These are friends of mine. I intend to introduce them to Maesteri Belamae." He leaned against the side of his wagon and smiled as though holding a secret from the two men.

"That's nice," Henny said, and bowed awkwardly before turning to pack his armload of instruments into the cathedral. Despite his rush, he handled them with great care. "Come on, Ilio, we've work to do."

Ilio didn't take his eyes off Wendra as he lifted two small boxes from the wagon. "Is she spoken for?" he asked, inclining his head toward the Ta'Opin, his stare still locked on Wendra.

"I don't think she heard you," Seanbea mocked. "Speak up and perhaps she'll answer you herself." He bent over to hide his laughter.

Ilio gave Wendra an embarrassed smile. His face flushed. Holding the boxes against his chest, he rocked side to side, seeming not to know what else to do. "If there's anything I can do to help . . ." Ilio said, leaning out over his boxes. "Rooms, rations, clothing . . . manners." The man scurried up the stairs after Henny.

"I'm sure you impressed her," Seanbea called after Ilio. He turned his smile on Wendra. "Pardon me, Anais, but I simply can't resist the opportunity to see Ilio's face turn that color. If I could duplicate it, I'd make a fortune in textiles."

Wendra and Penit climbed down from the wagon, just as Henny scurried back out.

"Will you see to the wagon and team?" Seanbea asked the man.

"Surely," Henny replied.

Seanbea patted the man's bald head, and led Wendra and Penit up the steps.

"It's a special place," Seanbea said, speaking as much to himself as anyone else.

At the top of the steps, the doors seemed much larger. The hard ironwood bore engravings Wendra couldn't read, and more than a few dents and scars. As they passed through them, cool air caressed her skin with the scent of cedar incense and oak and mild fruit rinds.

And underneath it all came the faraway echo of song. It seemed to emanate from the walls themselves.

"What is that?" Wendra asked, putting her hand to a pillar and looking up at the ceiling of the vestibule in which they stood.

"That," Seanbea said, "is the Song of Suffering." His voice carried a deep reverence. He moved further into the cathedral without any further explanation.

Wendra's heart began to race. *Suffering? My last god, Suffering.*

Penit trotted past her to follow Seanbea. Wendra lingered a moment, feeling the hum through the marble pillar. Under her fingers, the beautiful stone felt vibrant, imbued with life by the uttering of words and music deep within it. Pulling away proved difficult. But she sensed that the song touching her fingers came from voices somewhere deeper within the cathedral. She wanted to hear it. Every word. Every note.

Beyond the vestibule, three hallways sprouted, each passing beneath great stone vaults and housing a few cherrywood tables bearing silver urns. Intricate scrollwork had been carved directly into the stone walls. The doors were heavy and paneled. Candles and lamps burned in long glass hurricane tubes, lending the halls intimacy. Brass handles and fittings had grown dark with time. And footsteps echoed flatly down the clean marble floors.

Wendra caught up to Seanbea and Penit, who'd angled left. Down the hall they passed a series of oil paintings of men and women, all wearing long robes. A few held instruments in their laps, and a few sat reposed holding a kind of baton.

As they proceeded down the hall, Wendra thought the music grew louder. Each step excited her. Something in this melody felt familiar, though she was sure she'd never heard it before.

As she tried to remember, three women turned into the hall ahead. The one in the middle wore a thick white cloak, the hood up, her arms wrapped about herself as though she fought the shivers. On each side, the others supported her as if afraid she might fall.

"Sariah?"

The woman in the middle looked up. "Seanbea?" Her voice sounded weak and tired, but pleased.

"It's good to see you," he said. "You've just finished a turn at the Song, though. Our reunion can wait until you have rested."

Sariah hugged Seanbea anyway, allowing his strong arms to hold her for several moments. Wendra watched the young woman's face laid against the Ta'Opin's broad chest, and saw a kind of concern and frightful wisdom that didn't belong in the face of one so young—she was maybe twenty.

Then finally she drew back. "Therin sings now. He'll want to see you, too, before you go. Can you stay a while?"

"Of course," Seanbea said. "Now get some rest."

The young woman smiled and the two girls beside her helped Sariah continue on. Seanbea continued as well, and a few moments later they came to the last painting at this end of the hall.

Wendra gasped, and covered her mouth.

She knew this face: the paternal smile, the patient eyes.

It was the face of the man who had appeared to her in her fever visions near Sedagin. Seeing him in this portrait gave the memory a frightening reality.

Her song was more than mere melody. And the burden of it burned in her. Singing had forever been an escape and source of comfort. After everything that had happened, this one private pleasure and reminder had become something . . . more. She looked away from the painting.

Seanbea softly rapped at a nearby door. As she turned, she saw the door open, revealing the face of the man in the painting, the man from the cave. He looked out and past Seanbea, directly at her.

"You've found your way," he said, beaming.

She stared back, not sure what to say.

"Well, Seanbea," the man said, shifting his attention to the Ta'Opin. "Always good to see you. Am I to thank you for shepherding this young woman to us?"

"There's no fee on it, Maesteri," Seanbea said, smiling. He embraced the old man, who gathered the large Ta'Opin in his white-robed arms like a mother bear cuddling her cub. The gentleman stood an apple taller than Seanbea.

Releasing him, the man said, "And who's this?" He bent over to look Penit in the eye.

"I'm Penit. I'm going to win the Lesher Roon."

"Is that right?" The old man winked. "I like a confident tone. Well, you've arrived just in time, then. The race is tomorrow." The Maesteri then glanced at Wendra. "And you came along with Wendra, did you?"

Penit looked back at her. "We kind of watch out for each other."

She stepped beside the boy and put her arm around his shoulder. "Seanbea says you might let us stay a night or two. I can work to earn our meals."

Both Seanbea and the man in the robe gave Wendra a puzzled look.

"You're both guests here," the old man said, "for as long as you'd like. We'll talk more on that later. Now, you may call me Belamae, if you wish. I teach music here."

"He leads *all* music here," Seanbea corrected. "I see they've added you to the wall." He indicated the portrait. "A good likeness, I'd say."

Belamae gave a somewhat self-conscious smile. "Not my idea," he said. "And the placement is kind of conspicuous. But I'm honored to be numbered among the Maesteri. They were rather forgiving with my nose, don't you think?" He chuckled warmly.

Seanbea joined him. "She creates," Seanbea said a moment later, "new song such as I've never heard." He pulled a roll of parchment from an inner pocket and unfolded it before handing it to the old man.

With a gentle smile, Belamae began inspecting the sheet. Wendra caught a glimpse of the unique musical notation and knew Seanbea had transcribed for himself a copy of the duet she'd sung with him. Embarrassment rippled through her, with a tinge of anger.

Belamae's smile faded, the light in his eyes flickering like a candle. Wendra might have thought the man had just read a warrant or elegy. His eyes rose from the parchment and locked Wendra in a serious gaze. She returned the old man's stare, uncertain. After a long moment, he stepped back through the door and motioned her to follow.

"Take the boy to the kitchen and get him something to help him grow," Belamae directed. "Give us an hour. Then we'll join you."

In each corner of the room, stands and easels stood overflowing with large books opened to a number of different musical notations. Beside each, instruments lay carefully set on pedestals uniquely crafted to receive them. On the walls hung more paintings, smaller portraits and a few pictures of musicians in battle settings. In the middle of the room sat a large desk with twin lamps burning brightly, one at either end.

The entire study shone with a great deal more light than the hall, the several easels and pedestals casting washed shadows across the floor like veins under skin. Directly opposite them, another door remained closed. And the distant sound of Suffering, like a warm undertone, could still be heard.

Belamae took a seat behind his desk and folded his hands in his lap. "Please sit down," he said.

Wendra sat and surveyed the scattering of music sheets and quills and drawing graphite. Near one lamp lay a metal instrument like a small horseshoe attached to a handle. Seeing her interest, Belamae picked it up and struck it against the edge of his desk. The tines hummed and vibrated a single musical pitch.

"Can you match the sound?" Belamae asked.

Without thinking, Wendra hummed the sustained note.

"Harmonize with it."

Wendra shifted her pitch several times to sing different harmonies with the chiming fork.

"Can you name the separate harmonies you've just created?" Belamae asked, deadening the instrument with a touch.

Wendra shook her head. "A few. My mother taught me. But I can't remember all their names."

He struck the fork again and asked her to sing a higher note. He then added his own voice in a lower register. The three notes sang together in a unity she'd never heard, seeming to fasten together as one. Belamae doused the chime and ended his note. Wendra stopped singing with a bit of regret.

"You've come to study," the teacher said, hopeful.

"I don't know." Wendra glanced at the music stands and their sepia parchments scrawled with notes and signatures.

Belamae captured her attention, his kind eyes intent. "You've a gift, Wendra. I can hear it. It's probably brought you comfort and delighted your friends and family. But what you possess . . . it's got other purposes." His eyebrows rose as though asking whether she understood him.

Wendra remained silent.

"The warmth and enjoyment of a voice, a musician's hands upon his strings or fingering the notes on his flute," he explained, "these are joys for evening meals and to accompany a good tobacco pipe at day's end. But given to a few is something more. For these few, the fulfillment of that . . . gift can only be achieved by careful training. Training to learn Resonance. Training to sing the Song of Suffering. This is what I do."

"I can't stay," Wendra blurted. "I've friends to find, and my brother. There are things . . ."

"Child," Belamae said, his voice filled with patience and experience. "With everything you've seen, is there anything more important than learning to sing Suffering?"

Thoughts flashed in her mind: her child, Tahn, Bar'dyn, Jastail . . . but mostly she saw the chalked feet of women and children on the blocks, and the world cast in a relief of dark and bright and nothing more. She closed her eyes and listened to the distant lilt and rhythm of Suffering.

"Come with me," Belamae invited.

She followed him to the rear door of his office. He ushered her through, pulling the door shut behind them. All grace and flowing robes, he bustled down the hall. His white hair floated in the long bob of his stride. Wendra had to step lively to keep pace with the elderly Maesteri.

They passed more oil paintings. Many depicted recitals, musicians at the center of amphitheaters filled with listeners. Further on, the paintings showed battles. In some, a single man or woman stood before a terrible onslaught; in others, a chorus of men and women stood together.

They walked through another door, and left the intimate warmth of cherrywood for the relative coolness of marble. They strode into a large vaulted hall, their footfalls like small things in a great cavern. Striations of color shot through the smooth stone surfaces in crimson, cobalt, green, and a dozen other hues. It reminded Wendra of the play of light on the water's surface when viewed from the bottom of a shallow lake.

Up steps and across short mezzanines they went, the ceiling a full six stories above them. Statuary replaced the oils, as did great, wide, intricate tapestries four times a man's height, woven with obvious skill. Sunlight fell through windows set in the ceiling high above. And on the air wafted the smell of rosemary and peppermint. Soon, they passed small pools set into the floor and surrounded by low benches. Within the pools, shallow steps allowed one to dip her feet and relax them there. Warm mist curled over the water's surface.

To the left and right, arched passageways led out of sight. The glow of candles set on simple, but elegant pieces of ironmongery gave the marble a fleshlike quality.

At the center of the vaulted hall stood a much larger pool, twenty-five strides across, with a narrow walkway to its center. Belamae strode to the edge and looked back at her. "Walk to the center. Go slowly so you don't fall."

"What is it?" she asked.

His face showed a curious expression, part frown, part smile. "Resonance," he said. "Something about which we'll talk quite a lot. Today, it will tell us both a little about your song." He pointed to the small dais at the center of the pool. "When you get to the center, sing. Create something."

She gave him a puzzled look.

"The way we talked about in the cave beneath Sedagin. The way Seanbea says you can." He smiled warmly. "Water gives us reflections, doesn't it? Let's see where you're at with your own song."

"I'm not sure this is a good idea," she warned. "The last time—"

"Let me be the judge of that, if you will, my dear. I've some experience." Belamae gestured toward the pool.

Wendra nodded reluctantly and walked down the narrow path to the center of the pool. She peered into the depths around her for a moment; the waters were deep. Then she gave Belamae a last look, took a deep breath, and started to sing.

She began soft and low, sketching out a melodic variation to the tune of her song box. The sound seemed to ride fast along the surface of the water, and out into the wide chamber. Then she gave the song words, lyrics drawn from the events of the last several weeks. She didn't bother with rhyme. She sought the right *emotional* words.

The water rippled around her.

Belamae watched intently.

Wendra moved the song into a faster rhythm. Higher notes. *Rougher* notes. She sang of gambling tables and auction blocks and dark poets. She sang about Jastail. And the sound of it shrilled from her throat as anger got inside the song.

The bottom of her pain.

The water around her began to roil and churn. The ripples rose like small waves. The musical splash of water against the stone became frantic. It heaved over the edge of the pool like tide after tide.

She hardly noticed any of it. And gave more to her song.

Things turned dark and bright in her eyes. A mosaic. Like they had in the mountains, singing down a band of Bar'dyn. And the highwayman.

She sang that moment. The moment when he'd tried to sell her womb to the Bourne. The boy, too. Penit. She sang about the contrast in her eyes that turned the world white and black.

Something inside her resonated deep and angry.

Around her the water erupted upward in gouts, forming the mountain scene.

As she sang it, it came to watery life. Jastail striking her in the face. Bar'dyn figures ready to take what they wanted. Penit being pulled. Jastail negotiating even as he lost control.

And her song.

Dark and bright.

It tore from her throat like a controlled scream. Melody inside it, but filled with a torturous rasp.

The water moved in the air above and around the pool. Bar'dyn tried to flee, amazement clear in their faces.

And Wendra was there. A figure at the center of it all, standing above her as she related what had happened with the same sounds that gave it life the first time.

The chamber filled with the sound of rushing water, like a great falls.

She screamed it out until the memory of another voice joined her. And in moments her dark song ebbed. And the battle depicted in watery forms heaving through the air . . . lost form and fell down. It splashed over her, leaving her wet and cold. The chamber echoed with the sounds of a flood as water thundered home again to the pool.

Wendra dropped hard to her knees at the center of the dais, drenched. Her song retreated back inside, but left her heart racing. Panting, she lay down on the wet stone. Her vision swam with the same stark mosaic, until her eyes, slowly, focused again on the world and its color.

She was in Descant Cathedral.

She had sung for Belamae. And it had left her feeling feverish again.

The cool water helped, and she rolled over, placing her cheek against the wet stone.

A pair of feet came into few. The Maesteri hunkered down beside her. She looked up at him.

"That's one hell of a song, my girl." There was worry in his eyes. "My deafened gods . . ."

CHAPTER FIFTY

A Servant's Tale, Part II

It's not a prison if you choose to stay.

—*The Rigor of Choice,* an Emerit guide to self-discipline

I do," Rolen said with a quiet steadfastness. "I *choose* to stay bound here in the stinking bowels of Solath Mahnus. But with good reason."

The Sheason cleared his throat. "Several years ago the Recityv Council debated a new law known as the Civilization Order."

Tahn nodded. He'd heard Vendanj speak of it.

"The League called it a progression in civility. Only two days did the debate rage before it was ratified. The order was read into the Library of Common Understanding. Anyone rendering the Will is subject to execution."

A pained silence followed.

"The League claims what a Sheason does makes for a slothful working class, destroys self-reliance." Rolen shook his head, and smiled in disbelief. "They mocked us. Said ours is the work of scops, deceiving others for gain, manipulating them to our own advantage. Some even called us spies for the Quiet."

"You didn't fight back?" Tahn asked.

"Our call is to serve," Rolen said with halting speech. "Some of us thought we could do so without having to render."

"Obviously Vendanj wasn't one of them," Tahn said.

"Vendanj isn't posted in Recityv." Rolen's half smile suggested he knew Vendanj. "And so far, thank our abandoning gods, the Civilization Order hasn't moved beyond Vohnce. But it's nevertheless helped drive a wedge between Sheason."

Rolen sipped some water, and swallowed hard in the dark.

"Some Sheason ignore the law," Rolen continued, nodding as he spoke. "They use the Will as they please. They argue they're doing the ethical thing, even when it's not legal."

"Is that what brought you here?" Tahn asked.

Rolen became quiet for a long moment. "I don't agree with Vendanj, or others like him. I may not like the law, but I respect it. And I don't think it's always necessary to render the Will to help someone." Again he grew quiet. "And yet . . .

"Two months ago, a young girl came to my door. Leia. She's twelve. For months she'd been helping me hand out food and clothes down on 'beggars' row.' She was sobbing, and said her sister had suddenly fallen sick. Very sick.

"She pulled me through rainy, empty roads in the small hours of the night. Led me to a modest house in the merchant district. A thin lamp burned in the window. The rest of the street was dark. The one-room home was cluttered with boxes and sundries.

"Her little sister, only four years old, lay on a pile of rags and old clothes in the corner. Kneeling over her were her parents, speaking softly and wiping her brow with a damp cloth. The roof was leaking. And the smell of mold and wet wood were strong. Leia's home was one step from beggars' row itself. Her family worked hard to get by.

"Her father looked up as I entered. I could see concern in his face as he began to shake his head. But his wife's hand came to rest on his own. He looked back at her, then down at his little girl. Some internal debate waged for a few moments. Then he sighed and nodded.

"I removed my cloak and went to the little girl's side. Next to her father, I could see the man weeping silent tears. It's the kind of grief parents learn when their children are close to death. . . . I've seen it too many times.

"I felt for fever, listened to the child's breath and blood. It was too late. Leia's sister was dying and there was nothing I could do for her . . . unless I broke the law and rendered the Will to save her.

"That's when I saw it. Something familiar. A cloak tucked under the girl's head as a pillow. Pulling back one fold of the garment, I found the crest of the League emblazoned on russet wool. If there was danger in helping someone by use of the Will, then rendering on a leagueman or his family . . . was plain foolish.

"I understood the look in the man's eyes. He was a member of the League. My presence in his home was dangerous for him and his family.

"And for me, the law was clear. Using the Will meant death if I was caught.

"I cursed the law then. How could letting the girl die be an advancement in civility? All the arguments that our Order hindered self-sufficiency and promoted idleness fell away like so much wax from a spent candle. They'd fashioned hatred and mistrust of Sheason into a law that could bring me here to this prison." Rolen slammed his fist against stone. "For the crime of saving a dying child.

"I turned to the girl's father, whose name I never learned, and meant to tell him of my dilemma." Rolen's wheezing ceased. "But I never did. I saw the terror in his eyes at the prospect of having to watch his little girl die. The anguish of it got inside me. I'd seen too much suffering already. Suffering that might have been avoided if it weren't for this law." Rolen gave a dry laugh in the shadows. "I even had the audacity to think that helping a member of the League might somehow change their attitude about the Sheason.

"So, I leaned close and put my hands on her head. I spoke the words, and called health from myself into the child's fevered body.

"When the girl opened her eyes, her mother took her gently into her arms. Around the child, she reached and touched my hand, a strange mix of gratitude and regret in her eyes.

"I understood that look," Rolen said with sympathy, "since the woman knew what might happen to me if others found out what I'd done. But there was something more.

"When I put my hands on the girl, I learned of the deception that had ensnared me. This child burned from a poison fabricated by League hands. The truth of it passed into me as my Forda passed into her. This little girl had been poisoned to test her family's loyalty to the League and my obedience to the Civilization Order.

"At the moment of healing I still could have stopped, saved myself. But the child would have died." He came momentarily into the light, a satisfied smile on his lips. "She didn't die. So I'm able to suffer my irons just fine." Rolen jangled his chains.

"The rest happened very quickly. The door burst open and six leaguemen carrying swords surrounded me. Coarse oaths were uttered. They feigned jabs with their weapons, and laughed as I flinched. I remember asking only that they close the door; the cold air was bad for the child.

"They put me in cuffs, then turned on the family and asked which one had sought the Sheason to heal the girl. The question surprised the parents. Do you know why?" Rolen asked.

Tahn nodded. "Because how would they have known the girl was sick. You said it came on sudden."

Rolen took a deep breath and let it out slow. "But I knew this already. In healing the child, the poison had revealed much to me. The League had suspected the family of being sympathetic to the Sheason—Leia helped me pass out bread on beggars' row. Poisoning the child would either prove their suspicions, if the family asked me to heal her; or if they didn't ask me, and the child would die, proving the family's loyalty.

"The leagueman asked again who had conspired with me to commit treason by asking me to heal the girl. Leia backed into the corner, her face pale with the realization of her crime.

"The Civilization Order calls for the death not only of the Sheason who renders the Will, but anyone who seeks a Sheason to do so.

"Leia's father stood. 'It was me,' he said. 'I couldn't watch my daughter suffer.'

"I could see their suspicion as he took the blame. A horrible silence fell over the room. The girl's father shared a long look with his wife. A good-bye look.

"He gave his wife and youngest daughter each a kiss on the forehead, and then swept up Leia in a tight embrace. He whispered something in her ear, and left her weeping as the League escorted him and me from the room. As we left, I saw the woman crawl into the corner with her children, thanks and loss in her eyes.

"That very night I came here," Rolen said, his voice far away. "I've stayed precisely because they expected me to escape. If I rendered the Will, took myself out of here, I'd be saying I'm above the strong law."

The Sheason took several breaths. "Still the snare worked doubly well: confirming distrustful feelings many of the people hold for Sheason, and keeping them preoccupied with small, local strife while greater threats roll toward us."

When he finished speaking, Rolen backed into his corner and sat, wheezing.

Tahn shook his head and looked up at the door where another guard walked by, momentarily blocking the shaft of light. "But why sentence you to death? The punishment doesn't seem to fit the crime."

Rolen laughed quietly. "Because as the League will tell you, a small act of disobedience is the sign of a dangerous man, a man who will eventually undermine civility itself." His voice echoed with bitter amusement. "Not unlike you."

Tahn made the mistake of smiling. His cracked and swollen lips stabbed him with pain. "Me. And I haven't even had my Standing." He calculated the days in his mind. "It's tomorrow."

"Tomorrow?" Rolen's surprise came gilded with condolence.

"It's all right," Tahn said. "My father went to his earth years back. So I didn't have a First Steward, anyway."

Though I still wanted to mark the moment.

"Still not the place you must have imagined it would happen," Rolen offered.

"In a piss hole? No, not really." Tahn shifted, his bruised ribs needing some relief. "But I'll get older one way or another. I suppose even prison has no hold on time."

Filth. Cold. Indifferent rock. Shadow. Raw skin. The unmusical sound of chains. And an unhappy story of a Sheason choosing death. These would be his memories of his Standing.

Rolen crawled toward him in the darkness. The scrape of flesh over the stony floor, accompanied by the dragging of iron-link tethers, got inside Tahn. He raised his hammer scar to his face, to again feel the old familiar comfort. Not much this time.

Then a hand came into the yellow light that fell between him and Rolen. The manacle had rubbed a scar so deep into the man's skin that beneath it was a thick ring of scabrous flesh. Above the hand floated the blurred edges of the man's face. A kind face. Tugging at his own chain, and ignoring the burn in his shoulder, Tahn reached for Rolen, and clasped his hand in a pale wash of light from the barred window above.

• CHAPTER FIFTY-ONE •

Sodality and the Blade of Seasons

The Sheason were divided once—when some went into the Bourne with Maldea. We're only ever at odds with ourselves over one issue: use of the Will.

—From the Cautionary Lecture given to all Sulivon
—those training to become Sheason

Braethen's legs and back ached, his hands throbbed. But all the hours of riding couldn't steal the wonder of beholding the grandeur of Recityv. A few windows glowed with candles; others, high and dark, caught the long rays of starlight like heavenly winks.

Mira assumed the lead and turned left, following a series of narrow alleys and rear streets where garbage lay clustered outside back doors. Cobbled stone lay slick with the sour runoff of the refuse, a few stinking heaps steaming warmly in the chill air. More than one beggar curled close to these sources of warmth, using the waste as pillow and blanket. Even the stench of offal and human filth seemed not to bother the alley people.

Soon, they passed from the merchant district to a quarter dominated by large homes and inns with stables. Mira reined in at the rear of a multi-story house. A courtyard lay behind a wrought-iron fence that stood twice the height of a man. Into the fence, the ironmonger had worked the sigil of the Sodality.

Braethen's pulse quickened. Members of his own order. He'd never met one.

Mira swung down from her saddle and scaled the fence. She walked the inner court to the back door, and rapped softly. A moment later the door opened without the accompaniment of a lamp. The fellow followed Mira to the gate, keyed the lock, and motioned them all inside. The man still wore his bedclothes, but didn't seem discomfited by the intrusion. He locked the gate behind them and jogged to the small stable in one corner of the fenced yard. Again he opened the door and let them in.

When the horses had been tended, the man led them to the house, never speaking, and leaving lights off even once they sat to table in a dining area adjacent to the door. High windows admitted the neutral lunar light, paling the face of their host—a middle-aged man with thinning brown hair and a strong face. The moonlight cast shadows of the others across the table.

"I apologize for the caution of darkness, Vendanj," the man began. "But we're watched more closely since Rolen's arrest."

Vendanj turned to face the man. "Arrested for what, Malick?"

"The League laid a snare for him." The man shook his head in disgust. "They poisoned the child of one of their own men. Wanted to test the man, and Rolen, too. See if they'd keep the law. Rolen's being held in the pits beneath Solath Mahnus. He won't rescue himself, and waits there to be sentenced."

"The Civilization Order calls for death," Mira said.

"Sentence of *when* to die, not *whether* to die," Malick clarified.

Vendanj's anger was tangible. Mira seemed poised to attempt a rescue that very moment. Grant made an incredulous noise, chuffing air out his nose.

"Catching Rolen has earned the League support among the people," Malick added. "It doesn't take much to incite suspicion of a renderer. And a Sheason who breaks the law reinforces the *need* for that law."

"Has any appeal been made?" Grant asked.

"The Court of Judicature has voted on it," Malick said ruefully. "It's too late."

"Perhaps not," Grant replied.

"The leagueman was *also* convicted of treason. Sentenced to hang." Malick smiled bitterly.

"I would have liked to have spoken with him," Vendanj said.

"You still can," Malick said. "Before he dropped from the gallows, an arrow severed his rope."

Vendanj sat slowly forward. "By whose hand?"

"Don't know him." Malick hunched his shoulders. "The League claims he's not one of theirs. I believe them. The leagueman was set up to be an example." He paused, seeming to consider. "I suspect it wasn't someone from the city.

"Convocation has flooded Recityv with aspirants and countrymen claiming lower seats." Malick shook his head with mild disgust. "Few real seat holders have arrived. It'll be weeks before some can make their way here. Meantime, pretenders come in droves, following the scent of fortune and the promise of a name to be earned in war."

"There's talk of war?" Vendanj asked.

"War always follows Convocation." Malick sighed. "But it's not just politicians who come. You saw them beyond the wall. *These* men are sent by their mothers, their wives, landfolk who say that in the great stretches between Recityv and Con Laven Flu they've seen the Quiet. Men and boys sent here to prepare for war because they want to protect their families."

Braethen nodded. Over the past few days they'd passed fields where plows had been left in the midst of tilling, empty stock pens. People were fleeing for the protection of cities with walls.

"There are so many, that a writ was issued to restrict who can enter the city." Malick shook his head again. "Hay forks, crooked staffs, sharpened hoes, old plow horses, and cabbage boots, Vendanj. While inside, the streets teem with scion nobles and charlatans jockeying for a commission to raise their own esteem, the fields fill with unlikely soldiers come to defend their home."

Malick looked up at Vendanj. "The archer who rescued the leagueman is probably one of these fellows, who managed to slip through the gates. A noble wouldn't flirt with the law."

"Where's this archer who cut him loose?" Grant demanded.

"From what we've heard, he's been thrown in with Rolen—the League's idea of insult and justice, no doubt. They'll try it as a high crime—"

"Did this archer act alone?" Mira cut him off.

"He came with another. Both are down in the pits. Don't know their names. The one is cursed in the streets as simply the Archer. The other—"

"Did he wear a glove?" Mira pressed.

"The glove of the Sedagin," Malick said, nodding. "Do you know him?"

"We do," Braethen broke in. "Both of them. They're friends." For the first time Malick gave Braethen a long look. "I'm Braethen," he said, introducing himself and extending a hand toward Malick in the cold light of the moon.

As they clasped hands, Braethen instinctively folded his first finger back into Malick's palm. At the token, Malick's jaw dropped visibly. He likewise folded his first finger back, and squeezed Braethen's hand in an iron grip. "And we are one," he said.

Malick's gaze whipped to Vendanj, seeming to seek confirmation.

The Sheason nodded gravely. "And he wears the Blade of Seasons, Malick. I've entrusted it to him."

Malick's expression turned incredulous. "That so?"

"Perhaps there are things for the two of you to discuss," Vendanj suggested, then shifted in his seat, seeming to refocus. "The man they call Archer must be set free, both him and his friend."

Malick nodded as though receiving an assignment. "We could snatch them from the prison. We have friends among the ranks."

"No," Grant said, his voice soft but not to be argued with. "This is why you brought me, Vendanj." He turned on Malick. "Take a message to the Halls at Solath Mahnus. The note will say that justice demands a hearing on the conduct of this Archer. It will say that there's evidence this leagueman isn't guilty and was rightly saved from execution. It will claim the law of Preserved Will against any who try to deny the hearing."

For a long moment, no one spoke.

"Can this Dissent win?" Malick asked, uncertainty thinning his voice.

Grant didn't answer, but turned a determined look on Vendanj. The Sheason nodded agreement. "Mira, find the convicted leagueman's family. Bring them here. We'll need to speak with them before the Dissent."

Without hesitation, Mira slipped out the back door. Grant's determined eyes grew distant in the moonlight, as if filled with memory.

"You'll take the message to the courts yourself, Malick," Vendanj said, breaking the silence. "I'll need to speak with Helaina at some point, but we'll see to this Dissent first. Better to ask her favor as little as possible."

Malick nodded. "There are rooms upstairs, if you're ready to rest." He turned to Braethen. "I'll stay behind if you'd like."

Braethen nodded eagerly. "I would, thanks."

Vendanj and Grant followed a hall deeper into the manor and could be heard ascending the stairs. Braethen turned to face Malick. He'd longed for the day when he might speak with one who shared his ideals. He didn't know where to begin.

Malick spoke first. "You're new to the Sodality. That's plain enough. What would you like to know? First principles? Our history? How to—"

"No offense," Braethen cut in, "but I've probably read every book that describes all that."

"Use of a blade maybe?" Malick suggested, a bit of condescension in his tone.

Braethen shook his head. "Where I'm from we get some basic instruction. And I'm not going to master swordwork in an evening no matter how good you are with a blade."

Malick exhaled long and slow. "What then?"

"This Rolen . . ." Braethen struggled to frame his question. "It seems he's Sheason, and yet not Sheason—"

"Oh, he's Sheason, all right," Malick said with an easy laugh. "What you're feeling is the division in the Order. Two ways of doing things."

Braethen made a circular motion with his hand, encouraging Malick to explain.

"Rolen may not like the law hereabouts, but he keeps it." Malick turned and spat—not, it seemed, a comment on Rolen. "For the most part, anyway," Malick amended. "He saved that little girl, but he knew he was violating the Civilization

Order. His way of serving is to abide by the laws of those he serves. I admire it, even if it drives me shithouse crazy."

Braethen looked at the ceiling, beyond which Vendanj took his rest. "And what about Vendanj?"

A strange smile spread on Malick's lips. "Vendanj goes his own way. He's led only by his conscience. Couldn't give a good godsdamn for law. He's as sure as Rolen that the way he serves is the right way to help folk."

Braethen understood, but it led to a difficult question. "How does the Sodality decide which to stand beside?"

Malick fixed him with a tight gaze. "We stand beside a Sheason, Braethen, no matter how he chooses to serve. That's our calling. To step into the breach that allows a Sheason the time necessary to make his own sacrifice."

"What if his intentions are wrong?" Braethen challenged.

"I suppose he would cease to be Sheason, and would be called something darker."

Braethen nodded to that. "Are there many like Vendanj?"

"If you mean Sheason that follow their own mind, a few. And growing." Malick scrubbed his face as if to freshen himself. "But if you mean with the same ability, then no. Vendanj . . . I've heard other Sheason marvel at his gift. The authority to render is conferred on those deemed worthy, but it doesn't come in equal measures. Vendanj understands the blend of Forda I'Forza as naturally as you or I breathe."

One question remained.

Braethen stared straight at Malick. "And what of this?" He put his palm to the sword on his hip. Malick didn't follow the movement. It wasn't necessary. The man's face looked back, impassive, unreadable. The cords in Braethen's back and chest tensed.

Malick let a quirky half grin move his lips. "That, my friend, is more than I could tell you . . . more than I know, myself. It's got memory in it. I know that. But the blade is a blessing and a threat I don't really understand. Guard it. Raise it when you must. And learn by it as surely as you have your books." His eyes seemed to see something through Braethen, past him. "Lasting hell, son, I don't like your luck."

CHAPTER FIFTY-TWO

A Last Pageant

The great secret is that troupers don't perform rhea-fols as propaganda or sedition. It's all a rehearsal for our own lives. We're terribly unassured.

> —From the recorded confession of a convicted pageant
> wagon owner

They stared at Sutter, unspeaking, eyes wide as though amazed they could be seen at all. Or perhaps the glossy whites of those eyes were simply the hundred-league stares of the dead.

Mists licked at him, creeping across the stone floor, swirling around their feet. The ethereal creatures stood with yearning expressions like they wanted to talk with Sutter . . . but could not.

And it was cold. To the bone. Just as it had been on the night he'd seen a spirit from the window in Leagueman Gehone's house.

Sutter's heart raced. He pulled at his chains, trying to get further away. He wanted to cry out, but his voice failed. This time, neither Tahn or the leagueman were around to help. And these two . . . creatures stood staring at him, their wide eyes caught in that eternal look of surprise and need.

Nightmare? Fever dream?

The trembling in his arms and legs grew so violent that his chains began to rattle. The sound of it rose into the deathly scene.

I'm going to die. I'll never see Da again . . . tell him thanks. . . .

It was the chill of the grave. Had to be. He pressed himself into the floor, waiting to die, and heard distantly his own weak moan.

"Sutter." An intruding voice. "Sutter!"

He stared up into the face of Thalen, at the end of his tether, calling his name. In an instant, something changed. Sutter looked around the cell. The mists were gone. The figures were gone. He gasped a long painful breath, and let out a loud cry.

"He's having the tremors." It was one of the scops against the other wall. "Give him some water."

Thalen took up a bowl and wetted Sutter's lips.

"He'll be all right. Have him keep drinking, even the filth they're providing. It'll help." The man spoke with the assurance of a father who's had sick children.

Long moments passed, and Sutter began to feel normal again. "Thank you," he managed.

"No thanks necessary, my boy," the scop said. "Precious little to be done here." His chain rattled as he waved a hand at the room. "I figure what I can do, I must."

Sutter pushed himself up. "Why are you here?"

"We await trial on grounds of sedition."

Another scop piped in. "We played the cycle of the First Promise in the square south of Solath Mahnus. The League didn't take kindly to the subtle suggestion that its own order was not only unnecessary, but unfortunate."

A weak laugh came out of the dark from yet another of the beaten players.

On their left the door opened, spilling harsh light down on them. Sutter blinked back tears at the intrusion, then shaded his eyes so that he could catch a better look at the pageant wagon folk across from him. One of the women had buried her head in her knees, maybe shielding her eyes from the light, or maybe feeling hopeless. But the faces he *could* see still held the sloppy, exaggerated face paint their jailors had put on them to make them look like fools.

"Quiet down there," a voice barked. "You'll get yer chance to entertain us later. You'd best save yer strength for yer performance."

The door shut with a bang, echoing down on them.

"I am Niselius. Why are *you* here?" the first man asked Sutter in a whisper.

"A friend of mine saved a leagueman from his rope. I guess heroism has its punishment." Sutter smiled, but his swollen face twinged and he let it go.

"That'll be our fate, as well," a woman said. "They'll make an example of us to scare other troupes from their wagons. I'm Mapalliel. Nice to share the darkness with you."

The woman uttered a mild laugh—something he could appreciate in the bowels of this pit.

"I'm Sutter." He shifted to a less painful position. "If it's really so dangerous, why do you do it?"

Mapalliel answered. "For me, there aren't many choices. For most women, come to that. If you've no husband and no dowry, there are precious few things a man with coin will pay you to do." She thought a moment. "And the wagons have a kind of honor of their own. It may be true that some of the rhea-fols carry double meaning—lessons from the past. But execution for playing a pageant? The regent has lost the fist inside her glove if it comes to this."

"Isn't it the League?" Sutter asked.

"Sure, they're behind it," Niselius said. "But law requiring such severe punishment would have to be ratified by the High Council. The regent oversees its affairs. Something's amiss up there." Chains rattled as an arm pointed up toward the heights of Solath Mahnus.

"This then is civility." This was a new voice, softer. And its owner was too deep in the dark to be seen. But it came as through the swollen lips of one beaten badly in the face. "The League suppresses the stories they believe threaten their plans."

The silence resumed. Deeper for the darkness around them.

Pageant wagon players. Like his first parents. The ones who left him. Pity wasn't easy for Sutter to summon.

Though something about the maniacal, painted grins on the beaten faces of these simple pageant players left him with a bit of pity, all the same.

"Come, enough of this brooding," Niselius demanded. "Let's make a rhea-fol even here. This one for ourselves." He stood, extending a hand to Mapalliel to help her to her feet.

Sutter watched as the other two scops dragged themselves up. They all stood in a line.

Niselius bowed. "What will it be, my friends? What story would you have of us?"

Sutter could think of nothing, but didn't have to. Behind him from his nook, Thalen asked evenly, "*The Last Harvest of the Reapers*."

The troupe stood in silent reverence for a few moments. Then, with a grave nod from their leader, they began. They told an amazing tale of heroism at the farthest reaches of the north and west, of the time that gave name to the Valley of Sorrow. When the Quiet stood in awful might against a small army and a band of Sheason.

> *The Velle rained down fire and wind upon the surviving few of the Second Promise. And the advancing line of Quietgiven came as a dark wave that would roll them under in minutes. Near to utter defeat, with the trained, armored soldiers of Recityv all but destroyed, the small battalion out of Risill Ond arrived after a three-day forced march with no sleep.*
>
> *But the farmers, come with pole-length and short-handle scythes, did not pause. They marched past the Sheason, who needed enough time and relief to join their hands for a final rending of earth and heaven to bring an end to their battle. Directly into harm's path they went, creating a mighty line of men with little else but their sickles.*
>
> *Muscle hardened by long seasons of fieldwork held the Quiet at bay, cutting down the enemy in a hard wave. They gave the Sheason the*

time they desperately needed. And when the great calling of the Will went up, every last man from Risill Ond lay dead upon the ground, most with their tools still gripped tight in their fists.

It would always be said of them that they thrust their implements of harvest with strength and faith after crossing the world to buy a moment's time with their very lives.

The troupe finished, their own faces in awe of what they'd just played. A quiet pride filled Sutter's chest—the kind that made one see more valor in his own simple past. Behind him, Thalen sniffed. Sutter imagined the man's hand-sewn emblem on an old rug and the honor that brought him here to fulfill an oath made generations ago.

Above them, the door slammed open. Light intruded on the darkness again. Their turnkey bustled in and unfastened two of the scops without a word, herding them up the stairs toward the outer door. One of these was the woman who'd spent most of her time with her head down on her own knees. As she began to shuffle her bare feet over the cold stone, she looked down at Niselius and spoke in a broken voice, "Tell my children I love them."

Tears coursed down her face.

At the door she and her fellow scop looked back at their friends, and that's when Sutter knew their faces. Captured in the light at the door, the bruises and blood and garish paint faded to the true faces beneath.

They were the faces in his waking nightmare.

The faces of the dead.

It hit Sutter with a horrible certainty, just as he now realized that he'd seen the spirit of the woman burned at Ulayla in his window the night before her execution.

The door closed, leaving them to their troubled hush and obscurity.

Sutter wept silent tears, knowing that the woman would never see her little ones again. Nor would they see her.

And that too touched the old wounds. Sutter cried for each of them.

CHAPTER FIFTY-THREE

The Lesher Roon

The Roon was predicated on a Monderan race run by men over many days, with tests of strength and judgment along its path.

—From the League roster of "Potential Allies or Threats"

Wendra stepped into the street that fronted Descant Cathedral. Seanbea accompanied her on her right, Penit holding her hand on the left. The boy involuntarily squeezed her fingers as he took in the festive decorations of a city virtually transformed overnight. Even the streets in the cathedral district celebrated the Lesher Roon, streamers dipping in low arcs between shops, lintels and sills adorned in makeshift garlands fashioned from corn husks and dried vines. Men and women walked about with small sprigs fastened to a lapel or hanging from a breast pocket, showing their support for the race.

Penit started ahead, pulling her along. She smiled, and followed willingly.

Seanbea laughed at the boy's enthusiasm. "He might win."

"If he does, what happens next?" she asked.

"He'd be given rooms in Solath Mahnus. Tutors." Seanbea nodded at the value of it. "He'd serve as Child's Voice until his own Change. Pretty fair trade for winning a race."

It was precisely what she'd hoped. If he won, she wouldn't have to worry about him. She swung Penit's hand. "Do you think you can win?"

Penit gave her a sidelong glance. "Troupers learn to run fast. To keep our skins."

Wendra smiled, and as they went, began watching for Tahn and the others—her real reason for getting out into the city. She hoped her friends had gotten to Recityv safe.

But she already missed Descant. Belamae had shown her a few wonders of music, and hinted at techniques she could learn to master her song. The ways to compose and organize music astounded her. And she'd only been there a day.

Past the end of the street, the crowds thickened. Barkers called out food and drink for sale. Street performers sang songs about the Roon. Bystanders spoke excitedly to one another. Some placed wagers.

Carriages and wagons in the streets, bridles and wheels woven with yet more garland. And here and there a child near Penit's age received advice from parents or other adults as they streamed toward the Halls of Solath Mahnus.

They moved past men and women with entourages—standards raised on poles marked areas of the street for families of station. Penit occasionally jumped to see what lay ahead, his small hand slick and sweaty with anticipation.

As the time of the race drew near, movement became difficult, people jamming the thoroughfares and halting all progress except by foot.

Seanbea led them down two less-crowded alleys and brought them out onto a wide concourse that crossed to a wall separating Solath Mahnus from the rest of the city.

"This is part of the course," he explained. "The children follow the line engraved into the street. It takes them around the Wall of Remembrance and through a few of the old roads of Recityv where the first regents lived. The race passes beneath their verandas. Then back here, ending at the gate to the courtyard." He pointed across from them. "Families with runners are allowed to stand against the wall to cheer them on. The rest line the outer side of the square."

Wendra listened distractedly. She searched the crowds for signs of Tahn, Sutter, and the others. There were so many people. She soon realized the folly of hoping to chance upon them in such a vast city. But she looked anyway, as Seanbea led them toward a table set near the wall gate.

While they stood in a line of parents giving last-minute instructions to their children, others called cheers and encouragement to the kids.

"A regent's right lad," one yelled.

"The truest voice at the High Table, you'll be," called another. "Don't let them intimidate you."

"Hey, Simba's jaybird is small enough," one fellow bellowed. "Don't that qualify him to race?" Those around him wailed with laughter.

Wendra couldn't help but smile, naturally assuming the meaning of "jaybird." In no time, they stood at the table, where two men sat with pleasant, intelligent faces.

"Are you running today, boy?" one asked.

"Yes, please," Penit enthused.

"Very well. Is this your mother?" The man looked up at Wendra with thoughtful eyes.

Wendra froze. She stared back at the man blankly.

"That's right," Seanbea interjected. "She's a little overwhelmed here. First time in Recityv."

"Ah, well, don't let it frighten you. We're a little crowded these days, but Recityv citizens are decent. Isn't it so?" The man turned to his partner at the table.

"You speak truth," said the other. "May we have your names?"

Wendra gave her name and Penit's to the recorder, who wrote them in a ledger. After their names lay scrawled on the page, the man gave Penit a blue pin to place on his shirt. He then leveled a serious gaze on the boy.

"Run hard but run fair, son. The only loser is the one who doesn't give the Roon all he has. But the cheater disgraces the Roon, and earns himself a month in the regent's stables as a helpmate to Gasher." He turned to his partner. "Would you ever want to work for old Gasher?"

"Oh, my, no!" his friend said. "He's an awful crank. Every minute would be drudgery. Wouldn't want that."

"I won't cheat," Penit put in. "And I'll win. You'll see."

"A champion's attitude," the recorder said. He winked at Seanbea and Wendra and motioned for them to move to the left.

The children lined up behind a broad ribbon stretched from the gate to a building across the concourse. A line of guards held the crowd back on the far side. A man carrying a baton came forward and offered to escort Wendra and Seanbea to a place along the wall from which to observe the race. She looked down at Penit, the boy's eyes brimming with confidence.

"Just have fun," she said, and kissed him on the cheek.

Penit nodded and suddenly cried out, "Dwayne." He rushed to a boy amid a host of other children. He talked excitedly with the other boy, the two jabbering about things Wendra couldn't quite hear, though she knew the two had met in the slave town of Galadell. Then the man with the baton led her and Seanbea to a place along the wall near the gate to the inner courtyard.

More contestants gave their names and were herded to the ribbon. The mass of children stood a hundred across and perhaps ten deep. Some of those waiting there were no more than six years old, eager parents enrolling them in the Roon with vain hope. The largest boys bulled their way to the front. Girls made up nearly half the runners, some taller even than the largest of the boys.

The racers fidgeted and looked over their shoulders toward parents who continued to shout instructions to them over the din. Youthful faces wore unsure expressions but nevertheless nodded understanding; other children shook their heads side to side in confusion. Penit stood in the middle of the pack with Dwayne, the two still avidly talking.

The hum of the crowd rose suddenly to a roar, as trumpets blared into the sunny air over the wall. The men at the table closed their books and drew their instruments back from the street into the courtyard. A stiff-looking man with a thin mustache appeared from the inner gate door and began to speak. His first words were lost beneath the tumult, but the gathering quickly quieted.

". . . this running of the Lesher Roon for the Child's Seat at the High Table, to sit at council with those who speak for their constituents. So then, do we, by tradition and law, draw our Child's Voice from this worthy field of contestants."

Another roar rose from the throng. The man went on, but his words ended before the people quieted again. The gentleman walked in stately fashion to the head of the ribbon and solemnly cast his eyes over the runners. Above frenzied speculation and last-second admonitions from parents, Wendra could just make out the man's words—the same exhortation that the recorder had made of Penit: "Run hard but run fair."

Confetti and streamers began to rain down from windows and rooftops. Trumpets blazed a triumphant fanfare. And the children hunched, ready to run.

The man strode to the wall and lifted his baton, taking the ribbon in hand. At the far side of the concourse, another did likewise. Amidst colored confetti and shouts and horns, the two men dropped their batons simultaneously, letting go the ribbon. In a spurt, a thousand children dashed ahead to claim the coveted prize of the Lesher Roon.

Several fell as legs locked and intertwined, but each quickly jumped up and joined the lurching mob. The thrill of the race got inside Wendra as she watched the children find their pace. She could still see Penit, his head bobbing with quick steps. He ran firmly ensconced in the pack. She cheered his name. The shouts and exultation of the masses deafened Wendra's own, but she waved toward Penit as the children rounded the first corner.

When all the runners had disappeared, she looked up at Seanbea, who gave her a quirky smile. "Gets in you, doesn't it?"

She smiled back and nodded, turning to where the children would circle back through the concourse. The crowd simmered, their jubilation falling to murmurs and bubbling expectation. Men and women continued to fill the air with confetti and streamers as the crowd awaited the return of the runners from around the outer wall of Solath Mahnus.

In the distance, the roar of spectators rose in a moving wave as the dashers passed them in their course. The sound of it grew more faint as the race approached the far side of the hill.

"What will you do if the boy wins?" Seanbea asked.

"Did you see the size of some of the runners?" She smiled wanly.

His eyebrows lifted to mark his point. "The Roon chooses who bears the seat, Wendra, not the child. It's a race, yes, but after all the child can do, something more aids the winner in crossing the ribbon."

"Sounds like a legend, like the White Stag or the Pauper's Drum." She stood on her tiptoes and looked in the direction the children would come.

"Legends come to us for reasons, Anais," Seanbea said. "Like the legends of songs that do more than entertain."

Wendra gave him a long look. His smile never faltered.

Far away, the cheering from the crowd began to cycle back toward them. As the roar of the crowd drew closer, those around Wendra and Seanbea began to fidget and call. The excitement of the race came before it like leaves stirred by prestorm wind.

Moments later, a pack of children rounded a corner and broke into a sprint down the long concourse. Twelve youngsters ran, their arms pumping, their hair rippling in the wind of their own speed. Across the cobbled street they flew, feet pounding in an impossible rhythm. Hands and arms rose in support as the runners raced past.

Twenty strides behind them, a second group of children came around the corner and another surge of cheers rose.

The first grouping came into clear view. Wendra rose up again on her toes and scanned their faces. Sweat streaked their cheeks and temples, matting hair to heads.

Two boys led the group, sprinting effortlessly. A handful of girls made up the middle of the pack, ponytails flipping to and fro with each long stride. A few more boys flanked the girls, eyeing their counterparts as they drove their legs forward.

At the back of the pack, Penit and Dwayne labored to keep pace with those at the front, their strides shorter and quicker than the long, graceful strokes of the others.

Wendra yelled Penit's name, but she could scarcely hear her own voice. In the midst of the deafening noise, she suddenly wondered if an unheard song held any power. But the thought fled her mind in the exuberance of cheering Penit on.

The colored bits of confetti showered like a blizzard in the street, swirling around the bodies of the children as they passed. Some small bits stuck to the sweat on their faces and forearms. Whistles pierced the din, noisemakers popped and rattled, and a few celebrants blew horns of their own.

Then the first pack turned and followed the course down a narrow side street. The crowds lined the route there, too. The throng lifted its roar down the roads where the Roon snaked out into the city. The sound reverberated off stone buildings.

The last runners passed them and followed the course down the street to Wendra's left just as the return route began to thrum with the excitement of the lead pack. Wendra could feel her heart pounding. Every beat fell like the blow of a hammer.

The intensity of the crowd was nothing to what it now became. Every onlooker howled and cheered at full voice. The force of the volume pressed at her eyes, tingled in her skin, and raised every hair on her body. She felt simultaneously like one dropped into a winter river and roasting on an oven spit. Waves of heat and chill raced down her arms and up her back.

Then Penit appeared from the return avenue.

His shoulders were bent, his arms driving with sheer determination. He emerged from the byway ten strides ahead of Dwayne. He'd found his own sure stride, his legs churning like a champion horse in long, powerful rhythms. His feet glided across the cobblestone, his heels never touching the ground. Tears of pride welled in Wendra's eyes as she added her voice to the incredible chorus around her.

Through the wide concourse Penit sprinted, seeming to gain speed with every stride. The crowd knew their winner, and screamed in anticipation of the ribbon, now again raised by the men bearing the batons.

Through the riverbanks of shouting celebrants Penit ran. The crowd's frenetic energy became a counterpoint to the smooth, elegant pace Penit kept as he dashed down the open concourse toward the finish line. He came closer, a calm but determined look on his face. The same look she'd seen when he'd gone out to find her help from the cave. She held her breath and embraced the joy that raced her heart.

Then, a strange look passed over Penit's features, a kind of thoughtful concern. He looked back over his shoulder at Dwayne, now twenty strides behind him, and the rest of the lead pack just emerging from the far avenue. His legs carried him forward, but in his eyes was a realization that hadn't yet reached his feet.

Fifteen paces from the ribbon, Penit stopped.

CHAPTER FIFTY-FOUR

Winners and Wisdom

The largest known amount paid to buy a vote on the High Council is ten thousand full realm marks. The vote was on land usage and taxes beyond the city wall.

> —From a list of court trivia kept by Solath Mahnus historians in their private study

Penit came to a skidding stop, his breathing labored, his eyes on the ribbon so close ahead.

The crowd erupted with frustrated expectation. Some jeered, others roared in confusion. Wendra noted the pitch shift to something deeper, less appreciative. Violent gestures exhorted Penit to finish the race. A few heads shook in annoyance.

Penit could have jogged the remaining distance and still won. Instead, he quarter-turned and watched as Dwayne came racing on. His friend gave him a curious look. Penit nodded, and returned an encouraging expression.

A moment later, Dwayne broke the ribbon. A roar of victory followed, and the boy was snatched up and placed on tall shoulders. A winner! Other children buzzed past Penit to finish for honor's sake. Some slowed and stopped, moving off to rejoin parents.

The crowd filled the street, rushing to congratulate Dwayne. A few sauntered close to Penit and gave him bewildered stares or cursed. Wendra fought through the wall of people to Penit, silencing his critics with a scathing glare. Seanbea forged a path for them back to the wall near the gate, where she knelt and embraced Penit for several moments before realizing he was not crying or upset.

She drew back and gave him a guarded look. "Why did you stop?"

He peered over her shoulder at Dwayne, his face a study in contentment that slowly became a smile.

A moment later, the race coordinator and a number of attendants dressed in city colors surrounded Dwayne and began escorting him toward the gate. The man holding the baton was nearly past her and Penit with his brusque, sensible stride, when he abruptly stopped beside them.

"You will come with me, all three of you," he said, pointing at Wendra and Seanbea while keeping his eyes fixed on Penit. "I'll have no discussion about my race. The regent and her table will hear an account of it from both you and Master Dwayne, and we'll let her decide what to do."

He pointed at each of them with his baton, then stepped smartly away, heading for the gate. The men in bright Recityv crimson folded them into the circle they'd formed around Dwayne and a shifty-looking man. Wendra thought she recognized the man's face, but couldn't quite place him.

Together, the five of them passed through the inner gate and onto the smooth surface of the Solath Mahnus courtyard. The stone clacked beneath their heels. Long slate slabs had been meticulously fitted together, rendering the yard virtually seamless. Dark marble benches edged the perimeter, here and there occupied by men in full armor and women in neatly pressed dresses. Planters stood on both sides of each stone bench, where manicured trees offered little shade, but prim decoration.

On the far side of the yard, a large archway tunneled into the hill. Above it rose the sprawling courts and halls of Solath Mahnus. Each roof showed crenellated abutments more decorative than useful. The stone of the outer walls had been carved with various crests denoting houses and families.

Their steward ushered Wendra, Seanbea, and Penit into the tunnel lit brightly with oil lamps. They passed several intersecting passages until finally they came to a wide stair guarded by four men bearing halberds. The fastidious baton wielder did not even bother to acknowledge the guards, fussing past them and up the stairs at a sturdy clip.

Wendra's legs had started to burn by the time they stepped into a wide, vaulted chamber. The room was appointed with suits of armor and weapons resting on oiled wood stands, pedestals bearing glass cases where sepia parchments sat atop easels. Murals hung painted on canvases several strides to a side, and long drapes in solid, dignified colors depended from brass rods fastened in the climbs of the room's great height. All around, charcoal-colored marble set in feathered patterns announced the dignity of court, and the refinement of artistry.

Their guide led them through the hall into a second chamber bordered by doors and dominated by a narrow stair that began in the middle of the room and ascended past the second and third floors, issuing them directly to the fourth story. Marble balustrades ran along the edges of each level, though Wendra had no idea how people found their way to those floors.

At the top, several soldiers stepped into their path in a practiced manner, and waited until the race coordinator said something to them before they would withdraw. They pushed through a large set of double doors, and saw a number of maps and long scrolls on tables where sat men and women, harried looks upon their faces.

At the back of this room stood another set of double doors guarded by eight men. The race coordinator impatiently waved them away as he approached. The soldiers gave way and the doors were drawn back to reveal a winding stair.

At the top of these final stairs was a set of doors that stood unattended. Wendra's stomach churned. She took Penit's hand, and as an afterthought, took Seanbea's hand as well.

Their guide stopped at the door and turned to face them.

"I've sent ahead for an audience." He looked them over one by one, pointing at each person with a crooked finger as though taking count. "This is an interruption the regent will permit because it bears on the completion of her High Table, but it is *not* an invitation to speak. If you are asked something, you may answer. 'My lady' is quite appropriate when addressing the regent. Otherwise, keep quiet."

The fellow didn't wait on questions or protests, and with a small grunt pushed open the heavy doors to the regent's High Office.

Every surface shone in alabaster marble. Arched windows running from floor to ceiling let sun into the chamber. There were two hearths attended by a cluster of high-back chairs and flat benches. A table set before each fireplace held books, some open as though left while being used. At the back of the High Office, a brass tableau had been fixed into the wall. It showed a king in full regalia removing his crown. Upon it, inscriptions gleamed in the light. Beneath it sat an elegant elderly woman in a large, upholstered chair behind a broad desk. To the right of the desk sat an old man with a grey-white beard, wearing a patient smile.

At the sight of the regent, Wendra felt the sudden urge to kneel. The woman had a commanding gaze, and seemed to be waiting.

The race coordinator cleared his throat apologetically and stepped forward, nodding to both the regent and her counselor. "My lady, Sheason Artixan, I present you the winner of the Lesher Roon and his father."

The woman stood. Her mantle fell to the floor in flowing folds. She hunched a bit from age. Lines in her face told of a life of fret and laughter. Yet her eyes sparkled with fire and clarity.

"I'm told the winner of the Child's Seat isn't as evident as you suggest." The regent indicated both boys.

"The boy who crossed the ribbon first isn't in dispute, my lady," the race coordinator replied. "But the *winner* may be."

"Don't draw it out, Jonel," she urged.

"This child," he began, motioning Dwayne to stand beside him, "crossed the ribbon ahead of the rest." He looked at Penit and brought him forward with a glance. "But this child led the race to within a house-length of the finish before stopping and letting the ribbon-taker pass him by."

The regent held up a hand. "Is this true?" she said, looking directly at Penit.

He nodded. The race coordinator gently pressed a knuckle in his back. "Yes, Anais, I mean, my lady."

Penit immediately looked up to see what danger he'd caused for himself in referring to the regent in such a way. Helaina surprised them all by smiling graciously.

"A long time since anyone honored me so," she said, sharing a look with the Sheason. "Wouldn't you agree, Artixan?"

"I would," the old man said, still wearing his smile.

"We're concerned that the children may have conspired to thwart the natural delegation of the Lesher Roon, my lady," the coordinator said. "And I put the matter before you to decide whether another race must be run, or the results of this Roon should stand. I'll have the records reflect my diligence selecting the appropriate Child's Voice."

The regent nodded once. "So noted, and wisely so, Jonel. Thank you." She then stood and rounded her desk, making her way with a slow, deliberate step. No one moved or spoke while she came to Penit. The sound of her shuffling steps filled the silent chamber.

At last she stood before them. "Come to me," she said, proffering her hands to Penit and Dwayne.

With a gentle shove from Jonel, they did as they were told, each taking one of the regent's hands.

"Your names?" she asked.

Each boy gave it.

She looked down at Dwayne, her eyes gripping him in a solemn stare. "Did you conspire with Penit to win the Roon?"

Dwayne shook his head. "No, my lady. I ran my hardest. I didn't expect Penit to stop, but when he did I just ran past him."

The regent gave a nod of satisfaction before turning to Penit with her iron stare. "And you, son, if you were sure to take the race, why did you stop?"

Penit looked back at Wendra, his eyes pleading. She gave him a reassuring nod. He turned back to the regent.

"Dwayne is much smarter than me, my lady, much smarter." He tried to look at his own feet, when the regent took his chin and lifted it again.

"And what has this to do with deliberately losing the Roon?"

Penit shrugged. "I wanted to win. Wendra and I have come a long way, and I thought if I won I could get us out of trouble with the Quiet and Vendanj and everybody." Wendra caught a start in the regent, who tightened her gaze on Penit. "But after I got close to the ribbon, something kind of hit me. Whoever wins the race has to make important decisions for the whole city. Dwayne will do a better job of it than I could. He knows more; he figures things out better than I do. If it was surviving on the street, that might be different. But it's not. So, if the children are going to have someone to speak for them, it should be Dwayne before me."

The regent gave Dwayne another look. The other boy stood dumbfounded.

"How do you know this about Dwayne?" the regent asked.

"We met at Galadell, that's where—"

"I was lucky to get him back," Dwayne's father blurted. Sweat had gathered on the man's forehead, though it was cool enough. "Was worried half to death."

The regent showed him a suspicious eye, then gestured for the boys to sit at her desk. She slowly retook her own chair, resting her aged body in the cushioned seat and gathering a breath before speaking.

"Go on now, Penit. And mind you speak the truth. We've no leniency for lies." She settled her keen eyes on the boy again.

"Wendra and I got taken by a highwayman to Galadell. First he took me because Wendra got sick and I went out looking for help." Penit rushed ahead with his story. "Wendra came and rescued me, but before she got there, I met Dwayne. He was being held for sale, too. They made us run a lot, the faster kids separated from the slower ones. Dwayne and I got put together, and food was better after that.

"Dwayne is very smart. He doesn't know as many of the stories as I do, or how to place a bet on a roadside game of dice. But he had a whole plan for escape, and I saw how he helped the younger kids when they got scared. He even helped the men and ladies, teaching them how to deal with the traders. I'm just glad he finally got out." Penit shot a look at Dwayne's father.

The regent held a finger to her lips as she listened. Her sharp gaze didn't vary as she assessed Penit's words. "But you must know the Roon selects its own. It's not for you to decide who takes the Child's Seat." Helaina spoke with a dignified calm, but certain sternness.

"Yes, my lady," Penit said. "But maybe the Roon is what made me stop. That's what I think." Penit ran his arms across the gloss of the table. "The race doesn't have a brain, it can't think. I decided that what the Roon meant was a race where all the children run and do their best to select one to sit at this table. I might be the fastest, my lady, but the best thing I can do is be sure you get the smartest one to help you do your ruling. That's Dwayne, no doubt."

The regent smiled around her finger.

"And anyway, now maybe I don't have to worry about the Bar'dyn and Vendanj and the rest. *You* can help them."

Helaina's smile faded from her aged lips. "You've seen the Bar'dyn, boy? And Vendanj, you've spoken with him?"

"Yes. Vendanj helped us get away from the Bar'dyn. So did Seanbea." Penit turned and smiled at the Ta'Opin. "But we got separated from the others. And we haven't seen them since."

"We will speak of these things later," the regent declared in an authoritative voice. "For now, I'm left with the trouble of who will sit at my table." She scrutinized each boy's face. "The rightful winner should have been Penit, who shows wisdom and humility in forfeiting the race.

"Still, the people have witnessed the ribbon falling to Dwayne, and will claim him as the rightful Voice." She sat back into her chair, straightening her hunched shoulders. "More than this, young Penit reminds us of the *spirit* of the Roon, the spirit of the *table.* We dishonor ourselves to question his sacrifice." She looked at Penit. "Besides, son, though I would be glad to have you take a permanent seat here, I trust your judgment on young Dwayne." She offered him a grateful smile.

The regent then looked at Artixan, who'd been mostly quiet. The Sheason nodded with a look of satisfaction. Just then, the door opened and a page bowed deep in apology.

"Excuse me, Regent," the page said. "But the Court of Judicature has been convened to hear a defense of the Archer."

"What is this?" the regent said, standing with some difficulty. Fire burned in her eyes. "We can't open this to law, there'll be riots."

"Pardon, my lady," the page went on. "Against the protest of our magistrate, the right to Preserved Will has been claimed, and the law still holds in the annals. I've been asked to convey you there to hear the Dissent and rule upon it. Lord Hiliard of the Court of Judicature doesn't wish to rule without your endorsement."

The regent looked around, the ire clear and bright in her face. On her wrinkled cheeks color rose. She didn't speak, her mouth a thin, tight line. Finally, she nodded.

"Follow me, Artixan," she said. "The rest of you, too. We'll continue after I put this matter behind us."

She bustled past them, her steps more sure now. Wendra went to Penit and gave him a gentle squeeze as they all followed the regent through the door and down the many steps toward the Court of Judicature.

CHAPTER FIFTY-FIVE

Preserved Will

Being right only goes so far where a jurist's opinion is concerned.
Trials are won in private rooms before Dissent begins.

—*The Practical Advocate,* an unsanctioned volume kept in the
home office of Recityv's First Counselor

Grant stepped back into the court that had sent him to the Scar.
Twenty godsdamned years.

Guards stood stoically beside the entry. But the gallery buzzed with speculation. Attendants fluttered in and out of view, hastily performing errands and delivering messages. Discontent rose from sophists who hated that their judgment had been challenged. That part made Grant smile.

Vendanj and the others followed him onto the chamber floor.

On one side, a number of men sat behind a long, burnished hardwood table coated with a deep chestnut lacquer. These gentlemen wore high-collar coats woven in black tightcloth and trimmed with white epaulets. Before them on their table rested dozens of books and mottled scrolls in hasty disarray. Four of them sat in utter silence, their faces gaunt and unsmiling. Beneath the austere visages the look of a trapped animal wrestled their near impeccable control.

On the other side of the round chamber sat a second table identical to the first. This was their table. Behind it, against the short wall that rose to the first row of the theater, Mira and Braethen took seats.

Vendanj joined Grant at the challenger's table.

All around them rose circular rows, each bounded by a low balustrade. Not a seat was vacant. Even the aisles teemed with gawkers hunkered down or seated on the stairs. Men and women, old and young, pressed cloth and rumpled shirttails, sat beside one another. The smell of expectation and the heat of cramped bodies filled the air.

A moment later, the chamber doors opened again and the regent stepped in.

Dead gods, it's been a long time, Helaina.

A wave of chatter and noise rippled through the gallery and the entire assembly rose to its feet and bowed. The regent acknowledged the crowd with a wave of her hand, and came forward into the ringed theater.

She crossed between the two tables, and mounted a low set of stairs to a modest platform and an old wooden chair lined with a horsehair fabric. The chair was chipped and marred, but its stout legs didn't grumble or budge as she eased her weight into it. She took a moment to gather her breath, before settling her gaze on the men wearing the formal counsel gowns across from Grant.

With the inclination of her chin, all came to silence. The guards closed the doors to the Court of Judicature. The boom of it reverberated in the hall.

"This is a matter already written into the ledger," she began, directing her comments to the first counselor, who wore a white braided rope slung over his shoulders, its ends knotted above a series of thin fringes. "Why are we convened again upon it, First Counsel?"

The man stood and cleared his throat. He came around his table and assumed a posture of oration. "My Law," he said, addressing Helaina, "indeed this matter was heard and ruled upon. The offender sits this day in chains he has rightly earned. I, for one, have no desire to put the argument to the Court of Judicature again. And you may make an end of it here and now—"

"I know my authority, First Counsel," the regent said curtly.

"Your pardon, My Law." He bowed, and again cleared his throat, his thin, aged cheeks puffing as he did so. "Our ruling has found a challenge. An old one to be sure." He looked back at the dusty scrolls on his table. "But we've not found sufficient cause to disregard it. We may circumvent this, if you'll delay the hearing until we've the chance to read—"

"The Dissent?" the regent asked, her impatience rising.

"Preserved Will, My Law."

A sudden flurry of whispers and gasps rose like the soughing of wind.

The regent raised her eyes to the many circular rows, and brought the crowd to silence. Helaina then looked to the challenger's table. Her expression slackened with memory and guilt. He could see her surprise that he hadn't aged in the same way she had. And then her face tightened with anger.

"Can you prove this?" she asked, locking Grant with a strict gaze.

She could have him killed just for being here. But she waited, listening. As he knew she would. She might hate him, but throwing his Dissent out on personal grounds wasn't her way.

Grant came around his table and took a wide stance at the center of the chamber floor. He looked from his far right to his far left. Finally, he leveled his grim regard on Helaina. "We can, my lady. We will show you today how honest men suffer in the prisons you create for them."

She looked back with quiet intensity. "You will hoist yourself up on your own rope, Counsel, if you intend to disgrace this chamber."

"I intend no disgrace to the . . . *chamber,*" he said.

The insult was plain, but Helaina let it pass. She would hear what evidence he might have. But she wouldn't suffer many slights before her patience would run out. Grant took his seat.

"Your books," she said, returning her attention to the First Counselor, who had maintained his orator's pose. "What do they say on this? We've not had it spoken here in a very long time."

"That is the issue, My Law," the man replied, his thin cheeks uninvolved in the formation of his words. He spoke in a dour, pessimistic tone. "The use of it is well beyond the memory of most of those gathered here. Tradition holds that laws so long out of use are not always of particular relevance to our ruling body." He bowed again.

Grant rose from his seat again. "Tradition also holds that laws granted in the Charter supersede the wiles of crafty counselors or the reformations of government."

Helaina ignored him, continuing to hold the first counselor's eyes. "Have you established the rightness of this Dissent, then, Pleades?" The counselor seemed caught off guard by the use of his name. But he nodded. "Indeed, My Law, if you've no mind to controvert it, we've no reason to deny an audience to examine their argument." The man sounded defeated as he made his report. "But you may give us leave to review it more closely, and some things . . . pass away, as time permits."

Clever, Grant thought. Prisoners would likely be dead before the Court of Judicature reconvened on the topic.

"No." Helaina turned to Vendanj. "And you support this challenge, Sheason?" Vendanj nodded.

"You're aware of the strictures placed upon your Order within the walls of Recityv and throughout all of Vohnce."

"I am," Vendanj said.

She refocused her penetrating gaze on Grant. "What can you add to what we already know about this Archer? And don't trifle with our time or patience. We don't abide liars or miscreants here."

"I've no time for either, my lady, today any more than in years past."

The regent nodded primly, and signaled the entry of six men and six women through doors on either side of her chair. The jurors stepped formally down the stairs, men to the left, women to the right. From their shoulders flowed long robes in the colors of Recityv, a white emblem of the tree and roots over each breast.

Pant cuffs hung beneath the robes. Shirt sleeves and collars were visible, too. These people had donned their outer ceremonial garments in haste. They filed to separate rows of chairs similar to the regent's, set on the first ring from the hall floor, and sat with their hands in their laps.

When they had settled themselves, Helaina lifted a wood staff kept beside her chair and struck the marble with a loud crack, signaling the first counselor to begin. She then sat back into her chair.

Pleades strode the floor with a long gait, and clasped his hands behind his back, pacing before the men seated at his own table. Several moments passed. The first counselor's face held a scowl, the thick skin of his forehead bunched over his thin white brows. Abruptly he stopped and folded his arms. He squared himself to face Grant.

"The ledger needs your name," Pleades said, a subtle ridicule in the simple request.

Grant stared back, unblinking. Then he smiled and nodded appreciatively. "A fine gambit, First Counsel, worthy of every book of logic you've studied to earn your post. Adding my name hurts the credibility of our Dissent." He shook a finger at him in a playful mockery of scolding. "What say you put the name of the three-ring, Vendanj, on your ledger? I shall merely be the voice to this challenge."

Pleades began to protest.

"Ah-ah," Grant cut him off. "The records don't require that they be the same, so let's dispense with clever ploys to discredit me before we begin."

The first counselor threw up his hands, exasperated with Grant's disrespect for the court.

Grant kept a calm focus on the man. "You've arrested and imprisoned two young men for thwarting your effort to execute a leagueman accused of conspiring with a Sheason." He pointed a finger at the first counselor. "You now plan to execute these two boys for interfering with your rite of justice. And the leagueman, as I understand it, sought the help of a Sheason to heal his dying daughter. Have I my facts straight?"

"Facts, yes. Deportment, no," Pleades said tersely.

From the gallery, a murmured laughter.

Grant stood and stepped into the center of the chamber. "Our challenge is this: that the actions of this Archer are not punishable, because the leagueman is innocent."

A rustling hum flared in the audience: gasps, sighs, denial, speculation.

"In the rush to convict these young men," Grant pressed, "you overlooked the most obvious evidence available to you: a witness." He shook his head and began walking in a slow, tight circle, addressing the gallery of citizens.

"Let's start simply. You have a law known as the Civilization Order, which holds that any Sheason who renders the Will, or any citizen who *seeks* a Sheason to render the Will, is guilty of a crime. A crime that is punishable in many ways, including death."

Assent came with the nodding of heads.

"So," Grant submitted, "if the leagueman didn't ask or conspire with this Sheason to render the Will, then he's not guilty. And if he was spared the punishment of a false charge by this Archer and his friend, then these young men you've condemned did what any men of conscience should."

"Your logic is sound," the first counselor admitted with a tone of reservation, "but someone should have informed you—and spared us all a lot of time—that the accused leagueman confessed to this crime. He chose to not even speak in his own defense." The counselor then paced away, deliberately turning his back toward Grant in a show of contempt. "Something you'd have done well to observe yourself in your own trial many years ago."

Grant clenched his teeth, biting back his anger. He stared at the counselor's back, then turned to face the juror council in their crimson robes. "Mark me," he began, his voice filled with threat. "You hold three men accountable for crimes they did *not* commit. You've sentenced them to death. I will answer for my own sins . . . will you?"

No one spoke for several moments. The first counselor finally retook his seat and attempted to look busy reviewing parchments lying on the table. His hands shook as he did so.

Grant turned and nodded to Mira, who went to the door and promptly returned with a young girl. The child stood adorned in sooty rags, her hair pulled back in a frayed band to keep matted strands from falling in her eyes. At the urging of the Far, the girl hesitantly came forward. Grant gently took the girl's hand and led her to the center of the circle. He whispered into her ear. She cowered for a moment, until he put a reassuring hand on her shoulder.

"Go ahead," he said softly.

"My name is Leia," she began. "It wasn't my father who went to get the Sheason . . . it was me."

The gallery erupted in shock and shouts. For a full minute Helaina struggled to restore order. Finally, the pounding of her staff against the marble floor brought silence to the court. "Go on, child," she said.

"I know Rolen," Leia continued, "I help him give out food on beggars' row. I've done it for months. Makes me feel better for what *my* family has. And Rolen always gives me a loaf of bread for helping. When my little sister, Illia, got sick, and we had no money for a healer . . ."

"Go on," Grant gently urged.

"I thought of Rolen, because I know Sheason can use the Will to make people better. I knew Mother and Father would never go to him because of the law. Or, at least, I didn't think so. But I couldn't just let Illia die. And Rolen is so good to me—"

Before the girl could say more, another of the Recityv counselors stood. This one wore the emblem of the League below his epaulets. He steepled his fingers under his chin and showed the girl a fatherly smile. "Are we to reverse the dignified resolution of this council on the testimony of a family member? It's notable that she would lie to preserve her father, but hardly admissible."

Grant stared back at the man, confused. "Why are you so eager to execute a member of your own fraternity when I'm here to tell you he's innocent? That he did what any father would, accepting the blame to save his child?"

The League counselor thought a moment. "Let me answer with a question: Why are you so eager to substitute this child for her father?"

Again the gallery murmured with the turn of logic.

Grant put his other hand on Leia's opposite shoulder. He stood as a father might, in full support of what the girl was about to say. "You've not heard the end of it," he announced, and waited patiently on the girl to finish.

Leia trembled. She could look only at the floor, seemingly terrified of what must come next.

Her voice cracked with emotion as she spoke. "Mother asked us if any of our friends had been ill, or if any of the beggars on beggars' row had looked sick when I went to help Rolen pass out bread. She says you can get sick by being around them. But Illia and I told her no. It wasn't until after they took Rolen away that I remembered Mother telling us that eating too many sugared fruits could give us stomach pain . . . that, and the gifts Illia and I had gotten the morning she fell sick."

Grant watched the League counselor closely. He fidgeted. His eyes darted. And he finally got to his feet again. He addressed the regent. "My Law, the child is emotional and should never have been forced to come here. And, despite her love for her father, this is a waste of the court's time. We should—"

"You just ran the Lesher Roon in the city, did you not?" Grant asked, with a hint of sarcasm. "Surely the voice of a child isn't to be discounted in *this* hall." He gave Leia a reassuring pat on the shoulder to continue.

"Illia and I were behind our home playing. Some of father's League friends came into the yard. They come by all the time. But that morning, they brought Illia and me each a gift. They gave me a sheaf of flowers and told me I was growing into a fine woman. And to Illia they gave a box of sugared sweets. . . ."

Grant caught the eyes of the robed council. "The trial record of the Sheason Rolen states that he testified of a poison in the body of child Illia—"

The League counsel shot to his feet a third time. "Don't you dare suggest it!"

Grant stared back at the man as he said, "I submit that the conspiracy in this affair is not the imprisoned leagueman's, nor this child's solicitation of the Sheason to heal her sister. The conspiracy belongs to the League itself, who poisoned a child to force the family of one its members to make an impossible choice: death of a four-year-old girl or loyalty to its immoral law."

A torrent of speculation, rumor, shock, and jeering cascaded down from the gallery. Even the jury wore concern on their usually impassive faces.

The League counselor found his composure. "With all due respect, we still have only the word of a family member, one who's emotionally distraught with the imprisonment of her father. A girl, I might add, who appears to have been *prepared* for her testimony by our Dissenter. A man, as we know, who has no respect for this court." He smiled. "It doesn't take much to understand what is really going on here. And I can assure you any League confection is not only harmless, but actually quite tasty."

Mellow laughter rippled through the chamber.

Grant whispered again in Leia's ear. The girl reached into the pocket of her ragged smock and pulled out a small wrapped morsel. "Illia gave me one of her sweets before she ate them all. I was saving it for a special occasion." She extended it in an open palm like a piece of damning evidence.

Grant held back his smile. He knew the League had swept through the child's home and gathered in anything that could incriminate them. This League counselor had been confident . . . until now. Grant took the sweet from Leia's hand and walked to Pleades' table. He held it up. "Do you recognize the emblem on this wrapper? Unless things have changed in the last few decades, I'm going to guess that only members of the League can procure this confection."

The League counselor's eyes never went to the sweet. "Anyone could have tampered with it in the weeks since the crime," he argued.

Grant reset his feet. "The seal is unbroken. Let's make this even simpler. Eat this. Eat it and prove that a simple gift to a child was not the instrument of conspiracy and death."

Whispers rushed like seeping winds.

The leagueman waved a dismissive hand. "This is an author's tale. A child's fancy. Besides, where Sheason are involved, anything with this sweet is possible." The League counselor looked over at Vendanj.

Vendanj rose for the first time. He looked across the aisle at the leagueman. His countenance shone with a terrible frown. Genuine concern rose in Helaina's face. The air felt charged with threat.

"You won't make this suggestion again." Though spoken softly, Vendanj's words resonated in the very stone. "And I won't suffer it. Am I understood?"

The League counselor nodded, though he held a small bit of defiance in his eyes.

"Eat this," Grant repeated.

The leagueman picked up the sweet and turned it over once cursorily. "Enough," he said. "This is all speculation. I think we've heard all we need of this Dissent for the jury to render a decision."

"I'll have that back," Grant said of the morsel. With some hesitance, the man returned it. Then he turned to Helaina. "What's your confidence in your League counselor? Would *you* risk partaking of this confection? Prove that the court's trust in this man is justified?"

Silence crept over the entire hall.

She stared back at him with heavy disdain. "We are done here," she announced, and tapped her staff. "Make your final argument or let this matter lie."

Grant sent the girl back to Mira. He then shot Helaina a sharp look and turned to address the League counselor. Into the thick stillness he said, "The League has benefited from the imprisonment of the Sheason Rolen. The feelings of the people turned to your favor after hearing of his supposed crime and conviction. And with all this distraction, you've caused men to forget the threat out of the Bourne that rushes toward us."

The League counselor laughed. "There's no threat—"

"Don't interrupt." Grant turned back to the jury council. "The League knew that this family—or their daughter anyway—was sympathetic to the Sheason. So, they tested their loyalty.

"And now two more have been caught in this shameless plot, two boys who freed a man innocent of the crime that nearly condemned him. Set them free. They may have interfered with the execution of the regent's order. But in doing so they answered the higher law of the Charter. They're blameless."

"This is careful logic," the League counselor exclaimed. "We still have men defying the law—"

"The question before the Court of Judicature," Grant declared, "is this: A Sheason who saved the life of a poisoned child, an innocent man accused of conspiracy, and the two boys who preserved the life of that man are all caged in your pits."

Grant's voice fell to a whisper. "The only lawbreaker here is Leia, a brave young woman who sought out Rolen to save her sister. The law condemns her for seeking the Sheason's help. But I put it to you now: Is she truly guilty?"

A long pause stretched throughout the assembly.

Grant sat again beside Vendanj, who nodded a subtle thanks.

Slowly, low voices began muttering to one another. No one attempted to quiet them.

And that's when Grant saw it. Nothing more than a look passed between the League counselor and the jurors.

Bastard rigged the outcome.

The robed council sat still, their faces unreadable. Each would arrive at their own decision. Then individually they would stand and indicate their support. Majority ruled. And by law, even then, the regent could overturn a decision—though he couldn't remember it ever happening. Some Dissents had been known to have jurors sit for three days before rendering a judgment.

Abruptly, one of the council members stood. Her robe fell in long, deep folds. Then other members stood. One by one. Helaina nodded and the council juror on the far left raised an arm in the direction of the first counselor's table. The man next to her did likewise.

In turn, each lifted an arm, the wide sleeve hanging in a low arc beneath his or her wrist. Each arm pointed toward the first counselor and his companions. The chatter in the gallery grew with each vote. Gasps of surprise and delight and uncertainty escaped hundreds of mouths at once, followed by a renewed furor of speculation.

The accounting continued, council votes pointing toward the distinguished men in their fine black attire. Looks of self-assurance replaced the austere severity in their hollowed cheeks. Every hand confirmed the merits of their prior judgment. All save the last, whose arm lifted calmly toward Grant.

The court erupted. Shock stirred the chamber, all eyes falling on the final voter. This last juror looked directly at Grant, then at Vendanj, and then at Leia. She didn't seem to be seeking approval for casting her vote in their direction, more that she wanted them to know her disappointment with her fellow jurors.

Grant nodded appreciation.

A court recorder raced forward and produced a ledger into which he began to make an inscription.

"Your pardon," Vendanj called with his resonant voice.

The Court of Judicature quieted, and the diminutive recorder lifted his pen from his book.

Vendanj pushed back his chair and came around the table. He disregarded the counselors opposite him. He disregarded those still holding their arms to designate their votes. He approached the regent. He came to the foot of the marble stair and placed one boot upon the first step. He stood staring at Helaina, who returned his fixed gaze for several long moments. The two appeared locked in a contest of wills.

"Regent Storalaith, look past the judgment of this court. I appeal to your privilege as regent." Vendanj lowered his voice a note. "Set these men free. Trust me that it's the right thing to do."

"Sheason," Helaina took a long breath, "I respect your Order. I have championed its seat at my table. But this council is just."

"My lady," Vendanj persisted. "Isn't it possible that after all the words are spoken we've not yet arrived at the truth? Or that what is lawful is still not right?"

"I'll not argue philosophy with you, Vendanj." She spared a look at Grant. "But if you ask me to rule according to my conscience and ignore the mandate of this court, you'd not like my conclusion."

Vendanj didn't immediately reply, seeming to consider alternatives. He half-turned and looked at Grant. The flinty look in his eyes was unsettling. Then he turned back to Helaina.

"Will you follow us to this Archer's cell?" Vendanj asked. "Look upon the accused once before closing the ledger on this matter?"

Her eyes narrowed as she held Vendanj's gaze, seeming to search for his motivation.

"No," she finally said. She summoned the recorder, who rushed to her side with his book. As she signed the ledger she pointed to the First Counselor. "You're dismissed." She then looked up at the ascending circular rows of the assembly. "You've seen the work of justice and reason. Now go into your homes and keep it yourselves." Her voice rang like iron from a clear throat.

The hall began to empty. Vendanj didn't move. The council folded robed arms and passed back through the doors by which they'd entered. In moments the great round chamber had been vacated.

Wendra appeared from the crowd and rushed to Braethen, taking him into a firm hug. Penit stuck out a hand and greeted the sodalist in formal fashion. Braethen smiled and shook the boy's outstretched hand.

"You look well," Mira commented, eyeing Wendra and Penit.

"We're fine," Wendra said.

"Very fine," Penit added.

Braethen held on to Wendra's hands. "There's a lot to tell you."

"We've stories of our own," Wendra said, rolling her eyes in exhaustion.

"Enough time for that later," Mira cut in, turning as Vendanj and the regent crossed toward them.

A tall man with dark skin hugged Wendra and promised to see her later before taking his leave.

Helaina called the door guard to her. "Escort the girl home," she said, indicating the witness. "See that she's not bothered for her testimony here today." Leia bowed and followed Mira and two soldiers out of the chamber. Then Helaina turned to Grant. "I can't believe you came back here, Denolan. . . . You've hardly aged."

"Call me Grant," he said without any real anger. "And you've not changed either." He looked around at the empty court chamber, remembering their last meeting in this place.

"You're an ass," the regent said icily. "And don't either of you ever try to strong-arm me in my own court again." She gave Grant and Vendanj a withering look. "But I'll go with you to see this Archer, in deference to the Sheason."

"Now . . . Grant," the regent said, "take my arm and assist me to these strangers you care so much about. And if fortune favors you, I won't remind my guard that your return to Recityv warrants execution."

Grant extended his arm. She linked elbows with him and together they started out.

"What would have happened if I'd eaten the confection?" she asked, as they left the court chamber.

He had to smile, weary though it was. "Not a damn thing. League swept the house clean days ago. Your counselors couldn't be sure, though. Their reaction was what I wanted. But you know as well as I do that they poisoned the child."

Mira led Leia back to her mother before she would join the others. The girl's small hand in her own was cold and trembling. Through a narrow hallway the two soldiers led them to a dimly lit room beneath the raised court gallery. The weight of expectation hung heavy on the air as she and the child entered.

The woman, Leona, got up from a low chair, and her daughter ran to her. The two fell into a close embrace as Mira stood just inside the door.

Then the woman looked at Mira, a question in her eyes.

The silence enveloped them.

Mira steeled herself. "I'm sorry. The Dissent failed. The ruling on your husband stands."

"Papa," the child cried. "Papa." And buried herself in her mother's side.

Leona tried to hold strength in her face and deny the tears. But the finality of it all overwhelmed her and her tears came. She fell to her knees, unable to support herself against the grief, and continued to hold her little girl in her arms. Together they wept for the loss of a father and husband. Wept for the failure of the girl's honesty and bravery to convince the court that this was a mistake.

As Mira watched them grieve, she thought about their future without the support of the innocent leagueman. If they had no other family or means, the city had few options for them. And what they had to sell would be taken roughly by men with liquor on their breath.

The loss and sorrow of it swirled in Mira's head as she stood witness to this private scene of heartache and hopelessness.

Not this time.

Mira crossed the floor and dropped to one knee in front of the mother and daughter. She again took up the girl's hand and drew her attention. "Leia, listen to me, and mark what I say. You take heart and give your mother the strength you showed today in the court. Can you do that?"

With a bit of hesitation, the girl nodded. "Yes, I can." She looked at her mother. "I'll help you, Mama." Then she looked back at Mira. "What are you going to do?"

Determination filled Mira as she looked at the child. "I'm going to free your father."

The girl stared at Mira with large tears standing on her cheeks. "Can you really do it? Can you save Papa?"

From the distant past, Mira heard her own questions about her lost parents. And she thought about what she was preparing to do now to keep her promise to this young girl. There were costs. But the right costs. And Mira wasn't about to let doubt enter in.

She gave Leona a confident look, then took the girl's wet face in her hands. "I believe I can. You hope, and I'll hurry." And with that, Mira gave mother and daughter's hands a squeeze and left to catch the others, thinking through precisely what must be given to keep her word.

• CHAPTER FIFTY-SIX •

Standing

It's hard to say what happens at the time of Change. But ask any man and he'll tell you: mistakes weigh heavier in the years afterward.

—*Interpretations of Accountability,* a survey
of men sentenced to die

The ache of hunger woke Tahn. His mouth was sour and pasty. His bruises and cuts had oozed and swollen further while he slept. Breathing hurt his ribs. His muscles burned from rigid immobility. When he attempted to reposition himself on the hard stone, iron shackles scraped over raw scabs. And today was his Standing.

He could hear a sleeper's breath in Rolen's dark corner. In that, Tahn found a small comfort.

Tahn clenched his teeth and sat up. His chains rattled loudly in the cell.

"Today's your Change." Rolen sat up, too, his chains also rattling in the stillness. "I'll stand First Steward for you if you'd like."

Tahn had resigned himself to ending this day without the rite or ceremony meant to mark it. The Change meant less to him now. Whatever lay on the other side of this day could look no better from where he currently stood, bound and starving.

"No," Tahn answered. "Not here. It doesn't make sense to celebrate in this place. I'm not sure it matters now, anyway."

"It always matters. And perhaps here more than anywhere else," Rolen said, his voice mild and instructive. "Don't let your circumstances rob you of what you cherish. It's an unfortunate truth that in the midst of celebrations and food and song, the meaning of this day sometimes goes unrealized."

"*Unrealized?*" Tahn asked.

Rolen didn't immediately speak. But moments later, his voice rose in the stillness. "Every child becomes accountable, Tahn, each of us comes of age. But not all of us Stand. Standing requires a steward, and during those moments of change, the steward may impart a portion of his spirit to the one passing into adulthood. It's a unique gift. Something many are robbed of because they've no one to stand with them, or because their stewards have forgotten there's a gift to bestow."

Tahn stretched a cramped arm and winced against the scrape of iron on his tender skin. "You could be my steward?"

"Stand up," Rolen said, his chains rattling again.

The Sheason rose to his feet and began shuffling toward him. Tahn stood, biting back oaths as his muscles and skin stretched. A moment later a ghost of a man stepped into the light falling down from the cell door window.

White, smudged skin clung tightly to bone, revealing sharp features. Wavy brown hair hung in matted clumps, some spots on Rolen's head thin or bare. A wiry beard filled Rolen's face, covering his mouth. His robe hung from his shoulders like a sheet on a dry-line. Whatever meat there'd been to him before he came here was gone. Dark half circles under his eyes spoke of many sleepless hours.

A vague smile played on the man's lips. But the look in his eyes captured him most. Against the backdrop of slate darkness, hunger, and indignity, Rolen looked at him with gentle hope. He looked not at all like a man in chains or nearer his earth with every breath. He might have been standing at the head of a great feast, his children at his feet, his wine cup full, and surrounded by friends.

The Sheason beckoned him with a gesture, and Tahn scuttled forward. "Do you know which way is east?"

Tahn nodded. It was an intuition that never failed him—his daily ritual with dawn.

"Look that way, then."

Tahn turned and stared into the darkness as Rolen shuffled and took position on his left and half a pace back. The Sheason put his right hand on Tahn's left shoulder and looked east with him into the darkness where no sun would ever rise. Into the cool, stale air he spoke with a soft clear voice.

"From the cradle you came, through the march of a hundred days, a thousand, and more. You crawled. You walked. You ran. You clutched a mother's finger, then carried stones, then learned to write. But you did these things for yourself. And never *owned* them."

Rolen's warm tones deepened in his chest. "Your days walk out before you now like a string of pearls. Valuable and imperfect. These imperfect moments are the choices you'll make. Some good. Some selfish. And many times you'll know the difference by the ripples they cause in the lives of others. But good or selfish, they are now entirely yours."

Rolen paused. Warmth spread in Tahn's chest and arms and legs. Heat flushed his cheeks, and the cold of his prison receded for the moment.

"I pledge to be your marker." At this, chills swept Tahn's newly warmed skin. "To help you see the ends you might create. To be a memory, a companion. Because the ends you create will now prove or condemn you."

Tahn raised his hand and covered Rolen's fingers. He hardly heard the rattle of his chains. He stared into the blackness of the room and forgot the rasp of irons, the emptiness in his gut. All the hell of this place remained, but seemed of no consequence. He stood with his cellmate at his back and looked past this day.

"The inclinations of youth aren't gone. And the Change doesn't leave behind all that you have been." Rolen turned Tahn around, clasping his shoulders with both hands, chains dangling and rattling impertinently in the stillness. "So be careful. Your course is a deep river, Tahn, filled with currents that pull and rush. Those currents will sometimes seem separate from you. But they're not. They're yours. As surely as your own breath."

Rolen's voice now quavered, his words coming in snatches, as though he reported images flashing before his eyes. "Beware though, Tahn. The line that separates light from dark is an easy place to lose your conviction. It is the dark backward, the light upside down. It invites but confounds. It's a stupor of thought that eases you toward the Whited One. And the foulness beneath his façade will corrupt the soul you wish to preserve . . . your own."

Tahn frowned at the words. But Rolen only patted Tahn's shoulder, causing his chain to clink unmusically. "I might still have hoped for a roast goose to endfast with you today." He gave a crooked smile.

"Is this the Change?' Tahn asked. "Is this all?"

"What more would you have it be?"

"Sutter and I have waited for so long," Tahn lamented. "Girls . . ." An embarrassed grin flickered at the corners of his mouth. "We always just thought that . . ."

But secretly, Tahn had always hoped the Change would restore the childhood he couldn't remember, disclose the secrets of the words he was compelled to speak whenever he drew his bow, reveal the face of the man in his dreams. A heavy sadness crept into his heart.

"I know," Rolen said, mildness in his voice. He squeezed Tahn's shoulders to force his attention. "But it's no less important than you'd hoped. I've given you a gift of myself, one your own father surely meant to give. It can be a fire inside you, if you'll let it."

Tahn stared blankly.

Rolen looked back with understanding. "It's not something you feel right now, I know. But trust me." He dropped one arm, grimacing with pain as he did so.

Tahn remembered the moment of warmth that had come over him as Rolen had spoken, and wondered if that was the gift he meant. But he felt none of it now. Instead, he felt only a new burden.

Rolen chuckled warmly. "Don't despair, my friend. The Change isn't a revelation. It's not some granting of wisdom or strength." He took a breath and said simply, "It's the freedom to stand or sit in your chains. To bear the bite of steel on flesh. To endure your hunger. To feel peace at the thought of death."

That peaceful look returned to the Sheason's weary features. He looked like a man who'd suffered well. Tahn wondered if he'd ever again run through the Hollows' groves in autumn and kick at the fallen leaves simply because they heaped into drifts on the forest floor.

He felt very much in the country of Rolen's "dark backward and light upside down."

Rolen disappeared again into the darkness of his corner, dragging his chains after him. Tahn had no will to sit or even move.

Finally, he cast his eyes upward into the vaults of the darkened cell and pictured the creep of the sun into an ashen sky cloaked by bruised clouds and imminent showers. The image held for the time it took Tahn to gather the courage to sit back down on the indifferent stone. Once there, he curled into a ball and gathered his chains into a pile to rest his head.

With his face to the wall, carefully shielded from even the sallow light of the high window, he chased old memories down toward sleep. The last he thing he recalled was the image of Sutter ruffling the dresses of girls as they wandered too close to his and Tahn's concealed seats beneath the rear steps of Hambley's inn. He hoped Sutter was all right.

Sutter opened his eyes to the dark. *The day of my Change.*

He knew it because he'd been counting down the days for the last year. Always before, he'd imagined it would be the day he would set out from his root farm. But that day had come a bit sooner, and its path had brought him here.

To this cell.

It was still deep in the dark hours of night. And his cellmates were asleep.

Sutter sat up off the rough stone, his bones and muscles aching with every movement. Across from him, the two scops had not returned. He tried not to think.

He missed his father. Today more than most. No one would stand for him. No First Steward. He'd still leave his melura years behind him, but they'd go with a whimper, nothing to commemorate the occasion except the dank, cloying smell of filth and stone.

Maybe his cellmates, the pageant wagon players, could do something festive. But the dark irony of it hit him—more of the old wounds.

But he really only had one regret: unspoken gratitude. He'd like to have said thanks to his father and mother for giving him a home when his birth parents had not. A home and a feeling he belonged.

And just now he wondered if they'd be proud of him. He realized suddenly he wanted that. On the day of his Change, he wanted that most of all.

Then, his thoughts turned to Tahn. His friend had always treated him well, something many in the Hollows found difficult due to Sutter's constant jokes.

He hoped Tahn had survived the Recityv dungeon. If he had, what would Tahn be doing for his own Change? What would either of them do if they never escaped or were freed? Would the others find them?

All hells, he was tired.

He lay back down on the stone, wanting to escape in sleep for a few more hours. And sleep took him quickly, easing the many pains.

Until another face rose up with the mists.

Until another waking dream.

Though this time, Sutter didn't start or shiver quite so much. Perhaps because he grew more accustomed, or perhaps because the sadness of it tempered the fear.

He stared back for a long time into the vacant eyes of this one . . . who soon would die.

CHAPTER FIFTY-SEVEN

Quite a Price

The only true threat to a movement's success is the self-sacrifice of its opposition.

> —*Concerns of a Dictator,* a guide to negotiation
> —required League reading

The echo of many feet brought Tahn half awake. The hallway beyond his cell door stirred with an unusually large number of guards. Then the sound of a key turning in the lock caused Tahn to come fully awake. Always before, the sound had sparked a bit of hope. Today he didn't bother to turn. He only hoped the guards wouldn't beat him again.

A harsh wash of light fell across the cell. Tahn squinted, even with his back to the door. Murmuring voices interrupted the dark and quiet, and soft shoes carried their owners down the stairs. The guards wore hard soles. Who were these visitors?

He raised his head, and a stabbing pain shot down his neck. The bright light made his eyes water. From the corner of his vision he could see several dark shapes like the figures in his dreams.

"There," he heard one say.

A collection of feet, all shuffling toward him. Slowly, his eyes adjusted. He blinked away the water and attempted to focus. Faces swam in and out, seeming familiar before blurring again.

One of the forms began to bend down, when a man beside her clasped her arm. "Patience, Anais. There'll be time for reunion later. There's a dispute to be settled first."

Tahn knew this voice, but a haze remained over his mind. He struggled to sit up, managing only to roll onto his back. He panted from the effort.

"What are you staring at?" he said, unable to say it as bitterly as he'd intended. The words sputtered unevenly through his gasps.

No one replied. But one of the forms came toward him. The figure didn't pause at the chalked line drawn on the floor to mark Tahn's reach. The man stepped across it, fixed his eyes on Tahn, and dropped to one knee beside him. The figure's head blocked the light from the door, becoming a misshapen silhouette. Tahn blinked again, trying to clear his vision, and still saw nothing. The man took Tahn's hand, lifting it into the light from the door to study the hammer mark. Gently, the stranger placed his hand back on the floor, and turned to the rest.

"Take a look for yourself," the man said. And again Tahn thought he knew the voice, though it came with more rasp than he remembered, as though too much wind and heat had traveled through it.

A second figure then came fully into the light. She looked old, though not fragile. "Be sure he behaves," the woman said.

"He's in no condition to threaten you," the man replied. He stood and stepped aside, making room for her. "This Archer you've chained, Helaina, is the boy Tahn."

The woman bent over him. A look of understanding bloomed in her eyes. She dropped to her knees, taking Tahn's face in her hands. Tears welled over her lower eyelids, falling directly onto Tahn's chin. All in a moment, Tahn saw joy, relief, concern, and shame. The old woman thrust her face into Tahn's neck and cried in silent heaves. Hot tears rolled down his skin into his collar. He was confused, but grateful for the warmth of both the woman's tears and embrace.

The woman repeated something over and over, but Tahn couldn't make it out, her cheek muffling his ears. When the tears stopped, she drew back, looking through eyes rimmed with the lines of age. An expression of grief stood on her brow as she put her forehead to Tahn's and whispered, "Thank the silent gods."

The woman let go of Tahn's face, wiped her eyes and cheeks, and extended a hand for help in standing. The rough-voiced man came to her aid.

"Get him out of those chains," she said.

"What about the ruling of your court?" the man asked.

"It's like you said, we both know who poisoned the girl." The woman's voice came quietly. "But there's too much at stake right now to make an enemy of the League by overturning the ruling. The two boys will be released. And when they're found missing, it will be called a miraculous escape."

A moment later, the manacles simply fell off Tahn's wrists and ankles. Had to be a bit of rendering. *Vendanj must be here.*

"Take him to the Levate healers," the woman commanded. "I will join you shortly. Don't leave him until I come to you." She nodded, satisfied, and turned toward the stairs.

The man hoisted Tahn to his feet as easily as a father might a child. Tahn's muscles sang painfully at the sudden jostling, but he bit back his cries. The man ushered him toward the stairs, when a sudden shock of clarity filled Tahn.

"Wait," Tahn said. The man kept on. "Wait!" he yelled, the sound echoing around the cell. The man finally stopped.

Tahn turned toward the shadows where Rolen remained cloaked and forgotten.

"Free him, too," Tahn said. He clenched his teeth against pain drumming in every cut and sore. "If I'm innocent, if the man I cut free is—"

"Tahn." It was Rolen. His voice came like a calm out of the shadow-veiled corner. A moment after, the Sheason stepped slowly into the light. "Don't worry about me. Remember, I choose this."

"But Rolen," Tahn protested. "They see it was a trap. They're letting me go because the man I cut free was innocent. You shouldn't have to—"

"Tahn." Again a voice of serene assurance. "Whether a trap or not, I broke the law. I knew what I was doing. But I'll say this. I have new hope after what I've just seen."

"What do you mean?" Tahn asked. "This isn't fair. It isn't right." He wrestled to free himself from the man's arms, but his body held little fight.

"I won't accept a pardon from the regent. It would give her critics more ways to attack her." He turned to look at the woman.

It dawned on Tahn who the woman was, and he stopped struggling in the man's arms.

When he turned toward her, he also clearly saw for the first time the faces of those standing near the wall: Vendanj, Wendra, Braethen, Penit, and Mira. Even in the dark, even weakened, he could see Mira's grey eyes, and even now they lit fire in his loins.

A crash of emotions descended on him. His heart swelled to see his sister safe, to see his old friend. Even the sight of Vendanj was comforting. Soon Sutter would join them, too. Emotion tightened his throat. He raised a hand to Vendanj for help. For Rolen.

"You're weak," Vendanj said, taking a step toward him.

"Vendanj." Tahn's tongue clucked dryly. He licked his lips and swallowed. "Vendanj, don't let them do this, please. You have to know about Rolen. He's one of your Order. He was only trying to help a dying child. Please."

Vendanj gave Tahn a strange look, then stepped past him toward Rolen.

"Is this how you intend to serve?" Vendanj asked.

"If I try to avoid punishment for my crime, the tension between the League and the Sheason, not to mention the League and the regent, will grow." He smiled weakly. "The law's misguided. But I'm bound to it just the same. What kind of servant am I if *I* choose which laws to obey?"

"We won't agree about that," Vendanj said. "And since we don't, I can accept the risk for you, take you away from this place."

"No," Rolen said. "This is how it must be. I've no regret." He looked past Vendanj to Tahn. "I've found meaning in it beyond my oath."

The regent came forward in her resplendent dress and extended her hand to Rolen. He took it. "Thank you," she said.

Rolen offered her a weak smile.

The man then started leading Tahn away. At the door, Tahn grasped the wall, stopping them again and looking down into the pit.

Rolen turned and looked up at him. "It was an honor."

The man bore him away.

Tahn lay still while attendants worked swiftly but methodically through their ministrations. One woman wearing a scarf tight around her face applied a cool salve to his wrists and ankles. The cream smelled of peppermint and nut oils. It burned icily, soothingly. Afterward, she wrapped the areas with clean, white strips of fabric. A second woman soaked a rag in a pungent liquid and rubbed it over the purple bruises that covered his body. Another forced him to sip water from a glass, and mopped his head and face with a damp towel.

When they'd finished, another woman came and dismissed them. She walked around the bed, eyeing Tahn's naked body with observant detachment. He wanted to cover his nakedness. She made a small grunt and came forward, leaning over his bed and looking at each of his eyes by turns. She took her hands from the folds of her heavy robe and placed her thumbs beside Tahn's nose, her fingers cradling the sides of his head. A look of confusion rose in her eyes.

Just then Vendanj came in. "Thank you for your help. I'll see to what's left."

The woman didn't acknowledge him.

"Do as I say," Vendanj said firmly.

The woman removed her hands from Tahn. Her head bobbed up and a faltering expression passed over her face. "This one, he's not whole. He—"

"He's weak, Anais," Vendanj said, firmer still. "Thank you. I will tend to him." Vendanj motioned toward the door.

The woman tucked her hands into her robe and scuttled from the room, some pallor in her cheeks. Vendanj had that effect on a lot of people.

As the woman left, Mira and Braethen brought in Sutter, his arms holding on to their shoulders for support. One eye was swollen shut, and dried blood had caked on his collar. His friend wasn't using his left foot.

"What happened to you?" Tahn asked.

"I complained about my food," Sutter said as he was hefted into a bed. "I see you've had it pretty light." With his one good eye, Sutter looked around at the spacious room.

"Yeah, they just don't care much for rootdiggers here." Tahn chuckled, the laughter descending into his chest in a fit of wracking coughs.

"Save your talk for later," Vendanj admonished.

The Sheason came to Tahn's side as the first three women reentered and began dressing Sutter's wounds. "You've had your Change," Vendanj said. It wasn't a question.

"This morning," Tahn answered.

"Rolen stood for you." Again the Sheason spoke with certainty.

Tahn nodded. "Though I'm not sure why we get so excited over this day. I think I might prefer to stay melura. . . ."

Vendanj's lip curled ever so slightly into an honest grin. The Sheason drew his thin wooden case from inside his cloak and produced a sprig, which he handed to Tahn. Tahn put it on his tongue. The bit of greenery dissolved quickly, leaving a hint of something peppermint. Almost immediately, Tahn began to relax from the stiffness in his body.

Vendanj moved to Sutter's side and placed a hand on his friend's eye. He also gave Sutter a sprig, and shared a long stare with Nails as the three women finished their dressings and made a silent exit.

"You've had your Change as well," Vendanj said, looking at Sutter.

Nails nodded. "Quite a story."

"Let's have it," Tahn insisted.

His friend focused instead on the Sheason. "The League has arrested a seat holder under false pretense. They mean to assume the Seat of Risill Ond in his place."

"The Reapers," Vendanj said softly.

"I don't think they plan to just keep him down there in that pit, either." Sutter's words grew anxious. "Is there anything you can do?"

"I'll speak to the regent about it." Vendanj put a reassuring hand on Sutter's chest. "Now rest, both of you."

Just as the Levate women left, Wendra burst into the room and rushed to Tahn's side. "Thank the abandoning gods." She gave him as firm a hug as she seemed to dare, and kissed him on the cheek. "What a mess you got yourself into." Her mouth tugged into a smile that betrayed her scolding. "What happened?"

Tahn gave Vendanj a look. "Later," he said, lifting his hand to gently take hers. "I'm kind of tired right now."

"Of course." She kissed him again, and turned as Penit came in and stood beside her. "We're all safe," she added, putting her arm around Penit's shoulders.

Tahn noted the look Wendra gave the boy. It reminded him of Vocencia, their mother, but also something else. Something had changed.

Mira came to Tahn's side, freezing him with a look. "A lot of grit to cut a man loose from the gallows, especially a leagueman." She gave him her small smile. "A day in irons is worth a hundred in battle. A man once held captive fights with more purpose. Don't forget."

The sight of her helped his spirits as much as the healing Levate hands.

"I'm glad you're well," Mira finished. And she finally returned the impetuous kiss he'd given her some days ago, pressing soft lips briefly to his.

The kiss seemed wonderfully slow compared to how fast she did everything else. Then he saw Braethen holding Tahn's weapons and pack and cloak. He sat up and pointed at them.

"Easy, Tahn," Braethen said. "Your things are safe."

"Hurry. Bring them here!" Tahn insisted.

"All right," Braethen said. "Nice to see you, too."

Tahn shook his head. "It's important."

Tahn tore his cloak from Braethen's hands just as the regent entered the room. She walked carefully, placing her feet in a steady rhythm. Behind her strode the man who'd first knelt at Tahn's side in the cell. Everyone in the room bowed, except the man behind the regent, whose weathered face held little emotion.

The last to enter was an old man who wore at his throat the same three-ring symbol as Vendanj. A snowy white beard fell on his chest, and wavy white hair hung to his shoulders. Spectacles adorned his bulbous nose, and the man moved with the deliberateness of the regent, his steps careful. Once he'd entered, he closed the door, and smiled warmly at Vendanj before turning his attention back to the woman.

"I've called for the Convocation of Seats," the old woman began, her voice filled with authority. "Detractors accuse me of politics, but I'm too old for such nonsense. I sent the birds and criers because there are reports of Quiet south of the Pall. Every day the gate is flooded with people who've abandoned their homes for the protection of Recityv walls. I suspect it's much the same in cities all across the east."

She turned to the man with the weathered skin. "It even coaxes Grant from his Scar?"

"I'm not here for Convocation," Grant said.

Grant? His was the familiar voice Tahn had heard in his cell.

Vendanj added, "He's agreed to go with us to Naltus Far and on to Tillinghast."

"Are you telling me that Grant intends to stand at Tillinghast?" The old woman's voice held a hint of amusement.

Vendanj turned and came to Tahn's bedside, suggesting who would stand at Tillinghast.

The regent looked from the Sheason down to Tahn, understanding in her eyes. "My dead gods."

"We'll rest today," Vendanj said, looking at everyone. "We can't wait any longer than that. We've a long way yet to go."

"The mists of Tillinghast," the regent muttered, "to test his spirit."

"Because things are different this time." Vendanj looked at Grant. "The Quiet have chased us since the Hollows."

Tahn suddenly remembered the strange words he'd heard from the Bar'dyn as he and Sutter had fled the black winds from the North Face: *You run only from lies . . . your lies and the lies of your Fathers will we show you.*

"And against this you take a *child* to Tillinghast," the regent said, a hint of confusion and impatience in her words.

"Precisely because of his youth. But no longer a child," Vendanj explained. "Tahn's had his Change. We must reach the Heights quickly."

The answer seemed to satisfy her, but she didn't look pleased. "Very well, Sheason. How can we help?"

"We'd planned to visit Qum'rahm'se on our way here," Vendanj explained, "but we got separated. We need the scriveners' study of the Covenant Tongue and the Tract itself, to try and strengthen the Veil. Send General Van Steward's best hundred men. Armored wagons. And bring the entire library here where it can be kept safe until we return from Tillinghast." He paused a moment, then added, "It's possible someone, maybe the Quiet, is piecing together an understanding of the Language, and using it against us. If so, they could potentially bring down the Veil."

Tahn suddenly remembered his cloak. He thrust his hands inside, and sighed with relief at the shape of the sticks still concealed inside.

He pulled them out and held them up. "Sutter and I went there. To the library."

Vendanj took the sticks from Tahn's trembling fingers. The Sheason seemed to know the end of their story. He broke the seals and read the testimonies. Next he rolled open Edholm's parchment and looked it over. As his eyes scanned the lines, a still, calm anger settled in his features. Finally, he held up the fourth stick, but didn't open it.

"The library is burned. Everything." Vendanj replaced the scrolls into their sticks. "There's no copy now of the Tract of Desolation. What we'd hoped to learn about the Covenant Language is lost." Vendanj turned to the regent. "Send word to Descant Cathedral. They no longer have the protection of redundancy. I know Suffering is only a translation and only part of the Tract, but it's all we have left."

Everyone held their silence in the wake of the revelation. Tahn noted a kind of serenity in Mira's face that either welcomed death or wasn't concerned over the loss at Qum'rahm'se.

Vendanj continued. "Helaina, the hundred that you might have sent to Qum'rahm'se, send instead to keep watch over Descant. Dress them in common clothes, so they are obvious. They're to guard the cathedral."

Penit tapped Wendra, who'd pulled him so tightly against herself that when she released him, he drew an exaggerated breath. She smiled an apology, and he took her hand. She wore a grave expression. Tahn didn't like the look of it. Wendra had always, even at work—whether forking out the barn or washing the cook pots—worn a smile.

"What else needs to be done?" Grant asked. "I don't intend to spend one unnecessary moment in the marble arrogance of Solath Mahnus."

The regent stiffened. She rounded slowly to face him. "If it weren't more cruel to leave you in exile, I'd have you strung up this hour. What a waste of a man you are. I'll allow you to accompany the Sheason for his sake. But curb your tongue until you find yourself outside with the animals, or you'll wear stripes as easily as your boots."

A terrible authority filled the regent's voice as she spoke.

Grant replied in a soft, unmoved voice, "Doesn't all this show you that I was right even then?" He returned the regent's stare a moment more, then opened the door and slipped out.

"Go with him," Vendanj said to Mira. "We need to be ready."

In the silence that followed Mira's departure, Braethen walked a bundle of clothes to Sutter, laying his Sedagin sword at the foot of his bed.

"Sweet of them not to pawn my belongings," Sutter quipped.

Braethen smiled without conviction. The others ignored him.

Wendra turned to Vendanj. "Penit should stay here. He's a boy. Whatever needs to be done at Tillinghast can't possibly involve him."

Instead of responding to her, Vendanj walked around Tahn's bed and knelt in front of Penit. He peered into the boy's eyes. "It's a dangerous thing we do. If you come, you may be asked to do as the Prince of Strohn did. Quite a price. Do you remember?"

Vendanj obviously referred to some obscure rhea-fol. Penit seemed to consider it.

"It's your choice," Vendanj went on. "No one will force you."

"He's a boy," Wendra repeated, indignant. "Ten years old. How can you even ask him to decide?"

Vendanj turned impatient eyes on Wendra. "I would rather this wait, Anais. But it can't. Penit must choose this for himself. He's aware of the risk."

Wendra began to argue, but Vendanj pinned her with a stare. "Your concern is noble, but you're not his mother."

The Sheason returned his attention to Penit, and spoke more softly. "What do you think, my boy?"

Penit thought a moment more. If Tahn didn't know better, he'd have sworn Penit was muttering lines from a rhea-fol under his breath. Maybe gathering his courage. "I'll go," Penit said.

Vendanj gave the boy a grateful smile. "We'll talk more," he said. Then he stood, looking more weary. Stern, but weary. "Will you require a moment alone here?" he asked Helaina.

"No," she said, shaking her head. "I've much to do to prepare for the Convocation." She then moved to Tahn's bedside. Though her back stooped slightly, she remained regal. Her blue eyes peered down at him. Tahn thought he saw concern behind them.

She put a soft hand on his arm and said, "Be safe."

Then she turned and brushed past Vendanj. The older man wearing the Sheason sigil followed her from the room.

"Tillinghast is a long way from here," Braethen said as the door closed. "Weeks . . . months of travel."

Vendanj nodded toward Wendra. "When it's dark, we'll find your cathedral, Anais. The talents there will make our journey short." He drew a long breath, and tucked Edholm's fourth scroll into the lining of his cloak. "I'll return after evening meal. Eat well. Penit, walk with me. We have things to discuss."

Vendanj and Penit left the four from the Hollows alone in the room. Tahn rested back onto his pillow, and sighed.

"I want him at my next birthday," Sutter jested.

The rest stifled a bout of giggles that lifted the worry and fear they all felt. Soon they spoke hurriedly of all that had happened to them, sharing freely and shaking heads in amazement over incredible events. Tahn kept back a few things, unwilling to worry his friends, and unable to shake the Sheason's words to Penit: *quite a price.*

CHAPTER FIFTY-EIGHT

Tokens

Compulsion is at the heart of good leadership, whether by inspira-
tion or threat. Regarding the latter: not of the individual, but what
he cares about.

—*Statecraft and Diplomacy,* an examination of
necessary measures; regent's library

Vendanj strode the marbled halls of Solath Mahnus. He was on his way to
Helaina's High Office. There were private matters to discuss, and he would
no longer be patient or silent. So, he didn't notice the grandeur of the halls, the
history engraved in the marble, the sculpture and art depicting kings and war
and the beautiful promise of the land that filled the high, vaulted ceilings.

Mira walked at his side. Vendanj had told her he meant to visit Helaina alone.
But Mira had insisted.

At the final stair, two of the regent's Emerit guard stepped in front of them.
Other guards had deferred to the three-ring sigil at Vendanj's neck. These did
not.

"I've been in your lady's company today," Vendanj said coolly. "If I'd wanted to
harm her, she would already be dead."

The two shared a look, acknowledged the logic, and stepped back. Vendanj
climbed the long marble stair, this one windowless and dark. At the top he
didn't bother to knock, but simply opened the double doors and went in. Mira
slipped inside and stood like a shadow against the wall.

"Do join us," Helaina said.

Artixan gave a knowing smile. "I told you he'd come."

"Yes, but you didn't say he'd show such disrespect." She gave Vendanj a measured look.

"I don't have time for etiquette." Vendanj shut the doors behind him. "You
know of my respect, my lady. But we're running out of time."

"What did Jamis say?" Helaina asked straight out.

Vendanj shook his head. "He won't come. The memory of Convocation's betrayal is as strong now as it's ever been." He took a few steps into the High Office. "If the Quiet invade, the Sedagin will fight back. But they won't pledge to you or Convocation."

Vendanj spared a look at the greatroom, a sanctuary built atop the several halls and palaces that comprised a man-made mountain in the heart of Recityv. Here Helaina kept her precious books, strategic war maps, and other secrets a regent must have. It spoke, too, of her refinement—white marble, sparing decoration.

"What of Tillinghast?" Artixan looked northeast out a window.

"When the boys are rested, we'll go," Vendanj said. "They're still weak."

Artixan shook his head and looked back at him. The man had mentored Vendanj. Was more a father to him than any other could claim. "Do you believe he can stand there?" Artixan clarified.

Vendanj crossed the room and looked from the northwest window with his old teacher. "I don't know. All the others we've taken there have failed." He was quiet for a long moment. "Either way, the Quiet come. No amount of rhetoric in these halls can make that untrue. The League's denial is either naive or calculated. It's dividing our attention and leaving us unprepared."

"Our attention isn't all that is divided, Vendanj." Artixan put a hand on his shoulder. "The Sheason aren't whole. You know this. Your use of the others, of Tahn, isn't helping that. The schism is deepening."

With soft regret he said, "I know." After several long moments, he focused himself, and turned to Helaina. "There's more. The League has arrested the seat holder from Risill Ond. After all this time, they answered your call to Convocation only to be treated to the hospitality of your dungeons. The League will take that vote if you don't set the man free and make it right."

The regent's brow furrowed.

Artixan's question came low and sad and ominous. "And if the League did it with Risill Ond, how many others have been compromised?"

"I leave you to deal with the League. But as for the rest . . ." Vendanj walked to the long table that served as the regent's desk. He looked across its polished surface at her weary face, feeling some pity. Then he recalled a list of widow names, and an infant's grave, and indignation burned again inside him.

With steady fingers he drew open his pouch and tossed a snake's head and a swatch of a child's blanket onto the desk.

The regent recoiled in surprise, then studied the artifacts. Artixan came close.

"The disgrace you forced on Grant may have been warranted, but the sentence was not. This cradle at the edge of the Scar . . . is finished."

"You don't have the power—"

"I claim the power!" Vendanj railed. He composed himself. "I'm telling you,

I won't let it continue. I'm telling you . . . Put an end to this vile cradle that keeps Denolan there."

"You forget yourself." The regent stood.

Artixan came to stand at her right shoulder. "Vendanj, your passion makes you unwise."

"No," he said. "I see more clearly than you both because I walk in the places where people suffer. Where their cries go unanswered and unremembered." He took up the swatch of blanket, his heart aching at its very touch. The token brought quiet reverence to what he said next. "Three days ago I visited your cradle in the Scar . . . and found a babe dead, bitten by a viper brought down out of the Bourne. It's a sign. A message."

Helaina and Artixan looked at the snake's head, understanding in their eyes.

"The Quiet know how you punish Grant. They took this child's life to make a point." Vendanj stared them down. "It ends. Now."

They looked back, beginning, he thought, to bear some grief over the loss. They said nothing, their eyes distant as if seeing what had happened.

"Grant will stay in the Scar if you ask him to, if that's what you deem fit for his treason. But he will go with me to Tillinghast." Vendanj shook his head. "I don't know how long we'll be gone. But the one thing I would spare him—the one thing you should wish to spare us all—is the worry that a babe may die if he's not there to receive it.

"And mark me: I will not needlessly bury another forgotten child. The day I do, won't forsake my oath and make a mortal enemy of any who put such children at risk."

The regent heard the threat but didn't falter under Vendanj's hard glare; neither did she rebuke him.

"All this," Vendanj finished, "or when we return from Tillinghast, kill Denolan. Execute him as you do any traitor. You know him, Helaina. He would stand up for that."

The regent looked back thoughtfully. "You're right," she said, "he would."

Vendanj's wrath receded. He looked at these old friends. "I do this because it's right. If you search your hearts, you'll see the right of it, too."

Helaina reached out, and Vendanj put the portion of the child's blanket in her hand. She looked down. And in that moment, the regent was replaced by the mother who had lost her own child.

Without looking up, she nodded. "No more children will I send to the cradle," she said softly. "Please tell Denolan."

Vendanj reached out and placed his hand over the regent's, as she smoothed the child's blanket. "Thank you, Anais."

He looked up at Artixan, whose wrinkled face held a glint of pride despite the roughness he'd seen in Vendanj. *Each servant has his way,* the look said. And for his part, Vendanj had meant every word he'd uttered. In some things, you went all the way, or not at all.

Vendanj had turned to leave, his business done, when Mira stepped into the center of the High Office and took the regent's attention.

"Something to say, Mira Far?" Helaina offered a slight smile. "I hope you have better manners than your friend."

Mira stared silently for a moment, sparing a last thought for what she was about to do. "I have a trade to make."

The regent shared a look with Artixan and even Vendanj, whose eyes showed some surprise. "Go on," Helaina said.

"Your Convocation is going to need help," Mira observed. "Especially now that the Sedagin won't come."

The regent paused to consider before responding. "And what do you propose?"

"The Far have never answered Convocation's call," Mira reminded her. "Both prior requests of the Far went unanswered."

The regent leaned forward in her chair. "True. And yet Convocation has prevailed anyway."

There was challenge in the regent's words. But a hollow one. And Mira had already weighed what came next. She leveled her gaze. "My sister is the Far queen, or was until several days ago when she passed this life."

"I'm sorry to hear it," Helaina said.

"Thank you." Mira paused a moment. What she was about to commit had many ramifications. "I will guarantee that King Elan, or whoever the rightful successor may now be, will return here to take the Far Seat at Convocation."

Helaina stared, unbelieving. "And what would you have in trade?" she asked.

Without hesitation, "The freedom of the leagueman framed in our Dissent today."

The regent began to shake her head. "No, that would undermine the court and the trust I've built—"

"On the contrary," Mira argued, "freeing the man would show your people that you're not afraid to defy the League. It would also let them know you're not afraid to have Sheason in the streets, using their gifts."

"How can you guarantee the Far king will come?" Helaina asked.

"You'll have to trust me." Mira glanced at Vendanj. "But if you need a witness to my honor, Vendanj will speak to it."

Helaina finally stood, and came around her long table to stand in front of

Mira. She stared at one eye, then the other, and seemed to wait for some internal question to solidify. "Why," she asked. "What is it to you if he dies?"

It was a cold question, Mira thought. But not unexpected from a woman who'd had to send armies to war. Still, Mira wondered if Helaina would have asked the question if she'd seen the mother and daughter grieving in the small room beneath the gallery.

"He's innocent." Mira spoke with soft tones. "He's a father. And this injustice is affecting more than the man you wrap with chains."

The regent nodded understanding. "Very well. But not by pardon. It would put Roth on a hunt for my office, which he wants bad enough as it is." Helaina gave a tired laugh. "I'll have my own counselors prepare a Dissent. And I'll make sure the jury isn't strong-armed by the League. You can trust that I'll see him freed." She raised a finger. "And I will hold you to your vow, Mira Far."

As though she hadn't heard, Mira pressed. "I need your word on more than simple release. Assign a few of your Emerit guard to him and his family. If anything unnatural happens to him, I'll hold those responsible accountable. . . ."

"You and Vendanj practice a unique brand of diplomacy." The regent's words elicited a soft laugh from Artixan. "Very well, the leagueman shall be freed and protected. We'll find a place far enough from Recityv where no one will recognize them. Where they can live in peace. Will that suit you?"

Warm satisfaction flooded her. "Thank you."

She caught a look from Vendanj that suggested he'd never heard her say so much at one time. She also saw approval, and a new respect in his eyes.

Now she just had to convince King Elan to attend this Convocation. And it wasn't simply about a leagueman and his family—happy as she was to have helped them. If the Far Nation was ever going to rejoin the world of man, it had to be now. They could no longer remain aloof to the other races. Their commission to protect the Covenant Tongue had found its time. The power of the Language was needed. Now.

It was time to fight or die.

Vendanj opened the door. "We'll return for Convocation as quickly as we can," he said.

Mira followed the Sheason from the High Office, wondering if she'd see this place again.

CHAPTER FIFTY-NINE

Garlen's Telling

If you get the words right, you can go anywhere.

—Author proverb, taken as an expression of fancy

Beyond the window of the Levate healing room, darkness had fallen, interrupted only by the glow of lights from windows in the Recityv night. Braethen stared out, new knowledge weighing on him. The others had returned dressed in thick cloaks and high-collar coats. Vendanj and Grant spoke softly near the door. Mira hadn't yet returned.

An uneasy feeling tugged at Braethen's gut.

He'd spent hours reading all he could find on Tillinghast. It was an *end* place: at the other side of the Saeculorum.

Much of what he'd found had been written in other tongues, writings he struggled to decipher. But the closest he could discern was the idea of *atonement*.

And no story that took this idea as a theme ever ended well. None that Braethen knew, anyway.

He watched as Tahn and Sutter took turns rushing to a basin to disgorge the food they'd eaten. They'd consumed too much, too fast. Their tender stomachs couldn't bear it.

The door opened and Mira stepped in. She conversed with Vendanj and Grant in a low tone. She then opened the door, looked into the hall, and nodded to Vendanj.

"Let's go," Vendanj said. "No talking."

Mira led them down the hall and across a mezzanine. They descended a stairway into a second hallway. Recessed alcoves on either side of them harbored statues, empty suits of mail, and occasionally a door.

At the hall's end, another stair spiraled down. Mira led them, and in short order they arrived at a workroom. Large tables stood laden with mallets, steel rings, sharp shafts, and rolls of leather. Along the walls, pegs were hung with unfinished suits of armor, saddles, tack and harness rigs, lengths of hide still curing. To the right blazed a forge with water troughs beneath it to cool heated metal. Everything smelled of armor oil and rawhide. A dense, humid heat thickened the air. That and the smell of a man's labor.

At this hour, the room was empty save for three smiths. One held something in the fires of the forge. As Mira started through the armory, he put a piece of red-hot iron into the water. A gout of steam and a loud hiss rose from the trough.

The other men beat at folds of doubled leather, driving studs into them at even intervals. They worked without their shirts, thick stomachs glistening with sweat beneath corded chests and shoulders. Each hammer swing fell precisely where they intended it.

One of the men working his leather looked up as they passed two tables away. He continued to hammer, uninterrupted, grunting at a casual nod from Vendanj.

Broad doors at the far end of the armory were open to ventilate the fires and keep the men cool. The wind was blowing hard, sending strong gusts into the room. Ten paces from that open yard, Mira abruptly stopped, drawing her swords in an impossibly quick, dual motion. Braethen heard Grant pull his own weapon. Four leaguemen walked into sight, blocking their passage into the stable yard.

"His Leadership was right. Look what we've found." One of the leagueman laughed as all drew their swords.

"Stand aside," Vendanj said.

The leagueman shook his head in an exaggerated motion. "Sheason, you're going to the pit for this. And if you draw the Will, you'll be put to death. Do you understand your choices?"

Mira leaped forward, blades slicing. Sparks rose from the furnace in the wind, streaking the air like light-flies around her as she dashed. Before the leagueman could defend himself, she had her blade at his neck.

"Not another word," she said. To the remaining leaguemen, "We're leaving. If you try to stop us, your friend dies."

"Hurry," Vendanj called.

Braethen ran with the others into the stable yard, where they found their horses ready.

They'd all mounted, when the leagueman gambled on Mira's threat and began to shout an alarm. His cries rose on the wind. A moment later, running steps echoed toward them from every direction.

Mira struck the man in the back of the head, knocking him unconscious. He dropped like a sack of wheat. Then she jumped to her own horse. Vendanj clucked twice, sending his horse into a gallop toward the stable yard gates. The clop of hooves rose like applause across the stone mall.

They rode hard and fast, the cobblestone underfoot too slick for iron-shod hooves to stop. A horse-length from the barred doors, Vendanj shoved a flattened palm toward the gates, casting them aside like straw in a summer storm. Into the street they poured, turning south along the outer wall of Solath Mahnus. Warning cries rose behind them, but were soon lost to distance and the rush of blood in Braethen's ears.

Around a sharp turn, the cobbled road ended, passing to soil. Braethen breathed a sigh of relief as their horses' hooves quieted in the dirt.

They raced under a full moon. Around them, the city had begun to fall to sleep: fewer lights shone in windows, fewer dogs barked.

After just a few minutes, Vendanj pulled up abruptly, jumping from his saddle and taking two running strides to a modest door. He rapped lightly at the lintel as Braethen and the others came to a stop and looked down in confusion. This was no cathedral. Mira gestured them off their horses, gathering the reins and pulling the mounts into a covered alcove beside the house. Grant assisted her, his eyes searching the night with the same intense awareness as the Far.

The door squeaked, and an old face peeked out—sallow cheeks beneath a shock of snow-white hair. An expression of unhappy surprise was clear on the man's face. But the fellow opened the door to admit the Sheason. Vendanj half-turned and gestured them to follow.

All went in save Mira and Grant, who remained outside to watch.

Braethen had just cleared the door when Vendanj shut it fast and directed him to keep an eye on the street through the window. The Sheason then stepped into the direct glow of a lantern hanging from a rafter. He eyed their host carefully. The old, tired-looking man stared back with arched brows.

"I need a Telling, Garlen, and I need it quickly." Vendanj spoke fast but clear.

"What else," the man replied. "I should know the sound of rushing hooves by now. Each time they clatter to my stoop, you expect some words. And in a hurry." An obstinate tone entered the old man's voice. "As things go, just talking to you could get me horse-whipped. And beyond that, those bumble-fools at Council may decide an author's craft is like to yours. I barely make enough coin as it is."

Braethen stared. An author. He'd been so distracted that he'd completely missed all the books and parchments. In this home, tucked away in a squalid quarter of Recityv, tables overflowed with scraps of parchment and books of various sizes, some bound in animal hide, some in cloth, others wrapped in twine; crowded shelves bowed from the weight of their volumes, sagging like a series of thin smiles; trunks sat open on the floor, overflowing with loose sheets and other paraphernalia; and amidst the clutter Garlen seemed to bring a perfect order to it all.

"Please, Garlen," Vendanj said. "I don't have time to debate the decay of a society that doesn't esteem your skill. And I've always made generous payment for your work."

"You're the only one," Garlen shot back, wheezing as he climbed a short stair and perched behind a lectern which rose two full strides from the ground.

"We go north, and east," Vendanj hurried on. "The words must tell of the Soliel. Do you remember it?"

"Aha." Garlen smiled and winked. "To me you come when my age and experience suits your purpose, but younger pens dally at your scryer's beck—"

"Nonsense," Vendanj said. "Yours is the only pen in Recityv I trust. And we're in a hurry, my friend."

"Don't end there," Garlen sputtered through a laugh. "Say it all. We've Quiet in the land. Patient shadow-stuff that brings with it a taint. A taint not just of foulness but of secrets mankind has ignored for far too long. I've put it on parchment a thousand times."

"I know, Garlen. But enough! Can you write it?" Vendanj may as well have thrust his fist into the lectern. The force of his cry rattled in the wood.

Garlen raised his chin and squinted with one eye. Up on his writing perch atop the impossibly tall lectern, his white hair glowed in the light of the lamp hanging close by. His spectacles caught a glimmer of the flame inside. The author peered a dreadful moment at Vendanj, testing the Sheason's patience. Then he pointed a quill at him.

"You're going to Tillinghast." Garlen paused, twisting the quill in his fingers. "It's a dangerous place, my friend. Not a place to go gallivanting off to with a tribe such as this." The quill swept across the room to indicate the rest of them.

Vendanj opened his mouth to speak.

Garlen stopped him before he could utter a word. "Yes, I can write it. Or near to it. I've seen the Soliel. Wandered like a lost pup in places most men won't write about." The author became quiet, his gaze reflective. "But I've not written of such things. Ever. That region is better left alone." Then as though waking, Garlen spoke up, "But yes, I can write it. I'll take double on what you usually pay. And I'd have you make mention to your cathedral hootenanny, that we tone-deaf louts find plenty of song in the spoken word alone."

Vendanj said nothing to that. Finally, he added, "We need to get to Naltus Far."

A look of concern touched the author's face. "I've not been there. I'm not sure I can write that Telling accurately. But I can put you on the Soliel. From there—"

"Do you have *Hargrove's Collected Works*?" Braethen interjected.

A'Garlen looked down from his perch, squinting into the dimness near the window where Braethen stood watch. "Who's that? What do you care about my book collection?"

"Do you have it!" Braethen demanded.

"No author considers himself—"

"Where?"

The author began to point, and Braethen dashed to a bookcase on the far wall. Braethen scanned the books and found them quickly. There were eight volumes. He fingered the bindings in a blur, and pulled down the sixth book. With an audible crack, he opened the tome and flipped, from memory, a third of the way through the pages. He scanned, his mind and heart racing with re-membrance and urgency.

"Here!" Braethen passed the open book up to Garlen. "Halfway down the left page."

The author took the book with a look of skepticism, but read the printed page. His face took on a conspiratorial smile. And before he did anything more, he reached down. Braethen took the author's grip, one he knew well.

"I thought so," the old man said. "Thank you, lad. Of course, this is pedestrian language, and won't do for a Telling." He harrumphed. "But it gets me what I need."

He shook his head, and cast a gleefully wicked eye over Braethen and the rest. Then the diminutive man stretched his arm up to draw back his sleeve, and made a grandiose movement of dipping his quill in an inkwell. His gaze flitted over the top of his glasses toward Vendanj as he withdrew the stylus, seeming to ask if the Sheason really meant to use what the author was about to produce. Vendanj nodded gravely.

As Braethen returned to the window to watch the street, the Sheason caught his arm and gave him a grateful nod. That one nod went a long way to erasing the feelings of disappointment he'd carried for not becoming an author himself. He settled deeper into the skin of a sodalist.

Garlen looked down at his lectern, and began to write. The scratch of the quill against the parchment came loud. But Garlen never looked up. His hand moved with practiced ease to the inkwell, but so quickly that it scarcely seemed anything more than another stroke in his current word. No pause, no waiting on something more to write. The scribbling was feverish but not panicked. The author's eyes looked beyond the page under the quill to whatever he created. Braethen's skin prickled at the sheer thought of what the man might be creating inside his mind and committing to parchment.

No one spoke or moved. None wanted to break the spell of silence. In the quiet, the only sound was the solitary quill roughing its way with black ink over a patch of vellum. That sound seemed to Braethen immeasurably lonely, and in the same instant impossibly important. It reminded him of his father's work, and somehow, so far from home, his esteem for A'Posian grew.

He didn't know how long they'd stood waiting, watching Garlen create his Telling. However long it may have been, it seemed an instant. The author was creating words that Braethen—from his years of study—knew could be sung in order to bridge great distances. The legends of Tellings were like legends of Far.

Suddenly the door burst open. Mira swept past Braethen to Vendanj, who didn't look away from Garlen.

"A mob searches the next street," she said in a quiet, urgent voice. "They come here next. If we don't leave now, we'll be overmatched."

Vendanj appeared not to hear her. And Garlen could not be disturbed. The author was alone with his words in a room full of strangers.

"Shall I run a decoy south? Grant and I could lead them false long enough for you to reach the cathedral." Mira looked up at Garlen. "How long 'til he's done?"

Vendanj raised a hand to silence her. That same moment, fighting broke out in front of the house. Mira bolted from Vendanj's side and into the street as the clash of metal and heaving grunts told of swordplay beyond the door. Shouts of alarm rose up.

"Over here," one man called.

Rearing horses whinnied, and frantic hooves echoed toward them. Getting closer. Scuttling boots pounded the soil of the road. The clink of armor and blade jangled Braethen's nerves. The shouts and calls became furious. Oaths echoed down the hard-packed dirt of the street.

The Sheason looked up at Garlen again. The author's quill still leapt across the page, undisturbed by the combat outside his door, unperturbed by the intrusion of voices and the threat of weapons in his own house. The fight raged closer to the stoop, bodies slamming the outside walls. Panes of glass rattled in their frames, wall hangings jounced and fell. A shrill cry rose like the sound of a mortal wound. Still, Garlen wrote; still Vendanj watched him write. Neither could be disturbed.

Someone got to the door, shouting an oath of death. The words gurgled in his throat, Mira's blade cutting short the curse. A hollow thud followed as the man fell across the entry.

There was a maniacal look in Garlen's eyes. His lips worked over his yellowed teeth. The hair on his jowls and in his ears stood on end, as though he were chilled. He didn't stop. His quill worked now at such a pace that it sounded as one long stroke, the individual letters and words indistinguishable from the whole.

"Here!" another voice called from beyond the door.

Garlen dropped his quill into the inkwell and dusted the parchment with sand to dry it. Then he rolled the sheet with stubby fingers, lashed it with a braid of horsehair, and tossed it at the Sheason.

Vendanj caught the scroll with a deft hand, and swept it into the folds of his cloak in the same motion.

The lantern rocked slightly over Garlen's head. The author leaned out over the lectern. "Never forget that you *asked* this Telling of me, Vendanj. I'm glad I don't know the names of your company."

Vendanj pulled a small bag from his cloak and placed it on Garlen's writing perch. "Thank you, my friend. And take care of yourself." With that, Vendanj whirled and strode to the door.

The others followed. Braethen lingered a moment to note the strange look on Garlen's face. It was as though he'd just returned from another place, and found the world he'd come back to with relief. The author turned toward him. He didn't speak, but smiled thanks again to Braethen and nodded.

Braethen returned the nod and moved fast to the door. He stepped across the body lying there and onto the stoop. Eight men stood near Mira and Grant, wearing the emblem of the League.

Vendanj rushed into the center of the street and pointed splayed fingers toward the sky.

The wind began to stir.

Vendanj dropped his arm toward the men and the wind descended on them in punishing waves. Small pieces of wood from houses down the street tore loose from their nails, rocks and cast-off bits of iron rose from the ground. Panes of glass shattered, and shutters, barrels, everything light ripped into splinters, streaking through the air toward the men. A rain of debris struck them like a swarm. A few of the men fled, some fell to the ground under the assault, their bodies writhing beneath hundreds of pointed pricks and the bludgeoning of stone and metal.

Braethen and the others clambered onto their horses and bolted as the wind howled past them, tearing at their cloaks and whipping dust into their eyes.

CHAPTER SIXTY

Leaving Peace Behind

As a young man, I ignored the advice of my Maesteri and left Descant to stand with my family in war. I don't regret it. But I returned broken.

—From the diary of Maesteri Belamae, Descant Cathedral

More shouts followed them. Searchers, spotting them as they raced through the streets, called alarms and pointed accusing fingers, spurring their mounts to move faster. Shadows blurred past, smears of grey beneath a bright moon.

Then they turned into a broad street that ended at the steps of Descant Cathedral. The sight relieved Wendra. It rose like a monolith against the starry sky. Great domes marked dark half circles against the night. Upper windows showed the dim light of reading lamps.

They raced for the cathedral. Wendra glanced behind her. Grant and Braethen brought up the rear, strain and determination etched in their faces. She held Penit against herself with one arm, coaxing her mount on with her reins.

More lights flickered in windows at each side of the street; a few men coming to doorways as they notched sword belts over nightshirts.

"You there," a man called.

"Hey, slow down!" another demanded.

Ahead, the street began to line with more residents of Recityv's Cathedral Quarter. Mira pushed harder, pointing her sword at one man who stepped into the street with violent intentions. Her warning stopped him in his tracks.

Suddenly, behind them, a roar erupted. Wendra looked over her shoulder and saw a dozen horses burst into the street. A chorus of battle cries rose from men in League brown and Recityv crimson. Their pursuers bore down on them, bloodlust in their voices.

Looking ahead again, Wendra's heart fell as three horsemen emerged from the end of the street and blocked the cathedral steps.

Mira didn't slow. She pulled both her swords and rode with an easy grace, eyeing the men ahead. Grant rode past Wendra and took a position beside the Far, barreling down upon the three horsemen.

Two of the three sat in old saddles on horses as shaggy as meadow mares. They wore armor pieced together from whatever they had at hand, and bore sigils that looked handsewn by the men themselves. They were aspirants to low seats at Convocation.

They mean to earn a reputation by stopping us.

But they seemed little more than opportunists. The third one wore a plain suit of black leather and carried a flail forged of a metal equally black. And though he wore no cloak, a hood hid his face. This third man was unsettling.

And still Mira did not slow.

A cacophony of angry shouts rose all around them. Wendra lowered her own chin and followed the others into the fight.

The man in the hood stared, waiting patiently. The Far charged forward undaunted, driving her mount directly toward him. Grant angled right for the rider on the end. Vendanj leaned forward, urging his mount on.

Braethen passed Wendra on the left, whooping his steed forward and drawing his own blade as he raced to the front and arrowed toward the horseman at the far left.

On the sides of the street, lamps flared into life, the growing crowd eager to see the fight.

She checked behind them again. The mob now filled the street like a wall of men and horseflesh. The glint of fire in dull metal winked at her, and she realized she and Sutter now held the rear position. If the three horsemen stopped them long enough, the swarm would have them.

Ahead, the man in the dark hood lifted his flail and began swinging it at a dizzying speed, creating a wide whirling barrier. In the air an ominous, painful moan began to grow, like the deathbed sighs of a generation—this was no ordinary warrior. The sound stole Wendra's breath, and she began to choke. She clutched at her throat and looked over at Sutter, who was doing the same.

A squeal pierced the air, and Wendra snapped her attention forward to see Mira rein in hard and jump to the ground, rushing the man. The rider turned and whipped his flail at Mira. The Far thrust one sword up and caught the weapon in its arc, and with her second blade sliced toward the hooded face. The rider leaned back to escape the blow, and rolled from his horse to the ground, keeping hold of his flail.

Grant forced his mount into a collision with the rider on the right, who made a weak attempt to thrust a sword into Grant's chest. The man out of the Scar twisted his fist into the other's hair and wrenched him from his saddle. A jarring crunch of mismatched armor accompanied a snap of bone, and the man scuttled away on his knees, dragging one arm uselessly.

To the left, Braethen raised his blade. As he closed in, Wendra caught a flash of shadow to his left. At the corner of the last building, two men huddled with crossbows aimed at Braethen. Their heads began to settle to the stillness Wendra knew came just before firing.

"Tahn," she shouted, pointing at the crossbowmen.

Tahn saw it immediately, and fired his bow at the first man.

The arrow hit the corner of the stone building, striking sparks in the shadows there. But it was enough to disrupt the man's concentration. The bolt sailed high and disappeared into the blackness across the street. The second man turned his crossbow on Tahn.

Tahn couldn't nock another arrow in time. Sutter couldn't help. Wendra looked at the man and shot a burst of angry song. The sound filled the end of the street, the force of it pounding the crossbowman like a stone gavel, and he slumped down over his own weapon. The echoes of her short song began to fade into the din of the mob.

A scream broke the sound of her dying note.

Wendra followed the cry and saw one of the riders pulling a barbed sword from Braethen's leg. The rider then raised his blade to finish Braethen.

His sword never fell. His mouth opened in surprise, his eyes shut in mortal pain. Mira. She pulled her sword from the man's gut, and he fell from his saddle.

Maesteri Belamae drew back the wide double doors. Vendanj rode past the fray and up the cathedral steps. Wendra and Penit followed him, Tahn and Sutter close behind.

Hooves clattered noisily on stone. Roars of anger echoed from the tall face of the cathedral. The wall of pursuers bore down on Braethen, Mira, and Grant.

Again the moan of human sighs rose up. The final horseman had begun to swing his flail in crushing arcs toward Mira. The Far danced back a step, and brought her swords up in defense.

Less than twenty strides separated the charging mob and Mira. She could easily have escaped them all and mounted the stair. But she stood between the dark rider and Braethen, a hard look in her eyes.

Vendanj ordered Wendra and the others inside, where a handful of men waited, eyes wide. "Quickly!" he shouted.

Maesteri Belamae drew Wendra and Penit inside. Sutter jumped from his horse and began down the stair, both hands on his blade.

"No!" Vendanj commanded. "Your one sword means nothing against so many."

Sutter flashed angry eyes at Vendanj, but stopped and looked again toward Braethen.

The din of shouts and howls and hooves and clattering armor rang around them.

Then, as if from nowhere, Grant appeared. He swept in quickly behind the hooded man, who turned in time to partially block Grant's sword, the blade slicing the man's side.

The flail slowed, the moan dimmed. A scream of anger lifted above the noise. The shadow inside the cowl focused on Grant, who pulled back, waiting for a counterattack.

Mira didn't hesitate. She took Braethen's reins and her own and raced up the steps. Grant took his own and followed, as the hooded rider disappeared into the darkness of a nearby alley. A rain of arrows began striking the steps about them, chips of rock flying, sparks leaping where metal met stone. But none found its mark, the arrows slipping from their trajectory by fractions, parting around their targets.

It was then that Wendra heard the melody. Like a battle song. But low, directed. She turned to see Belamae singing just under his breath.

The leaguemen and city guard reached the cathedral steps. They brought their horses to a skidding halt. Several voices shouted commands and warnings. But they faded as Vendanj ushered the last of them through the doors, which Belamae closed with less haste than she might have expected.

As soon as the door shut, two men and two women dropped crossbars through great iron rings to hold them. Belamae gave some quiet instruction to these men and women, who quickly led away their horses.

Then Belamae turned his clear, patient gaze on Vendanj, looking a question at him.

"A Telling," Vendanj said. "And quickly." He paused, pulling the scroll from his cloak and handing it to Belamae. "And my apologies for bringing this to your door, Maesteri. This won't go easy for you, even with Helaina's help."

Belamae took the Telling parchment and smiled, unconcerned. "You may be right." His voice rang deep and clean. "But while our gables and spires are tarnished, our purpose is not." He gave Wendra a warm but expectant look.

Vendanj drew her aside. Belamae joined them.

The Sheason's eyes grew solemn. Softly, he said, "Wendra, when I came to the Hollows, I asked you to come with us. To come here and study music. I knew your parents." He paused briefly, seeming to consider what to say. "I sensed a song in you. But only Belamae should—"

Wendra held up her hand to stop him. "I found some of that song." She looked a sad smile at Belamae. "The Maesteri and I have met. I know I have Leiholan gifts."

Vendanj seemed glad. "Then you know you're needed here, to learn to sing Suffering."

The Sheason shifted to look at Belamae. "The Quiet have burned Qum'rahm'se. Descant now has the only copy of the Tract of Desolation."

"Ours is a partial translation," Belamae clarified.

Vendanj nodded. "Yes, but it carries the spirit of the Tract."

"Belamae?" Wendra said.

The Maesteri showed her patient eyes. "The Song of Suffering is the singing of the Tract of Desolation. To sustain the Veil that holds the Quiet inside the Bourne, the Song is sung without end." He paused, his eyes momentarily distant. "We have so few Leiholan . . . and they tire."

Vendanj gathered her attention. "You're the reason we came to Recityv, Wendra. The rest of us have to go. But your place is here."

A flutter of panic stirred in her chest. "What about Penit?"

"He's coming with us." Vendanj gave the boy a knowing look. "You'll have to let him go."

Desperation filled her. She felt trapped.

It was impossible. . . . Then she thought of her lost child, and all she'd done to rescue Penit after she'd lost him, too.

Something stern and calm got inside her. She looked back at Vendanj, returning his stare.

"She's chosen." Vendanj didn't sigh or shake his head. "She'll go with us. But I give you my word, Belamae, that I'll protect her."

The Maesteri's demeanor changed, not to anger but concern. He smiled with disappointment, nodded, and led them down a dim hall.

No one spoke. Mira and Grant came last, supporting Braethen between them. Distantly, she heard the same melodic humming she'd heard before: the Song of Suffering, being sung deep within the cathedral.

Belamae led them through several halls, where small lamps burned on shallow shelves. They went past closed doors, catching phrases of song, musical passages played on citherns, flutes, and violins.

The Maesteri strode to a closed door. He produced a key, turned back the tumbler, and admitted them before he himself entered and locked the door behind them.

He then went round the room and lit several lamps. Gradually the shadows receded, showing an oval chamber with a ceiling fifty strides high. Murals had been painted there whose detail faded to the eye at such a distance. A great oval rug of blue-and-white interlocking patterns stretched to the walls, but left bare a smaller oval of stone at the room's center. The stone there was seamless, and shone like a dark, placid pool. At the back of the chamber stood a lectern like Garlen's, wrought from the same sleek stone as the floor.

The Maesteri went to Wendra and stood quietly before her. He gently took her hand, cupping it between his own. He let out a sigh and smiled wanly. "You'll never know how difficult it is for me to see you go." His voice caught with emotion. He swallowed and patted her hand.

"Go safely, young one," he added. "Remember that when you open your mouth to make song, there's responsibility in it. Please, come back to me. So much depends—" The Maesteri stopped, though it appeared he wanted to say more.

Wendra realized as the words died that they did so after a slowly fading roll of echoes. The chamber resounded with the cast of Belamae's voice, making each word larger than itself, a quality of depth and dimension Wendra hadn't heard before.

She smiled appreciatively at the old man, but in her heart she held reservations . . . a child had been ripped from her womb, Penit nearly sold on the blocks, her own chance to save him wagered in a game of chance.

The Maesteri left her and walked around the black oval to the lectern. He climbed a stair behind it, and soon stood overlooking the room from several strides above them. Carefully he untied the scroll and unrolled it. His eyes scanned the words. He looked up. "This is A'Garlen, I can tell." He smiled.

Then the Maesteri began to hum in a rich, deep voice, the sound of it resonating in the chamber until the entire space seemed filled with it. The sound came at Wendra from every direction, washing over her like her most vivid dream. The music thrummed with a life of its own, so that she couldn't be sure the Maesteri sang it at all.

Then the man began to sing the words. The Telling unfolded in glorious detail, the language fitting together as naturally and rhythmically as any lyric Wendra had ever heard. The dance and play of each phrase gave life to the words and what they described. From the lips of the Maesteri, the music soared as though it might stretch outward and upward without end.

In moments, the words ran together with the song and became something more. It touched Wendra deeply, resonating inside her.

Above the brilliant oval, the air began to draw itself into threads like the weave of a loom. Tendrils of space with the color of what lay beyond it reflected in thin wavy lines. Hundreds, then thousands of these strands shimmered together and grew until they filled the space above the dark stone.

Through the weave, she saw the face of Belamae as if through rippling water, but in slow vertical lines, and thin, like strands of hair.

As the song unwound itself, she glimpsed the gift that lived inside her. She might have been afraid, but in the embrace of Belamae's song, she felt safe.

The Maesteri sang a crescendo that wove itself in a shifting, scintillating pattern. Garlen's words given voice here began to create a picture. The threads moved, changed color, wove in new patterns. Wendra felt a pull as though the physical space of the chamber was realigning itself. The strands danced to the song, the words gave direction, and thousands of hairline rents in the air obeyed, moving and reshaping what she saw.

The weave coalesced, pulling tight and firming. The strands began to disappear from view, creating a new order in place of the old. On the Maesteri sang. And the picture became complete. She could feel a wind and smell the plains she looked upon, and heard the sound of thunder in a dark sky.

"Step through," Vendanj said, his voice soft so as not to disturb the song.

Mira and Grant went first. In a moment, they passed through this new curtain in the air and appeared on the soil of the scene rising up from the black oval floor. Then Vendanj, and Braethen. To her left stood Sutter, who gave an enthusiastic salute to Tahn, and stepped through himself. Then Tahn. And Penit.

Wendra looked up at the Maesteri, who continued to sing, but gave her a reassuring nod. With a rush of sound, Wendra stepped into the tapestry. With a sudden sadness and doubt, she left Descant behind.

• CHAPTER SIXTY-ONE •

Children of Soliel

When the Framers abandoned the world, they left their Language with the thought that one day it might be used, should the Quiet bring down the Veil.

—From *The Apocrypha of Shenflear,* thought to derive from his historical period

Tahn crunched shale underfoot as he emerged onto the vast dark plain. A damp wind pulled at his hair as he quickly took visual count of his friends. All had arrived safely. He looked back through a window torn in space and saw the Descant room, heard the Maesteri ending his song. The weave of strands began to unravel, pulling back to a previous form and distorting the picture behind it. In moments, the chamber was gone, replaced by unbroken terrain that met dark clouds at the horizon.

Vendanj helped Braethen lie down, rolling his cloak for a pillow to cushion his head.

"Breathe easy," the Sheason said.

Then Vendanj put a hand over the wound in Braethen's leg and said something that Tahn lost in the wind's flapping of his cloak. Braethen's face relaxed. Vendanj applied an ointment, and carefully wrapped the wound.

As he finished, a shearing sound startled them. They all turned as the strange weave of threads opened another window on the Soliel and their mounts walked through onto the shale. The Far gathered the horses, handing reins to each of them as the second weave disappeared.

A distant flash of light blazed near a range of jagged peaks, followed by a muted roll of thunder. The charcoal darkness of the shale blended gradually with the darkness of the mountains and the storm clouds that closed them in.

"The Soliel Stretches," Mira said evenly. "Garlen is full of surprises." She jumped into her saddle, and looked around in a full circle. "Naltus is close. We should get there before the storm comes."

Another flash lit the night. And soon the grumble of thunder cracked and boomed around them. Far away coyotes or wolves raised howls of protest to the sound.

As they traveled, Tahn caught glimpses of Grant watching him.

They passed tangles of bleached bone in the shale. Small prongs of calcified skeletons jutted up from the earth. The size of the bones was alarming. Nothing Tahn could identify. More than once, they passed rows of shale piled in mounds like graves, and several dolmens besides.

Then in front of them, as if from nowhere, a city.

Massive walls formed of the same shale around them made the city hard to discern, especially in the shadows of twilight. He couldn't see a single watchman, or gate. The walls looked seamless and abandoned.

And there were no merchants or pilgrims or even homes outside the walls.

"Strangers are seldom admitted past the gate." Mira sounded unapologetic. "Be respectful."

The walls of Naltus Far were much taller and broader than they'd appeared from further away. Tracking the parapets proved difficult in the dark, but their tops were clearly visible each time the sky erupted in flashes of lightning.

Drawing closer, Tahn saw that the walls rose in smooth, sheer planes. No joints or extruded rock offered a foothold. And there was no gate. Mira led them to the base of the great wall. With sure movements, she traced a design on the smooth surface with her fingertips. Then again she made the pattern. And a third time.

When she'd completed her last pass, a whisper of escaping air came from the wall and a large door swung inward. Tahn strained to see what the Far had done, but there was no marking, or latch. The door moved in a slow, deliberate arc, but made no sound, no grinding of rock or squeak of hinges. An entry large enough to admit a horse opened in the wall.

When they'd all ridden through, Tahn found Mira standing silently before a male Far. She lifted her right hand and placed her middle three fingers on the other's lips with a tenderness Tahn envied. While her hand still rested there, the male Far returned the gesture. Neither spoke a word. Mira withdrew her hand and motioned them to follow.

All the city rose in sleek lines of shale. In some places a dark wood augmented the architecture in the way of support posts or window dressing. But the impenetrable dimness of black slate prevailed in almost every structure.

"It's kind of ugly," Sutter muttered.

"I don't know," Braethen said from behind them. "There's a stark beauty in it, I think, a kind of simplicity if nothing else. Besides, I don't believe the slate is used because it's all they had."

Nails turned in his saddle to look at Braethen. "What do you mean?"

"I mean that I think the Far chose the Soliel Stretches *because* of the shale." Braethen looked back at Sutter.

"Must be hell for farmers," Sutter observed.

Braethen smiled as he explained. "Shale's noted as an element without Forda. Or at least, so little that it possesses no value to—"

"Velle." Grant started them with his intrusion, casting a look at Mira. "How the Far thrive here . . . is a wonder."

Hooves beat at cobbled shale bordered by countless homes and shops and storehouses, but Tahn didn't see a single Far. Not in the street. Not peering from windows. No music from taverns. No laughter or shouts from men drinking fast toward inebriation. Everything was still. Though many windows burned with light, even at this late hour.

An entire city like Mira. Are they all as beautiful? Tahn wondered.

They stopped before a large rectangular building with round, fluted pillars supporting a roof that covered an outer walk. It stood three stories high. Long terraced steps rose in groups of two from the street to the first story. Mira dismounted and handed her reins to the man who had conveyed them there.

"Thank you, Secretary Bridgoe," Mira said softly, her words barely carrying to Tahn's ears.

"They convened when you arrived on the Soliel," the secretary said. "You're expected."

Tahn and the others stepped down to the street. Bridgoe took their reins as well, escorting the horses away while Mira led Vendanj and the rest toward the large building. Near the stone wall she went to one knee. She bowed her head in the direction of the inner hall and held her unguarded pose for what seemed a long time. *A long time for Mira.*

The sound of their passage came like a rustling. The folds of cloaks. Footsteps kept light. The small hours of night held sway in the quiet shadows.

They mounted a stair that gave onto a mezzanine. The light of large lamps showed Tahn a view of bookcases set in long rows. Ahead of them were several closed doors. Over each portal hung a different weapon as if an indication of what could be found within.

Immediately to Tahn's right, a broad wall was covered by an enormous map that stretched from floor to ceiling. Across it, names had been written in a tight, fine hand: places he'd never heard of, battles, wars, and leaders. Beside many were dates as one sees on a gravestone.

So many names, the map was crowded with ink. Names Tahn hadn't heard. Surnames showed a trailing serif on the last stroke denoting gender, female, which Tahn surmised by finding Helaina's name near Recityv.

The name on Naltus: King Elan. It appeared in many places along the Saeculorum mountains above the city. Then Tahn's heart sped when he saw above the mountains the scrawled words: Rudierd Tillinghast.

Reading the words gave Tahn chills. That's where they were going. That's where he'd face whatever mistakes he'd made. Memories. Closer now to their reason for coming, cold dread opened low in his belly.

Tahn got moving, following Mira down another stair that descended in long steps to the level below. Coming to the edge of the mezzanine, he looked down on a small assembly of Far sitting in rows divided by a center aisle. Before them stood a young man who held a short crook in his hands.

Lightbearers stood stoically around the group, lanterns hanging from poles only slightly taller than their owners. The lamps glowed small in the vastness of the hall. Their presence felt symbolic. Perhaps they were a welcome.

None of the Far looked up at them as they descended the stairs. Flat footsteps echoed into the hall. On the floor, Mira held up her hand to stop them. She crossed to the Far standing at the front of the others.

A pace from him, she stopped and bowed her head. She didn't raise it again until he'd softly touched her shoulder with his crook.

Mira spoke to him, her words inaudible to Tahn. Then she stepped back, and Vendanj strode forward, his tall frame commanding even in the depths of the great hall. He humbly bowed as Mira had, likewise receiving a touch of the Far's crook.

Vendanj looked up for only an instant before turning to the assembly. He didn't immediately speak, his gaze passing over each Far.

Not one of those here was older than Tahn. Some were several years younger. All wore a kind of experience and confidence in their youthful faces that he couldn't explain.

Vendanj pushed his cloak back over his shoulders, exposing the three-ring pendant that hung around his neck. A rustle of movement swept through the

Far. No words. But the stirring of feet and straightening of backs spoke the same surprise.

"Children of Soliel," Vendanj began. "Not many days ago the Quiet found the library at Qum'rahm'se."

More rustling.

Vendanj held up a hand. "They got nothing. The scriveners burned it all before the Quiet could take it. As they should have. But generations of scholarship on the Covenant Language is now ash." Vendanj paused. "And the library contained the only complete copy of the Tract of Desolation."

The Far became still.

Vendanj stepped closer, capturing them with a serious gaze. "What knowledge man had of the Covenant Tongue is gone. Your stewardship over the Language is now more crucial than ever. More at risk. Even in this shale valley you aren't safe. You know this." Vendanj looked past them, his eyes growing distant. "You've kept your promise, kept the Language safe. But the time has come. You must prepare to *use* the Language."

"Vendanj?" It was the Far leader.

"Men bicker. Even Sheason are not all of one mind. And Leiholan tire as they sing Suffering." Vendanj nodded, distance still in his eyes. "The Quiet come, and . . ."

It was the only time Tahn could remember Vendanj not finishing a thought.

The Sheason stepped back beside Mira. The young Far with the crook placed the small staff on the table behind him. The Far assembly rose as though formally dismissed and quietly took their leave. The lightbearers placed their staffs in holes in the floor before likewise exiting the room. Moments later, the hall stood empty save for Tahn's companions and the one Far who'd held the crook.

He sat on the edge of the table. "It's good to see you, Vendanj. But I wish you had better news."

"So do I, Elan." Vendanj rubbed at his eyes.

"But there's more to say," Vendanj added, "without your captains."

"I suspected as much," the king replied. "Water?"

"They need it," Mira answered, nodding to Tahn and the others.

Elan turned to the table behind him and poured several glasses from a carafe, inviting them all to drink. As Tahn drank, he stared at Elan, realizing this was the Far who wanted Mira to bear him an heir. Vendanj paced to the center aisle of the chairs and turned to look back at Elan and the rest of them.

He pulled out the list of names he'd created with Ne'Pheola, and handed them to Elan. "I think someone's learned how to nullify the vow, and probably by using the Covenant Tongue."

Elan's brow creased as he reviewed the altered names. "The Quiet."

"We don't know. Maybe." Vendanj took a few steps back toward Elan. "But what's clear is that the Quiet are trying to better understand the Language.

Which will lead them here. If the Quiet take possession of the Covenant Tongue, our fight is over."

Elan poured a glass of his own and drank. "Naltus will hold."

"It's not about holding," Vendanj countered. "You have to prepare the Language for battle."

"Vendanj," Elan said, his tone grave. "We've fought the Quiet before. We've never needed—"

"It's different this time." Vendanj was shaking his head. "They walked into the Hollows, Elan. Something's changed. There's no time for half measures."

Vendanj grew quiet for a moment, his eyes downcast in his own thoughts. "We'd thought to strengthen the Veil, bring the Tract of Desolation here. Retranslate it. The Tract is gone. The regent has recalled Convocation to build an alliance. But not all will show." He turned toward the king of the Far. "We need the Language as a weapon, Elan."

Elan finally nodded. "We'll go into our own library. Start to prepare. But I don't think that's the only reason you're here." The king looked down at Penit, a disconcerted look on his face.

Vendanj looked up from beneath a lowering brow. "We're on our way to Tillinghast."

Elan frowned at the news, and kept a cold silence. Then he turned to stare in the direction of the mountains where the storm raged. "What do you hope to gain?"

Vendanj followed Elan's gaze. "This time . . . when the Quiet comes . . . it's different. This time I think we're going to need someone who's looked back at his choices. Good and bad. And remembers it all when the Bourne is set free."

Elan put his glass down. "You've tried this before, Vendanj. What makes you believe these will fare any better?" He glanced at Tahn and the others. "And why do you think this is how we must meet the Quiet?"

For a long time, Vendanj said nothing. Into a heavy silence he finally spoke. "Just a feeling."

Elan raised a sober eye. "I hope you're right. Forgetting may have been the only grace given to man. No one should have to remember all his choices."

The Sheason didn't disagree. Uneasiness filled Elan's face. Vendanj looked up at Tahn with grim resolve.

A peal of thunder reverberated around the great hall.

"The blood of many stains my hands," Vendanj said softly. "I've asked families to walk painful paths. I won't let these sacrifices go unremembered." His voice turned cool and even. "So few are willing to answer the threat of the Bourne. Our great 'civility' breeds indignation at the thought, or worse, disbelief. And complacency." Vendanj stopped, and cast his eyes upward. He took a long inward breath. When he lowered his head again, an indomitable expression lit his face. "It will not be so *this* time."

Goose bumps rose almost painfully across Tahn's skin. Mira looked at him, a kind of empathy in her eyes he'd not seen before. It both comforted and frightened him.

The Sheason pulled his cloak about his shoulders and weighed the looks of those around him. Only Grant showed no expression. The exile out of the Scar sniffed and waited.

"You'll have rooms at my home," Elan finally said, shattering the silence. "Vendanj, I'll insist that you take attendants into each room."

"To sleep with us?" Sutter blurted.

The Far king half-smiled, seeming grateful for a change in mood. "Not to sleep. It's our custom that visitors be watched over, even at rest."

"Of course," Vendanj agreed. "I'd like Mira to sit with Tahn."

The Far king nodded, took up his crook, and strode away. Vendanj went with him, the two conferring as Mira motioned for the rest to follow her.

On their way out, Tahn looked back over his shoulder at the great hall, seeing the light standards, the rows of chairs, and the mezzanine where he'd first seen the map showing Rudierd Tillinghast.

At the door, Grant put a reassuring hand on his shoulder and urged him through.

• CHAPTER SIXTY-TWO •

One Bed, the Same Dream

A good parent touches eternity. But so does a bad one.

—Colloquial saying; scriveners place its origin
in the Kamas Throne

Tahn surveyed the bedchamber: table and chair set beside the window, chest of drawers, a bed. *One* bed. A thrill raced through him, followed quickly by anxiety. Slowly, he shut the door. When he turned, Mira had already seated herself in the chair beside the window and taken out her oilcloth to work her blades. As she set to wiping down one of her swords, Tahn unshouldered his bow and threw off his cloak, tossing it over the foot of the bed.

Beyond the window, lightning still flashed against the darkness to the north. Gouts of wind buffeted the eaves, whistling like thin reeds. A single lamp burned on the table, its wick so low that the oil threatened to extinguish the flame.

Tahn turned up the wick, brightening the room, and put his hands near the glass as though to warm them. He then sat beside his cloak, and watched Mira. She seemed not to notice, evenly running her cloth over the edge of her weapon, which caught reflections of the flame.

Questions spun in his head, things he wanted to ask but didn't dare: *Did she think it was possible that a boy from the Hollows and a Far girl . . .*

Tahn regarded her in the lamplight. No delicate square-neck blouse on *her* bosom, as the women of the Hollows wore when spring came. Mira's cloak remained clasped at her neck, the grey folds cascading around a tight shirt that stretched when she moved. No tincture colored her lips or eyes. But the glow of the flame gently touched her skin, lending warmth to her determined features. White flashes burst from the sky, starkly lighting half her face for brief moments.

"Something on your mind?" she said, turning over her blade to inspect both edges.

Tahn groped for words. "I don't know. Yes."

"You should tell me, then get some sleep."

"All right. Why me?"

Mira sheathed one sword and withdrew the other. Without a look, she said, "You don't really need me to answer that, do you?"

"I know, I'm not the first." Thoughtfully, he touched the mark on the back of his hand. "All right, why me *this time*?"

"Will that make it easier for you?" Mira said, folding over her oilcloth.

Tahn's fist tightened into a ball. "Wouldn't it make it easier for you?"

Mira continued to work. "No."

"Well, that's fine for you," Tahn said with mild irritation. "You're a Far."

"Keep your voice down," Mira said calmly. "Others are trying to sleep."

"It's got something to do with all the years I can't remember, doesn't it?"

Mira went on with her careful cleaning of her weapon.

"What Elan said . . ." Emotion caught in his throat. "I'm afraid, Mira."

She stopped cleaning her blades, and showed him compassionate eyes. "I don't have answers, Tahn. And even if I did, I don't believe hearing them would ease your heart. But I do know a little about remembering."

He nodded for her to continue.

"I told you Far die when we come to our Change. It gives us the freedom to do and say what's necessary to guard the Language left behind by the Framers. We never have to account . . . for anything.

"My sister's passing leaves me the sole remnant of my family line. She was Elan's wife. And before I go he'll ask me to stay. To take up her crown. And to bear him an heir. It will be an honor to be asked. And our people need this." She paused, staring. "But I don't want to be the queen. I don't want to have a child that I'll never hear say my name. A child—like me—who'll never have the chance to know her mother. A child who'll remember a handful of 'mothers,' but not the one who gave her life." She shook her head. "I don't remember my true mother. And I'd rather forget the rest."

They shared a long look, anguish in her eyes.

Tahn let out a slow breath. "You remember a childhood you'd rather forget. And I can't remember a childhood I wish I could."

The Far looked back thoughtfully. "Why do the memories matter so much to you? Who you are is defined by the choices you make *now*."

Tahn considered her words. "Perhaps you're right." Then he added, "And the same would hold true for you and any child you bear."

They sat looking at one another. He wished he could wrap his arms around her, but didn't know how not to do it clumsily. The hiss of the lamp seemed suddenly very loud.

Maybe there was a lesson for him in her commitment to this journey to Tillinghast, where she would give so much of a life that would end so soon.

Considering it, Tahn felt selfish.

Neither of them spoke again until he asked her the question that had been on his mind ever since he'd met her in the Hollows. "Has a Far ever married a man?"

Mira smiled her glorious lopsided grin, but didn't answer.

He had one more question, but she answered it before he could ask.

"I will sit vigil. You'll have the bed to yourself."

"Draw your bow," the man said.

Tahn looked out from the ridge in the cool blue of morning and raised his bow.

"No arrow today," the man said.

Tahn glanced at the man and put the arrow away.

"Focus on yourself. Steady aim. Breathe slowly. Feel the energy of your draw."

Tahn pulled deeply and held it, letting out his breath in a long exhale.

"Why did you lie about what Meche did?" the familiar voice asked.

Tahn tried to turn and explain to the man.

"Focus!" the other said. "Keep your aim. Keep your draw."

Tahn looked back out over the chasm, leveling his eyes.

"You took a second helping of stew on the day of Lile's third combat test," the man reminded him. "He went to bed hungry that night."

"But I thought—"

"Don't talk," the man said. "Your draw is the only thing you should care about right now."

Tahn's arms began to burn. His chest and shoulder and fingers, too. It was getting hard to hold his bow steady.

And as he stood, trying to breathe calmly and hold a focused draw, the man went on. The ways Tahn had harmed his friends by negligence or small deceits. The unkind words he'd said in anger. And more.

Tahn's aim began to waver.

"Hold your draw steady," the man scolded.

"I can't," Tahn said.

"You can," the man insisted. "Think past everything I say, everything I remind you of."

It went on minute after minute. He could see the canyon rim swaying beyond the line of his bow. He was losing it.

Then the man pointed to the canyon floor. "You missed it. On patrol you lost focus. And Devin—"

Tahn started to scream, drowning out the man's voice. His aim swayed violently until he could no longer hold his draw and dropped his bow. He fell to his knees beside the weapon, his body aching, still screaming—

Tahn sat up in his bed, slick with sweat and breathing heavily, images and words fading with the nightmare. For a moment he didn't know where he was. He frantically looked about. Mira was watching him.

She said nothing, but came to his bedside and took hold of his hand. Her touch helped, but dread still pounded in his chest.

The world beyond the window was still dark. But not for long. Slowly, he lay back down and turned his head east, his hand still held in Mira's. He managed to imagine a sunrise briefly before even that image mattered too little to remain in his mind's eye. He focused on his breathing and soon regulated the rhythm enough to calm himself.

If only for a while.

Tomorrow they left for Tillinghast.

CHAPTER SIXTY-THREE

Leavetaking

It's remarkable that Far pray, given their assurances beyond this life. Maybe this explains man's lack of prayer, since he's been given no such assurance.

—Discussion topic during the Fourth Congress on Faith, an exploration of prayer

Mira knelt at her sister's tomb in the Hall of Valediction. The dark shale dimly caught the glow of braziers, which lit the names and dates inscribed on the stone.

It pained her to say good-bye.

Saying good-bye to a Far wasn't supposed to be a sad thing. They went on to a next life where they'd meet family. And Lyra had lived well, ruled well, earning a rare esteem.

But she'd not produced an heir.

All Far shared stewardship over the Covenant Language, but to only a few were the gifts of that tongue given. Mira was the last of her bloodline that could produce such an heir.

And child-bearing years for a Far were short.

It wasn't law that she take her sister's place. But if she was honest, it *was* a fair expectation. More than that, it might prove to be an absolute need.

There was another need, though, one she'd joined herself to many months ago. Meeting Tahn had been a pleasant surprise. He had courage. And she felt comfortable around him. . . .

It was a dream. She had less than two years to live. She shouldn't be thinking beyond that.

But over the tomb of her loving sister, she argued with herself. *Lyra, what should I do?*

As if in response, footsteps sounded on the hard floor. She didn't need to turn to know their owner.

"Can't I have an hour to pray for my sister?"

"Prayers aren't needed, Mira. You know this. And I wouldn't ordinarily interrupt the respects you pay her. She was my wife. I loved her. But your companions are preparing for the Saeculorum, and I need your answer."

"Mankind wouldn't find your proposal terribly tender." Mira ran her hands over the inscribed name of her sister.

Elan's voice softened. "We're not mankind."

"Better?" Her voice rang with accusation.

True to his nature, Elan replied, "No. But the Far made a promise to keep the Language. And I'm not a year from my own earth."

Silence settled in the Hall of Valediction. Elan neither pressed nor departed. Mira continued to kneel, searching.

"Tell me what to do," she whispered over her dead sister's body.

She stood and turned to Elan. He was a good king, strong, and a better strategist than any single person she'd met in all her travels. He approached gently. He touched her face. His eyes held compassion for her struggle with this choice.

"It's not so easy," she said.

"The mantle of leadership never is." He smiled, a wan look touching his face. Perhaps to sit at his side, produce an heir, *would* be a happy last chapter to her short life.

"I'm honest and kind," he said, a hint of humor in his voice. "That's as true as our need of an heir. In case that helps you."

Mira looked back at him and gave her own wan smile. "Subtle," she said.

A confused expression rose on his face.

"Never mind," she said.

Elan walked her to the stable yard. There in the bright sun, as her companions began to file out of the king's manor, she kissed his cheek. "I must see this through to the end before anything else." She looked away toward the Saeculorum. "But I have a request of my king."

Elan raised an eyebrow, waiting.

"You must take your place at Convocation," she said firmly. "The regent needs your support."

Moments passed before Elan answered. "Mira, you're asking me to leave Naltus without a king *or* queen."

"I believe Convocation will fail if you don't go." Mira thought of her sister's tomb. "Our covenant must be to more than our commission. We're part of this world; our fates are joined with man's."

Elan's brow drew down. He was fair, but he wouldn't be manipulated. "You aren't thinking clearly, Mira. Our best help to others is to keep our commission."

She looked back at him with calm defiance. "Elan, if you won't go, then I'll take my place as queen and go myself."

Mira didn't want to undermine him. But she wouldn't let this pass. "Think on it, Elan. But don't think long. They already assemble at Recityv. Two, maybe three weeks. From Naltus, it should be *you* who goes."

Her king smiled softly. "It seems we each have something to consider."

He then held up Mira's hand and passed her a small fold of parchment. She knew what it was—her sister's last message for her. "Read it when your journeys are at an end."

She nodded and led Vendanj, Tahn, and all the rest from Naltus. Toward the Saeculorum. And Tillinghast.

• CHAPTER SIXTY-FOUR •

Rhea-Fol Reprise

Who is fiercest in battle? He with the most to lose, or he with the most to win? Neither; it is he with nothing to lose.

> —*The Gearworks of Motivation,* a field manual
> for Alon I'tol officers

They rode for eight straight hours, taking only brief breaks to rest their horses.

Late in the day, shale gave way to russet earth broken by an occasional oasis of long green grass around pools of water. Thorny flowers grew across the earth, crawling over the ground in a huge network of interconnected creepers. And stout trees with long thin leaves dotted the land, their shade giving rise to bloodred ferns and yellowed bushes with leaves that rustled together like dim rattles.

Ahead, the mountains loomed closer, reaching up with suddenness from the basin as though thrust into the sky in a violent quaking of the land.

Behind them, the sun began to set, aureate hues fading to russet and finally to the muted blues of twilight. With the passing of the light, they finally stopped to rest.

Grant perched on a rock, his back to them, watching the southern horizon where stars flickered into view against the spread of dark. Mira set off to scout the surrounding area. Vendanj sat a short distance from them, looking over a book.

Sutter sat gingerly, grimacing against the pain in his thighs and buttocks. Once down, he promptly pulled a hunk of salted meat from his daypack and took a large bite. Around it he said, "No need to stop just yet. I still have feeling in my ass."

Tahn and Wendra laughed weakly, and found patches of ground on which to lay out their bedrolls. Braethen managed the fire.

"Hey, I know," Sutter said, "let's have a story. Penit, give us one of your fancies. I'm paying." He tossed a rock in the semblance of a coin into the center of the circle they'd formed. "And spare not the wit."

Penit didn't stand up this time, as he'd done at the Sedagin feast. But he sat up straighter, as though preparing himself. Tahn looked over at the boy, wondering why Vendanj had allowed him to come.

"Have a story in mind?" Penit asked.

"Anything," Wendra said. "Something stirring. Something familiar, perhaps. Oh, you choose."

"How about *The Great Defense of Layosah*. It's one of my favorites." Penit nodded. "Layosah it is," he said, keeping his voice low.

Wendra looked eager with anticipation of the tale. Vendanj sat back, his features thoughtful. Braethen nodded appreciatively, seeming to remember the story.

"And so it goes," Penit said.

With a tilt of his head, and various turns and expressions, he told the story of a woman receiving news of yet another of her sons dying in the war of the First Promise. She'd lost several other sons, and her husband besides.

Something had to be done. Things had to change.

Layosah had gone to the general of the army. But got no satisfaction.

She'd gone to a Sheason. Still no help.

So, in desperation, she'd mounted the steps of Solath Mahnus, carrying her newborn child. There she railed for three days, calling on the king to do something.

"Don't you see what's happening," Penit said as Layosah. "The Quiet are making refugees of the people, and they flood every safe town and city, seeking refuge. Granaries are ravaged, the food runs out and the people starve. City arbors reek of the unbathed. The streets are filled with low men and every unsavory practice. Children are forced into whore dens. All to survive while you send unprepared armies to die!"

Penit looked rueful in the firelight, gesturing and pacing, pointing and covering his heart with his hands.

"And now the largest legions out of the Bourne march into the east." Penit's voice was soft, but filled with worry and anger. "And so I ascend these stairs of the great Halls of Solath Mahnus in the free city of Recityv, as one of King Baellor's Wombs of War—whose grandmother's sons, and mother's sons have gone to fight this enemy . . . and fallen.

"And I stand here," Penit said, resolute, "on these chiseled steps with my babe." He raised his hands high as though holding aloft a small child. "I stand here, denied an audience by King Sechen Baellor the Swift. Denied an audience, though my family's blood has purchased this city's freedoms. I lift my child here and call upon our king to form a council to represent *all* the people of the east. Send word. Bring *every* king here. Build an army to *end* this fight."

Penit's voice grew thin, tremulous. "Or else I would rather dash my babe on this stone stair and snuff his life, than see him grow and send another generation to war."

Tahn watched in amazement, holding his breath as Penit stood poised with his hands held aloft.

Silence stretched, as they waited to see what would happen. The fire burned in the quiet between them.

Penit took a long breath and lowered his arms, ending his tale. A kind of self-reflection rested in his face. These were clearly more than sketches for the boy. Something of the valor and integrity in them seemed to mean something to him. Or maybe it was this one story.

He gathered himself and sat again next to Wendra.

"Any particular reason for this one?" Braethen asked.

The boy looked up, appearing old beyond his years. "The willingness to sacrifice a child. Seems almost unbelievable," he said, and gave a sad smile.

"You tell it well, Penit." Braethen's voice was soft, reverential. "Layosah's speech brought about the Convocation of Seats that ended the First War of Promise. She was a remarkable woman."

Wendra seemed not to hear them. Perhaps the subject was too raw for her. Tahn's heart ached seeing her in pain.

Vendanj looked away into the hills behind them, his brow a tangle of deep furrows over dark eyes.

A moment later, the sound of rushing air rolled toward them. Grant jumped to his feet and took a step into the night, his sword a flash in his hand. In an instant, Mira sprinted out of the darkness toward them. Over her head streaked arrows, humming past her and flashing through the air above their circle.

"On your feet!" she yelled, drawing to a quick stop beside Grant and turning to face the way she'd come.

Tahn jumped up, nocking an arrow and pulling a deep draw in one fluid motion. But he pointed the tip aimlessly toward the darkness beyond the fire, unsure of a target.

Out of the night more arrows slipped swiftly by them.

Sutter and Braethen took positions a few strides behind Mira, and Wendra placed herself between the arrows and Penit. Vendanj walked to stand beside Grant.

Grant spoke with a loud, calm voice, never looking away from the south. "They won't have moved this quickly with an entire collough. It's an advance squad."

The approach of feet came louder—labored, heavy steps, but not clumsy or careless. The sounds bore down on them from the dark.

Then in the distance, a glint of light reflected from two orbs bobbing in the darkness. A second set of eyes appeared, catching the light. Behind these first two Quiet, came two more. Then all four Bar'dyn emerged from the night at a full run, their stout legs carrying their considerable forms at impossible speeds. No crazed look of ambush or bloodlust lit their faces, as maces and swords were raised to meet Grant and Mira.

Arrows continued to streak through the air around them, but they seemed more an attempt at confusion than attack.

And just as the Bar'dyn came within three strides of Mira, the sound of footfalls fairly shook the ground behind them.

Surrounded!

Tahn pulled his draw around, but still saw nothing. Wendra shuffled her feet, trying to decide which direction to shield the boy from.

Then, out of the dark, two Bar'dyn came barreling in from the north. Wendra shot Tahn a worried look. She stepped forward to meet the flank attack, and Tahn aimed at the first Bar'dyn coming in from behind.

He thought the old phrase in an instant, and let his arrow fly.

His arrow struck the lead creature in the arm. Without slowing, the Bar'dyn plucked it away and let it fall beneath his feet. As Tahn drew again he heard weapons and bodies clash behind him. He thought he heard Sutter cry out, but had no time to check on Nails. He released again, aiming for the Bar'dyn's head. The arrow caught the creature just below the eye. It pulled this arrow out as it had the first. Never a sound.

The second Bar'dyn raced past his wounded fellow and surged into their camp, closing on Wendra and Penit. Tahn raised a draw on this one. Before he could release, Wendra sang a quick set of rough sounds. Sharp, dissonant. The air shimmered, looking like a horizon baking in heat. Her voice grew louder and more angered. The camp swirled. Blood began to flow from the Bar'dyn's eyes and nose and ears. But it pushed on as though fighting a river current, moving with deadly intent toward Wendra. A moment later it grasped her around the throat.

Her song abruptly stopped. The shimmer in the air stopped. And the Bar'dyn's sluggishness ended. Wendra struggled against the beast's grip. Tahn fired and hit the creature in the neck, blood oozing out as though he'd hit a vein.

The Bar'dyn threw Wendra to the ground on top of Penit and turned. Tahn tried to retreat a few steps. But the two Bar'dyn slipped behind him and began to drive him away from the firelight. Tahn began to fire his arrows in a blur. Some deflected off the Bar'dyn's tough skin. Others found home, sticking in the creatures, who now simply ignored the arrows.

These Bar'dyn held their swords low, not rushing or threatening. Just advancing on him slow.

They're isolating me from the others.

And he was out of arrows.

Tahn looked over at Wendra. He couldn't tell if she was breathing. Had the Bar'dyn crushed her throat? Penit struggled to free himself from beneath her. Behind the Quiet herding him, Mira and Grant descended on a Bar'dyn simultaneously, swords flashing in the weak light; it dropped in a heap. At their side, Sutter swung his longsword in a huge sweeping figure eight. His arms worked with intensity as he drove one Bar'dyn back several paces, this one also with its sword held low.

Braethen fought beside Vendanj. Four Bar'dyn had formed a rough circle around them. They were far from the fire. Hard to see. But one by one the creatures were falling.

Mira and Grant parted and drew the advance of two more Quiet. The whistle of steel sliced toward the Far. One sword went up, deflecting the blow, the other came directly after, catching the Bar'dyn in the neck. A gout of blood splashed Mira across the face.

A second, more cautious creature waited on Grant's attack. It held a menacing ax, ready to swing. Grant outlasted the Bar'dyn's patience, his sword held dangling at his side. The creature bolted, its great ax descending like a judgment. Grant anticipated the move and leapt close to the Bar'dyn's wide chest. In a furious thrust, Grant swung his sword up through the underside of the creature's chin. The creature's body went immediately limp.

Tahn looked back at the Bar'dyn pushing him now far from his friends. They appeared unconcerned about the deaths of their comrades.

"I am I!" Out of nowhere, Braethen flashed into Tahn's view. His battle cry caused Tahn's skin to tingle. With fury, the sodalist came at the Bar'dyn that were trying to separate Tahn from his friends. Sutter rushed to Braethen's side. But before they could be of any help, arrows hit them in the legs and they both went down in a tumble.

Tahn stood alone. He was getting further from the rest by the moment. Further into the dark. Without any arrows.

Then something occurred to him. Something from a dream. Something he'd done on instinct in the wilds of Stonemount.

He drew his empty bow, rehearsed the oldest words he knew, and aimed.

A look of recognition caught in the Bar'dyn eyes.

"We did not choose this, Quillescent," one said. "Beware your own destruction if you first seek ours." It spoke with a soothing intelligence that caught Tahn off guard. Then, they nodded, the movement seeming like a signal.

In the next moment the camp grew still. Quiet.

All light dwindled. The fire guttered. Tahn's own wakefulness seemed to ebb . . . when an apparition parted the two Bar'dyn that separated Tahn from the others. It moved with a strange grace, wore no great cloak, no dark hood. Its clothes were plain. His fear of it was the disregard it held in its face when it looked at Tahn. The indifference.

Tahn had only the vaguest sense that it had no body of its own. Though it had a kind of gravity about it, thickening the air, muting the glow of the fire. Even the stars flickered, their immutable light straining in the shadow that surrounded the figure. It came toward him, walking slow, inviting Tahn to release his arrowless draw.

Tahn's heart hammered. He thought the old words. Doubt flooded through him. Icy fear paralyzed him, and he dropped his bow.

A willowy hand rose. It pointed at Tahn.

He thought he heard whispers, countless voices, rushing in his ears. Something inside him stirred. Vibrated. It was like a string resonating when being played. Tahn lost all strength in his legs and fell face-first to the ground. His body trembled, his nose and mouth filling with dust as he gasped for breath.

And yet beneath it there seemed an invitation. A desire to be resonated with. This apparition, or man, wanted . . . *He wanted me to fire at him.*

A moment later Tahn thought he could hear a vibrant note. He was locked in some kind of connection with the creature. And when it began to feel a dark vibration inside it, Tahn felt it too.

It came like a howl of wind heard at a distance. A deep note. It raced outward from inside the mind of this Quiet, a scouring rush. Its form began to quaver. And a long moment later it exploded like a collection of vapors. And there behind it stood Vendanj, one hand raised, a grim look on his face.

The Sheason grimaced and swept his hands up toward the sky. A wave of soil swallowed the last two Bar'dyn. The creatures fell, snatched down into the earth amid the grinding of rocks and twisted roots. They struggled against the Soliel, their throaty voices grunting with the effort, until their mouths filled with dirt and sand that seemed to flow there intentionally.

Before their mouths were of use to them, one of the Bar'dyn stared up at Tahn with a look of disappointment. "You still don't understand, do you?" it said, turning a brief eye toward the ground where his dead comrades had been swallowed up.

Vendanj stepped between Tahn and the dying Bar'dyn.

The creature looked up at him. "You can't win a war against an enemy who hasn't anything left to lose."

Then its mouth was full and its eyes went blank.

"Are you all right?" Vendanj asked Tahn.

Tahn nodded. The aching resonance inside him had ended when Vendanj destroyed the apparition.

Vendanj then rushed to Wendra's side. He took his wooden case from the inner lining of his cloak, and removed a sprig. He opened Wendra's mouth, and put it on her tongue. Then he took her hand and placed his fingertips to her throat.

Penit sat close, watching Vendanj with fascination and concern. As Vendanj worked, the others remained still, watching and hoping.

A few moments later, Wendra convulsed, and took a long, ragged breath. Her eyes shot open, immediately searching for Penit. Seeing him, she settled beneath Vendanj's hands, still gasping.

The Sheason made her comfortable, then tended to Braethen and Sutter, whose wounds were not so severe. Sutter limped back into camp, his sword held loosely in his hands. Sweat ringed his armpits and collar. Between heavy gasps he muttered, "Had . . . them . . . worried."

Still shaking from his encounter with the apparition, Tahn crawled his way back to the fire. His face felt raw and dirty, but he didn't bother to brush the dirt away. He propped himself up on his hands and stared through the flames at the Sheason, whose face showed heavy concern.

"This wasn't just a band of advance scouts," Vendanj said. "They came to test us. To take stock." Then he sat on the ground, and laid back against a fallen tree. He looked gaunt and pale. Older, maybe. In the firelight, sweat shone on his brow like tiny pearls.

"They've reached the hills ahead of us. And they know there's only one reason for us to travel north. It doesn't matter." Vendanj shook his head, and looked at Wendra. "But they know about you now. That's clear. It's why they tried to silence you." Vendanj then settled a heavy gaze on Tahn. "And they've learned more about you now, too."

My empty bow. Tahn caught his breath, wondering what he'd meant to do with an empty draw.

"Rest a while. We'll ride north when you've collected your strength." Vendanj closed his eyes and breathed deeply, taking a sprig from his wooden case for his own tongue.

Sometime later they mounted again, and rode into the Saeculorum.

• CHAPTER SIXTY-FIVE •

Lineage

Genealogists ask us to remember people who are often better left in the past. Sadistic bastards.

—From the pen of satirist Sech Galen, on
"How to Remain a Happy Orphan"

It was dark hour when Vendanj woke him.

They had ridden several hours to put distance between themselves and the Quiet, then found some shallow caves high on a defensible ridge. Tahn had barely fallen asleep.

"Tahn, come with me. There are things we must discuss."

It was the heart of night. Tahn crept from his cold bed and joined the Sheason far from the others under a hard moon and starlight. Vendanj waited as Grant joined them in the shadows. For several long moments, they kept silent company.

"It's time to restore your memory," Vendanj began in a low voice. "It won't all come back at once. May take a few days. But we want you to remember so that these things don't surprise you at Tillinghast." Vendanj reached out and gave Tahn's arm a reassuring squeeze.

"Some of it will be painful," Vendanj added. "Which is why we've waited 'til now. Too many things to get through before coming here. But now's the time."

Tahn didn't argue. He'd had plenty to deal with.

"Are you ready?" Vendanj asked.

Tahn spared a look at Grant, then took a deep breath. He'd spent years in the Hollows wanting to remember his first twelve years. Feeling a bit lost because of it. And now, there was a rock in the pit of his stomach. Some of this was going to go badly. He thought about Mira, how she wished she could forget her own childhood. But *he* still had to know. He nodded to Vendanj.

The Sheason put his hands on Tahn's head and began to speak in a tongue Tahn had never heard. The touch of Vendanj's hands warmed his skin, relaxed him, made him feel safe and comfortable. He couldn't understand the Sheason's words, but somehow understood their *feeling*. Then slowly, what Tahn could only think to call a veil slipped from his mind. As it did, memories returned to him, memories from his youth, before the Hollows.

A strange weight crushed down on him. Tahn fell to the hard rock.

In his mind, he was still falling. Falling down a long tunnel of forgotten things. Images and thoughts and feelings that for years had made him feel odd or sometimes even sick . . . now made sense. And the memories continued to rush through him.

He shut his eyes.

And he knew without seeing that the shadow behind him was the man Grant.

And he knew Grant was his father.

Grant was the faceless man from his dreams and nightmares. The man who had taught him that he might one day stand on a cliff at Tillinghast and draw. The man who had taught him that what mattered was the *intention* of his pull, since there would be no target. The man on the barren plain—the Scar—the man with the wind-tortured voice. The man who'd taught him how to recognize his latent gift to hear the whispering of the Will and bring it into harmony with his weapon by reciting words with every bowstring he'd ever pulled.

I draw with the strength of my arms and release as the Will allows.

Words that had defined him in ways that often made him feel quite mad.

Words that had stayed his hand when he should have defended people who needed his help. A woman being burned. A sister and her child.

Tahn's eyes shot open, and he glared at Grant. "You bastard! Wendra. Is she even my sister?"

Grant rushed to Tahn.

Tahn shoved him back. "Answer me!" But he knew the answer.

The wind soughed around the cliff's edge under the brittle moon. "No," Grant said. "She's not."

Tahn stared out at the long dark plain of the Soliel far below. "Balatin, why?"

He saw in his mind a hundred memories of singing and dancing and hunting and playing and eating and celebrating Northsun and feeling the warm love of the man . . . and it was all *false*. The life he had clung to when he couldn't remember the long past had been nothing more than a hoax, a scheme, conceived by people who claimed to love him. People who meant to use him.

And now, underneath it, he could see and feel his years of dry, lonely hopelessness spent in the Scar with Grant. He had learned to fight and examine and live, all in anticipation of the day he would come into this place of last things. Come here to what? Become a sacrifice for a Sheason and his martyr's quest? Murderous thoughts rose in Tahn's mind.

The Sheason must have sensed it, because he took hold of Tahn again, imparting a measure of peace to his troubled heart. Again Tahn felt warmth.

But it wasn't enough to quench his anger. Not completely. When Vendanj removed his hands, Tahn knelt under the harsh glare of the moon and swore an oath. "If there's something that qualifies me to stand at Tillinghast, why send me away?" He looked up into the vaulted heavens. "You stole everything from me. You took it when you sent me into the Hollows. And now you've taken the life I had there, too."

He collapsed again and wept.

He understood so much now. He was Grant's son. He'd trained for years in the barrenness of the Scar. He'd prepared for a time none of them hoped would come. And then he'd been sent away.

Tahn cried out again, anger and frustration and sadness competing in his heart. He'd been an instrument. That's all his life had been about. The days since his forgotten youth, the days of the Hollows, had been his to live and remember. But even they were a disguise to hide the purpose Vendanj and Grant thought might one day come, and for which he had been removed from the company of the one . . . who should have loved him.

As he lay beneath those same stars that had once been the far points of dreams, he realized that the man who should have loved him first and best, his real father, had been the one who sent him away.

But he also wept for the loss of the life and family he'd believed were his own. For Balatin, his mother, Vocencia . . . and Wendra. His heart broke most because of her. He'd not even been able to defend her because of these things they'd put in his head about the Will.

He hoped that this man, Grant, remained forever in the Scar where the endless sun and lifelessness could beat on him until time passed him by.

"Tahn?" It was Grant.

Tahn waved his hand for Grant to leave.

Vendanj hunkered close and spoke softly. "I asked Grant to come with us, Tahn. I needed his help. Still do. But he came because you're his son. At least listen to him."

Tahn glared up at the exile.

Grant stared back, his eyes hard to read. "You'll remember living with me in the Scar. Training. And you'll remember I sent you away." He sighed. "I could tell you it was to give you a better life. And that wouldn't be a lie. But it's not the real reason. I would have sent you there regardless."

Grant looked up at Vendanj, then up to the stars for a moment before focusing back on Tahn. "Early in your life it became clear that you possessed a gift, a certain bond with the Will. It's a subtle thing. Small, maybe. But you sense things." Grant scrubbed his cheeks. "You're not the only one. Vendanj has told you as much. And I'd say this sense you have isn't all the time. Not for all things. But with time, it did grow. In slight ways. And I knew I couldn't hide it. Even in the Scar. There are some who'd seek to abuse it. Or just kill you flat. Not to mention the Quiet. That's why I sent you to the Hollows. That place was once hallowed, set apart by the First Ones, as a safe haven from the Quiet. I thought you'd be safe there, especially in the care of my closest friend . . . Balatin Junell."

A fresh wave of anguish thickened in Tahn's chest and throat. He bit back more tears. Grant tried to touch Tahn, to console him, but he jerked away. The man withdrew his hand.

"But from the beginning, we suspected this sense of yours might one day be needed in the way it now is. That's why I taught you to 'draw with the strength of your arms, but release as the Will allows.'"

Hearing the words spoken by this man . . . it was almost more than Tahn could bear. He shut his eyes and waited for this nightmare to end.

"You see, Tahn, when you go to Tillinghast, all your choices will return to you. Even for a young man that's a grave risk. But you . . . your choices have been guided by your perceptions of the Will. You possess less guile. It'll still be painful. But you stand a better chance there than most."

Tahn opened his eyes again, and glared at Grant. "And what happens if I survive?"

"We don't know," Vendanj interrupted softly. "None I've brought here have lived. But I believe if you do survive, and the Veil fails, you can help us against the Quiet. Really help us." There was the faintest hope in his voice. "But you must make your peace with what we've shown you. Not this instant, but soon."

Tahn took a deep, bracing breath, trying to gather his composure. But it was no use, not tonight, anyway. To endure these things, he could only harden his heart. He'd suffered a long time with doubt of the deepest kind—missing pieces of himself. And here on this ledge he'd lost the rest.

He crawled over the rough stone back to the shallow cave and lay down, wondering if the dreams that came would at last be truly his own.

As he fell down toward nightmare, he shivered not from the cold of the Saeculorum, but from wounds he felt deep inside. Wounds he didn't know how to heal.

The guilt descended on Grant in a rush.

He sat at the edge of the cliff, as his son crawled away, and let the self-hate come. The gentle but firm hand of the Sheason on his shoulder did little to reassure him. The Vendanj left him to find his own place. In the dark solitude, his own remembrance came full and bitter.

He still believed that sending Tahn away into the Hollows had been the right thing. The boy had learned enough, he thought, to serve him all his life. But the Scar and being in Grant's company hadn't been healthy for the lad. More importantly, he'd been safer in the Hollows.

Still, he'd sent away his own son. And the thought of it had hurt every day. If being exited held any real punishment, it had been that.

He'd not stood beside his son through it all.

He'd done the next best thing, convincing his closest friend, Balatin, to leave his life in Recityv and take his young bride into the Hollows to raise Grant's son. Balatin had been a good father, and Vocencia a good mother. They'd given Tahn a good, simple, safe life. But right now that was small comfort.

Abandonment. Something he'd done to Tahn. *I'm a bastard.*

He stared into the distance, considering. The long years of placing children from the Forgotten Cradle into homes that might better care for them had been a kind of personal atonement. Not because Helaina had sentenced him to it. But because he'd wanted to redeem his own act of desertion.

And if he was honest, he even resented his old friend Balatin a little. Resented him despite the immense favor the man had done him. Resented him because he could imagine the moments his friend had shared with Tahn that Grant would never know.

But those many years of rearing wards in the Scar, of protecting those he'd placed into homes here and there, gave him confidence that he knew what was best for a child, for a young man. He'd have to find some comfort in that knowledge. He might even have to use it to guide Tahn yet later in the Saeculorum.

Or afterward, if Tahn survived Tillinghast.

And though the Scar hadn't gotten into Tahn as it had gotten into him, he nevertheless saw much of himself in his son: honesty, doggedness for the right things. It pleased him in the same way it would any father. But those traits had also caused Grant a lifetime of sorrow. He hoped it wouldn't be the same for Tahn.

He couldn't undo what he'd done. He'd do it again. He'd tried to prepare his son for what lay ahead. But he wasn't deceived. Even if Tahn survived, Grant would never truly be the boy's father.

He'd given away that honor.

The Sheason's restoration was double. Grant's own lifetime whirled back on him, and left him as completely in the Scar as if he had never left it.

Grant needed the stoniness of his heart to return, to relieve the pains of memory and choice.

If there was any blessing to his life in the Scar, it was the emptiness it inspired. And there were times Grant could call on it to soothe him.

Here at his own Tillinghast, he hoped it would come to him.

• CHAPTER SIXTY-SIX •

Waking Dreams and Forgiveness

Forgiveness is fitting, but forgetting is foolish.

—The last line in "The Old Saw of Penitents,"
oft repeated following avowals

Tahn woke to the crush of dirt under Sutter's boots. His friend was up before the sun, and walking away into the night alone. A moment later, Tahn followed.

Frigid winds swept down the face of the mountain, tamed by the heat that rose off the Soliel. On the face of the short, sheer bluff, Tahn hunkered down next to Sutter, who'd found a crag to sit in. Out of the wind, everything became suddenly quiet, and he stared with his friend into the predawn dark.

They shared a long companionable silence.

Tahn used to love this time of day back home. The smell of sweetroot and eggs would fill the air as they sizzled over a griddle on the hearth. Strong warm tea brewed in Balatin's pot, and from the yard came the sound of wood being split to fuel the endfast fire, and feed being thrown down for the animals. Then a race through chores before he took to the trees and discovered a new way through the woods to Sutter's house, where he'd hope to find his friend stooped over his furrows so he could peg him in the ass with a dirt clod.

As he peered deep into the darkness from the Saeculorum ridge, he imagined a sun that shone weakly over the crests of these far mountains. The promise he'd always felt when imagining the sun . . . was somehow gone.

Tahn shut his eyes and rested his head against the rock, grateful for only one thing: his friend, Sutter. Nails was the only person he could talk to about the horror of his last few hours. And Sutter, perhaps better than anyone, would understand.

His friend had himself been abandoned.

Finally, Tahn broke the silence.

"You've been a good friend," he said. It came out sounding lame.

Sutter, still staring into the darkened plain, gave a wan smile. "You, too."

"Then can I ask you something? Something about your parents . . . *all* of them?"

Sutter turned, and nodded.

"Last night Vendanj restored my memory."

Sutter's brows went up.

Tahn waited a long moment. "I'm not Balatin's son. The dreams and loss of memory, everything that's bothered me, it's all because of my real father . . . Grant."

In the dark, Sutter's eyes widened. But he didn't interrupt.

"I spent years with him in the Scar, but then he sent me to live with Balatin and Vocencia." Tahn shook his head. "They knew, Sutter. They knew and never told me." Tahn choked the words out. "Why didn't he want me, Sutter? Why do parents not want their children?"

Sutter took Tahn's hand in a firm Hollows grip. He spoke through the tears.

"Tahn, Grant isn't your father. Your father is Balatin, your mother is Vocencia. I don't know all the reasons why they made the mistake of not telling you the truth, but they loved you. Don't doubt it. I was in your home, I knew your father. I saw it. Hold to that."

"How do you do it? How do you put a parent's abandonment aside?" Tahn waited, hoping for some truth that would help him. If anyone would have it now, it would be Sutter.

His friend looked back, his eyes distant. "Maybe you never do." A calm touched his face. "I think you have to find a way to live past it. For me . . . I consider myself an orphan. Not because the parents who bore me were already dead. They weren't." Sutter looked out on the vista before them. "They just didn't want me." He paused a moment.

"I hated them. I thought for a long time that I wanted them to die." Sutter nodded to himself. "I remember wishing I could watch it happen. They were pageant wagon players like Penit. They didn't want to be burdened by a kid as they traveled town to town. My true father—the one who raised me—saw them in a field one day when they'd come to the Hollows with their wagons to play the rhea-fols."

Sutter's eyes stared into the past. "They were alone in the high grass, hidden. But my father walks the field every day. Accidentally found them. They'd just had me, Tahn. There in a field under a summer sun they'd brought me into the world between sketches on the wagon."

Then Sutter looked back at Tahn, his eyes brimming with tears. "The man who gave me life was about to put me in a bucket of water. End my life before it started."

The revelation stole Tahn's breath. How long had his friend lived with this knowledge? Tahn ached just hearing it. Dead gods, the image of it.

Sutter went on in a low voice. "He rescued me, Tahn. Filmoere took me in as his own. Raised me. Gave me a life. And he told me the truth of it because he said truth was the only way." Sutter wept silent tears. "He told me the *better* truth was that he was proud of me, and that none of that business in the field meant a damned thing. Told me he loved me."

Sutter gave Tahn a determined look. "So your father is still Balatin. He made mistakes. Should have told you the truth. But he didn't abandon you. And I'm a witness to that."

They sat together for a time in the dark of the crag, staring out over the Soliel. Tahn's spirits rose a little. And he imagined the dawn, but briefly.

Sutter kept his friend company for the better part of an hour before breaking the silence.

"Tahn, have you ever dreamed with your eyes open?" he asked.

He let the inquiry hang. In his mind he stood again at a window seeing unearthly things that he didn't want to believe were real.

A gust of wind howled around the bluff above them, and with its passing, the breezes vanished altogether. In the distance, the earliest trace of the new day touched the sky in shades of deep violet.

Tahn shook his head.

"I've seen some things," Sutter continued. "Like the kind of dreams you have before you're fully asleep. I don't know what to think of them. Maybe I'm tired. No harvest ever worked me so hard as this." He stuck a thumb toward the horses and the others. "But I think it's more than just dreams. I see them when I *know* I'm awake. And I need to tell someone about them, Tahn. I need to tell *you*."

Tahn waited without speaking.

Sutter looked away at the horizon. Traces of light streaked the sky in dark violet. "Last night it was the strongest. But I've seen it every night since the prison at Recityv. . . ."

Tahn shifted his weight. "What is it?"

"I see faces, Tahn. All the time, and not like you do when you just think of them and remember. It's not like that." Sutter's voice began to tremble. "Sometimes I think they're looking at me, trying to tell me something. But their eyes are empty."

"Who?" Tahn prodded. "Who do you see?"

Sutter gave Tahn a fixed stare. "I think I see the spirits of people who are about to die. I think I see death before it comes." With a quiet tone he finished, "And I think it walks with us to Tillinghast."

Sutter looked away from his friend again.

Tahn patted Sutter's leg. "I think you just need some sleep, Nails. I know I could use some."

"Maybe," Sutter agreed, unconvinced. He tugged at the leather loop around his finger that the Sedagin had given him. It reminded him of a different strength he thought he could possess. He clenched his fist and sat straighter. "The night we stayed at the leagueman's home," Sutter began slowly. "Do you remember?"

"Of course. You spent half the night under your bed with fever dreams."

Sutter corrected him. "Not fever dreams. I don't know *what* it was. I was tired but still awake when I began to get cold. I got up to close the window a little. When I got to the sill, a face came up out of the dark beyond the glass."

"You were pretty sick," Tahn offered. "Maybe you saw your own reflection?"

"That's what I thought at first. I even remember laughing at myself for spooking at my own face . . . until I moved . . . and the image didn't."

"But this all sounds like a fever dream," Tahn reasoned. "You could have imagined it, and then fallen out of bed and rolled beneath the mattress."

Sutter stared at him. Even now he dreaded saying it out loud. "The face I saw that night beyond the window belonged to the woman they burned the next day."

His friend's face went slack, and Sutter's own heart pounded.

"Dead gods, Nails, are you sure?"

"And it's not the only time."

Silence settled over them. Sutter turned and stared thoughtfully into the cold of dawn.

Death walked with them to Tillinghast.

"That's not all of it, Tahn." Leaves stirred by a cold breeze whispered a warning, as Sutter prepared to tell Tahn the rest.

It was such a burden. The anguish and loss and confusion and regret in the faces of these spirits. And drawn to Sutter. Was this thing in him permanent? How would he live with this? How would he ever find love and have a family, knowing that he would see their souls before they died, and then have to spend those last days with them knowing what would come?

And what of his parents, Filmoere and Kaylla, who'd given him a life and home? Already Sutter dreaded the day he might see their spirits.

It was too much.

He wanted to return to his roots. Just till the earth and leave Tillinghast and everything else behind. No waking nightmares anymore. No shadows of death that came to him. Not his friends. Not his parents.

But he gripped Tahn's hand and looked him in the eye. Because somewhere inside him he wanted to believe that the things he saw could be changed. "The face I see now, every night since Solath Mahnus . . . is Mira's."

Tahn sat in silence.

Forgotten was the hammer scar on his hand—a brand he knew now belonged to the children of the Scar.

Forgotten were his misgivings about Grant.

His eyes ached from sleepless nights and the endless stream of days that had preceded them.

He thought about a Bar'dyn in his home, a leagueman on a gallows, and others he'd aimed at, uttered words for, and felt something about their life. What did he feel about *Mira's* life? Was *she* meant to die?

Tahn shook away the thought when Sutter spoke again. "Do you think it'll be like this forever? Will I see them all my life? Will I see my own . . . ?"

"I don't know, Sutter." Tahn gave his friend a sturdy look. "But I'll tell you what I do know. For as long as you need me, I'll help you however I can."

Sutter's jaw set with determination. "I don't know what's at the end of these mountains, Tahn. I don't know what waits for us at Tillinghast. But whatever it is, I'm with you. And we'll go there for our fathers. The ones who stood by us when others would not."

He gave his friend a strong embrace and stood, his head still filled with the ache of revelations.

He left Sutter sitting low against the rock, and went to saddle his horse.

As he fidgeted with the saddle belts, Wendra drew up beside him.

"How are you?" she asked, her voice sounding bruised.

"I've had better days. How are you?" He pointed to her throat.

Wendra gingerly touched her neck. "Still hurts," she managed. "Just talking is a strain." She coughed lightly.

"Then don't," Tahn said. "We can talk later. But at least you're on your feet. I guess I've one reason to thank Vendanj." Tahn looked up the hill, where several strides away Vendanj cast his hawkish gaze back over the same vista he'd watched with Sutter. "You ever feel like it might have been better if we'd just stayed in the Hollows?"

Wendra followed Tahn's gaze, then pointed toward Penit, who methodically rubbed his mount's legs. The boy was singing soft snippets of a song Tahn had often heard Wendra singing.

She whispered, "Sometimes. But mostly I'm grateful to have come along. I'd never have met Penit otherwise. And in spite of everything, it's been a kind of . . . blessing for me to watch after him." She turned back to Tahn. "And Balatin would have wanted us to stay together." She took his hand. "I love you. You're my only family now."

Tahn fought the emotion clenching his throat. He still loved her as a sister. But she didn't know they weren't truly related. Tahn shot a look at the Sheason, wondering if he should tell her. He decided to leave it be for now. She'd been through too much already.

"Besides, when this loveliness is over, we'll go back, and Hambley will keep our plates full for the stories we'll have to tell his patrons." Wendra playfully rolled her eyes. "It might even fetch me some attention from eligible men . . . besides Sutter." She coughed again, quickly stifling the noise with her palm.

Tahn marveled at her resilience. And he was grateful for this moment. A normal kind. Like the days before the Bar'dyn who took . . . He wanted suddenly to tell her. Tell her that he hadn't fired because of the old words and the feeling that came. He might not be ready to tell her that they weren't related, but by hells he could explain why he hadn't helped her that night.

So he did. He told her his oldest secret, the need to seek the *correctness* of every draw, the words he recited. And he explained how he'd spoken those words when he'd aimed at the Bar'dyn who'd come into their home to take her child.

"I had the feeling I shouldn't shoot," he said. "I can't explain it. It doesn't make any sense. But I'm sorry. If there was ever a time in my life when I wish I hadn't listened to those feelings . . ."

She smiled wanly.

"I want that shot back," he went on. "Even if I couldn't save the baby, I want that chance again."

In his heart of hearts, he didn't know if he could do it differently.

Wendra shook her head and placed her hands on his cheeks. She turned his face fully to her own. She looked at him tenderly, and Tahn saw in her the might of his father, Balatin: a desire to forgive.

With an intent gaze, Wendra whispered, "Give me time."

He wished for a bit of her strength. He pulled Wendra close and folded her in a tight embrace.

"Revelations have been part of this whole journey, haven't they?" she said. "I've learned a little about myself, too. Apparently, gifts run in the family." She smiled at him, and explained about the power of her song. She shared more than she had before. She told him about Jastail, and the slave blocks, and the terrible song she'd sung down on the Bar'dyn. She told of Seanbea and Descant Cathedral and the Maesteri.

"Belamae wanted me to stay and learn to sing Suffering." A look of regret crossed her face. "But I couldn't, Tahn. I had to make sure Penit stays safe. I disappointed Belamae. Vendanj, too, I think. The reason we went to Recityv was because of me—"

"While you're working on forgiving me, do it for yourself." He offered her a smile.

She nodded her thanks, and then took him by the shoulders. "Now, to more important matters." She looked around. "There are rumors that you have feelings for Mira. True?" A playful smile spread on her lips.

Tahn shook his head and smiled again. "You've been talking to Sutter."

"No, I *overheard* Sutter. He has one volume. Hard not to pick up a thing or two."

He took her hands. "If I ever choose to do anything with regard to Mira, you'll be the first to know."

"Good enough," she answered. Then she kissed his cheek and went to Penit, the two of them returning to her horse with arms intertwined.

"She's a strong woman."

The voice startled him. He turned to find Grant at his side.

"Wendra, your sister." Grant nodded toward Wendra. "She'll be your greatest ally, if you keep faith with her."

Bile rose at the back of Tahn's throat. His anger thrummed inside him.

"Tahn, I want—"

"I don't care what you want." He spoke sharply.

The stoic look in Grant's eyes flickered. Another man might have risen to the bait. This man stared back with the patience of long isolation. "Whatever you decide to think is your choice. But you'd better search your newfound memory. You have a task at the end of these mountains and you need to be straight in your heart and mind to do it.

"I didn't want to send you away. It was the best, safest thing for you. And I convinced my best friend and his wife to go into the Hollows to raise you and their young daughter, because I wanted you to have the best possible life." Grant's words came as though he'd thought them over.

They had the tone of a father.

And Tahn hated him for it.

"Yet you kept some wards in your Scar," Tahn said. "How did you decide that *they* were worthy of your care and protection, but I wasn't?"

"It wasn't easy . . ." Grant started and failed.

Tahn held no sympathy. "You stole my childhood from me twice: once when you used it to prepare me for your own purpose, and again when you wiped it from my mind and sent me away. If I survive Tillinghast it will be because of the decency of another man, not the secrets and lies of an exile."

Grant stood a moment, as if he might say something more, but finally just walked away.

• CHAPTER SIXTY-SEVEN •

Stain

Man has eighteen years to learn accountability. There's no reason— or means—to transfer guilt.

—*Discourse on Sacrifice*, authored by the Second Prelate of the Church of Reconciliation

Winds drove the clouds from the Saeculorum, turning the air brittle cold under clear skies. Tahn and the others climbed for two days. The wind through the pines and over the crags was a constant moan.

Tahn kept his own company.

On the morning of the third day, glittering points of sunlight sparkled like gems on a blanket of snow. The clean, bright vista relieved the sullenness that had settled in since they'd entered the Saeculorum.

Tahn rode up beside Mira. "We're close, aren't we?"

Her eyes continued to search the tree line. "Yes. And how are you?"

"I'm still headed to Tillinghast," he answered.

She nodded as if it was the only answer.

He looked down then at the ground. "The snow will make make it easy for the Quiet to track us." Tahn had often gone immediately to the woods after a good winter snow. It made hunting easier.

"Yes, but there's no mystery about where we're headed. The Bar'dyn know it. And the Velle have probably counseled their scouts to find a good place to make a stand." She looked out over the delicate green-and-white blanket of pine and frost spread below them.

A couple of ravens were startled from their branch on a dead hemlock.

She noted the birds, then leaned over and put a hand on his own as it rested on his saddle horn. "I have faith in you."

Then she spurred her horse and disappeared into the pines.

He couldn't explain or deny it.

He might not be ready for Tillinghast, but he was as ready as he'd ever be. Mira's confidence helped.

He loved her.

Then he remembered what Sutter had said, about Mira's spirit. . . .

They moved with caution over the blanket of snow. Towering pines rose around them, many with an ivory bark Tahn hadn't seen before. Patches of sunlight fell through the trees, producing shards of light. With the scent of pine needles and snow, the air smelled clean, free of the molder of last year's leaves. The crunch of hooves broke the silence, louder than usual in the stillness. But even Grant seemed at relative ease.

Until boots pounding through the crisp snow shattered the morning air.

The sound spooked the horses. Several of them reared up. Their shrill whinnying filled the morning with panic. Footfalls ahead. Down slope. Upslope.

They were trapped.

Tahn pulled his bow and nocked an arrow. Braethen already had his sword in hand, touching the blade in a thoughtful way.

Mira dismounted and pulled Tahn from his saddle. They ran into a clearing, just up the hill from the path they'd been taking.

Vendanj and Grant already stood at the northern edge, kicking back snow and clearing a wide circle in which to fight.

Wendra sheltered Penit behind Sutter and Braethen, as she strode into the small clearing and shot worried glances at Tahn.

Sutter drew his sword, looking anxious.

The ground shivered with the pounding of so many heavy feet, snow sifting and crusts of ice cracking. Birds took to the air, calling as they went.

It sounded like a stampede. The splintering of wood cracked loud, and Tahn imagined small trees being snapped like kindling beneath the bodies of towering Bar'dyn. Movement caught his eye, and he looked up to see treetops bristling as the Quiet crashed toward them. The air grew thick with the expectation of violence.

Then into the clearing on the left came six Bar'dyn. Grant waited patiently in the small area he'd cleared. Vendanj smote his hands together, calling a whirlwind from the ground that twisted ice and snow and the hard, cold rocks beneath it into a maelstrom. He then thrust both hands at the coming Quiet. The whirlwind leapt at the Bar'dyn. Three were drawn into the tangle of roots, stone, and ice, and lifted from their feet, tumbling over as they were battered and slashed.

Two Bar'dyn turned on Grant, the remaining one fixing his eye on Tahn and heading for the center of the clearing. As it did, six more Bar'dyn emerged at a full run from the east. But these were different; they wore charcoal tunics with a dark grey insignia in the center of their chest: the symbol of a single tree whose roots spread and grew downward to become several smaller, withered trees. These six each carried a heavy pike in one hand, and a spiked shield in the other.

Sutter turned toward the six, as Tahn loosed his first arrow at the leftmost. With his shield, the Bar'dyn batted Tahn's arrow away as if it were a slow fly.

Braethen started toward Vendanj, but the Sheason shouted at him to stand with Sutter against their flank.

The three Bar'dyn caught in Vendanj's swirl crashed down in a dead heap. The two spoiling for Grant came into the exile's circle. They fanned out to opposite sides of the man. But before they could strike, Grant drew a small hidden knife from his belt and threw it at the first Bar'dyn's sword hand. It pierced the creature's wrist, and the Quiet made a low sound in its belly. Tahn felt it in his gut. The second Bar'dyn threw itself at Grant, and went tumbling with him to the ground.

Vendanj turned his attention to the dark-clad six, and began gesturing at them with one hand, then the other. Bits of the bark tore from tree trunks and hurtled toward Bar'dyn eyes as sharp as tiny daggers. Two lost their sight. The others pushed against the onslaught, covering their eyes as they came.

The single Bar'dyn heading for Tahn slowed as it came near Mira. It drew a second sword, and began swinging each in tight looping figures. The swords created a wall of whistling blades as the Bar'dyn pushed toward Mira.

She sprang forward, dropping low at the last moment and thrusting her sword with savage intent. She caught the Bar'dyn in the lower belly. The creature staggered backward, and fell, bleeding fast.

A flail clipped Sutter, spinning him around and dropping him. The attacking Bar'dyn lifted its weapon to deal a death blow. Tahn let fly an arrow. The missile caught the Bar'dyn in the neck. He fired a second, and a third. All three hit the Bar'dyn in the same place, driving it backward.

A second Bar'dyn leapt at Sutter, who lay in the snow. Before it could strike, a cry filled the air: "I am I!"

The call raised the hair on Tahn's neck. Braethen surged into the space between Sutter and the Bar'dyn, whipping a blow at the creature in a tight, vicious arc. His sword hummed in the morning light. Then the steel found home, and tore open the flesh of the beast's chest.

Grant escaped the Bar'dyn that had wrestled him to the ground. As he did, Vendanj raised his hands again, sending the creature skyward thirty strides. Then the Sheason fell to the ground, breathing heavily.

The two remaining Quiet ran past Braethen, heading for Wendra. Nothing lay between them and Tahn's sister, and he knew he wouldn't reach her in time.

He nocked and fired another arrow. It stuck in the Bar'dyn's side, but hardly slowed the beast.

Wendra pulled Penit behind her and stared savagely at the creatures as they bore down on her. She opened her mouth, as though to sing. Alarm lit her face as she found she hadn't the voice for it. She tried again, but managed only a husk. She began to back away, pushing Penit along.

Tahn fired again, this time missing completely. An airy rasp rose from his sister's throat as she pushed harder to vocalize something. The Bar'dyn closed in.

Wendra turned to Penit, trying to get him to flee. The boy shook his head. Wendra pushed him in a safe direction. Penit began to sprint away.

She wheeled and headed in another direction, hoping to draw the Bar'dyn's attention from the boy. The Bar'dyn Grant had stuck with his knife was up again, and took off after her, pointing for his fellows to stay on Penit.

As Wendra dashed away, the last two Bar'dyn followed Penit. And they began to gain on the boy.

Only Mira could catch up to them. Tahn shouted to her, and she gave chase. In eight strides she looked like she would rescue Penit.

On the other side of the clearing, Braethen and Grant took down the Bar'dyn pursuing Wendra. She turned back, watching helplessly as Mira streaked toward the lad.

One of the Bar'dyn pursuing Penit turned suddenly to meet Mira. She lost her footing in the snow and fell. A menacing grin spread on the thick, rough features of the Bar'dyn as it jumped and planted its foot on Mira's arm, kicking the sword from her other hand.

In unison, Tahn and Wendra lifted their cries: "No!"

Vendanj lay spent in the bright snow several paces away.

Grant and Braethen started to plow toward Mira. But they were too far away, and spent besides.

Sutter was down.

Only Tahn could help. He raised his bow and nocked an arrow.

He drew down on the Bar'dyn pursing Penit, then shifted his aim to the Quiet hovering over the woman he loved. The moment lengthened, and the world grew dreadfully still. Plumes of labored breath hung in the air.

Tahn looked at the exhausted Sheason, his face gaunt and as pale as the snow. Then to his sister, who'd taken the boy as her own. Wendra gave Tahn a pleading look, and his mind filled with the memory of his own suspended action when another child had been taken from her.

The memory seared him still.

He'd not truly stood passive in her moment of need, had he? Not the son of Balatin. Not Tahn.

But he also thought of the face in Sutter's visions, Mira's face. Nails had seen the haunted, anguished expression of a woman burned by the League the night before her death. At least he thought he had. But Sutter believed it, and so Tahn believed it.

Tahn spoke his words in his mind as cries and yells sounded all around him. He recalled Rolen standing for him in a dank prison cell, and was reminded that he was now accountable for his choices.

Then Tahn narrowed his aim. And between the towering pines and over the fallen snow, he released his shot.

The arrow sailed true, slicing the brittle morning air, and whistling toward its target. As it struck the Bar'dyn down, Wendra raised a cry that broke Tahn's heart. The Quiet pinning Mira fell back, releasing her. A moment later, Penit was caught and whisked away into the forest.

Tahn dropped to his knees. He caught the tortured look on his sister's face before tears blurred his own eyes.

The quiet sound of sobs came to him sometime later. Tahn looked up into the impassive face of Vendanj. Over his shoulder stood Mira. The Far wore a mixed expression of gratitude and concern.

Vendanj heaved a weary sigh. "You made your choice. You must own it."

To one side Braethen stood with one arm heavily bandaged and blood on his neck. The sodalist looked too weary to stand, swaying as he attempted to steady himself with his sword. Sutter winced every few moments and finally sat on a large rock to roll up his pant leg, revealing a purpled bruise that ran from his calf to his knee. Nails placed tentative fingers on the crown of his head, and pulled them away bloody. The exile seemed to have no injuries and kept his distance.

Wendra sat collapsed at the far side of the clearing. She wept softly, hiding her face deep in her garments. The sound rasped from her bruised throat.

He'd chosen to save Mira instead of the boy, a boy Wendra had virtually claimed as her own.

Putting words to it, Vendanj said low and even, "It was a selfish draw."

Tahn snapped his head in the direction of the Sheason. His anger flared. And he was grateful for it. The anger replaced the ache growing inside him for Penit. For Wendra. For failing her twice. What use were the old words, if he chose to serve himself instead?

And yet, he was glad Mira was safe. The ache inside ebbed as he imagined the possibility that they could be together. The thought calmed his deepest grief.

"Sutter, Braethen, gather the horses," Vendanj ordered. "Be quick and quiet. If they've wandered too far, leave them to their instincts."

Tahn shook his head. "Why was Penit here in the first place?" he asked, mostly to himself.

Vendanj turned back to Tahn and exhaled slowly before explaining. "The child was a contingency, in the event you made a poor choice."

Tahn shook his head, failing to understand.

"He was to be a sacrifice, Tahn. Not a blood sacrifice," Vendanj clarified. "But to Penit we could have transferred the stain of some misstep. He's far from his Change, and could have taken on himself whatever mistake you might have made."

Understanding dawned in Tahn's mind. He'd known he should have shot to save Penit.

"You not only chose selfishly, you also let slip the one to whom we would have moved the blemish . . . to keep you ready for Tillinghast." Vendanj drew back and looked about him, appraising the situation. When his eyes rested again on Tahn, he reiterated in a soft, defeated voice, "It was a selfish draw."

The Sheason crawled a few strides away, and rested his back against a rock. He fell deep into thought and weariness, leaving Tahn staring at Mira. She returned his gaze for several long moments, her grey eyes sympathetic but sorrowful.

Then she took a small step and touched Vendanj's shoulder lightly. They shared a long look, ending with a mutual nod. Mira drew near to Tahn again, and knelt in the snow beside him. She searched one eye, then the other. Without a sound, she mouthed the words, "Thank you."

It was all the reward Tahn needed.

Then she spoke. "'Melura' is a word from the Covenant Tongue, meaning *first inheritance*. The blessing given to the Far is that they remain in this condition all their short life." She gave Tahn a reassuring look.

The realization of what she was about to say hit him.

"As one who stands spotless in her first inheritance," Mira said with firmness, "I will take Penit's place."

The snow creaked as Grant wheeled about, his impassive, sun-worn face now taut with concern and admiration.

Tahn didn't know how to respond. He stole a look at Wendra, who was still lost in her grief.

Looking back into Mira's eyes, he searched for direction. "What would it mean for you?"

"It's not yours to count the cost, Tahn. It's only yours to accept or deny my gift." Her voice fell to a whisper. "But there is no choice. If you won't allow it, then all we've done may have been in vain. If you go to Tillinghast burdened. . . ."

He'd shot to save her. Because he loved her. Now she needed to try and save him from what he'd done. And somehow he sensed it would have painful consequences for her.

What do I do?

Sutter and Braethen were nowhere to be seen, on an errand the Sheason had put them, to take them away from here. Vendanj offered no council. Tahn wished Balatin were here; he'd have wisdom to share.

Unable to decide, he simply said, "I don't know what to do."

"Then let me do this for you," Mira said, "For all of us."

"Isn't it selfish of me to be saved from my own mistake?" he asked.

"You didn't seek it." Mira leaned closer. "I offer it freely." She noted his reluctance with a kind smile.

The sight of it eased Tahn's concern, but only slightly. "Tell me what it means if you do this?"

This time, she didn't hesitate. "I forfeit my first inheritance."

Tahn's eyes grew wide. "Your next life? Reunion with your family? . . . Your mother?" He shook his head. "I can't let you do that. Not for something I've done."

She smiled again her slight, nearly imperceptible smile. "People often do such things for those they care about."

The revelation spread through Tahn, and made him certain he couldn't allow it. As he began to protest, she interrupted.

"There isn't time to argue about this," she said. "This is right. Trust me."

Tahn thought of his compulsion to await sunrise, his lost memory, and all the things he and Sutter had shared in recent days.

"Trust me," Mira repeated.

Again Tahn began to argue.

"Tahn, even if you were a *stranger* traveling to Tillinghast, I would insist."

He stared into her grey eyes a long time.

"So much easier that you are not," she finished.

Tahn felt like he was again unable to defend someone he loved, like in his Hollows home at the start of all this madness. But the truth was, he did trust Mira. Slowly, he gave a simple nod.

Vendanj stood and came to them. He placed Tahn's hand on Mira's and bound them with a silken cord he drew from his cloak. Clasping the union in his hands, he began to speak in a soft, calming voice. Words Tahn didn't understand. Warmth spread up Tahn's arm.

In his mind, Tahn saw his moment of choice. He saw it from high above the clearing where he now sat, his bow drawn toward the Bar'dyn. He watched in terrible clarity the release of his arrow. The moment came like a knot in his throat, suffocating him. He felt his deliberate betrayal of trust in the appropriate shot. And while Mira had been spared, he realized something more: new repercussions in the life of the child, Penit . . . were now Tahn's.

Soon to be Mira's.

A wave of dread and dismay overcame him as he realized the consequences of his mistake would touch many lives. He saw flashes of burning pages, the rending of the air, and a bloodied figure leading an army out of a dreary place.

Then, a moment later, Tahn felt lighter, new. He opened his eyes and saw Vendanj staring intently at Mira. Her eyes still shone with razor awareness. But her brow furrowed now with a concern, a weight, he'd never seen in her before.

It's done.

Mira crept away on her hands and knees. Over the snow she went, assuring the others she was fine, but wanting to be alone.

Where she could feel the stinging tears of relief and regret.

Carrying Tahn's stain, she could no longer bear an heir for Elan, for her people. Her long fear of loving a child for the few short months before she moved beyond this life . . . was gone. And that eased her heart in a way that surprised her. But blemished, she would also not inherit the promise of the Far. Whatever awaited her beyond this life, she wouldn't rejoin any of those she'd known and loved.

Then an awful realization hit her. The end of her bloodline was now certain. That might mean the end of the covenant itself to safeguard the Language. She looked away from the others and wept. And hoped Tahn stood well at Tillinghast.

Vendanj slumped back onto the snow and lay down, staring up into the deep blue. His body and spirit were weary. And not just from the use of the Will. This flight across the Eastlands had reminded him of a past he'd tried to forget. The closer they came to Tillinghast, mounting losses brought that past to mind in starker relief.

His breath plumed in the frigid air above him as he thought of Penit, now gone—just like his own wife and child. He shut his eyes and gave himself up to a more recent memory. In the Halls of Solath Mahnus he and Penit had walked together. Vendanj had learned what a remarkable young man Penit was. Then Vendanj had told him how he thought the boy might help them on their way to Tillinghast—bearing Tahn's mistake, should that occur.

Even asking Penit had been hard. It left Vendanj feeling ashamed. But the Will had provided a failsafe against Tahn's possible lapse, and Vendanj had known he must ask. It had been for the boy to choose.

And Penit had stayed committed to them, in the same way he'd stayed committed to the stories he played. *Like* The Great Defense of Layosah, *a story about the possible sacrifice of a child* . . .

Still, the consequences of all these choices bore down on him. He twisted fists of snow in his hands.

The Quiet had marked them. They knew the boy was the key to controlling Wendra. And they knew of Wendra's Leiholan talents. They might also know that Mira carried one of the last covenant threads of the Far bloodline. So, the Bar'dyn attack had almost certainly targeted others besides Tahn.

And still, Tillinghast awaits.

Wendra sat in the snow as Tahn crawled toward her. She made no effort to move, or to acknowledge him. He stopped a stride away.

"Wendra . . . I'm sorry," he said.

She didn't look at him.

"I don't expect you to forgive me. . . ." Tahn faltered, searching for words. "I couldn't save them both."

"He's not dead," she said flatly.

Tahn waited a moment, then went on. "I sensed I should help Penit. . . ."

Wendra gave him a withering glare. "I like Mira, but you let the Quiet take a *boy*." She swallowed hard down her bruised throat. "If I had my voice, I'd sing. . . ."

Finally, he said simply, "I had to do it, Wendra. . . . I love her."

Wendra ignored his apology, and turned away. Eventually, Tahn crawled back toward the others, leaving her alone.

Before he'd gone to his final earth, Balatin had told her to hold to Tahn no matter what happened. Twice now, Tahn had abandoned her and the young ones she'd sworn to love and protect.

I'm sorry, Da, I can't do it anymore.

It hurt to let Tahn go. But she hated him right now.

Visions of helpless children in the hands of slavers plagued her. It was one thing for an adult to suffer at the hands of another. But it was something else entirely for a child, who looks to adults for safety, to have their cries unanswered.

She remembered moments when she'd lain and felt her child moving inside her. That child, taken.

She remembered Penit's courage, going to try and find her help. Then put up to bid on an auction block. And now . . . taken.

The song throbbed inside her, and she ached to give it voice. Color fled her sight. All looked white and charcoal in her eyes.

She drew handfuls of snow and washed her face, its icy sting bracing her.

• CHAPTER SIXTY-EIGHT •

A Blade of Grass

When Maldea was sent into the Bourne, a few Sheason followed. In time, they became elder leaders. In time, they became Draethmorte.

—Drawn from rubbings of glyphs taken at the
Tabernacle of the Sky

Braethen helped Vendanj into his saddle, wincing from the effort. The Sheason slouched over his saddle horn, looking more drawn than ever. The man had lain in the snow for a long time, unmoving, Braethen doing what he could to help him.

Most of the others were also unsteady in their saddles, fighting the pain of their own wounds.

But they turned toward a narrow pass to the northeast, and trudged toward Tillinghast.

As they rose higher into the Saeculorum, it got harder to breathe. The air was thin. But it wasn't only that. Tillinghast was close.

It was a place mentioned in authors' tales. But actual historical accounts couldn't be found. It wasn't a place men were meant to visit.

The dark stone of the mountains struck Braethen with its stark beauty. Cliffs rose hundreds of feet, defying anyone to pass. Small clouds floated near, and were pulled into the coursing updrafts, becoming wisps, then nothing. The sweat on their horses' shanks began to freeze. By the time they cleared the trees and became fully exposed to the wind, ice crystals hung from their mounts' hair.

By midafternoon, the sky itself had begun to thin. Through the light of midday, Braethen could faintly see the stars, glimpse the very vault of heaven.

As they crossed into the shade and shelter of a towering cliff, Mira stopped them. "The horses will die if we push them further," she said. "We'll leave them here and go the rest of the way on foot. Take a moment to gather your breath and drink." She then sat with her back to the cliff, and took her oilcloth to her blades.

Wendra wandered down their backtrail, and sat watching the way they'd come. Twice, Tahn started toward her, before abandoning the effort and returning to his horse. Vendanj and Grant sat conferring, arguing quietly. Up the cliff's face, the wind howled around sharp outcroppings.

Favoring his arm, Braethen huddled over his book, passing one finger of his good hand under each successive line he read. The Sheason came and took a seat next to him.

"Learn anything useful?" Vendanj asked, nodding at Braethen's book. The Sheason wore his hood up, shading his hollowed cheeks. He spoke quietly, as though conserving energy.

Braethen stared ahead at the page, his finger stopped, lost in memory. "I used to sit on my porch and watch the rain. My father taught me that a story could be born of every drop, and that the chorus of their landing on a Hollows roof was a lifetime of revealed truth."

"Sounds like a bit of poetry," Vendanj observed.

"He used to say such things when I grew impatient to understand something." Braethen turned to look at the man. "Or when I pushed to know more about the Sodality. Or how to use a sword."

Vendanj kept quiet, nodding.

"One night, he woke me," Braethen said, remembering. "We went by lantern out to our well. We sat in wet grass in front of a rosebush.

"I remember the birds starting to call just before dawn. Smoke from chimneys lit with endfast fires. It was damned cold until the sun came up. But even then, the roses remained closed. It wasn't until late morning that the petals finally opened. We sat there, in the wet grass and cold, to watch a rose until it opened to the sun."

Vendanj put a hand on Braethen's arm. "Your father's a good man. I know he wanted you to be an author. And I know your desire to become a sodalist caused strain between you."

Braethen nodded. "But now I *am* a sodalist. And each time I lift my sword, I fear the darkness will consume me." He hefted his book and dropped it back into his lap. "And even with the books, I don't seem to glean what's necessary."

"You helped Garlen get us to Naltus," Vendanj reminded him. "Damned quick thinking, too."

Braethen nodded, unconvinced.

Vendanj looked down at the book in Braethen's lap. "Perhaps you're not reading the right stories," he suggested. "What are you hoping to find?"

"Something to help Tahn when he stands at Tillinghast," he answered.

Vendanj made a small, appreciative smile. "Tahn will have to figure that out on his own. Best thing you can do is help us get there."

Braethen touched the blade the Sheason had given him. "I took the oath. I believed in the stories, that the Sodality honored what was best about the Sheason, standing beside them to record and remember. To place themselves in the way of whatever risk. To take up weapons. . . ."

Vendanj listened, but didn't interrupt.

Braethen's breath came fast and shallow, the late-day sun streaking the cold plumes that billowed from his lips. "But I was naive. I've idealized the tales of heroism, the banner . . . even war. And now I've steel of my own. I'm not much good with it. And when I raise it, I usually find myself in darkness." Braethen's breath faltered, catching in his chest. He paused. "I'm a small, foolish scholar who belongs in the Hollows."

Vendanj stared back at him, his face reassuring. "Taking up a weapon is black business. You'll grow used to it with time."

Braethen tried to stop his trembling fingers. "I don't want to grow familiar with it," he managed.

"I spoke nothing of familiarity," Vendanj corrected. "But it's still true that now more's expected of you."

Braethen nodded, no less comforted than when Vendanj had sat down.

"Put your book aside a moment." Vendanj gathered Braethen's full attention. "Do you have a sigil of your own?"

"I wear the crest of the Sodality. It's—"

"A worthy emblem," Vendanj finished. "But it's not individual. Do you understand?"

Braethen nodded. "I've no family mark. And in the Hollows everyone knew my name—"

"That's not the purpose of a personal mark." Vendanj paused, studying Braethen closely. "A sigil speaks of a man's purpose. His intention."

Braethen thought for several long moments, then reached down and plucked a blade of grass growing from a patch between his feet. He held it up, a slow smile touching his lips.

"Ja'Nene," he said. The widow with the ruined face who walked each day to pluck a few blades of grass.

Vendanj gave Braethen an appreciative look. "Your own story. An important one." He then stood up and returned to the others.

Braethen fetched the needle from his pack, and managed to pull several threads from his shirt. He removed his cloak and fashioned the likeness of a blade of grass over the left breast. The color was even right, dark green. It wasn't an expert job, but clear enough.

Moments later, Mira called. "Gather your things."

Braethen shrugged into his cloak. "Let's go see Tillinghast."

Once through the pass, the air warmed. A shallow valley stretched before them, the mountains rising again at its far side.

Across the valley floor, trees had fallen heavily to the earth, their trunks half buried in the soil. Elaborate root systems stood exposed in twisted knots. It struck Tahn like a garden of stone statuary tumbled by a quake. The trees were a hundred strides long, and more.

Vendanj stopped, frowned, his expression edged with despair. "The Cloudwood." His words sounded like an epitaph.

After several long moments, the Sheason followed Mira onward. They wove through the fallen trees, scrub oak, low cedars, and grasses brown as from an early autumn.

"What's wrong?" Tahn asked Braethen.

"I think this is what the histories call the Eternal Grove. These trees"— Braethen pointed at one as they passed it—"are cloudwood trees. Their wood is said to be impervious to the ax."

Tahn stared at the fallen forest, skeptical.

"The stories say the First Ones created the grove to be a source of renewal," Braethen explained. "Its roots are said to crawl into the mists and form new earth."

"Mists?" Tahn remembered Je'holta, off the plains of Sedagin, and turned back to Braethen. "That's where we'll find Tillinghast, isn't it?"

Braethen nodded. "That'd be my guess." Then he looked around him again at the fallen trees. "But it looks like the Cloudwood is dying. Maybe this helps explain how the Quiet are crossing the veil. How they came into the Hollows."

They descended into the midst of the fallen sentinels, the girth of the trees twice and three times as tall as Tahn.

From several strides ahead, Vendanj spoke. "We've not been good stewards. We share the blame for this." He looked across the valley of dead cloudwood. "But it's also the Quiet. They take for themselves and leave the costs for us to pay."

Vendanj stopped and turned. "There's only one thing that is ours. Truly ours. To give or use." He paused a long moment. "Our will."

His voice softened. "It can be used to tear down. As the Quiet have." He looked again at the fallen trees. "But it can also be used to build up. And we're here . . . because the Quiet want to take it from us."

He then pointed to a range of peaks on the far side of the valley. "Beyond the valley lies Tillinghast." Vendanj looked at Tahn. "It's a mirror for your will. All of it."

Vendanj turned and led them on. Hours later, they neared a narrow canyon pass at the far end of the valley. The sun slid behind the mountains behind them, casting everything in blue shadow. With it came a deep quiet. No whir of crickets. No larks taking to their nests. Every footfall seemed loud in the silence. Sutter started a fire to ward off the chill. And the silence.

As Tahn was tending to his horse, Grant cornered him near a fallen cloudwood. "I know you don't want to talk to me, but this once, please listen."

Tahn stood, waiting.

"I didn't come along with Vendanj expecting to just pick up as your father." Grant's face was hard but earnest. "And I'll be honest with you, I don't know if there's anything we can do to turn back the Quiet this time. I sit in the middle of Quiet desolation every day."

He paused, seeming to search for the right words.

"But whatever you end up thinking or feeling about me, I want you to understand, especially as you go to Tillinghast . . . that I'm proud of you. It wasn't an easy decision to hide you in the Scar. Hell, it wasn't easy to go to the Scar, at all. I'd have preferred hanging." He shook his head. "But I wanted you to be safe. And if it came to it, I wanted you to have the strength of body and character to stand at Tillinghast."

He put a hand on Tahn's shoulder.

"And by every absent god, Tahn, I'll stand behind you with anything that is mine to give . . . anything."

He removed his hand and left Tahn without another word or look.

Tahn didn't know how to feel. But he'd noticed something he hadn't before—maybe because Grant hadn't been wearing his gloves. A brand on the back of the man's left hand . . . in the shape of a hammer. More similarities between them? Tahn put it out of his mind and took a seat at the fire.

Vendanj regarded Tahn across the flames. He rubbed his eyes before starting to speak. "Tomorrow we'll come to Tillinghast. It's a place where Forda and Forza meet. A place of potential. There's no deception at Tillinghast, Tahn. You'll remember all that you've done. You've the shield of melura to answer for most of it. But you'll remember it just the same—every misgiving, every ill thought. That'd be painful enough. But you'll also see the effects of it all." Vendanj shook his head. "That part's not so easy."

Vendanj fell quiet for several moments.

"But Tillinghast is more than remembrance," Vendanj added. "More than a scale to measure worth or value. It'll show you who you've become, who you're capable of being."

"That's our purpose," Vendanj explained. "The Quiet are restless. Their influence grows. They would use that influence to convince you of lies. To help them." He looked at Tahn. "Better you die than do so."

The words chilled Tahn.

"We need those who can bear all the mistakes they've made," Vendanj said, "and become more. Become changed in whatever way Tillinghast would change them. And use it to stand *against* the Quiet."

From the crevasse, a deep wind rose up, shrilling into the night air. "When will you tell the boy the truth, Sheason? He is Quillescent."

Tahn whipped around as a figure floated up from the crevasse. The air grew thick, pressing at Tahn's skin.

Vendanj threw back his cloak, and rose in a single, graceful motion. Mira, Grant, and Braethen jumped to his side, brandishing their blades as Vendanj crossed his arms and stared into the deep cowl of the floating form.

The figure rose up three strides above the edge of the crevasse, and peered down at them. "This is the hope to which men cling?" Its voice chafed the very air, and shook the stone all around. "Quillescent or not, the Will here is feeble." The cowl shifted noticeably, facing Tahn.

"You've no dominion here," Vendanj shouted above the howl of wind still rising from the crevasse.

"No dominion? I am Zephora, Draethmorte," the creature declared. "My authority is as old as the injustices of the Placing." Zephora's voice grew quiet, menacing. "I am more lord here than all your councils, I am more enduring than all your restored choices."

His words resonated inside Tahn, sad and bitter, like the voice of the damned. They prickled his skin in a painful rash of goose bumps. They sounded like the soughing of winter winds through dead trees. His words even seemed to move in the soil beneath them all.

Tahn raised his bow, nocking an arrow as Sutter drew up alongside him, his sword gripped firmly in both hands.

Zephora descended to the edge of the crevasse, landed softly, yet never stopped facing Tahn. On the ground, he stood as tall as Vendanj, though thinner and frailer looking. "You don't understand the Charter. Or you wouldn't try to keep us bound inside our prison. You're as guilty as your abandoning gods."

Anger flared, and Zephora's next words bristled the air. "And we grow tired! The prattling of generations will come to an end. No more will we be bound by your tethers." The Draethmorte quieted. "You are done."

Zephora's cloak began to unfurl, his arms reaching out. Vendanj drew back his hands and thrust them at the Draethmorte. An immense burst of energy shot from the Sheason. Not just from his hands, but all of him. A few paces away, it felt like the raw power of lightning. But there came no light. Just a rushing sound like the roll of thunder. It seemed to gather strength as it went, too, drawing energy in from rock and soil and the air itself, everything pulled into its stream.

The attack swept Zephora back. But briefly. The rush of force began bending around him, unable or *unwilling* to touch him any longer.

Vendanj dropped his hands and grabbed Mira's shoulder, pulling her close, focusing his eyes on hers. She nodded, as if hearing something unvoiced. She broke past Vendanj and Grant and grabbed hold of Tahn. "Follow me."

Tahn didn't hesitate, and dashed with Mira to the far side of the pass. He pushed himself to keep from slowing her. At the base of the next climb, Tahn stopped and looked back. The others had positioned themselves between him and Zephora.

The Draethmorte didn't make any great or hasty counterattack. No flames or shifting of earth. Instead, Zephora slowly, almost lovingly, opened his arms as though to receive them all unto his embrace. And with that graceful gesture, a cold silence settled across the pass, stealing sound and replacing it with an ineffable sadness. A deep and mortal grief chilled Tahn to the bone. It stopped him in his tracks. That feeling bore down on everything, pressing the stone and sand, weighing heavy in the air. And it laid hold of Tahn's heart, resonating inside him like a string drawn too tight, vibrating and ready to snap.

The moment lengthened, threatening to consume them all, when a triumphant cry shattered the silence: "I am I!" The resounding scream erupted into the stillness, sending shivers of hope down Tahn's back. The spell broken, Mira yanked him, and up the mountain they raced. He realized with a sudden sense of dread that she was taking him to Tillinghast.

As they sped over star-shadows and stone, Tahn looked back over his shoulder at the fight unfolding at the rim of the pass. Wendra's head bobbed as she retreated and tried to force song from her injured throat. He wondered if this would be the last time he'd ever see her, and wished he'd tried to speak to her again. Grant and Braethen danced in close to Zephora, attempting to use their dual attack to confuse and cripple the Quietgiven. With a casual pass of his hand, Zephora sent them both skidding across the rough ground like scarecrows ravaged in an autumn wind.

Vendanj spared a look up the mountain at Tahn before calmly turning toward the Draethmorte and raising his hands. The rock itself came to life and licked at Zephora with shard tongues and clutched at him with stony fists. One lashed his chest before he dropped to one knee and drove a bony hand into the hard soil. With frightening speed, the earth took on a deathly pallor that began to spread around them.

Tahn and Mira swept over the rise and found level ground. Behind them, the world lit in an explosion of darkness as searing and painful as live coals. The concussion thrust them forward, driving Tahn to the ground. The blast echoed past them in long, diminishing waves, leaving in its wake an emptiness that might have claimed the shrieks and suffering of friends. Tahn heard only his own labored breathing, and the sound of his boots grinding Saeculorum gravel as Mira hauled him up and they turned again toward Tillinghast.

The sky above shone dark, revealing stars brighter than Tahn ever remembered. He'd hoped to have time to consider Vendanj's words, consider everything that led him to this moment. But now all his thoughts clouded in his mind. And distantly came the sound of footsteps. Far down the mountain, someone was climbing after them. Whoever it was came with a steady, purposeful rhythm.

Perhaps Vendanj . . . perhaps not.

Tahn fought to climb faster, pushing Mira to quicken the pace.

• CHAPTER SIXTY-NINE •

Rudierd Tillinghast

Many of us would take back things we've done. But how many of us would do things we didn't do the first time?

—The central question in the *Concept of Omission, or the Law of Unintended Consequences;* first-year reader, Aubade Grove

Sweat drenched Tahn's face, stinging his eyes. The higher they climbed, the tighter his chest, the pressure making him gasp. Deep breaths sent piercing shards of pain through his lungs.

But they pushed harder up the mountain.

Twice Tahn looked back and saw nothing. But holding his breath for a moment, he could hear the pursuing steps down the rocky way.

He attacked the path again, sliding in behind Mira as they forged through dense brambles. At times, the steep pitch of the mountain made it seem like they ran up walls. But the Far's sure steps showed Tahn where to place his feet.

The sound of his own heart pulsed in his ears, behind his eyes, and in his wrists. He'd never been so aware of his own blood. Never felt so close to his own final earth.

Rushing up a steep leftward jag, he thought of his Hollows friends, Sutter, Braethen . . . Wendra. The dark explosion . . .

His concentration lapsed, and he missed a step, crashing to his chest and slipping toward the edge on loosened dirt and flat stones. He clutched at dry grass and sharp, buried rocks that ripped at his hands, tearing rough wounds.

He slid over the edge of the path, catching some withered roots before falling. He dangled in the emptiness that cut away a hundred strides to a spray of jagged rock. Hanging by his hands, he stared up past the mountain at the sky, flooded with bright stars that blurred in his vision. He hadn't the breath even to scream. And his hands were weakening.

He smiled, finding irony in failing this way after coming so far, after all the expectations he was supposed to meet at Tillinghast. He slipped closer to disaster. He fought the momentum, and tried to pull himself back up. He'd almost gotten his legs over the edge, when he dropped back again. One hand slipped, losing purchase. A weak moan escaped his lips.

Where's the tragedy in this? he thought, looking down at his imminent fall. *My family's gone. My friends are gone. And I don't think I can do this. I'm not who they want me to be.*

As he began to slip further, he wasn't sure his fall was entirely due to weak hands.

Dead gods, I'm tired.

Then a hand flashed down and took hold of his arm before his fingers could give out. His head lolled back, and he saw Mira's furrowed brow. Her hair hung down around her face, but Tahn saw something new in her eyes. She took his wrist with her other hand and hauled him up in one powerful effort.

He sat a moment, wind stirring his hair, and tried to gather enough breath to thank her. Before he could say anything, she put his bow in his hand, and helped him to his feet. She nodded and resumed their climb, the resolve in her features rivaling the Sheason's.

He cast a look backward around several tight switchbacks, and caught a glimpse of a dark figure gaining ground. His skin rippled with warning, and he raced after Mira.

As the slope leveled off, the air thickened with mist, as if a storm were close. Moving through it, the mists parted, coursing smoothly over his forehead, cheeks, and the backs of his hands. The clouds seemed alive somehow. Aware. His skin felt *caressed*. And a moment later, the mists thickened, slowing their pace.

Mira paused, getting her bearings. They stood together in the dense earthcloud, with the rasp of leaves stirring around them. Mira locked on a direction and grabbed Tahn's shoulder. She gently thrust him forward, coming a half stride behind.

Then, out of the mists, a ridge appeared. They headed directly toward it, angling for a break to their right. They passed through a rim of black rock that let out abruptly on a few strides of soft loam before a sheer cliff fell away to nothingness.

Mira stopped. "Tillinghast."

The mist roiled in slow patterns, turning back on itself and folding endlessly together. Looking skyward, Tahn could see more of the same, though thinner.

Beyond the ledge the mist thickened to obscurity. He took a tentative step, and his foot sank into the rich-smelling soil. He looked at his sunken boot, then peered right along the cliff to the vague silhouette of one cloudwood, rising at the edge of the land. Its roots grew partially into the abyss, twisting down into the clouds like bony, scrabbling fingers. The tree disappeared up into the mist, its top lost completely to view. At its base, a single branch lay fallen as though broken away in a storm.

He looked once at Mira, whose eyes shone with confidence.

Then Tahn crept to the ledge, wanting to look down, his boots tracking deep in the loam. Halfway across to the edge, he heard Mira draw her steel, and turned to see Zephora ease from the rim of rock. The mists parted around his black cloak as though in aversion.

The Quiet disregarded Mira, looking past her to Tahn. "Quillescent."

Mira didn't wait. With blinding speed, she set upon the Draethmorte. Her blades sliced through the fog so quickly that it didn't stir. Several blows appeared to land directly on the creature, but Zephora didn't flinch. Blades seemed to have no effect on him. Mira sprang back, landing in a defensive posture.

"Your life is larger than the race of man allows." Its words rang darkly. "You are more than they know. Their arrogance and greed have opened a way to put right the abominations and abandonment of the First Ones. You can erase ages of neglect and cruelty."

"He lies, Tahn," Mira shouted. "Don't listen to words that make darkness light and light dark. The trick of the Quiet is to lead you *gently* into chains."

With a slight gesture, Zephora pushed a burst of dark light that hit Mira full in the chest and shoved her to the very edge of Tillinghast.

"She can be yours, too," Zephora said in a silken tone. "In Maldea's care, you'll have restored to you only what *you* wish, remember only what is helpful. You may even *undo* things you have done. This is true power. This is what we offer you. It is not villainy, Tahn."

Zephora's use of his name unnerved him. But those words: *undo things you have done*?

Tahn relaxed his grip on his bow. "Why do the Sheason fear you, then? What have they to lose?"

Mira groaned, struggling to get up, but Tahn focused on the Draethmorte.

"Their own power. Their own control." Zephora took a casual step toward him. "It has always been so. Your histories are incomplete. They tell a flawed version of history and demonize all those trapped inside the Bourne."

"Bar'dyn and Velle have tried to kill me. Quiet took my sister's child. And you speak as though *you* are the casualties. Mira's right, you lie."

Zephora's voice softened, deepened. "We have not sought your life, Quillescent. In ignorance, you are filled with hatred and fear. Don't let it be so. I can give you answers." Zephora's voice resounded in the loam beneath Tahn's feet, and crept up into his body.

The Draethmorte drew back his cowl, revealing skin drawn so tight over his bones that it might tear from a smile. "Or," Zephora added, "I can end the life that never belonged to you."

Uncontrollable shivers wracked Tahn. He struggled to ask, "Why do you call me 'Quillescent'?"

The Draethmorte laughed, the sound of it dry and hollow.

A loud clanging interrupted the laugh. Tahn turned to see Mira kneeling beside a boulder. In one hand she held a broken sword. In her other hand she held the rock she'd just used to snap her blade in two. Fury raged in her eyes as she stood and pointed the broken blade at Zephora. "In the name of the Far, I rebuke you. By our covenant, I call you out."

Tahn had no idea what Mira had just done, but Zephora's face registered a brief glimmer of concern. Just as quickly, the expression passed, and he turned to face her, lifting his robed arms.

"Oathbreaker," the Draethmorte said to Mira, an awful delight in its voice.

Then a deep howl rose from him, emanating from his mantle, his pores, his eyes. It touched the air with a bitterness that coalesced into a palpable form Tahn believed would tear skin from muscle. It rushed at Mira, streaking through the mists. She leapt out of the way, the wail passing into the mists and losing its power to silence. Mira danced to her feet, and came nearer Zephora with the jagged stump of her sword.

"You waste my time." Zephora turned toward Tahn, leveling him a thoughtful stare.

Tahn drew his weapon. Blood from his wounded hands seeped between fingers tightly clenching his bow. But he aimed and drew back the string.

This time, with certainty, he used no arrow.

The bow was always just a way, when the time came, to focus. He remembered, from years ago, standing with Grant in the Scar, that only the *intention* of his draw mattered. And along his path from the Hollows, he'd learned something new about himself, some deeper ability when he drew an empty string.

In his mind he began to speak deliberately the words. . . .

I draw with the strength . . .

"Don't be a fool, Quillescent. You've no understanding of what you do."

Mira circled closer to the Draethmorte.

A low hum began in Tahn's head. In his chest.

. . . of my arms . . .

"Don't make me destroy you. There's so much that may be done. To help men be what the gods had hoped." Zephora raised a beseeching hand. "I would rather not render your soul to nothing. That is a pain you don't ever want to know. But I would rather you die than see you help the Sheason."

Vendanj said the same thing of the Quiet.

He drew deeper yet, his body still quivering, his flesh weak and cold. Questions and grief plagued Tahn as the hum inside him grew loud, like the faster and faster turning of a potter's wheel. A deep vibration inside him.

Mira raised her truncated sword and began to say something in a low whisper. Her body looked less substantial, perhaps a trick of the mist.

. . . and release as . . .

"Will you serve injustice, Quillescent? Will you honor those gods who placed us in the Bourne, and didn't try to set things right?" Zephora took a step forward. With it, Tahn's body shook, his mind filled with shapeless fears and doubts. "A doleful little archer come to Tillinghast without his own childhood. You raise your aim, and would become like those gods, abandoning us, instead of delivering us."

Tahn held his draw, focusing.

Zephora turned his palms out, toward Tahn. And when he spoke, the resonance shook Tahn to his core. "I defy you. I name you unforgiven. The ravages of time I invoke upon you. All of you. The Bourne will fall on the east." He paused, his head inclining. "Now enough."

Zephora loosed a wave of darkness from his outstretched hands. It shoved Tahn to the loam. His flesh felt as though he'd fallen into the rough stones of a winter river. But the silent pulse also throbbed in his flesh. He could hear nothing. But he saw images: burning pages falling like cinders from the air; rivers of blood coursing from the Sheltering Sky; men and women stumbling with their throats ripped from their necks as the last notes of the Song of Suffering ended; and great mountains in the deep places of the Bourne beginning to thrum.

These terrible scenes flowed in his mind. His soul ached. And he hoped for solace. Instead he saw himself seated in the dark of predawn awaiting a sunrise . . . that never came.

And that was something he knew he couldn't bear.

He remembered those moments of training in the Scar with no arrow. He remembered recent days when he'd drawn his bow the same way. What had he intended to release?

He remembered Sutter's ramblings in the wilds: *The spirit isn't whole, Tahn. It's not whole. It can be divided. Given out. Taken. Small portions separated . . .*

Tahn stood and drew his bow again. The words flashed in his mind. And he released. Something unseen, something of Tahn, shot from his string and struck Zephora in the chest. The Draethmorte wailed, a cry like a chorus of mourners.

Tahn stood in awe. Almost unbelieving. He'd fired his heart. A small portion of his spirit.

But Zephora wasn't done.

The Draethmorte had a heart of its own. It rent its garment and exposed its awful flesh. From the earth and abyss and heavens all at once came a thunderous ovation that Tahn knew was only ever heard in his mind.

There came to him a taste of the Quiet.

Not malice. Or hatred.

But a lack of empathy.

Tahn fell, his body numb. His spirit numb. He was still aware. Still awake. He lay in the deafening silence of lament and regret that followed the rain of dark applause. His will had been bled from him.

In that moment, he forgot his name and all the history—good and ill—that had been his own.

Accountability no longer even mattered.

And suddenly he watched himself fading into a canopy of white so immense and stark that he couldn't be sure he wasn't blind. The world was as empty as new parchment.

He was ceasing to matter.

At the far side of his consciousness something rang. Another blade being broken in the air of Tillinghast.

Then came the soft words of a familiar voice speaking in an unfamiliar tongue.

It gave him enough mind to cry out for help: *Rolen.*

The scream filled his head, echoing out to silence, where he heard simply: *Be still, Tahn. Remember standing in the dark, waiting on the light of the sun.*

He opened his eyes. Mira stood between him and Zephora, invoking some ancient promise and holding the Draethmorte at bay, if only for another moment.

Feeling returned painfully to his body. And mind. He had little left to give. And little time. Slowly, he pushed himself to his feet and drew his bow. As Zephora's dark resonance reached out again, Tahn finished his own prayer:

. . . the Will allows . . .

And released an empty string.

Not at Zephora.

But into the abyss.

With it, he was swept away, carried into the roiling mists, the arrow of his own shot.

A great roar erupted behind him, making Tahn think of the dying of nations. Then it was quickly gone, shut out by Tillinghast.

He disappeared into the clouds, seeing not himself, but only the rush of forms gathering and dissipating all around him in the empty mist. He sensed that he had left his body behind, becoming something more pure, more vulnerable. A feeling of motion captured him, but not physical movement, movement through time. Through possibility.

Faces appeared before him, as though sculpted from the mist. Some of the faces were smiling, some frowning, others talking, though Tahn couldn't hear them.

His mind raced on, streaming through the abyss, light and dark swirling in close and flitting away again. Each time, he saw a choice, a word, a deed, a way of responding that directed him to other choices. He marveled at the winding of his own path through this matrix of interconnected moments.

Some moments brought him shame. Most painful were those when he could have helped, but did nothing. These brought a cascade of images showing the tumble of consequences resulting from his unwillingness. He felt the raw pain of those who struggled with sadness or loneliness because of his neglect, even when unintended. Opportunities to make a difference cascaded in wild succession before him, opportunities he'd passed up.

Other moments made him laugh, especially those with Balatin and Sutter. The feelings of love and togetherness felt as strong as when they'd first occurred. Tahn tried to speak with the memory of his father—it was so real. And though he thought he spoke, he heard nothing.

But he gloried in the recollections, so many lost to him. He reveled in the carefree smile Wendra so often used to wear. He watched Balatin smoke his pipe and sing and tell stories. He watched Hambley put down another contender in a game of shoulder-wrestling and then help the man up to buy him a cup of bitter. He saw light falling through the aspen trees on the Naghen Ridge during a hunt years ago.

Then the mist shifted, and Tahn watched the journey that had brought him to Tillinghast. He felt his own worry, those first stirrings at the sight of Mira, the bite of manacles in a prison cell. He recalled an empty city and the unexpected defense he'd made for Sutter with an empty bowstring.

Most of all, he remembered his failures to Wendra. The first time because he hadn't believed he should release on the Bar'dyn. The second time because he believed he was in love. The latter was his most painful single memory in Tillinghast. But the choice didn't sting as it had before, and Tahn knew it was because of Mira's sacrifice.

Then a great rushing began, mists flowing in toward him, gathering speed as they came. He watched in astonishment as a thousand varying paths from a thousand different choices sped through his mind. He saw countless versions of himself that he would never be. He felt gratitude for small victories, and guilt for missed opportunities.

With it all came a sense of the meaningless measurements of time and space. It was like standing atop a grand mountain where he could see countless trails all leading toward the summit. Or perhaps he was standing atop a thousand mountains all at once.

The mists produced flashes of light and wellings of darkness. Frightening images emerged, interleaved with peaceful moments. The many moments became less difficult to experience, and Tahn relaxed at the center of the storm. Everything began to gather close—his memories, his choices—touching his mind with possibilities, some things sure and inevitable, others unlikely but understandable.

The mists licked at him, through him. They invaded his senses and lulled him to acceptance. It all became deafening, filling him until he was no longer capable of thought. There was only a resonance inside him. A vibration down deep.

He floated in the abyss and simply was.

And that was enough.

Then it ended, and the silence shocked him. His eyes already open, he could suddenly see again. He found himself where he'd stood to shoot toward Tillinghast, his feet still rooted in the loam.

He felt . . . peace. Then collapsed and fell unconscious.

• CHAPTER SEVENTY •

A Solitary Branch

The Sheason wear the three-ring. But it was not their first sigil.

—Notes from Estem Salo symbology and semiology studies

The smell of rich soil awakened him, as fresh as a pot of brewed cloves. For a moment, Tahn imagined Sutter holding a handful of roots beneath his nose in jest. The thought of his friend brought a weak smile to his face, and he held it there a moment. He sensed if he opened his eyes, the fancy would shatter. He breathed deeply, and felt the cool density of the air as it rushed into his lungs: mist.

The abyss.

Tahn opened his eyes. A few strides away, Tillinghast. The graceful billow of the clouds. He didn't rush to get up, and stared vacantly outward. Ripples in the mist threatened to coalesce into familiar shapes, as though drawing on his thoughts. But the mist swirled onward.

Then, like a pail of river water poured over him, he remembered Zephora and *Mira*. He pushed himself up, a wave of nausea and unsteadiness sweeping up from his belly to his head. When his vision cleared, he searched about him, frantically looking for Mira, remembering her last stance as she created a barrier between him and the Draethmorte.

Silent gods, I left her here alone with him.

He struggled to his knees and crawled to where he'd last seen her standing. A form came into view. The figure lay motionless. He tried to hurry. His arms gave out, and he went face-first into the soft dirt. He took a mouthful of soil.

He spat it away. "Mira!"

Tahn got to his knees again, slowly moving toward the body. Closer, he saw it wasn't Mira. But he still tugged the shoulder to turn it over: Zephora's gaping maw and vacant eyes stared back at him. Tahn's hands began to burn. He thrust them into the loam, scrubbing them as with soap. The pain subsided.

But Mira was nowhere in sight.

He tried to stand, but his legs wobbled, and he collapsed back to his knees. His mind filled with panic. The Draethmorte must have killed Mira before dying himself.

They're all dead. All his loved ones. Tahn turned a hateful eye toward Tillinghast.

The sacrifices—most of them by others—raced in his head. All to bring him here. To remember.

But something more had happened. Something he couldn't explain. Something he could feel at the center of him.

Did it get inside me?

After a moment, Tahn crawled back toward the cloudwood tree. He meant to get the fallen branch and use it like a cane. At the base of the tree he found a shallow makeshift basket woven of nearby brush. In it were a few dozen stones.

You're not the only one.

And yet none had survived. A stone for each of the dead.

Tahn picked up a rock and tossed it in. "Seems fair."

He grabbed the branch and struggled to his feet. After retrieving his bow, he shuffled toward the edge of Tillinghast. He felt ashamed and angry that so much had been lost on his behalf. One way or another, he wouldn't let those offerings go unrewarded.

He moved to Zephora's body. Paused there. With sudden fury, he rolled the dead heap toward the ledge with his makeshift cane. Though tall, the Draeth-morte weighed very little. Just before he pushed it into the mists, a silver neck-lace bearing a pendant fell onto Zephora's pale, thin neck.

Using his knife, Tahn moved it around, trying to make sense of the glyph. A single hoop of dark metal hung from the necklace, and at its center lay a small disk, creating a sort of bull's-eye. But nothing connected the inner piece to the outer ring. Tahn thrust his dagger into the emptiness around the center disk—it passed through unimpeded. When he tapped the centerpiece itself, it didn't budge from its place.

Tahn pulled the necklace off the dead Draethmorte and dropped it in his tunic pocket. Then he pushed Zephora into the abyss with his branch. The body fell soundlessly, dropping away from the ledge and out of sight.

Tahn pivoted and began to ease away from Tillinghast. Just past the ridge, he thought he heard, far off, the sound of leaves being trampled underfoot. He paused, unsure if it was the stirrings of the wind. The crunching became louder.

Hope leapt in his breast, and he began to hurry. "Wendra, Sutter . . . Mira?" he hollered as he stumbled forward, his legs threatening to drop him.

From the other side of the field, voices rose in response. He couldn't under-stand the words, but the meaning was clear enough. At least some of them had survived!

He hurried on, ignoring the burn in his chest as he fought for breath. He came around a tangle of roots from a fallen cloudwood and saw his friends running at full stride. He collapsed, exhausted, but with relief and a smile.

Their boots kicked up the hard leaves, crackling others underfoot. Mira reached him. She took him in a tight embrace, and held him for long moments. She then dashed past him toward Tillinghast. He assumed she went to check on Zephora, but he hadn't time to tell her what he'd done with the body, or ask her how she'd killed the Draethmorte.

Then his friends were there. Sutter fell into a slide, shoving a pile of leaves between them and into Tahn's lap. "Woodchuck, my skies, I never thought I'd be so glad to see you." Sutter planted a big kiss on Tahn's cheek, and flung some leaves in the air as if showering him with festival streamers. The leaves plunked down on Tahn's head like small stones.

Tahn grinned. "And I've never been so glad to bear the company of a man who plays in the dirt."

Sutter laughed, but then his face drew taut. "When I saw you disappear from the pass, I wasn't sure I'd see you again." His friend took Tahn's hand in the familiar Hollows grip, clasping him tight. "Not that I doubted you. But I wish I could have come. . . ."

"You'd love it," Tahn said. "The loam there is six inches soft, and rich with the smell of growth." Then Tahn gave Nails a mischievous grin before wrapping him in an embrace.

Braethen came up as the two broke their hug. "It's good to see you, Tahn." The sodalist hunkered down on Tahn's other side. "It would seem you've proven yourself at Tillinghast."

Tahn took Braethen's hand in the same Hollows shake.

Wendra came next, slowing to a stop a few strides away. She held his gaze long enough to say, "I am glad you're alive, Tahn."

Even with her words hanging between them, Tahn's throat closed with emotion at the sight of her. He wanted to stand and take her in his arms, apologize. He wanted the closeness they'd always shared.

Wendra moved aside as Vendanj came up next, Grant trailing him close behind.

The Sheason looked deathly ill. He sweated as they all did, but his flesh hung slack on his face, dark circles ringing his eyes. His hood was back, revealing dark hair slick with perspiration that clung to pallid skin. His shoulders hunched deep as though the weight of his own cloak was too much to bear.

He stopped, and made no quick attempt to speak. Looking at Tahn, he leveled his eyes, which never seemed to dim, even now. Again, Tahn had the feeling he was being measured, weighed, by the penetrating gaze of the Sheason.

Then Vendanj asked Grant's assistance in helping him to sit. The exile eased him to the ground, and propped a large fallen branch behind him so he could recline.

Standing straight again, Grant gave Tahn a look both proud and relieved, but said nothing.

When Vendanj had recovered his breath, he folded his hands in his lap. His first question caught Tahn off guard. "What stick is this you carry?"

Tahn looked into his hand, finding he hadn't let go of the cloudwood branch.

"A walking cane," Tahn answered, confused.

"It's cloudwood," Vendanj stated. "But not greyed yet." Without lifting his stare, he pointed at the tree behind Tahn.

"There's a live cloudwood at the edge of Tillinghast," Tahn explained.

A look of relief showed on the Sheason's face.

A small silence stretched between them all, broken by Mira returning from the ledge.

"Tahn rolled the body into the abyss," she said, as if answering a question Tahn hadn't heard.

"Good," Vendanj replied. "The Quiet have their ways of reclaiming their own. In the abyss, Zephora is forever lost."

Shifting, Tahn looked up at Mira. "Why did you break your sword? And why did it call you oathbreaker?"

"It's not important right now," Mira said, then shared a strange look with Vendanj.

Clearly it *was* important, but Tahn hadn't the energy to pursue it. He did have one question, though. "How did you kill him?"

The Far stared back with her bright grey eyes. "I didn't kill Zephora, Tahn. You did. When you fired into the abyss, things started to change around us. The mist pulsed with reflections of light like lightning streaking inside a cloud. At the ledge, each pulse changed the landscape, the position of rocks and trees. One moment, the air was fragrant and new, the next burnt and sharp. The ghosts of cloudwood trees flickered around the edge as though showing the possible gardens that might have grown there. At times, the ledge itself extended, leaving me and Zephora standing in a dense wood. In other moments, our feet hung over the abyss, the cliff far behind as the mist swirled around us."

Mira looked back in the direction of Tillinghast. "In some moments, Zephora wasn't there at all. In others, he lay dead in the loam."

She stopped, turning her gaze directly at him. "And in some moments . . . I wasn't there. Or if there . . . *I* was dead in the loam."

Mira went on. "But *you* were always there, Tahn, staring into the clouds as though you saw things I couldn't see.

"Then the flashes of light quickened. The mist began to whip and lash over the ledge, stabbing at Zephora. I jumped away as the clouds rushed in a thick streamer and wrapped around him. They shot through his cloak and skin. They wove in and out of his mouth and nose, streaming from his ears and seeping from his eyes. The mist seemed to find every pore, passing through him as though he weren't there.

"Zephora cried out. His howl shattered stone and made my body ache. He was trying to transfer the pain of what was happening to him. The ground shook. Dark light began to shoot from every part of him. He blazed a bright darkness and then stopped. Fell to the ground." She shook her head. "You never moved.

"The mist became still and drew back. The wind was gone. The ground quiet. No flashes of light or dark. Only the soft light of the mists.

"Then you collapsed. I couldn't revive you. So went to look for Vendanj."

"What happened in the pass?" Tahn asked. "The last I saw, there was some kind of explosion. It pushed me to the ground."

Sutter chimed in, his eyes eager with a tale to tell. "Zephora shoved his hand into the soil. A circle began to spread, stripping color from the ground. His eyes blackened and a great burst threw us back. It felt like . . ." Sutter swallowed hard. "It felt like that time when Haley Reloita, Shiled's son, got trapped in the well just before the rains came. Do you remember?"

Tahn nodded. No one had been able to get Haley out. The well was too narrow for men, too dangerous for a child. Haley's fall had brought loose well stones down on him, half burying him in the stagnant, shallow water at the well's bottom. Hours later, it began to rain, swelling the river, and from an underground tributary, the water in the well, too. They watched as the water rose, and Haley cried. Frantic men lowered ropes that Haley couldn't hold firm enough to pull him from the stones. Eventually, the water covered him completely. . . .

Nails smiled weakly. "Just give me my roots back."

Vendanj caught Tahn's eye, and looked like he had a question. But he didn't ask. Instead, he said, "Give me your cane."

Tahn handed the branch of cloudwood to the Sheason, who took it and hefted it twice in his upturned palms. He then clasped his fingers around it and closed his eyes. The wood began to reshape itself, coming alive in Vendanj's hands. Slowly, it turned, moving as though alive, drawing itself into a definable shape. Within moments, the branch had become a sleek bow, fashioned of the ebony cloudwood.

"The branch still courses with Tillinghast." He handed the bow to Tahn. "That might prove valuable to you." Vendanj then took a deep breath and slumped back, closing his eyes.

Tahn admired his new bow for a moment, then patted his tunic where he'd pocketed the necklace he'd lifted from Zephora's dead body. Both reminded him of choices he'd witnessed at Tillinghast. And the way one choice echoes forward to the next.

CHAPTER SEVENTY-ONE

A Refrain from Quiet

If you look long enough, the stars will seem as familiar as friends. Because they are. They're your possibility.

—Common expression for astronomers from Aubade Grove

The stars still held sway when Tahn stirred awake. Gentle dew coated his face with freshness he took a moment to enjoy. Around him, the hulking shapes of fallen trees rose up. Tahn folded back his blanket and crept past his companions to the end of a nearby fallen cloudwood. There, he used the snakelike roots to climb atop the tree, where he stood and surveyed the world around him.

In that broad valley, he became the highest point, and quietly mourned for the forest now blanketing the ground. The sky shone with stars Tahn didn't remember ever seeing. They were comforting all the same.

Standing there, he imagined the coming of the sun, a slow, beautiful dawn that turned the vault of heaven a hundred shades of blue.

He shut his eyes and took deep, deliberate breaths. He didn't let other thoughts in, and felt a bit of the peace these moments used to give him.

"There's a kind of glory in it, isn't there?"

Tahn's eyes snapped open, and he turned to see Vendanj standing a few strides behind, watching him.

"Glory in what?" Tahn asked.

"The coming of another day."

Tahn turned back to his view of the valley. "A small comfort, yes."

"And why small?" Vendanj asked, his tone calm, fatherly.

Taking a moment to survey the dead forest around him again, Tahn said, "I used to love the morning sun. The look of it on a planted field. The hazy way it falls through leaves."

He waited, feeling suddenly ungrateful. "But now . . . now it just warms the air, helps me see my feet so I don't trip."

"And where's the smallness in that?" Vendanj persisted.

Tahn exhaled a deep breath, watching it cloud the chill air. "I don't know why I get up for sunrise. I used to feel I wasn't watching it alone."

"But now you don't?" The Sheason kept silent for a long moment. "The Council of Creation is said to have ended with the First Ones abandoning their work on behalf of men. They thought the work was lost. Once Quietus had been Whited and sealed inside the Bourne, they left it all behind. Left us few protections. But even among ourselves . . . we war." Vendanj turned to Tahn. "So perhaps you wonder if we deserve another day."

Tahn nodded. "And what difference can the bow of a simple hunter make when added to the armies of nations . . . against the Bourne?"

Tahn saw something in Vendanj's eyes: knowledge, perhaps comfort. The Sheason spoke of neither. "There's more to you than your bow, Tahn. You know this."

His mind turned back to something Zephora and other Quiet had called him. "What is Quillescent?"

Vendanj's brow furrowed with concern. "I'm not sure. But I heard Zephora say it. We'll see if we can find its meaning in Naltus."

Tahn didn't have the energy to pursue it further, and let it lie for now.

Vendanj stood in Tahn's company for some time, before adding, "And keep safe the token you hide in your tunic. It may serve us at some point."

Tahn kept the surprise off his face. He should have known Vendanj would sense the Draethmorte glyph.

The eastern horizon warmed faintly with the hint of sunrise. "Was this all worth it?" Tahn asked.

Vendanj stared toward dawn. "At the end of it, we came here to see about a possibility."

"We did all this for a *possibility*?" Tahn wasn't angry. Just tired.

Vendanj took a deep breath and smiled. "I'm glad for possibilities. And really, what more could you want?"

"Certainty," Tahn answered. They shared a quiet laugh over that.

Vendanj showed Tahn a look of gratitude. "You survived Tillinghast, Tahn. We believe one who can do so stands a much better chance against the Quiet."

"We've already been—"

"No," Vendanj interrupted. "Not like they'll come if the Veil falls. And your time at the ledge will have changed you. Not in any way you probably recognize yet. So, in some ways," he put his hand on Tahn's shoulder, "your survival of Tillinghast has just begun."

"That's comforting," Tahn said.

"That, my young friend, is a possibility."

The evening of the second day after Tillinghast, they spotted the Soliel Stretches beyond the lower peaks of the last range of mountains. Their rations gone, Sutter dug some roots he recognized, and they drank from a nearby stream. Tahn sought an opportunity to talk with Wendra, but his sister kept her distance, speaking only occasionally to Braethen. Like Wendra, Sutter was changed, too, but Nails seemed to fight the change, turning their minds toward home.

"Can you imagine the welcome we're going to get from Hambley?" Sutter licked his lips. "I can taste his roast duck already. Hey, Woodchuck, maybe you can hunt us up something good for him to roast in those magic Fieldstone ovens. This time, we'll be the ones everyone buys spiced bitter for. I think I'll take a glass of warmed cinnamon and some plum brandy to wash it down with." As he spoke, Sutter casually rolled his own sword in his hands, its use seeming to have become more familiar to him.

Tahn laughed. "Well, so long as you put some fine roots beside that duck, root-digger, I'll spare not the carafe."

Distantly, Wendra sang as she drew more water from the stream. If nothing else, it gladdened his heart to hear her sing again.

Braethen wore a quizzical half smile, his books for once put away, and only his sword in sight, lying near to hand. "Place another plate at that table, and a handful of cups for me alone."

Sutter gave Braethen a look of pleasant surprise. "And when Hambley sets the glasses down, will our resident scop favor us with an emotional retelling of the events of Tillinghast?" Having baited him, Sutter waited expectantly to see how the sodalist would respond.

Braethen cleared his throat, preparing to orate something, but with his first word broke down laughing. His laughter was contagious, and soon they were all doing it.

"That's all right, Sodalist, after all," Sutter said, standing and drawing a deep breath as though he meant to issue a battle cry, "you are you!"

That got them all laughing again. Tahn rolled off his rock, holding his stomach, while Sutter struck a noble pose.

King Elan shifted around abruptly, and returned Vendanj a despairing look. "Zephora? Then the Veil is thin, indeed." He glanced over them all in his forum hall, quickly searching their faces. Lighting on Tahn, the king asked, "But you made it to Tillinghast?"

"I wouldn't have if it wasn't for Mira," Tahn said.

Elan nodded gratefully to Mira, a silent acknowledgment passing between them.

"They failed to stop us at Tillinghast. Now they'll likely seek the Covenant Tongue," Vendanj said matter-of-factly.

Concern rose in the Far king's face.

That night, after all the details had been shared, they were treated to hot baths, assigned beds, and allowed to sleep. This time, though, they slept without the company of standing guards—an exception the king made to give weary companions some privacy. Braethen went with Vendanj, a kinship forming between the two. Grant went with Mira to the training yards, where immediate preparations began to defend Naltus, in case the Quiet came. Wendra took her own room, saying a soft goodnight to them all before retiring. Tahn and Sutter bunked together, opening their window to let the night air touch their chests as they'd always done on hunting trips into the Hollows.

"What's next?" Sutter asked, staring over the foot of his bed at a bright moon through the open window.

"I'm sure they'll tell us," Tahn remarked, lending both contempt and humor to his words.

Sutter raised his hand that bore the unique glove of the Sedagin. "Do you suppose I'd be welcome back into the High Plains again?"

"Sure. You make a wonderful impression wherever you go." Tahn chuckled and turned likewise to view the risen moon.

Sutter laughed.

It felt good to banter with his friend again, even if the familiarity of that banter didn't put him completely at ease. Looking at the moon, Tahn recalled the last room he remembered sharing with Sutter, and the disturbance at their window that had caused Nails to take refuge under his bed. The memory of the leagueman's charity and his friend's vision sent a chill down Tahn's back, and he drew his covers up over his chest.

"Do you think Wendra will ever forgive me?"

Sutter exhaled into the cool, comfortable air. "I've never seen her this way," Sutter said thoughtfully. "But I have faith in her. And why not, as I intend to marry her one day."

Tahn gave his friend a playfully quizzical look. "Do you suppose she'll return to Recityv?"

"I think Vendanj would like that," Sutter replied. "But I've a feeling Wendra will make up her own mind. What I want to know is if Braethen intends to tag along with Vendanj to Estem Salo. That's a place I'd like to see."

"Not me," Tahn shot back. "That's a secret I'll gladly let them keep."

"The real question," Sutter said, a smile audible in his voice, "is what you intend to do about Mira. I mean, a Hollows boy finding romance with the elusive Far. I'm starting to think you're keeping things from me."

"I'm no good at secrets," Tahn said.

"Well, don't delay, that's my advice. A ripe root goes soft if left in the ground too long." Sutter belly-laughed.

Tahn joined him, unable to resist Sutter's infectious laughter. When they'd finished, Sutter wiped his eyes of mirthful tears, and asked, "What do you think happened to Penit?"

The mention of the boy's name caught Tahn off guard. "I hope he gets away," Tahn said. "If there's a lad in the world who could do it, it's Penit."

They both nodded at that.

"And what have you decided about Grant?" Sutter asked, treading lightly.

Tahn didn't immediately reply. "There's a lot to think about."

Sutter nodded at that, too. "I don't know. He's just so full of fun and love. You know, if the exile career doesn't work out, maybe we could put in a word for him at the tenendra. I hear they have a few empty cages to fill."

They went back and forth for some time, their jests and laughter resounding in the room, and pealing through their open window toward the moon.

When they'd calmed down, and Tahn was starting to feel sleepy, he turned his head on his pillow. "Thanks for coming along, Nails."

Sutter shifted in his bed and returned Tahn's grateful look. "And thanks to you, Woodchuck. You got me out of the fields."

"Well, you may thank me the day we dine on that duck and plum brandy. Until then, simply call me . . . master."

Sutter sat up and bowed his head in jest. "Especially now that you've passed your Standing, right?"

"Of course, boy," Tahn said in a kingly tone.

"Woodchuck, that might have worked out fine, but it's common knowledge that a master's generosity springs from his loins. And when we shared a room tonight for our baths, I noticed that despite what you might have hoped, in that regard the Change hasn't been terribly kind to you, has it?"

Again their laughter rose, even louder this time, so that they almost feared a knock on the door to quiet them. Just as Balatin had often done when they were boys. Forgotten were Sutter's greatsword and Tahn's new bow.

Down the hall, Vendanj sat up, quietly placing an herb on his tongue. With Braethen fast asleep, Vendanj reflected on the brightness of the moon, and listened to the laughter echoing from a few doors away. His first thought was to quiet them, afraid their noise would draw undue attention from the sober-minded

Far. But easing into his pillows, he let them alone. If they could find even small joys here and now, then perhaps there remained hope for them all. Perhaps it was that one quality that most suited them to this endeavor. Perhaps the very thing that gave Tahn success at Tillinghast. With that thought, Vendanj nodded silently to himself.

So with their laughter in his ears, Vendanj drifted to sleep with belief ever more alive in his heart.

Read on for a preview of

TRIAL OF INTENTIONS

by
Peter Orullian

Available in May 2015 by Tom Doherty Associates

Prologue
A Third Purpose

After long years in the Scarred Lands, Tahn Junell realized their patrols held a third purpose.

First and most obviously, they were meant to provide early warning when visitors or strangers came into the Scar. Patrol routes held long sight lines of the wide, barren lands. From a distance, newcomers could be easily spotted and reported.

On a second, practical level, patrols were used to build and maintain stamina for fight sessions. Every ward of the Scar—age three to nineteen—spent no less than six hours a day in ritualized combat training.

It wasn't until later that Tahn finally came to realize a third, more subtle reason for patrols. They were a way for wards of the Scar to monitor themselves and guard against one of their own wandering from home, alone.

With the purpose of self-slaughter.

Tahn and Alemdra ran fast, arriving at Gutter Ridge well ahead of sunrise. They slowed to a walk, catching their breath and sharing smiles.

"You're starting to slow me down," Alemdra teased. "I think it's because I'm becoming a woman, and you're still a boy."

He laughed. "Well, maybe if we're going to keep running patrols together, I'll just put a saddle on you, then."

She hit him in the arm, and they sat together with their legs dangling from one of the few significant ridges in the Scar. Alemdra was twelve today, barely older than Tahn. And he intended to kiss her. From the glint in her eye, he wondered if she'd guessed his intention. But if so, the unspoken secret only added to the anticipation.

Casually wagging their toes, they looked east.

"See that?" He pointed at the brightest star in the eastern hemisphere. She nodded. "That's Katia Shonay, the morning star. It's really a planet."

"That so." She squinted as if doing so might bring the distant object into sharper focus.

"Katia Shonay means 'lovelorn' in Dimnian." He liked few things better than talking about the sky. "There's this whole story about how a furrow tender fell in love with a woman of the court."

She made no effort to conceal her suspicion of his timing for sharing the story of this particular planet. "You might make a good furrow tender someday. If you work hard at it, that is."

"Actually," he countered, smiling, "the story's only complete in the conjunction of Rushe Symone—the planet named after the god of plenty and favor. You know, bountiful harvests and autumn bacchanalia." He nearly blushed over the last part, having learned the richness of bacchanal rituals. "Rych is the largest planet—"

She was giving him a look. *The* look. "You seem to think you're smarter than us now."

"What do you mean *now*?" And he started laughing.

She broke down laughing, too. "You really liked it there, didn't you? In Aubade Grove."

"I'd go back tomorrow if it didn't mean leaving you behind." It came out sounding rather more honest than he'd intended, but he wasn't embarrassed. He stared off at Katia. "It's amazing, Alemdra. No patrols. No fight sessions. Just books. Study. Skyglassing to discover what's up there." He gestured grandly at the eastern sky.

She smiled, sharing his enthusiasm for the few years he'd been away before being called back here. "Do you think you'll ever leave the Scar for good?" There was a small, fatal note in her voice.

He turned to see her expression—the same one she always wore when they talked about Grant. While all the wards were like Grant's adoptive children, Tahn was the man's actual son. He supposed someday he might leave this place, especially if he were ever to learn who his mother was. If she was even still alive.

"Eventually. After my father goes to his earth. I don't think I could leave him here alone." Tahn threw a rock out into the air and listened for it to hit far beneath. In his head he began doing some math to determine the height of the ridge. *Initial velocity, count of six to the rock's impact, acceleration due to gravity—*

"He'll never be alone, Tahn," she said, interrupting his calculations. "Not as long as the *cradle* is here."

Tahn nodded grimly. The Forgotten Cradle. It served as a big damn reminder of abandonment to all the wards of the Scar. And it was the way most of them came to this place. Every cycle of the first moon a babe was placed in the hollow of a dead bristlecone pine. Orphans. Foundlings. And sometimes children whose parents just didn't want them anymore. Grant retrieved the child, tried to find it a proper home outside the Scar. Those for whom no arrangements could be made came to live with them *inside* the Scar. Not knowing their actual day of birth, wards celebrated their *cradleday*—the day they were rescued from the tree. Like they were doing for Alemdra today.

"I don't know why you feel any loyalty to stay, either." She looked away to where the sun would crest the mountains to the east. "Not after what he's done to you."

His father put more pressure on him. Tahn's lessons were less predictable. Harder. One might wonder if being his son, he bore the brunt of his father's exile to the Scar. A sentence he'd earned for defying the regent. And his father could never leave; otherwise who would fetch the babes from the cradle.

Their special morning had struck a somber note. But he couldn't let her comment lie, even though in his heart he agreed. "He just has a different way of teaching."

Alemdra seemed to realize she'd touched too close to private insecurities. "If you go, will you take me with you?"

Tahn smiled, grateful for a change in the direction of their morning chat. "You think you can keep up? I mean, I *have* been off to college and all."

This time she hit him in the shoulder, soft enough to let him know she wasn't offended, hard enough to let him know she was no rube. Then they fell into another companionable silence. The sun was near to rising. They wouldn't speak again until its rays glimmered in their eyes. This was Tahn's favorite time in the Scar. Morning had a kind of wonder in it. As if the day might end differently than the one before it. That moment of sun first lighting the sky was something he made time every day to witness. And he liked these sunrise moments best when Alemdra was with him.

He wanted to kiss her when the sun began to break. Sentimental, maybe, but it felt right anyway. As the time drew closer, his left leg began to shimmy all on its own.

What if he'd misread their growing friendship? What if she rejected his kiss? He'd be ruining future chances to run with her on morning patrol.

When the sun's first rays broke over the horizon, he turned to her, his mind racing to find some words, debating if he should just grasp her by the shoulders and do it.

He neither spoke nor grasped. In the second he turned, Alemdra inclined with a swift grace and put her mouth on his. Her eyes were open, and she left her lips there for a long time before closing them and uttering a sigh of innocent delight.

The sound brought Tahn's heart to a pounding thump, and he knew he loved her. The other wards would tease him; maybe try to convince him he was a boy who couldn't know such feelings. Let them. Because even if he and Alemdra never knew a more intimate moment than this, he would always remember her kiss, her sigh.

Sometime later, she pulled away, her eyes opening again. She smiled—not with embarrassment, but happily. And together they watched the sun finish its rise into the sky.

Then an urgent rhythm interrupted the morning stillness. Distant footfalls. Someone running. Together they turned toward the sound. A hundred strides to the east, from a behind a copse of dead trees, a figure emerged at a dead run toward the cliff's edge. They watched in horror as their friend Devin leapt from the edge. Her arms and legs pinwheeled briefly, before she gave in to the fall, her body pulled earthward toward the jag of rocks far below.

Alemdra screamed. The shrill sound echoed across the deep, rocky ravine as their friend fell down. And down. Tahn stood up on impulse, but could only watch as Devin stared skyward, letting the force of attraction do its awful work. *Initial velocity, acceleration due to gravity . . .*

A few moments later, Devin struck the hardpan below with a sharp cry. And lay instantly still.

"Devin!" Tahn wailed, wanting his friend to take it back. Angry, frustrated tears filled his eyes.

Alemdra turned to him. They shared a long, painful look. They'd failed their third purpose. They'd been so caught in Alemdra's cradleday, in the peace of sunrise, in their first kiss, that they'd missed any signs of Devin. One of their closest friends.

Tahn sank to his knees, sobs wracking his body. Alemdra put her arms around him and together they wept for Devin. At Gutter's Ridge, in the first rays of day, with Pliney Soray still rising in the east, they wept for another ward who'd lost her battle with the Scar.

The third purpose. Tahn understood the feeling that got into those who made this choice. Every ward had some kind of defense against it. Or tried. His defense was morning and sunrise. The sky. Those moments gave him something to look forward to, to find hope in.

Sometime later, they started down to gather the body, keeping a griever's silence as they went. The sun had strengthened in the sky by the time they got to Devin. They stood a while before Alemdra broke the silence. "She turned fifteen last week."

Wards who found their way out of the Scar often did so soon after their cradleday.

Alemdra sniffed, wiping away tears. There was a familiar worry in her voice, when she whispered, "She was strong. Stronger than most."

Tahn knew she meant in spirit. He nodded. "That's what scares me."

They fell silent again, knowing soon enough they'd need to build a litter to drag the body home. There'd be a note in Devin's pocket. There was always a note. It would speak of apology. Of regret. Of the inability to suffer the Scar another day. There'd be no blame laid on Grant. Actually, he'd be thanked for caring for them, for trying to teach them to survive in the world, such as it was. But mostly, the note would be about what wasn't written on the paper. It would be about how the Scar somehow amplified the abandonment that had brought a ward to the Forgotten Cradle and the Scar in the first place.

The notes were all the same, and were always addressed to Grant, anyway. Patrols usually didn't bother looking for them.

Alemdra went slowly to Devin's side and knelt. Hunched over the body, she brushed tenderly at Devin's hair, speaking in a soothing tone—the kind one uses with a child, or the very sick. Her shoulders began to rise and fall again with sobs she could no longer hold back.

Tahn stepped forward and put an arm around her, trying this time to be strong.

"It gets inside." Alemdra tapped her chest. "You can't ever really get out of the Scar, can you? Even if you leave." She looked up at Tahn. Her expression said she wanted to be argued with, convinced otherwise.

Tahn could only stare back. He'd gotten out of the Scar—a little bit, anyway—during his time in Aubade Grove. Maybe.

This time, Alemdra *did* look for the note. It wasn't hard to find. But when she unfolded the square of parchment, it was different. No words at all. A drawing of a woman, maybe forty or so, beautifully rendered with deep laugh lines around the eyes and mouth, and a biggish nose. Devin had talent that way. Drawing without making everything dreamlike.

The likeness brought fresh sobs from Alemdra. "It's what she imagined her mother looked like."

That tore at Tahn's fragile bravery. He could see in the drawing shades of Devin as an older woman. Simple thing to want to know a parent's face. *Dead gods, Devin, I'm sorry.*

The Right Draw

Tahn Junell raced north across the Soliel plain, and his past raced with him. He ran in the dark and cold of predawn. A canopy of bright stars shone in clear skies above. And underfoot, his boots pounded an urgent rhythm against the shale. In his left hand, he clenched his bow. In his mind, growing dread pushed away the crush of his recently returned memory. Ahead, still out of sight, marching on the city of Naltus Far . . . came the Quiet.

Abandoning gods. The Quiet. Just a few moon cycles ago, these storied races had been to Tahn just that. Stories. Stories he'd believed, but only in that distant way that death concerned the living. *Their* story told of being herded and sealed deep in the far west and north—distant lands known as the Bourne, a place created by the gods before they abandoned the world as lost.

One of his Far companions tapped his shoulder and pointed. "Over there." Ahead on the left stood a dolmen risen from great slabs of shale.

Tahn concentrated, taking care where he put his feet, trying to move without drawing any attention. The three Far from the city guard ran close, their flight over the stones quiet as a whisper on the plain. They'd insisted on bearing him company. There'd been no time to argue.

Through light winds that carried the scent of shale and sage, they ran. A hundred strides on, they ducked into a shallow depression beside the dolmen. In the lee side of the tomb, Tahn drew quick breaths, the Far hardly winded.

"I'm Daen," the Far captain said softly. He showed Tahn a wry smile—acquaintances coming here, now—and put out his hand.

"Tahn." He clasped the Far's hand in the grip of friendship.

"I know. This is Jarron and Aelos." Daen gestured toward the two behind him. Each nodded a greeting. "Now, do you want to tell us why we've rushed headlong toward several colloughs of Bar'dyn?" Daen's smile turned inquiring.

Tahn looked in the direction of the advancing army. It was still a long way off. But he pictured it in his head. Just one collough was a thousand strong. So several of them . . . *deafened gods*! And the Bar'dyn: a Quiet race two heads taller than most men and twice as thick; their hide like elm bark, but tougher, more pliable.

He listened. Only the sound of heavy feet on shale. Distant. The Bar'dyn beat no drum, blew no horn. The absence of sound got inside him like the still of a late autumn morning before the slaughter of winter stock.

Tahn looked back at Daen. They had a little while to wait, and the Far captain deserved an answer. "Seems reckless, doesn't it." He showed them each a humorless smile. "The truth? I couldn't help myself."

None of the Far replied. It wasn't condescension. More like disarming patience. Which struck Tahn odd, since the Far peculiarity was an almost unnatural speed and grace. A godsgift. And their lives were spent in rehearsal for war.

Endless training and vigilance to protect an old language.

"I wouldn't even be in Naltus if it weren't for the Quiet." Tahn looked down at the bow in his lap, suddenly not sure what he meant to do. His bow—any bow—was a very dear, very old friend. He'd been firing one since he could hold a deep draw. But his bow against an army? *I might finally have waded too far into the cesspit.*

"We guessed that much," said Daen.

Tahn locked eyes with the Far captain, who returned a searching stare. "Two cycles ago, I was living a happy, unremarkable life. Small town called the Hollows. Only interesting thing about me was a nagging lack of memory. Had no recollection of anything before my twelfth year. Then, not long before my eighteenth year . . a Sheason shows up."

The Far Jarron took a quick breath.

Tahn nodded at the response. "First day I met Vendanj, I realized stories were true. I saw him render the Will. Move things . . . kill. With little more than a thought."

"Vendanj is a friend of the king's," Daen said. "Not everyone distrusts him."

Tahn gave a weak smile at that. "Well, he arrived just before the Quiet got to *my* town." He then looked away to the southwest, at Naltus, an elegant, magnificent city risen mostly of the rock that dominated the long plains—black shale. In the predawn light, it was still an imposing thing to look at. It would never gleam. It didn't light up brightly with thousands of lights as Recityv or any other large city. It didn't bustle with industry and trade. It didn't build reputation with art and culture. But the city itself was a striking place, drawn with inflexible lines. It had a permanence and stoicism about it. The kind of place you wanted to be when a storm hit, where you wouldn't fear wind and light storms. And where rain lifted the fresh scent of washed rock. Altogether different than the Hollows with its hardwood forests and loam.

What Tahn wouldn't have given for some roast quail, hard apple cider, and a round of lies in the form of Hollows gossip. "Vendanj convinced me to follow him to Tillinghast."

This time it was Aelos who made a noise, something in his throat, like a warning. It reminded Tahn that even the Far people, with their gift for battle, and their stewardship over the language of the Framers . . . even they did not go to Tillinghast.

"Did you make it to the far ledge?" Daen asked.

Tahn turned and looked in the direction of the Saeculorum Mountains, which rose in dark jagged lines to the east. Impossibly high. Yes, he'd made it there. He and the few friends who had come with him out of the Hollows. Though, only he had stood near that ledge at the far end of everything. A place where the earth renewed itself. Or used to.

He'd faced a Draethmorte there, one of the old servants of the dissenting god. More than that. He'd faced the awful embrace of the strange clouds that hung beyond the edge of Tillinghast. They'd somehow shown him all the choices of his life—those he'd made, and those he'd failed to make. It was a terrible thing to see the missed opportunity to help a friend. Or stranger. Wrapping around him, those clouds had also shown him the repercussions of those choices, possible futures. The heavy burden of that knowledge had nearly killed him.

It ached in him still.

But he'd survived the Draethmorte. And the clouds. And he'd done so by learning that he possessed an ability: to draw an empty bow, and fire a part of himself. He couldn't explain it any better than that. It was like shooting a strange mix of thought and emotion. And it left him chilled to the marrow and feeling incomplete. *Diminished.* At least for a while. Maybe something had happened to him in the wilds of Stonemount. Maybe the ghostly barrow robber he'd encountered there had touched him. Touched his mind. Or soul. Maybe both. Whether the barrow robber or something else, something had helped him fire himself at Tillinghast. Though he damn sure didn't want to do it again, and had no real idea how to control it, anyhow.

"Yes, we made it to the far ledge," he finally said.

He could tell Daen understood plenty about what lay on the far side of the Saeculorum. But the Far captain had the courtesy not to press.

Tahn, though, did find some relief in sharing some of what had happened. "Near the top, Vendanj restored my memory. He thought it would help me survive up there."

Jarron glanced at the Saeculorum range. "Did it?"

Tahn didn't have an answer to that, and shrugged.

Daen put a hand on Tahn's shoulder. "The Sheason believed if you survived Tillinghast, you could help turn the Quiet back this time. Meet those who've given themselves to the dissenting god . . . in war." He nodded in the direction of the army marching toward them.

Twice before—the wars of the First and Second Promise—the races of the Eastlands had pushed them back, avoided the dominion the Quiet seemed bent toward. Now, they came again, seeming as content now to destroy as they'd once been to control.

"Mostly right," said Tahn, "and now I've got a head full of awful memories. I've done nothing but remember for two damn days, sitting around in your king's manor." His grip tightened on his bow, and he spoke through clenched teeth. "Better to be moving. Better to hold someone . . . or something, accountable for that past."

"Idleness makes memory bitter." Daen spoke it like a rote phrase, like something a mother says to scold a laggard child.

Tahn forced a smile, but the feel of it was manic. "Vendanj was the one who took my memory in the first place. Thought it would protect me . . ."

"From the Quiet," Daen finished. "So you're here with a kind of blind vengeance. Angry at the world. Angry at what you see as the bad choices of people who care for you."

The wind died then, wrapping them in a sullen silence. A silence broken only by the low drone of thousands of heavy feet crossing the shale plain toward them. Into that silence Tahn said simply, "No."

"No?" Daen cocked his head with skepticism.

"I'm not some angry youth." Tahn's smile softened. "I'm no irate mask like the pageant wagon players use so watchers in the back know who's onstage." He leveled an earnest look on the Far captain. "If I'm reckless, it's because I'm scared. And angry. Do I want to drop a few Quiet with this?" He tapped his bow. "Silent hells, yes. But when I saw them from my window in your king's manor this morning . . . I'll be a dead god's privy hole if I'm going to let the Far meet an army without me." He pointed to the Quiet army marching in from the northeast. "An army that's probably here *because* of me."

Daen studied Tahn a long moment. "It's reckless . . . but reasonable." He grinned. "Well, listen to me, will you? I sound as contradictory as a Hollows man." His grin faded to a kind of thankful seriousness. "I'm glad you were awake to see them from your window, Tahn. Somehow our scouts failed to get us word."

He'd been up early. He always was. To greet the dawn. Or rather, imagine it before it came. Those moments of solace were more important to him now than ever. Because images plagued him night and day. Images from Tillinghast. Images from a newly remembered past. Sometimes the images gave him the shakes. Sometimes he broke out in a sweat.

Tahn looked again now into the east, anticipating sunrise. The color of the moon caught his eye. Red cast. *Lunar eclipse.* By the look of it, the eclipse had been full a few hours ago. Secula, the first moon, was passing through the sun's penumbra. He'd seen a full eclipse in . . . *Aubade Grove!* The memories wouldn't stop. He'd spent several years of his young life in the Grove. A place dedicated to the study of the sky. A community of science. This, at least, was a happy memory.

Does the eclipse have anything to do with this Quiet army?

An idle thought, and there wasn't time to pursue it further. The low drone of thousands of Quiet feet striding the stony plain was growing louder, closer.

"We'll wait until the First Legion joins us on the shale." Daen spoke with the certainty of one used to giving orders. "Anything we observe, we'll report back to our battle strategists."

They didn't understand Tahn's need to run out to meet this army, any more than his friends would have. Sutter and Mira, especially. Sutter because he'd been Tahn's friend since he'd arrived in the Hollows. And Mira because—unless he missed his guess—she loved him. So, he'd sent word of the Quiet's approach, and slipped from the king's manor unnoticed.

"I won't do anything foolish," Tahn assured Daen, and began crawling toward the lip of the depression.

The Far captain grabbed Tahn's arm, the smile gone from his face. "What makes you so eager to die?"

Tahn spared a look at the bow in his hand, then stared sharply back at the Far. "I don't want to die. I don't want *you* to die, either. And if I can help it, you won't die *because* of me."

The Far captain did not let go. "I've never understood man's bloodlust, even for the right cause. It makes him foolish."

Tahn sighed, acknowledging the sentiment. "I'm not here for glory." He clenched his teeth again, days of frustration getting the better of him—memories of a forgotten past, images of possible futures. "But I must do *something*."

The Far continued to hold him, appraising. Finally, he nodded. "Just promise me you won't run in until we see the king emerge from the wall with the First Legion."

Tahn agreed, and the two crawled to the lip of the depression and peeked over the edge onto the rocky plane. What they saw stole Tahn's breath: more Bar'dyn than he could ever have imagined. The line stretched out of sight, and behind it row after row after row . . . "Dear dead gods," Tahn whispered under his breath. Naltus would fall. Even with the great skill of the Far. Even with the help of Vendanj, and his Sheason abilities.

We can't win. Despair filled him in a way he'd felt only once before—at Tillinghast. And on they came. No battle cries. No horns. Just the steady march over dry dark stone. A hundred strides away, closing, countless feet pounded the shale like a war machine. Tahn's heart began to hammer in his chest.

Beside him, Daen spoke in a tongue Tahn didn't understand. The sound of it like a prayer . . . and a curse.

Then he saw something that he would see in his dreams for a very long time. The Quiet army stopped thirty strides from him. The front line of Bar'dyn parted, and a slow procession emerged from the horde. First came a tall, withered figure wrapped in gauzy robes the color of dried blood. *Velle! Silent hells.* The Velle were like Sheason, renderers of the Will, except they refused to bear the cost of their rendering. They drew it from other sources.

The Velle's garments rustled as the wind kicked up again, brushing across the shale plain. Tahn's throat tightened. Not because of the Velle, or at least not the Velle alone, but because of what it held in its grasp: a handful of black tethers, and at the end of each . . . a child no more than eight years of age.

"No," Tahn whispered. He lowered his face into the shale, needing to look away, wanting to deny the obvious use the Velle had of them.

When he looked again, two more Velle had come forward. One was female in appearance, and stood in a magisterial dress of midnight blue. The gown had broad cuffs and wide lapels, and polished black buttons in a triple column down the front. The broadly padded shoulders of the garment gave her an imposing, regal look. The third Velle might have been any field hand from any working farm in the Hollows. He wore a simple coat that looked comfortable, warm, and well used. His trousers and boots were likewise unremarkable. He didn't appear ill fed. Or angry. He simply stood, looking on at the city as any man might after a long walk.

And in the collective hands of these Velle, tethers to six children. The small ones hunched against their bindings. Ragged makeshift smocks hung from their thin shoulders. Each gust of wind pulled at the loose, soiled garments, revealing skin drawn tight over ribs, and knobby legs appearing brittle to the touch.

Worst of all was the look in the children's faces—haunted and scared. And scarred. A look he knew. A look resembling the one worn by many of the children from the Scar. A desolate place he'd only recently remembered. A place where he'd spent a large part of his childhood. Learning to fight. To distrust. Lessons of the abandoned.

Not every memory of the Scar had been bad, though. A name and face flared in his mind: Alemdra. But the memory of her bright face quickly changed. Old grief became new at the thought of a ridge where they'd run to watch the sunrise, and watched a friend end her days. *Devin.* Some wounds, he realized, simply couldn't be healed. No atonement was complete enough.

The Velle yanked at the fetters, gathering the small ones close on each side. The children did not yelp or complain, though grimaces of pain rose in some few faces. Mostly, they fought to keep their balance and avoid going down hard on the rocky plain.

Then the Velle reached down and wrapped their fingers around the wrists of the young ones.

The Far king's legion hadn't emerged from the city wall. The siege on Naltus hadn't yet begun. But Tahn knew the stroke these Velle were preparing, fueled by the lives of these six children, would be catastrophic. Naltus might be destroyed before a single sword was raised.

Beside him, the Far captain cursed again and crept down to the dolmen to consult with his fellows. *What do I do?* His grip tightened on his bow. The tales of lone heroes standing against armies were author fancies. Fun to read, but wrong. All wrong. He could get off a few shots at the renderers before any of the Bar'dyn could react. But that wouldn't be enough to stop them, or save the children.

Each Velle raised a hand toward Naltus. Tahn had to do something. Now.

Without thinking further, he climbed onto the shale plain and stood, setting his feet. He pulled his bow up in a smooth, swift motion as he drew an arrow.

Softly he began, "I draw with the strength of my arms, but release as the Will—"

He stopped, not finishing the words he'd spoken all his life when drawing his bow, words taught him by his father, to seek the rightness of his draw. The rightness of a kill. His father and Vendanj had meant for him to remain blameless of wrongfully killing anything, or anyone, because they'd thought one day they might need him to go to Tillinghast, where his chances of surviving were better if he went untainted by a wrong or selfish draw.

For as long as could remember, he'd uttered the phrase and been able to sense the quiet confirmation that what he aimed at should die. Or if he felt otherwise, he shifted his aim. Usually it was only an elk to stock a meat cellar. But not always. In his mind he saw the Bar'dyn that had stood over his sister Wendra, holding the child she'd just given birth to. He saw himself drawing his bow at it, feeling his words tell him *not* to shoot the creature. He'd followed that intimation, and it had cankered his relationship with her ever since.

He was done with the old words. The Velle should die. He wanted to kill them. But he also knew he'd never take them all down. He'd never be able to stop their rendering of the little ones.

More images. Faces he'd forgotten. Faces of older children—thirteen, fourteen—reposed in stillness. Forever still. Still by their own hands. The despair of the Scar had taken all their hope. . . . Like Devin, and his failure to save her.

And what of the young ones in these Velle's hands? The ravages of *their* childhood? Long nights spent hoping their parents would come and rescue them. The bone-deep despair reserved for those who learn to stop hoping. He also sensed the ends that awaited each of them. The blinding pain that would tear their spirit from their flesh and remake it into a weapon of destruction.

Sufferings from his past.

This moment of suffering.

A terrible weight of sorrow and discouragement.

Then a voice in his mind whispered the unthinkable. An awful thing. An irredeemable thing. He fought it. Silently cried out against it. But the dark logic would not relent. And the Velle were nearly ready.

He took a deep breath, adjusted his aim only slightly. And let fly his awful mercy.

The arrow sailed against the shadows of morning and the charcoal hues of this valley of shale. And the first child dropped to the ground.

Through hot, silent tears, Tahn drew fast again, and again. It took the Quiet a few moments to understand what was happening. And when they finally saw Tahn standing beside the dolmen in the grey light of predawn, they appeared momentarily confused. Bar'dyn jumped in front of the Velle like shields. *They still don't understand.*

Like scarecrows—light and yielding—each child fell. Tahn did not miss. Not once.

When it was done, he let out a great, loud cry, the scream ascending the morning air—the only vocal sound on the plain.

Bar'dyn began rushing toward him. Tahn dropped to his knees, unhanded his bow, and waited for them. He watched them come closer as he thought about the wretched thing he'd just done.

It didn't matter that he knew he'd offered the children a greater mercy. Nor that he had decided this for himself. In those moments, it didn't even matter if what he'd done had saved Naltus.

These small ones, surprise on their faces—*Or was it hope when they saw me? They thought I was going to save them*—before his arrows struck home.

The shale trembled with the advance of the Bar'dyn rushing toward him with their calm, reasoning expressions. Tahn found himself already wondering what he'd do if he could go back and undo it. The bitterness overwhelmed him, and he suddenly yearned for the relief the Bar'dyn would offer him in a swift death. Then strong hands were dragging him backward by the feet, another set of hands retrieving his bow. Down into the depression, into the safety of the dolmen Tahn was cast. He flipped over and watched the Far captain and his squad defend the entrance to the barrow as Bar'dyn rushed in on them.

Jarron fell almost immediately, leaving Daen and Aelos fighting back three Quiet.

Tahn couldn't stop trembling. It had nothing to do with the battle about to darken the Soliel with blood. It was about the way the Quiet would wage their war. About what men would have to do to fight back. Choices like he'd just made.

Abruptly, the Bar'dyn stepped aside. The two Far shared a confused look, their swords still held defensively before them. Then one of the Velle came slowly into view. It stopped and peered past the Far, into the dolmen.

"You are too consumed by your own fear, Quillescent. Rough and untested, despite surviving Tillinghast." Its words floated on the air like a soft, baneful prayer. "Have you learned what you are? What you should do?"

Its mouth pressed into a grim line.

Tahn shook his head in defiance and confusion. Whatever Tillinghast had proven to Vendanj about Tahn being able to stand against the Quiet, the thought of his own future seemed an affliction. He'd rather not know.

"You are a puppet, Quillescent. Or were. But you've cut your strings, haven't you? Killing those children. And for us, you—"

A stream of black bile shot from the creature's mouth, coating its ravaged lips and running down its chin. A blade ripped through its belly. As it fell, it raised a thin hand toward him, and a burst of energy threw Tahn back against one of the tall dolmen stones. Blood burst from his nose and mouth. Shards of pain shot behind his eyes. In his back, the bruising of muscle and bone was deep and immediate.

He dropped to the ground, darkness swimming in his eyes. But he saw Daen and Aelos and the Bar'dyn all look fast to the left, toward the whispering sound of countless feet racing across the shale to meet the Quiet army—the Far legion come to war.

Read on for an exclusive bonus story
set in the world of The Vault of Heaven,

STORIES AND MUSIC

Kett Valan waded knee-deep in the muddy water of the dredge farm. He bent over a row of mud-onion, methodically rooting up the ripe ones and dropping them in his canvas satchel. All across the broad and shallow waters of the farm, other Inveterae did the same. Beneath a cloudy sky, only the sound of hands and feet slowly stirring the water . . . until a gasp and splash far to Kett's right.

He turned to see his mother fallen near the bank. She clutched at the lower side of her belly. *The baby.*

To Kett's left, rushing steps churned through the mud. His father. But the Quiet overseer of the farm was already there—a Bar'dyn named Rall. The lash of his whip rained down on Kett's mother, goading her back to work. She turned away from the beating, taking the brunt of it across her back. She fought to give an explanation, but it came out incompressible, choked by the pain.

"Stop!" Kett's father cried, falling in his haste. "She's with child."

The overseer didn't seem to hear him, and laid on with his whip again. More earnest now.

Kett was closer, and mad, besides. He raced toward his mother, his hands waving wildly. "Stop it! Stop!"

All the Inveterae stood up from their onion stoop and watched. They'd seen this scene before. Kett's family was Gotun. Of the Inveterae races, the Gotun were among the largest. Broad shoulders, broad waists, broad faces. Two and a half strides tall, and heavily muscled. They were a thick-bellied people. Impossible to know when a female was pregnant. But whippings weren't reserved for Kett's kind alone—the overseer was liberal with his encouragements.

Kett dodged those who stood and gawked, as he pushed through rows of onion root.

Rall's arm rose again, as Kett splashed closer. "She's got a baby inside," he cried out. "Hit her again and I'll kill you!"

Rall paused, his whip poised. He looked down at Kett for the boy he was.

454 • PETER ORULLIAN

Fourteen. Not even full in his chest or loins yet. The Bar'dyn smiled at the impertinence, the look of it twisting with a bit of impatience.

"Another water hound, is it?" The overseer looked back at Kett's mother and thrashed her once more for good measure. "Get it out and get back to work." He then ambled in the other direction, coiling his whip, as if beating Kett's mother had been as normally inconvenient as taking a piss.

Kett's father, Elam, raced past him and dropped beside his wife. Her back bled freely, the muddy bank coated red.

"Sala, I'm so sorry," Elam apologized. "I should have taken the bank today." Bank rows held a higher risk of whippings. Easy to do without Rall having to get wet and muddy.

She shook her head. "My choice. Closer to home if I needed to get there." She clutched again at her lower stomach.

"Let's go," Elam said, making as if to pick her up.

Again she shook her head. "No time. The baby's coming."

"Here?" Elam's surprise seemed hollow. Maybe defeated.

Kett crept up beside his mother, whose eyes shifted to him with regret, as though sorry he'd had to see it. "It'll be all right," she tried to reassure him. "Hold my hand."

He took her hand as his father helped her prepare. The other Inveterae returned to their onion rows before they received a whipping of their own.

Elam removed his shirt and made a makeshift bandage for Sala's wounds. It was a poor thing, and did more to keep the mud out of her opened back than blood inside her body.

For three hours she worked at getting the baby out. Kett watched her bite back her pain, as she tried not to alarm him or invite any more of the overseer's attention. It was the most heroic thing he'd ever seen.

And as the hours passed, she grew weak. Really weak. Worry rose in his father's face. If she lost strength to birth the child, it would die inside her. Or his father would have to cut the child free.

That's when Kett stopped *hearing the music.* That's what the older ones called it. He'd felt it coming for some time. A slow ebb. Like when irrigation slowly tapered in the autumn, eventually leaving the dredge farm dry and cracked.

Harvesting mud-onion and other root crops had been until now more like play, or sport. Sploshing through the water, digging in mud. Even the beatings he'd witnessed over the years hadn't left permanent impressions on him.

Young ears hear the music.

The kind that suggests one's choices are his own.

But eventually, he'd learned, all Inveterae stop hearing the music. They awaken to who and where they are. Trapped inside the Bourne. Slaves to the Quietgiven.

Harvesting crops to feed them. Shepherding camps of prisoners. Sometimes forced to fight, sent as the first line of attack. Expendable.

His mother squeezed his hand. "I love you, Kett. You're mindful of others and kindhearted. Those are good things. Don't let anything or anyone take them from you." And then, as if knowing his mind, added, "Don't stop listening for the music."

She smiled at him, then looked at his father and nodded. Elam leaned down and kissed her forehead, lingering a long time before drawing back. It had a good-bye feeling.

Then she tensed, and seemed to bear down with everything she had left to give. A few long moments later, Elam received the child. A little girl. He brought her around for Sala to see. A look of rare satisfaction spread on her face. They huddled together on the bank of the dredge farm. And sometime later, his mother closed her eyes. For good.

The ache that bloomed inside Kett threatened to stop his heart. Beneath it, far away, was anger. He sensed there'd be time for that later. He put his face against his mother's side. And wept. He wanted her back. He wanted to hear her voice. He wanted to hear the music.

But it remained quiet on their dredge bank. Quiet in his heart.

The night sky shone bright with stars against a deep black. No moon. Clear skies were uncommon in the Bourne. At least what Kett knew of it. He took it as a good omen for the request they were on their way to make. He followed his father, their boots grinding the dirt loudly in the stillness.

Rall's house rose before them, yellow light seeping out around a few shuttered windows. Elam didn't hesitate. He knocked, not hard but not soft.

Heavy steps came, and their overseer opened the door. The Bar'dyn's face, usually unexpressive, held a hint of surprise. Inveterae didn't come here. Certainly didn't knock at his door. Then, Rall looked down at the child in Elam's arms.

"Your woman died." It was said matter-of-factly. "You want to avenge her."

Elam shook his head. "I want a new obligation. Move me and my family to a camp to watch over prisoners."

"You don't want to avenge your mate?" Rall asked, sounding eager for an excuse to test himself.

"Without milk, I only have a day or two before the child dies," Elam replied, and waited.

Rall heaved a long breath. "Have one of the other dredge-hands suckle it. Many have young."

"I've asked," Kett's father explained. "They would help. But their teats scarcely produce enough for their own."

"Hmmmphf. I tire of Inveterae weakness." The Bar'dyn looked down again at the child in Elam's arms, his face as indifferent as if he stared upon a rock. "If the child dies, it dies."

Elam held a long, tense silence. Kett had seen this look in his father's eyes before. He fought not to take a step back.

"And if Inveterae children keep dying, who will dredge your roots?" Elam finally asked. "I think your farm is harder on its harvesters than most."

"Sedgel leaders like that I produce twice as much with the same size ponds," Rall countered. "And besides . . . who would complain." It was a clear challenge. The Bar'dyn still wanted his fight.

"Just until the child can take hard food," Elam pleaded. "Then we'll return."

Several long moments passed, Rall unmoved, before Kett's father added, ". . . please."

There was a pain in the plea. A pain of asking the favor of the man who'd killed his wife. A favor to keep a child alive so they could all return to the wet fields and harvest mud-onions for the bastard.

Silent gods, one day . . . Kett left that thought unfinished.

"A year." Rall pointed to the northeast. "Take the Ailanthus road. Day's walk to a camp." He held up a hand for them to wait. A few moments later he returned with a brand. He motioned for Elam to hold out his arm.

His father shifted the babe to one side and put out his hand. Rall placed the hot brand on Elam's skin, burning a symbol beside the brand all his workers already bore. The new mark was a line with a horseshoe shape at each end. A sign for temporary property. The two marks together would make it clear who owned them, and that they were expected to return.

Rall held out his hand to Kett, who didn't hesitate, and gave the overseer his arm, staring defiantly into his eyes as the Bar'dyn put the hot iron on his skin. It burned like all hells. And the stench of burning flesh made his stomach churn. But Kett didn't let the pain touch his eyes or face. He showed Rall the same godsforsaken indifference he'd shown when killing Kett's mother.

Without asking, Rall took the little girl's arm and burned the same brand there. As the skin sizzled, the child began to scream in pain. The Bar'dyn ignored it, ducked back into his home, and returned with his personal brand, and burned the child again, marking it as he did all his dredge hands.

Rall didn't bother to give them each a last look before going back into his house and closing the door.

They walked all night under the same clear skies. Getting away from the mud-onions, Kett thought he could almost hear the music again. Not sound music. More like an inner motion. Or resonance.

As they went, Elam's gait soothed the babe to sleep eventually. And just before dawn, they crested a hill and looked down on an encampment that stretched far up a river valley. From the hilltop, Kett could see them. Pens. More than he could count. Filled with humans.

He'd seen a human once. Rall had tried to use one as a dredge hand long ago. But the southern race simply didn't produce fast enough. They hadn't the strength or stamina of the Inveterae Houses that Rall used in his ponds. The human man had been sent back after a single day's work.

But here. *Dying gods, there must be thousands of them.*

They showed their brands at a small stone gatehouse before entering the encampment proper. The Bar'dyn guard gave them each a worn leather coat. A uniform of sorts. He pointed them to a command house, and by evening they had a new obligation, watching a pen of humans on the eastern side of the valley. A pen of *female* humans, at Elam's request.

After setting a fire in the hearth of the small hut given them for quarters, Kett broke his silence. "Why do Quietgiven herd the humans? Why keep them in pens?"

Elam stood up, rubbing arms that had held his little girl all day—the child now gratefully slept. "I'm not sure I know."

"Father?" Kett pressed.

Elam sighed, casting a look at his babe before turning toward Kett. "The Velle use some of them. Has to do with the power they have to move things. Change things. The humans are like wood for them to burn."

"But why so many?" Kett questioned.

Elam seemed only able to shake his head, evidently having no answer.

And there are so many camps. . . .

They lingered only a few minutes in the warmth before his father said, "Come," and headed out into the night again.

Elam went directly to the adjacent pen. The fence had been built of thick iron rods that rose twice the height of the tallest human. The top of each rod ended in a sharp point. And the fenced-in area was easily fifty strides on a side. Like stock, the captives could mill about if they wanted. Beneath a shabby lean-to on one side, more than thirty women huddled together to keep warm.

His father unlocked the gate and went in, heading for the lean-to. As he neared, they grew restless, pushing back against the bars beneath the slanted roof of their shelter.

Elam held up his hands to try and ease their anxiety. "Do any of you speak a Bourne tongue?"

Most of the women nodded. They'd been here long enough to learn.

"Good." His father looked them over. "I need a woman who has her milk. To nurse my child."

None answered, though several reflexively covered their breasts.

"You'll be given a place to sleep. Inside." Elam gestured toward his and Kett's new home. "A fire. And extra food." A moment later he added, "And no beatings."

"Do we have to fuck you, too?" one woman asked, her words filled with hatred and hurt.

"Nurse the child. That's all," Elam assured them.

For a long while, none of the women spoke or moved. Elam could force one to do it. But Kett knew his father wanted a volunteer. Someone Elam could hopefully trust with his little girl.

The silence stretched in the dark pen. Far behind them, the child woke and began to cry from inside their home. The sound of it was like a song sung with just two notes. Distant and faded.

The human who finally raised a hand wasn't the oldest and saltiest, nor the youngest and most brave looking. Getting to her feet was a dark-haired woman with a mild face. "I still have my milk," was all she said.

Elam nodded in gratitude and turned back toward the gate. The woman wove her way through her sister prisoners, and followed.

Back inside their home, the woman found the baby in a floor cradle, and took it immediately to her bosom. On her knees, she rocked back and forth in a practiced motion, feeding the babe, who still hadn't a name. Elam and Kett sat in low-slung chairs and watched, listening to the small sucking noises, which reminded Kett of the sound his feet made pulling out of dredge mud.

The woman never looked up. Never complained, as the hungry infant fed on-and-off for the better part of an hour.

Afterward, both the woman and the little girl looked spent. Elam gently took his child from the human's arms and put her back in the floor cradle. He then went into the shed behind their home and returned with an iron-bar cage that he set in the corner of the hearth room.

"It's better than the cold outside," he remarked, as he opened the door for the woman.

"My name is Asha," she said, and crawled inside her cage.

His father handed her two wool afghans before closing the door and securing it with a lock. "I'm Elam. This is Kett."

"And the child?" she asked.

"No name yet," his father replied. "Hasn't needed one."

"We all need a name." She stared at the child asleep in its cradle. "What was her mother's name?"

A long moment later, Elam answered, "Sala."

"Sala, then," the woman said, speaking it firmly. "Sala Cotlyn," she amended.

Before either Kett or his father could ask, Asha explained. "The name of my daughter before they took her away."

She didn't wait to hear comment or argument about it, and curled into the corner of her cage, losing herself in afghans oversized for her.

For three months, the same routine. Day and night. Elam tended the larger pen outside, seeing to the women—new ones, those who died or killed themselves, those who gave birth, the transfer of the get of their wombs to unknown Quiet intentions. And Kett watched after Asha—let her out to feed Sala Cotlyn, locked her back up afterward, got her warm stews and cups of water, took her into the field to shit or piss, fetched her buckets of water to sponge away the stink on her skin.

And they talked a lot.

"Father says humans are used by Velle to render the Will," Kett said, probing Asha to learn more about her kind.

"Some," she said, adjusting her breast in little Sala's mouth.

"And the others?" he asked.

Asha looked up. "How do you not know?"

"I'm a dredge farmer." He hunched his shoulders. "I know onions."

"Mating," she said without emotion. "I can't tell if it's for pleasure or something else. But there's lots of it. Seems they like to keep us pregnant. Some of us, anyway. The human men they hold in other pens, entire camps of them. They forge iron. Build. They're worked until they can't work anymore."

Kett shook his head, trying to figure it out. "They don't use humans much to farm; I know that."

"Different kind of farming, I suppose," she said. It was the first time he'd seen her smile, though it was rather mirthless. "But some . . . some they take north and west. I hear up there they aren't kept in pens at all. That they don't do much of *anything*. But those are rumors whispered at night, when the wombs get hopeful."

"Wombs?"

"You'll learn the language of it," Asha chided mildly. "We are what we do."

Kett considered it. "They called us 'dredges.'" He nodded with new understanding.

She nursed Sala Cotlyn in silence for a time. And Kett regarded her cage. She had several more blankets now, to make it more comfortable. And there was a small basket of food—nuts, dried meat, a few edible leaf stems—and a few utensils. She also had a small set of mouth pipes. She sometimes played to little Sala when the babe grew irritable.

In Asha's cage, there was even a small sketch she'd made on a scrap of parchment. She'd woven her image in and around the words written there. Drawn mostly with charcoal, the picture had been brushed in here and there with a russet color. Kett guessed at where she got that "ink," but never said anything.

He finally asked her. "Why are you helping us?"

"Nurse the child?" She laughed. This had mirth, but it came out somewhat coarse. Maybe she was just tired.

"Father could have forced you. But you volunteered." Kett looked back at her. "After losing your daughter, too." He paused. "Honestly, I'm not sure why *any* human would help us."

"You're Inveterae," Asha said, as if that explained everything.

He showed her a puzzled expression.

"You're a captive here as much as I am," she clarified.

"But we herd you like animals," he argued. "We keep you caged so the Quiet can do with you as they please. And the little ones you *do* have . . ."

The woman stared back him, her gaze far away. "I want to go home. I want to leave the Bourne." She pointed at him. "I want to leave it as much as you do."

Kett gave her a narrow look. "As much as *I* do? *I* didn't say that."

"You will," she followed. "You're still young. You haven't learned the cage of it yet."

But he had. Some of it, anyway.

The music is mostly gone.

That's when he understood why she was helping them.

"Make a friend of me. Of father." He made his own smile. "That's why you did it." His smile faltered, and he held up his arm so she could see his brands. "We're going back to the dredge farm as soon as little Sala can take hard food. We don't have a choice about it."

Asha stared back at him, and spoke with a quiet voice, "There's always a choice." Her words had a cold feeling in them. And they left Kett with a mix of emotions. Because he and Asha had become friends. Or so he thought. But now he also felt an unnamed fear.

A fear he understood as he watched her pull from her sleeve a spoon sharpened into a shiv. The bowl of it had been wrapped with lengths of wool to form a handle. The other end had been ground to a point. She rather gracefully brought it up to little Sala's throat.

Kett held up his hands. "Asha, no. We trusted you."

"Tell me why I should care about that." She didn't yell. Her face never tightened in anger. "After what everything your kind has done, tell me why."

"But you said *we* were prisoners, too—"

"The worst kind," she cut in with her even tone. "You do the Quiet's bidding to curry a dog's favor. What does it get you? And what does it cost *us*?" She nodded toward the outer pen, where other women were being held.

Kett looked down at the baby. "You want to avenge Cotlyn. But killing Sala isn't going to bring her back. All you'll be doing is murdering a baby. Taking the last part of my mother away from my father and me."

Asha nodded. "That's right. And maybe then your godsdamned ears will be opened." Silent tears fell from her eyes. "Maybe our cries won't go unanswered by a people who should stand up against the Quiet. Lead us from this place."

She began to tremble with anger. Or fear. Whatever it was, her shiv swayed and pricked Sala, who began to cry loudly in her arms. A drop of blood welled beneath the baby's chin and ran down her neck.

Asha's eyes widened. She appeared surprised and panicked and filled with indignation. She quivered like a string ready to snap. Her silent tears came faster, running over her placid cheeks. It was strange to see.

But not uncommon.

"Bourne sickness" the humans called it. Many wound up this way. Fragile minds broke from the strain of captivity. Only this human, Asha, held a shiv to Kett's sister, his mother's namesake.

His anger bloomed. But came tempered by something else. Empathy.

He held up his hands. "Asha, you don't need to do this. Please."

Her trembling hands caused the shiv to prick Sala again. The child wailed now, the sound loud in the room. And soon running steps approached from outside. The door was thrown open, and Elam burst in, another Inveterae behind him—a roaming pen-hand.

Kett's father took in the situation at a glance, and leveled a hard stare at Asha. "If you're going to kill the child, do it quickly. Don't make it suffer."

Asha snapped from her daze. "The same as you do for us?" she said with icy sarcasm.

"I'll make yours quick, if you do the same for my child," Elam replied. "You have my word."

She laughed again. There was something loose-sounding in it. Still cold, but unsteady.

Elam didn't wait a moment longer. He started toward her. Kett saw her hand flex on the shiv; her shoulder rose as she set to plunge the homemade knife deep into little Sala's throat.

And in a moment of clarity, Kett knew she would go through with it. Not from lunacy or anger. Something had gone lost inside Asha. He'd watched it ebb over the last three months.

Do you humans hear music, too?

She would have her moment's justice, and then be glad to die herself.

But looking at his little sister, Kett felt more than a brotherly urge to save her. It somehow seemed suddenly important for reasons that were different. Larger.

Before his father's presence could force Asha to murder the babe, he called out to her. "You named her Cotlyn."

That brought his father's attention, and Asha's, too. They stared at him in a long moment of suspended action.

Kett continued. "Whether she lives . . . or not, you can decide with your knife. But it's not vengeance if you kill her. And her death won't change my heart, or my father's heart, into something you think it should be." He swallowed. "You'll just be killing a child you saved from death. Which makes her yours, every godsdamned bit as much as she's ours."

A long moment later, Asha began to sob, and lowered her knife. She bent over and kissed Sala Cotlyn, whispering an apology as she did so.

Elam sent his extra pen-hand away, and sat into his chair, where he buried his head in his hands.

Kett stared at Asha and his father and thought about cages.

That evening, as Asha slept in her cage, and little Sala slept in her cradle, Kett sat near the fire trying to drive out the chill that had gotten inside him. It was a foolish thing to do. His chill wasn't from the cold.

"We're more like the humans than we are the Quiet," he said to his father, who had just returned from securing the pen and the rest of his day's end chores.

"Because we're slaves to Quietgiven?" Elam said, rubbing at his hands.

"No," Kett replied. "Because we can't leave the Bourne."

His father's eyes narrowed. "I've been told humans can walk right through the Veil. Has no hold on them."

Kett smiled darkly. "Which is why we keep them penned up."

"That's at least part of it," his father answered. "Kett, don't let what happened today get inside you—"

Kett shook that off. "We weren't meant to be here. But we are. The stories say the gods didn't believe in us. Easier for them to send us into the Bourne with the dissenting god's own. So we don't belong here. And we don't belong south of the Pall, either." He gave his father a long look. "Where should we be?"

His father smiled. Not a tired or ironic kind. "You still hear the music, don't you?"

"I'm not sure what that means anymore," Kett answered.

"Your mother would be pleased," Elam added.

Then his father sat back, taking a moment to regard his daughter, the woman who nursed her, and finally Kett. "A long time ago," Elam said, "just a few generations after the Placing, many of us left the Bourne."

Kett turned sharply toward his father, a flicker of hope in his belly. "What?"

"We don't speak of it—breeds false hope. And false hope will kill a content Gotun." Elam smiled again. "Five Houses. All of them Mor peoples. They escaped through the Veil. Used a kind of song to tear through. Some say they went to get out of the Bourne. Some say they went to keep their song from Quiet hands. Whatever the truth, they got away."

The wind stirred in trees outside. Wood creaked in the yard behind their home.

"No one has this Mor song anymore?" Kett asked.

"Not on *this* side of the Veil." His father must have seen his disappointment. "But they aren't the only ones to get through."

Kett felt another spark of hope.

Elam sat forward in his chair. "The Lul'Masi, another House, they pierced the Veil. No song that time."

"Then how?" Kett quickly asked.

"No one knows," his father said, "but the Lul'Masi were sky watchers. Better at it than other Inveterae, or even the Quiet, so the story goes. Must have learned something in the stars."

Again wind murmured and wood creaked beyond the walls of their home. Kett might have found it less random, if he hadn't been so excited by what he was hearing.

"Then we could do the same," he suggested. "There are ways to get out." He looked over at Asha. "And the humans could come with us."

Elam put his hands up in a slowing motion.

But Kett's mind was racing forward. "Maybe the Mors and Lul'Masi have something in common. We can study—"

"We'll have to keep it quiet," his father said. "It's dangerous talk. And don't ever share any of it with someone you wouldn't trust with your life. Don't even repeat the stories I've told you unless the Inveterae you're with will guard them—"

The door to their home opened. The camp overseer walked in. A Bar'dyn more heavily muscled than most. His eyes moved over every surface, assessing, before fixing on Kett's father.

"Telling stories?" the Bar'dyn asked.

"A small slip," Elam admitted. "Probably brought on by the human woman. It won't happen again."

"Tales of music and stars," the Bar'dyn said without passion. He looked down at Kett. "Inciting sedition in one so young."

"Told to discourage," Elam lied. "To warn. We know our obligations."

The overseer didn't immediately reply, and walked the room, brushing near Elam, Kett, the cradle, and Asha's cage, where he sniffed twice. He then ambled back to face Kett's father, staring at him with blank disregard.

"You're borrowed. Here for a wet nurse." The Bar'dyn leaned in, his voice low. "A dredge. Come to me when your children lost a mother. Come into my camp and telling stories of escape."

Elam lowered his eyes, a sign of respect and submission. "Please," he whispered.

In his low, rough voice, the overseer went on. "I'm here because I heard there was an incident today. I thought I might be of help. Imagine my surprise to hear from beyond the walls of this home, your voices, sharing entirely the wrong kind of stories."

Elam didn't dare look up. He stood, waiting.

The overseer turned and looked down at Kett again. "And what about you, little dredge. What do you think of what your father was saying?"

Kett felt a fire inside. *Is this the music they speak of?* He wanted to shout back with bright defiance. He wanted to take Asha's shiv to the Bar'dyn. He did neither. Instead, he stared up. Spoke like a child. And lied like a thief.

"I don't understand." Kett screwed on a confused expression. "We're *all* in the Bourne."

The overseer patted his head with Quiet condescension. He strode back abreast of Elam, but facing the other direction. He turned his head and spoke into Elam's ear. "Say good-bye."

Kett's father shut his eyes a long moment. When he opened them, Kett saw failure there. Elam took half a step toward Kett, stopped. "You're old enough," his father began. "You don't need my help any—"

Elam's mouth gaped open at some unseen pain. He slipped to his knees, and Kett saw the overseer's blade pull from his father's back, slick with blood.

"*No—*"

"Stop, dredge," the Bar'dyn said. "Your father was right about one thing. You're old enough to walk a muddy row on your own. I don't want borrowed goods here anymore. The child is old enough to stomach hard food. Take it back to the ponds with you."

The overseer briefly stared at Asha in her cage. "And get that womb back into the pen."

Then the Bar'dyn left, shutting the door gently on his way out, as if he'd been visiting a friend.

Kett went to his father, who tried to say something to him. But his words were husky and garbled. There was no final wisdom or expression of love. His father died in front of him for telling a story of escape from the Bourne.

Blinding hate and anger and loss pulsed behind his eyes. The same ache as he'd felt for his mother came, too. But this time it stood at a distance. He wanted to scream and pound on something. He finally went out into the night to try and cool the heated thoughts racing through his head. *Sedition. I'll give you sedition. I'll take every gods-abandoned Inveterae and human out of this place!*

But he had no knowledge of how to do so. No plan. No help.

He had what? A couple of stories. He had dead parents. He had a little sister still sucking a teat for her meals.

The only long familiarity he had left was back at the dredge farm, walking a row of mud-onions.

The music was vibrant in his head. Not an echo of sound. A different vibration. One of life. Of living. But he couldn't do anything with the music just now. He also knew he couldn't dredge through mud forever, either.

For a while. But not forever.

He went back inside, and unlocked Asha's cage. Then he picked up Sala Cotlyn from her cradle and sat again in his low chair until the human woman came out.

"What will you do?" Asha asked.

"The three of us are going to walk back down the Ailanthus road, past the gatehouse," he explained. "If they ask, you're my personal womb. And wet nurse to Sala. She and I are going back where we belong. And you," he gave Asha a nod, "you're going to try to get home."

He handed her Sala, then spent half an hour bending a thin knife into the shapes of his own brands before heating them in the coals of their fire.

"It's a long walk to the Pall. I've no food. No—"

"Come here," he said.

Asha put little Sala down for a moment, and came close. She didn't waver as he put the brands to her arm. They weren't exactly the same dimensions, but they were close. They'd serve.

And the smell wasn't quite so unsettling this time. Maybe because the brands held a different purpose.

"You look like chattel now." Kett thought the rest through for her. "As you travel south, tell anyone who asks that you've been loaned out to a border post. A year's time. The Quiet will believe you've been whored out to lonely troops. When you get to the Pall, you'll have to take your chances getting over the mountains."

"And leave the others behind?" Asha asked, her tone belying the answer.

"Alone you might make it."

He picked up his sister, and they left their shepherd's home. In the yard, he bent and scooped up a handful of cool mud, and coated Asha's brands with it.

"It'll ease the burn. And dirtied up, they won't look so fresh," he explained.

She nodded, walking beside him as they made their way from the encampment.

Half a league beyond the gatehouse they stopped. She gently caressed the crown of little Sala's head, before doing something that shocked and pleased him. She took Kett in a full embrace. Young as he was, he was still taller and thicker than the woman, but she managed to give him a tight squeeze.

Then she turned and cut south along a narrow road, leaving Kett alone with his sister-child. Sala would be hungry soon. He thought he could get back to the dredge farm and mash something up for her by morning.

He would have liked there to be stars as he walked the Ailanthus road back to the ponds. But there weren't. It was dark. Extremely dark. But both moons shone a filtered light through the high clouds. Enough to travel by for a dredge.

But he didn't really go back just a dredge.

Now, he had stories.

And music.

Abandonment, the: The cessation of Creation at the hands of the Framers, and their subsequent abandonment and absence from the lives of men.

Aeshau: From the Language of the Covenant, meaning "gathered."

Age: A reckoning of time roughly equivalent to a thousand years.

Anais (Ah-NAY): An honorific used for women, derived from Anais Layosah Reyal.

Ars and Arsa (AHRS and AHRS-ah): Alternate terms from the Covenant Language for "body" and "spirit," denoting also the beauty and elegance of both sides of Creation individually and as a unified whole.

Artificer: See Quietus.

Ayron (EYE-rahn): A Far drink made of plain yogurt and water.

Baenel (Bay-NELL): Covenant Language term meaning "eternally left behind."

Bar'dyn: Creatures created at the hands of Quietus to balance the efforts of the Council of Creation, and consigned to the Bourne at the Abandonment. Three heads taller than a tall man, they have a thick, fibrous skin as resilient as most armor. Due to its roughness, the skin often appears to move independent of the muscle and bone beneath. They have protruding cheekbones and long arms ending in hands with a thumb on each side of three taloned fingers. Still, they make use of weapons, and possess an unsettling intelligence belied by their brutish appearance. Their strength is expressed in a common folk myth that with their bare hands they could crush stone.

Blade of Seasons: A blade forged from a block of metal folded a thousand times. It is said to have the power of remembering.

boards, the: A term referring to the platforms where the human auctions take place.

Bourne, the: The great area north and west of the Eastlands where the races given life by Quietus were sent and sealed behind the Veil.

Castigation, the: When Regent Corihehn of Recityv sent the Sedagin people to almost certain death, the Randeur of the Sheason sent his Order into the court and council of every nation and caused them, upon threat of death, to reassemble in Recityv to honor Corihehn's lie and go to help the Sedagin.

Chamber of Anthems: A great round hall in Descant Cathedral, where the Leiholan sing the Song of Suffering.

Change, the: See Standing.

Charter, the: A legendary code of principles and dictums, said to have been authored in the Language of the Covenant by the Council at Creation, it sets forth the fundamental covenants of life, the model for joyful living, and the universal laws that govern all Forda I'Forza. It is said to be the mind of the Great Fathers, the hope of man. Yet it remains largely a myth, with but a few of its tenets still uttered on the lips of men, and these known only by oral tradition too old to be reliable. Still, invoking the very name of this treatise inspires silence and reflection.

Children of Soliel: See Far.

Civilization Order: Order authored by the League of Civility that makes rendering the Will, or asking a Sheason to do so, a crime punishable by death.

Convocation of Seats: A council called first by King Sechen Baellor to answer the threat of the Bourne in the war of the First Promise. The convocation seated rulers from almost every nation known to Baellor. Its unified efforts helped bring the war of the First Promise to an end.

court wastery: Sewage area of a big city or palace.

Covenant Tongue (or Language of the Covenant): A language used by the Framers to put the world in place.

Cradle of the Scar: A dead, white tree not far inside the Scarred Lands. The tree bears a hollow at a height just above the head of an average-sized man.

Craven Season: The age that followed the High Season. Known as craven because the designs of the First Ones seemingly came to naught, leaving the land in a state of debility. During this period, the Veil weakened and gradually let slip those hidden up in the Bourne, resulting in the Convocation of Seats and the War of the First Promise.

crest of Mira Far: White banner with two red swords described in vertical lines, one pointing up, the other down.

crest of the Sodality: A quill dancing on the flat edge of a horizontal sword, typically rendered in white and black.

crest of Vohnce: A tree with as many roots as branches, typically white upon a crimson field.

collough (Kul-LAW): A term defining the standard military complement of the Bar'dyn; typically numbering about a thousand.

dark hour: Midnight.

Dissent: A legal term for a case or issue brought before a court.

Dissenter: A legal term for one who brings a Dissent or dispute before the court.

Draethmorte: Those first Adherents to the cause of Quietus, given the right and privilege to direct the Will by Maldea himself. Some believe they were created when the Artificer knew he would not be allowed to finish his work and at great personal cost formed from his belly and mind these sacred few to aid him in the ages that would follow.

Drum of Nicholae: A mythic instrument that, when played, it is said, causes the hearts of all those fighting beneath its drummer's banner to beat in unison, effectively creating one great heart to thrust upon the enemy. The legend tells that the drum is an inelegant thing, with a dark origin.

dust gone up: A phrase used by traders and highwaymen to refer to the auctions held to sell human stock. It is derived from the chalk put to the feet of those to be auctioned. Alternately, the phrase refers to mortality, dust being the reduced Forda of mortal flesh, life.

earthsky: A common term, meaning horizon.

Emerit (EM-ehrit): A warrior with sworn fealty to men and women of station. His feats of prowess might only be surpassed by his keen intellect. It is a title bequeathed on only the greatest fighter by only the highest mantle of government.

Estem Salo (EH-stehm SA-low): The seat of Sheason leadership, inhabited primarily by those of the Order and their families. It is said to be a small city of energetic thought and applied principle.

Far: A race that lives in the Soliel Stretches and is known for exceptional speed and weapons handling. Legend holds that they live a shortened life, having been given a commission by the First Ones ages ago. Little is known about them, to the point that distant nations consider the Far nothing more than an authors' story. Few have ever seen a Far, as they remain a reclusive and well-protected race in the harsh terrain of the Soliel.

final earth: Euphemism for either death or a grave.

First Fathers: See Framers.

First Ones: See Framers.

First Promise, the: A covenant to answer every injustice with an equal measure of justice. The First Promise was entered into by nearly every nation, kingdom, principality, throne, and dominion with a government to be represented at the Convocation of Seats. It was the beginning of the end of all things craven, and gave men hope again after the Abandonment. Fealty and honor meant something between friends and countrymen. Equity and fairness were the highest law, and scarcely anything needed to be codified or written, one's word being as certain a thing as the dawning of another day.

First Steward: The honorific given to one who stands as witness to a melura's Change.

Fleetfoot: See Far.

Forda (FOHR-dah): From the Covenant Language, meaning "matter" or "body," and sometimes "earth."

Forda I'Forza (FOHR-dah ee-FOHR-zah): The union of matter and energy, body and spirit, earth and sky, that makes up life. Even the First Ones are bound by the laws of this governing dynamic. One without the other collapses, and is brought to unhappiness or stasis. It is a delicate balance, upset by Maldea during the creation of the world and for which he was Whited and bound.

Forgotten Cradle: See Cradle of the Scar.

Forza (FOHR-zah): From the Covenant Language, meaning "spirit" or "energy," and sometimes "sky."

Framers: The gods who created the world of Aeshau Vaal.

gave me the crawls: A colloquial phrase meaning "it was creepy."

handcoin: Worth ten jots or plugs. Sometimes called simply "a coin."

Hargrove (HAR-grohv): A renowned poet, whose work often took historical themes.

High Council: A body of select representatives empowered to enact change and provision for Recityv in particular and the nation of Vohnce in general.

Hollows, the: A small town in the Hollows Forest. It's name changed over time, as it was once known as "The Hallows," consecrated to protect those residing therein from the Quiet, should they come into the land.

hostaugh (Hoh-STAW): A poisonous serpent from the Mal.

Inner Resonance: See Sheason.

Inveterae (In-VEHT-er-eye): If the stories are to be believed, the Inveterae are those creatures given life at the hands of the First Ones (not Maldea, but the others of the Creation Council), yet still consigned to the Bourne alongside the Quiet. Most Eastland folk consider this folklore created to keep children in line.

jaybird: A euphemism for the male genitalia.

Je'holta (Jeh-HOHLT-ah): A gathering of thought, feeling, and languor from things tangible—even if inanimate—and given form in a dark fog that coaxes those enveloped within it to experience their own fears. It carries voices that belong to souls lost while serving Maldea, tainted and languid because there is no redemption for them. They cry, their hollow voices audible within Je'holta, like a touchstone of awful remembrance. It is a unique instrument of the Quiet. It may be called spontaneously anywhere, having no imprisonment behind the Veil. See also Male'Siriptus.

Jo'ha'nel (JOE-hah-nell): Legend holds him to be the presiding member of Quietus's servants. Rumors abound of diaries held deep in the libraries of Estem Salo that bear the handwriting of this Quietgiven. It is said that he was the first to follow Maldea. There are old stories about his first fight with Palamon for the lives of men.

Jurshah (JER-shaw): A compliment of four Leaguemen in which each of the four League disciplines is represented. Originally, each branch of the League represented simply the four directions on a map. Now, these disciplines pursue separate fundamental skills deemed needful by His Leadership: politics, justice and defense, history, and finance and commerce. Just as the directions on a map combine to indicate middling courses, so too are their factions with covert purposes unspoken of by His Leadership.

Kaemen Sire (KAY-men SIGH-er): The second organized entrance into the Eastlands by the Bourne was led by a creature of unknown origin. Some believed Kaemen Sire to be one of Maldea's first creations, others a Draethmorte, and still others are sure it was Inveterae. Whatever the truth, its madness and rage was said to blind men for merely looking upon it. The defeat of the Quiet during the War of the Second Promise did not claim this creature, which escaped back beyond the Veil.

King Sechen Baellor (SEH-shen BAY-lohr) the Swift: The king of Vohnce—which later moved to a more representative government—at the beginning of the War of the First Promise. Baellor called the first Convocation of Seats.

Latae: Used with "dance" or "stance" to describe a series of battle motions learned by the Far for battle.

Layosah (LAY-oh-saw), the Great Defense of: Referring to one of the Wombs of War who shamed King Baellor into calling the First Convocation of Seats.

Leadership, His: Euphemism for the leader of League of Civility, currently Roth Staned.

League of Civility: An association of presumably civic-minded militants who believe that enlightenment trumps all. Self-appointed administrators of the law, they are dedicated to the quelling of insurgency that runs counter to their described goals: peace, equality, and prosperity. In the interest of their creed, they have made strict enemies of the Sheason by forcing ratification of a "Civilization" order (death) executable upon evidence of a Sheason's exercise of the Will. The League holds that rendering the Will is at best an arcane practice with unnatural and unholy origins, smacking of stories that assume the reality of the Great Fathers, and ultimately becomes nothing more than a cover for deception and manipulation of the working class. With four branches—politics, justice and defense, history, and finance and commerce—the League has evolved to have political representation in almost every nation. Their sigil is four arms in a circle, each gripping the wrist of the next, now extolled as a metaphor for unity of the people, though originally a symbol of its four branches, each branch coming to emphasize particular goals in the interest of the League.

Leiholan (LAY-ih-HOH-uhn): From the Language of the Covenant, meaning "Wrought by Song." An inborn ability to exercise the Will through song. It is a gift of Resonance. The term is also used to refer to one who possesses the gift.

Lesher Roon (LESH-uhr ROON): A race run at Recityv by children ages twelve and below. The winner occupies a seat at the regent's High Table as the Child's Voice, and is thus a member of the High Council, able to cast a vote in all decisions that relate to Recityv and the nation of Vohnce.

Levate (LEH-vuht): One who practices the healing arts.

Library of Common Understanding: A repository of laws and codified principles by which all residents of Recityv, and to a larger extent Vohnce, may be reasonably expected to be held. It is also the immense library that serves the nation of Vohnce.

light storm: Also sometimes known as a Forza storm, this phenomenon appears as a series of light bursts with no apparent source.

Loneot: A renowned architect from the flourishing years of the Dispensation of Hope.

longblades: Euphemistic name for Sedagin. See also Sedagin.

Low Ones: A disparaging term applied to those born with abnormalities. Also sometimes used to refer to any not highborn.

Lul'Masi (Lull-mah-SEE): A race of Inveterae escaped from the Bourne during the War of the First Promise. Similar to the Bar'dyn in stature, they stand three full strides tall, and have broad, flat features. Most notable is the sheer size of their legs, which cause them to move in more of a gallop than a run, swinging each leg out around the muscled bulk of their thighs. Known for their stoic natures and generally reclusive tendencies.

Lyren (LEER-uhn): Music students at Descant Cathedral. Typically describes students early in their studies and those without Leiholan abilities.

Maesteri (My-STAIR-ee): Instructors of music at Descant Cathedral.

Mal i'mente (MAHL ee-MEHNT): An imprecatory prayer offered in battle by Maere Quietgiven that holds the power to alter the substance and fabric of its adversary's life. It is an unhallowed phrase of the Covenant Language.

Mal Wars: A series of wars focused west of the Divide in the Mal lands during the Age of Disdain, giving evidence to the thinning of the Veil along the Rim. The failure of the Second Promise left the Sedagin unwilling to commit itself. And most rulers had no desire to see the Convocation of Seats re-called.

Male'Siriptus (Mahl-eh-Sih-RIP-toos): Most often referred to as "the caress of Male'Siriptus," it is sometimes used in place of Je'holta. Though it is a singular term, giving a single, unending voice and hand to a host of shadows and dark fates. Male'Siriptus is what Je'holta can do, by surfacing darkness of fear to the individual.

Maere (MAYR): A servant of Quietus, these are wraithlike creatures. It is believed that the Maere are the final state of those who've lost their physical lives in service to Maldea, living a fate they wish to extend to those still alive in the flesh.

melura (Meh-LOOR-ah): The term used to describe someone who has not yet reached the age of eighteen and undergone the Change.

meridian: Midday, noontime.

Mor Nation Refrains: A mythic set of songs held safe by the Mor Nations. Said to bear more power even than Suffering.

Noble Ones: See Great Fathers.

Northsun: A festival now largely observed only in rural communities where the League has yet to exert any real control. It is a celebration of the sun's northernmost passage through the sky, and a time of reckoning one's age. It is likewise often attended by a Reader, who brings news and recites histories and stories to entertain and remind.

Ogea (OH-gee-uh): A Reader who comes to the Hollows at Northsun to relate the stories of ages past.

Opawn, Hambley (oh-PAWN, HAM-blee): Proprietor of the Fieldstone Inn located in the Hollows.

Ophal're'Donn: The bridge crossing the Lesule River into Stonemount.

order, the: See Sheason.

pageant wagon: A large traveling wagon on which a troupe plays rhea-fols (plays) for communities large and small.

Palamon (PAL-uh-mahn): Often regarded as the first Sheason, he is a hero to those who oppose the Bourne.

Passat (Puh-SAHT): A reverent festival held at Midwinter in the Hollows to commemorate the spark of life and light within, and the hope for a return from the long nights of winter to the long days of summer. Hollowed gourds are fitted with candles emblematic of both observations.

Pauper's Drum: See Drum of Nicholae.

penaebra (Peh-NAY-brah): A ghost of the dead.

pinchcomb: A kind of barrette used for a woman's hair.

Placing, the: Thought to refer to the consignment of Inveterae in the Bourne. Alternately meaning the dire days when all things were sealed behind the Veil. Some believe it refers to secrets even Quietus does not know that are held at the farthest reaches beyond the Rim.

Preserved Will, law of: A law understood as existing in the Charter, in which any action that might be shown to harmonize with the design of the Will cannot be prosecuted as unlawful.

Quiet, the: The name, singular or plural, given to those who follow Quietus.

Quietus: One from the Council of Creation, known then as Maldea, given responsibility for establishing balance in the world. His vaulting ambition and exceeding ability toppled the delicate scales of harmony as he brought forth unimaginable darkness and creatures out of madness to harrow the races given life in the land. For his crime, the Council Whited him, binding him in a far place where there would be little opportunity to stretch forth his hand to exercise the Will.

Qum'rahm'se (Coom-rahm-SAY): A library established ages ago to gather and study any and all available documents relating to the Language of the Covenant.

Randeur (RAN-djeeoohr): A title given to the leader of the Order of Sheason. In the Language of the Covenant, it is thought to mean "descended below them all."

Reader: A branch of the Scola given entirely to the study of history and books for the purpose of relating the stories to others. Readers are often considered to be seers and scryers, as well as historians and fanciful storytellers.

Resonance: A principle that underlies a Sheason's ability to render the Will, just as it also underlies a Leiholan's ability to render song with power and influence.

Reyal, Layosah (LAY-oh-saw Ray-AL): One of the Wombs of War during the War of the First Promise, and the one who stood on the palace steps in Recityv and called for a council to do something more concerted to combat the Quietgiven, resulting in the Convocation of Seats.

rhea-fol (RAY-fohl): A dramatic presentation with actors typically inspired by a historical event.

Right Arm of the Promise: Name given to the people later known as the Sedagin for the zeal and loyalty of their service in the War of the First Promise. See Sedagin.

Rudierd Tillinghast (ROOD-yahrd TILL-eeng-ghast): From the Language of the Covenant, meaning "return of all things."

Scar, the: Abbreviated term for the Scarred Lands.

Scarred Lands: An area east and slightly north of Recityv where the last battle of the War of the Second Promise took place. That battle is also known sometimes as the Battle of the Scar or the Battle of the Round. The Scarred Lands have lost their vitality due to being raped by the Velle, who drew their essence and life to darkly render the Will during that great last stage of the war.

scriveners: A highly literate association whose purpose is to assist in the collection of ancient documents and genealogy, with emphasis on studying the Covenant Language and its applications.

Season of Rumors: Name some have given to the current age.

Second Promise: An attempt to renew of the First Promise, added upon by a spoken commitment to end, once and for all, the shedding of blood by emissaries of Quietus. It was forsaken by some governments, either because they never attended the Second Convocation of Seats, or because they did and simply didn't keep their word.

Sedagin (Sehd-ah-gin): Name of the people living in the High Plains whose mastery with a greatsword is legendary. They live by the principles of the First Promise.

SeFeery, Denolan (she-FEER-ee): See also Grant.

Sento, Belamae (BELL-ah-may SENT-oh): Chief Maesteri at Descant Cathedral.

Sheason (SHAY-son): From the Language of the Covenant, meaning "servant." Members of this Order possess the ability to render the Will—influence

Forda I'Forza. When the First Ones abandoned their work in Aeshau Vaal, they conferred the authority to direct the Will in the interest of men to Palamon. The right and privilege to render has since been passed down only after vigorous training. Though the Order was conceived on the principle of service and sacrifice, they are often disliked or distrusted. Much of this has grown under the influence of the League of Civility. The Sheason are also sometimes known as "three-ring" for the emblem that signifies their order: three rings inside of each other, and all meeting at one point. This same symbol also describes another name the Sheason bear: Inner Resonance.

Shenflear: An acclaimed writer of the early years of the Craven Season.

Sky, the: The overreaching, never-ending constant of life. Often used interchangeably with the word "life," it connotes assurance, stability. The sky holds the sure patterns and procession of the stars, and the unvarying, necessary return of the sun and daylight. It represents that which is known without being touched or proven. "The Sky" is also the shortened term for "Tabernacle of the Sky."

Slope Nyne: Tenendra word for Bar'dyn. See Bar'dyn.

sodalist: A member of the Sodality, and one given to the study of the Authors as well as the crafts of war. Ancient diaries define the sodalist as both Author and Finisher, though the meaning of the phrase is unclear. See also Sodality. By virtue of a sodalist's study, he or she often serves in a community as teacher, Levate, and counselor.

Sodality: A brotherhood of men and women aligned to protect the integrity of Authors' words, and to bring them to bear in conjunction with the bite of steel. The Sodality's highest call is as protectorate to the Order of Sheason, to which it holds a solemn oath.

Solath Mahnus: The buildings and castle constructed on a risen hill in the center of Recityv, where governing activities are held.

Song of Suffering (also called just "Suffering"): The musical rendering of the Tract of Desolation, performed in the Chamber of Anthems of Descant Cathedral. Sung entirely in the Language of the Covenant, a single performance has but one refrain and lasts seven hours.

song of the feathered, the: Colloquial phrase referring to morning time.

spine-root: A low-lying plant which grows barbs and needles.

Standing (or to Stand): A rite of passage which takes place at the first full moon after a melura's eighteenth birthday. The ceremony is witnessed by a First Steward, typically the child's father or mother. Beyond this time, the child becomes an adult, and is considered responsible thereafter for his or her actions.

Staned, Roth (STAN-ed, ROTH): Defender of Civility himself, Roth is the Ascendant of the League of Civility, its ranking officer, and often referred to as "His Leadership."

Stem: A paper rolled with tobacco inside to be smoked.

Stipple toes: A common cooking root similar to rhubarb.

Stonemount: An abandoned city near the Valley of Lesule almost entirely constructed of stone: granite, marble, and other indigenous rock. Legend holds that the inhabitants simply vanished, no war or disease accounting for their disappearance.

Storalaith, Helaina (Hel-AY-nah Stohr-uh-LAY-eth): Regent of the nation of Vohnce, who wields discretionary power of the High Council and all other governmental powers of Vohnce and Recityv alike.

Stranger: See Quietus.

straw-drift: Backstreet folk; moneygrubbers, informants, thieves, etc.

Strong-wagon: A large, heavy wagon with thick walls used to convey important cargo.

sword and quill: Emblem of the Sodality. See Sodality.

Ta'Opin (Tah-oh-PIHN): One of the Mor races. Rumor and myth surrounds their origins. Some believe them to be a lost race escaped from the Bourne, one of the Inveterae. A race unusually strong with song, they are generally unwelcome around others, though their outward geniality and fierce loyalty belies this social estrangement.

Tabernacle of the Sky: A set of great, tall buildings and theaters in the heart of the Divide where it is believed the First Ones worked to bring about Creation.

Table of Blades: The ruling body of the Sedagin people.

Teheale (Te-HEEL): From the Language of the Covenant, meaning "earned in blood." It is the High Plain risen by the power of the Order of Sheason as a gift and home for the Sedagin.

Telling, a: Written by an Author, a specialized document used to travel from one place to another through a kind of portal. Most Tellings are made usable by the gifts of the Leiholan.

tenendra (Tuh-NEHN-drah): A large traveling carnival where feats of strength, acrobatics, strange sights, merriment, games, and exotic foods can be had for a price.

tent folk: Euphemism for those who work the tenendra.

Therus (THEER-uhs): The Quietgiven name for a Sodalist.

three-ring: Euphemism for a Sheason, due to the sigil they bear of three rings— one inside the next—all touching on one side.

Tillinghast: A place on the far side of the Saeculorum Mountains, where the earth falls away into clouds, and it is said one has all their choices returned to them.

tongue-money: Common term referring to money used to buy someone's silence.

Tracker: A Quietgiven that moves upon the land with ease, possessing an unearthly skill to follow anything that lives. Some believe the tracker's capability is to see or smell the passage of Forza, the residue of which remains in a place much longer than physical—Forda—traces. Their skin is hairless and translucent, showing striated lines over jutting bone, and their eyes protrude like a dead, bloated animal's.

Tract of Desolation: The written account of what transpired when Maldea was Whited and all those given life by his hand were sent into the Bourne.

upright dust: See walking earth.

Veil, the: The boundary between the Bourne and the races of the Eastlands of Aeshau Vaal, maintained (it is thought) by the Song of Suffering.

Velle (VEHL-uh): These renderers of the Will serve Quietus. Some came to their dark path through the baser, self-gratifying motivations of avarice and vanity. They sully the authority to direct the Will by transferring the personal cost to other living things. By so doing, they cheat death a long time, their own Forda hardly depleting. In every age since the Abandonment, there have been Sheason impatient and wanton enough for their own gain and comfort to reject their covenant and embrace the reward of the Quiet. Most, though, are descended from other Velle inside the Bourne who grant the power—usually too soon—to others to grow their ranks. From the Covenant Language, meaning, "my wish, my desire, or my will."

Walkers: When the Abandonment took place, there remained a few Inveterae "untabernacled"—without a physical form in which to live or experience joy and adversity. Forgotten by the First Ones, they were not herded into the Bourne with the rest. Thus twice forgotten, these lonely children of Forza seek a suit of flesh to wear. With no authority to command living things, they attempt to claim the lost bodies of others to make themselves finally whole. Over time, their bitterness and their own dark arts have grown, as has their understanding.

walking earth: Used to refer to one who is alive, but doomed.

Wall of Remembrance: The wall surrounding the Halls of Solath Mahnus to provide privacy and protection, but more importantly to chronicle the history of Recityv and its place in the events of the family of man.

War of the First Promise: During the Craven Season, the Veil weakened and Quietgiven escaped the Bourne. The war to press them back to their confinement lasted four hundred years and brought into existence the First Promise and the Convocations of Seats.

War of the Second Promise: The Quiet again descended into the Eastlands. From several points beyond the Veil, they came, more purposeful and more studied in their use of the Will. Individual nations could not alone fight back the threat to their people, so the Convocation of Seats was re-called. The Right Arm of the Promise, the Sedagin longblades, was called to march into the breach. Responding promptly, they did so, losing every man when the Army of the

Second Promise—supposedly comprised of battalions from every nation in the Second Convocation—never arrived to relieve them. This Second war lasted two hundred and sixty years before the Quiet were pushed back.

we are made: A colloquial expression meaning "it's a deal."

went to his earth: Euphemism for death.

Whited One: See Quietus.

Whiting, the: The marking and punishment of Maldea for his overreaching ambition. This describes the event where the Creation Council stripped all color from Maldea and gave him his new name: Quietus.

Widows' Village: A dreary settlement where surviving spouses of Sheason reside, having been robbed of the Undying Vow of their marriages by the Velle—and some by other means.

Will, the: The power whereby all things are created, and without which there can be no growth or progression. Rendering the Will, causing change in Forda I'Forza, has a price, which is nothing less than the same, Forda I'Forza. For matter and energy cannot be created or destroyed, only changed, transubstantiated, rendered. Balance can be maintained if the renderer offers his own matter and energy, body and spirit, to the exchange. Transference of the personal cost to a secondary source of Forda I'Forza deepens the wound of disharmony between the two sides of Creation—matter and energy.

winter's pen: The writing an Author completes during the winter.

womb: Derogatory term used to refer to human females by the Bar'dyn.

Wombs of War: A term the women of the First War of Promise gave themselves, when wives and mothers gave up their children to the army ranks to defeat the Quiet. It resulted from generation after generation of women giving birth to yet another generation of children who went to war.

• ABOUT THE AUTHOR •

Peter Orullian has worked at Xbox for over a decade, which is good, because he's a gamer. He's toured internationally with various bands and been a featured vocalist at major rock and metal festivals, which is good, because he's a musician. He's also learned when to hold his tongue, which is good, because he's a contrarian. Peter has published several short stories, which he thinks are good. *The Unremembered* is his first novel, which he hopes you will think is good. He lives in Seattle, where it rains all the damn time. He has nothing to say about that.

Visit him at www.orullian.com.